HOOKSETT PUBLIC LIBRARY
HOOKSETT, NH 03106
603.485.6092
http://hooksettlibrary.org

ABOUT THE CREATOR

Maximilian Uriarte is an artist based out of Los Angeles, California.

Growing up in Corvallis, Oregon, Maximilian enlisted in the United States Marine Corps at the age of nineteen in 2006. After two combat deployments to Iraq between 2007 and 2009, Maximilian started the world's most popular military comic strip, *Terminal Lance*, in 2010.

Maximilian graduated with a bachelor of fine arts in animation in 2013 utilizing the Post-9/11 GI Bill and has been a working artist and creator ever since. When not writing and illustrating epic graphic novels or hilarious Marine Corps comics, Maximilian is actively working in the film industry.

Maximilian currently lives in Santa Monica with his beautiful wife, Rachael, and his dog, Charlie.

 @tlcplmax

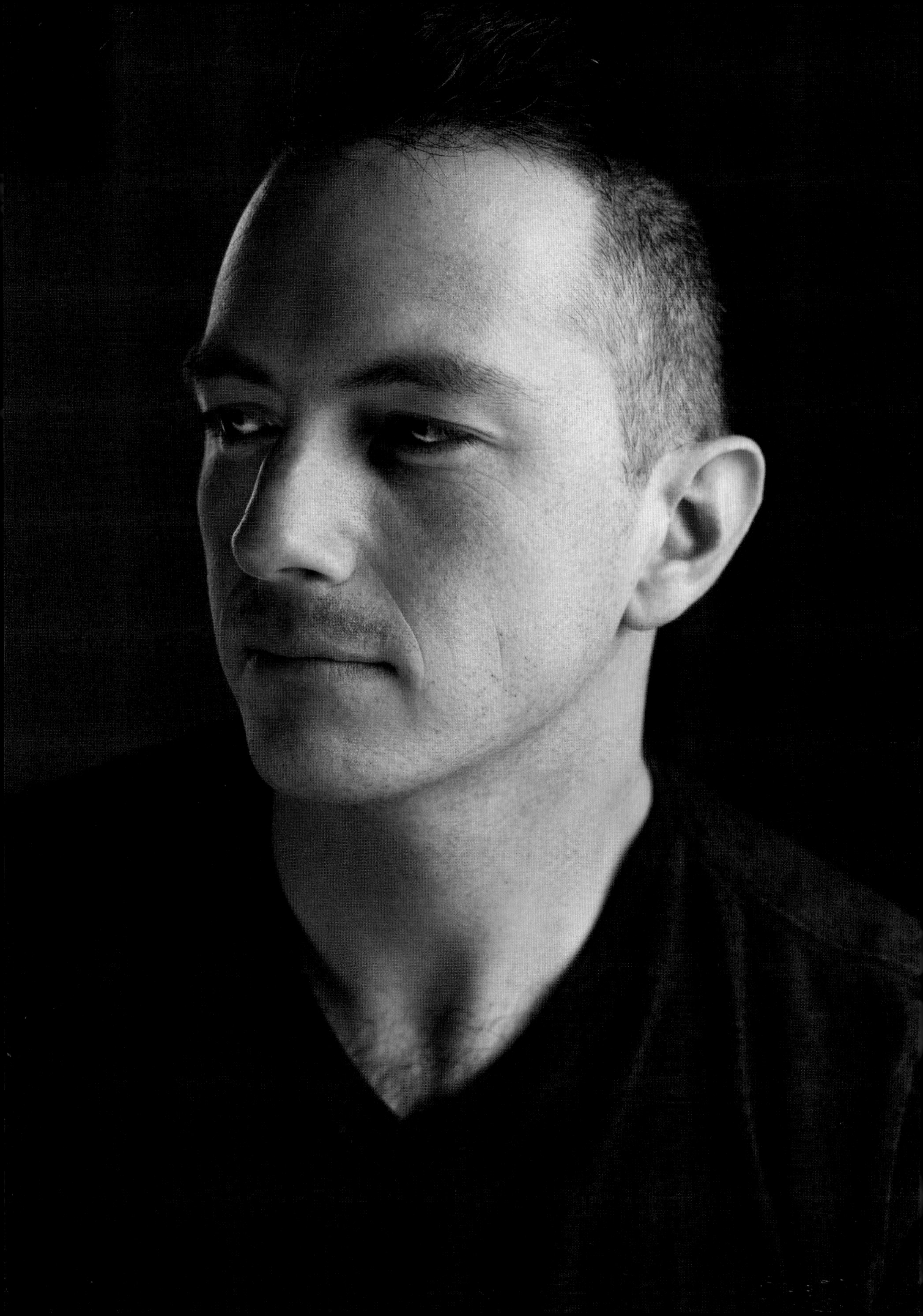

Rest assured, Sergeant King will return.

In addition to writing King's story, I also illustrated this entire thing from start to finish. Coming off of *The White Donkey,* I wanted to do something that was bigger, bolder, and more visually driven than my previous graphic novel.

Color is something that I grew into later in my life as an illustrator, as it was always intimidating to me. However, I didn't think I could tell this story without it. The deep blue of the lapis lazuli, the opulent mountain vistas, and the rich world of Badakhshan demanded to be illustrated in full color. As well, this is a different kind of story than *The White Donkey* before it. King is a much less talkative character than Abe or Garcia; he's driven by his passion and deep emotions rather than quips.

I wrote the script to this story with this visual approach in mind, knowing that I would spend much more space on imagery than words. As a result, this book is nearly one hundred pages longer than *The White Donkey*, but with significantly less dialogue. With its roots in medieval high fantasy like Conan, *Battle Born* was always intended to be a more visceral experience than a heady one.

To research this book's visual style, I embedded with a few infantry companies at the Marine Corps Mountain Warfare Training Center in Bridgeport, California. The winter warfare gear was something that I never got to experience as an Iraq veteran, so I used the opportunity to study and soak it up. If nothing else, I'll never look at buckets the same way again.

This book was a labor of love and a long time in the making. It was a massive undertaking as a graphic novel, and I hope that the journey is memorable.

AFTERWORD

I originally came up with the idea for *Battle Born* when I was working on *The White Donkey* back in 2014. In fact, the first thing I ever wrote in the universe of *Battle Born* was the scene where Forrest kills the child in the farmlands, which was originally written as a short film.

In a way, *Battle Born* was designed to be a kind of modern reinterpretation of Robert E. Howard's Conan the Barbarian character. I wanted to create a kind of modern mythical hero like Conan in a contemporary realist setting. Sergeant King became that character.

When I began the journey of writing *Lapis Lazuli*, all I knew was that I wanted the story to be set in the mountains, which I thought would be a unique setting for a modern war story. I started doing research on mountainous areas of the world and came across the Badakhshan Province. I was immediately awestruck by the natural beauty of the region. It came across as rugged, wondrous, and ancient.

In my research, one of the things that immediately stood out to me was that the Sar-i Sang Valley of Badakhshan had been home to lapis lazuli mining for millennia. I didn't know much about lapis lazuli, but I recalled from my time at the California College of the Arts that it had been used to make ultramarine pigment for painting. This simple fact led me down the rabbit hole of the very real-life conflict surrounding the mineral and the region occurring today. In 2016, after the Taliban and local warlords took control of the region, a watchdog group known as Global Witness classified lapis lazuli as a conflict mineral.

Given my background as a Marine twice deployed to Iraq, with many friends that have been to Afghanistan, I was shocked at the seeming lack of interest in this particular conflict in the northern province.

Looking deeper into the history of Afghanistan and the Anglo-Afghan wars, I was further intrigued by the British colonialist history of Afghanistan. It seemed sad to me that such a beautiful part of the world had been reduced to little more than a political set piece in the game of the British empire, through multiple Anglo-Afghan wars. This echoed into the modern day, as we watch America continue its escapades into the land for nearly 20 years, as of writing.

This ultimately led me to the major themes of this story: the civilized and the savage in the shadow of colonialism, driven by racism. The people of Afghanistan are not viewed as people at all, but collateral pawns. It was former British Prime Minister Lloyd George, who presided over the United Kingdom during the third Anglo-Afghan War, who famously said, "We insisted on reserving the right to bomb niggers," in regard to the 1932 World Disarmament Conference. As well, it was Winston Churchill who defended the use of chemical weapons against the Afghans in 1919, or as he called them specifically, "uncivilized tribes."

While not necessarily my initial motivation, I found that writing a black protagonist gave me a unique literary opportunity to tie the themes of racism and colonialism from this story into America's own bloody, racist history. To be clear, it was never my intent as a white-hispanic man to try and capture the experience of being black in America. However, I found that the further I delved into King's character, the more it became impossible to separate his blackness from his worldview and his story. Empathy is the writer's most powerful tool, and the experience of writing the book through the eyes of King had a profound impact on me, while I also grew increasingly attached to him as a character.

WRITTEN AND ILLUSTRATED BY
MAXIMILIAN URIARTE

THE END

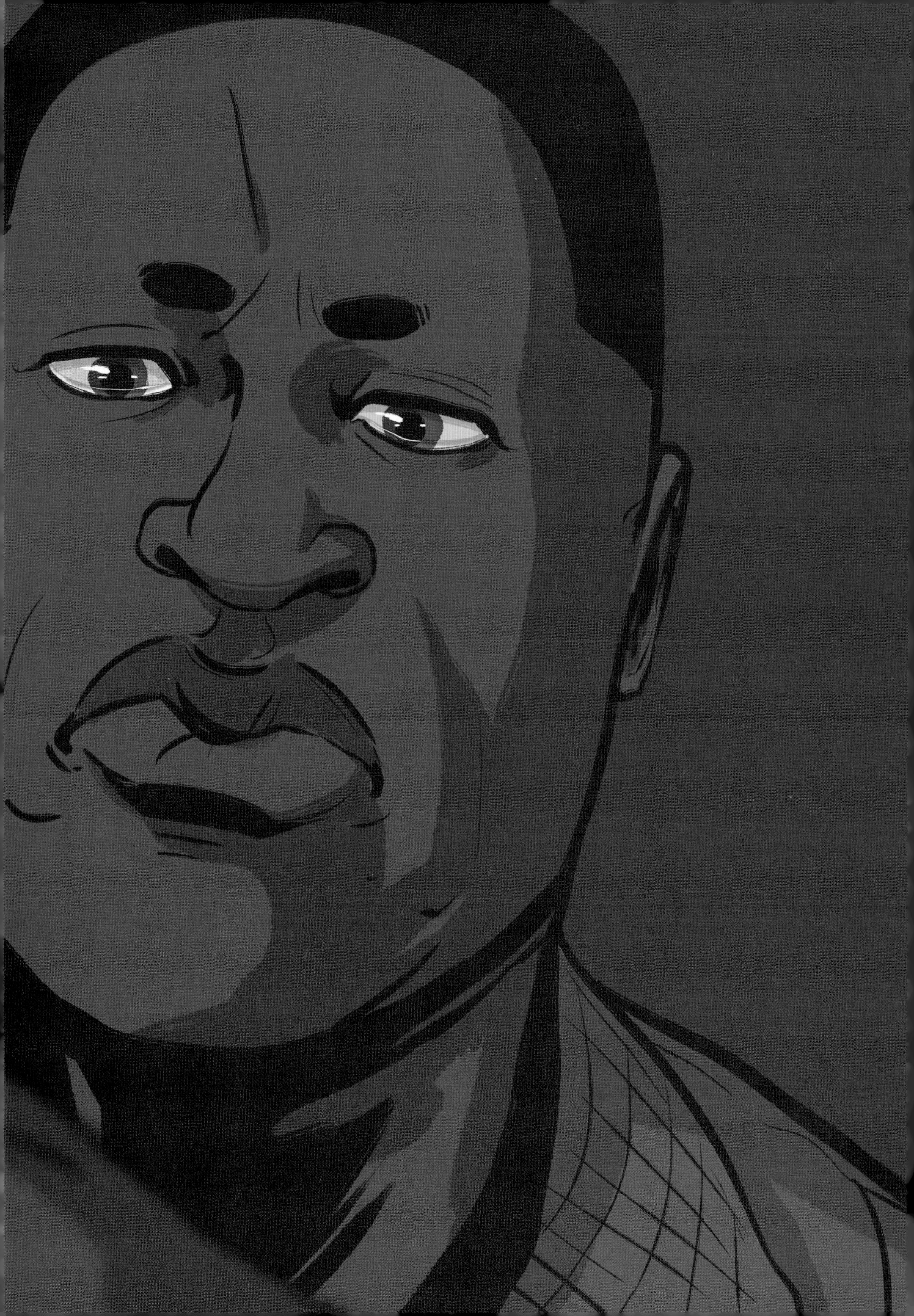

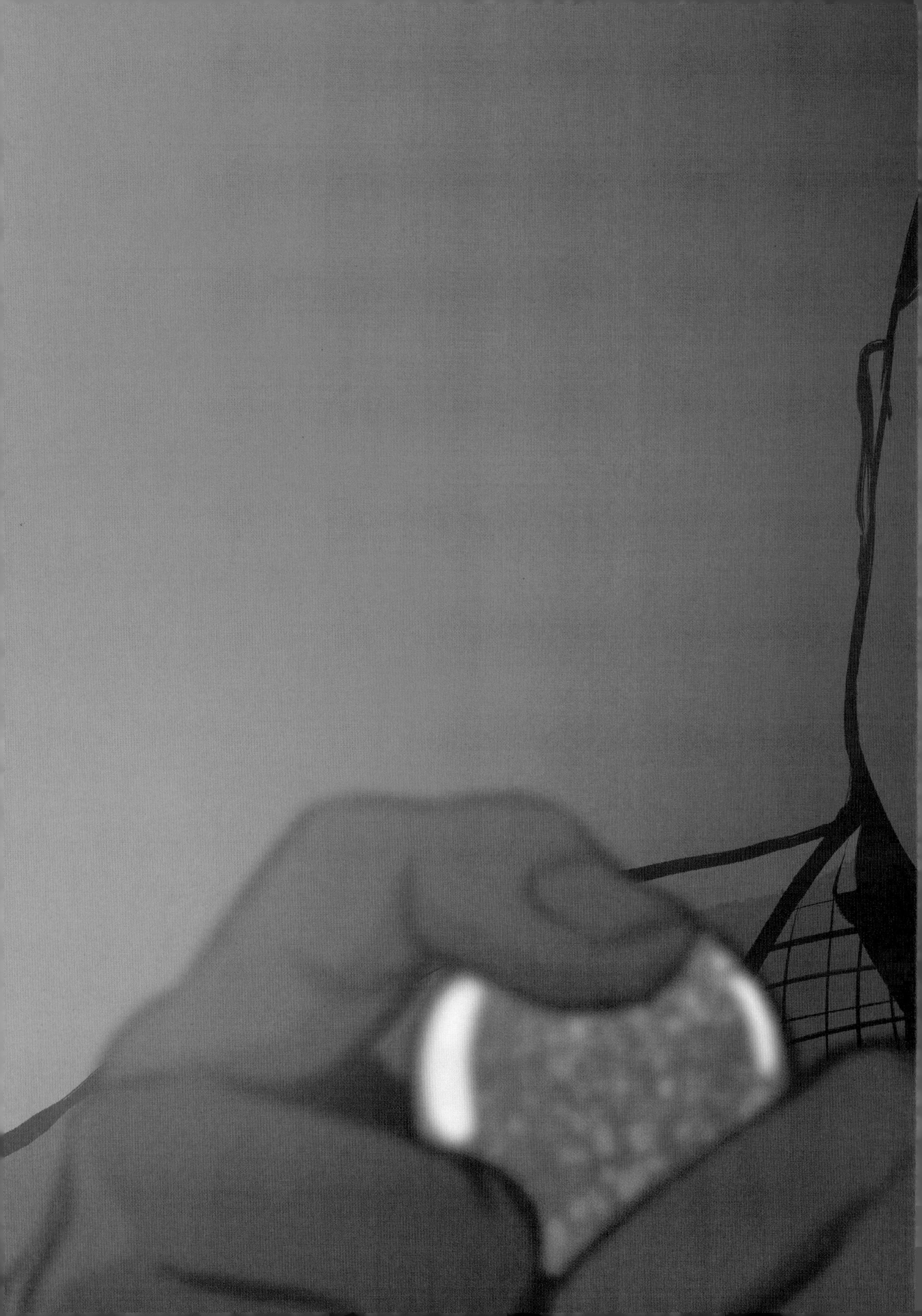

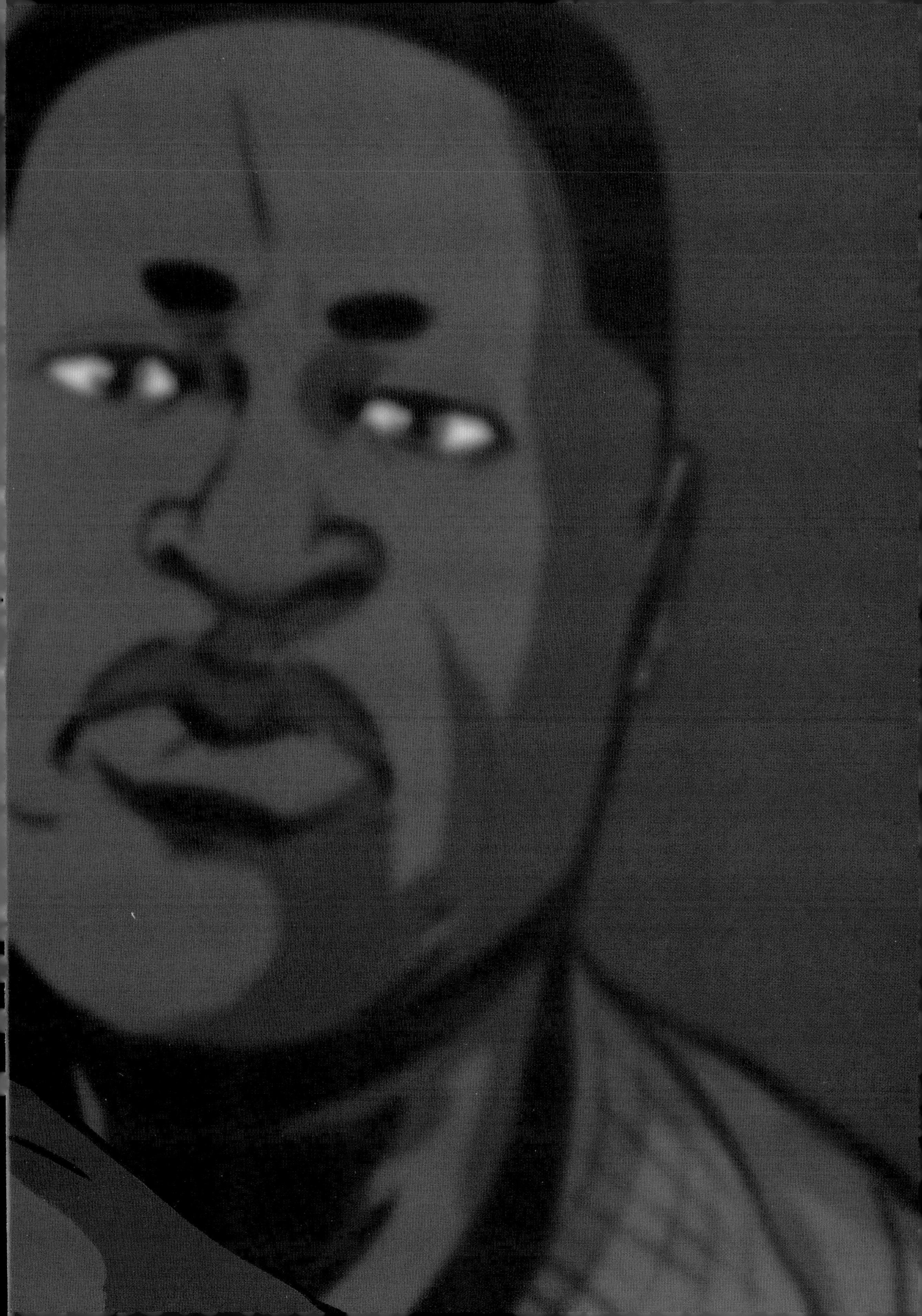

DEDICATED TO RACHAEL

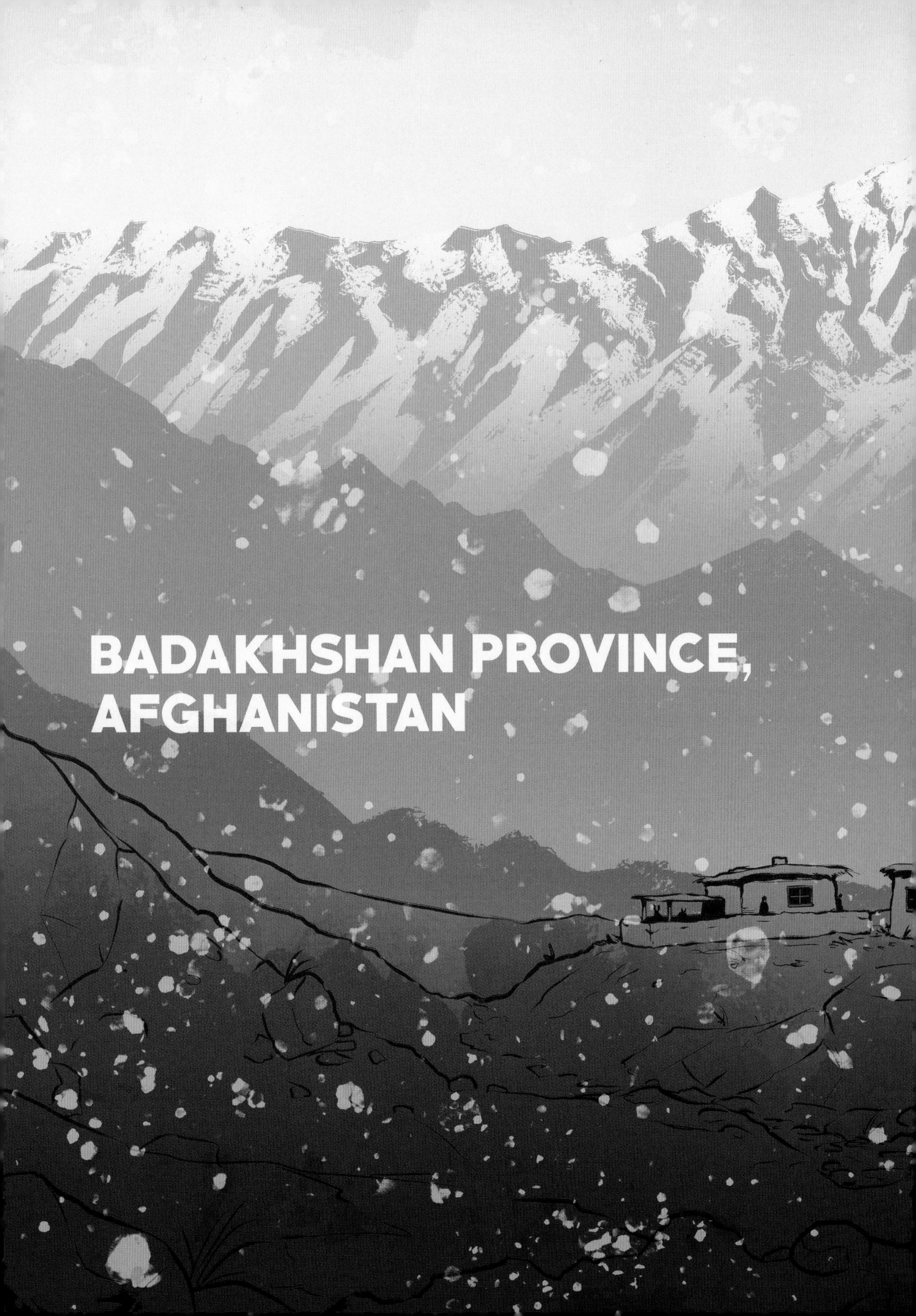
BADAKHSHAN PROVINCE,
AFGHANISTAN

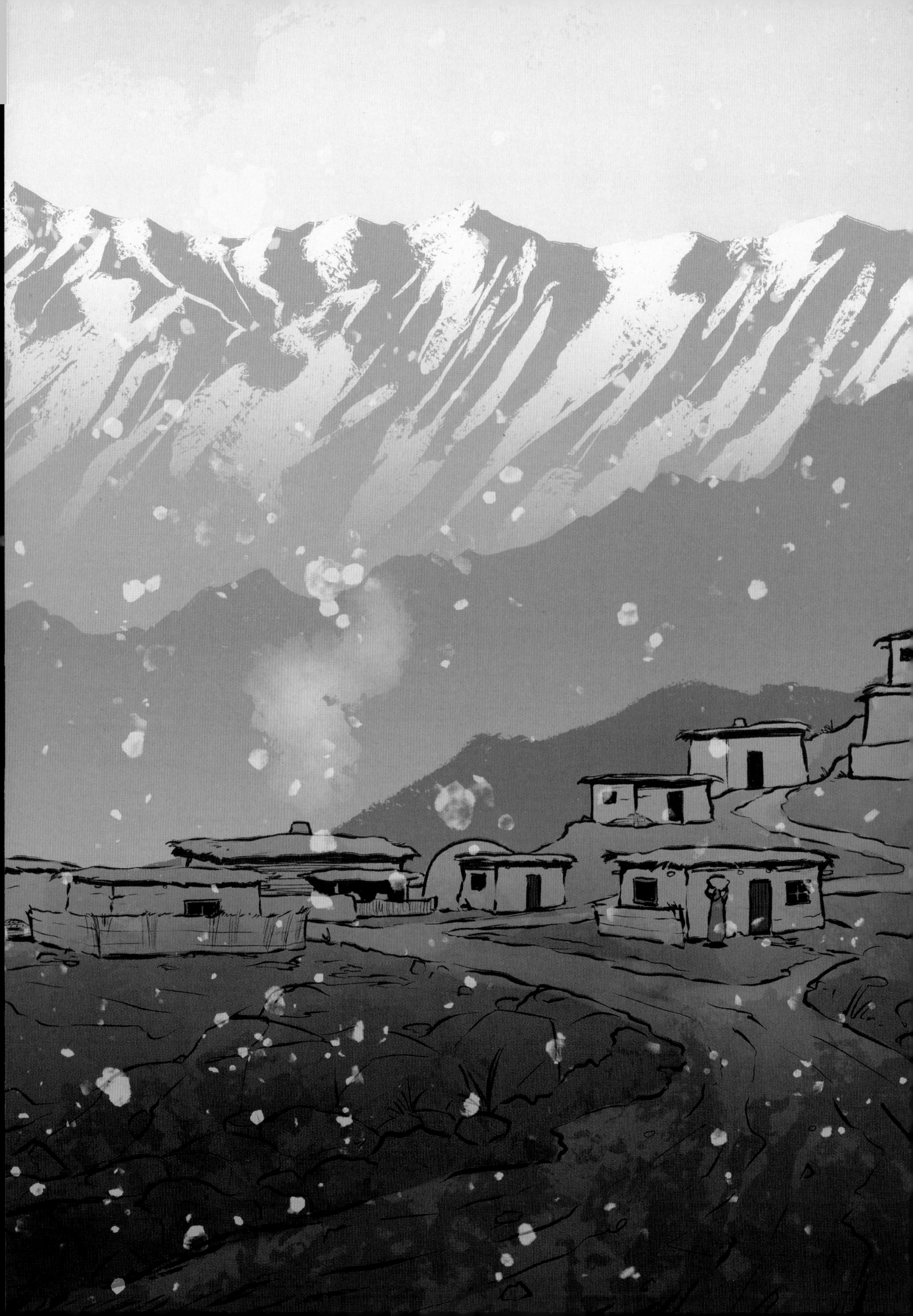

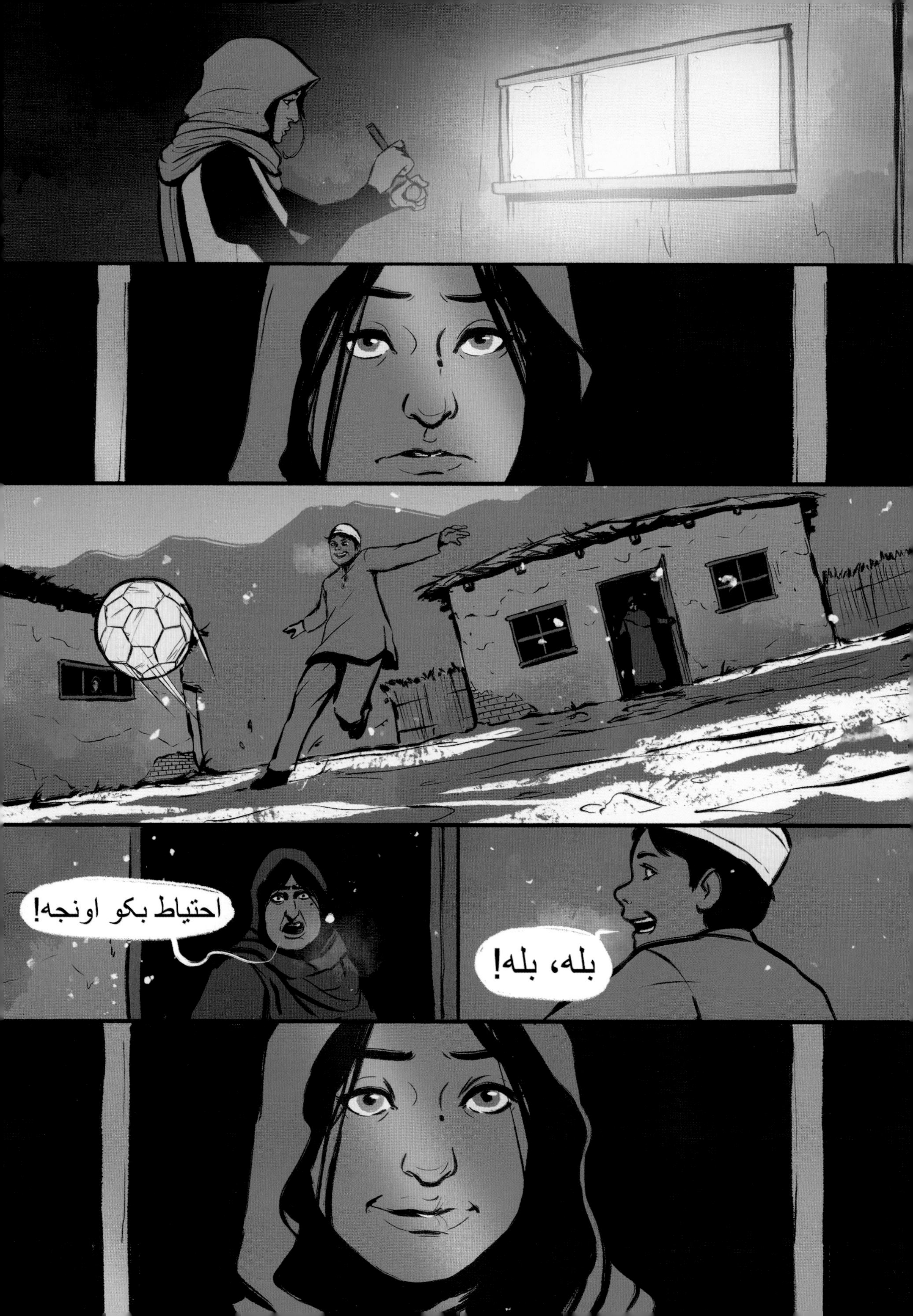
احتیاط بکو اونجه!
بله، بله!

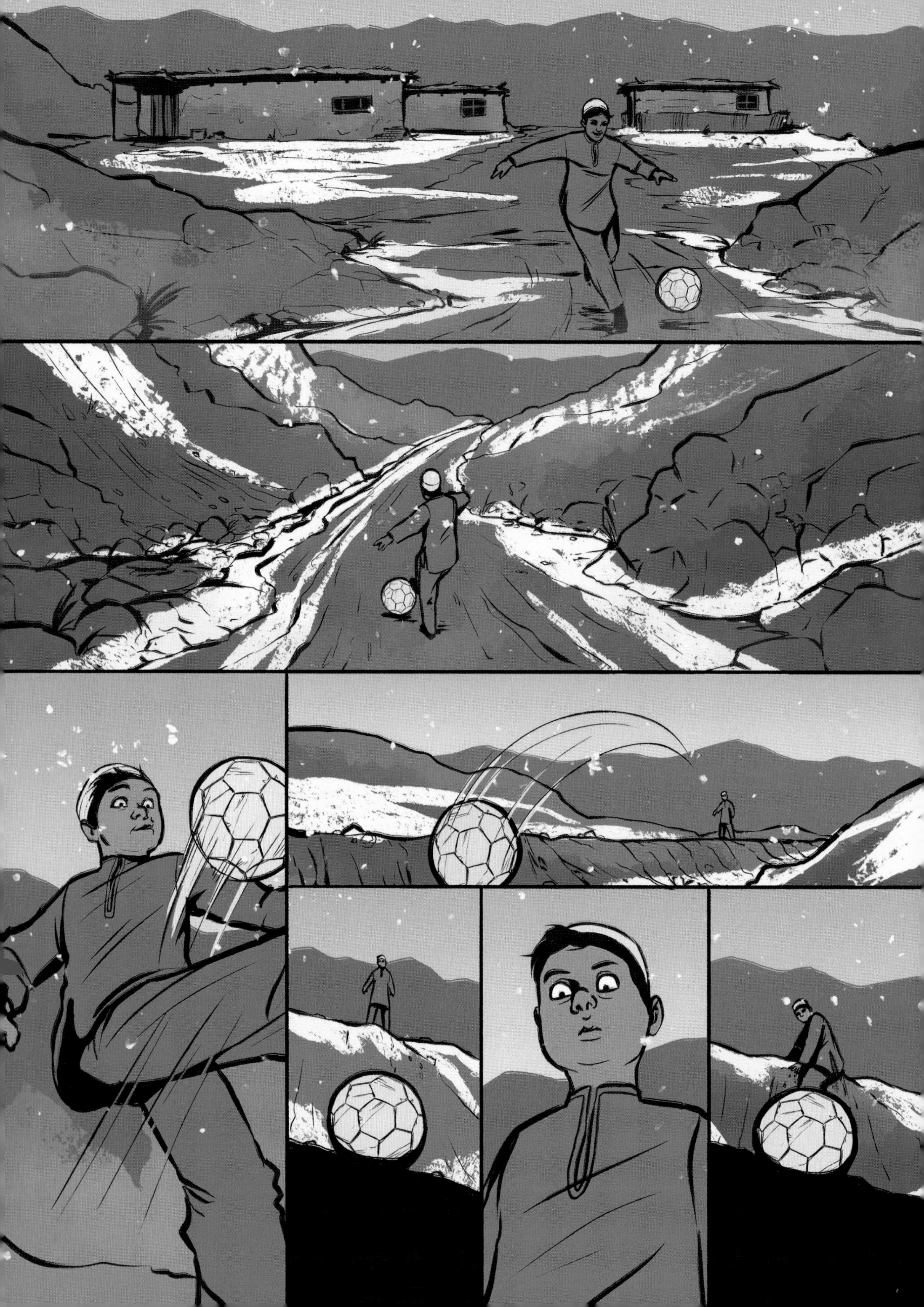

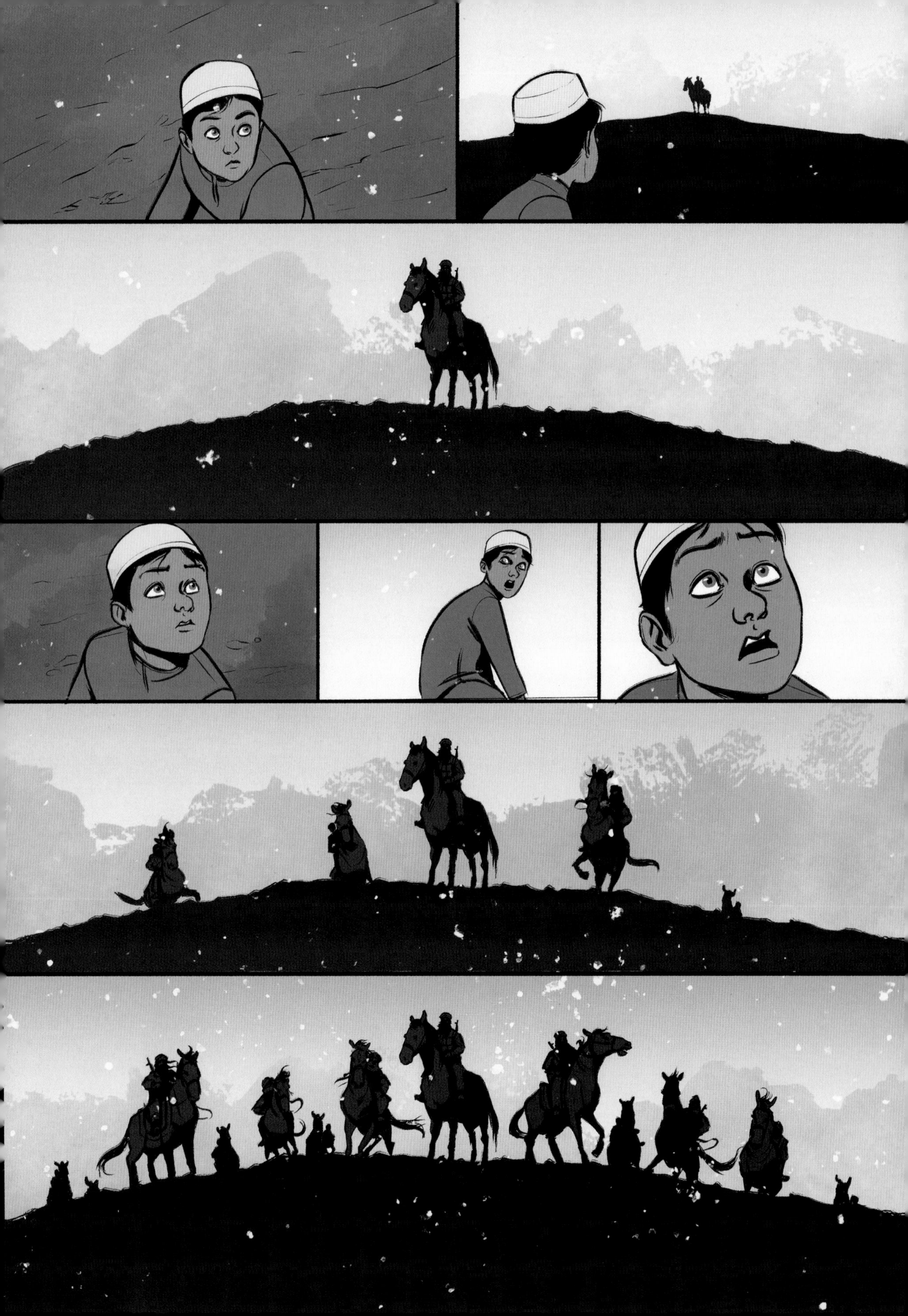

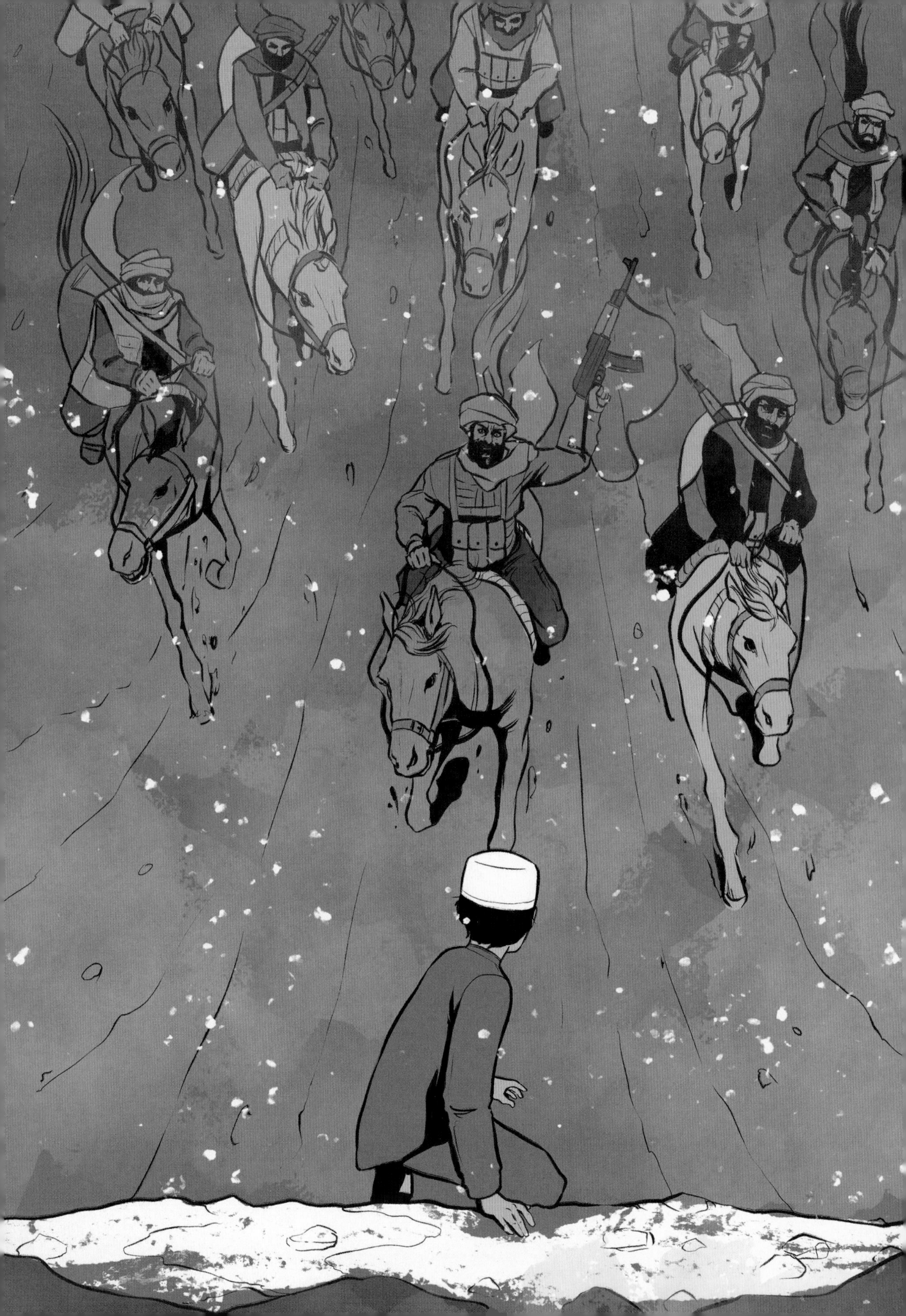

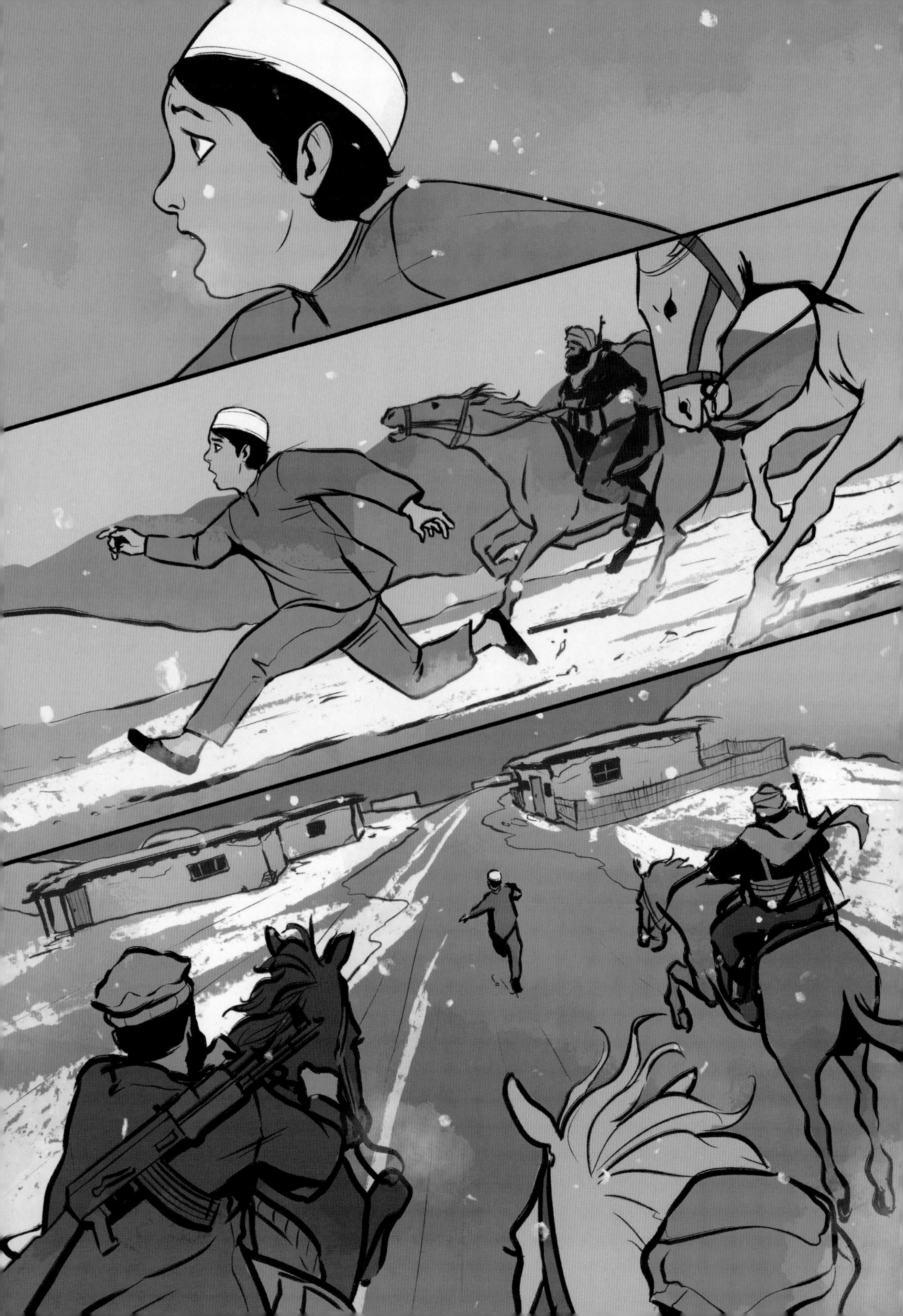

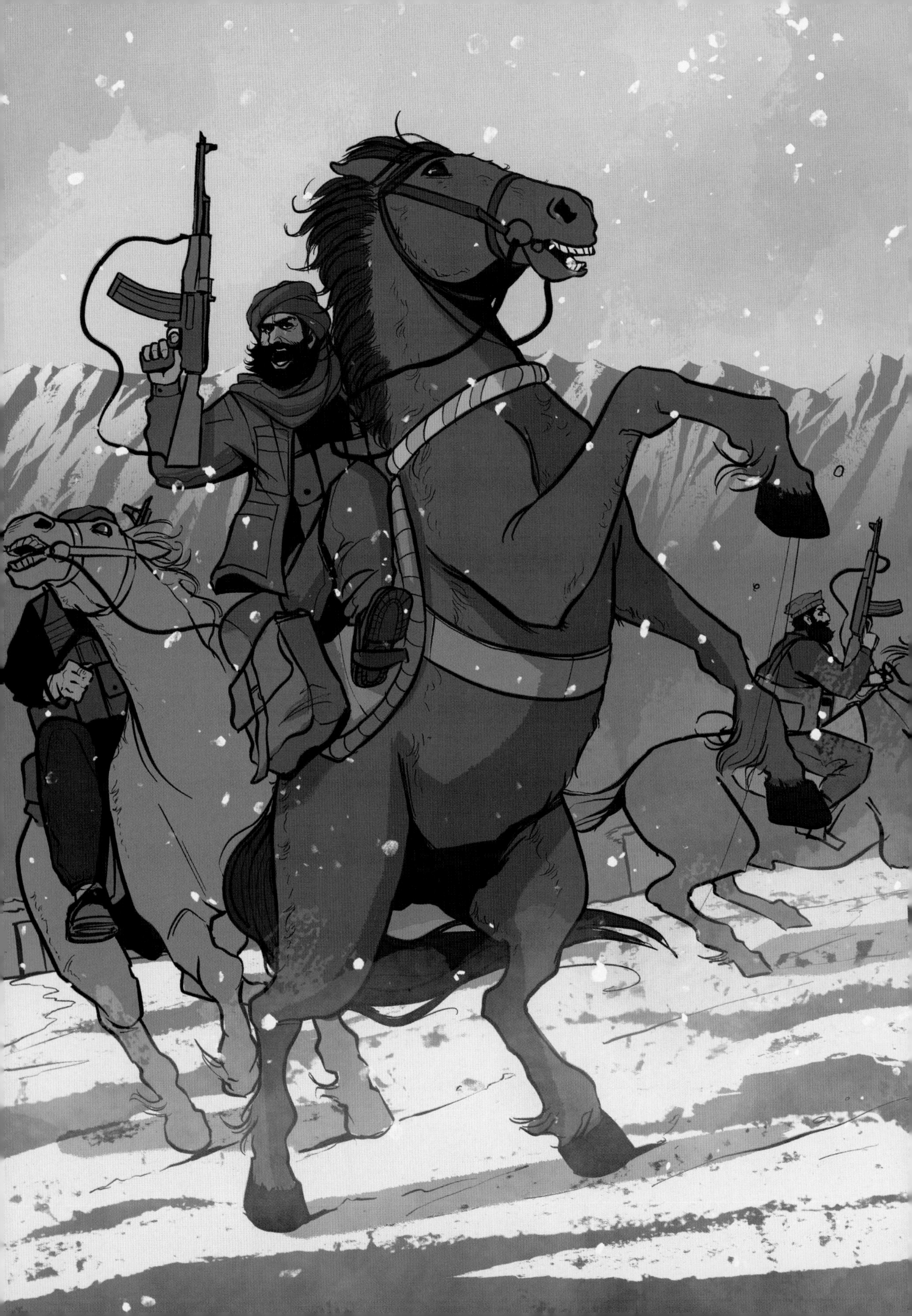

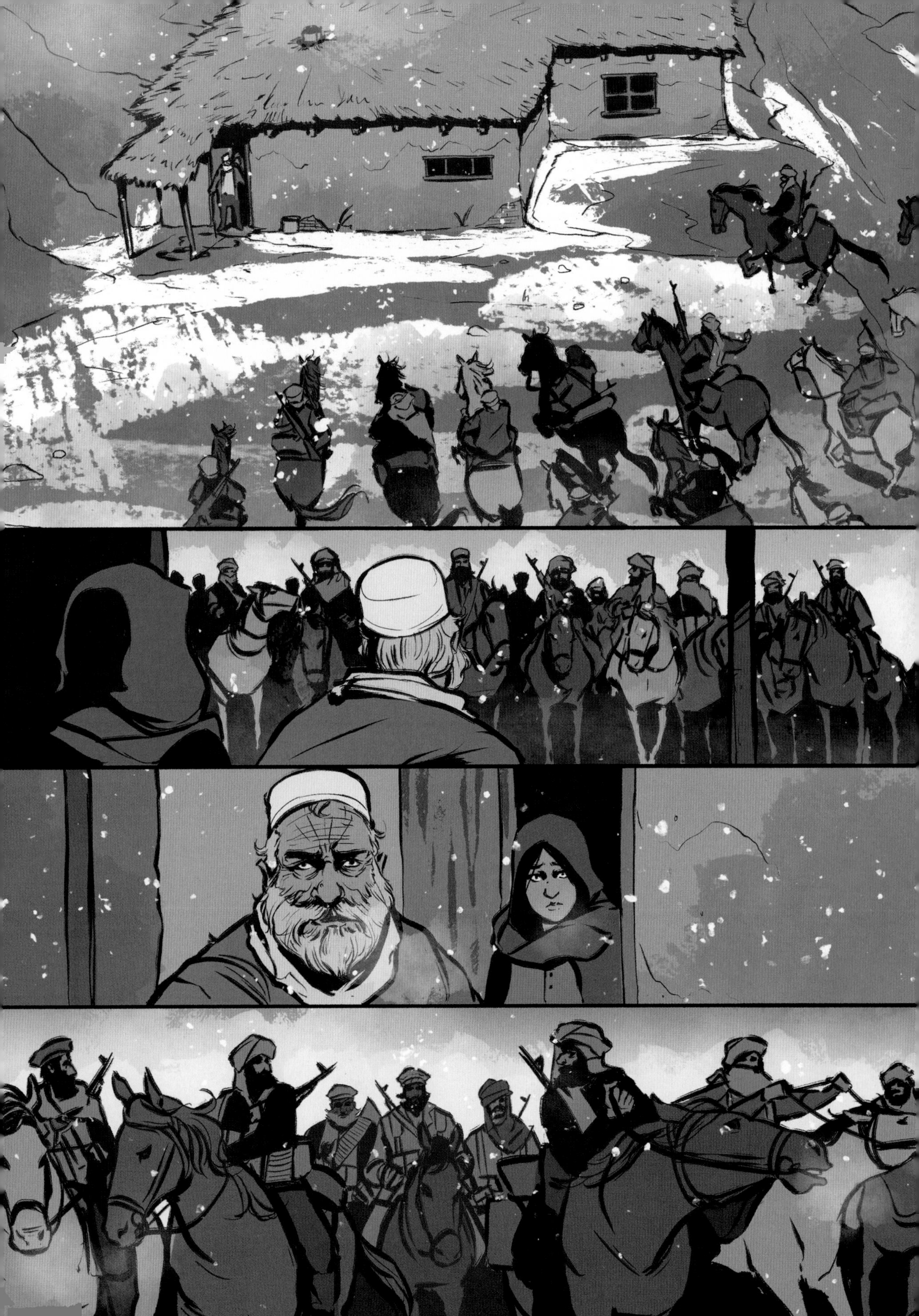

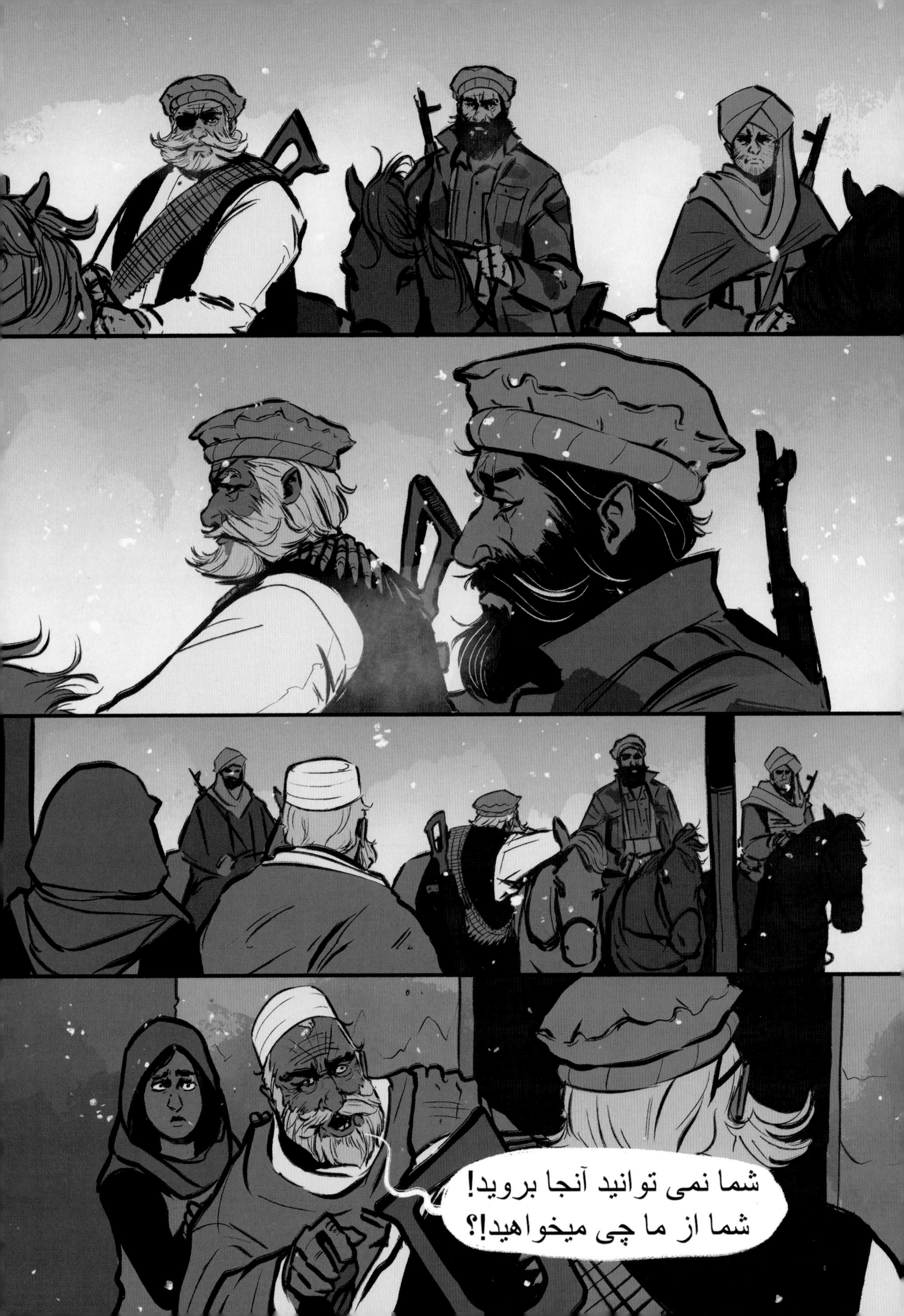
شما نمی توانید آنجا بروید! شما از ما چی میخواهید!؟

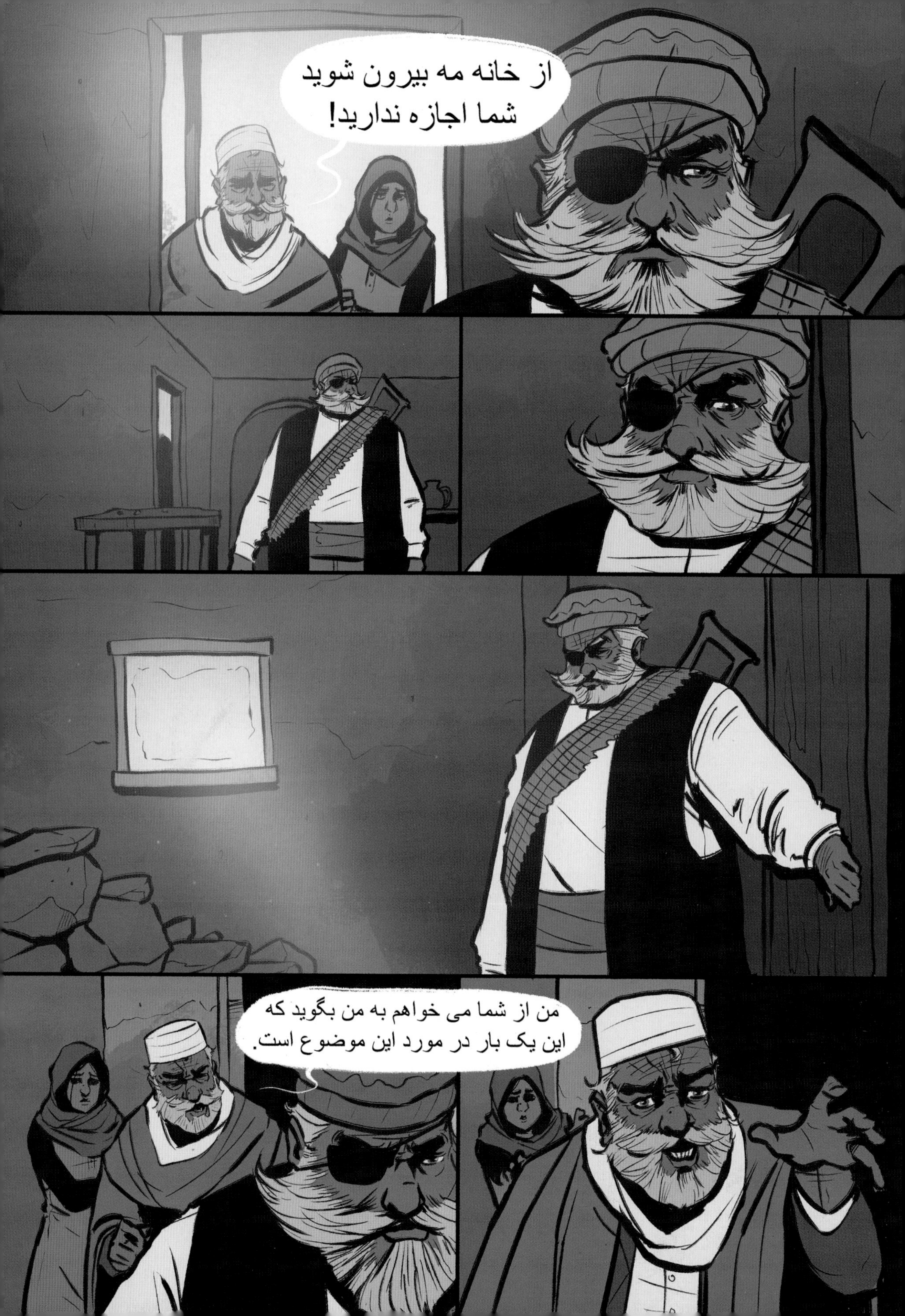
از خانه مه بیرون شوید
شما اجازه ندارید!
من از شما می خواهم به من بگوید که
این یک بار در مورد این موضوع است.

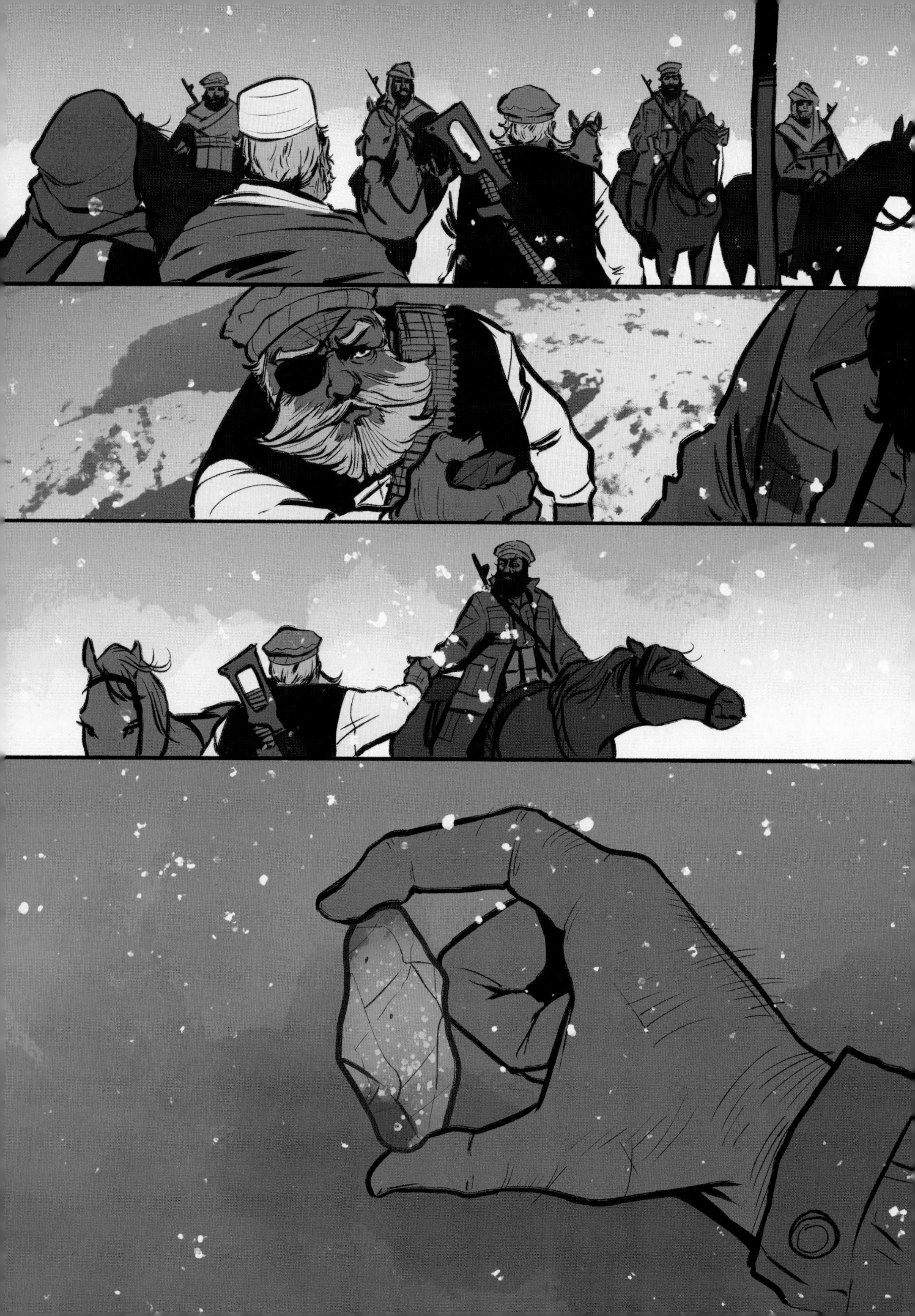

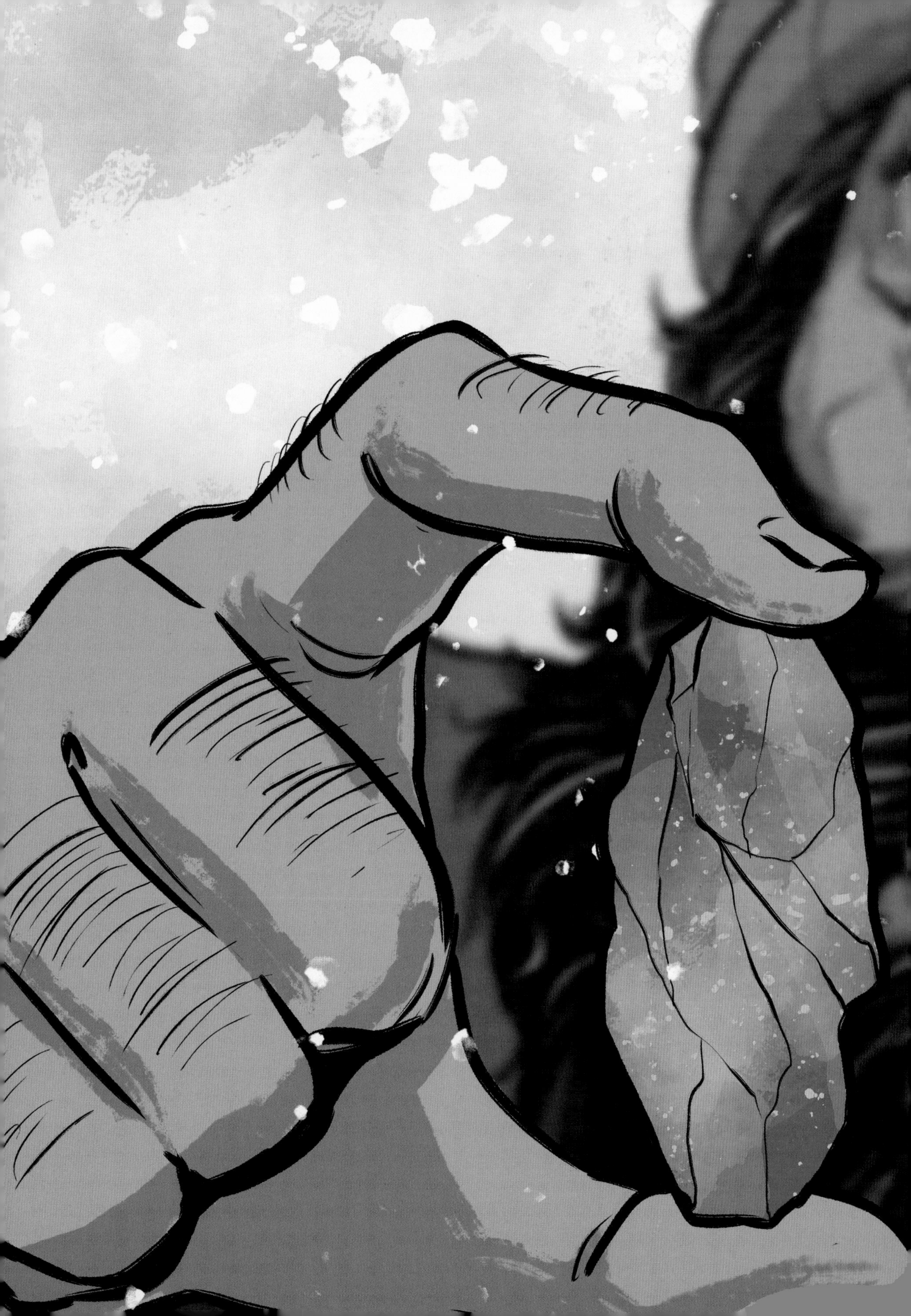

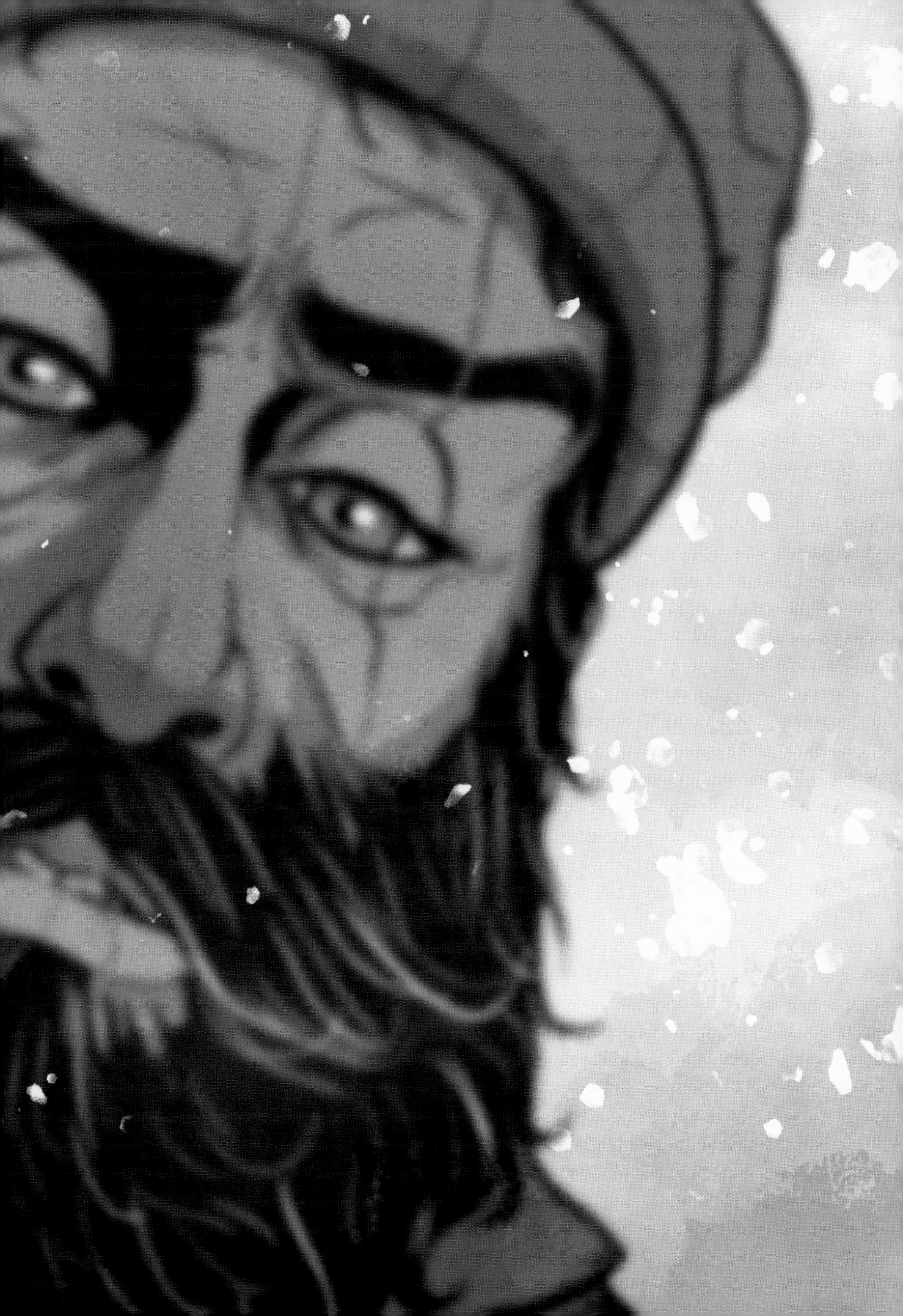

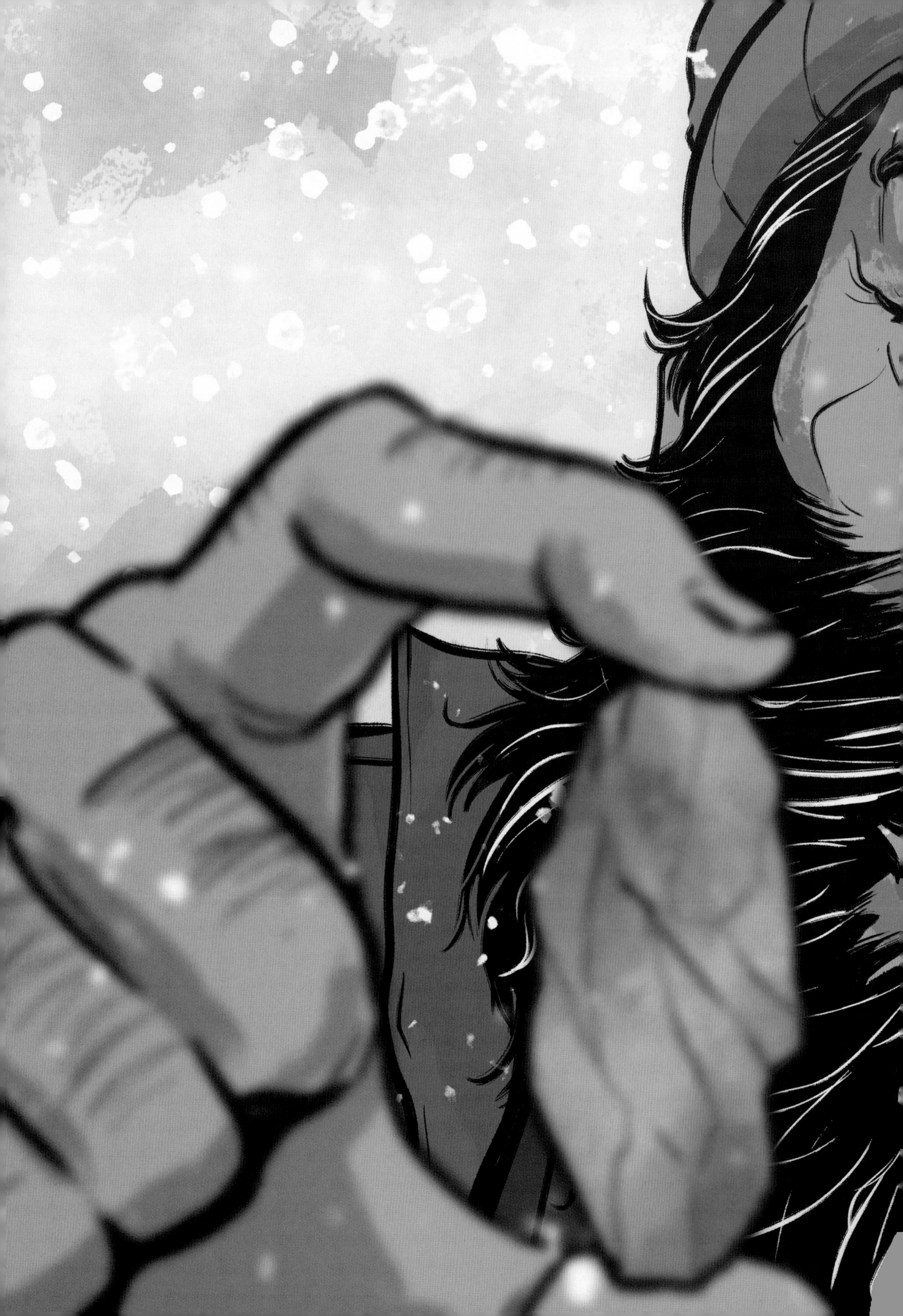

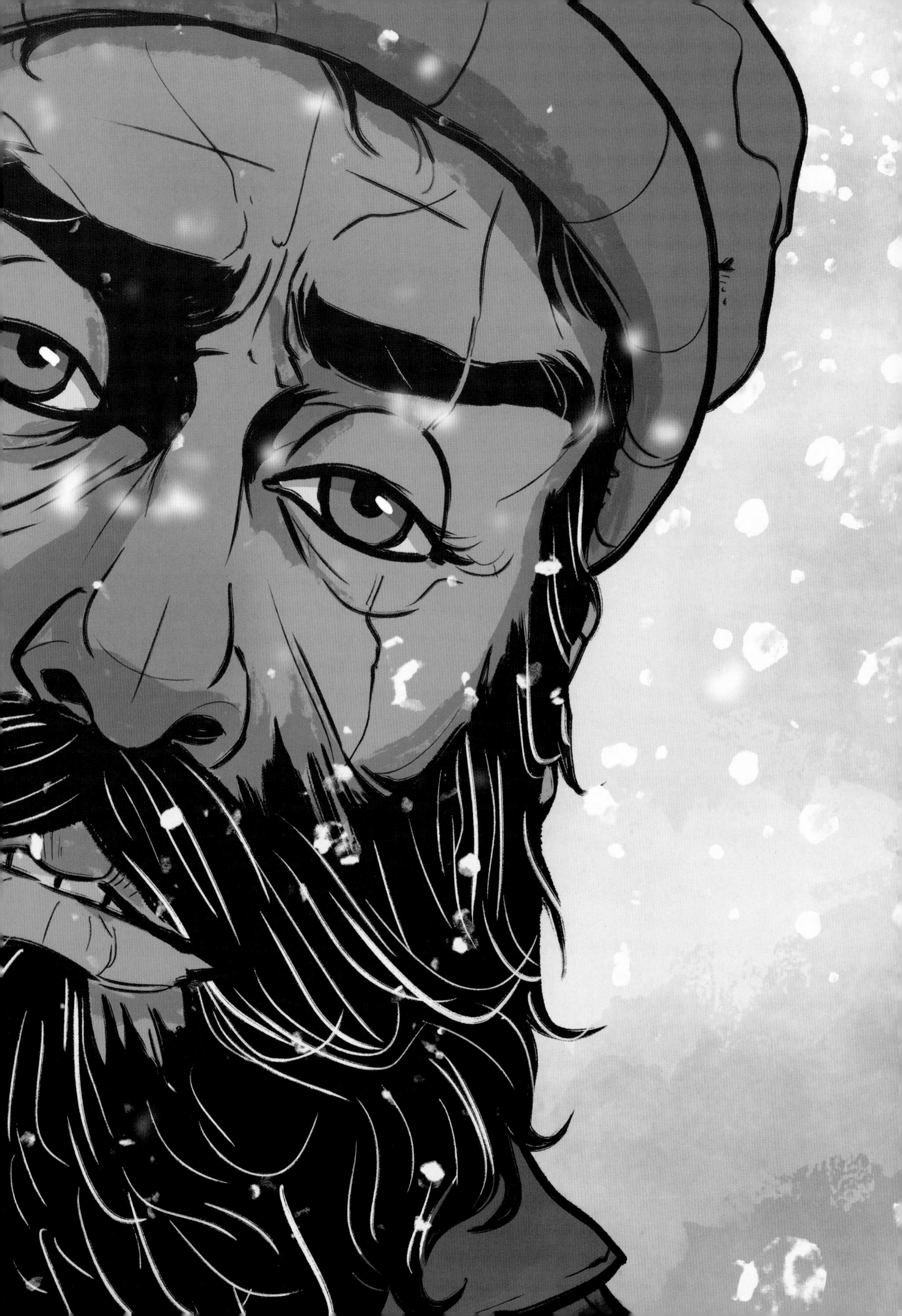

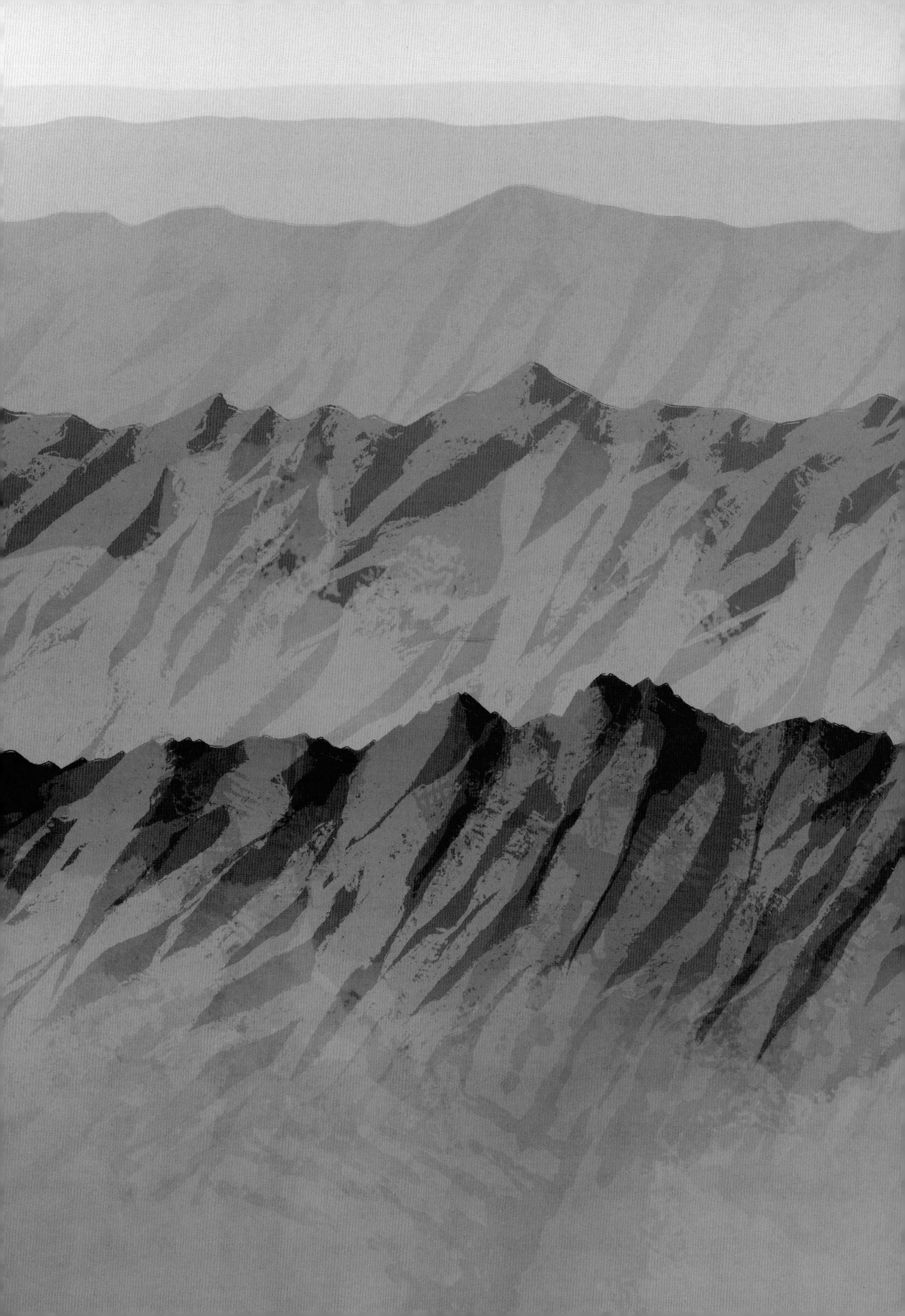

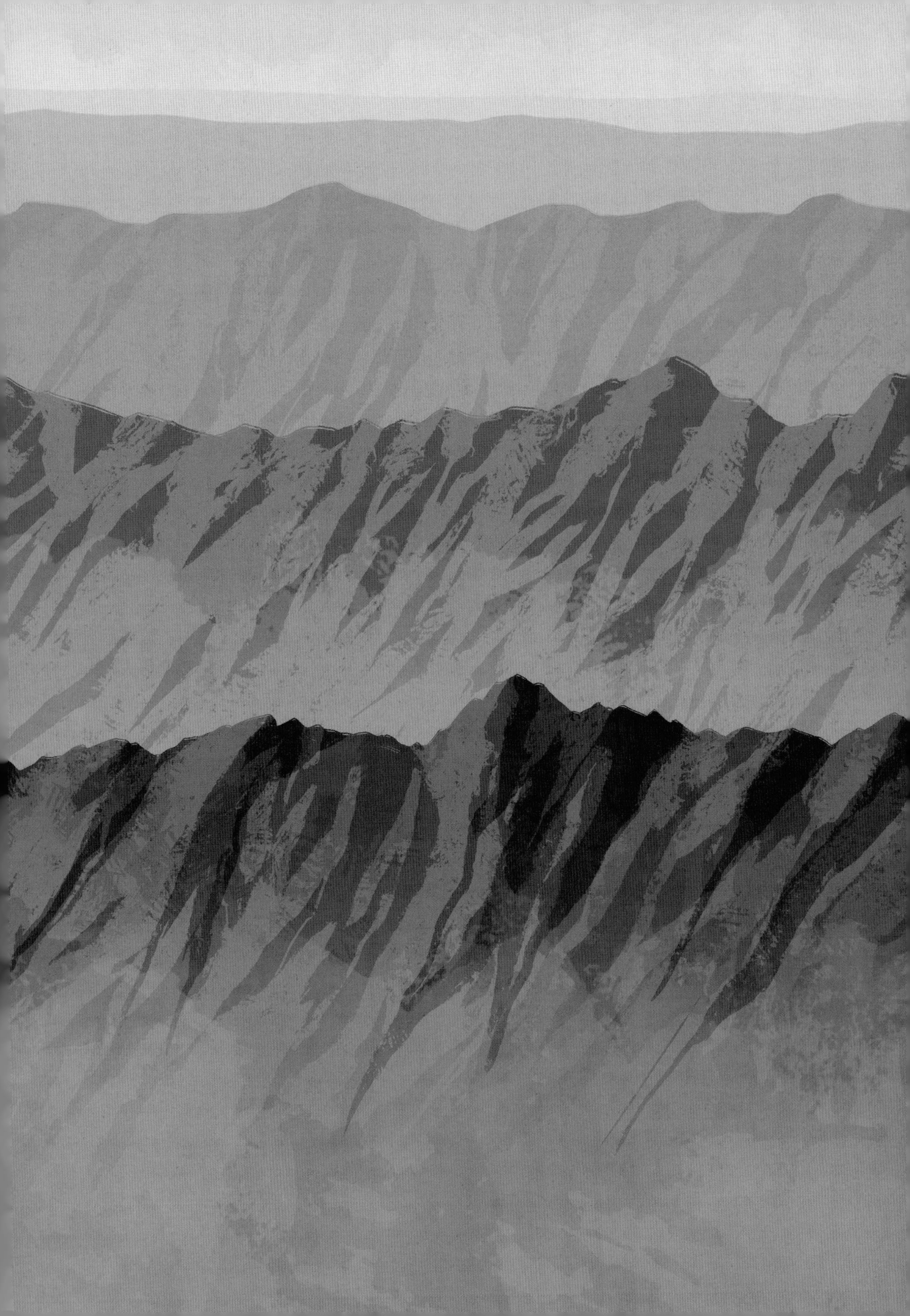

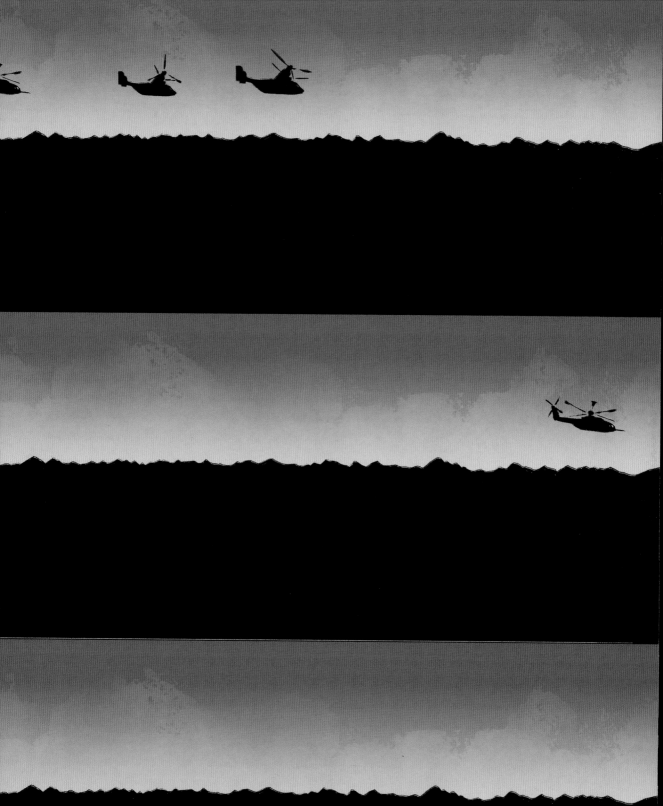

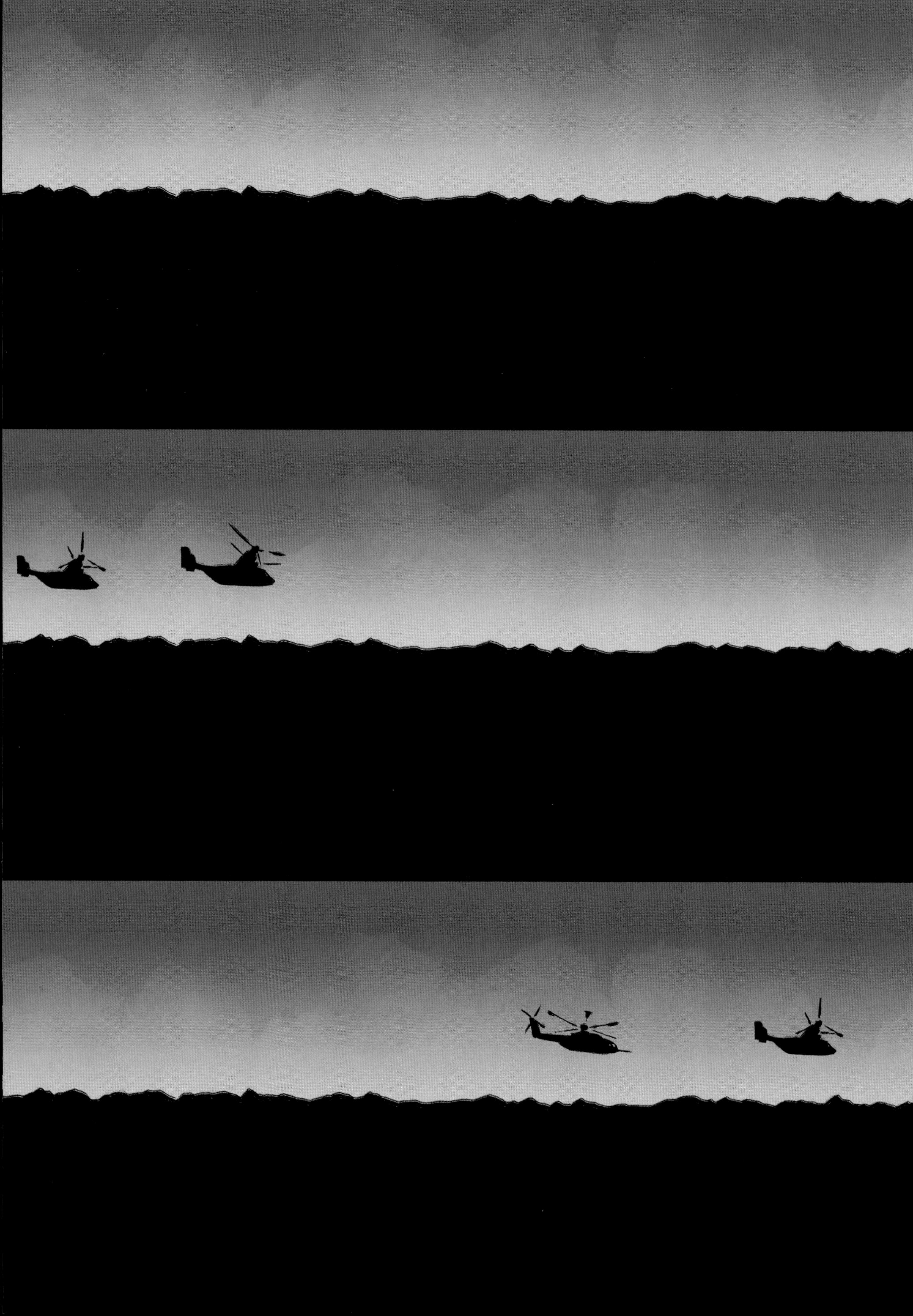

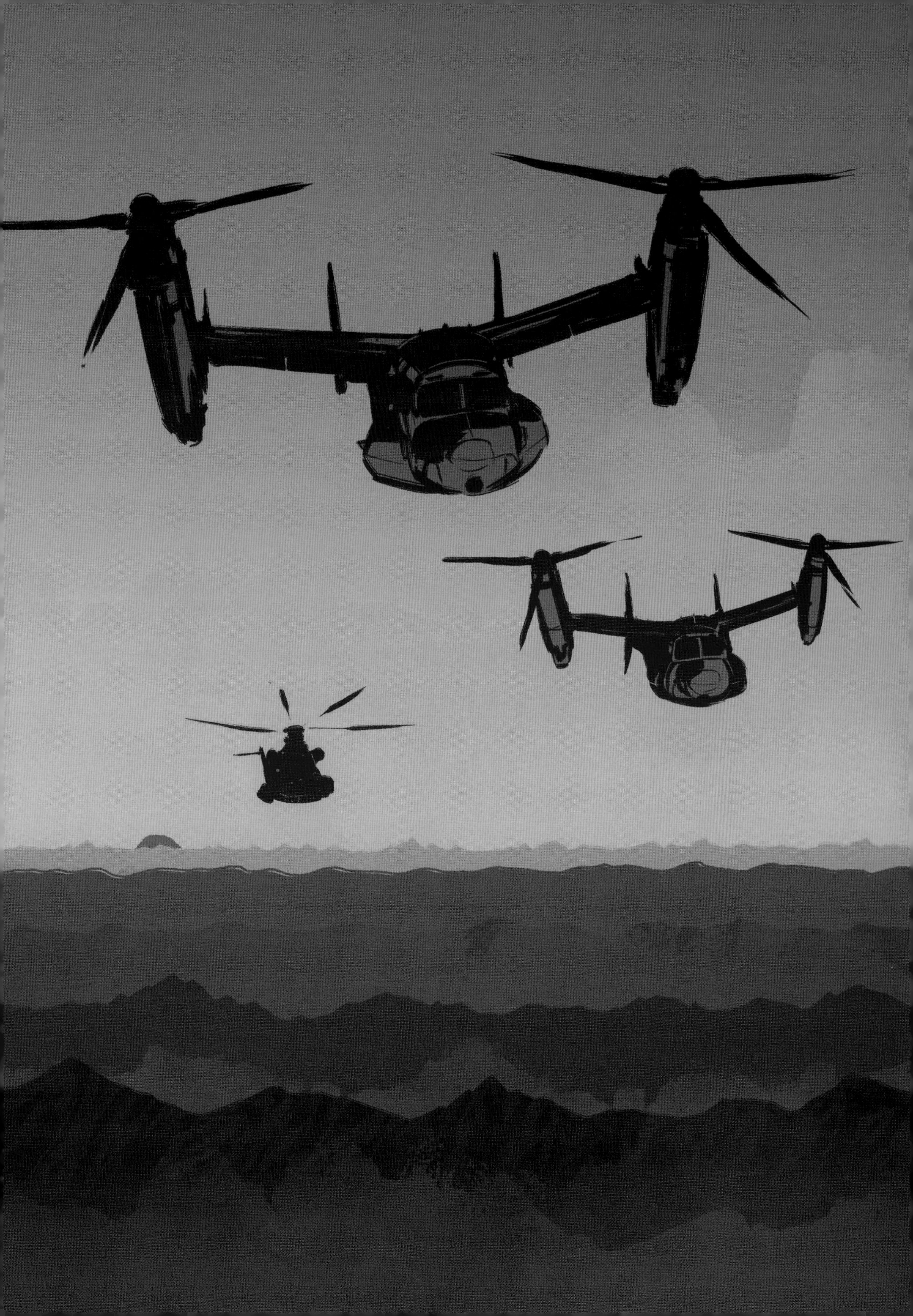

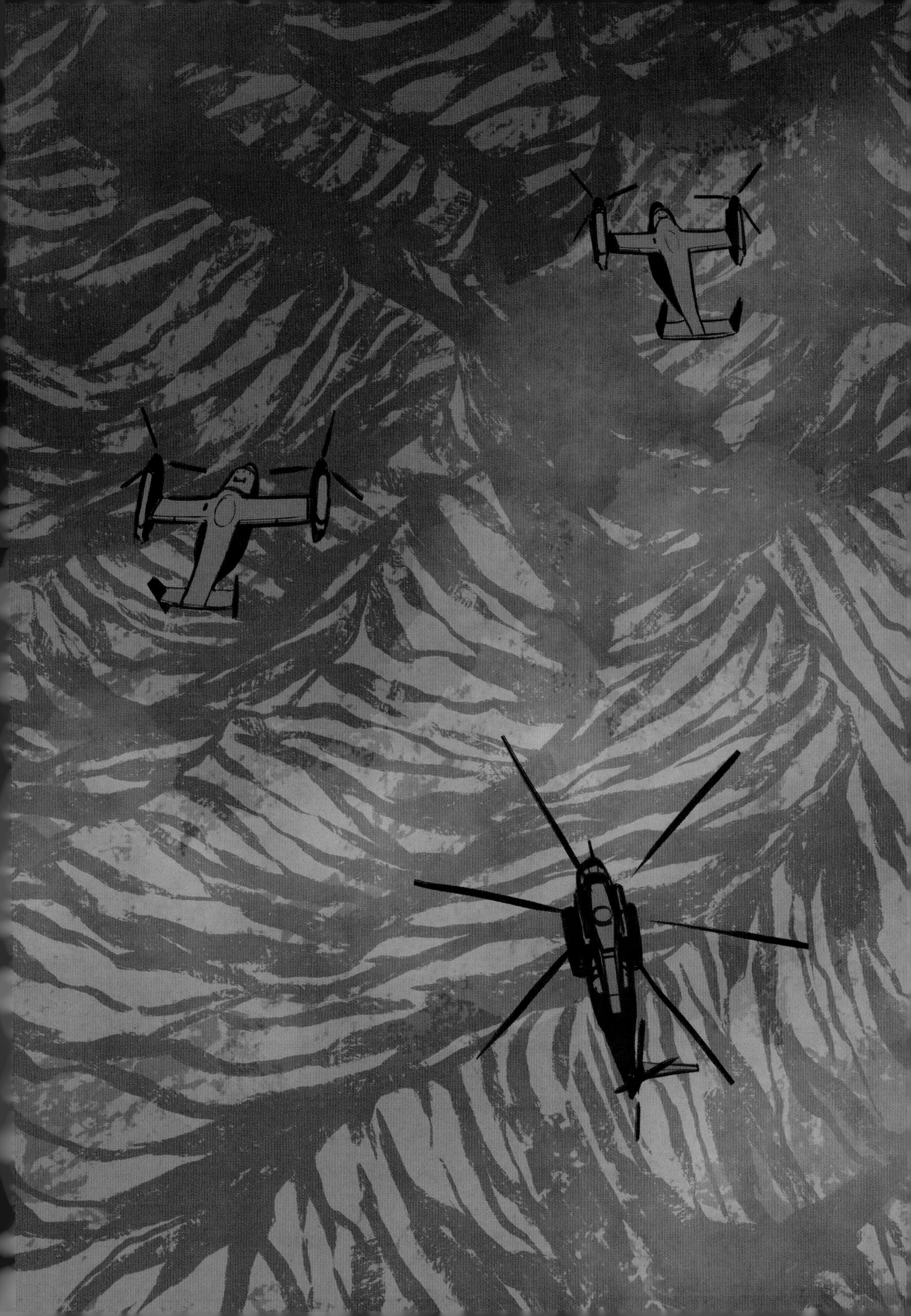

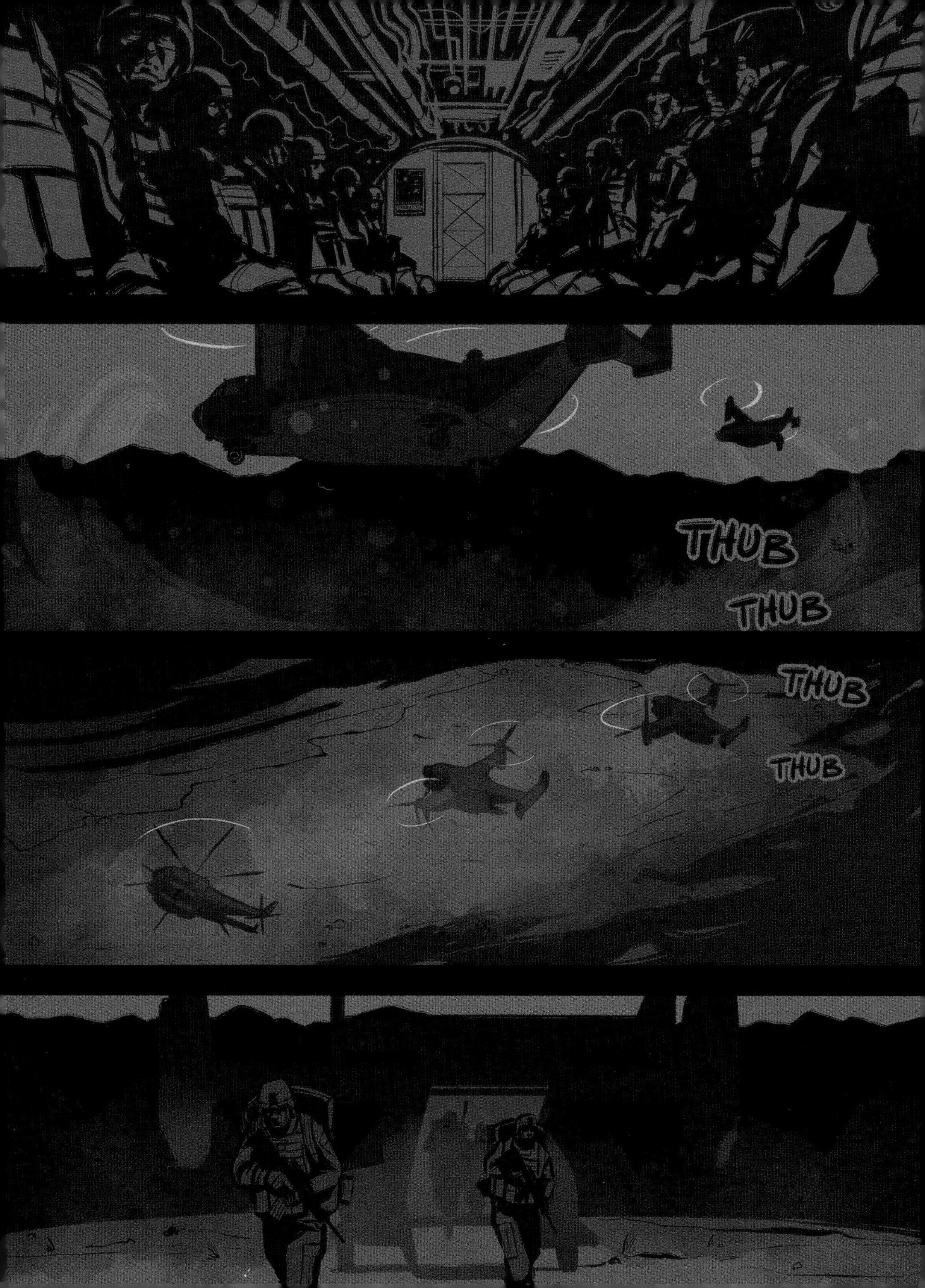
THUB
THUB
THUB
THUB

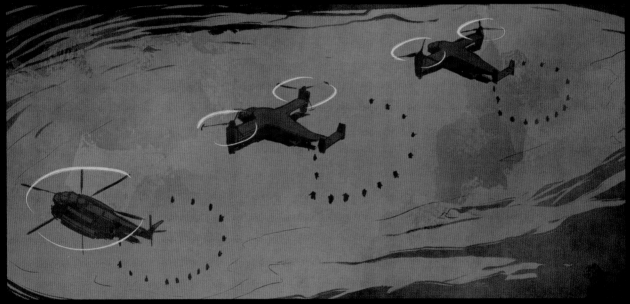

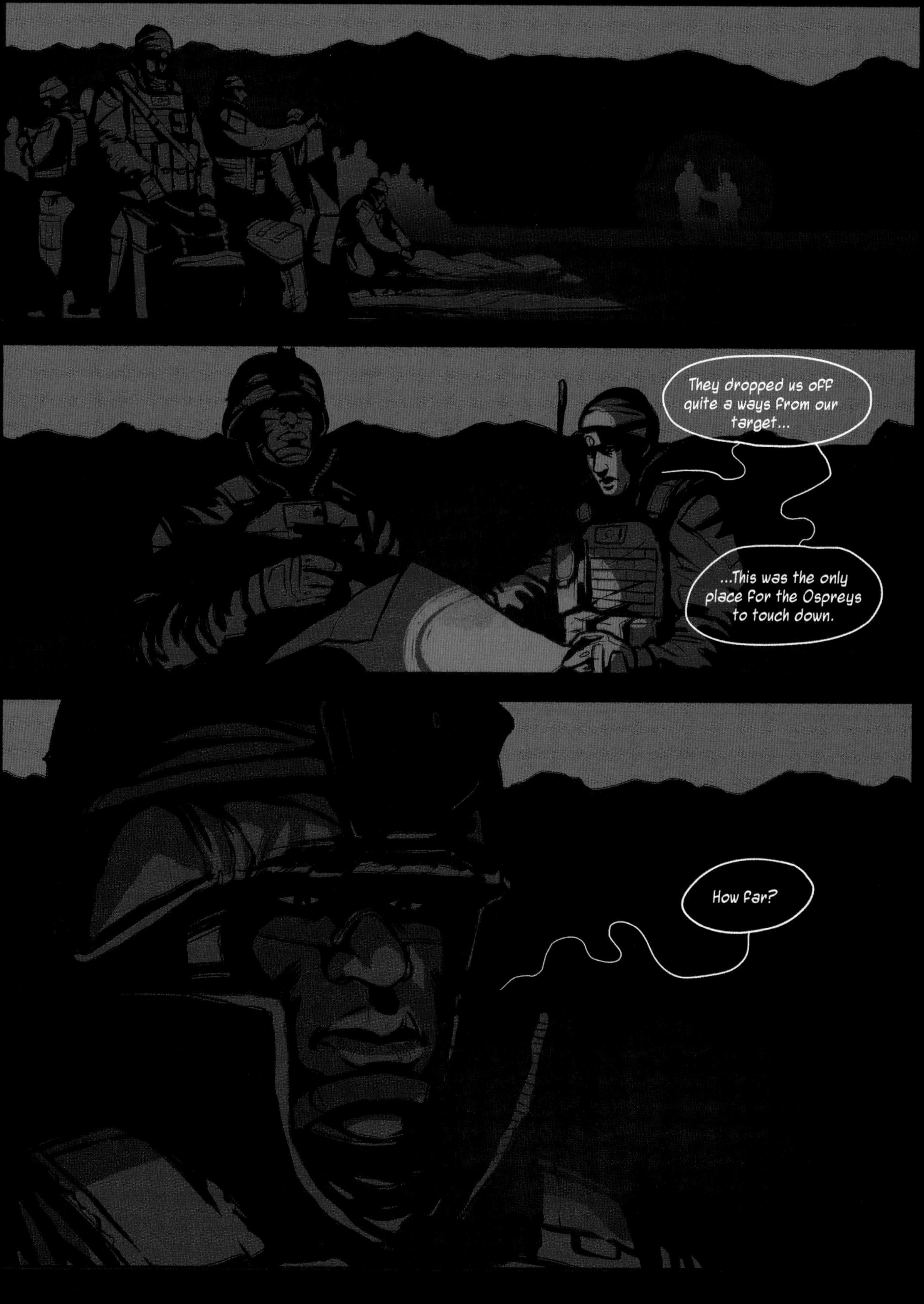
They dropped us off quite a ways from our target...
...This was the only place for the Ospreys to touch down.
How far?

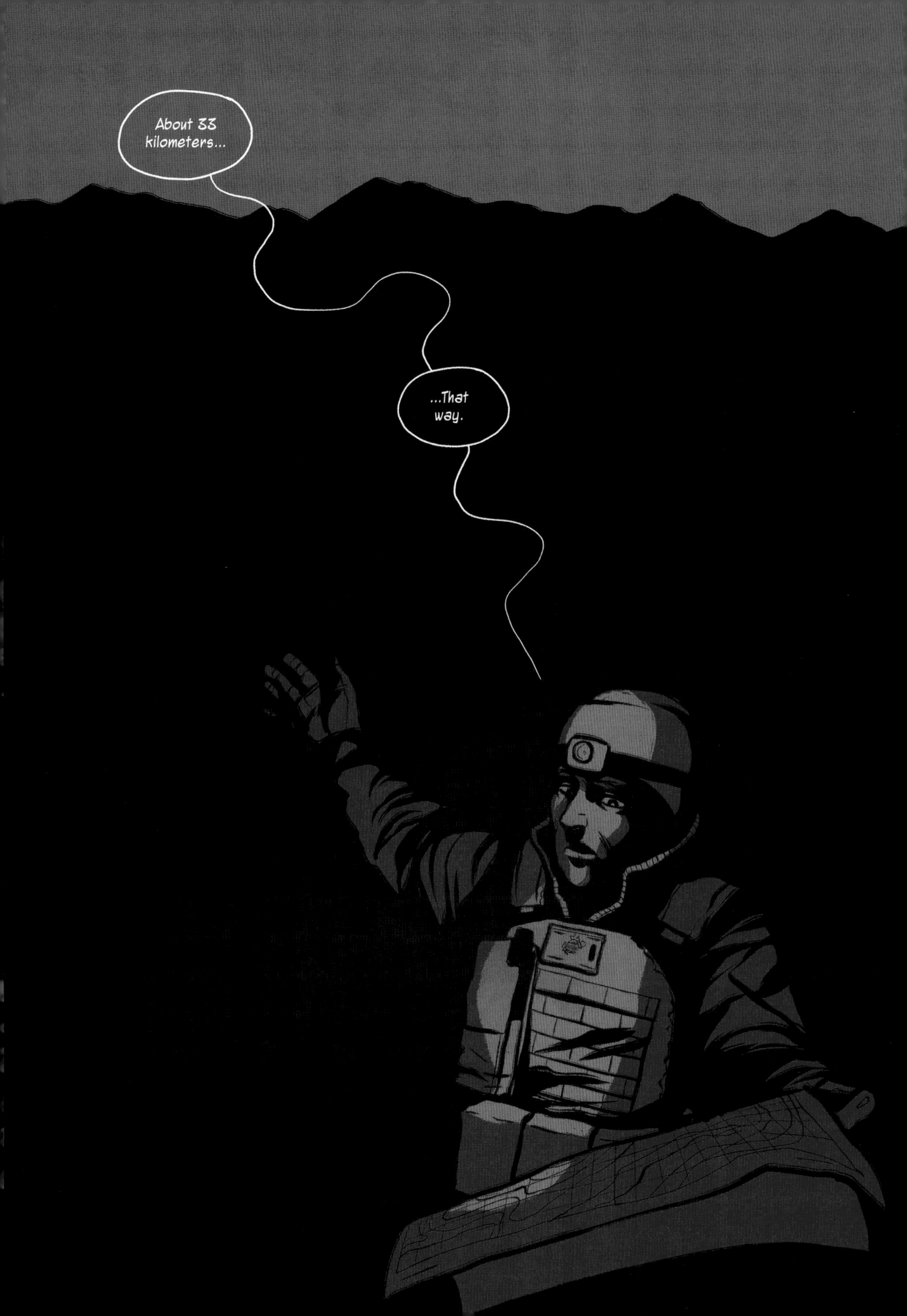
About 33 kilometers...
...That way.

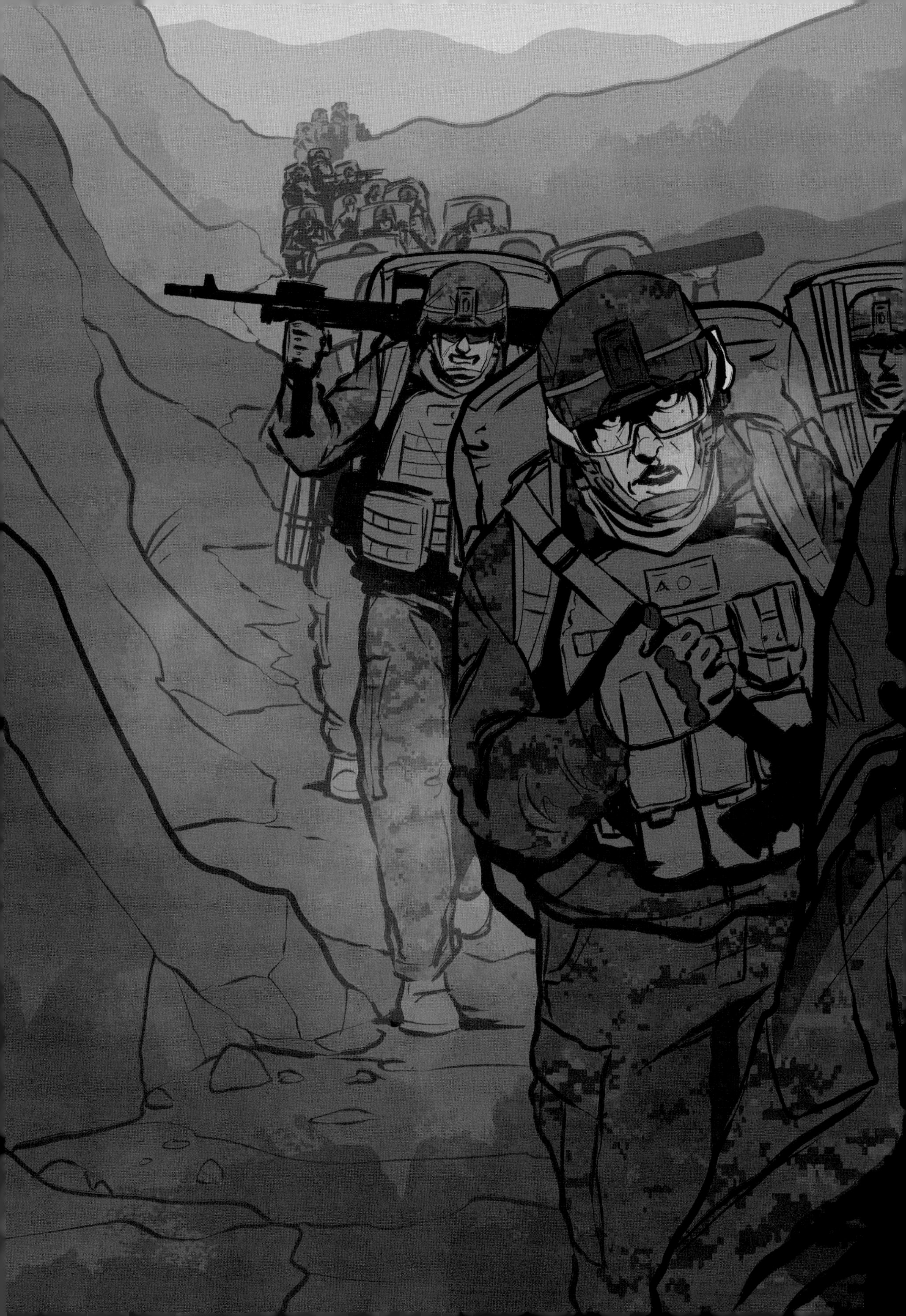

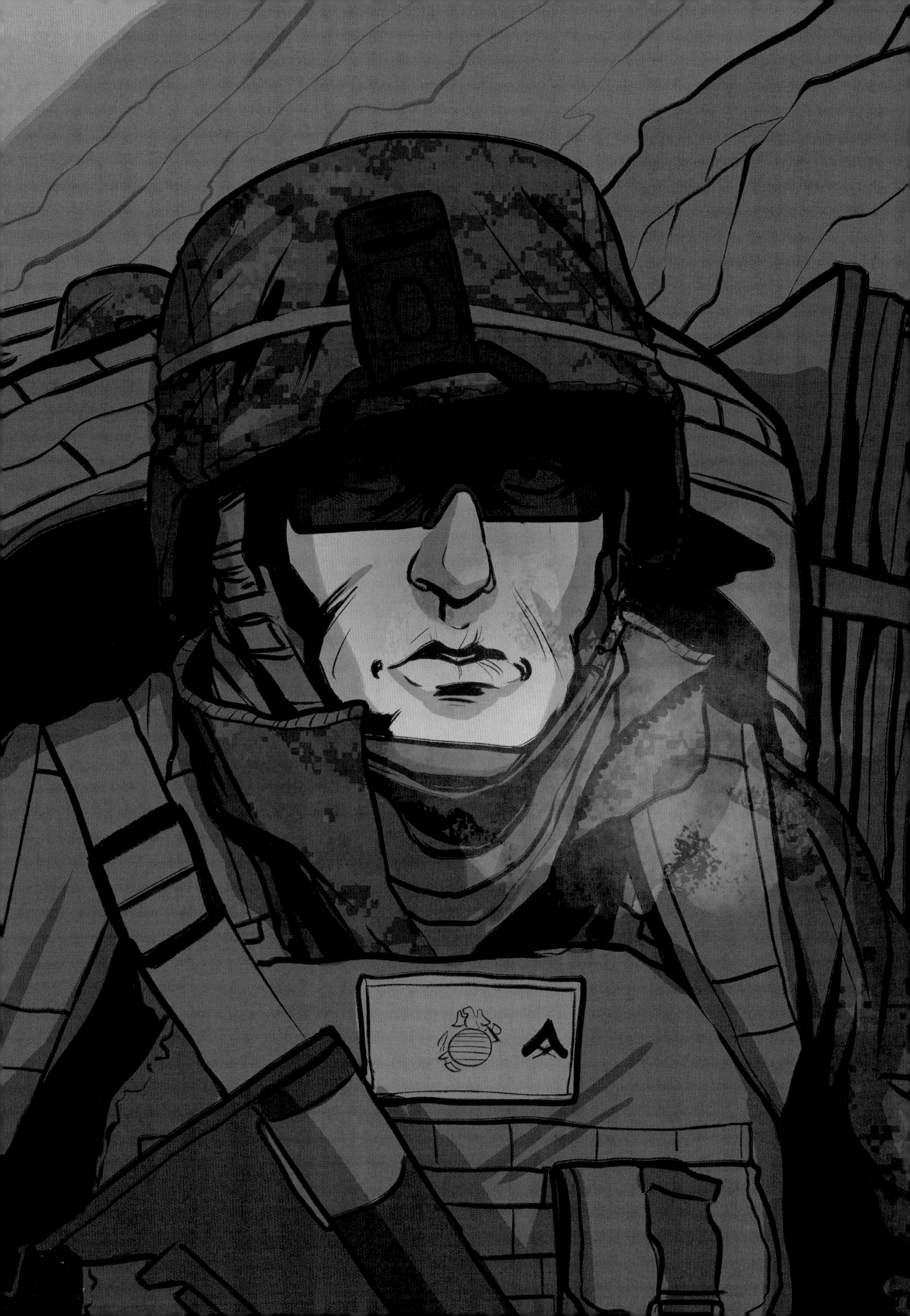

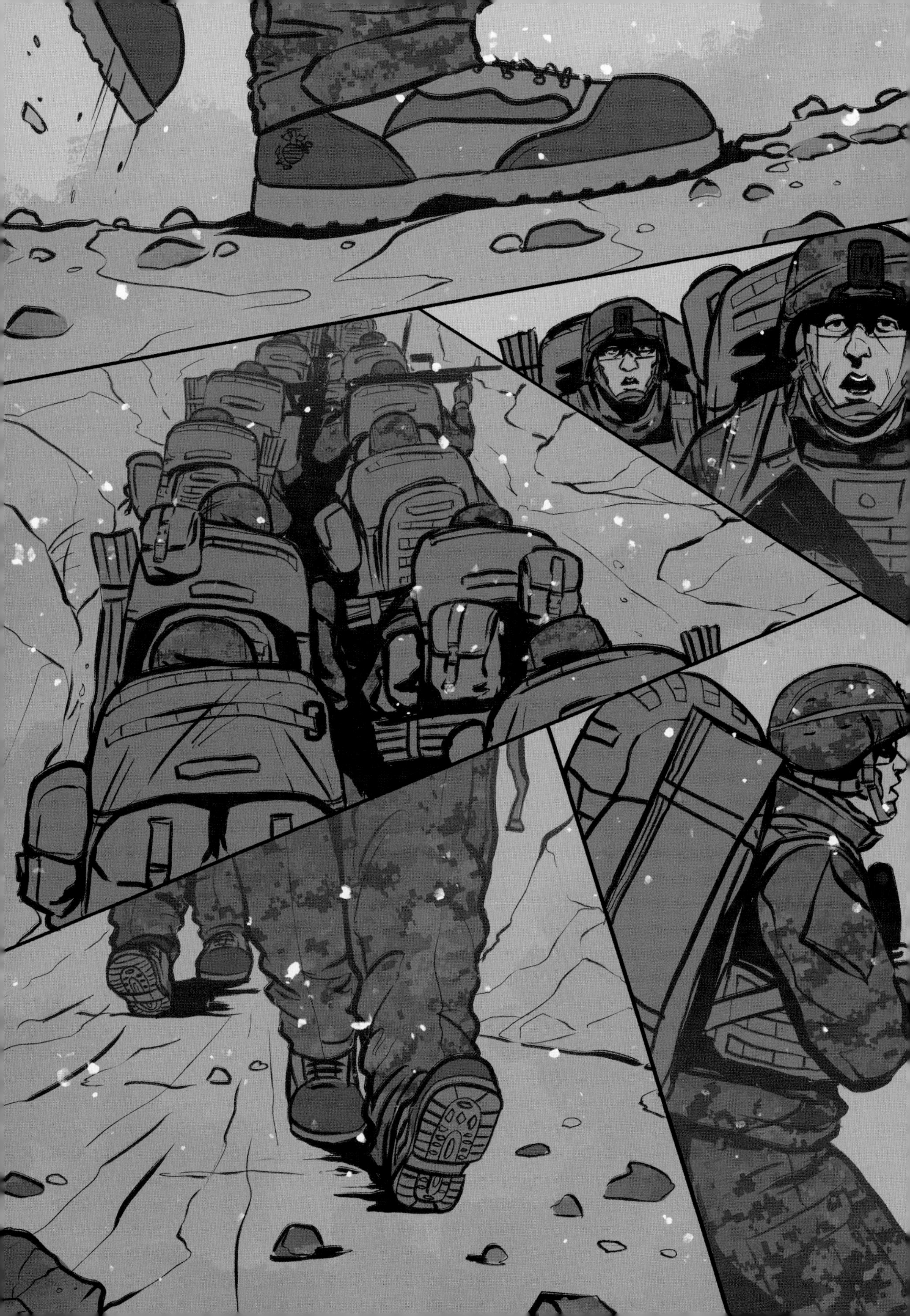

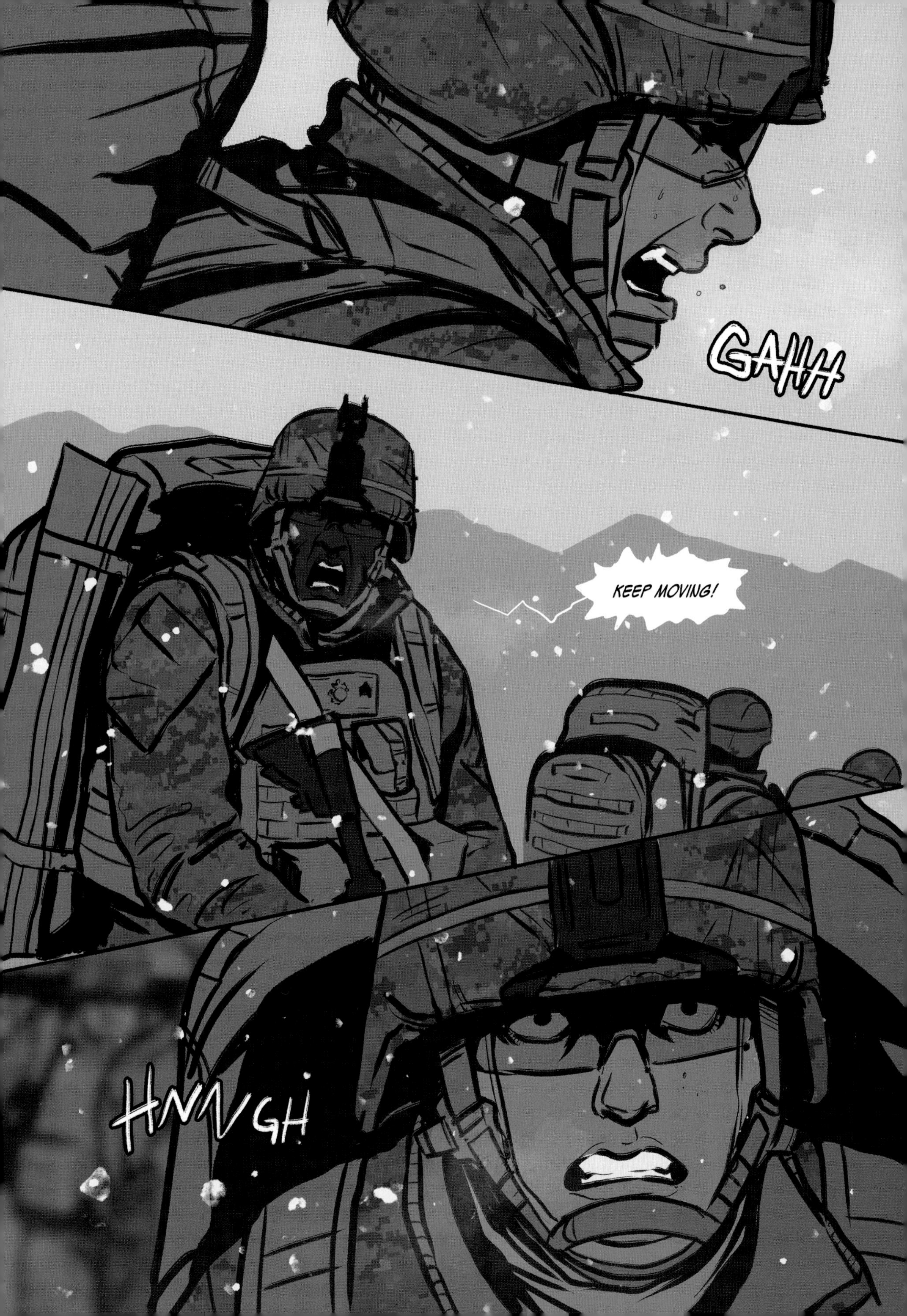
GAHH
KEEP MOVING!
HNNGH

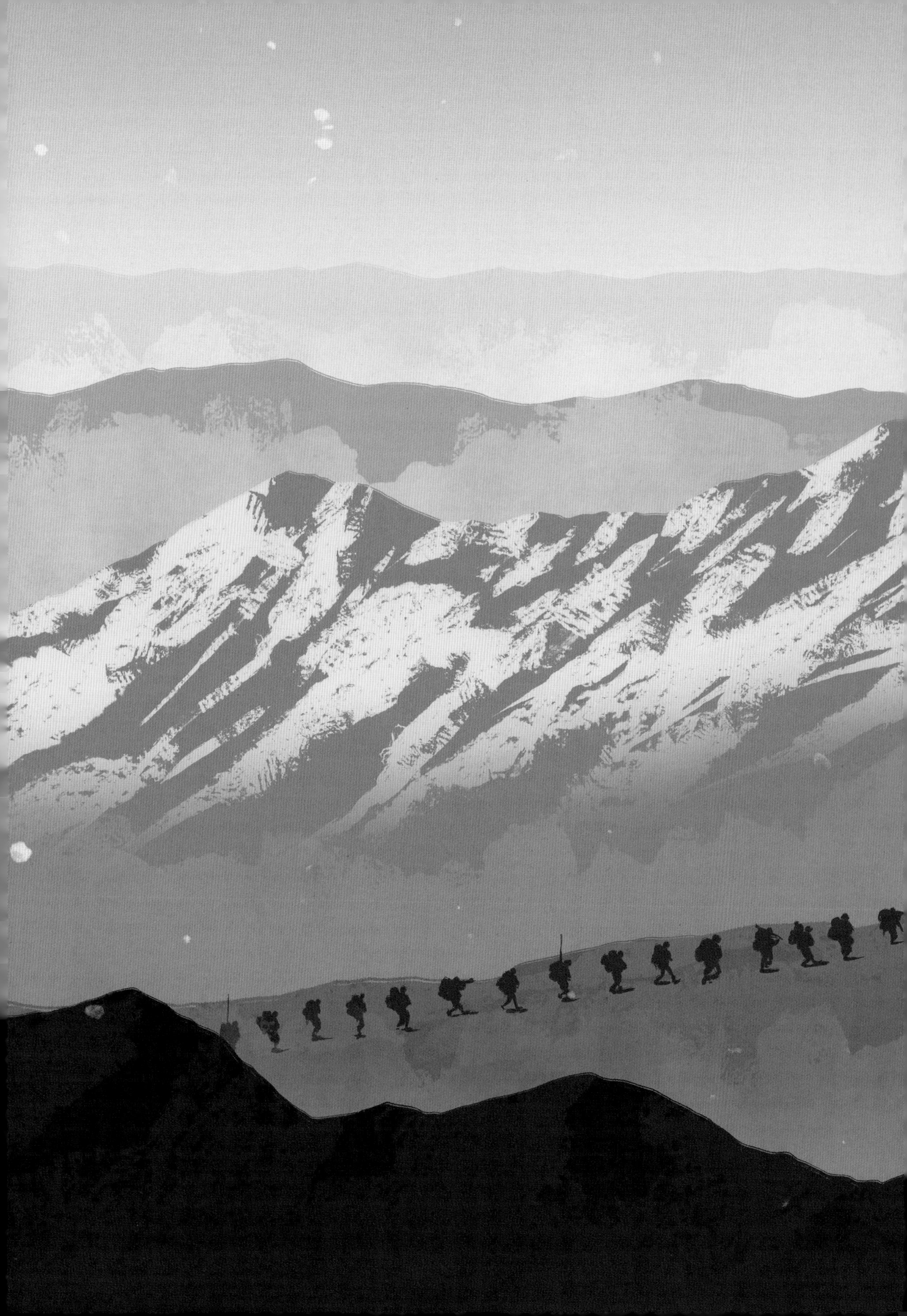

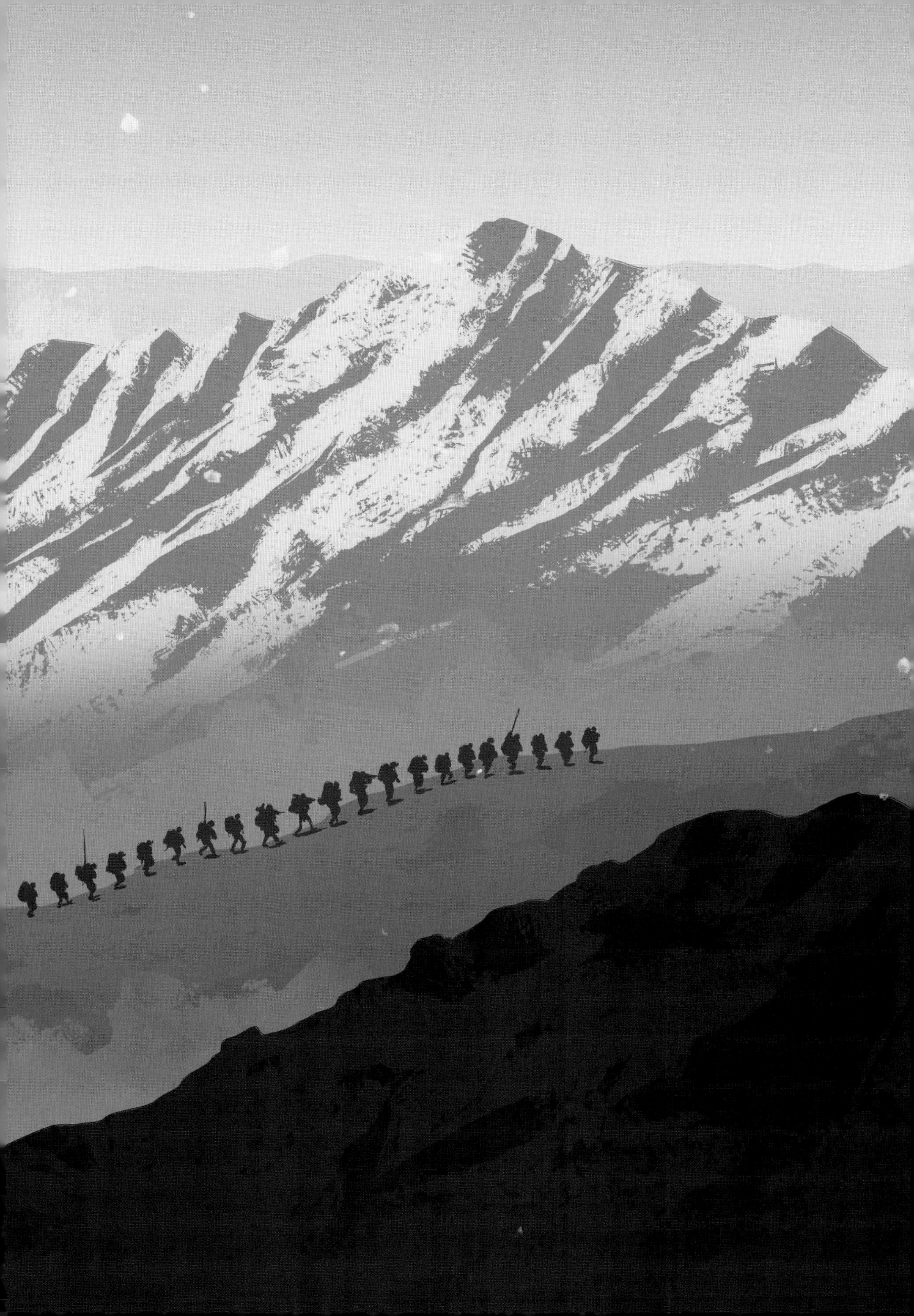

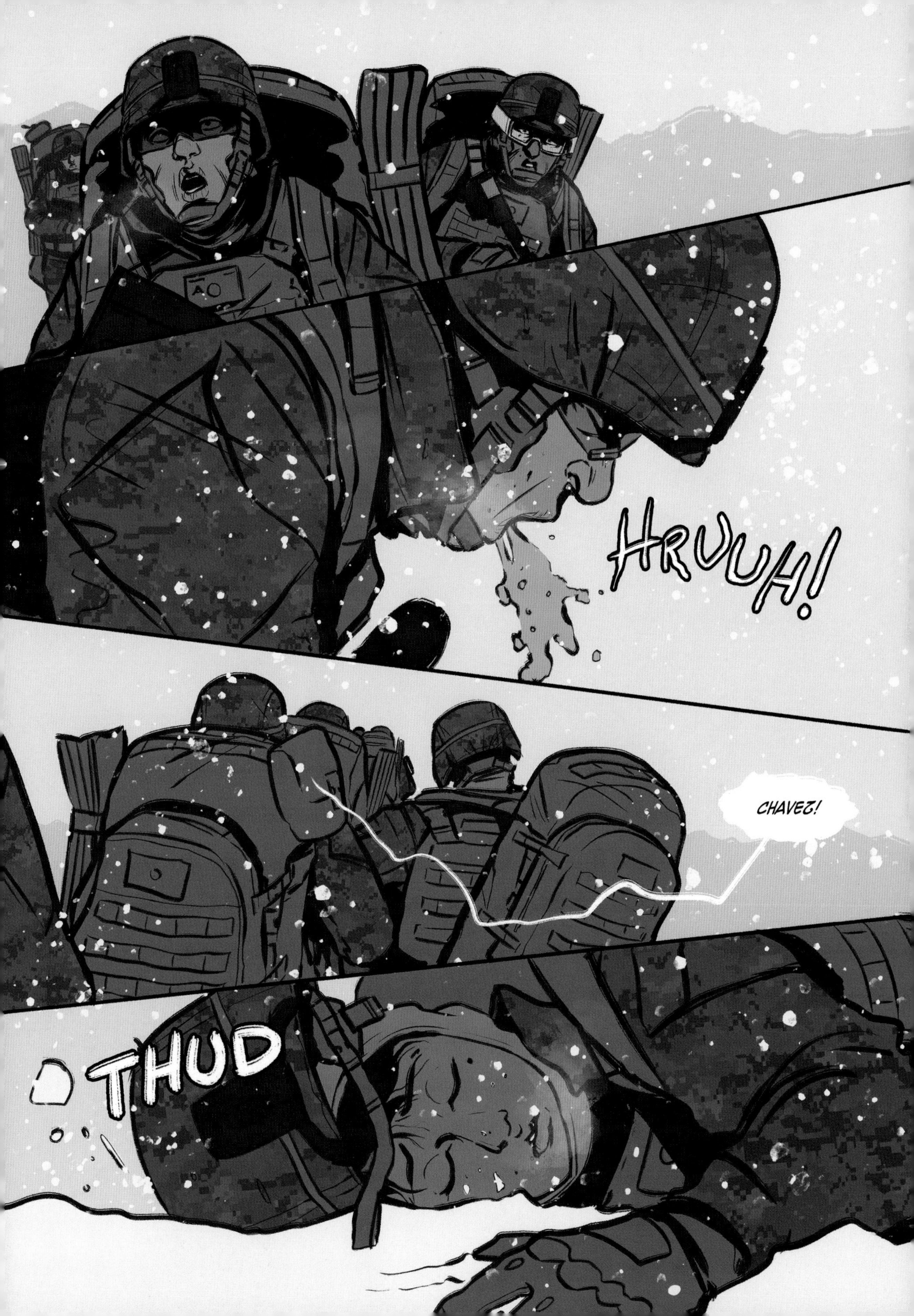
HRUUH!
CHAVEZ!
THUD

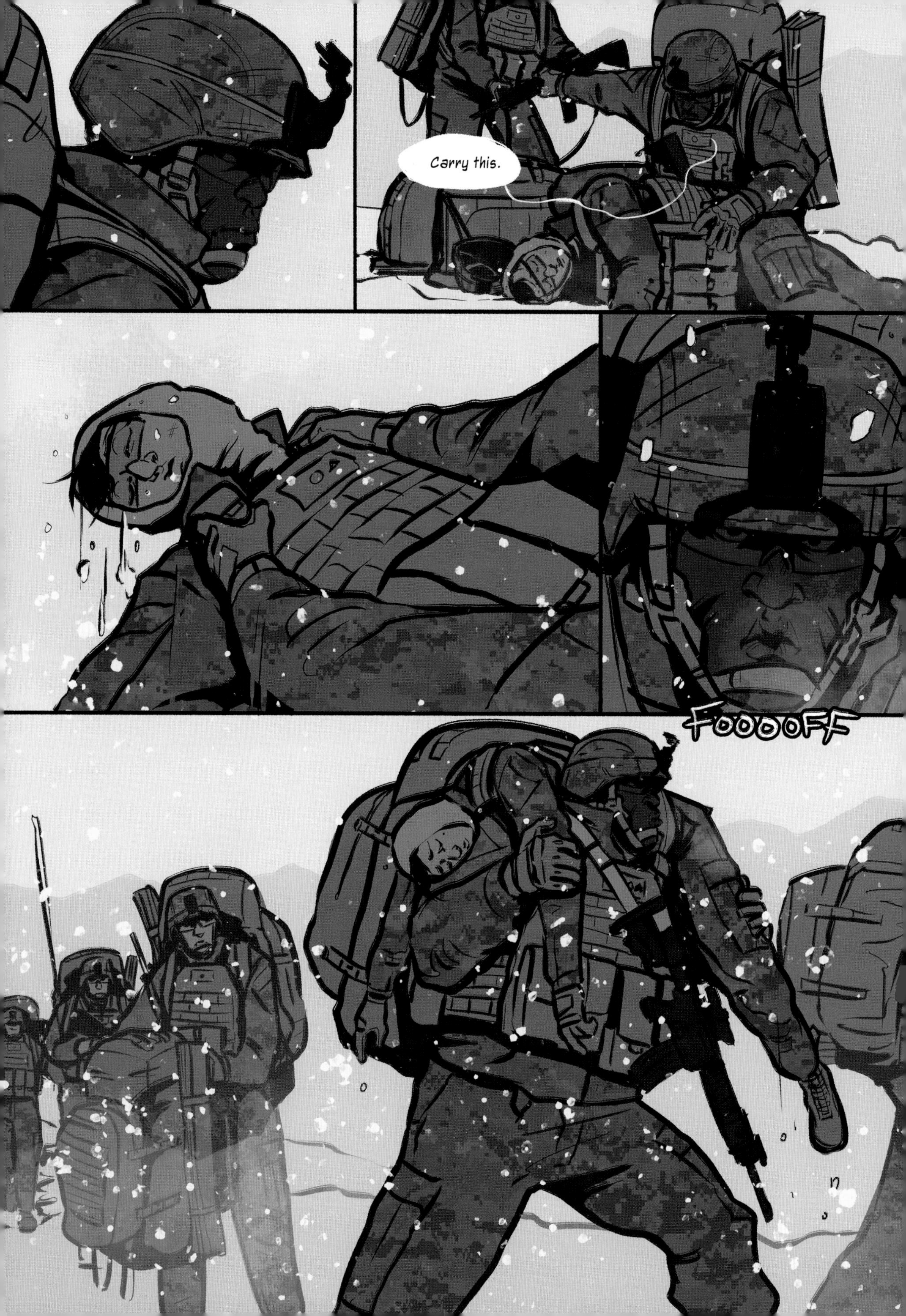
Carry this.
FOOOOFF

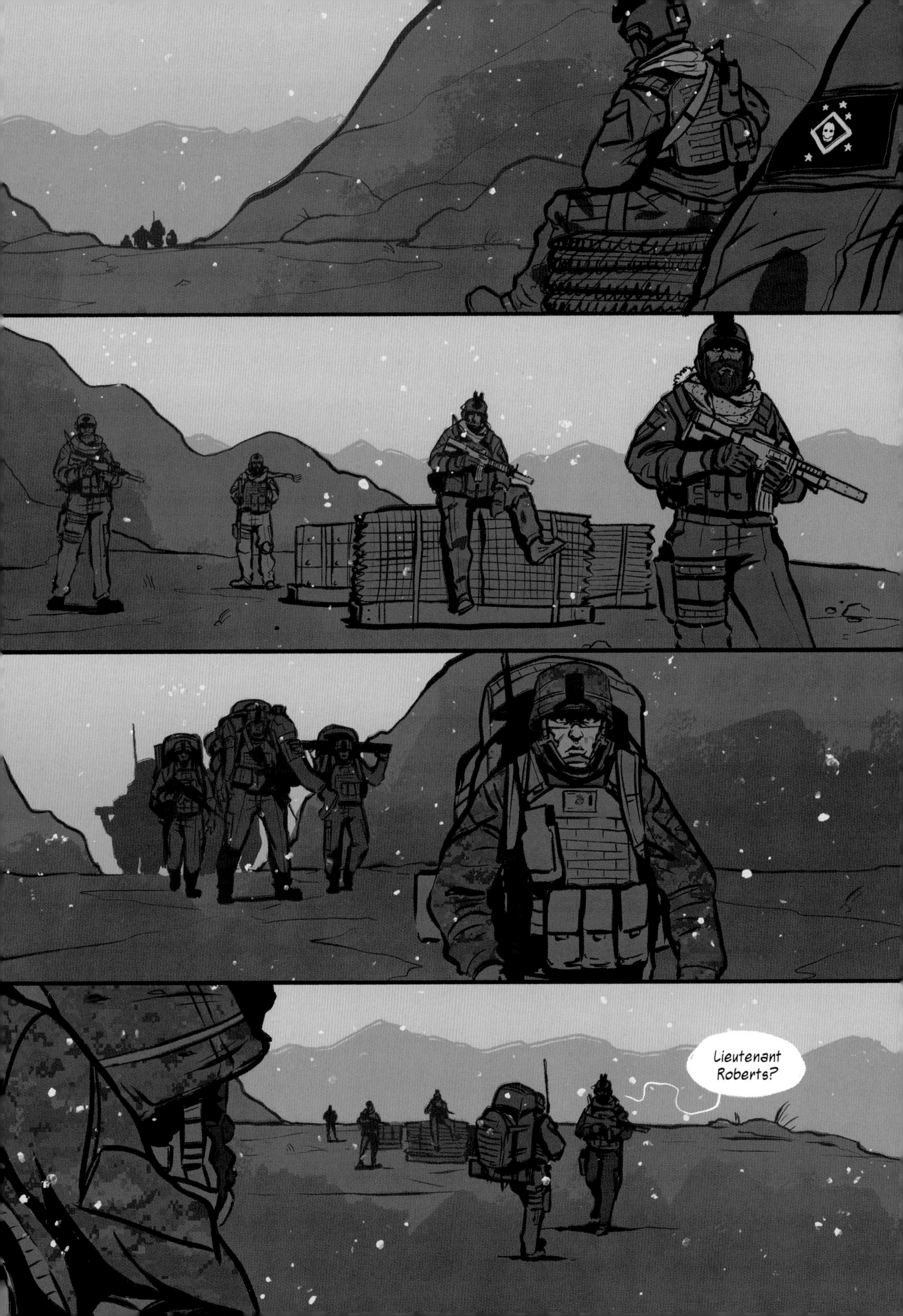
Lieutenant Roberts?

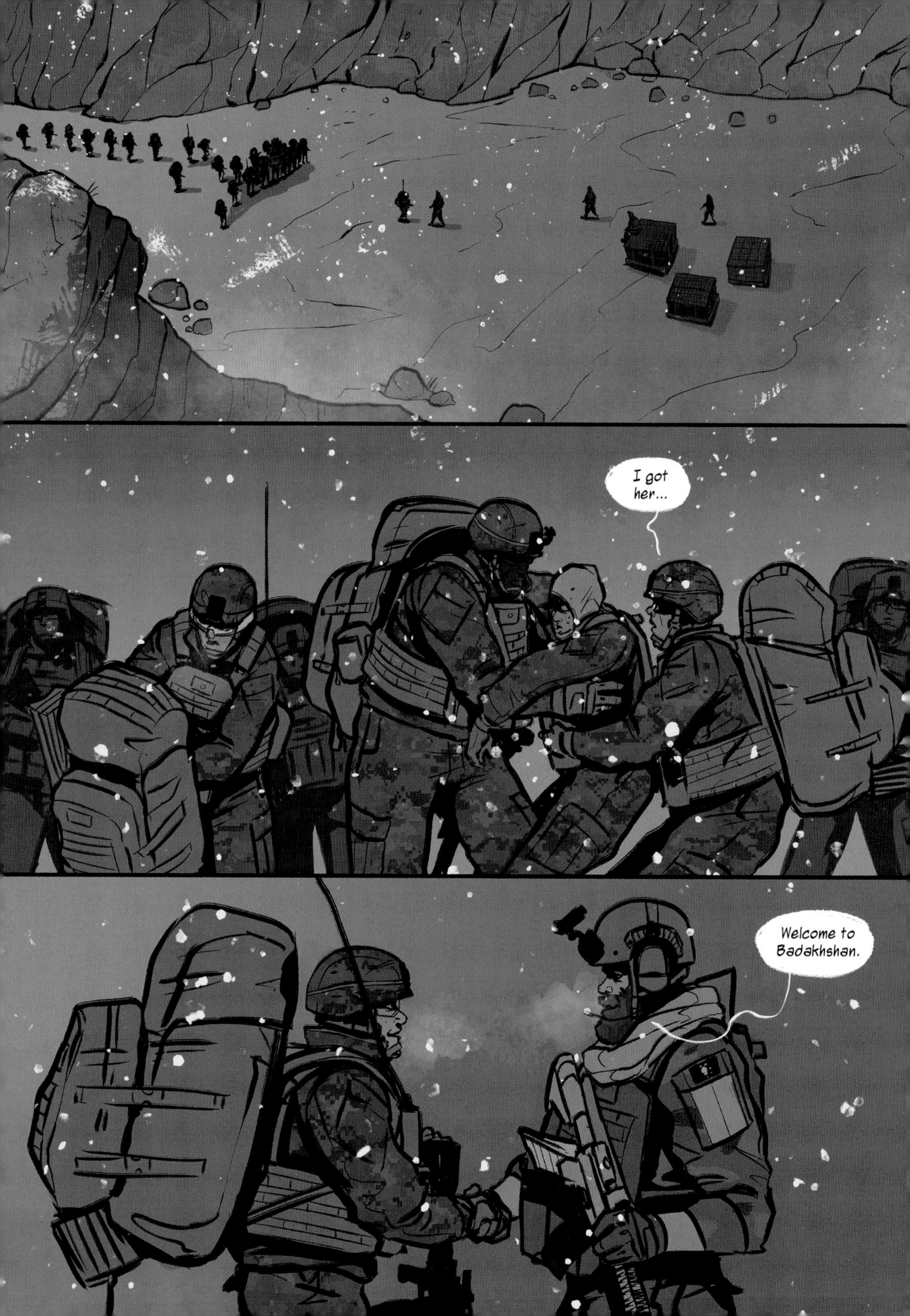
I got her...
Welcome to Badakhshan.

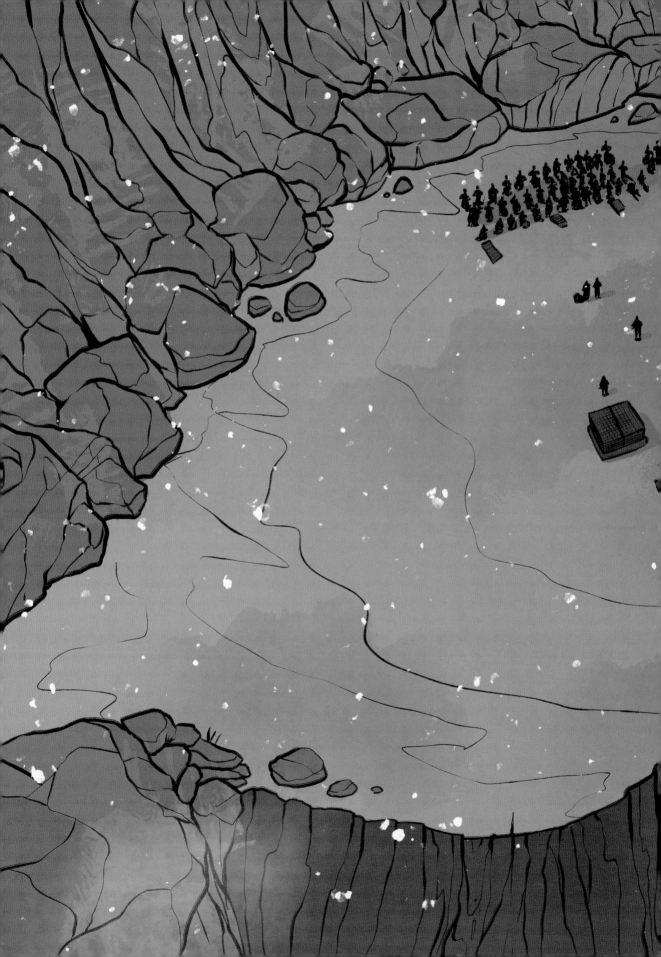

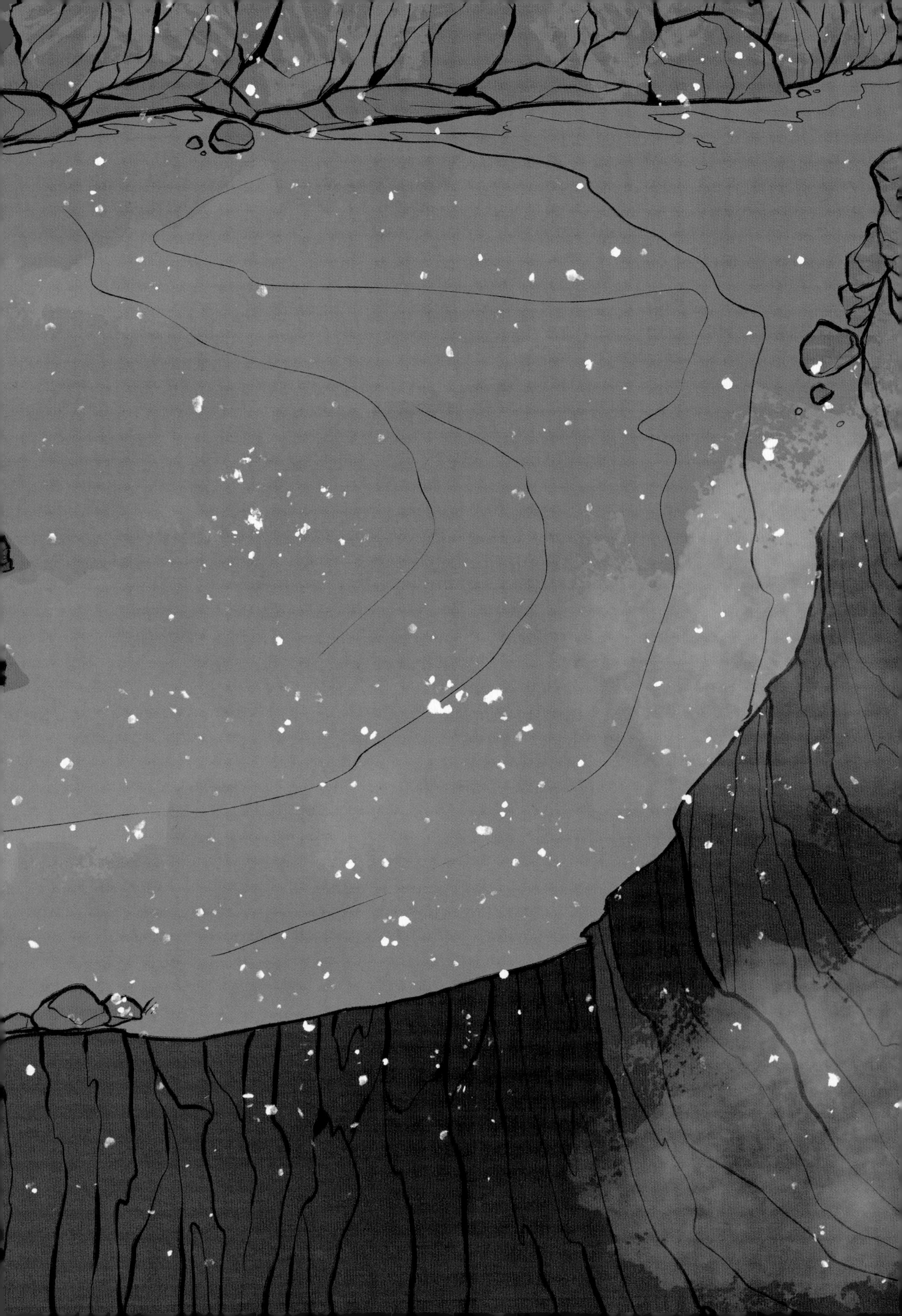

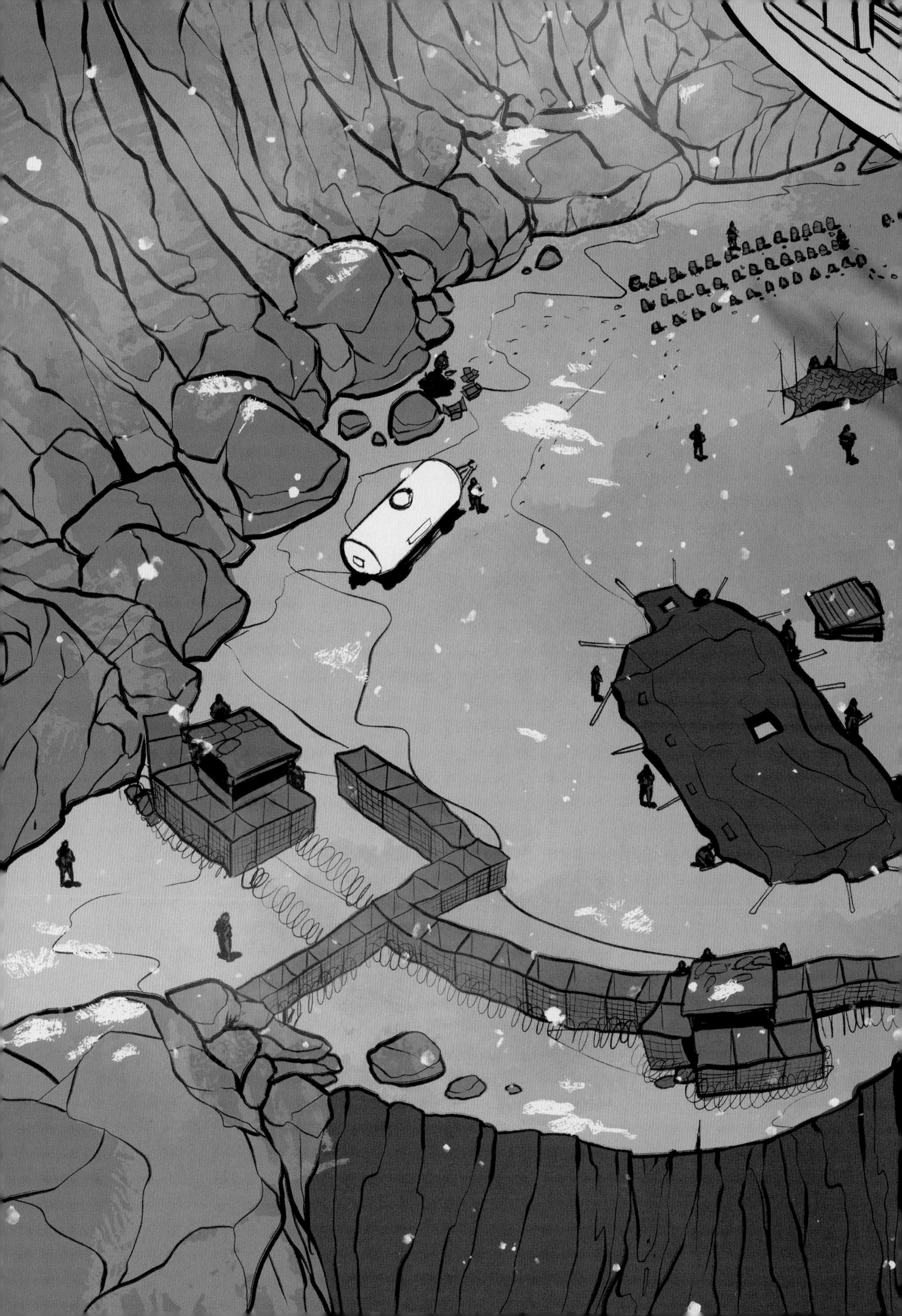

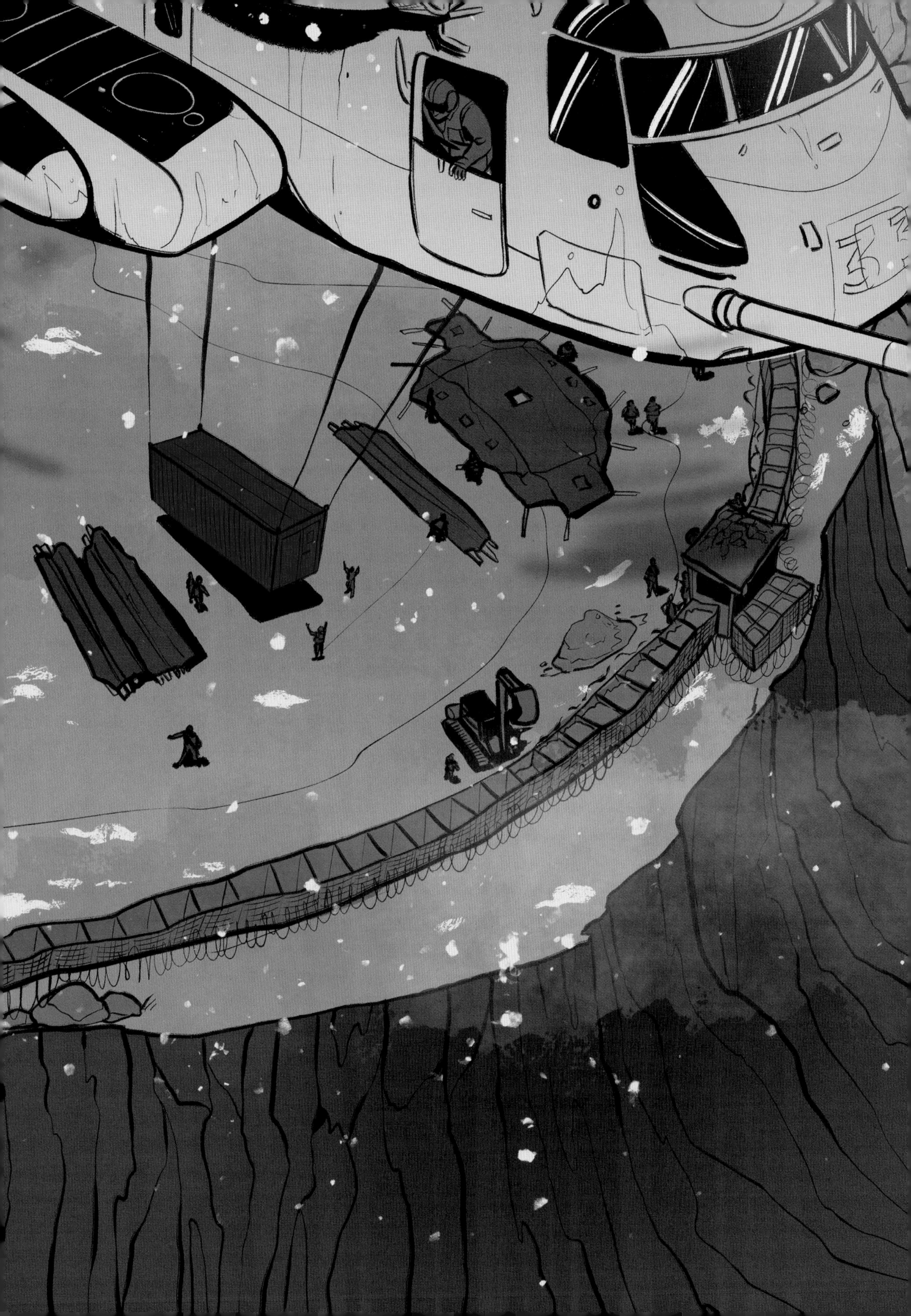

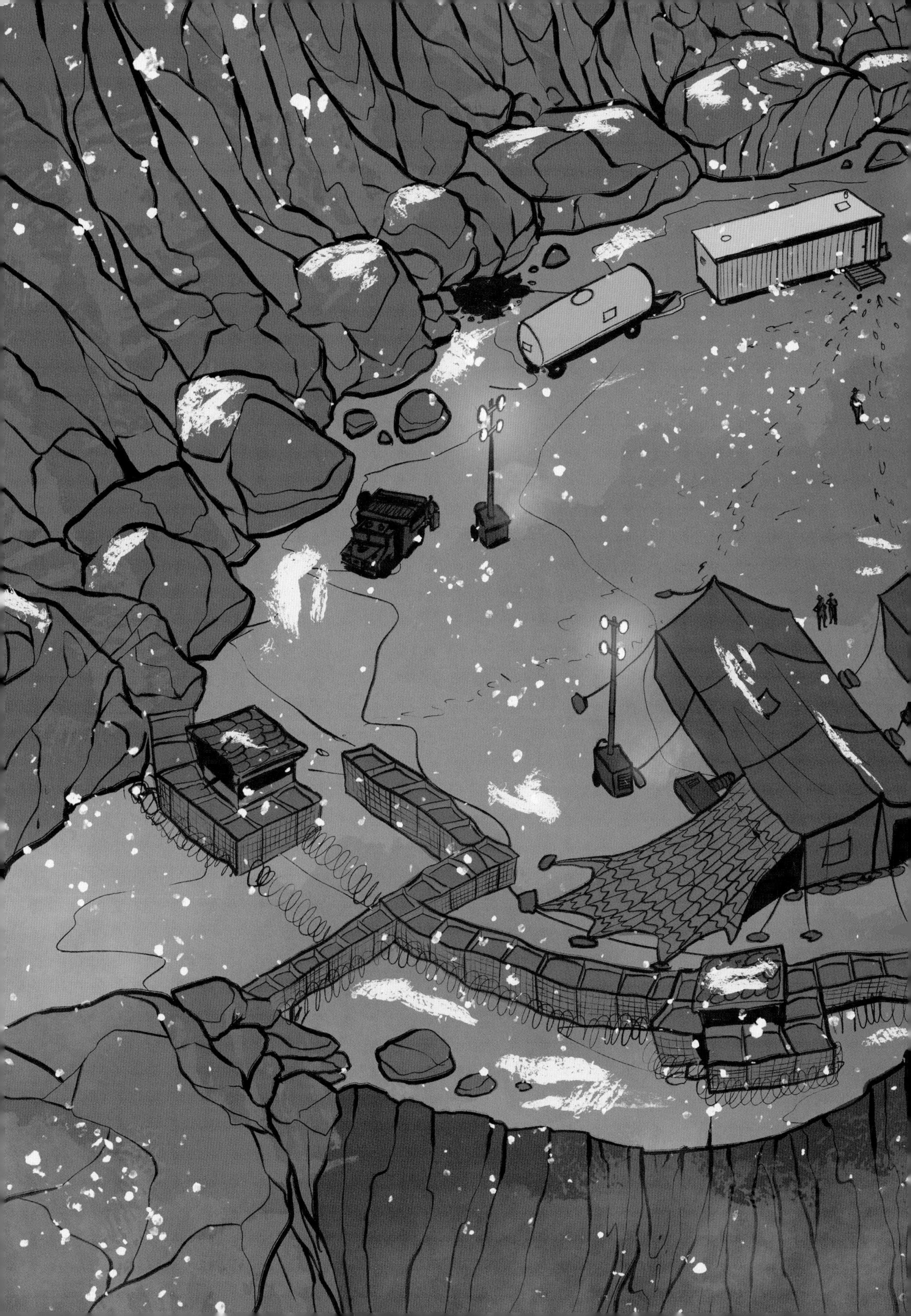

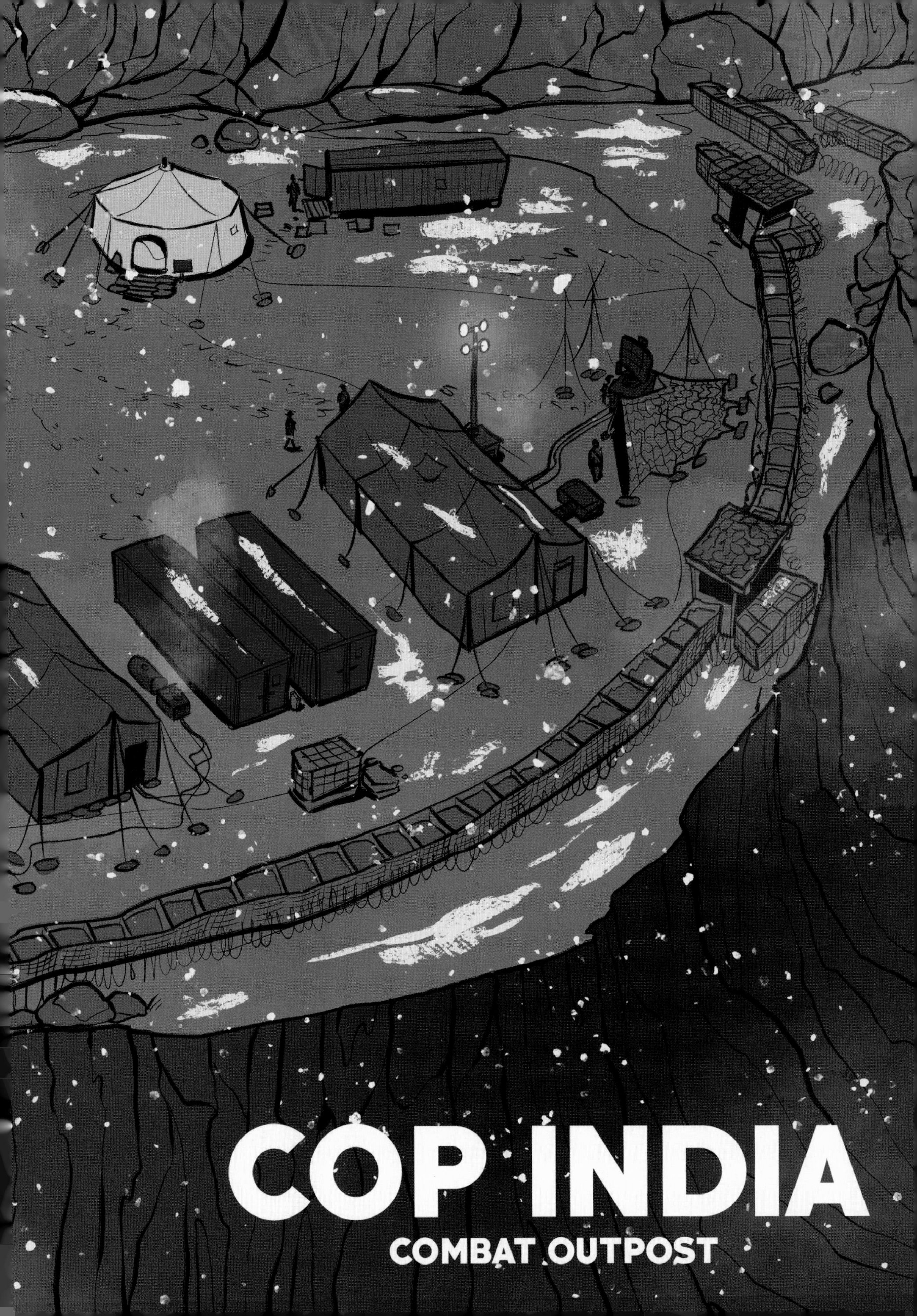
COP INDIA
COMBAT OUTPOST

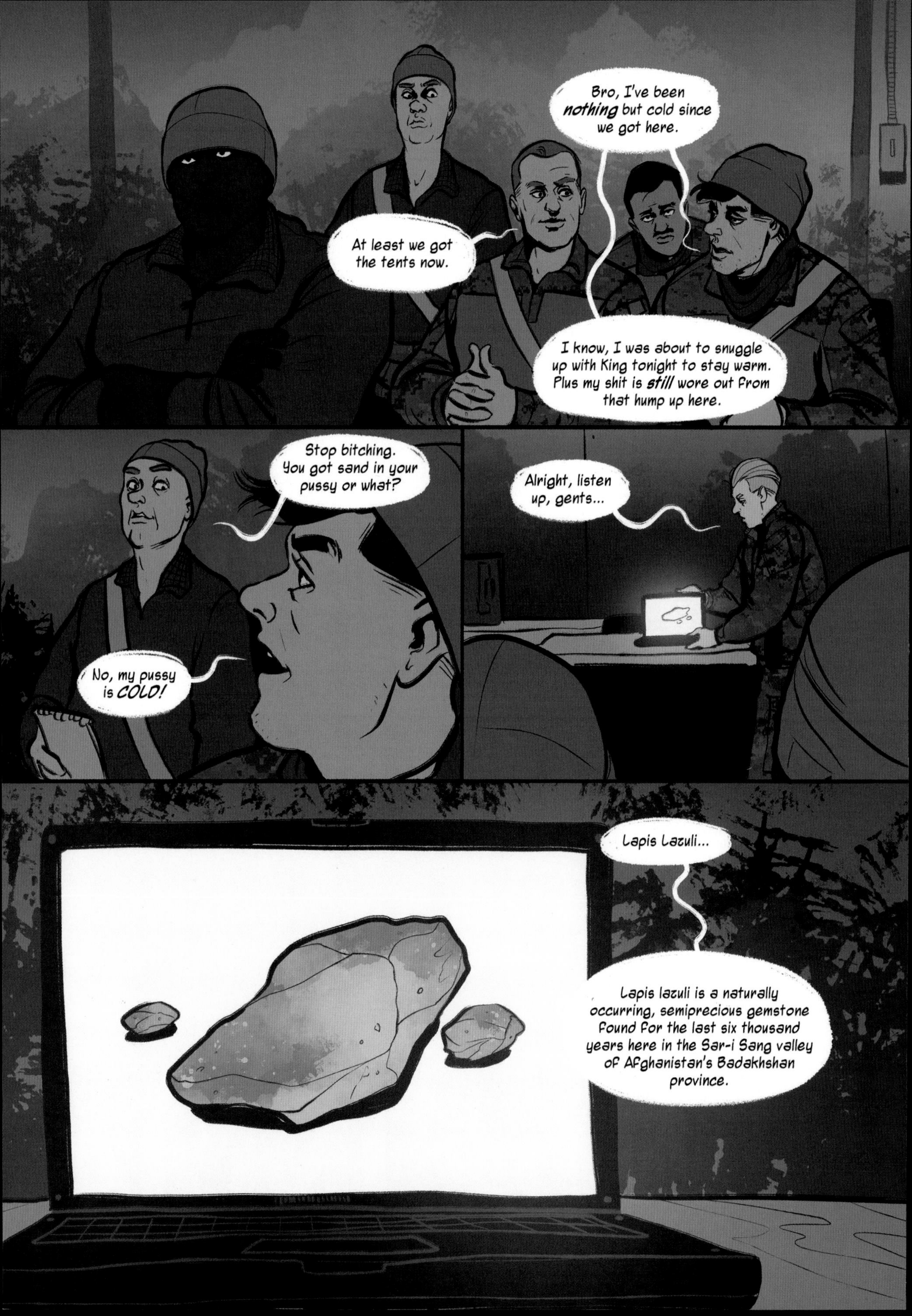
Bro, I've been *nothing* but cold since we got here.
At least we got the tents now.
I know, I was about to snuggle up with King tonight to stay warm. Plus my shit is *still* wore out from that hump up here.
Stop bitching. You got sand in your pussy or what?
No, my pussy is *COLD!*
Alright, listen up, gents...
Lapis Lazuli...
Lapis lazuli is a naturally occurring, semiprecious gemstone found for the last six thousand years here in the Sar-i Sang valley of Afghanistan's Badakhshan province.

More importantly though, lapis lazuli is one of Afghanistan's biggest exports, and an important part of the Afghan economy, along with other minerals and gemstones. Until recently, this region had been relatively untouched by the war...
However, in the last couple of years, the Taliban discovered the treasure trove of gems here and have been strong-arming the local population for the stones and selling them on the black market. It is estimated now that up to twenty-five percent of the Taliban's annual revenue comes from illegal mining and gem sales from Badakhshan province, and most of that is lapis lazuli.
The Afghan government has requested the help of the United States military with the situation, which is where we find ourselves today. Our mission is to deter the Taliban from the lapis mining operations and restore order to the local officials. Unlike other parts of Afghanistan, the people here haven't really been exposed to Americans. They don't have a reason to love or hate us, so let's start off on a good foot...
Any questions?

Sir?
Are we getting porta-shitters or are we gonna keep shitting in buckets like savages?
...No word on that for now, Sergeant Doughtie. Rest assured, we're doing our best to bring some comforts of the first world to you all. We may even have hot chow within a few weeks.
If there's nothing else, you guys should get some rest. We officially begin operations tomorrow. We need to find out as much information as we can about the gemstone trade here. I think the market is a good place to start.

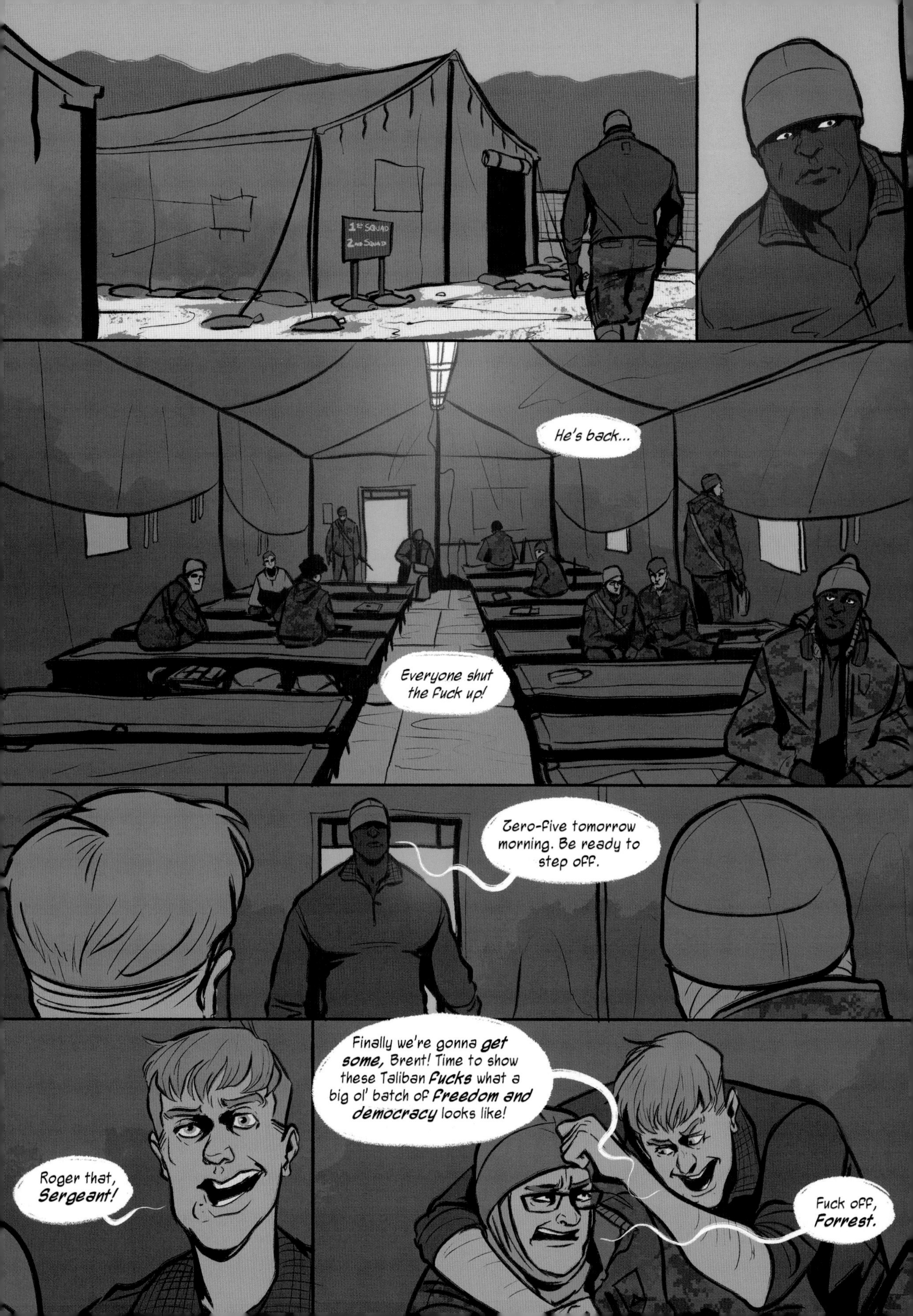

1st SQUAD
2nd SQUAD
He's back...
Everyone shut the fuck up!
Zero-five tomorrow morning. Be ready to step off.
Roger that, Sergeant!
Finally we're gonna get some, Brent! Time to show these Taliban fucks what a big ol' batch of freedom and democracy looks like!
Fuck off, Forrest.

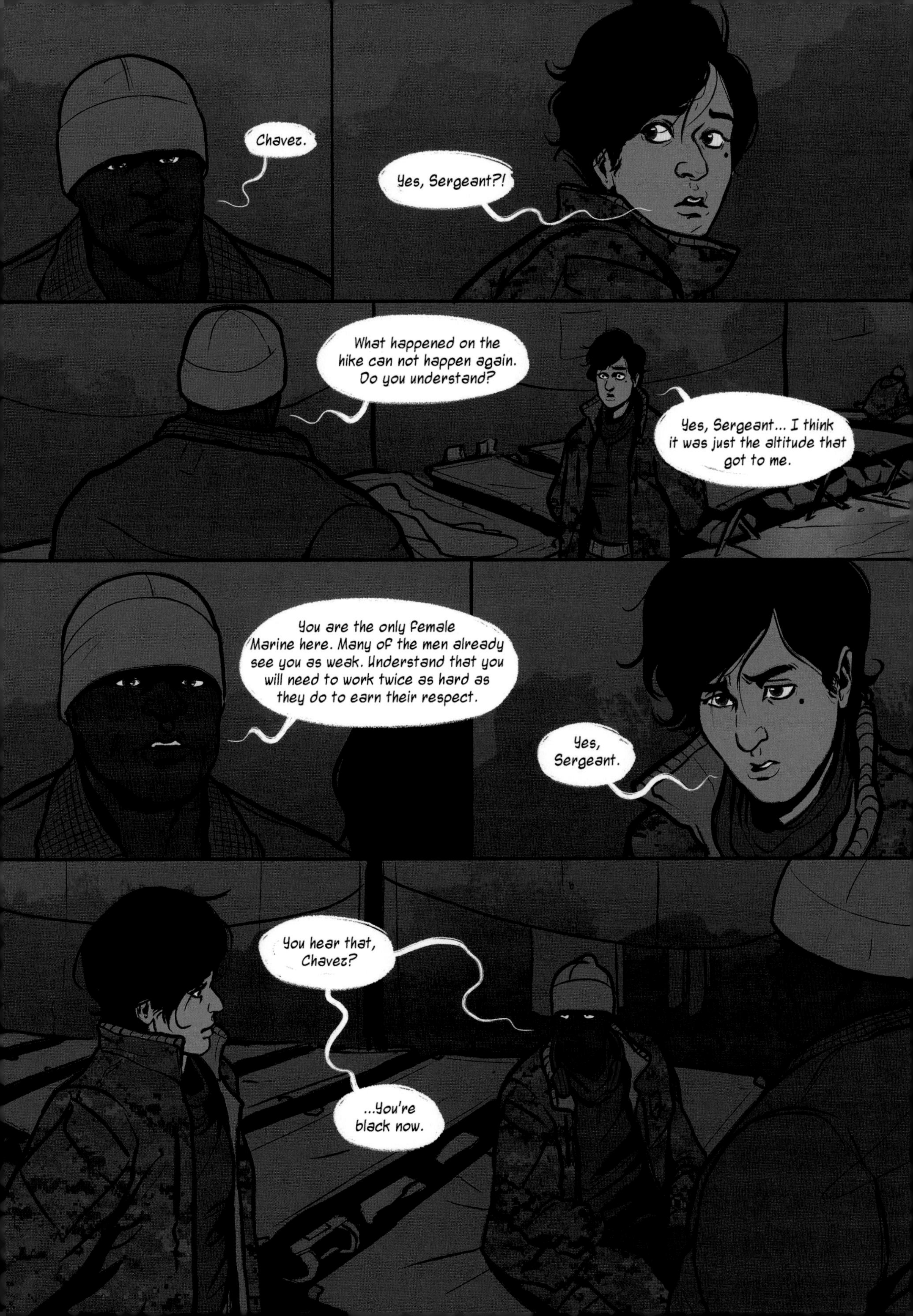
Chavez.
Yes, Sergeant?!
What happened on the hike can not happen again. Do you understand?
Yes, Sergeant... I think it was just the altitude that got to me.
You are the only female Marine here. Many of the men already see you as weak. Understand that you will need to work twice as hard as they do to earn their respect.
Yes, Sergeant.
You hear that, Chavez?
...You're black now.

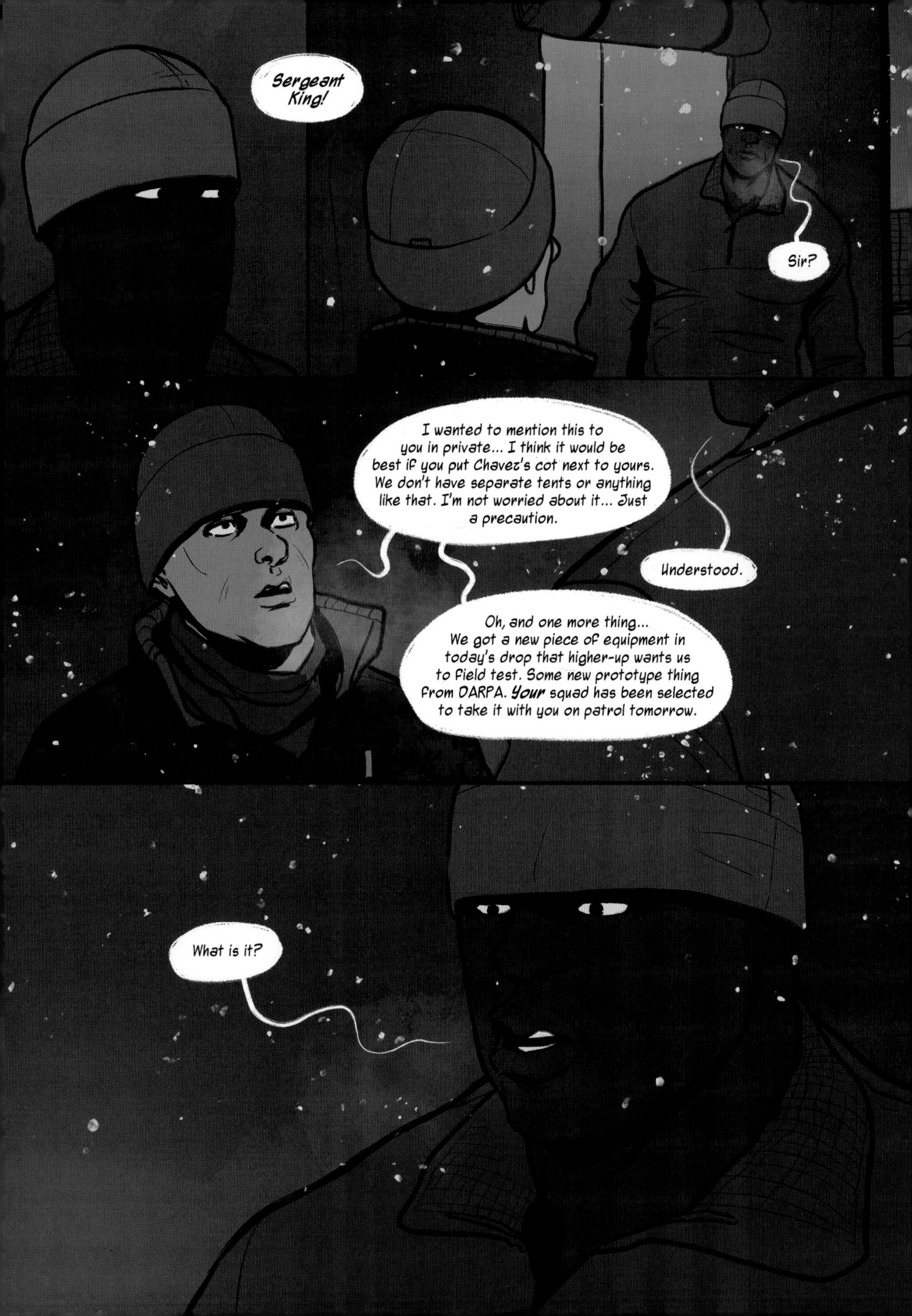
Sergeant King!
Sir?
I wanted to mention this to you in private... I think it would be best if you put Chavez's cot next to yours. We don't have separate tents or anything like that. I'm not worried about it... Just a precaution.
Understood.
Oh, and one more thing... We got a new piece of equipment in today's drop that higher-up wants us to field test. Some new prototype thing from DARPA. ***Your*** squad has been selected to take it with you on patrol tomorrow.
What is it?

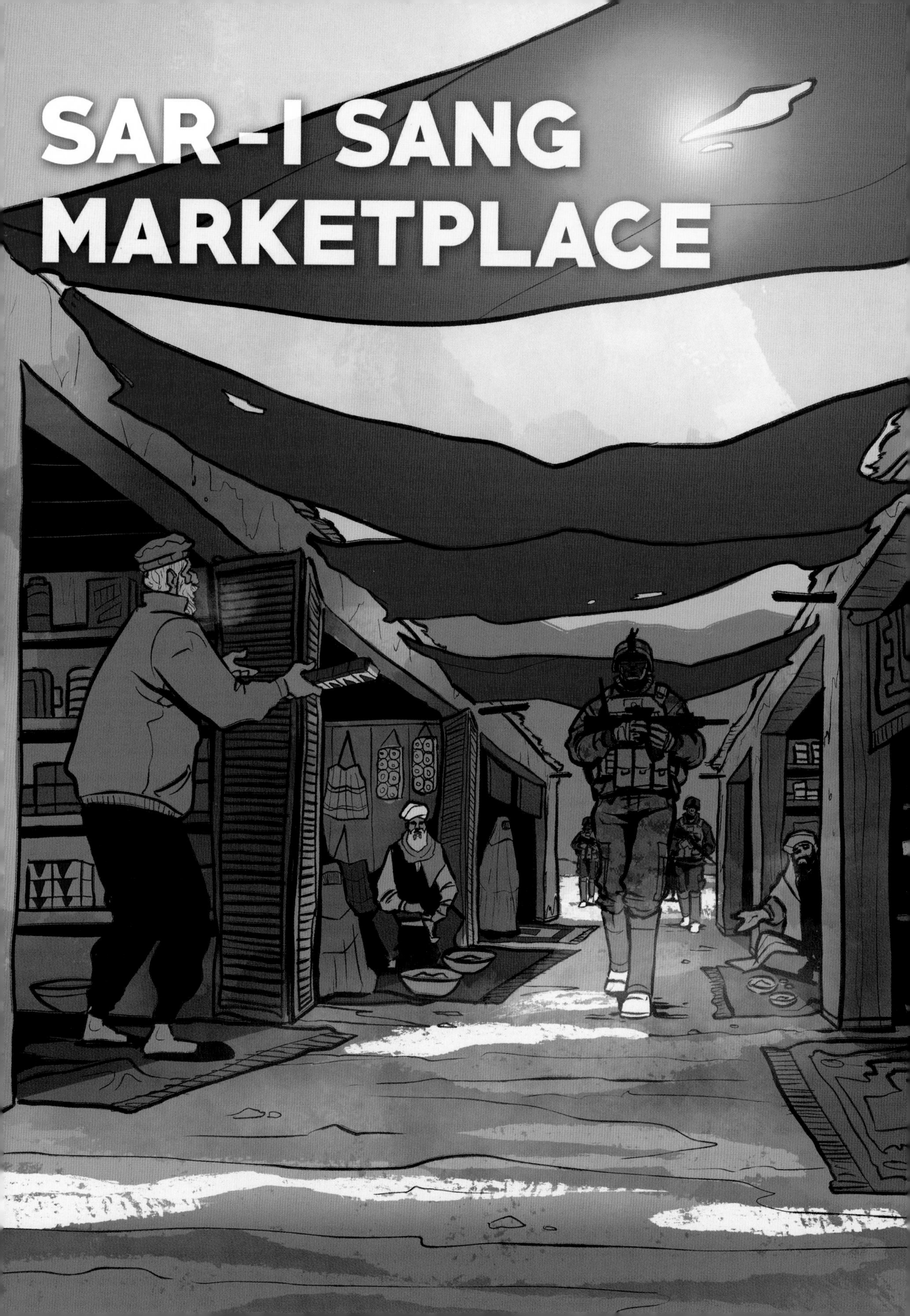
SAR-I SANG
MARKETPLACE

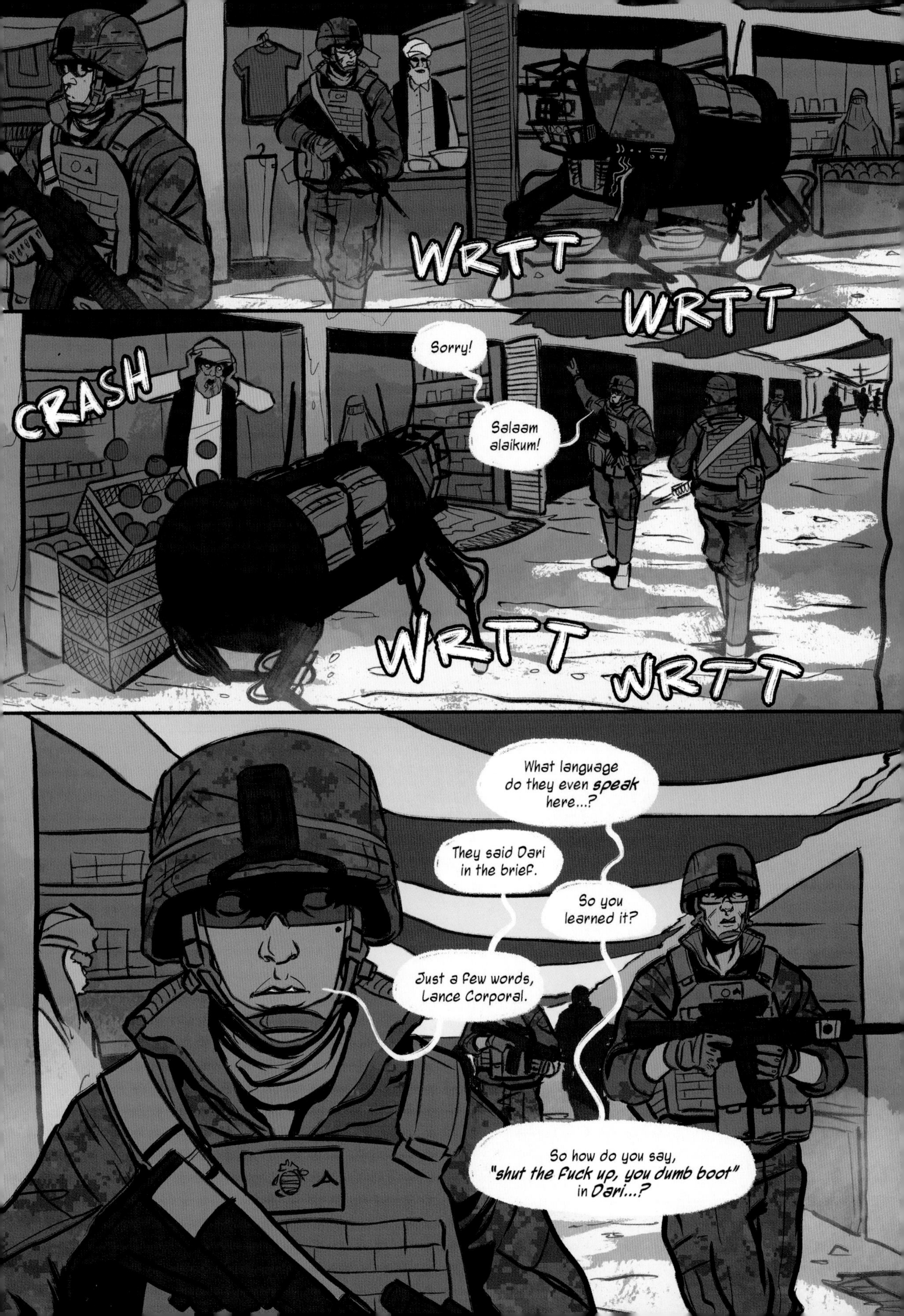
WRTT
WRTT
CRASH
Sorry!
Salaam alaikum!
WRTT
WRTT
What language do they even *speak* here...?
They said Dari in the brief.
So you learned it?
Just a few words, Lance Corporal.
So how do you say, ***"shut the fuck up, you dumb boot"*** in ***Dari...?***

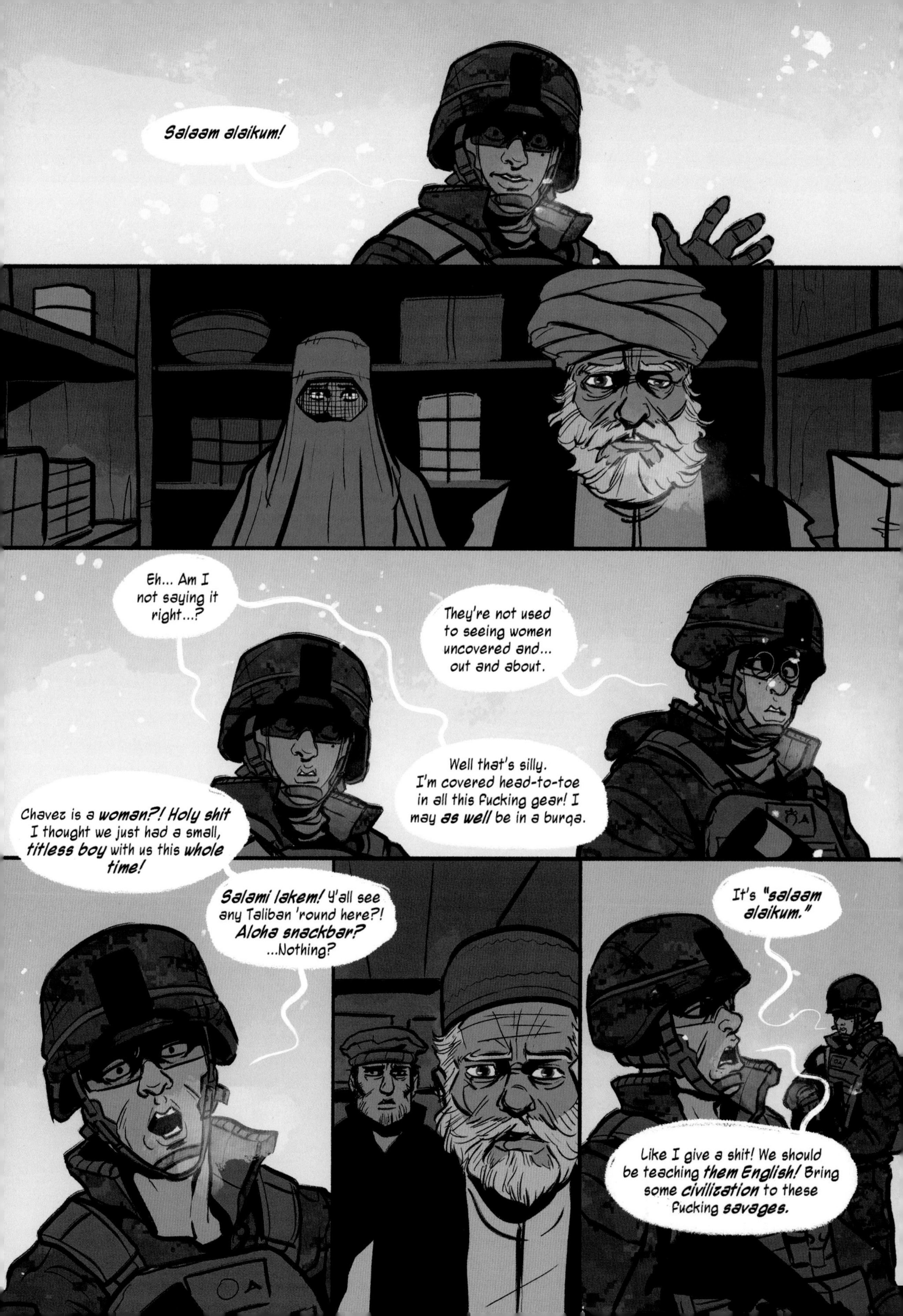

Salaam alaikum!
Eh... Am I not saying it right...?
They're not used to seeing women uncovered and... out and about.
Well that's silly. I'm covered head-to-toe in all this fucking gear! I may as well be in a burqa.
Chavez is a woman?! Holy shit I thought we just had a small, titless boy with us this whole time!
Salami lakem! Y'all see any Taliban 'round here?! Aloha snackbar? ...Nothing?
It's "salaam alaikum."
Like I give a shit! We should be teaching them English! Bring some civilization to these fucking savages.

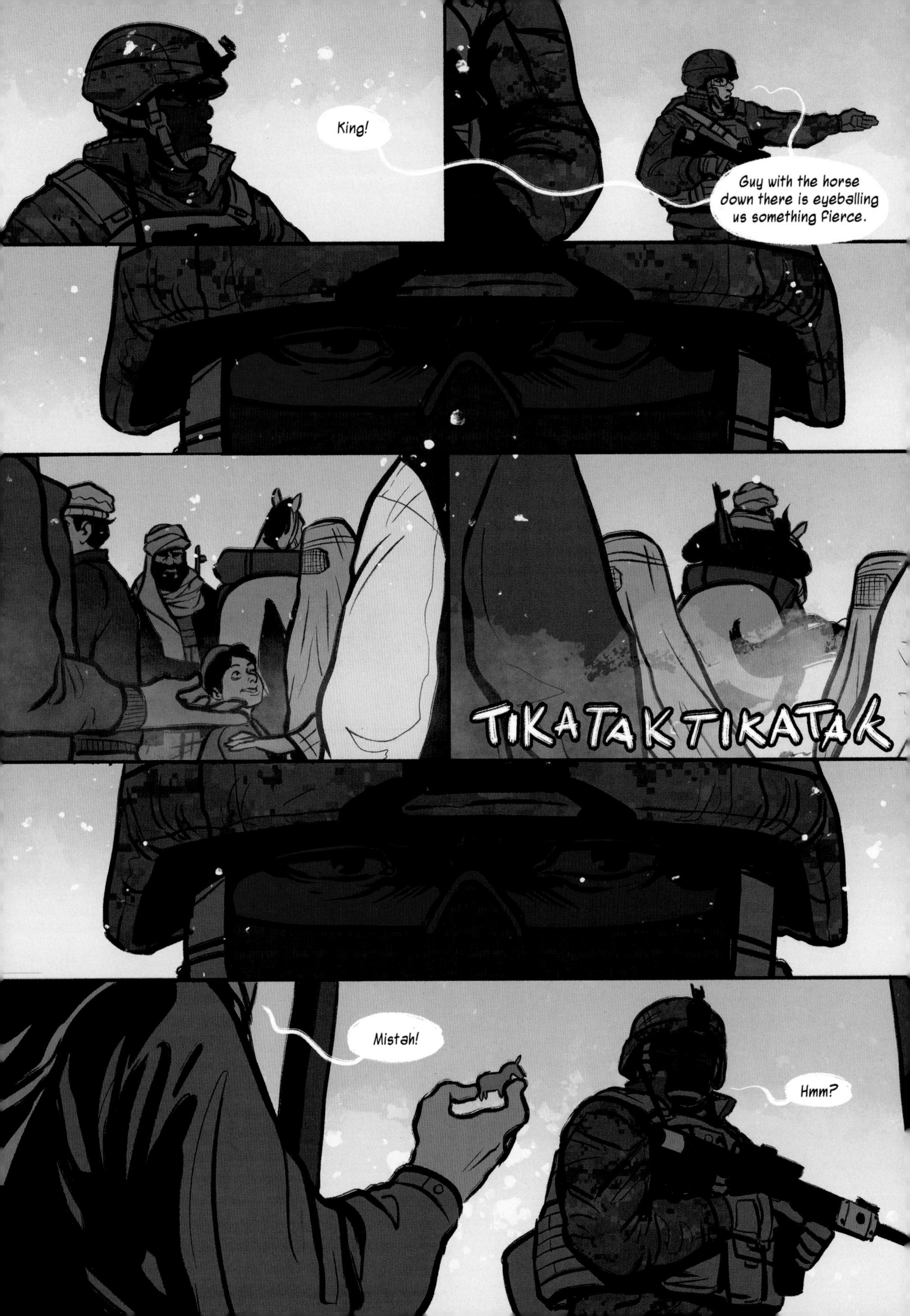
King!
Guy with the horse down there is eyeballing us something fierce.
TIKATAK TIKATAK
Mistah!
Hmm?

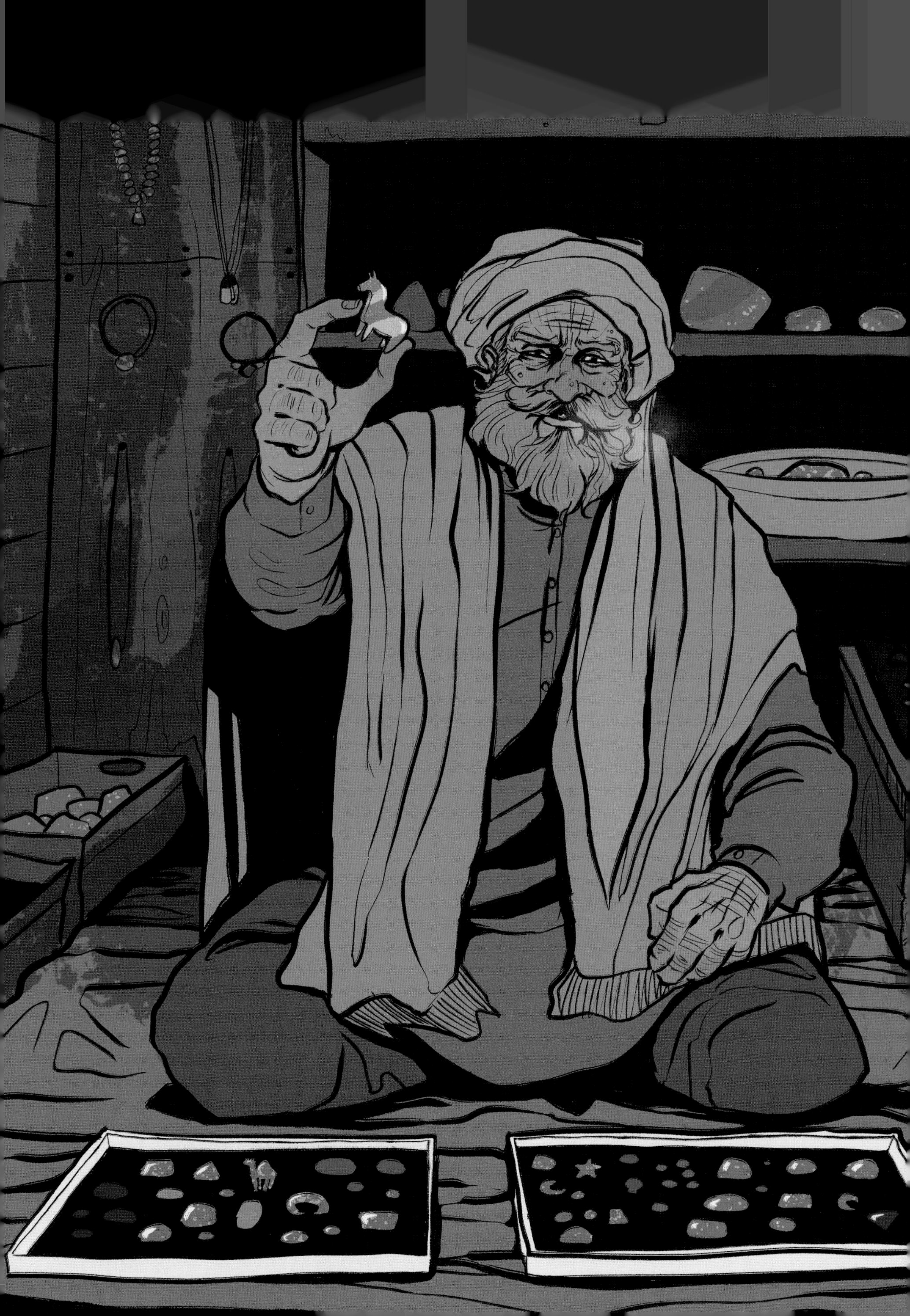

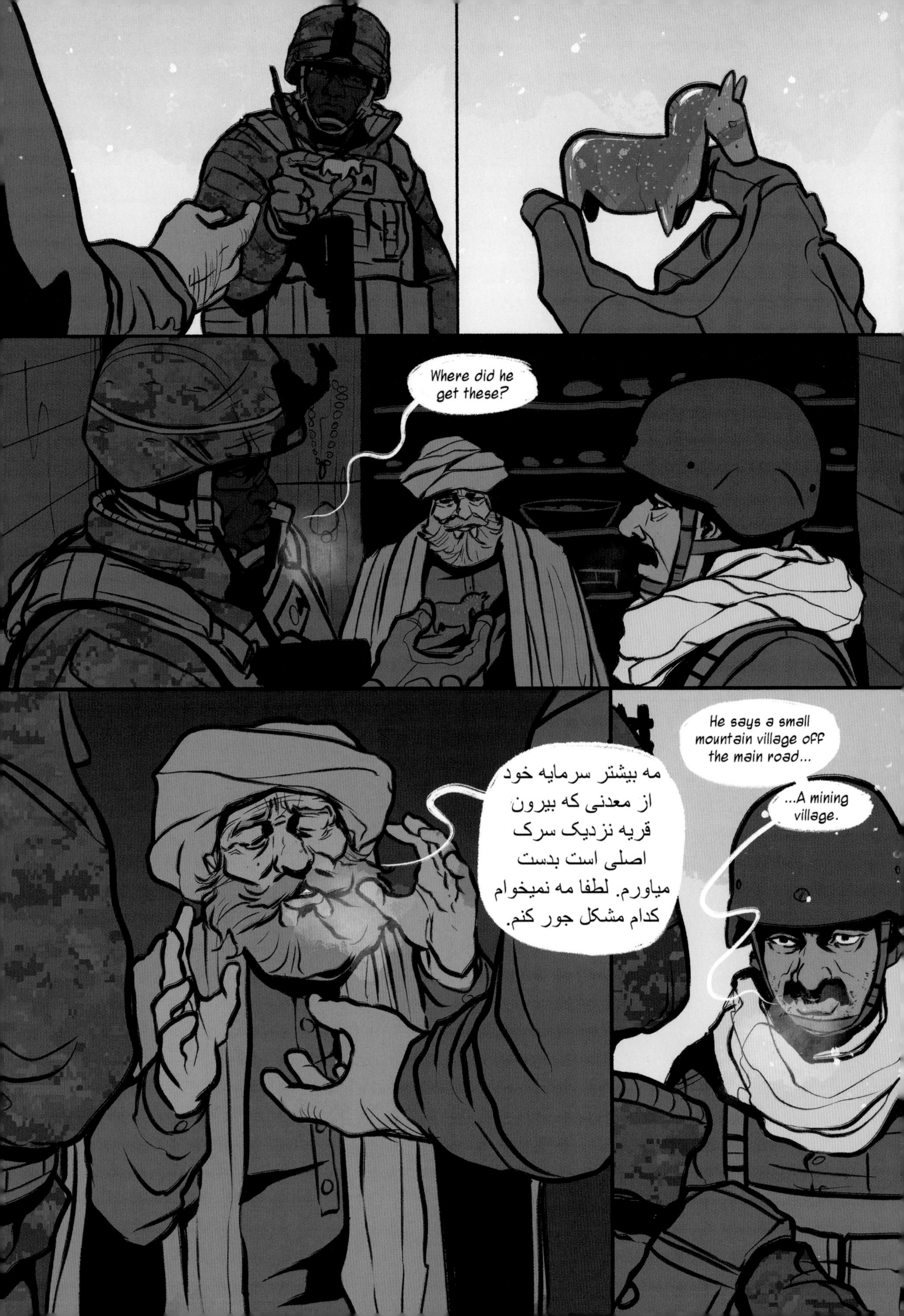
Where did he get these?
مه بیشتر سرمایه خود از معدنی که بیرون قریه نزدیک سرک اصلی است بدست میاورم. لطفا مه نمیخوام کدام مشکل جور کنم.
He says a small mountain village off the main road...
...A mining village.

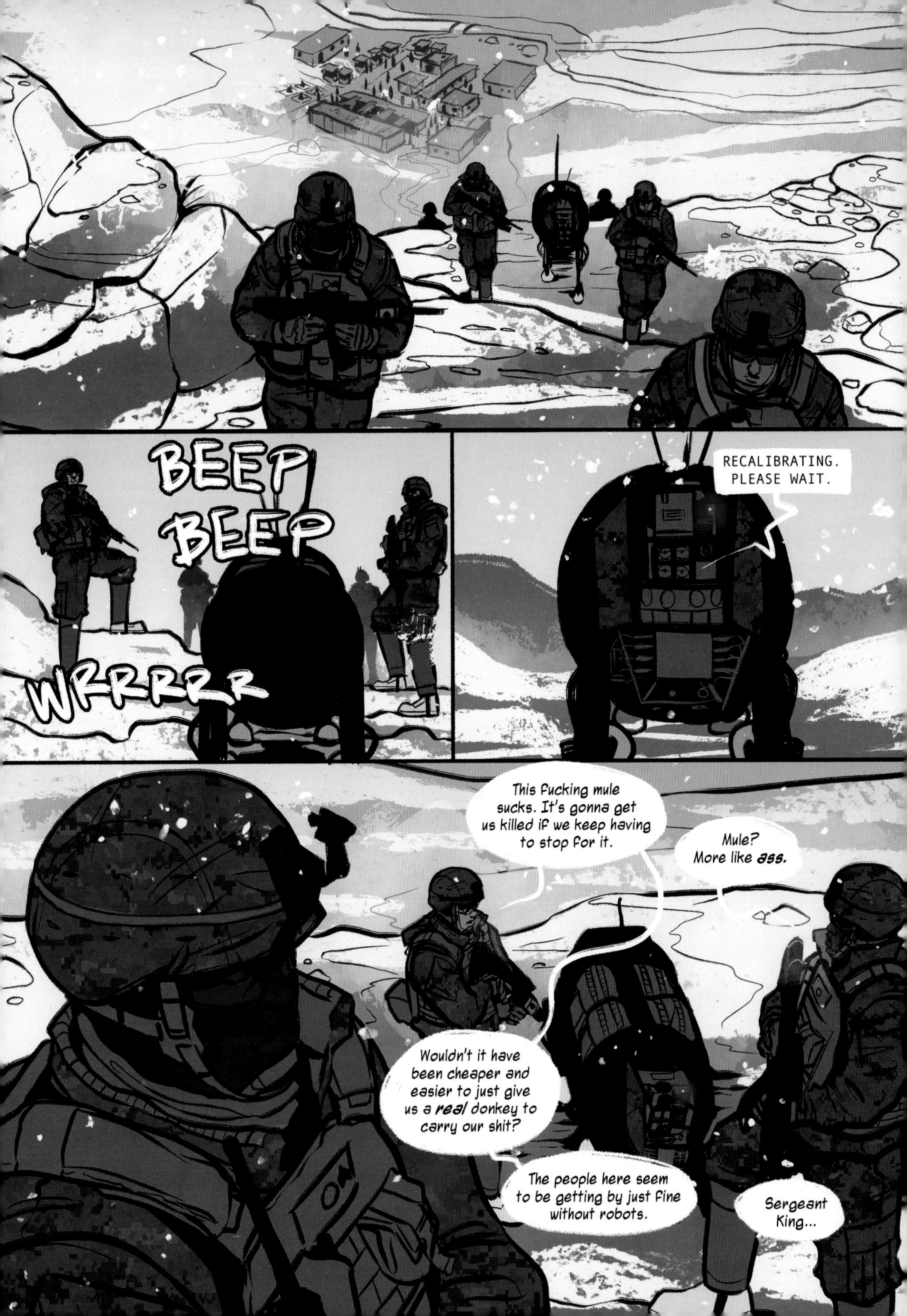
BEEP
BEEP
WRRRRR
RECALIBRATING. PLEASE WAIT.
This fucking mule sucks. It's gonna get us killed if we keep having to stop for it.
Mule? More like *ass.*
Wouldn't it have been cheaper and easier to just give us a *real* donkey to carry our shit?
The people here seem to be getting by just fine without robots.
Sergeant King...

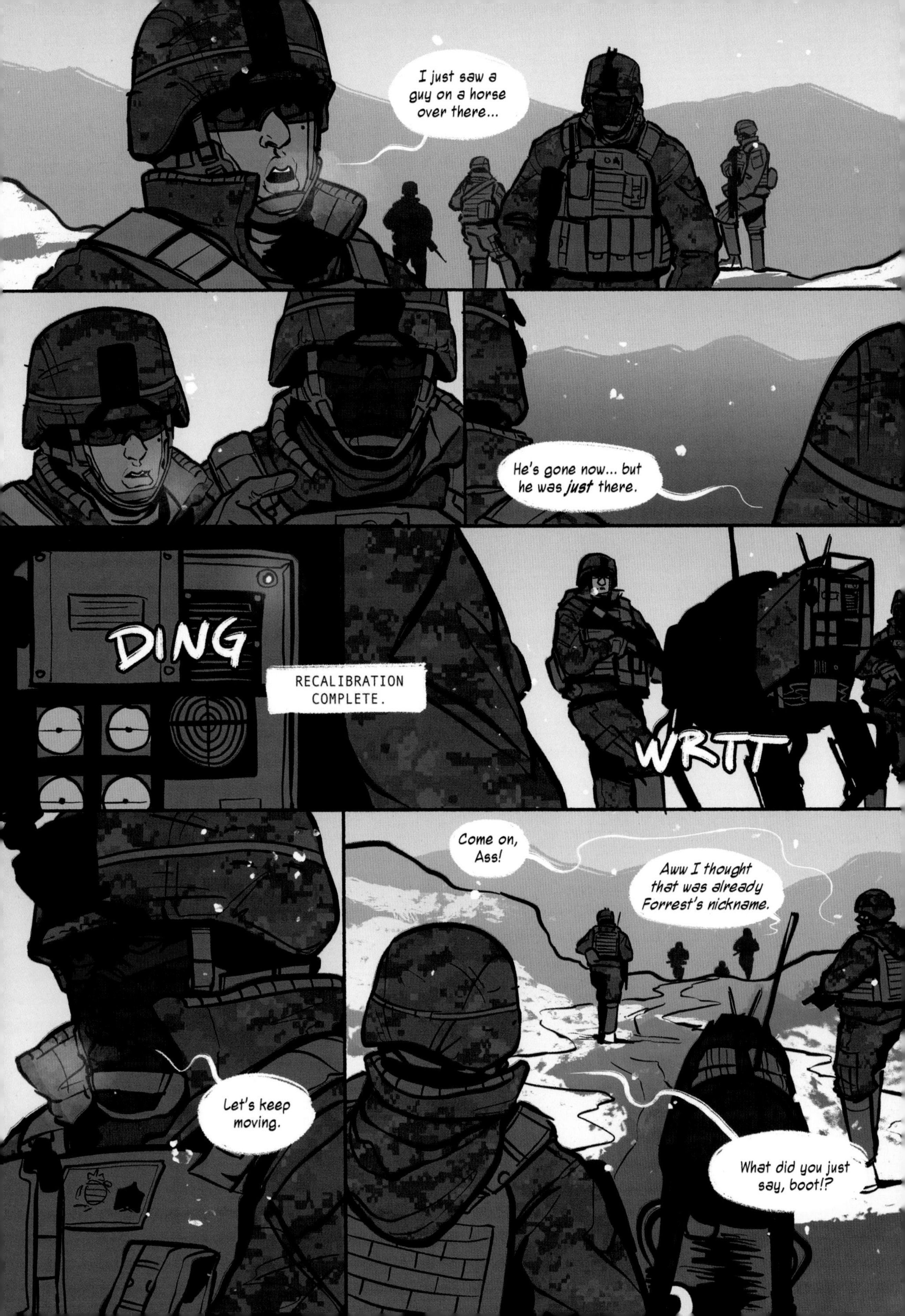
I just saw a guy on a horse over there...
He's gone now... but he was *just* there.
DING
RECALIBRATION COMPLETE.
WRTT
Let's keep moving.
Come on, Ass!
Aww I thought that was already Forrest's nickname.
What did you just say, boot!?

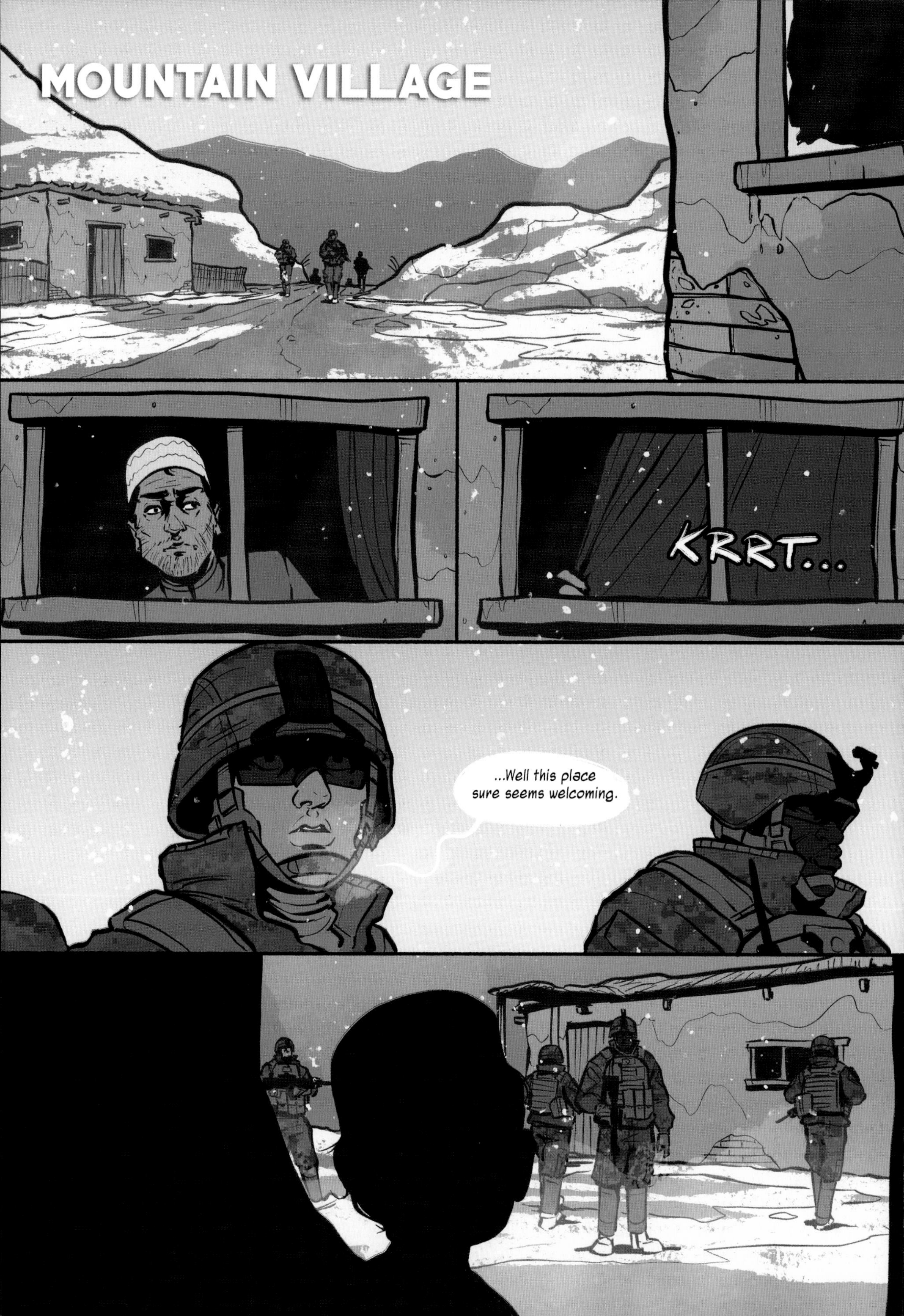
MOUNTAIN VILLAGE
KRRT...
...Well this place sure seems welcoming.

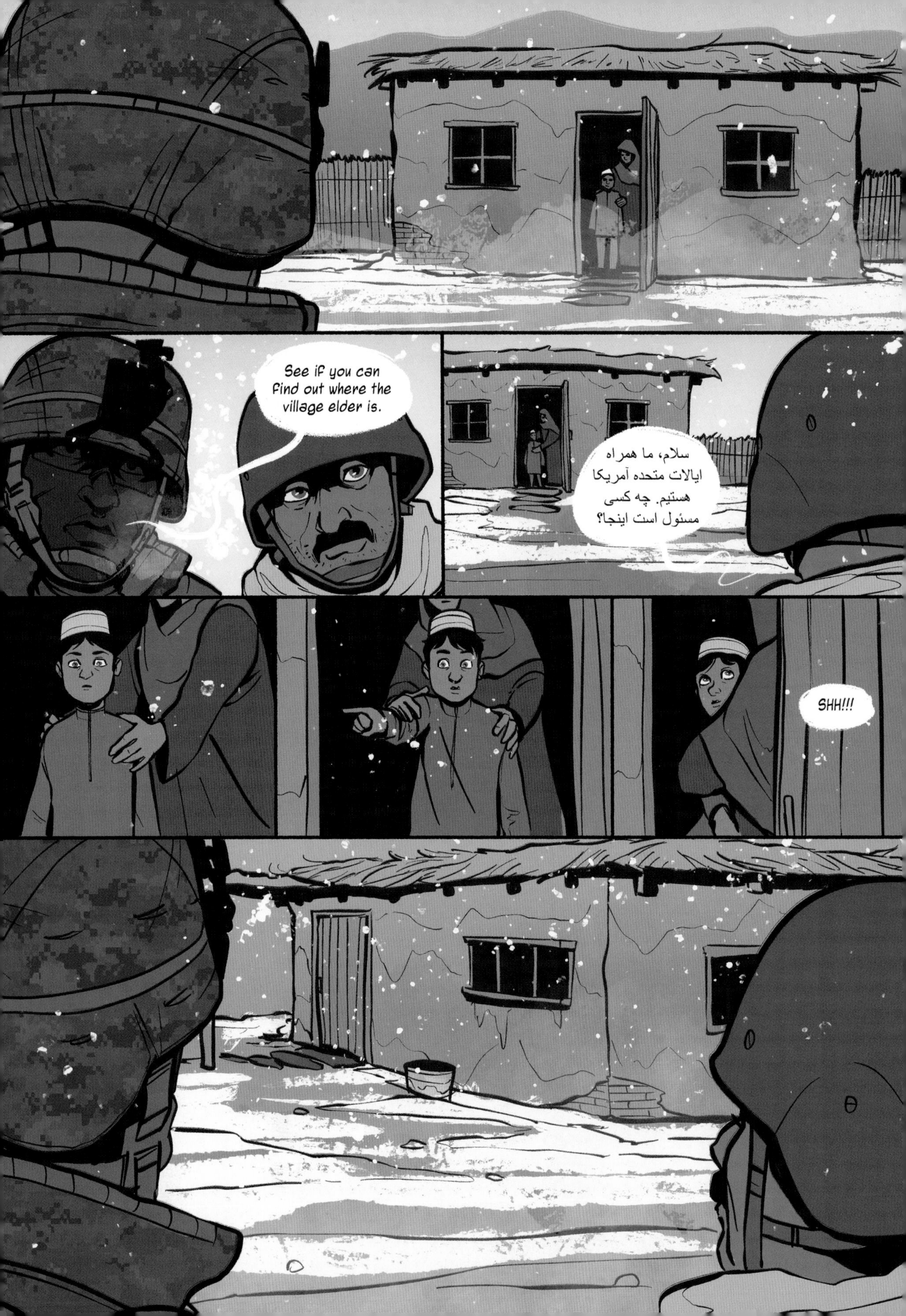
See if you can find out where the village elder is.
سلام، ما همراه ایالات متحده آمریکا هستیم. چه کسی مسئول است اینجا؟
SHH!!!

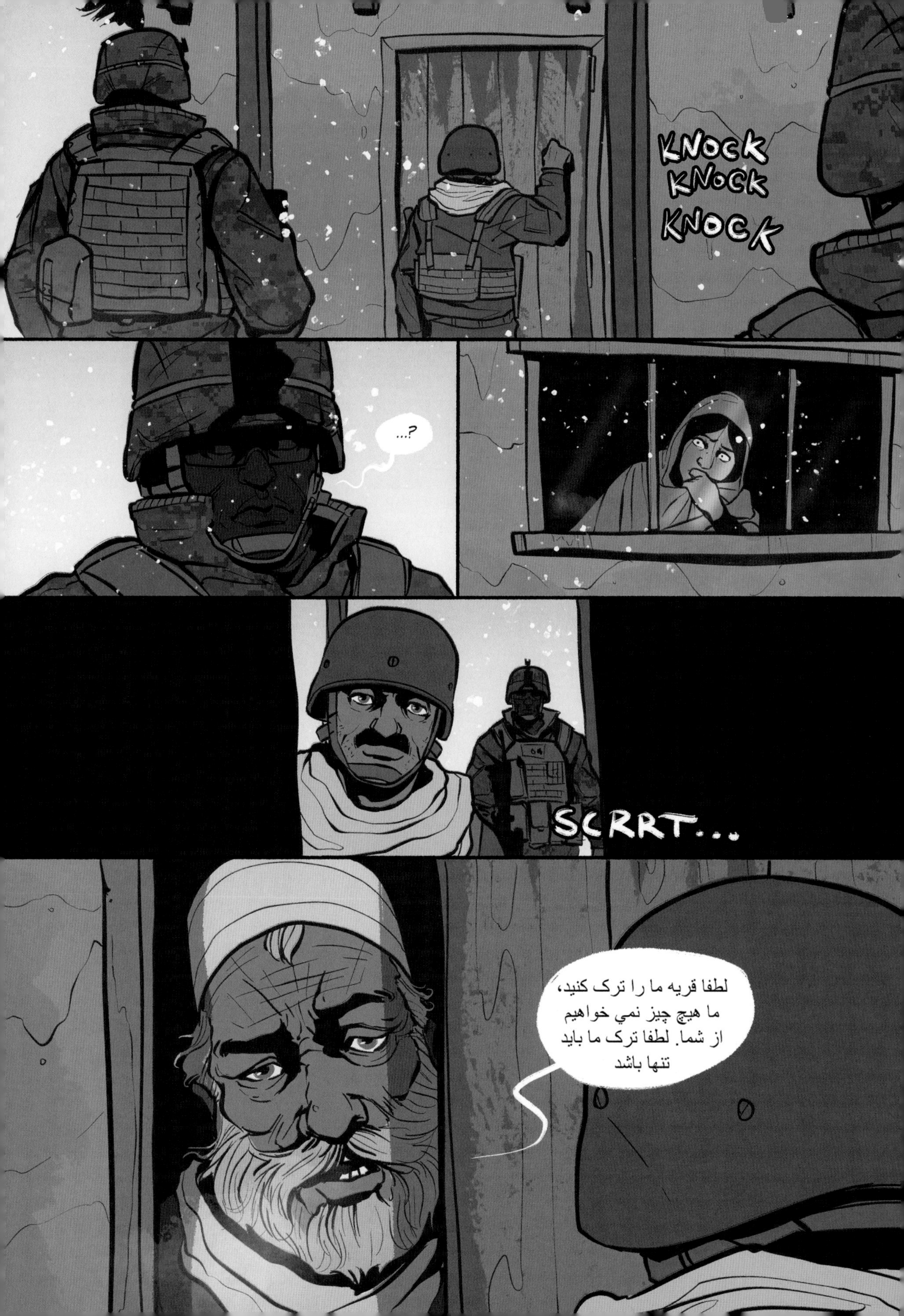
KNOCK
KNOCK
KNOCK
...?
SCRRT...
لطفا قریه ما را ترک کنید،
ما هیچ چیز نمي خواهیم
از شما. لطفا ترک ما باید
تنها باشد

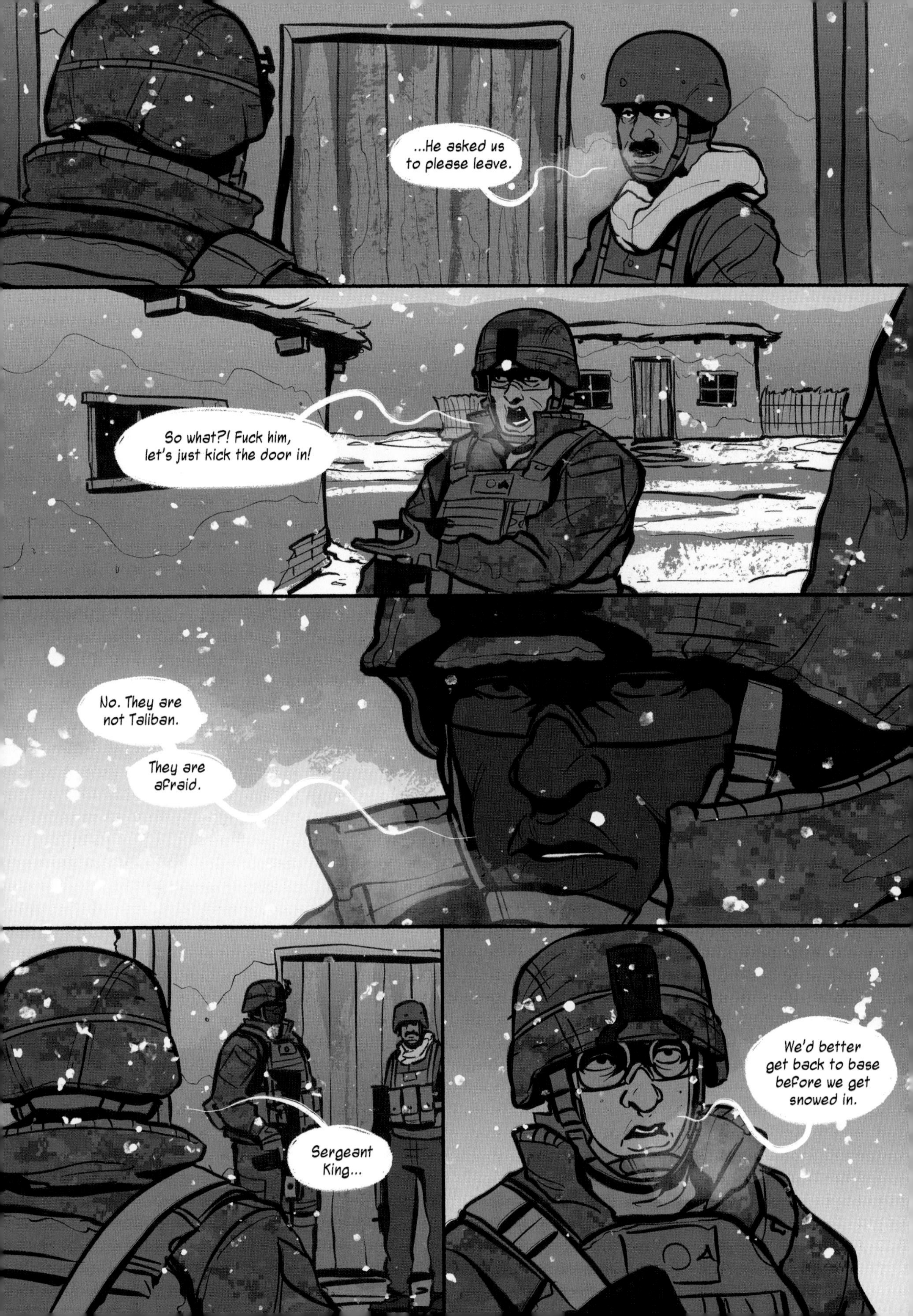
...He asked us to please leave.
So what?! Fuck him, let's just kick the door in!
No. They are not Taliban.
They are afraid.
Sergeant King...
We'd better get back to base before we get snowed in.

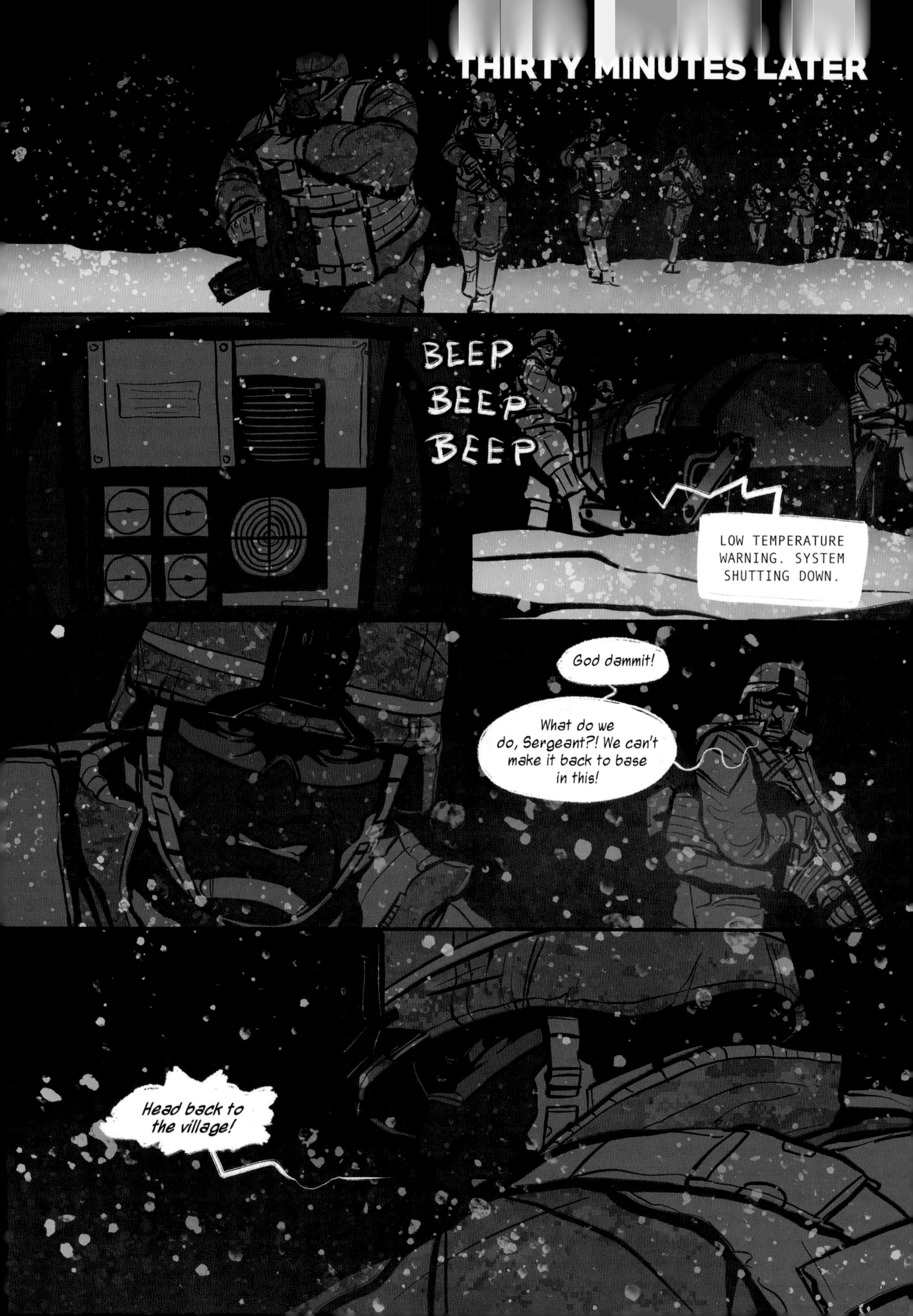
THIRTY MINUTES LATER
BEEP
BEEP
BEEP
LOW TEMPERATURE WARNING. SYSTEM SHUTTING DOWN.
God dammit!
What do we do, Sergeant?! We can't make it back to base in this!
Head back to the village!

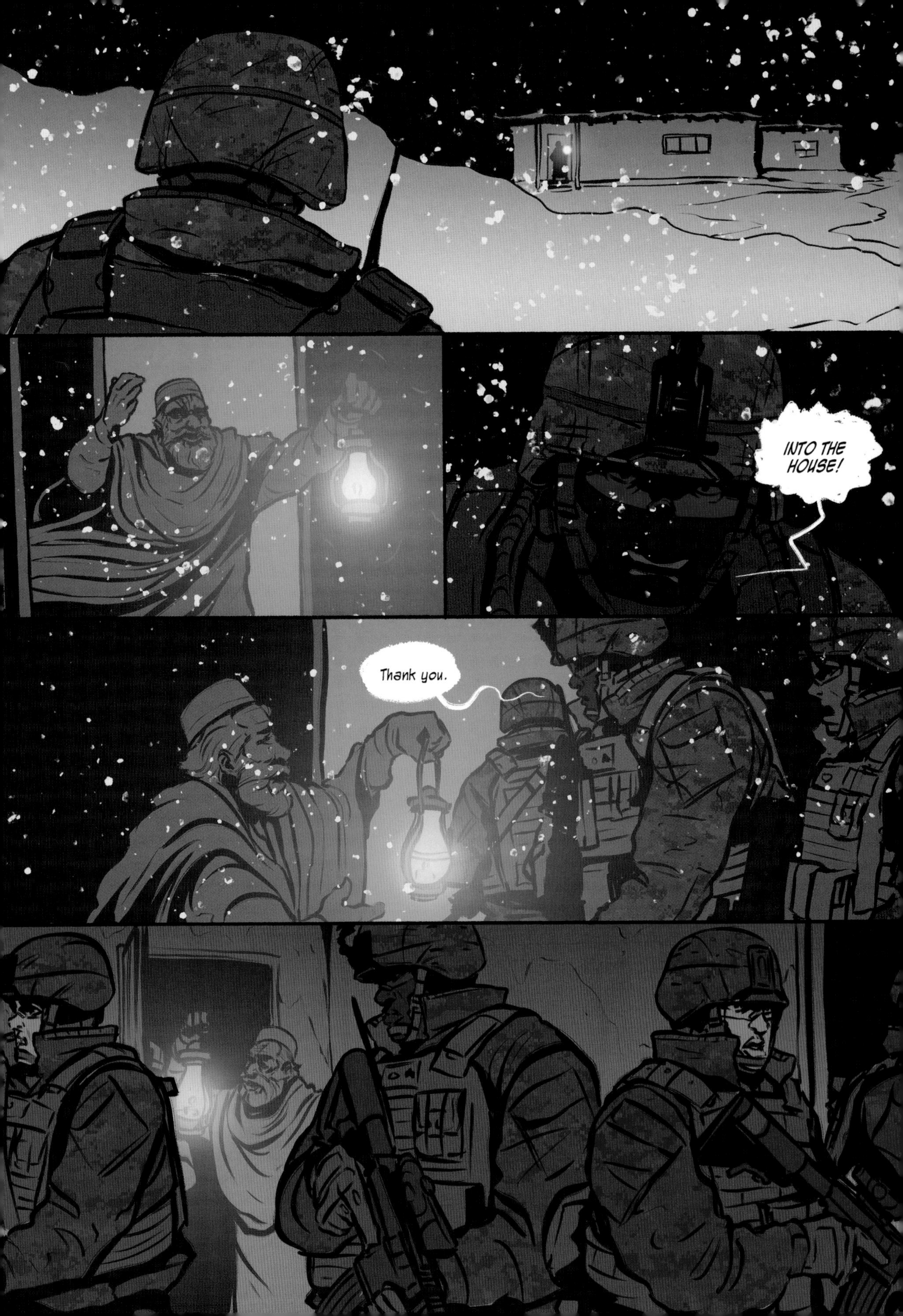
INTO THE HOUSE!
Thank you.

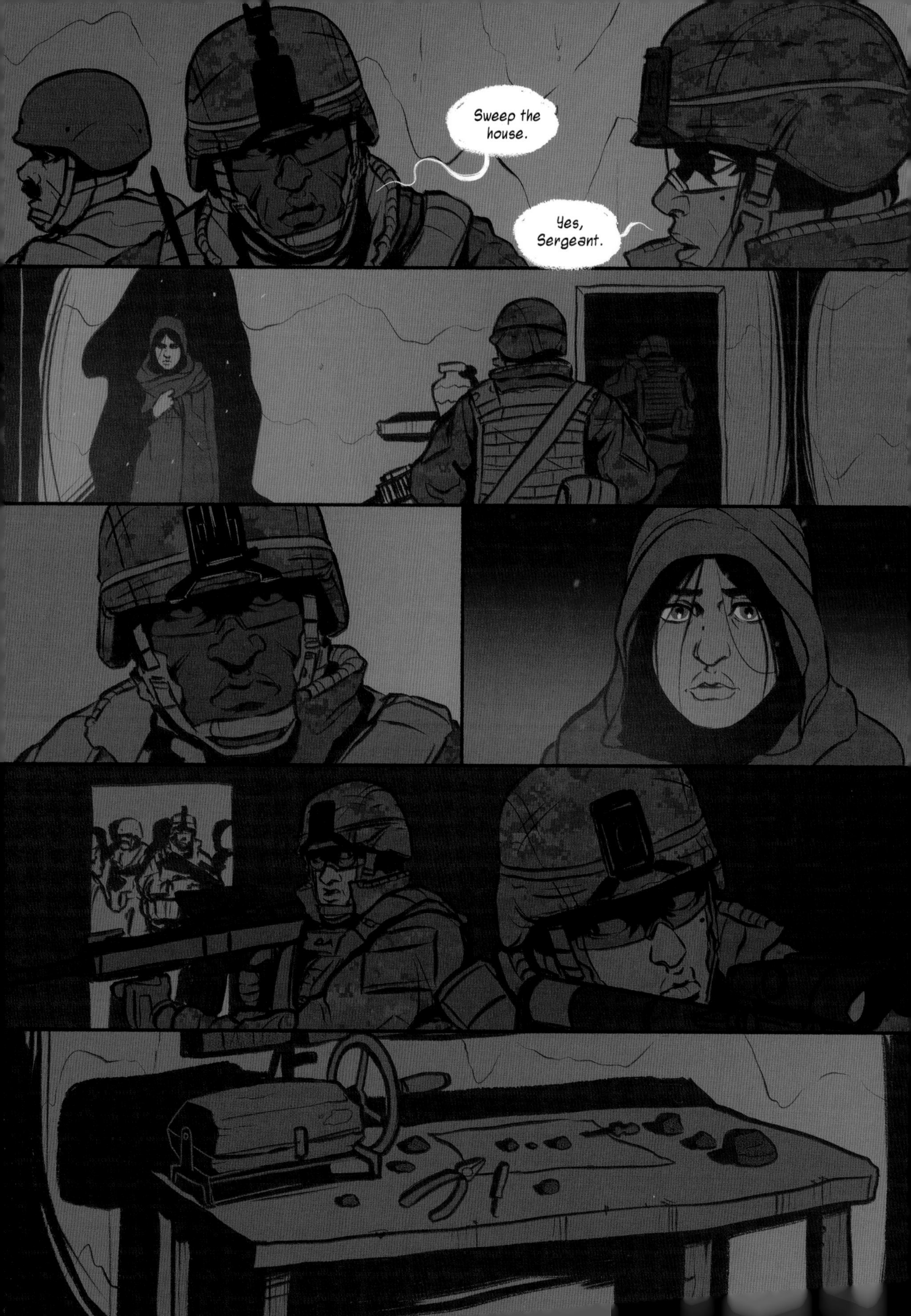
Sweep the house.
Yes, Sergeant.

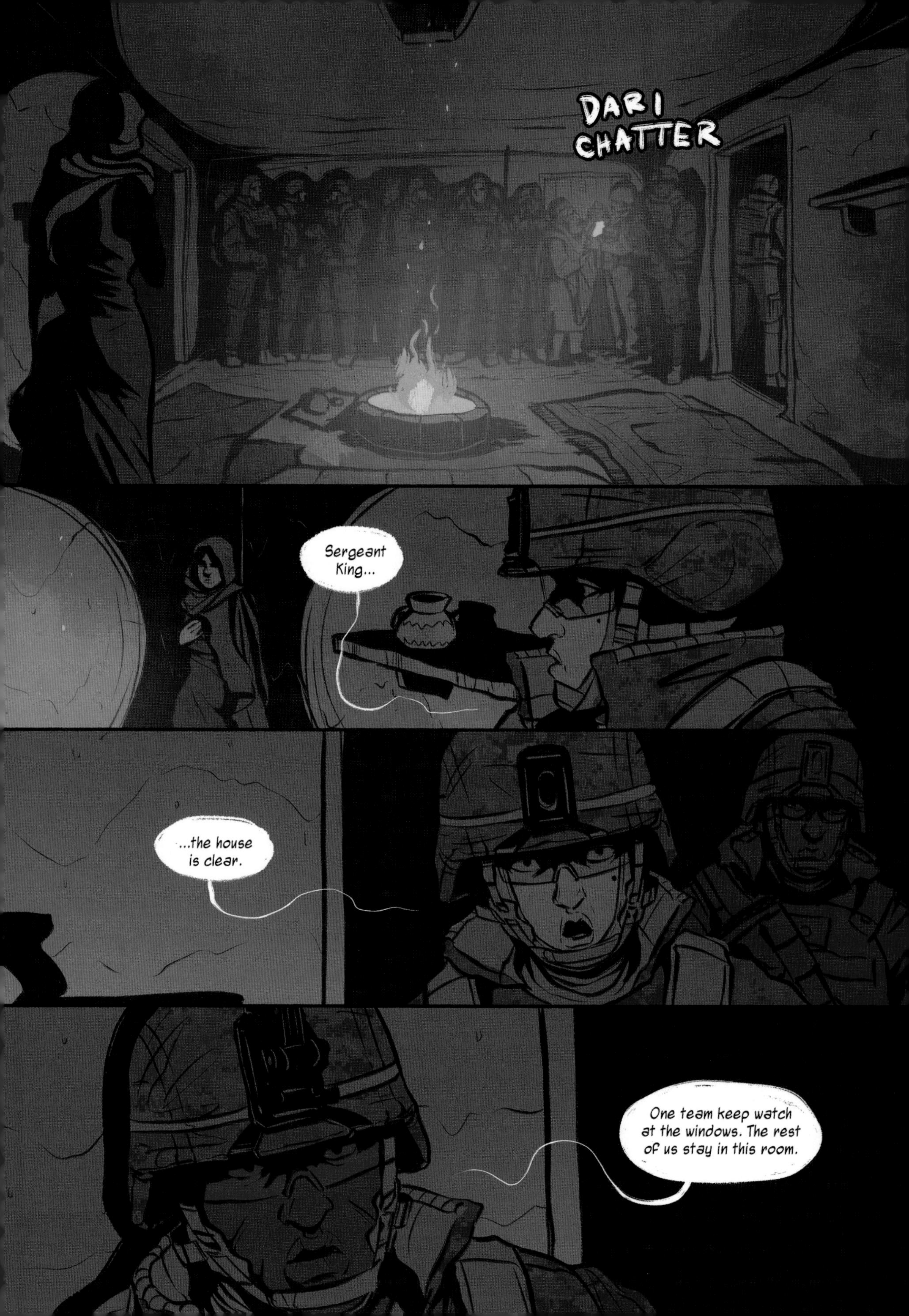
DARI CHATTER
Sergeant King...
...the house is clear.
One team keep watch at the windows. The rest of us stay in this room.

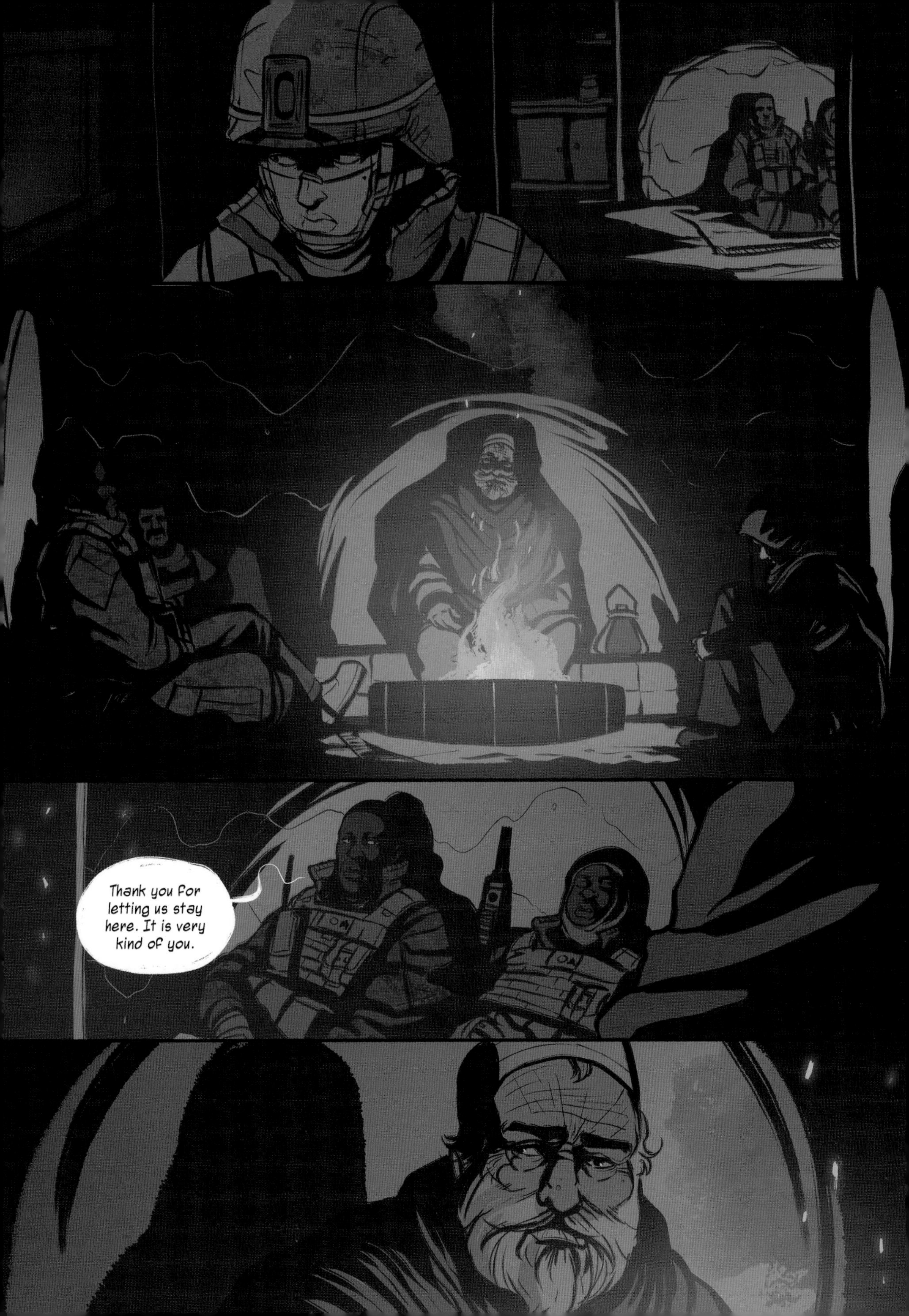
Thank you for letting us stay here. It is very kind of you.

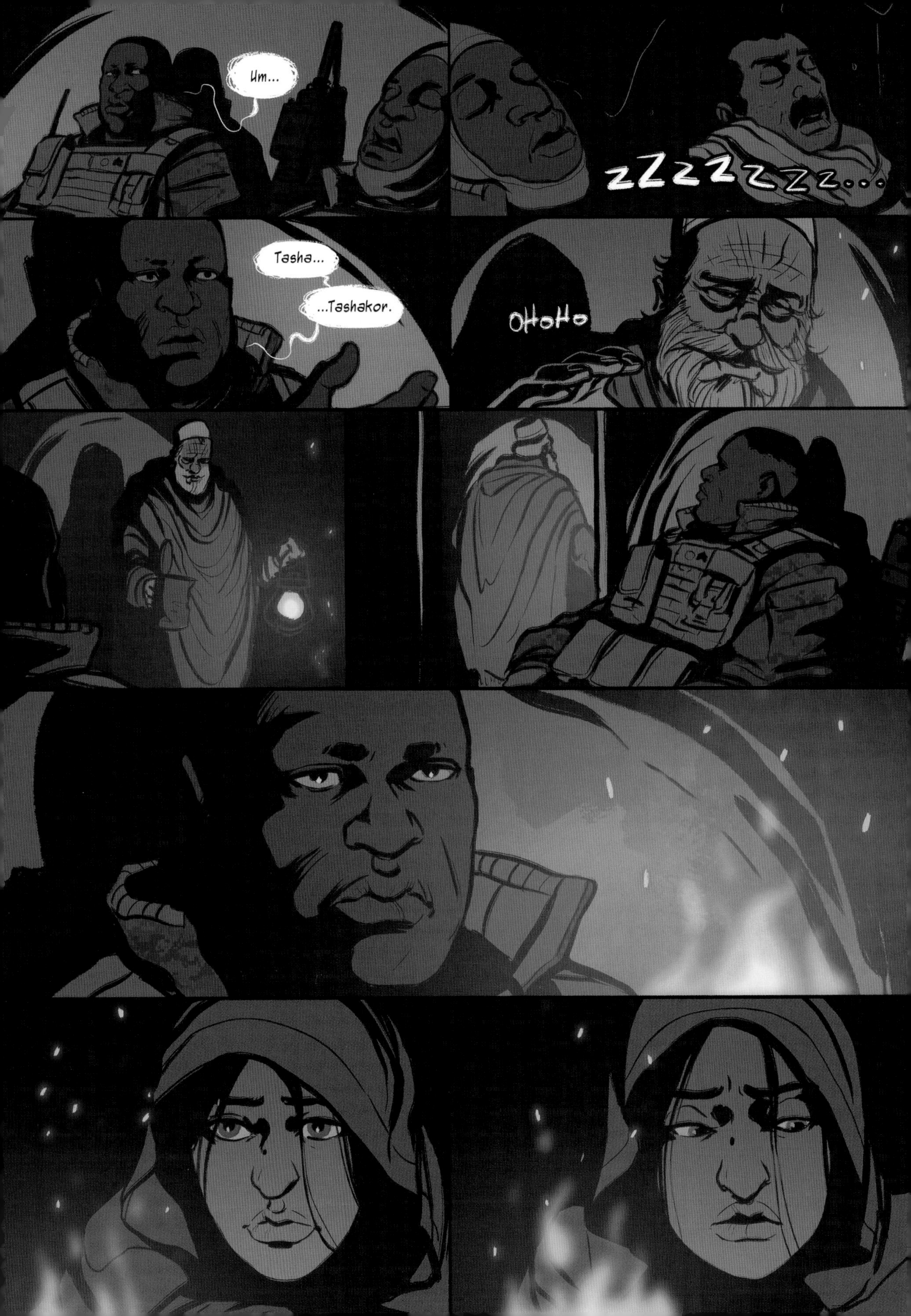
Um...
ZZZZZZZZ...
Tasha...
...Tashakor.
OHoHo

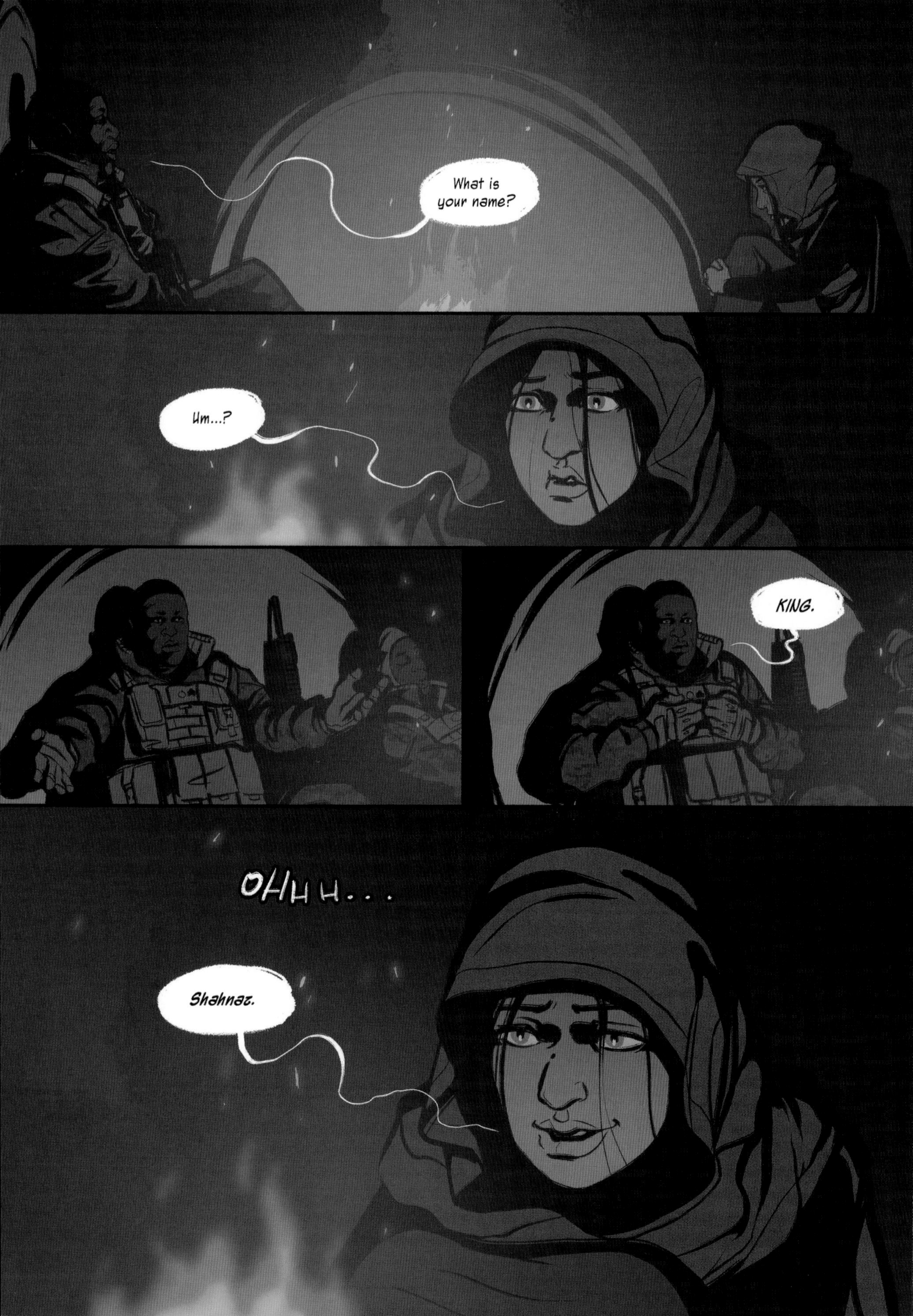
What is your name?
Um...?
KING.
OHHH...
Shahnaz.

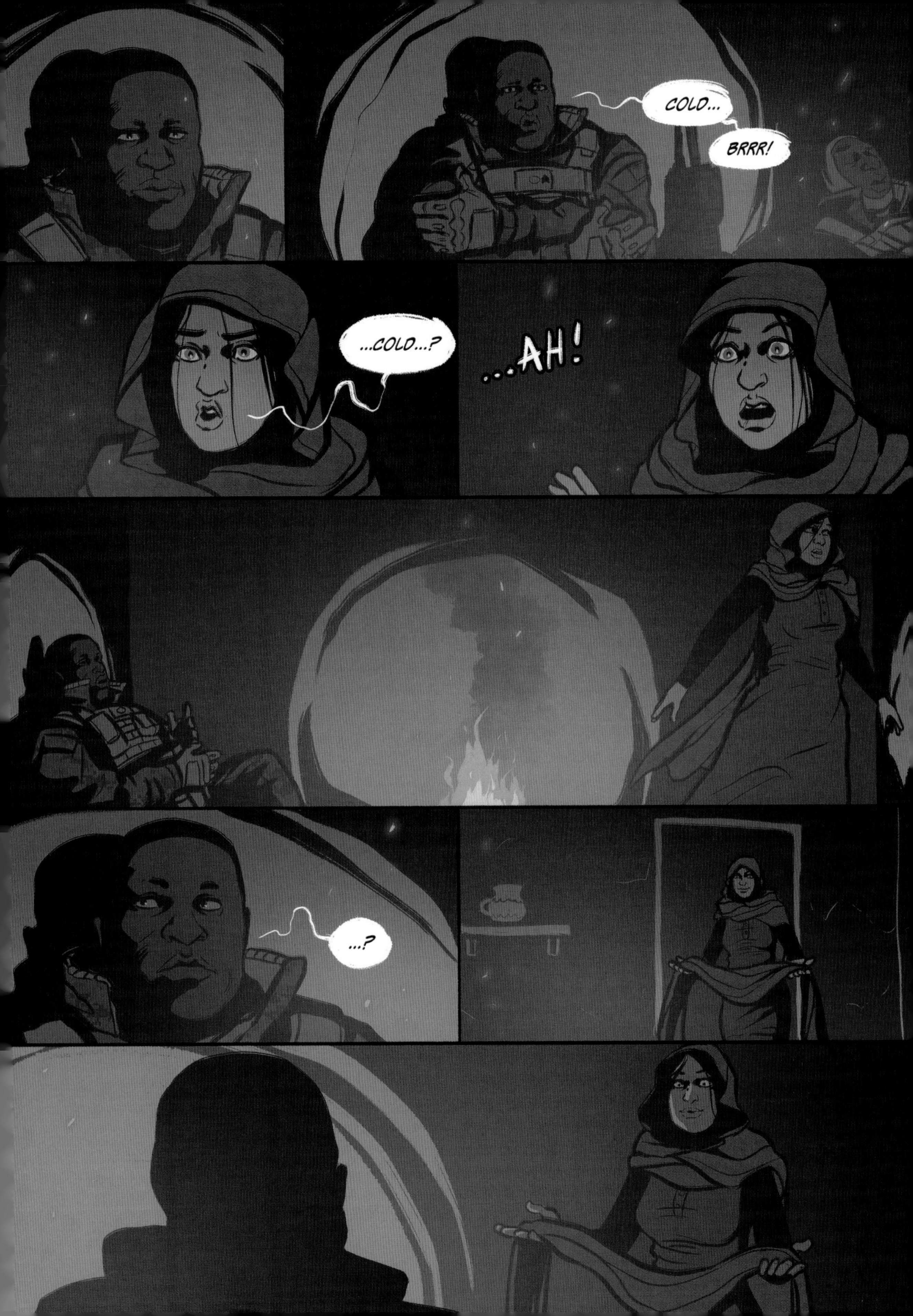
COLD...
BRRR!
...COLD...?
...AH!
...?

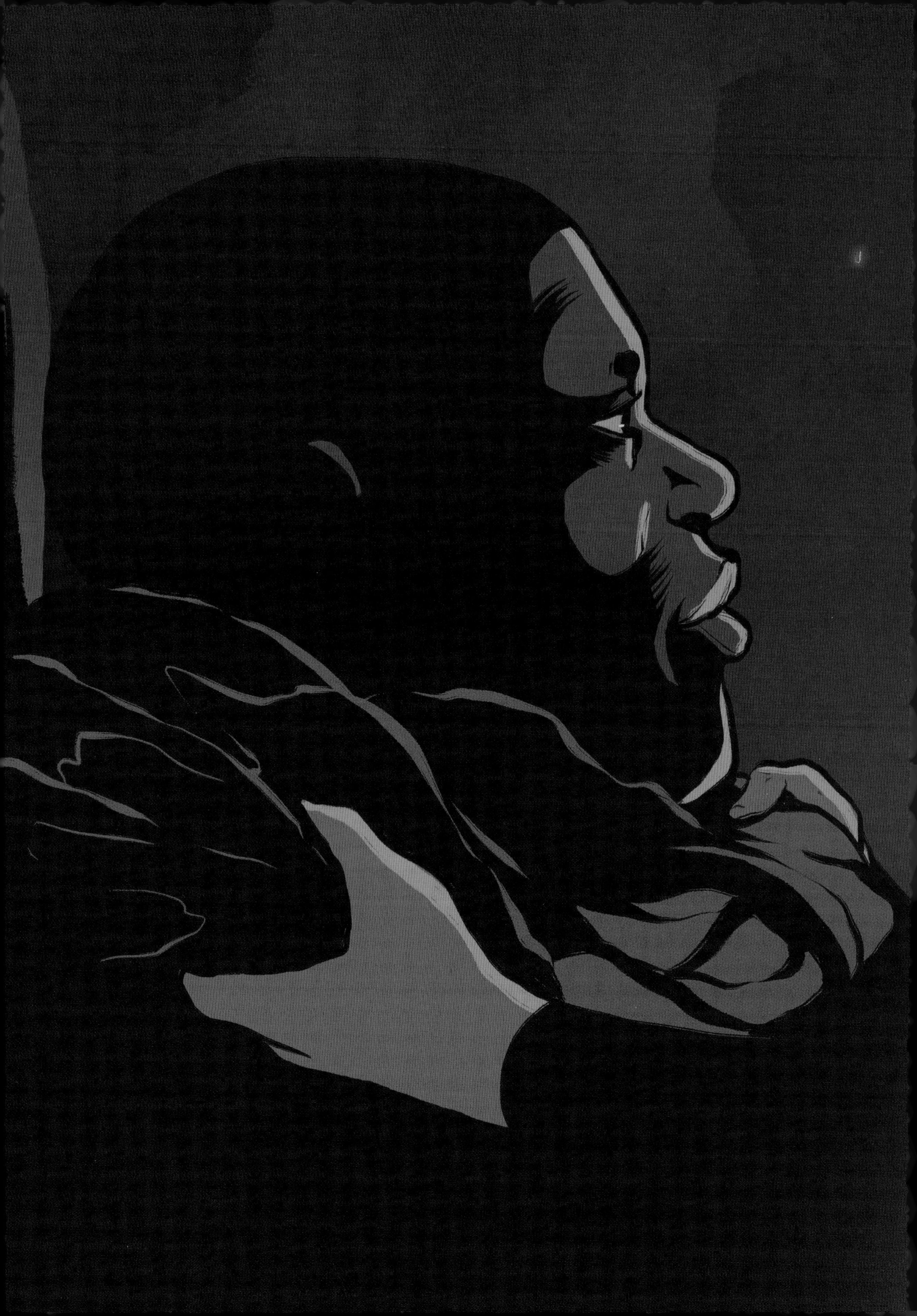

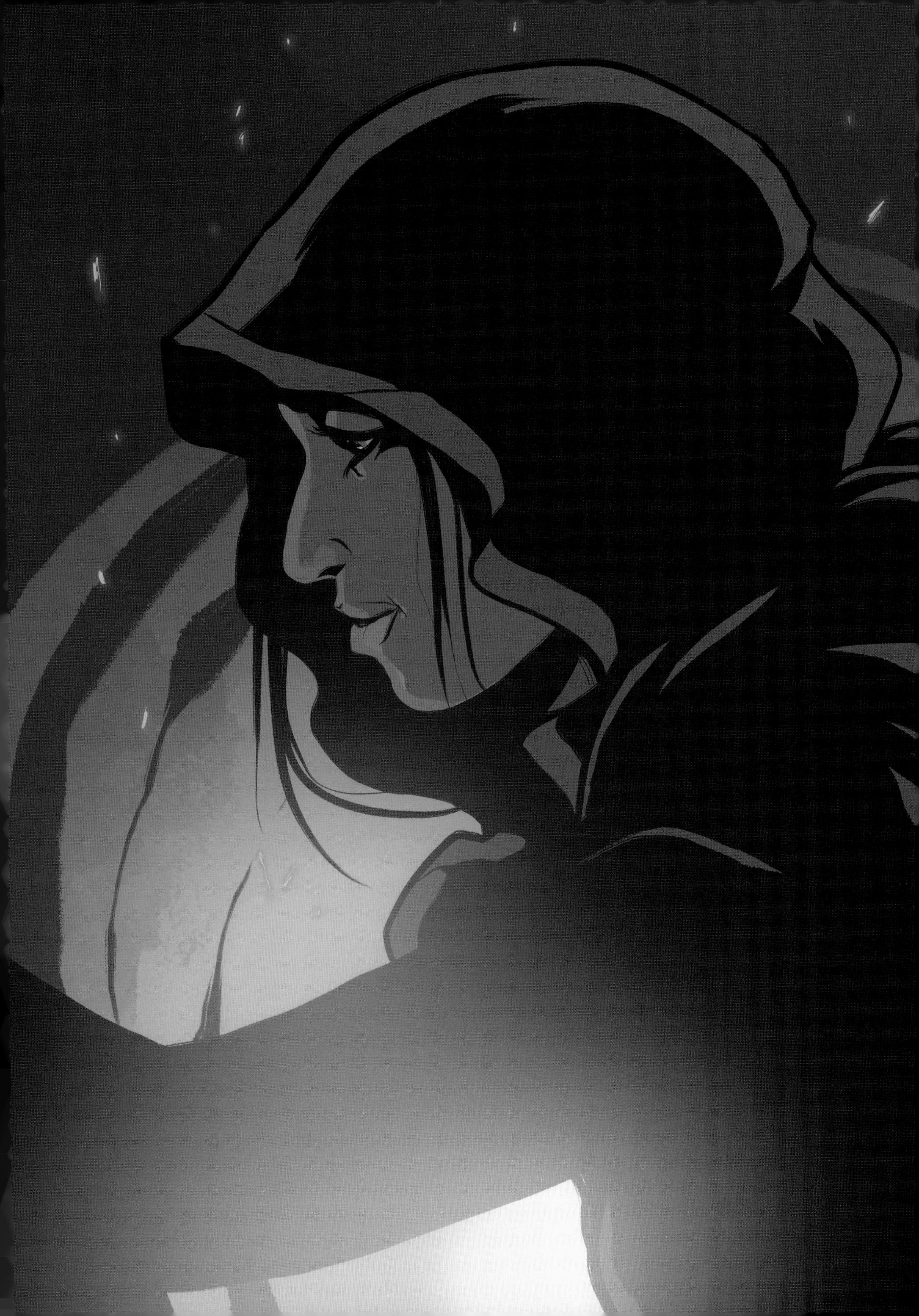

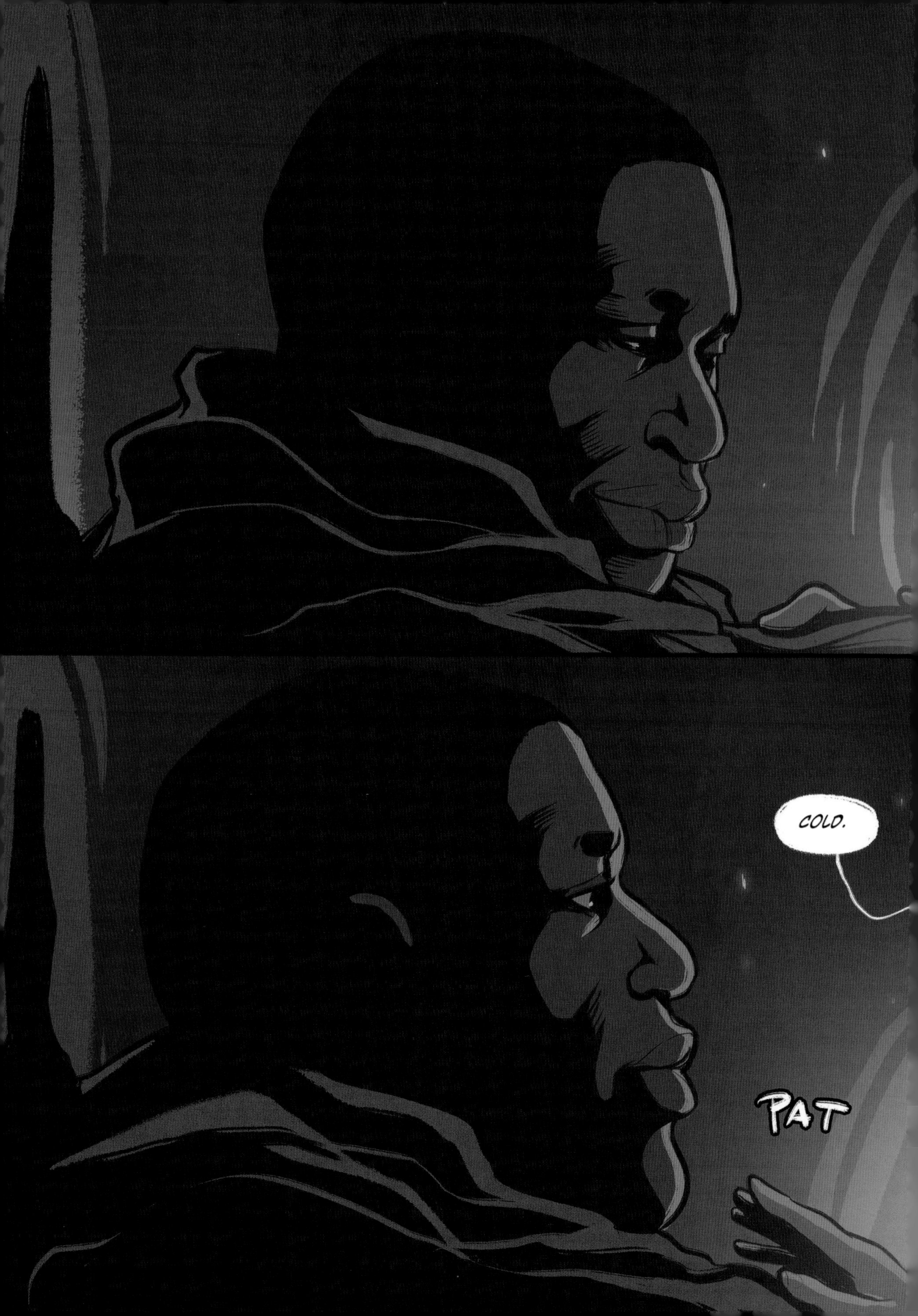
COLD.
PAT

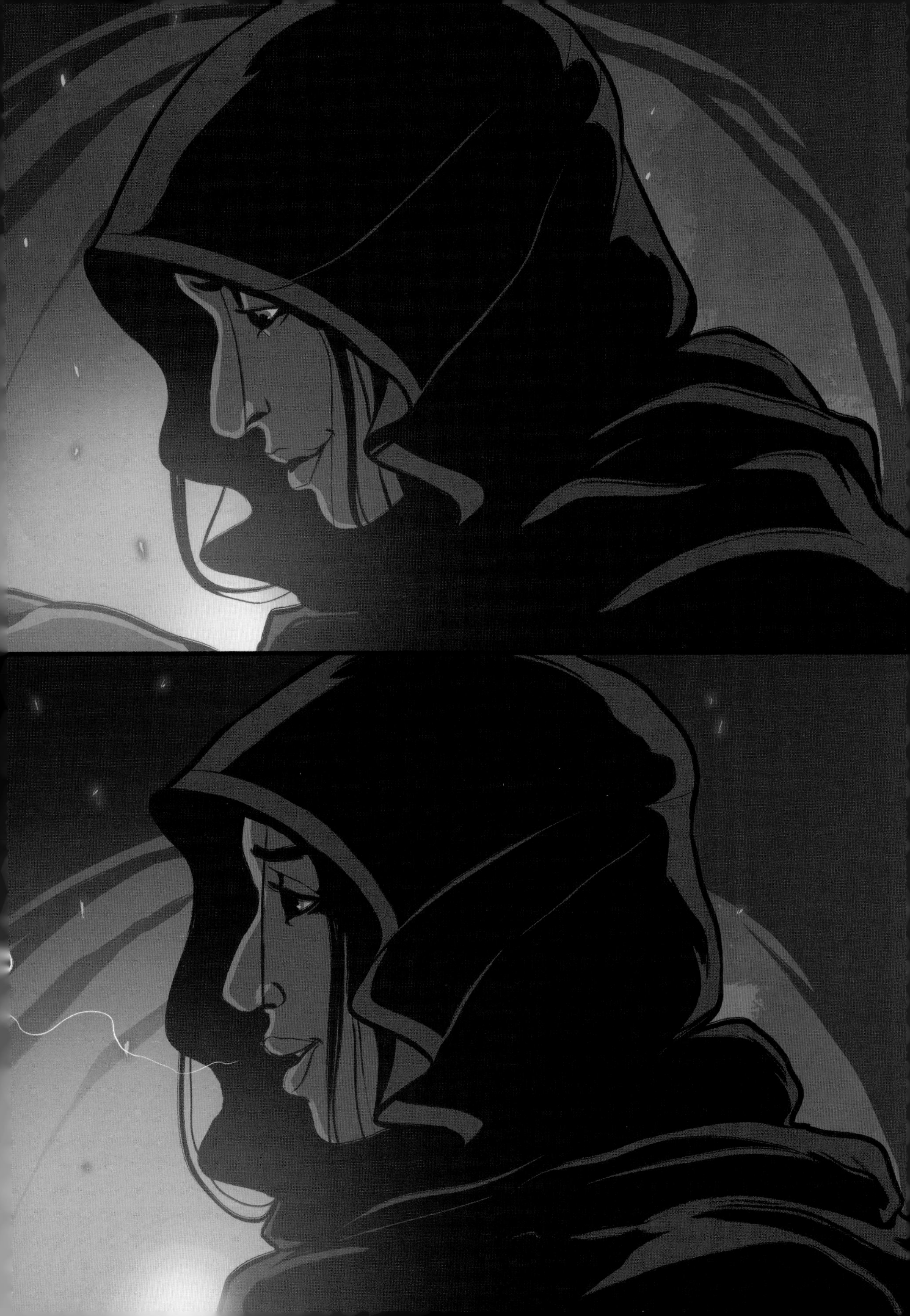

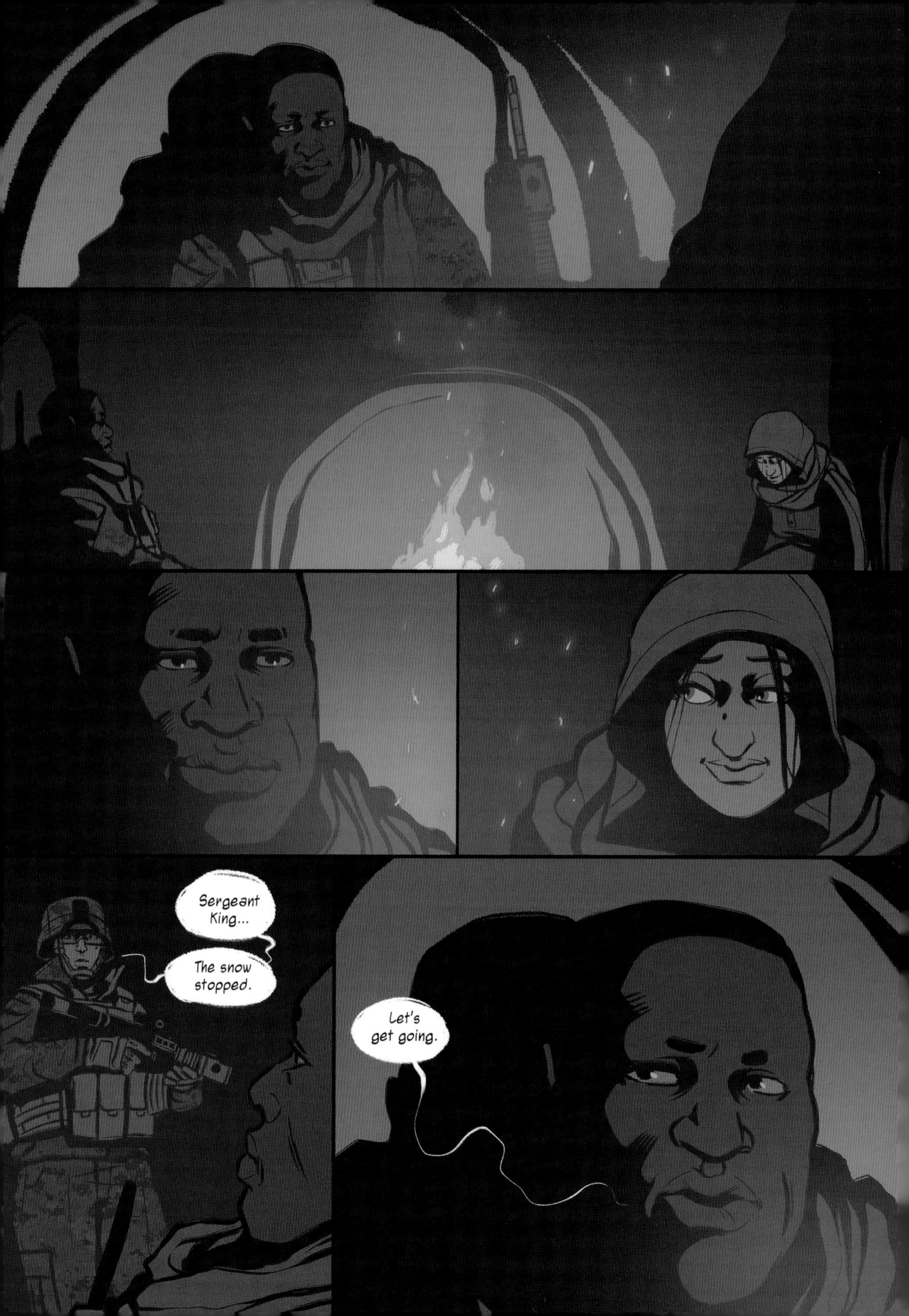
Sergeant King...
The snow stopped.
Let's get going.

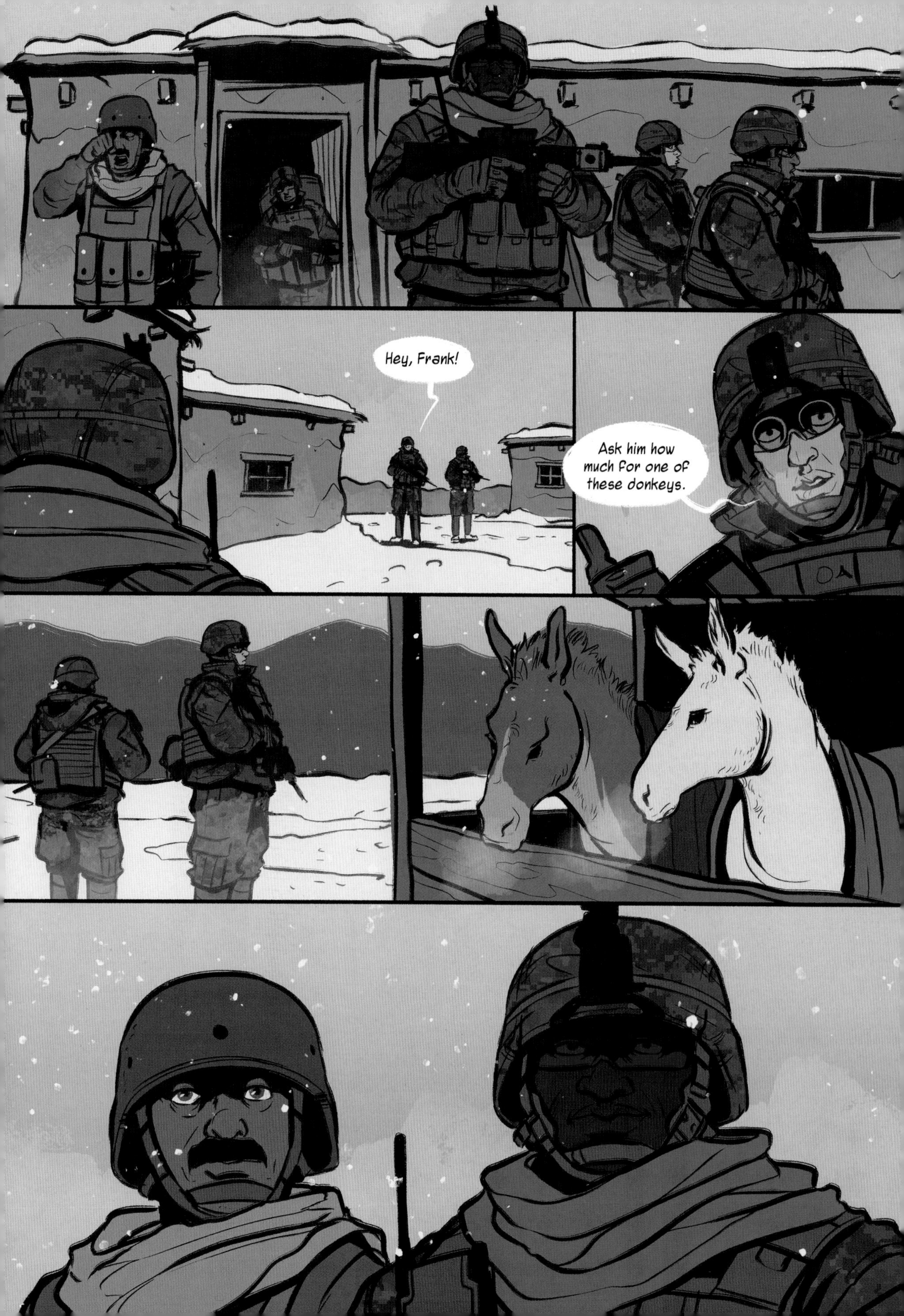
Hey, Frank!
Ask him how much for one of these donkeys.

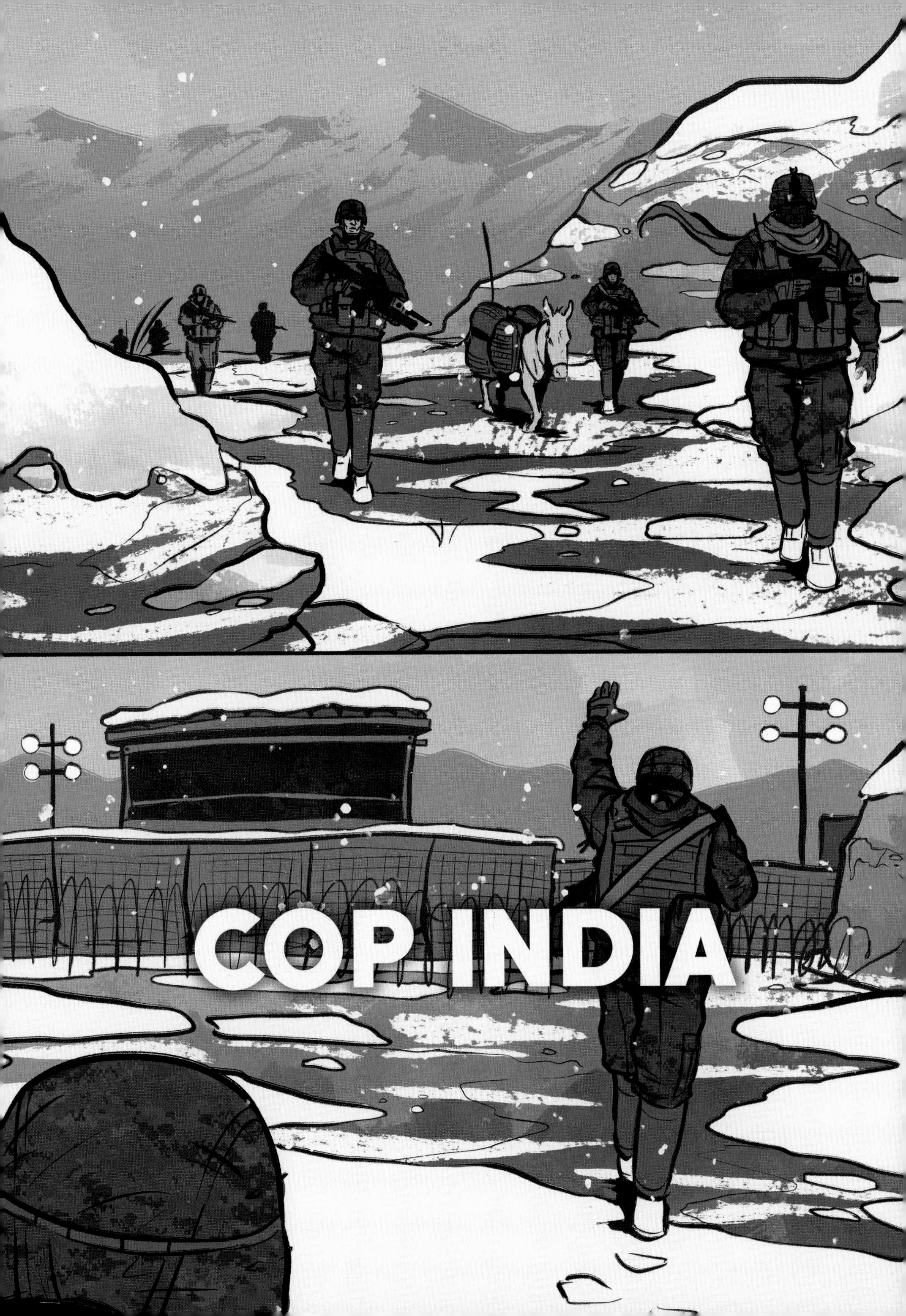
COP INDIA

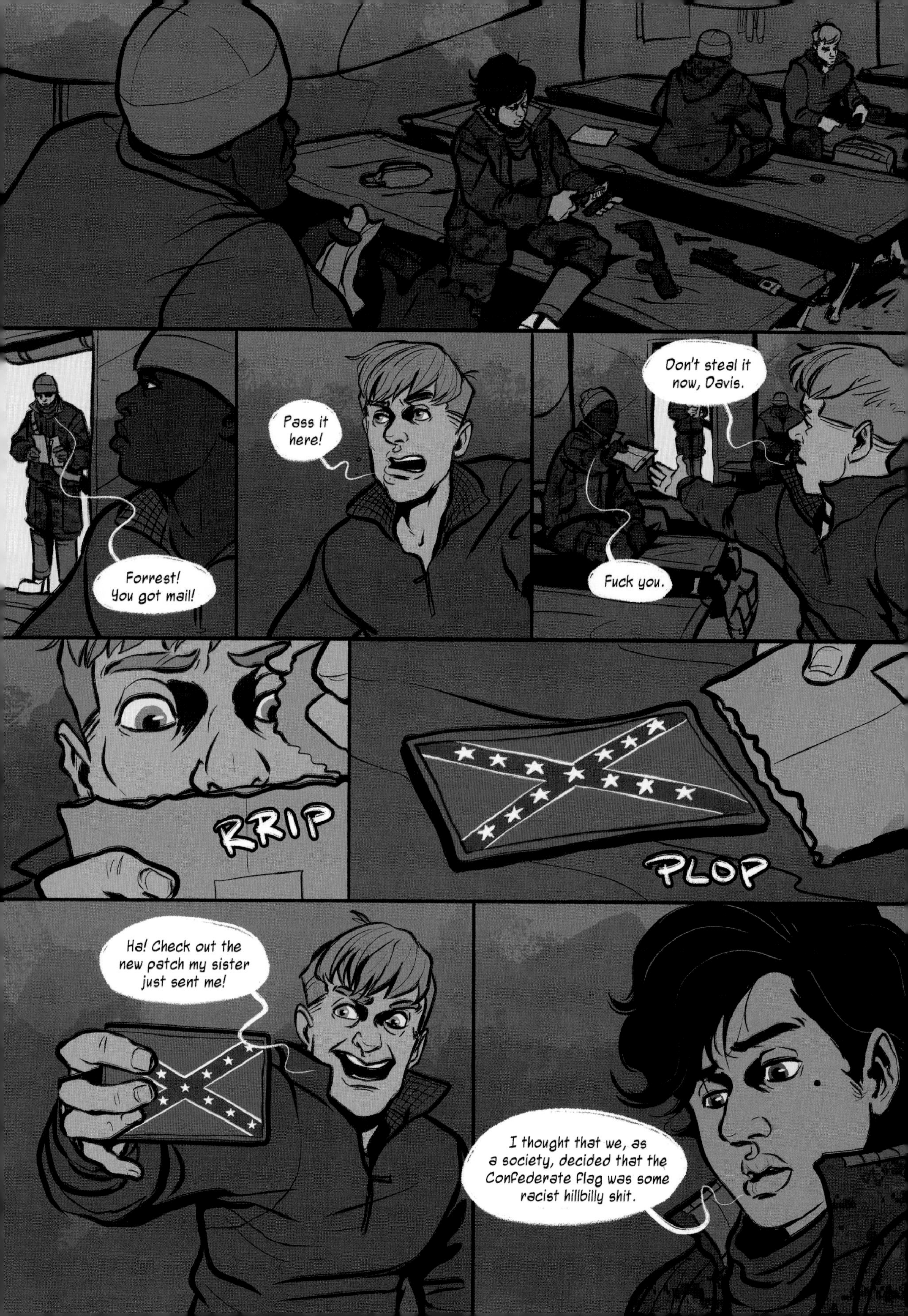
Forrest! You got mail!
Pass it here!
Don't steal it now, Davis.
Fuck you.
RRIP
PLOP
Ha! Check out the new patch my sister just sent me!
I thought that we, as a society, decided that the Confederate flag was some racist hillbilly shit.

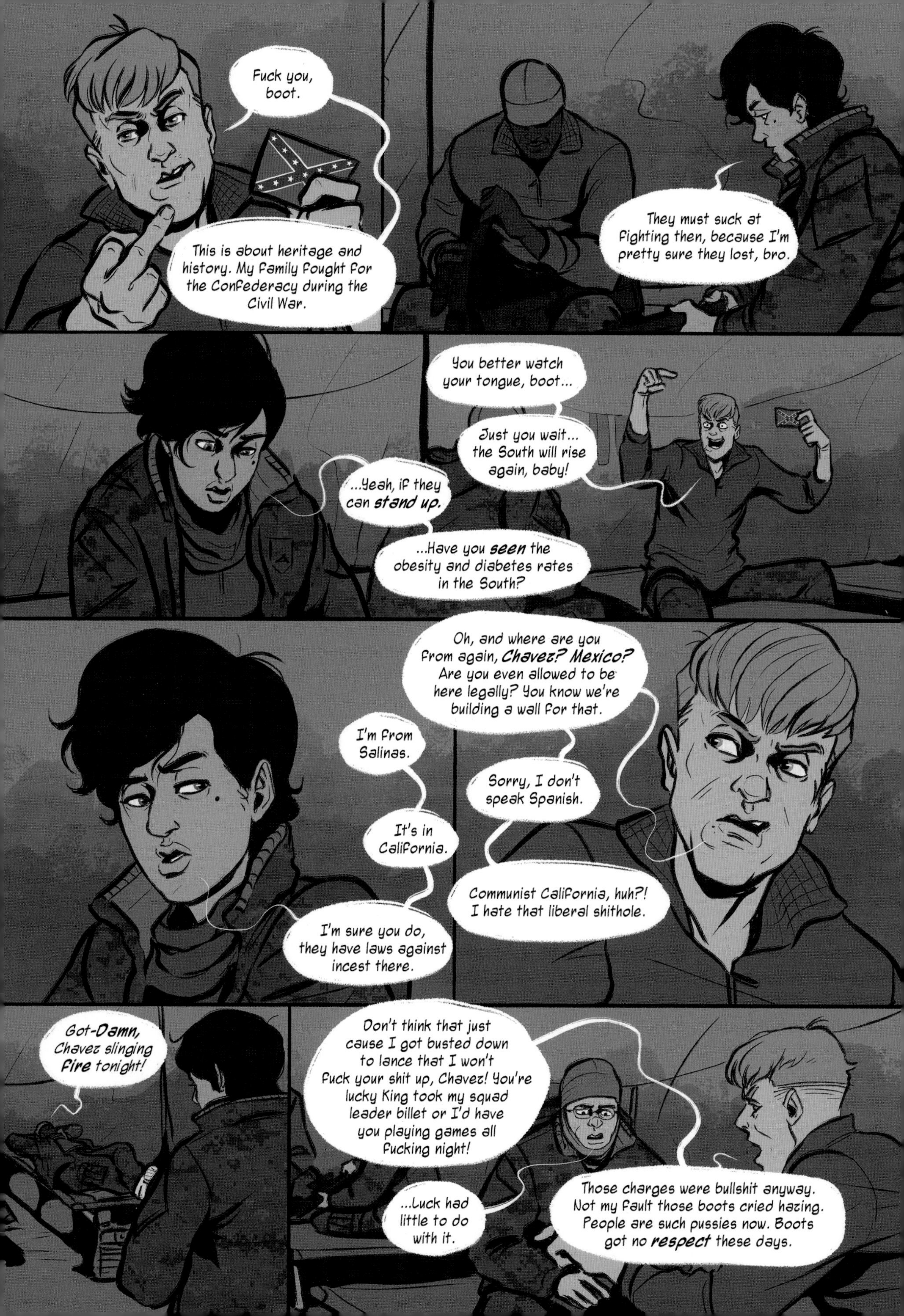
Fuck you, boot.
This is about heritage and history. My family fought for the Confederacy during the Civil War.
They must suck at fighting then, because I'm pretty sure they lost, bro.
You better watch your tongue, boot...
Just you wait... the South will rise again, baby!
...Yeah, if they can **stand up.**
...Have you **seen** the obesity and diabetes rates in the South?
Oh, and where are you from again, ***Chavez? Mexico?*** Are you even allowed to be here legally? You know we're building a wall for that.
I'm from Salinas.
Sorry, I don't speak Spanish.
It's in California.
Communist California, huh?! I hate that liberal shithole.
I'm sure you do, they have laws against incest there.
Got-***Damn,*** Chavez slinging ***fire*** tonight!
Don't think that just cause I got busted down to lance that I won't fuck your shit up, Chavez! You're lucky King took my squad leader billet or I'd have you playing games all fucking night!
...Luck had little to do with it.
Those charges were bullshit anyway. Not my fault those boots cried hazing. People are such pussies now. Boots got no ***respect*** these days.

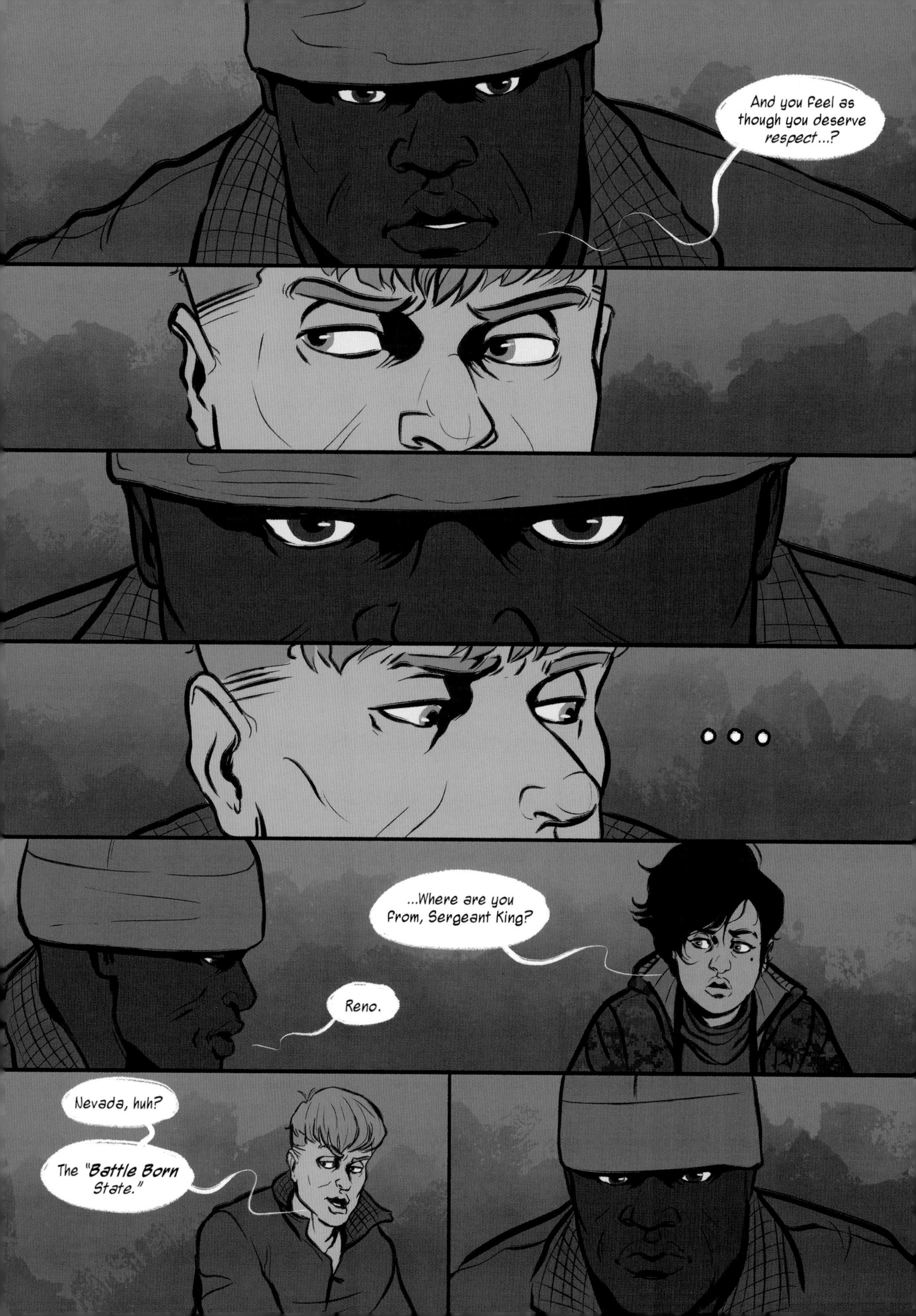
And you feel as though you deserve respect...?
...Where are you from, Sergeant King?
Reno.
Nevada, huh?
The "Battle Born State."

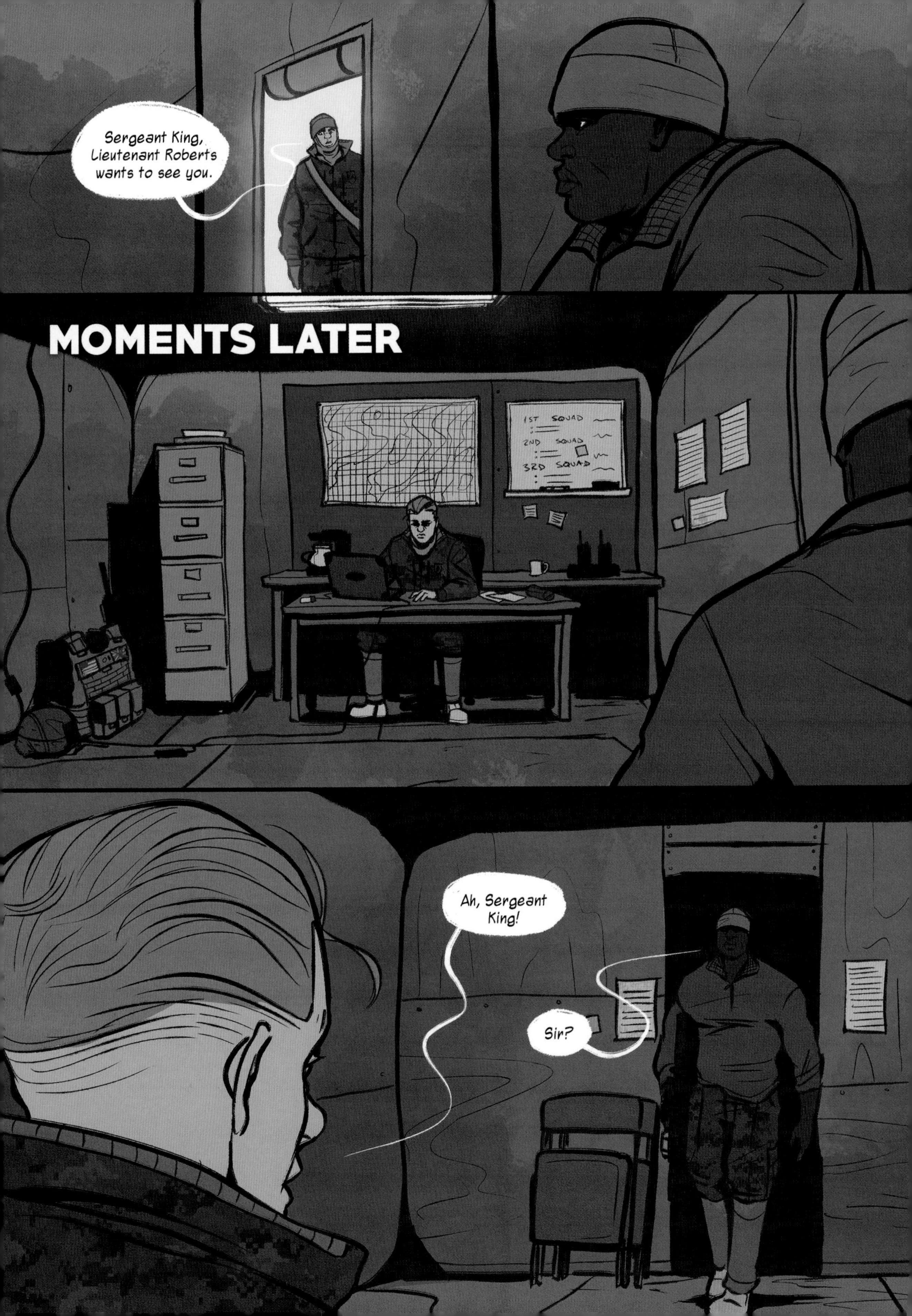
Sergeant King, Lieutenant Roberts wants to see you.
MOMENTS LATER
1ST SQUAD
2ND SQUAD
3RD SQUAD
Ah, Sergeant King!
Sir?

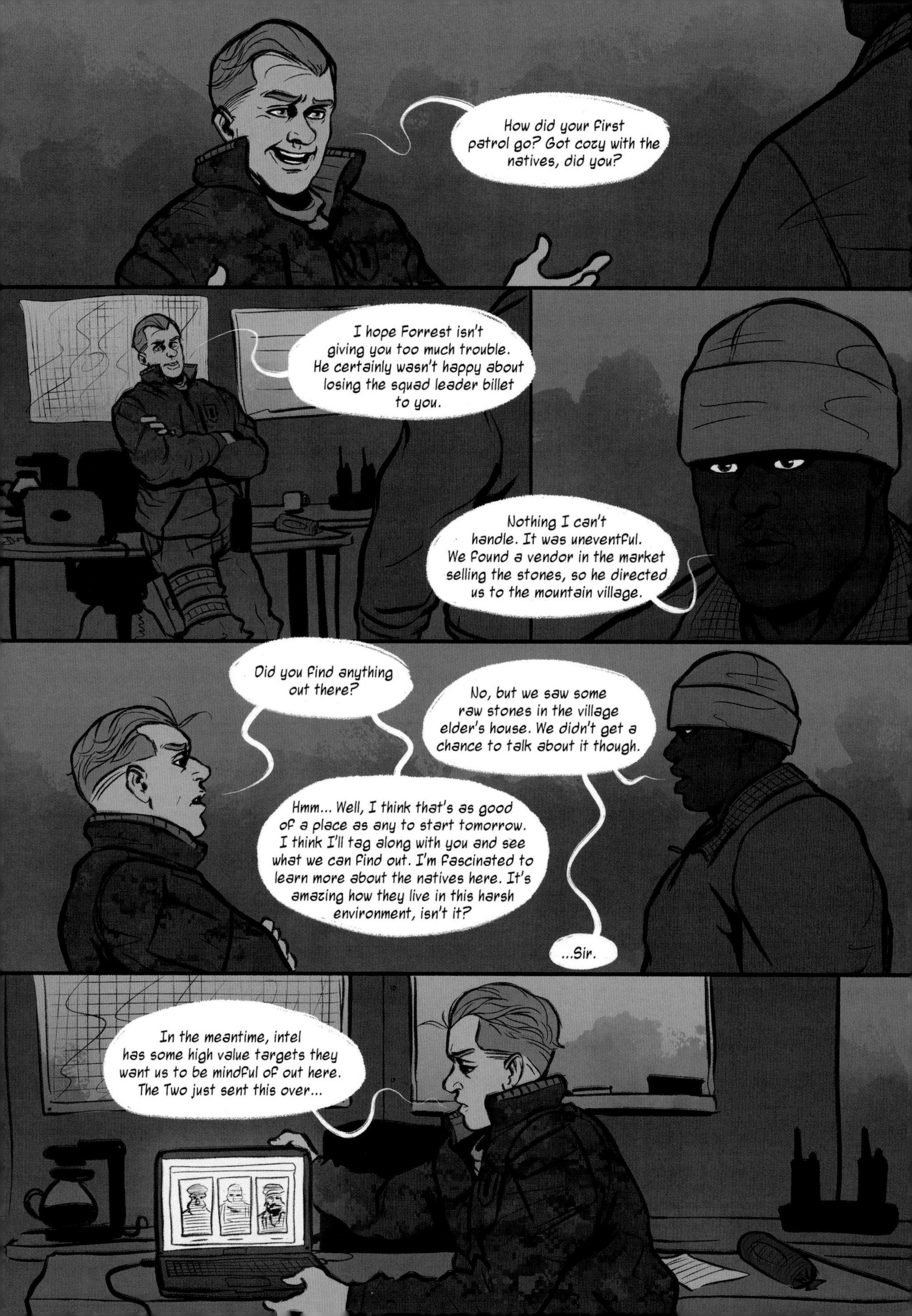
How did your first patrol go? Got cozy with the natives, did you?
I hope Forrest isn't giving you too much trouble. He certainly wasn't happy about losing the squad leader billet to you.
Nothing I can't handle. It was uneventful. We found a vendor in the market selling the stones, so he directed us to the mountain village.
Did you find anything out there?
No, but we saw some raw stones in the village elder's house. We didn't get a chance to talk about it though.
Hmm... Well, I think that's as good of a place as any to start tomorrow. I think I'll tag along with you and see what we can find out. I'm fascinated to learn more about the natives here. It's amazing how they live in this harsh environment, isn't it?
...Sir.
In the meantime, intel has some high value targets they want us to be mindful of out here. The Two just sent this over...

ALPHA
BRAVO
CHARLIE
For our AO, we're not entirely sure which one of these guys is in charge of the Taliban here, but we've narrowed it down to these three.
We're leaning toward Charlie here... Mohammed Nadir.
He calls himself the *Shah of Badakhshan...* The *king.*
I'll let you know when we find out more. I just wanted you to be aware. I'll link up with you guys before your patrol tomorrow morning.
Sir.
Oh hey, got these in the mail today...

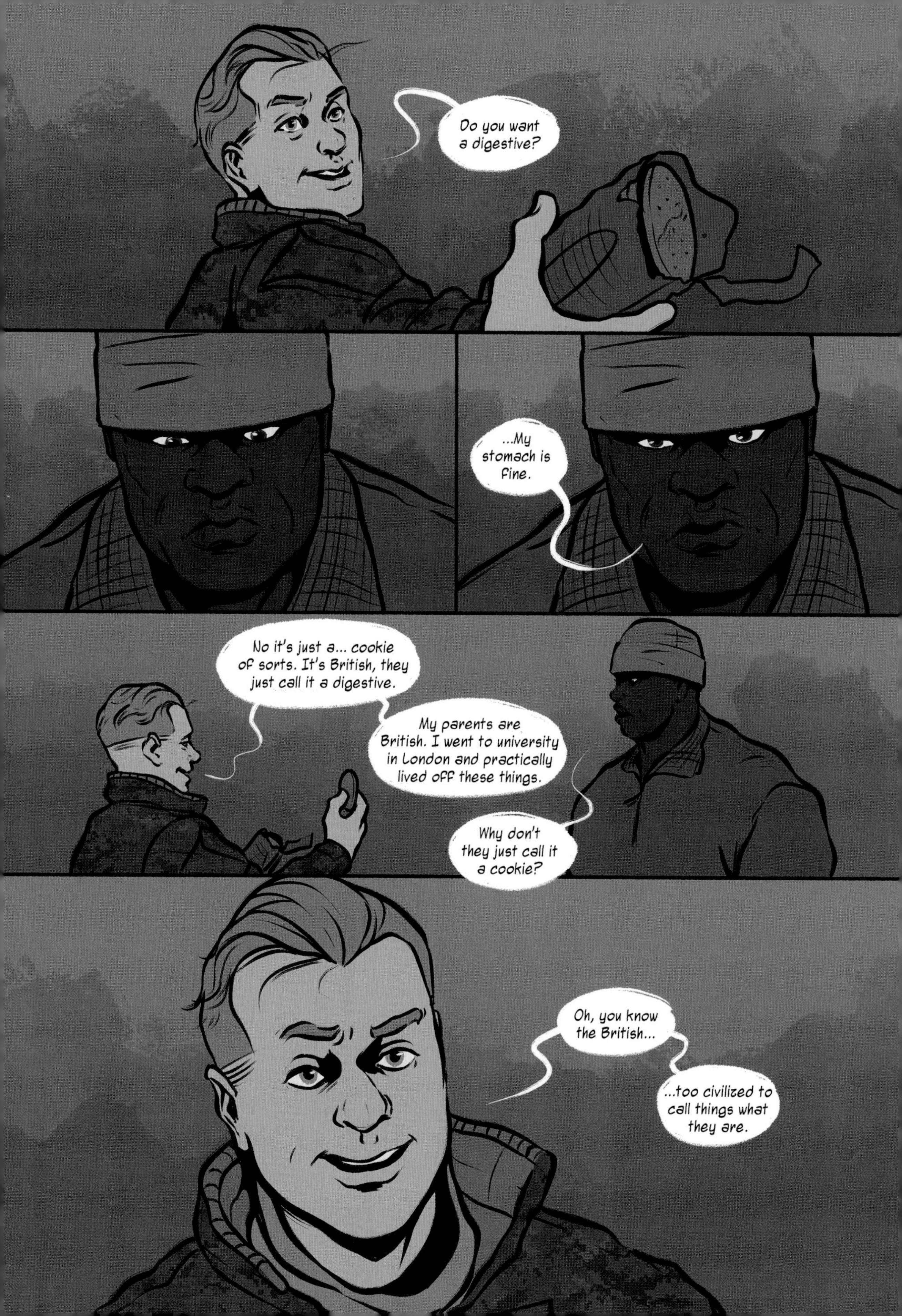
Do you want a digestive?
...My stomach is fine.
No it's just a... cookie of sorts. It's British, they just call it a digestive.
My parents are British. I went to university in London and practically lived off these things.
Why don't they just call it a cookie?
Oh, you know the British...
...too civilized to call things what they are.

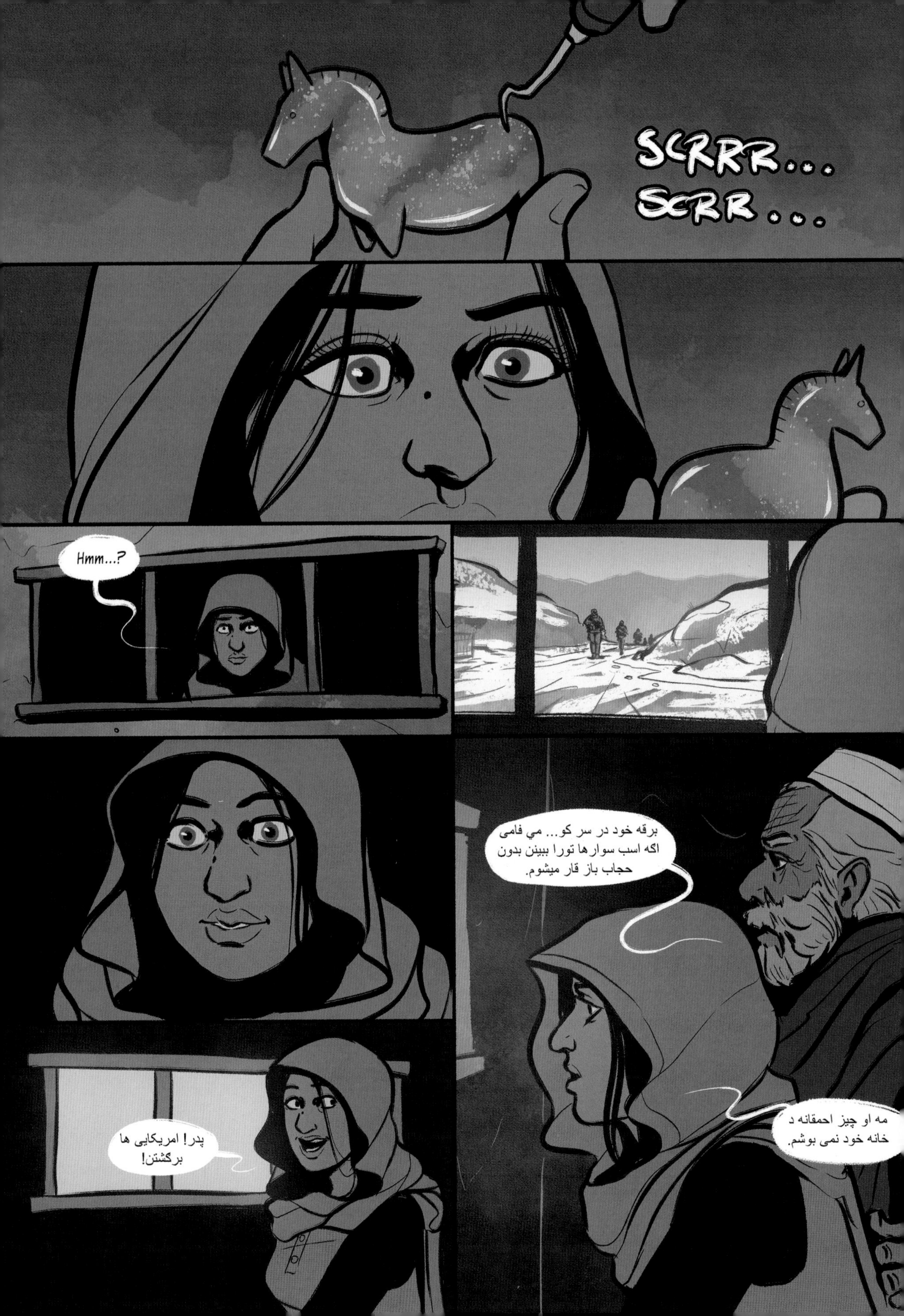
SCRRR...
SCRR...
Hmm...?
پدر! امریکایی ها برگشتن!
برقه خود در سر کو... مي فامی اگه اسب سوارها تورا ببینن بدون حجاب باز قار میشوم.
مه او چیز احمقانه د خانه خود نمی بوشم.

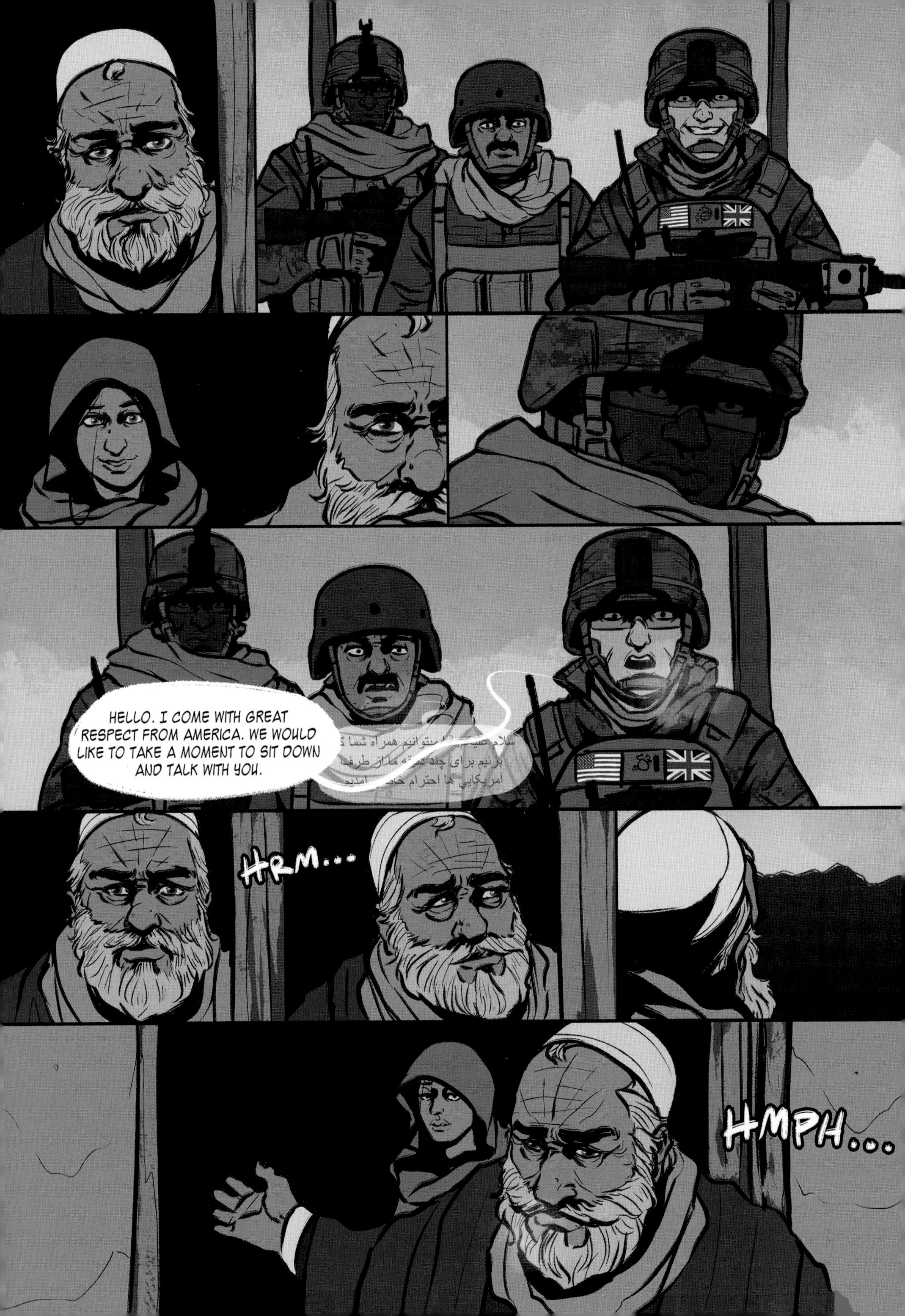
HELLO. I COME WITH GREAT RESPECT FROM AMERICA. WE WOULD LIKE TO TAKE A MOMENT TO SIT DOWN AND TALK WITH YOU.
HRM...
HMPH...

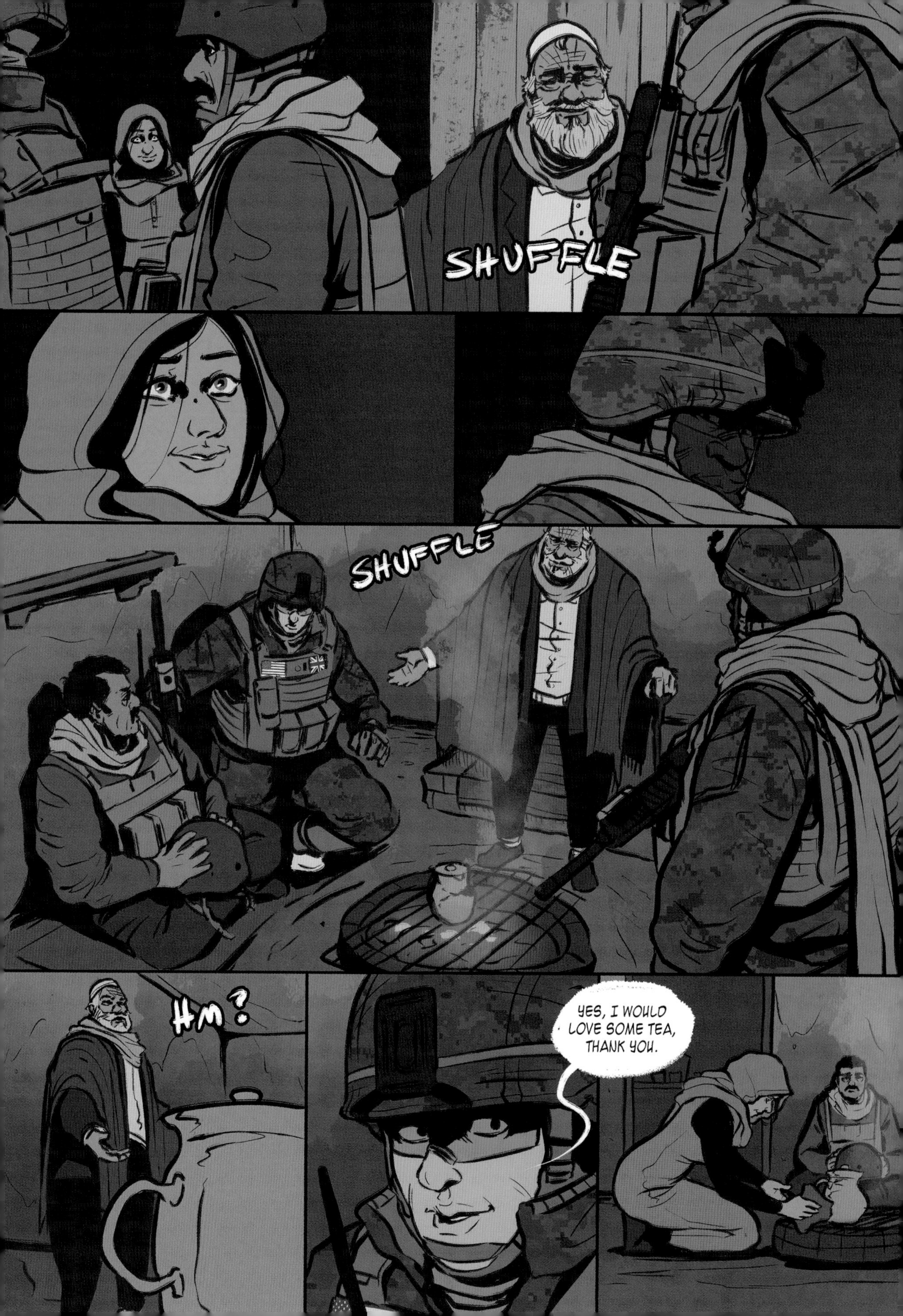
SHUFFLE
SHUFFLE
HM?
YES, I WOULD LOVE SOME TEA, THANK YOU.

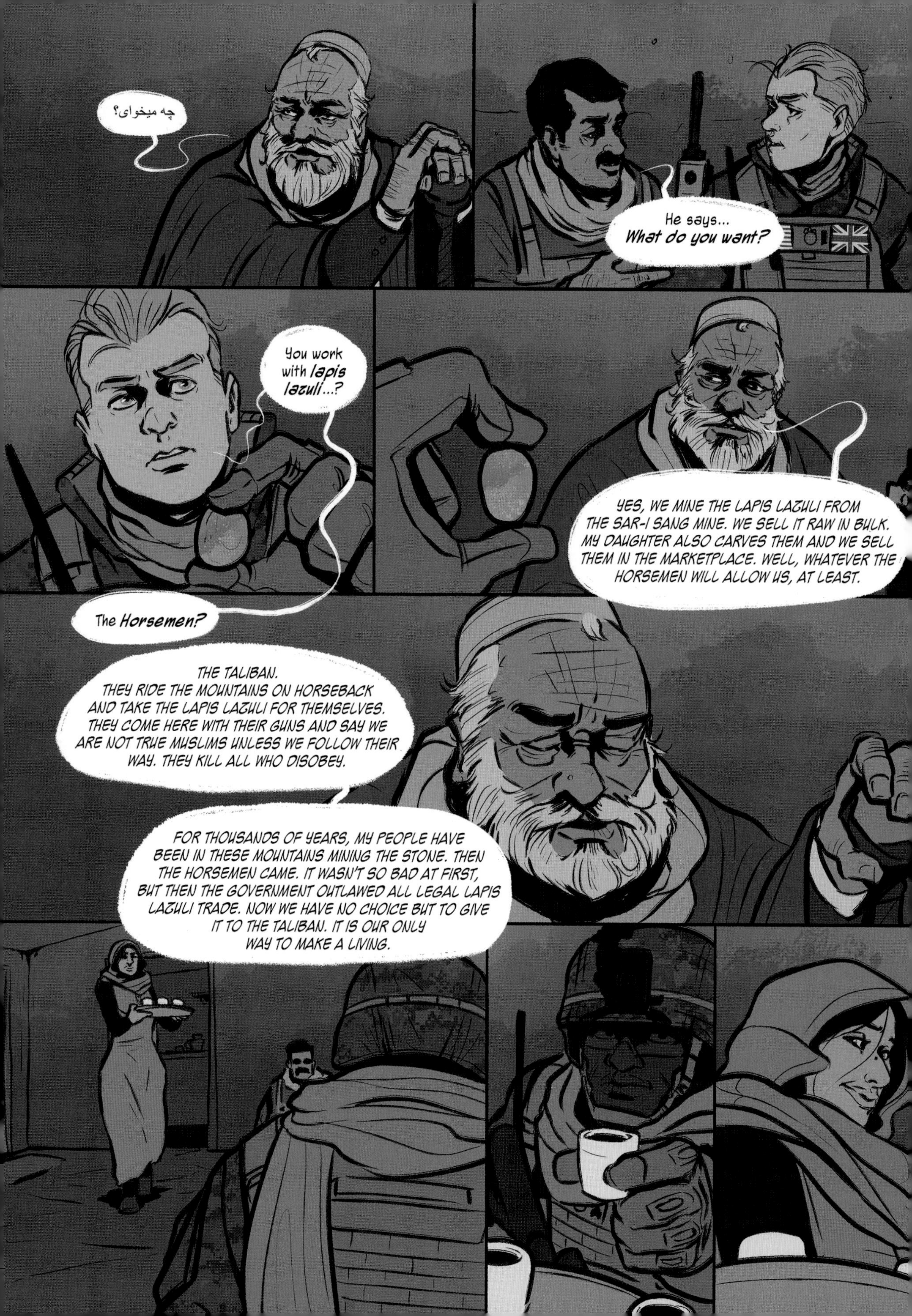
چه میخوای؟
He says... What do you want?
You work with lapis lazuli...?
YES, WE MINE THE LAPIS LAZULI FROM THE SAR-I SANG MINE. WE SELL IT RAW IN BULK. MY DAUGHTER ALSO CARVES THEM AND WE SELL THEM IN THE MARKETPLACE. WELL, WHATEVER THE HORSEMEN WILL ALLOW US, AT LEAST.
The Horsemen?
THE TALIBAN. THEY RIDE THE MOUNTAINS ON HORSEBACK AND TAKE THE LAPIS LAZULI FOR THEMSELVES. THEY COME HERE WITH THEIR GUNS AND SAY WE ARE NOT TRUE MUSLIMS UNLESS WE FOLLOW THEIR WAY. THEY KILL ALL WHO DISOBEY.
FOR THOUSANDS OF YEARS, MY PEOPLE HAVE BEEN IN THESE MOUNTAINS MINING THE STONE. THEN THE HORSEMEN CAME. IT WASN'T SO BAD AT FIRST, BUT THEN THE GOVERNMENT OUTLAWED ALL LEGAL LAPIS LAZULI TRADE. NOW WE HAVE NO CHOICE BUT TO GIVE IT TO THE TALIBAN. IT IS OUR ONLY WAY TO MAKE A LIVING.

I see.
SO FIRST THE HORSEMEN CAME. NOW THE AMERICANS ARE HERE. WHAT IS IT THAT YOU WANT FROM US? HAVE YOU COME HERE FOR THE STONE, TOO?
No. We came here to help you. We can build you guys schools and roads. We can help improve your community and make Badakhshan part of the modern world. All you have to do for us is work with us and trust us to fight the Taliban.
I DO NOT CARE FOR YOUR MODERN THINGS, AMERICAN. I JUST WANT TO BE RID OF THESE TALIBAN MONSTERS AND LIVE IN PEACE. THIS VILLAGE WAS ONCE A HAPPY PLACE. IT IS NOW SAD AND SCARED...
MY FATHER USED TO CALL THIS STONE THE HEART OF AFGHANISTAN... AND NOW THE TALIBAN HAVE TAKEN IT FOR THEMSELVES.

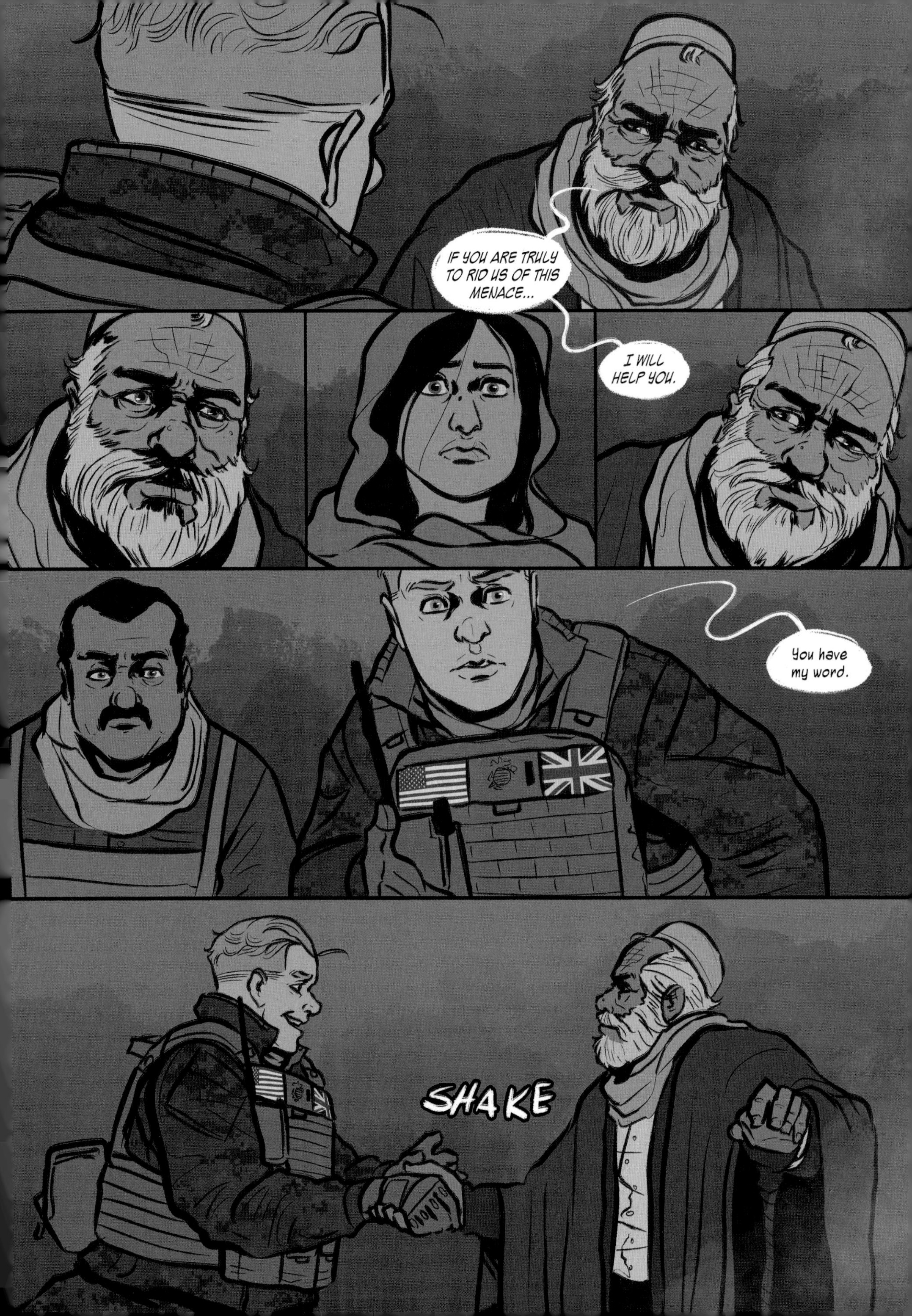
IF YOU ARE TRULY TO RID US OF THIS MENACE...
I WILL HELP YOU.
You have my word.
SHAKE

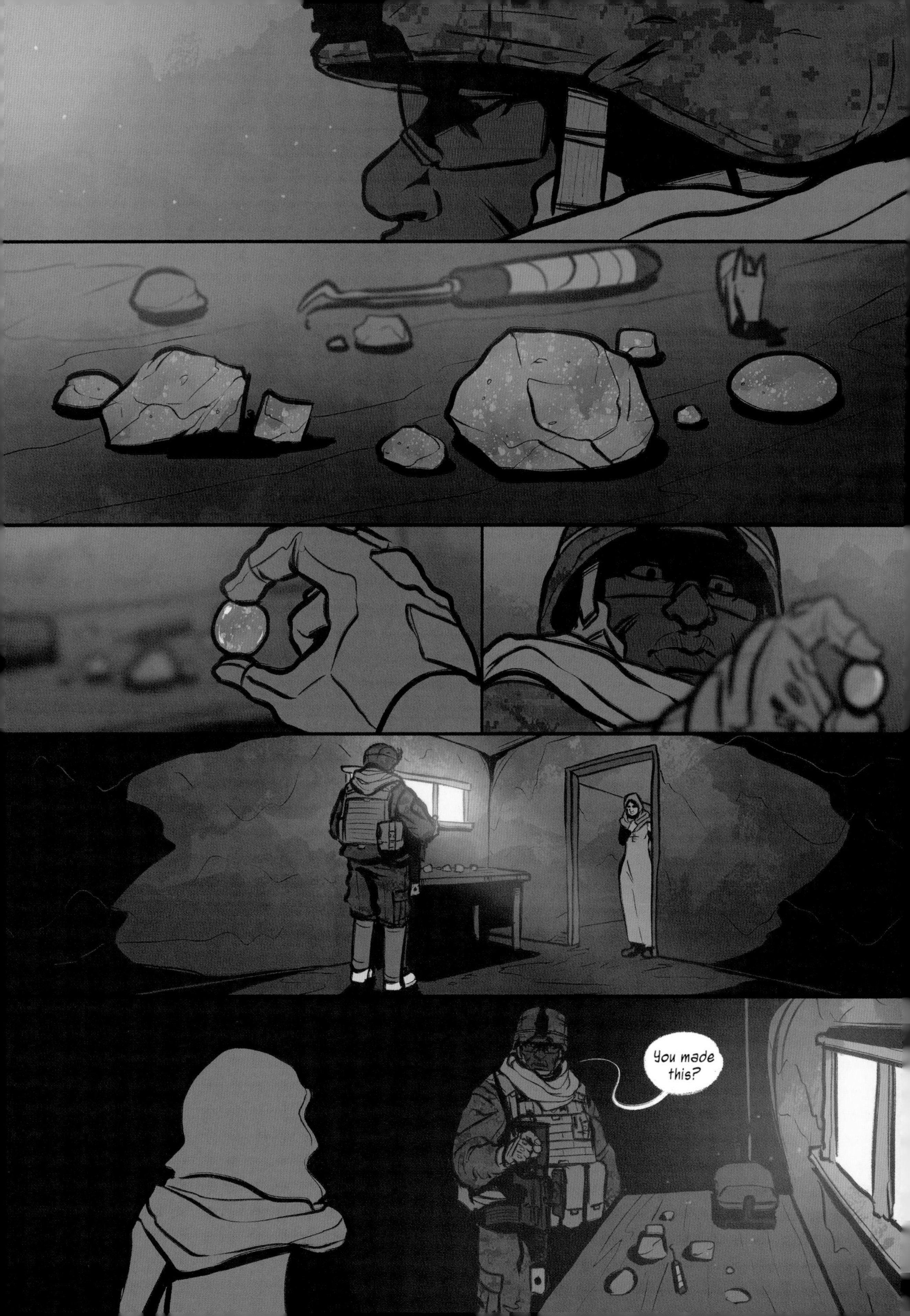
You made this?

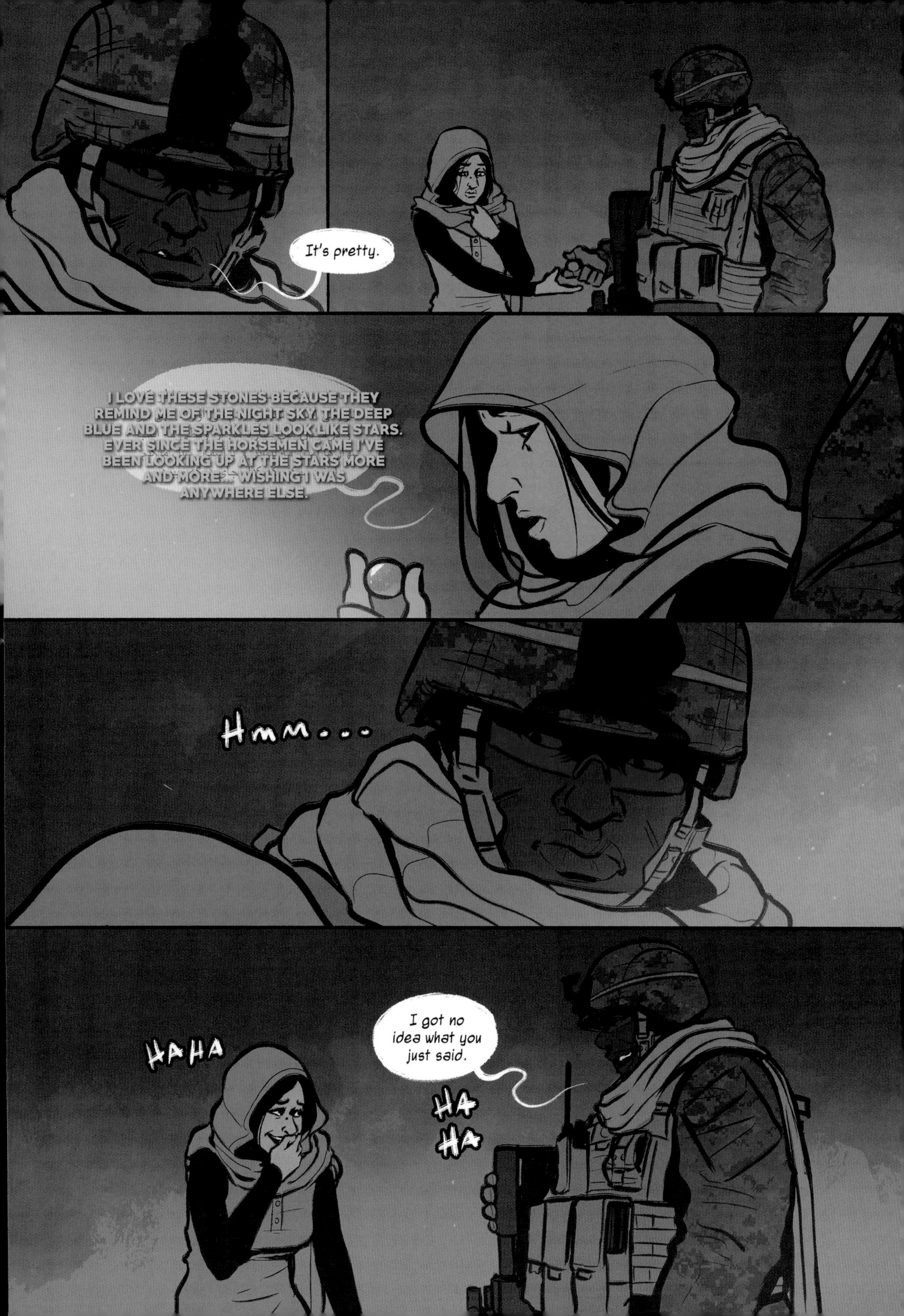
It's pretty.
I LOVE THESE STONES BECAUSE THEY REMIND ME OF THE NIGHT SKY. THE DEEP BLUE AND THE SPARKLES LOOK LIKE STARS. EVER SINCE THE HORSEMEN CAME I'VE BEEN LOOKING UP AT THE STARS MORE AND MORE... WISHING I WAS ANYWHERE ELSE.
Hmm...
HAHA
I got no idea what you just said.
HA HA

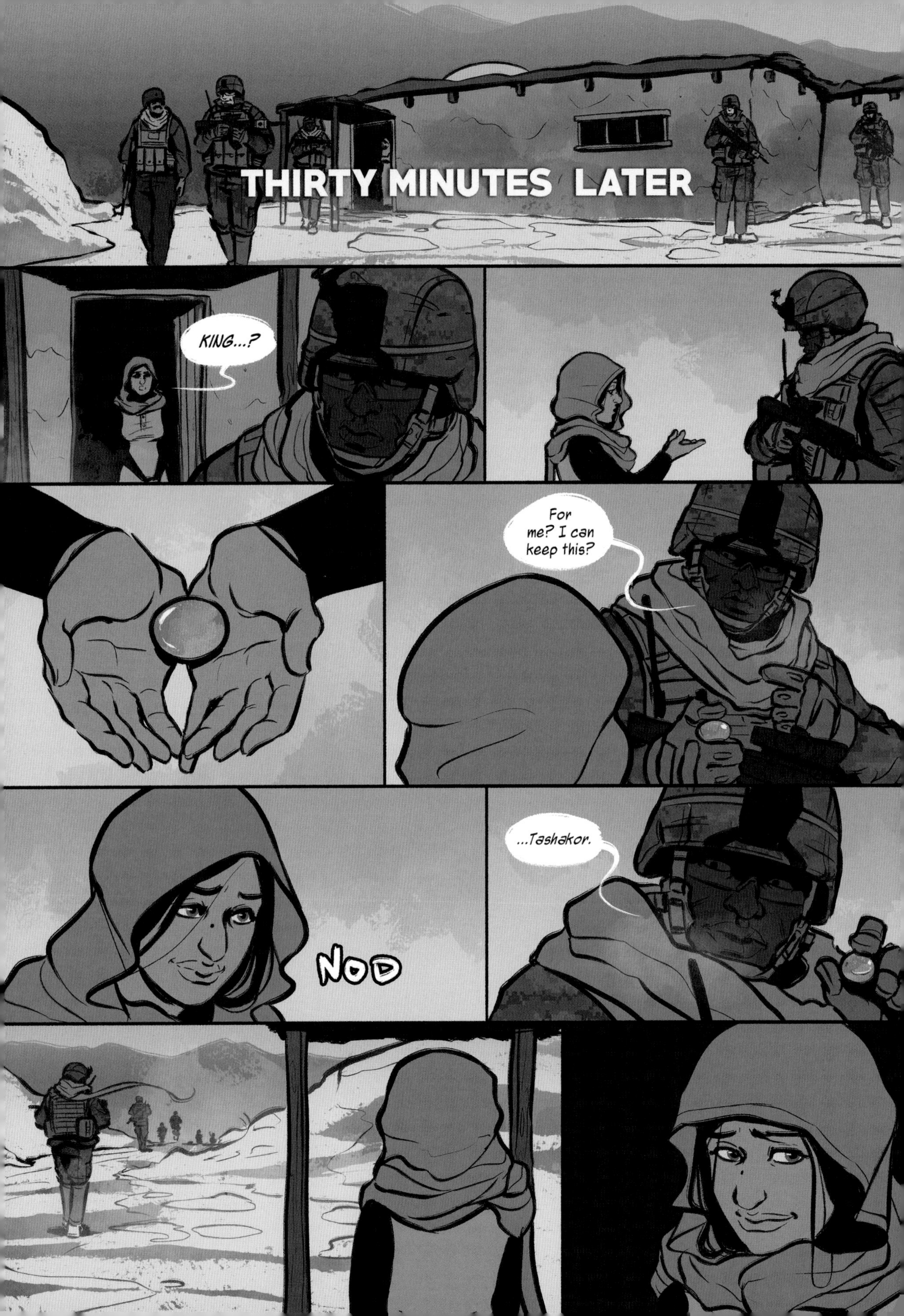
THIRTY MINUTES LATER
KING...?
For me? I can keep this?
NOD
...Tashakor.

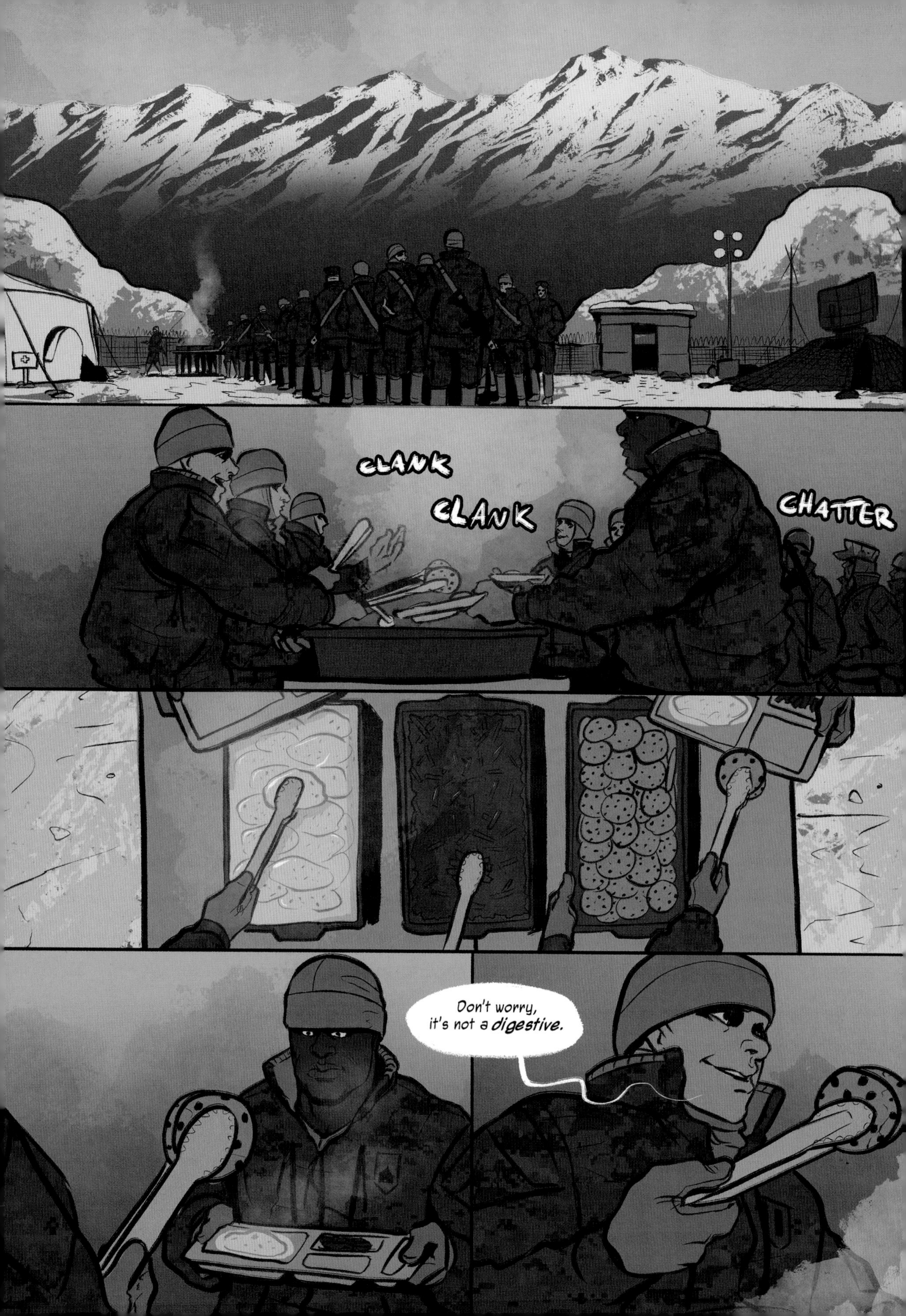
CLANK
CLANK
CHATTER
Don't worry, it's not a *digestive.*

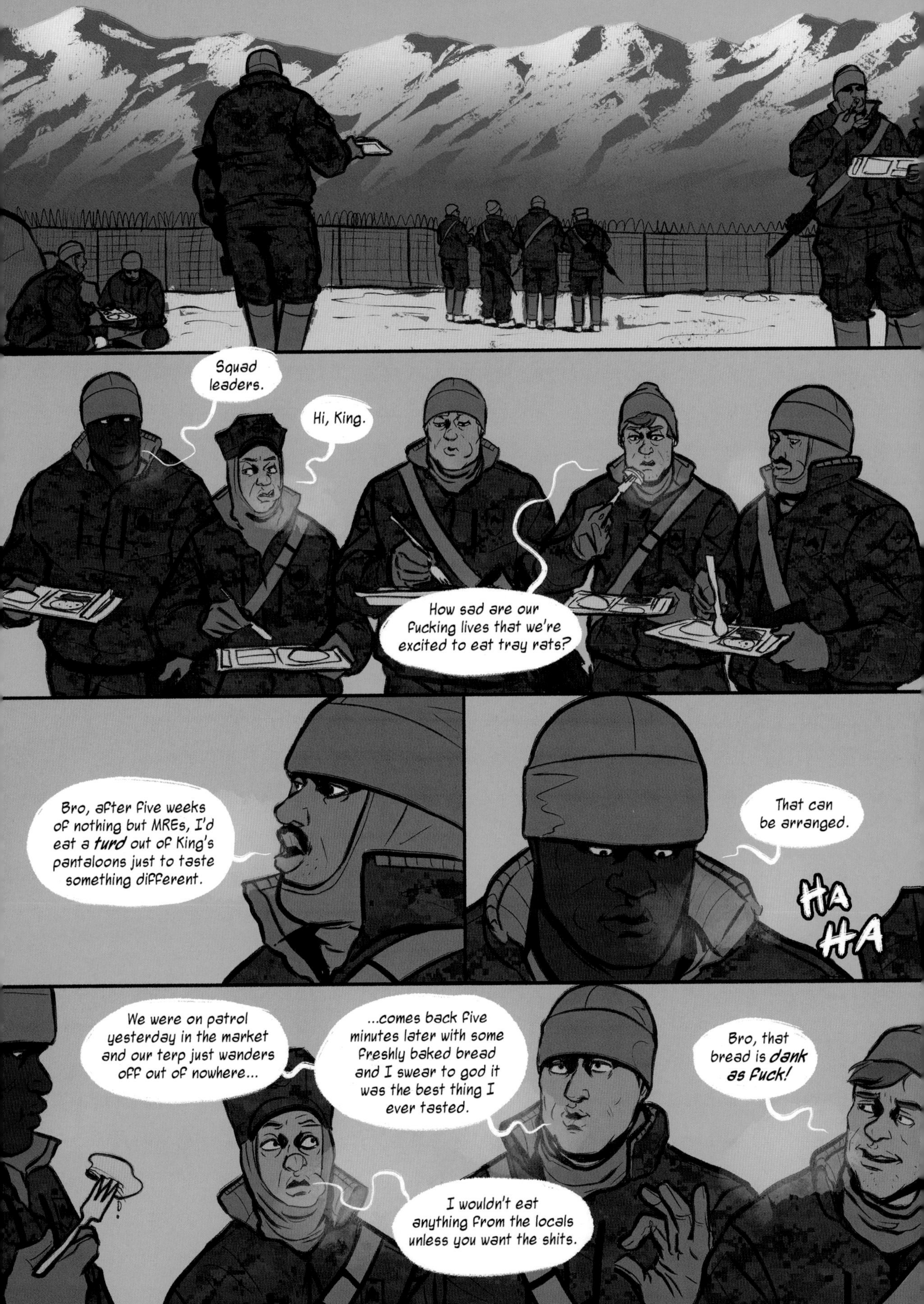
Squad leaders.
Hi, King.
How sad are our fucking lives that we're excited to eat tray rats?
Bro, after five weeks of nothing but MREs, I'd eat a *turd* out of King's pantaloons just to taste something different.
That can be arranged.
HA HA
We were on patrol yesterday in the market and our terp just wanders off out of nowhere...
...comes back five minutes later with some freshly baked bread and I swear to god it was the best thing I ever tasted.
Bro, that bread is *dank as fuck!*
I wouldn't eat anything from the locals unless you want the shits.

It's **bread,** bro. It's not like you're eating it out of someone's butthole.
You may as well be! I was out in a village the other day and, swear to god, this guy comes out and takes a shit right out in the open. Wipes his asshole with his hand and then just moves on. These people are goddamn savages.
Personally I think there's a lot to like about this place. Look at how beautiful it is.
Yeah but it's the people that make the place. Do you think we'd be here if these Afghans had their shit together? The entire Middle East is a shit-show. The world would be better off without it.

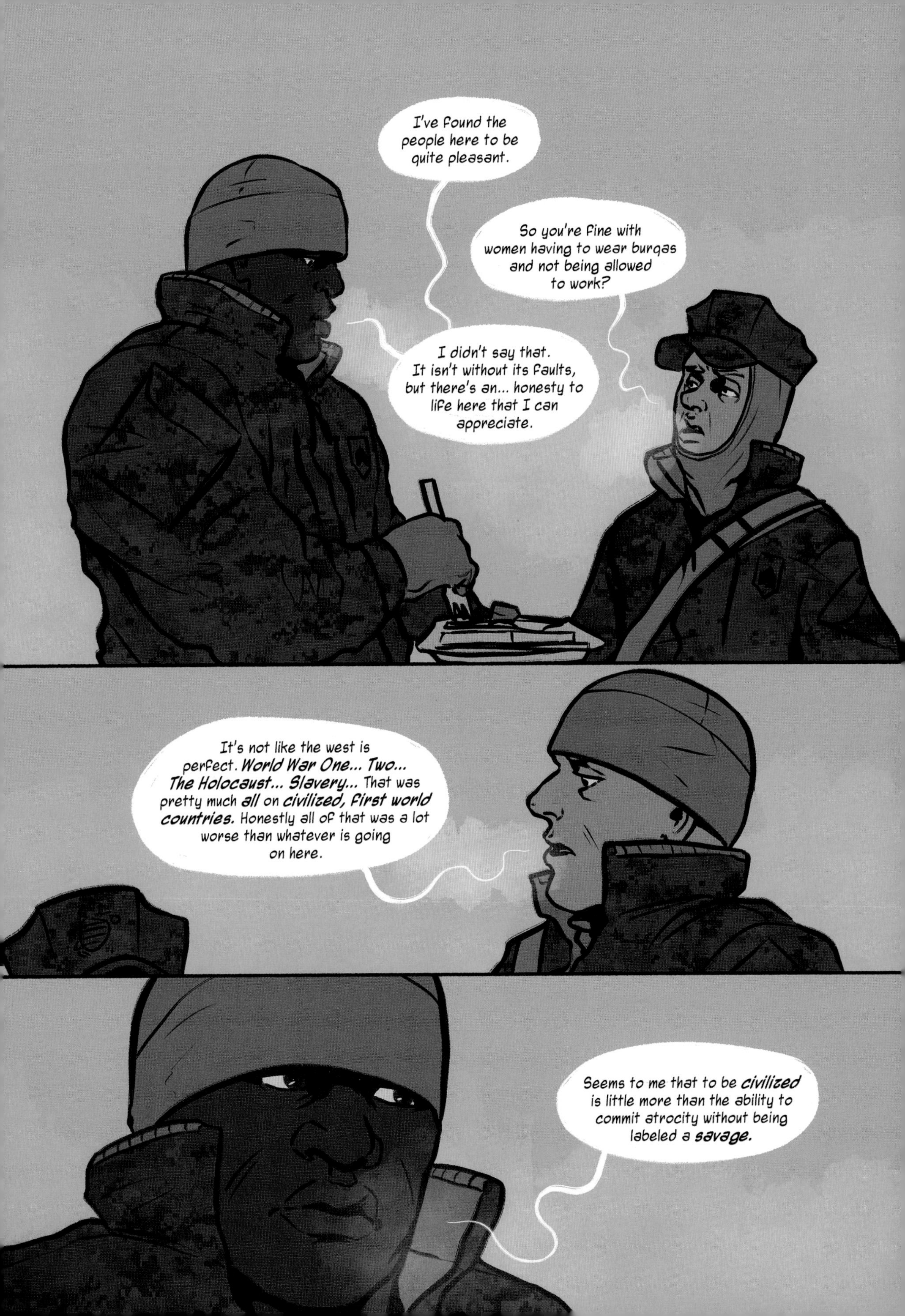
I've found the people here to be quite pleasant.
So you're fine with women having to wear burqas and not being allowed to work?
I didn't say that. It isn't without its faults, but there's an... honesty to life here that I can appreciate.
It's not like the west is perfect. *World War One... Two... The Holocaust... Slavery...* That was pretty much *all* on *civilized, first world countries.* Honestly all of that was a lot worse than whatever is going on here.
Seems to me that to be *civilized* is little more than the ability to commit atrocity without being labeled a *savage.*

No, civilized is not trying to fuck every farm animal you come across...

FRANK!

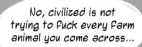

I SEE YOU THERE! LEAVE THAT DONKEY ALONE! IT AINT FOR FUCKIN'!

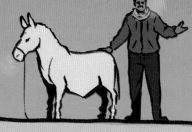

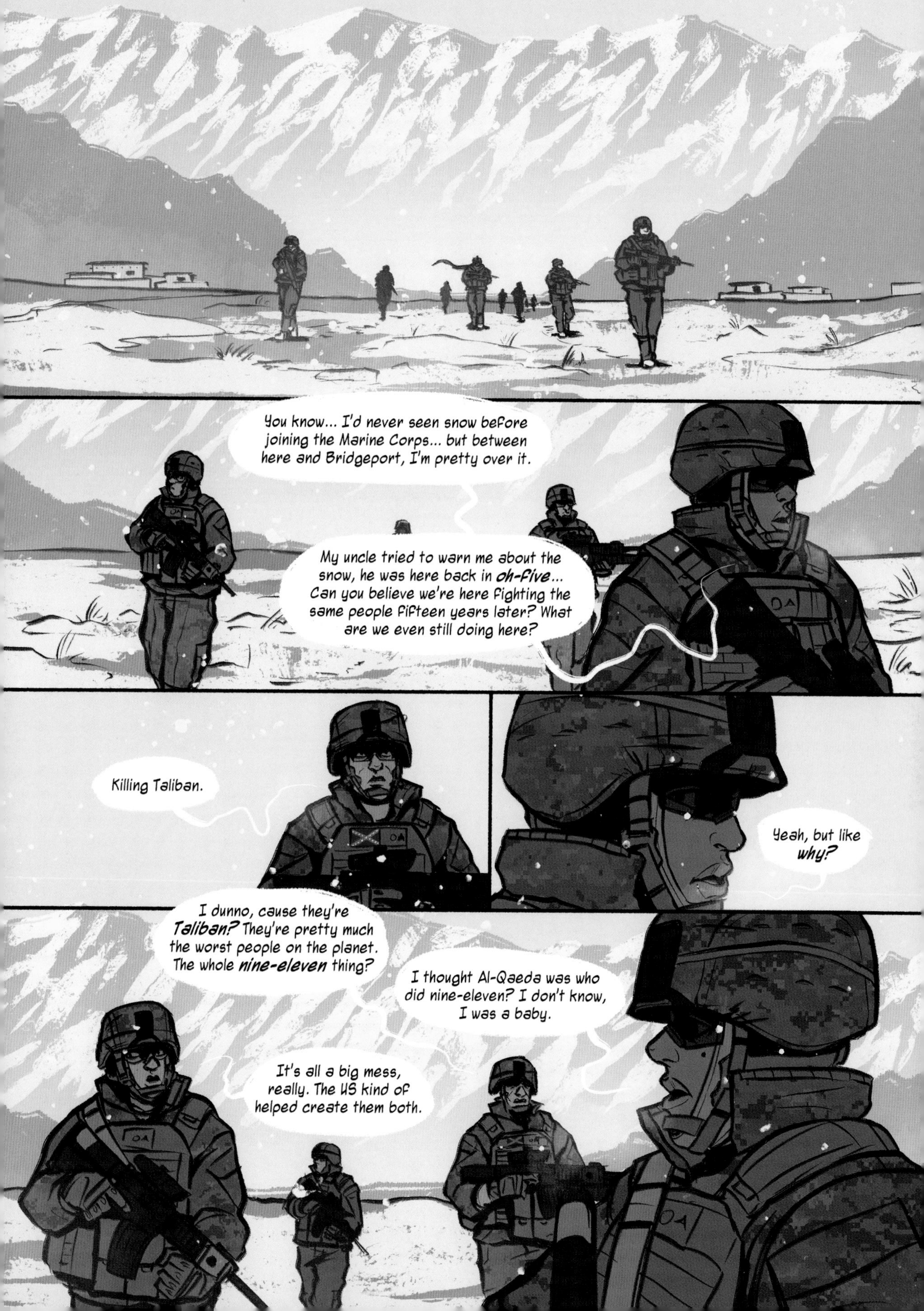
You know... I'd never seen snow before joining the Marine Corps... but between here and Bridgeport, I'm pretty over it.
My uncle tried to warn me about the snow, he was here back in *oh-five*... Can you believe we're here fighting the same people fifteen years later? What are we even still doing here?
Killing Taliban.
Yeah, but like *why?*
I dunno, cause they're *Taliban?* They're pretty much the worst people on the planet. The whole *nine-eleven* thing?
I thought Al-Qaeda was who did nine-eleven? I don't know, I was a baby.
It's all a big mess, really. The US kind of helped create them both.

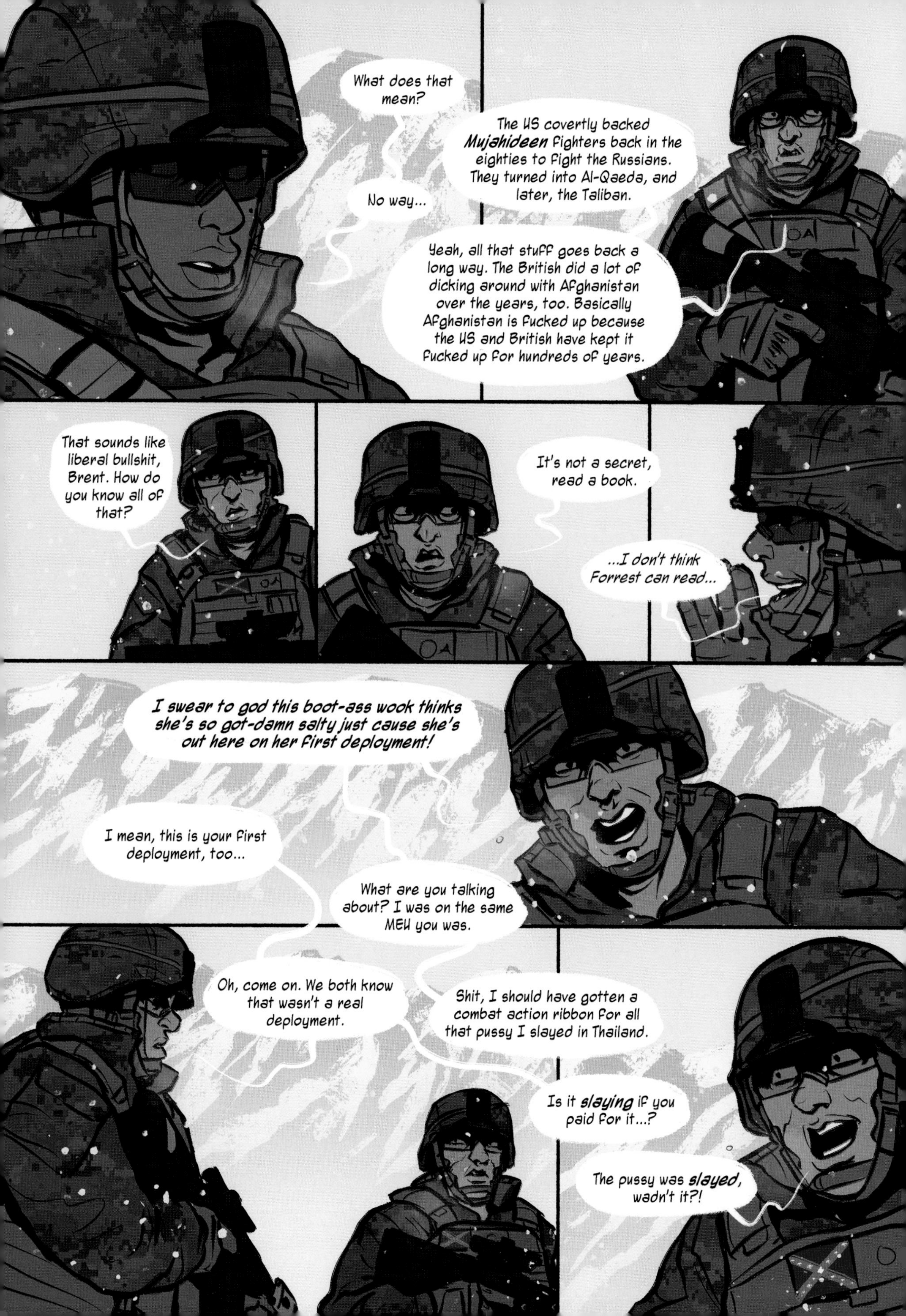

What does that mean?
No way...
The US covertly backed **Mujahideen** fighters back in the eighties to fight the Russians. They turned into Al-Qaeda, and later, the Taliban.
Yeah, all that stuff goes back a long way. The British did a lot of dicking around with Afghanistan over the years, too. Basically Afghanistan is fucked up because the US and British have kept it fucked up for hundreds of years.
That sounds like liberal bullshit, Brent. How do you know all of that?
It's not a secret, read a book.
...I don't think Forrest can read...
I swear to god this boot-ass wook thinks she's so got-damn salty just cause she's out here on her first deployment!
I mean, this is your first deployment, too...
What are you talking about? I was on the same MEU you was.
Oh, come on. We both know that wasn't a real deployment.
Shit, I should have gotten a combat action ribbon for all that pussy I slayed in Thailand.
Is it ***slaying*** if you paid for it...?
The pussy was ***slayed***, wadn't it?!

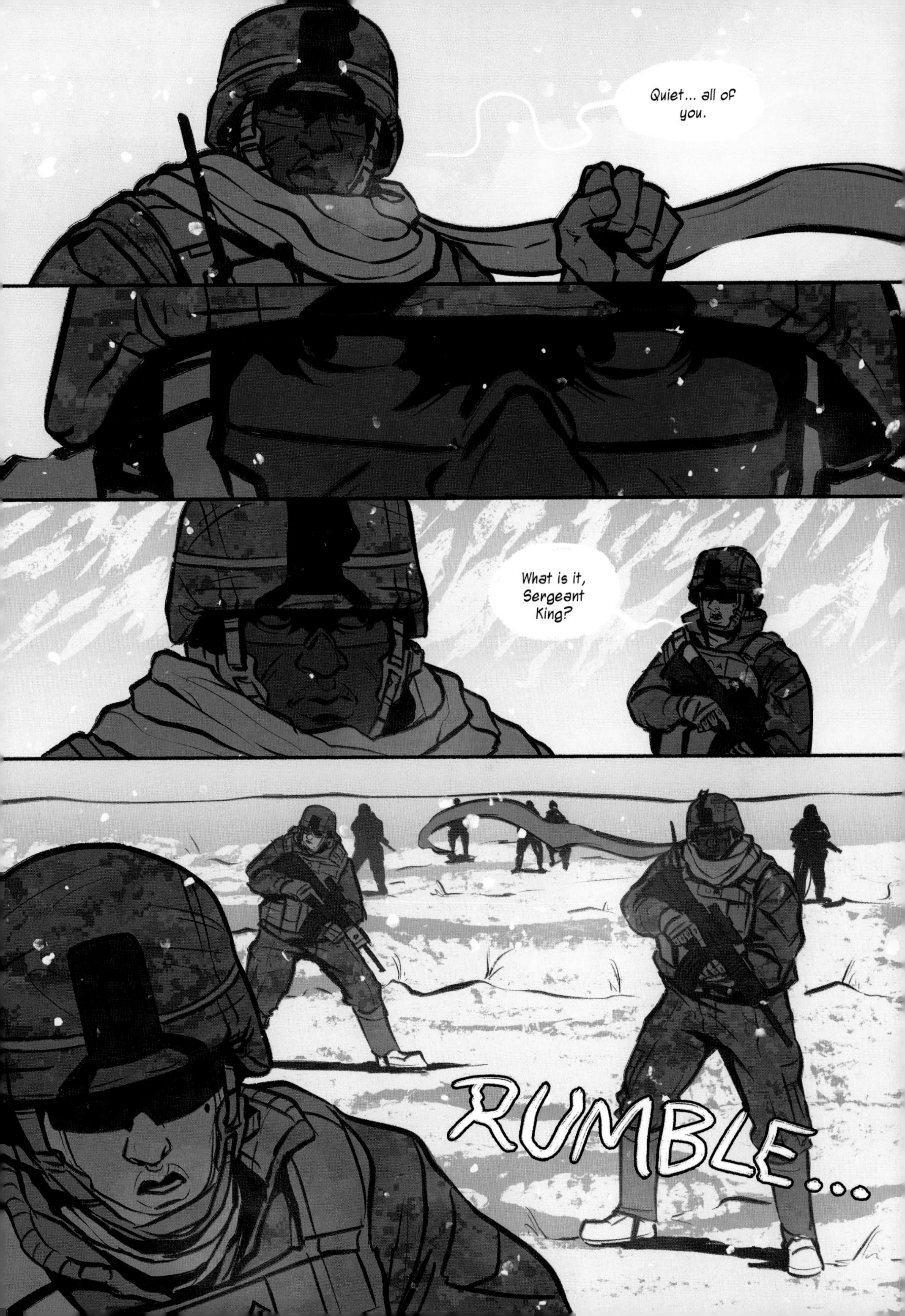
Quiet... all of you.
What is it, Sergeant King?
RUMBLE...

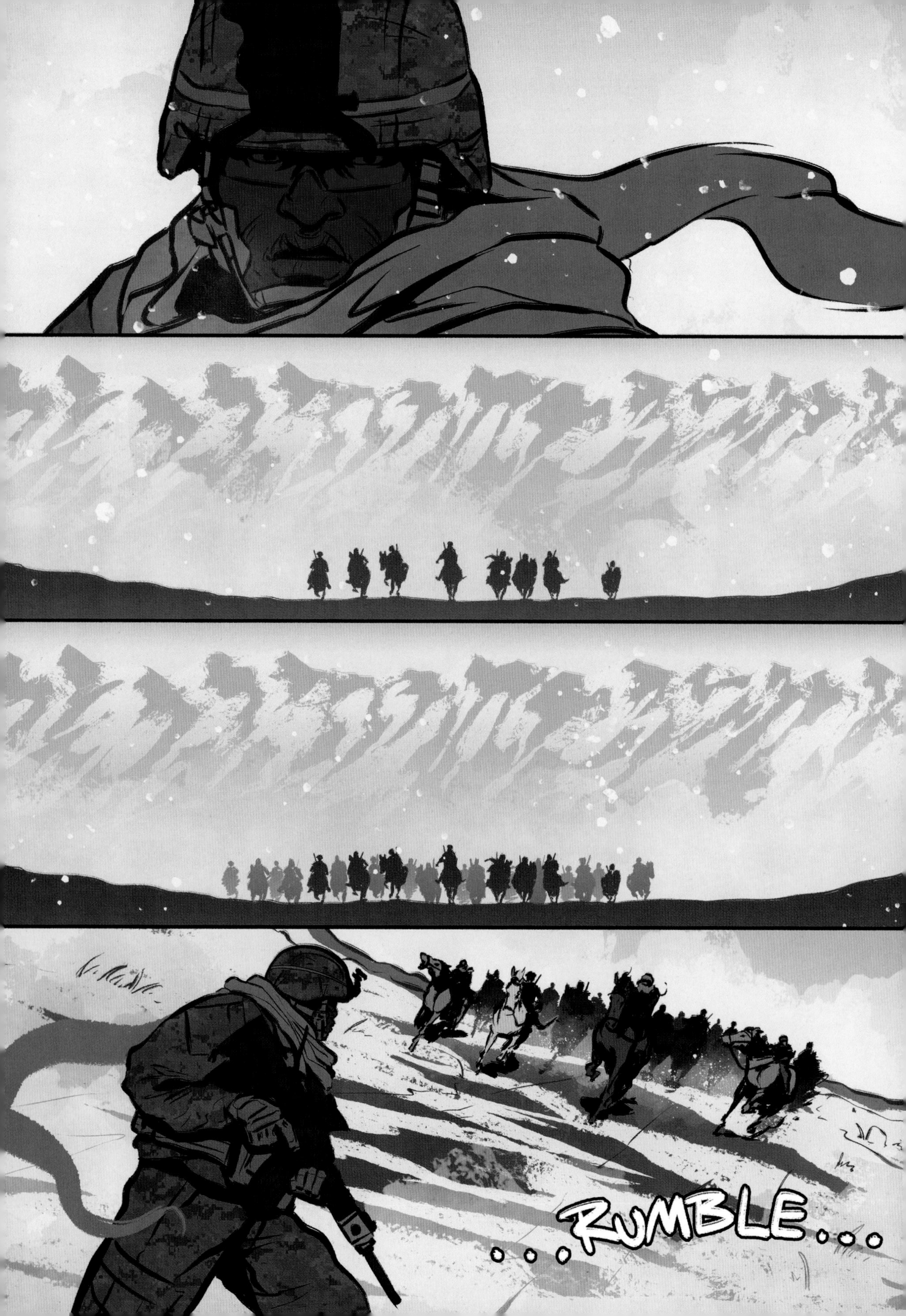
...RUMBLE...

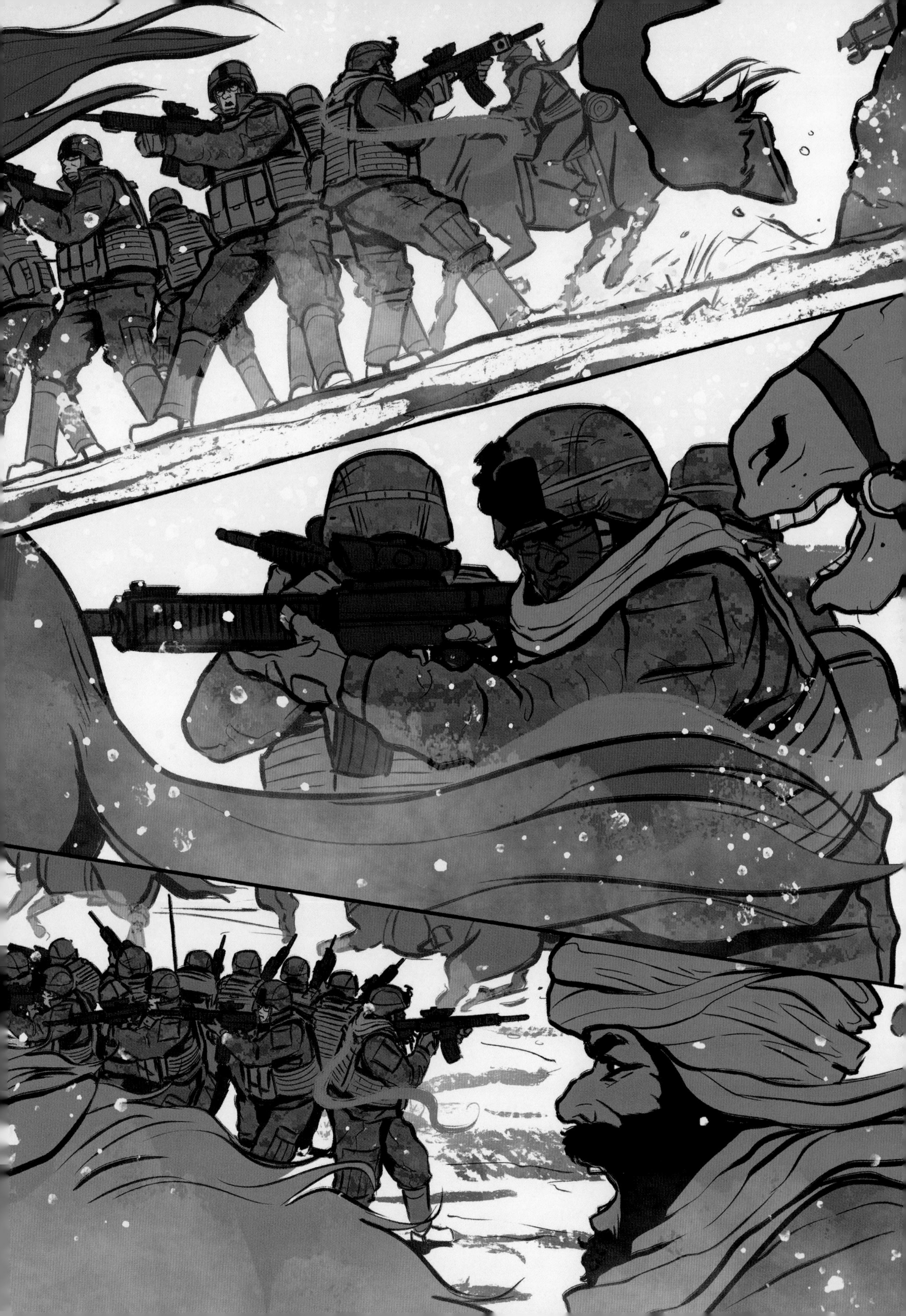

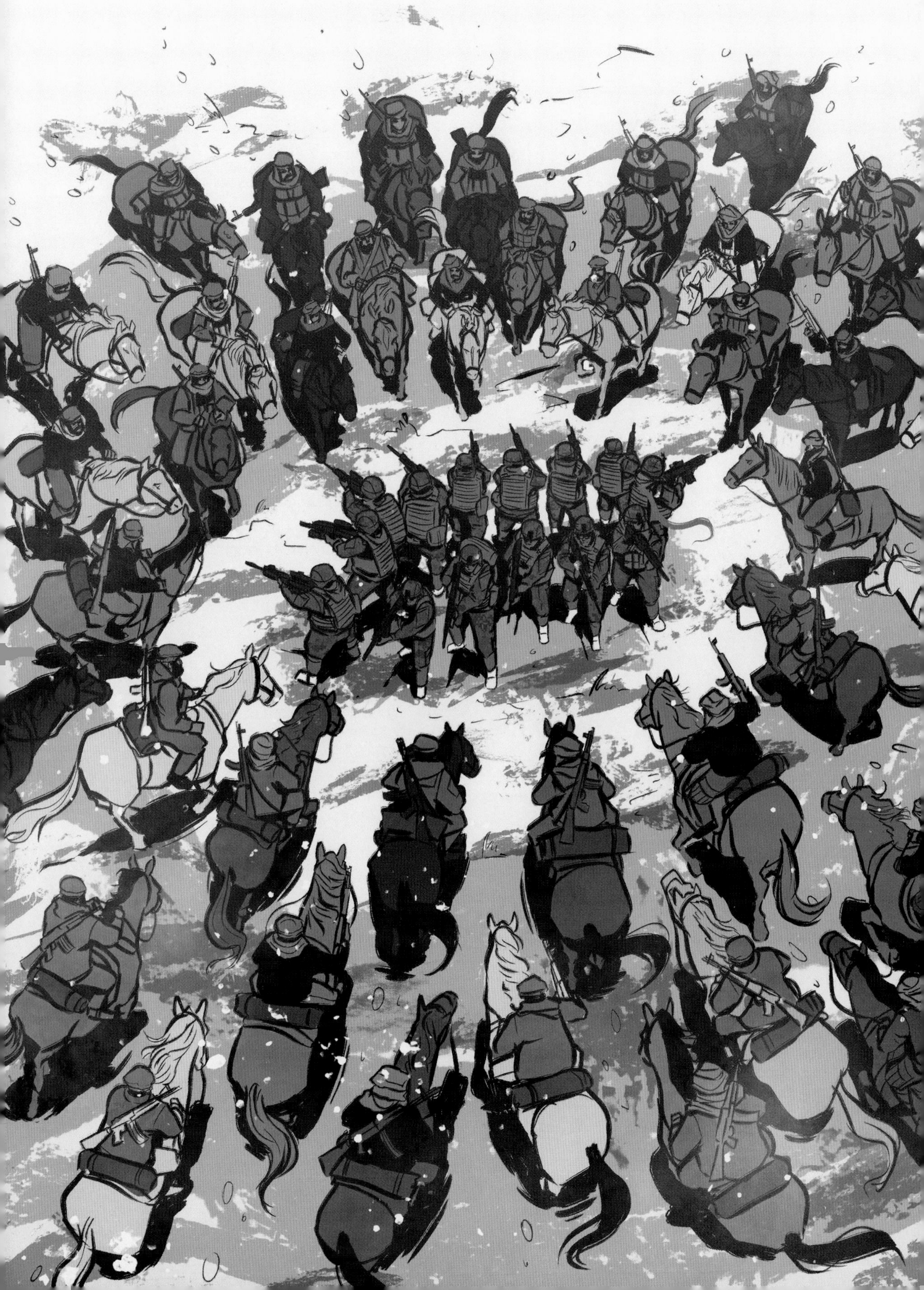

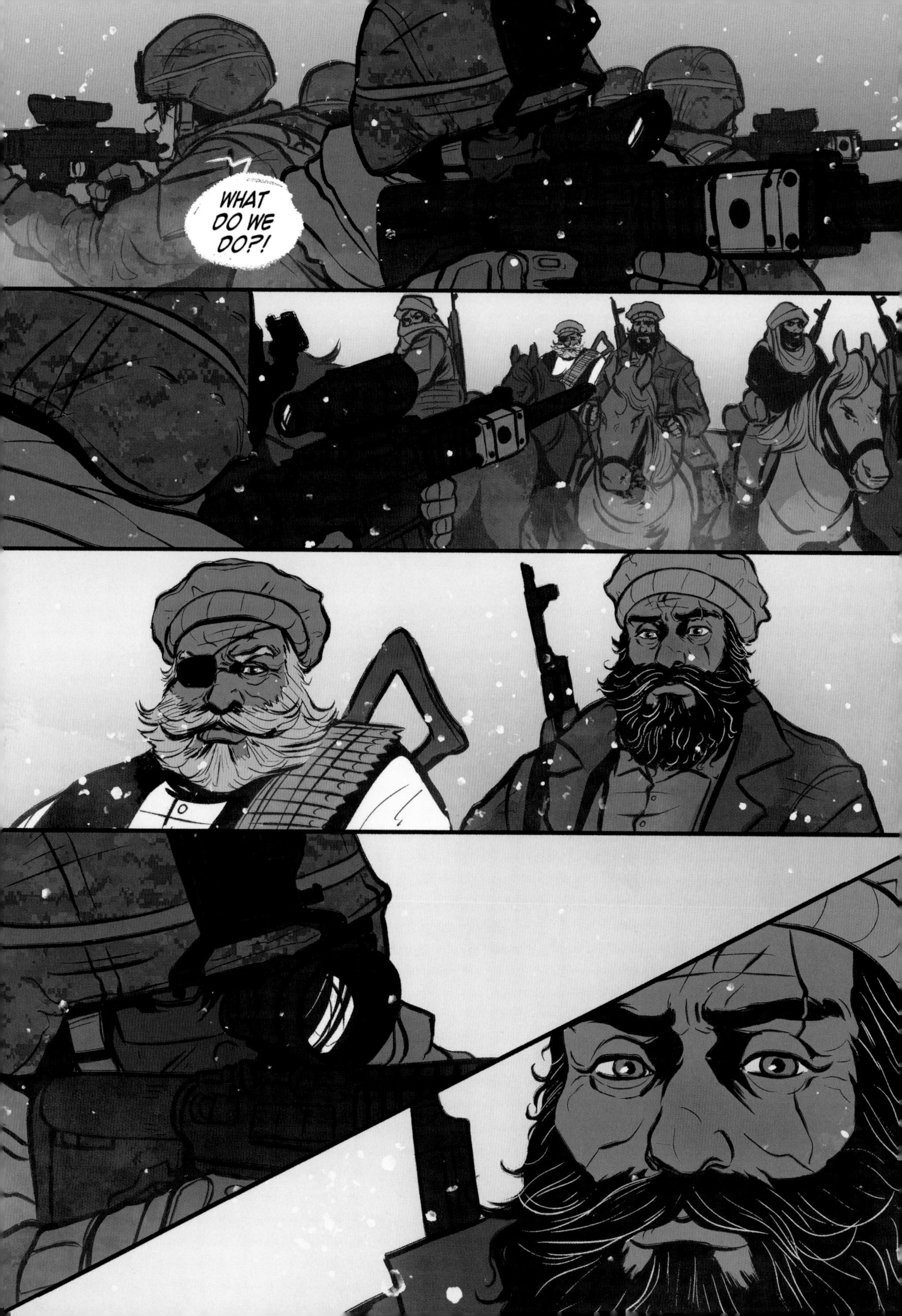
WHAT DO WE DO?!

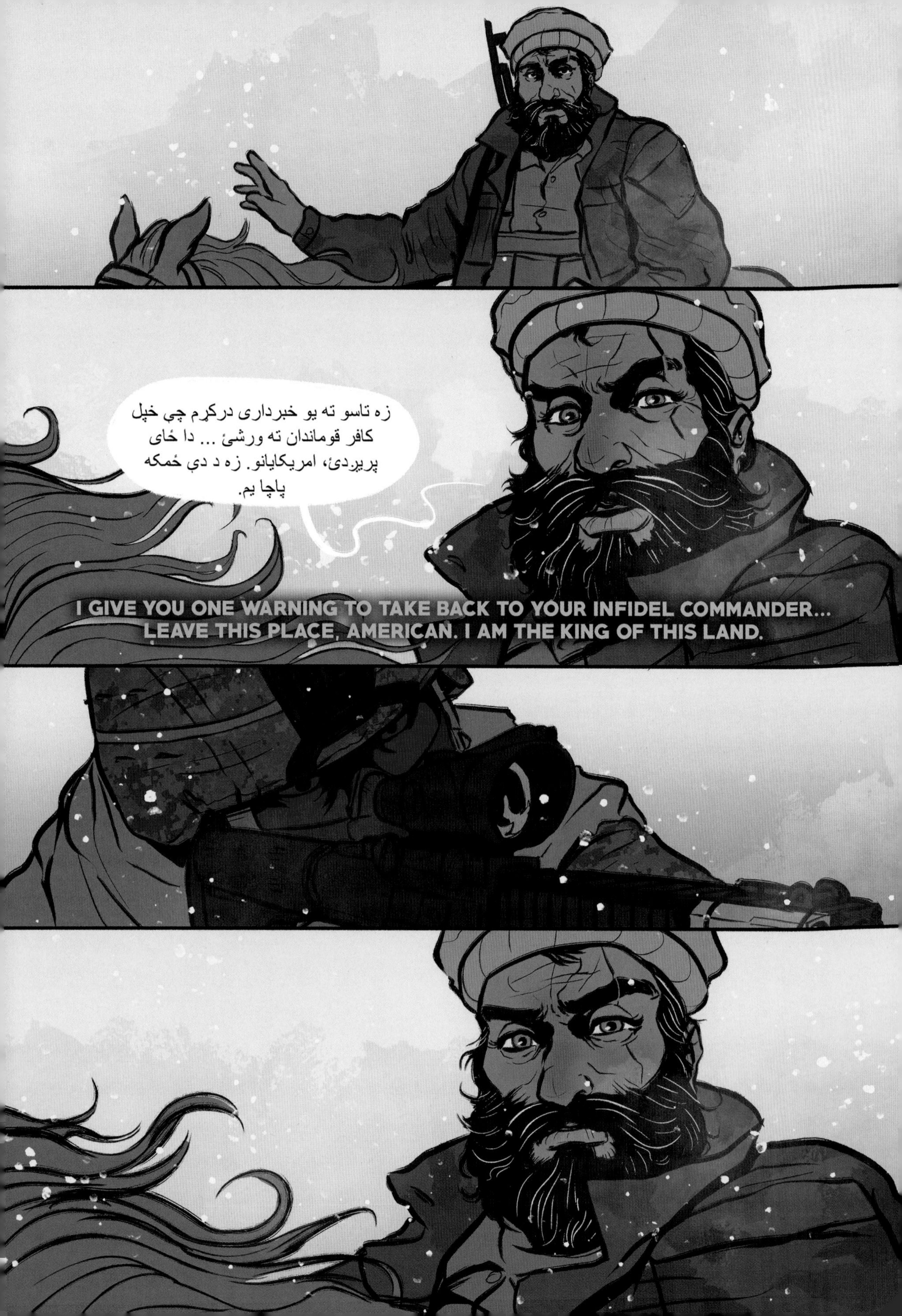

زه تاسو ته يو خبرداری درکړم چې خپل کافر قوماندان ته ورشئ ... دا ځای پرېږدئ، امریکایانو. زه د دې ځمکه پاچا یم.
I GIVE YOU ONE WARNING TO TAKE BACK TO YOUR INFIDEL COMMANDER...
LEAVE THIS PLACE, AMERICAN. I AM THE KING OF THIS LAND.

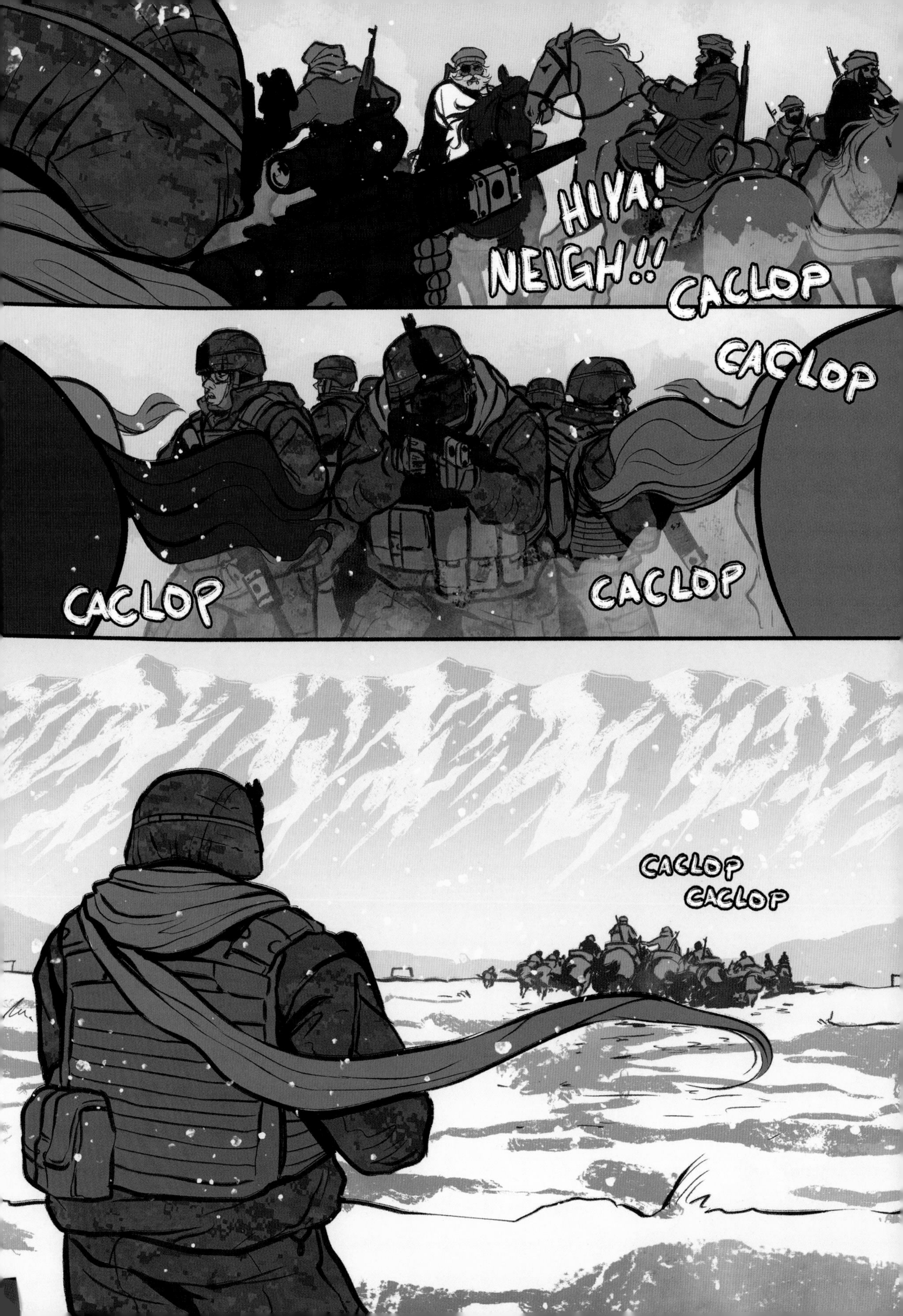
HIYA!
NEIGH!!
CACLOP
CACLOP
CACLOP
CACLOP
CACLOP
CACLOP

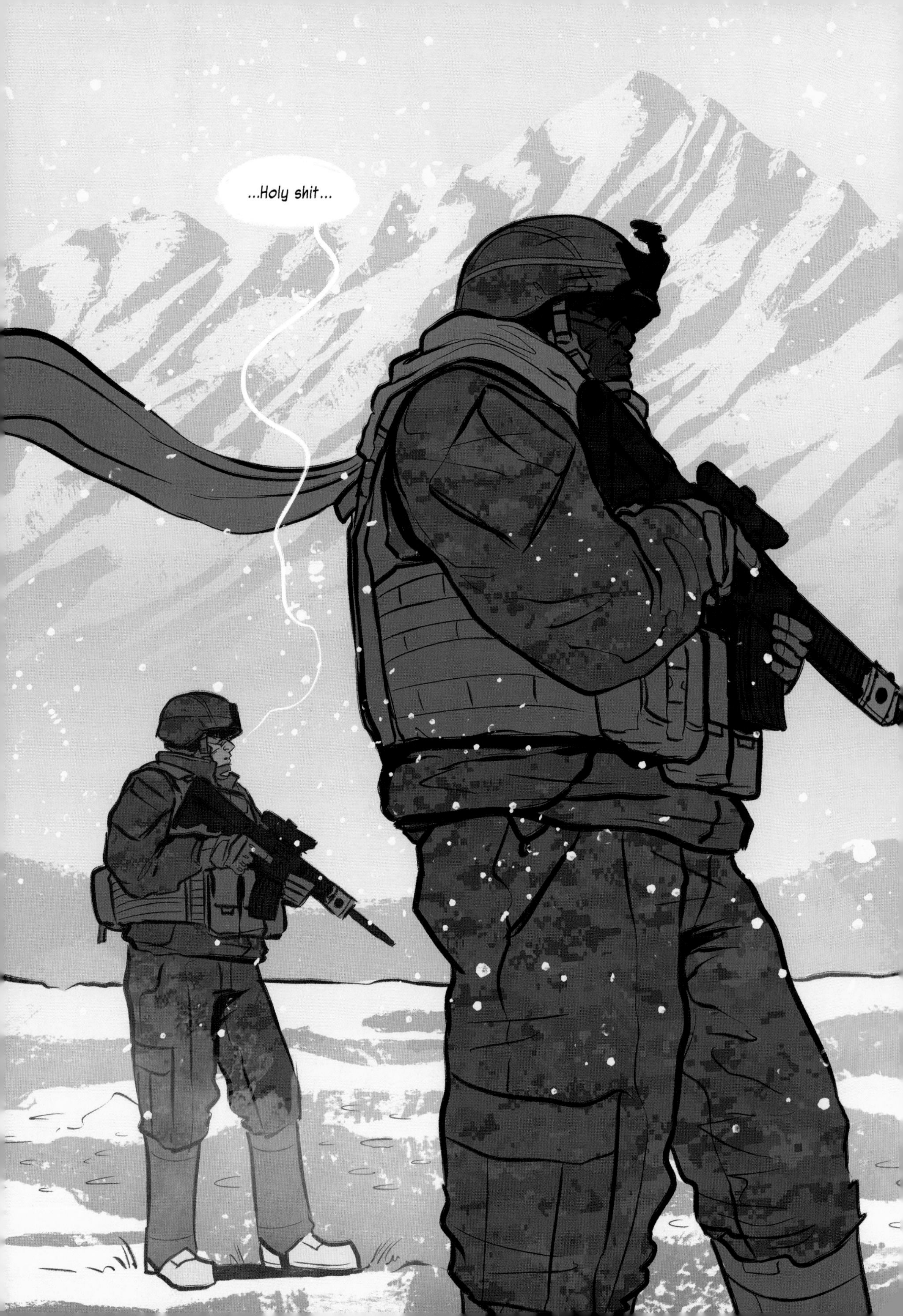
...Holy shit...

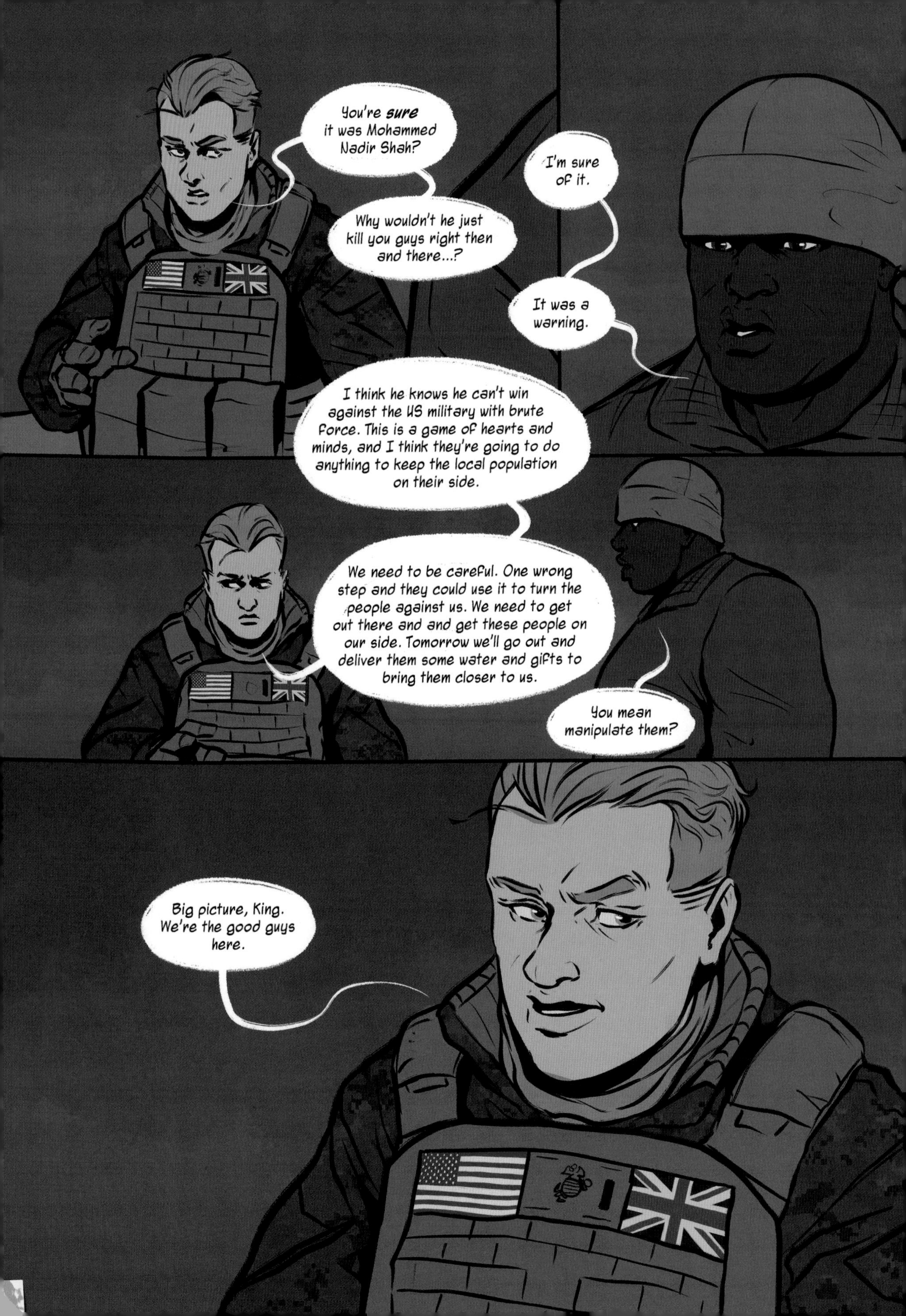
You're **sure** it was Mohammed Nadir Shah?
Why wouldn't he just kill you guys right then and there...?
I'm sure of it.
It was a warning.
I think he knows he can't win against the US military with brute force. This is a game of hearts and minds, and I think they're going to do anything to keep the local population on their side.
We need to be careful. One wrong step and they could use it to turn the people against us. We need to get out there and and get these people on our side. Tomorrow we'll go out and deliver them some water and gifts to bring them closer to us.
You mean manipulate them?
Big picture, King. We're the good guys here.

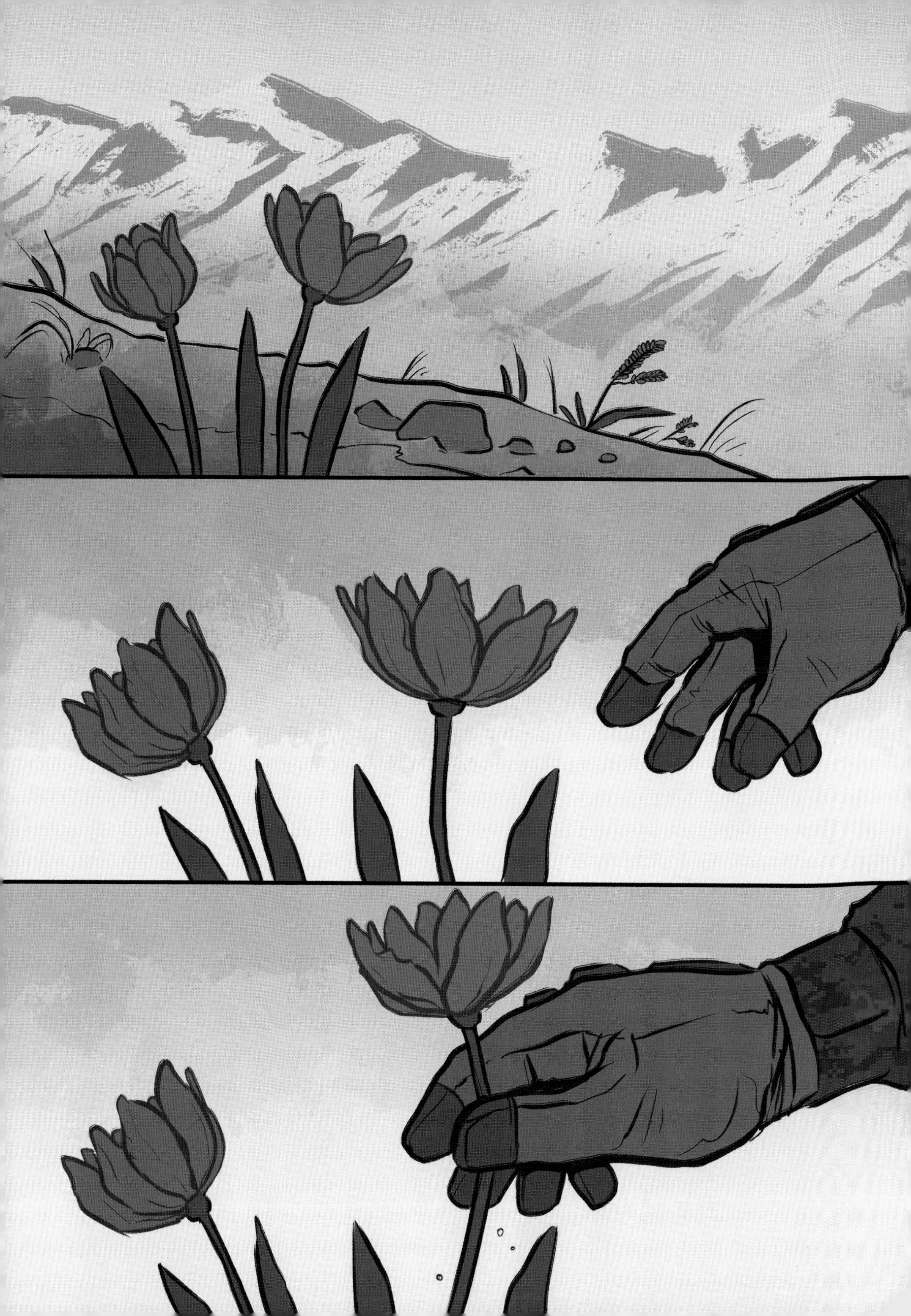

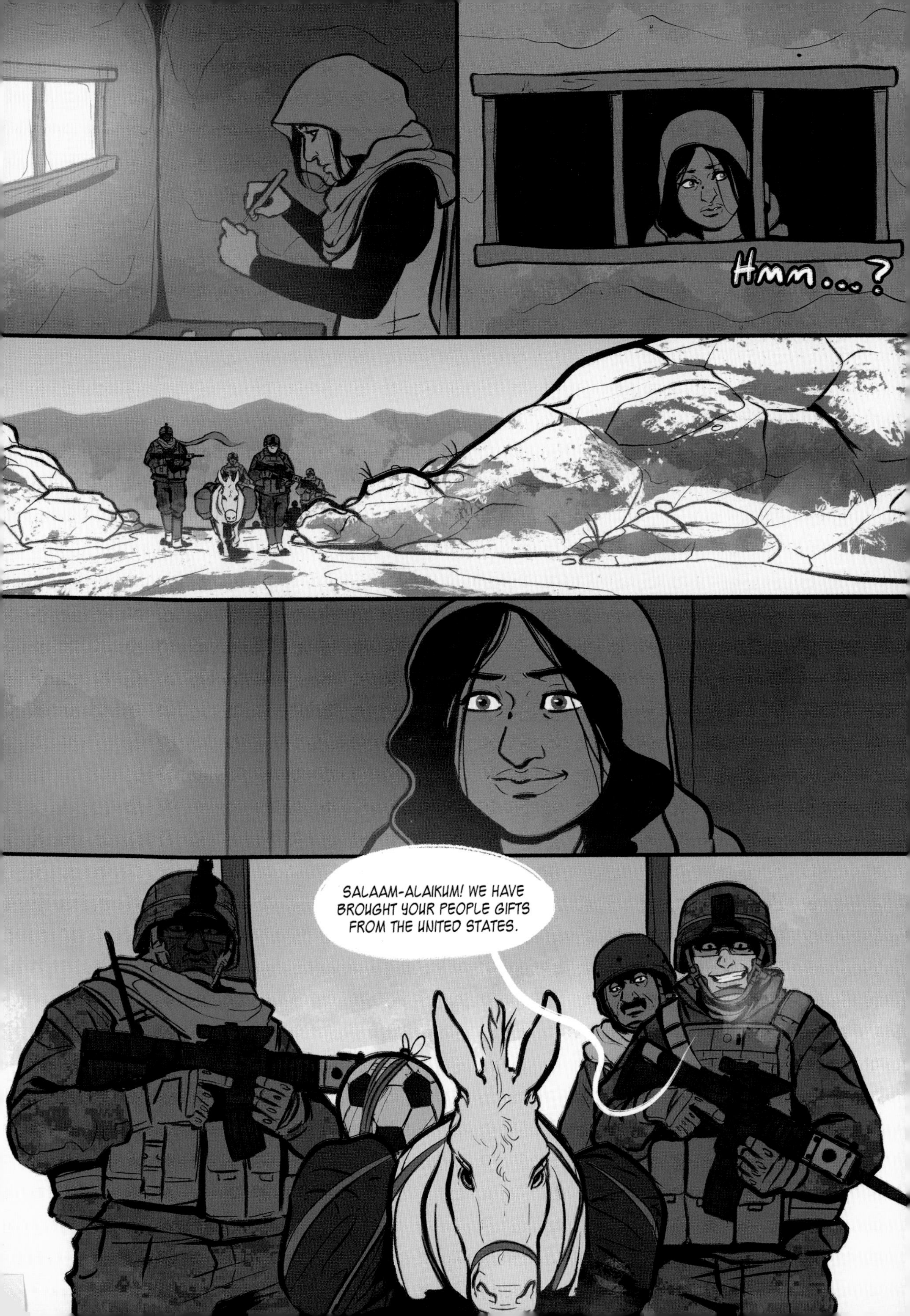
Hmm...?
SALAAM-ALAIKUM! WE HAVE BROUGHT YOUR PEOPLE GIFTS FROM THE UNITED STATES.

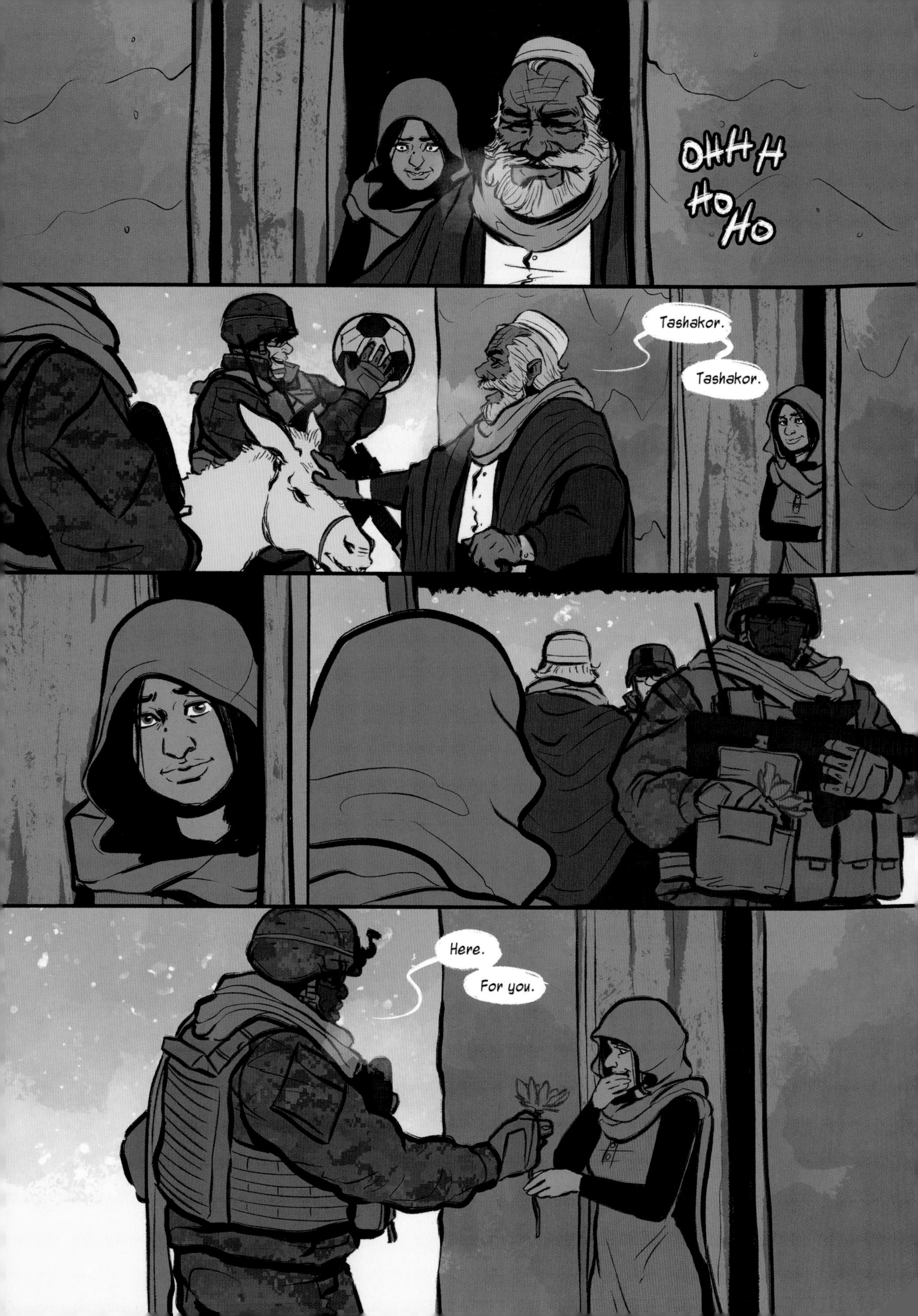
OHHH HO HO
Tashakor.
Tashakor.
Here.
For you.

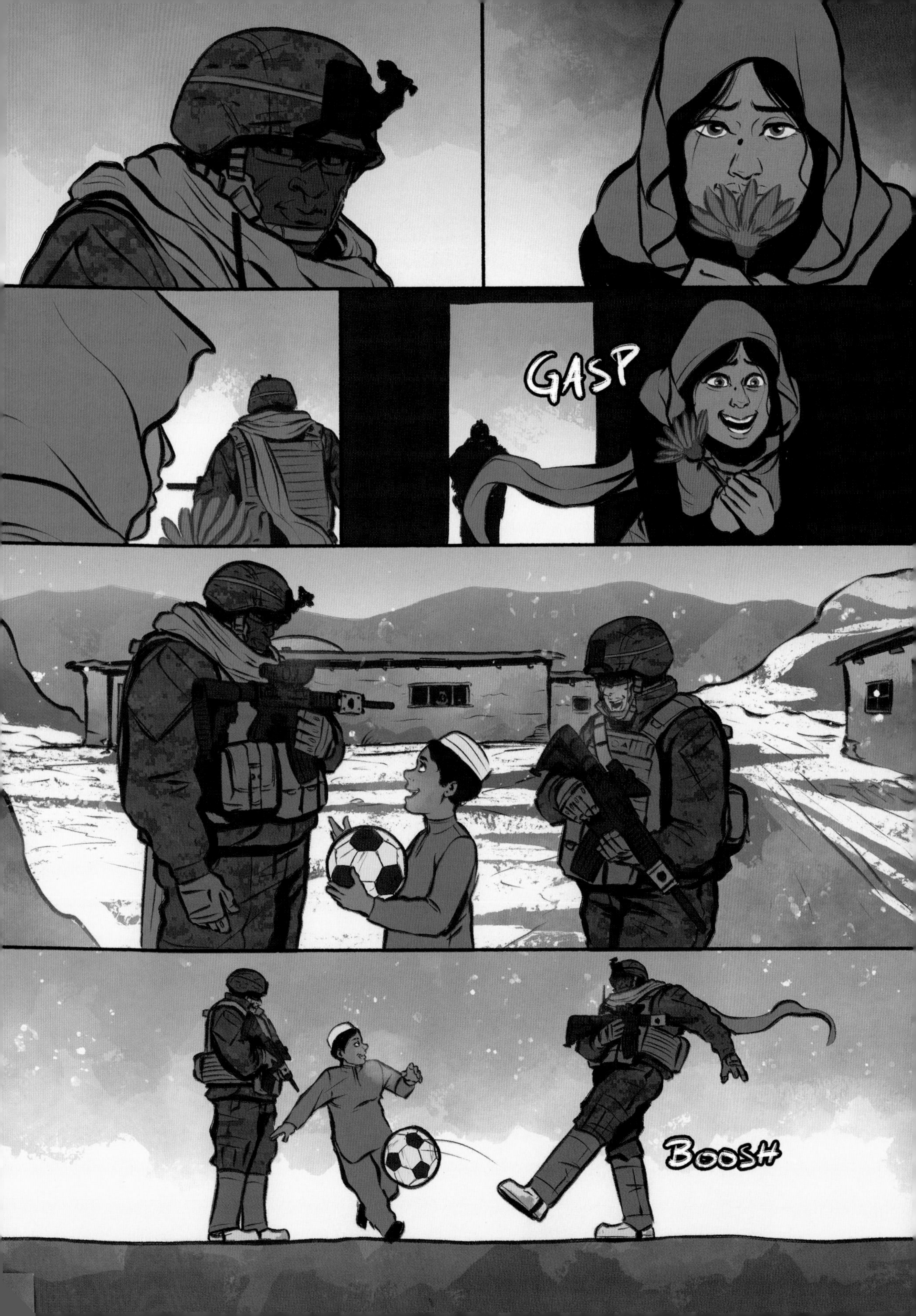
GASP
BOOSH

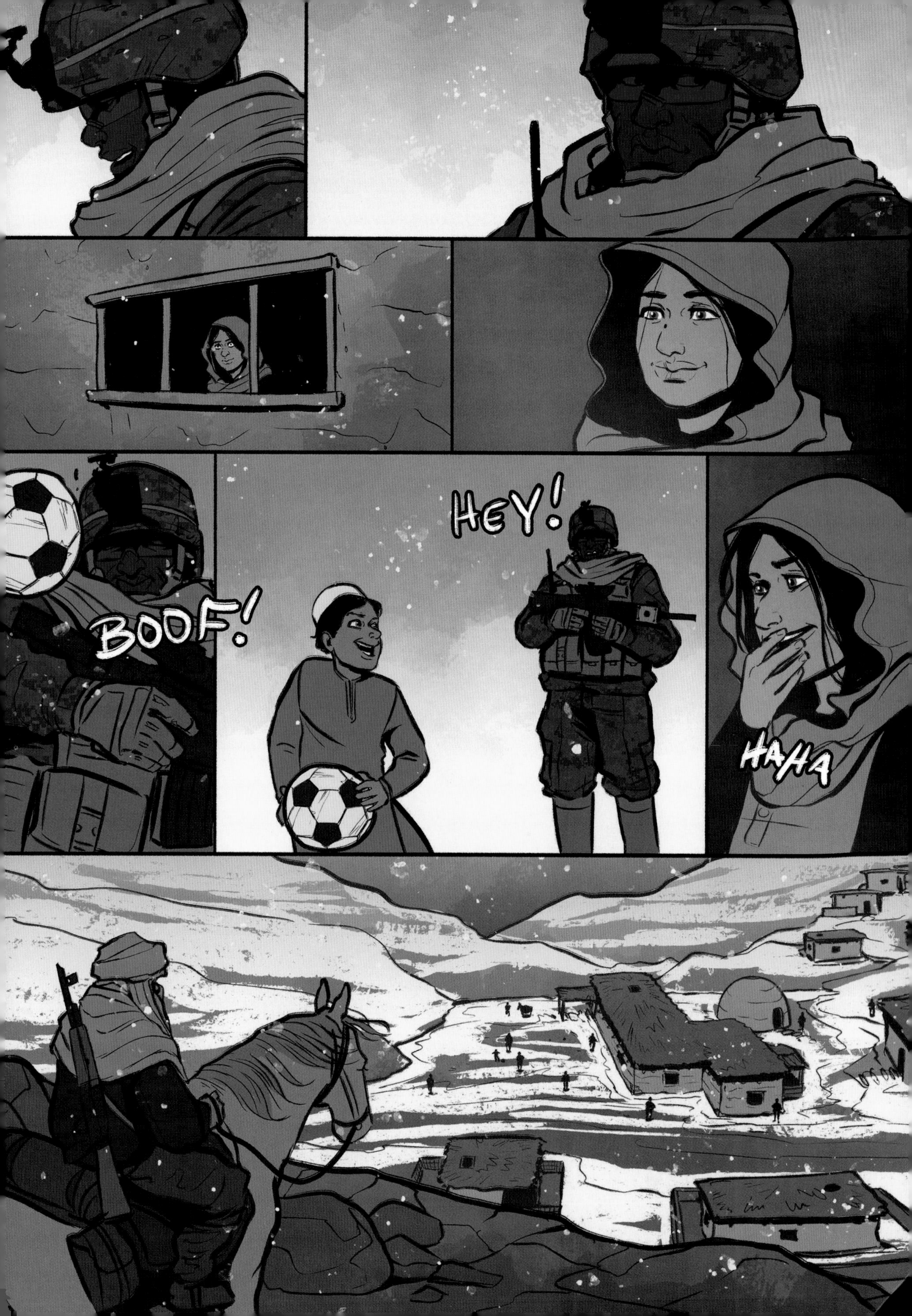
BOOF!
HEY!
HAHA

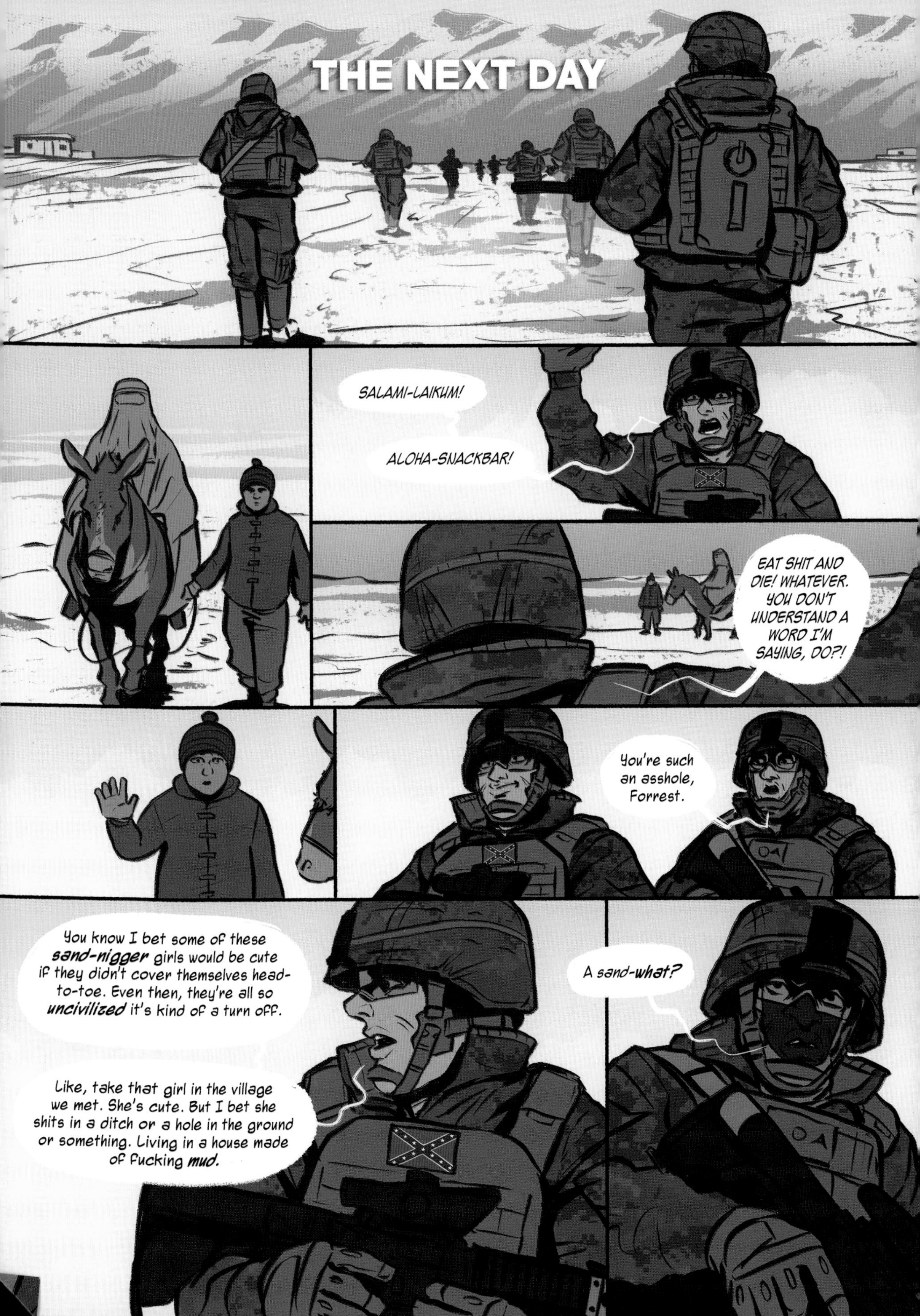
THE NEXT DAY
SALAMI-LAIKUM!
ALOHA-SNACKBAR!
EAT SHIT AND DIE! WHATEVER. YOU DON'T UNDERSTAND A WORD I'M SAYING, DO?!
You're such an asshole, Forrest.
You know I bet some of these sand-nigger girls would be cute if they didn't cover themselves head-to-toe. Even then, they're all so uncivilized it's kind of a turn off.
Like, take that girl in the village we met. She's cute. But I bet she shits in a ditch or a hole in the ground or something. Living in a house made of fucking mud.
A sand-what?

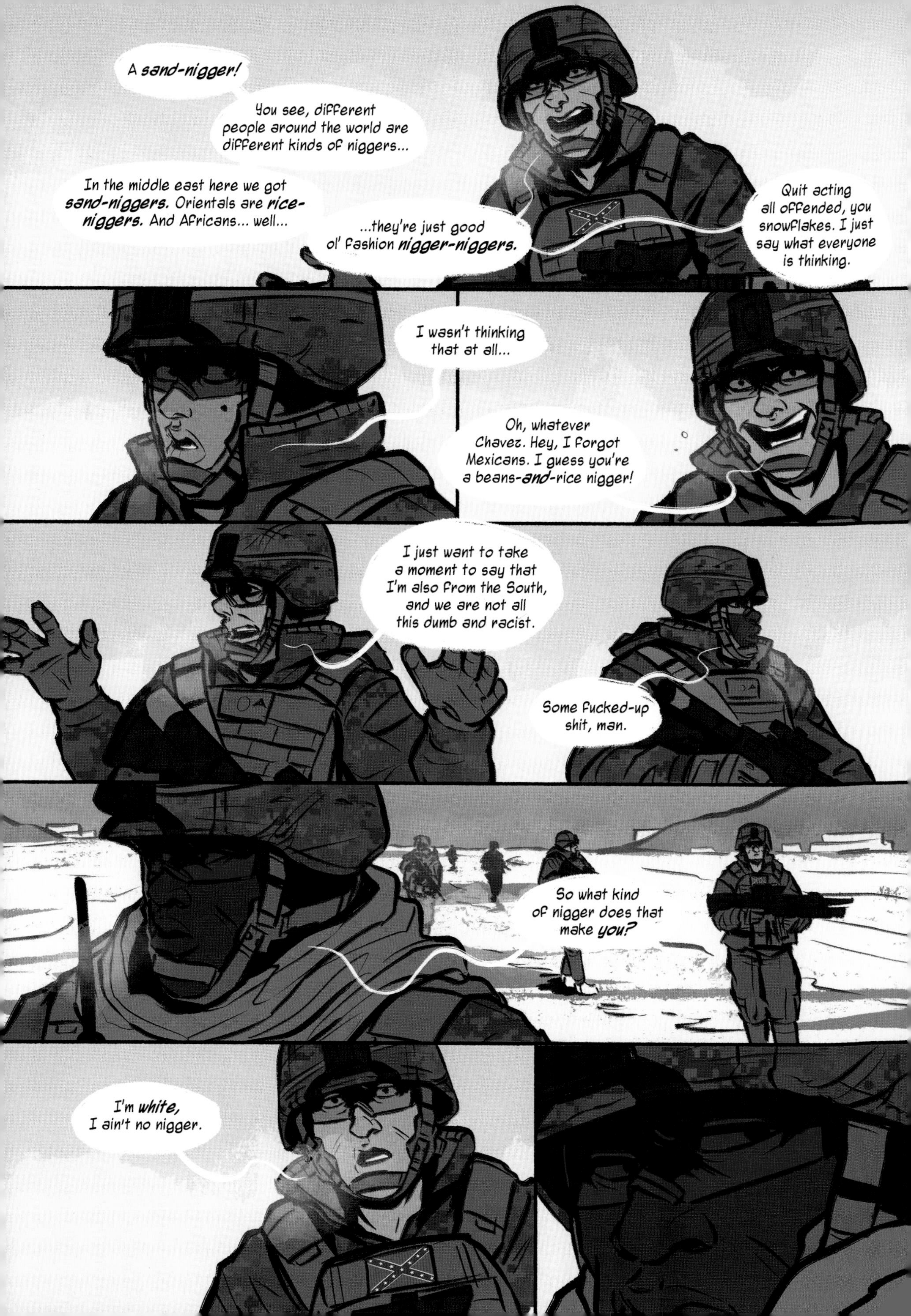
A sand-nigger!
You see, different people around the world are different kinds of niggers...
In the middle east here we got sand-niggers. Orientals are rice-niggers. And Africans... well...
...they're just good ol' fashion nigger-niggers.
Quit acting all offended, you snowflakes. I just say what everyone is thinking.
I wasn't thinking that at all...
Oh, whatever Chavez. Hey, I forgot Mexicans. I guess you're a beans-and-rice nigger!
I just want to take a moment to say that I'm also from the South, and we are not all this dumb and racist.
Some fucked-up shit, man.
So what kind of nigger does that make you?
I'm white, I ain't no nigger.

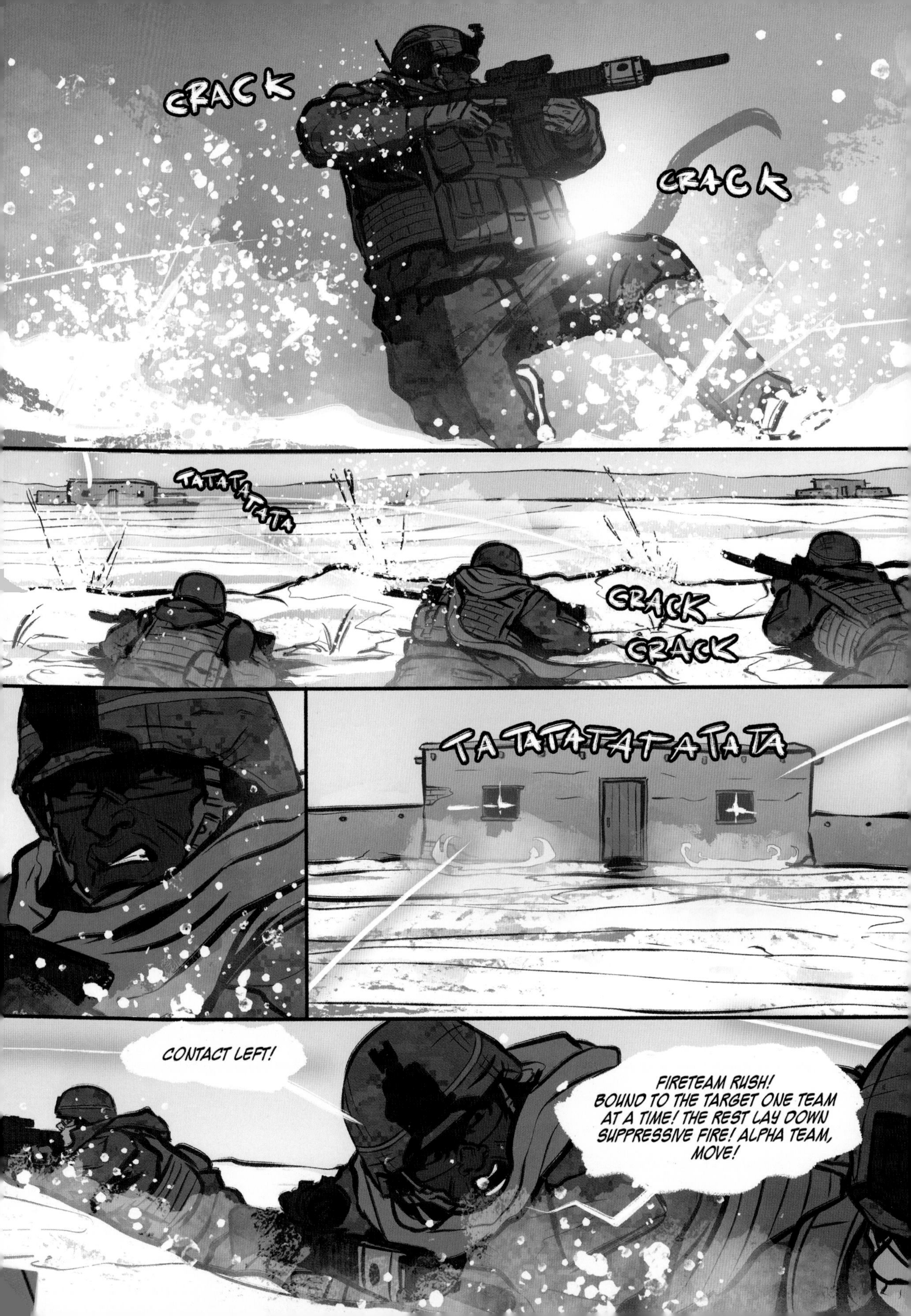
CRACK
CRACK
TATATATATA
CRACK
CRACK
TA TATATATATATATA
CONTACT LEFT!
FIRETEAM RUSH! BOUND TO THE TARGET ONE TEAM AT A TIME! THE REST LAY DOWN SUPPRESSIVE FIRE! ALPHA TEAM, MOVE!

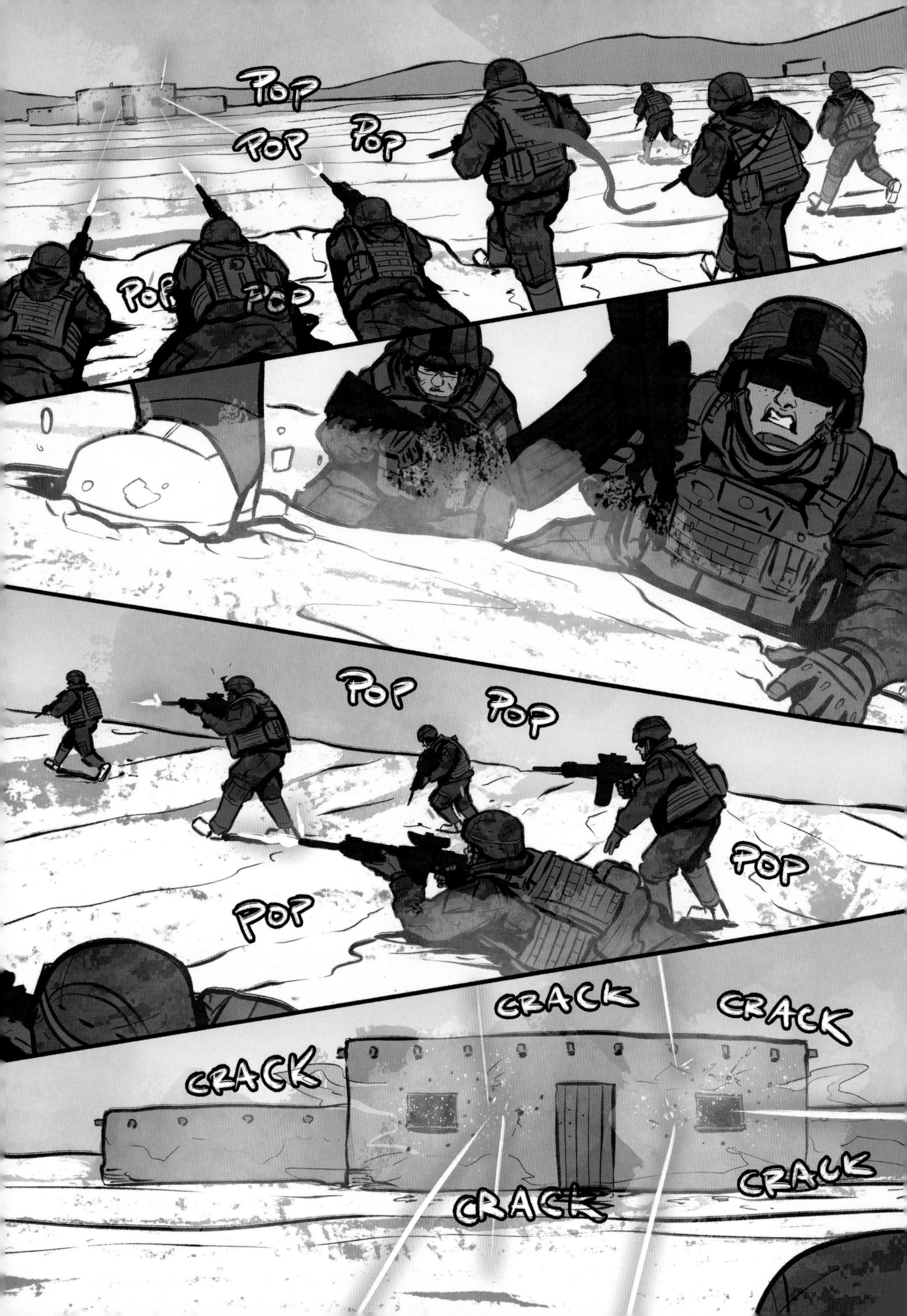
POP
POP
POP
POP
POP
POP
POP
POP
POP
POP
CRACK
CRACK
CRACK
CRACK
CRACK

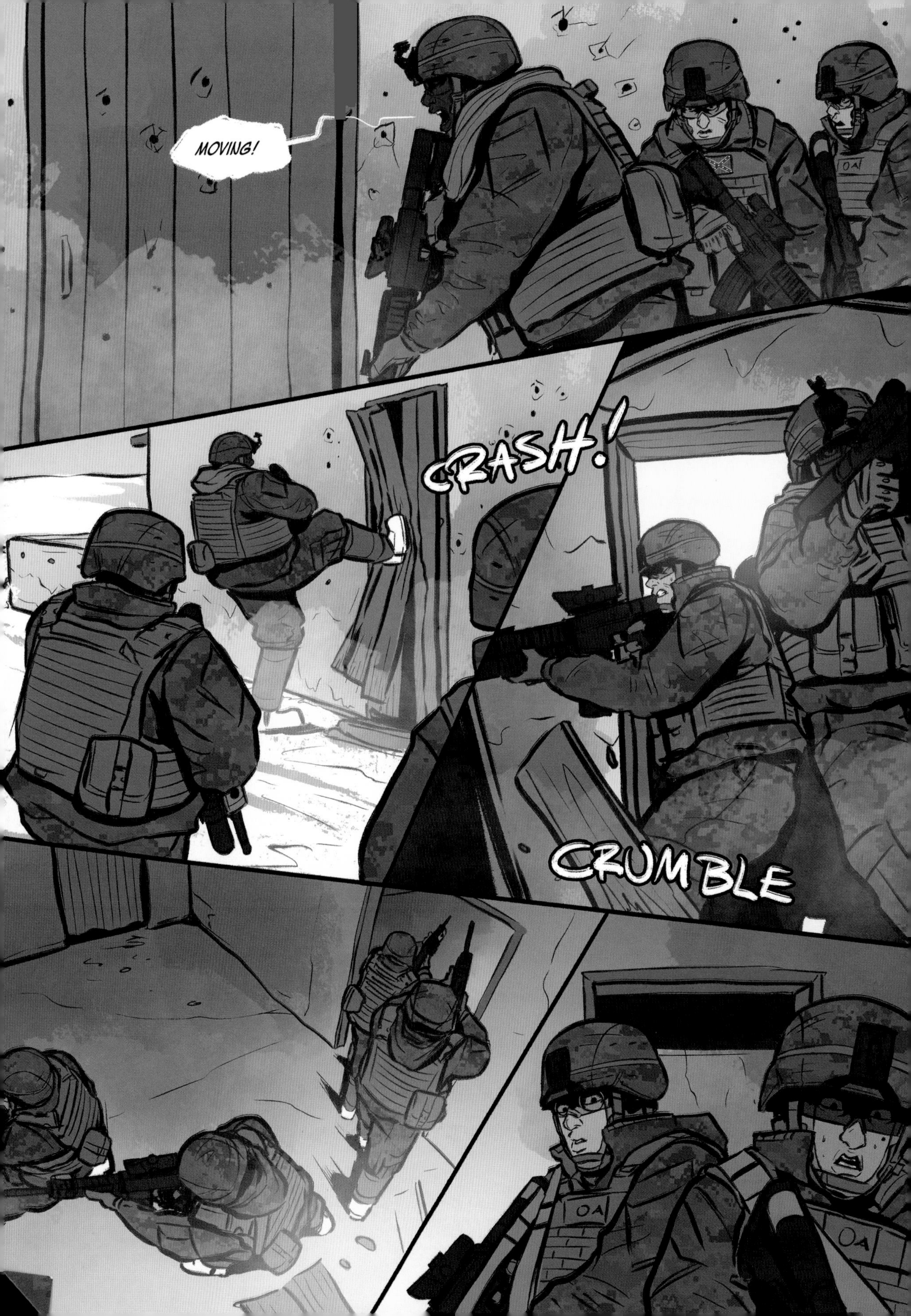
MOVING!
CRASH!
CRUMBLE

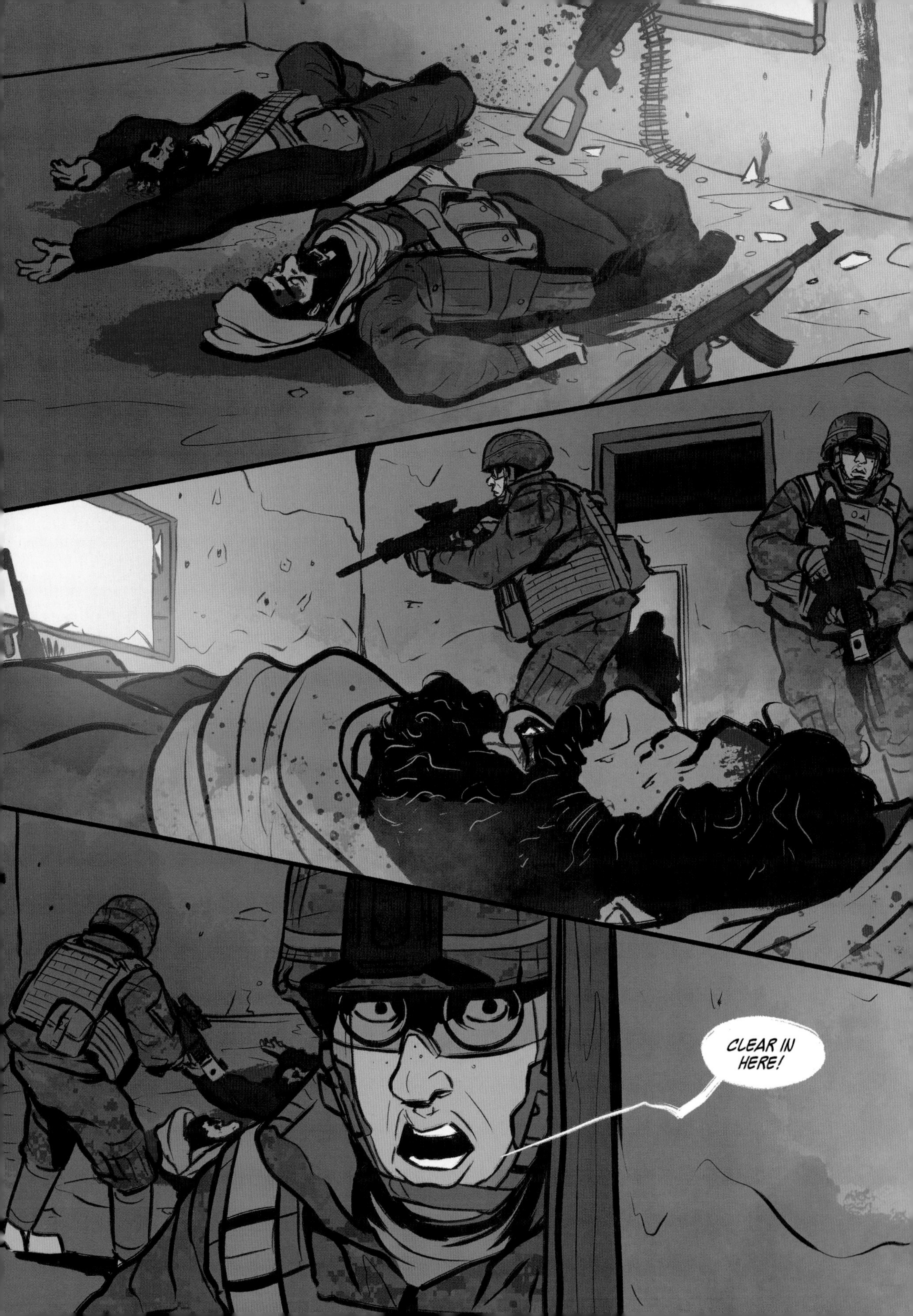
CLEAR IN HERE!

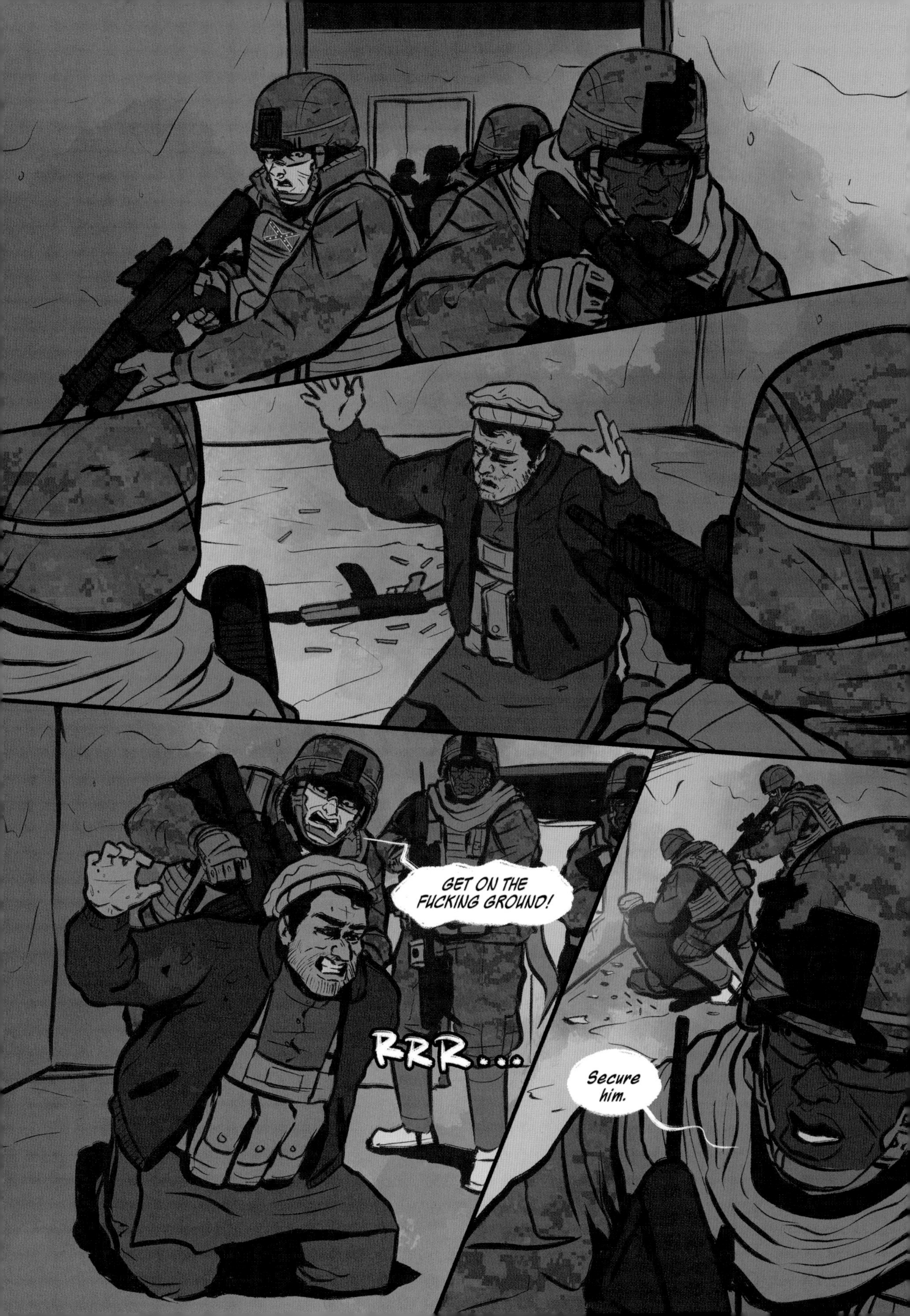
GET ON THE FUCKING GROUND!
RRR...
Secure him.

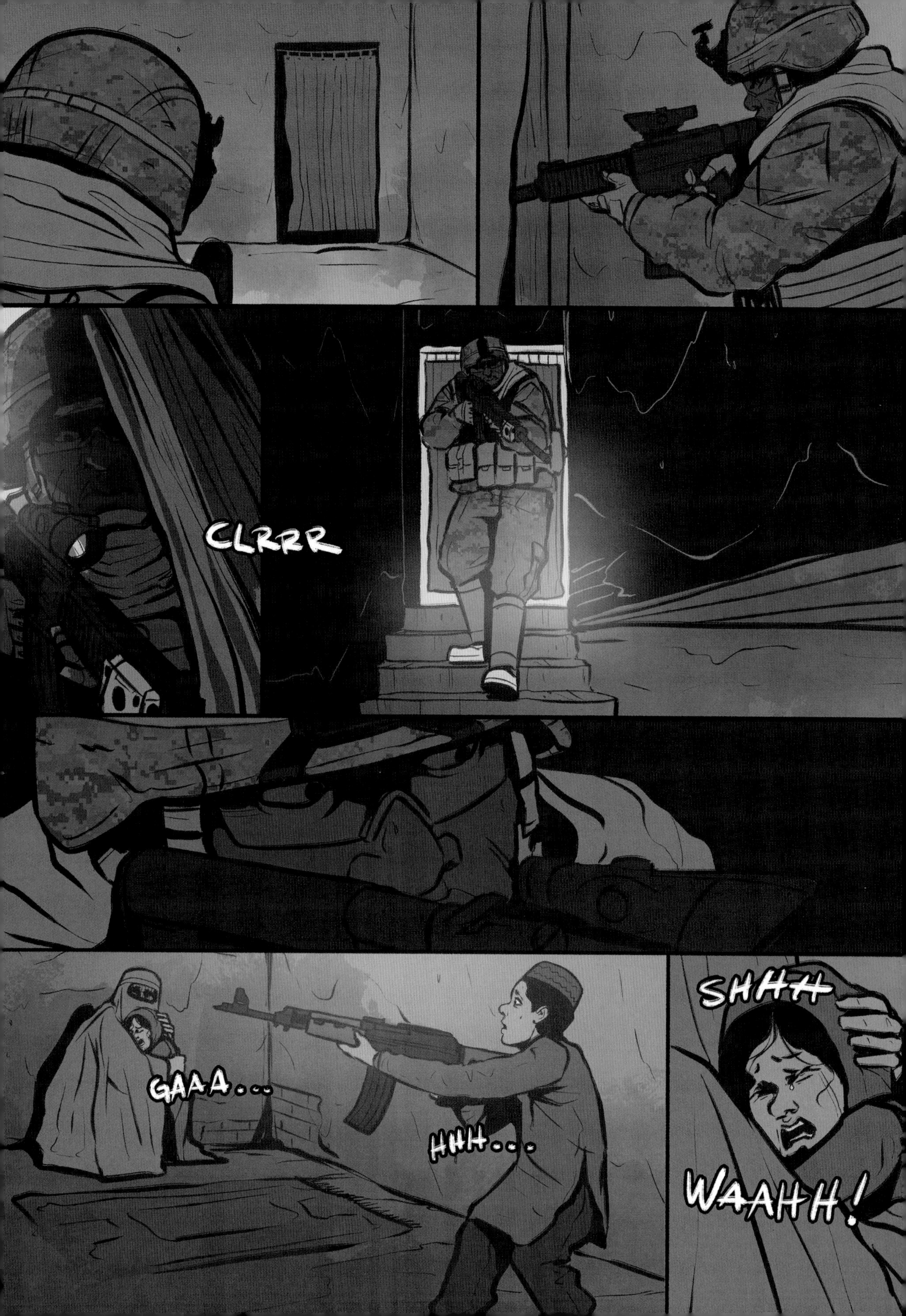

CLRRR
GAAA...
HHH...
SHHH
WAAHH!

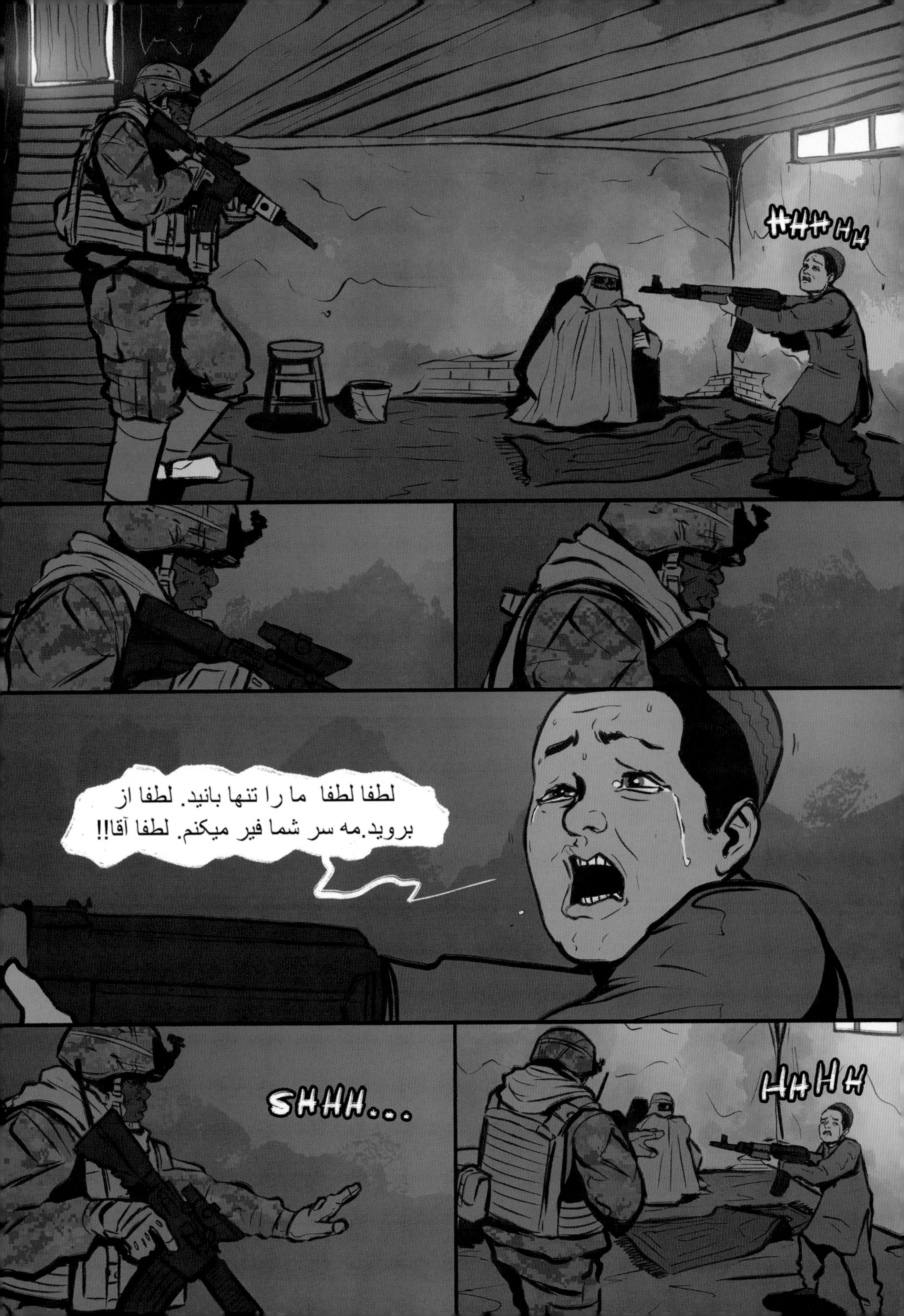
HHHHH
لطفا لطفا ما را تنها بانید. لطفا از
برويد.مه سر شما فير ميكنم. لطفا آقا!!
SHHH...
HHHH

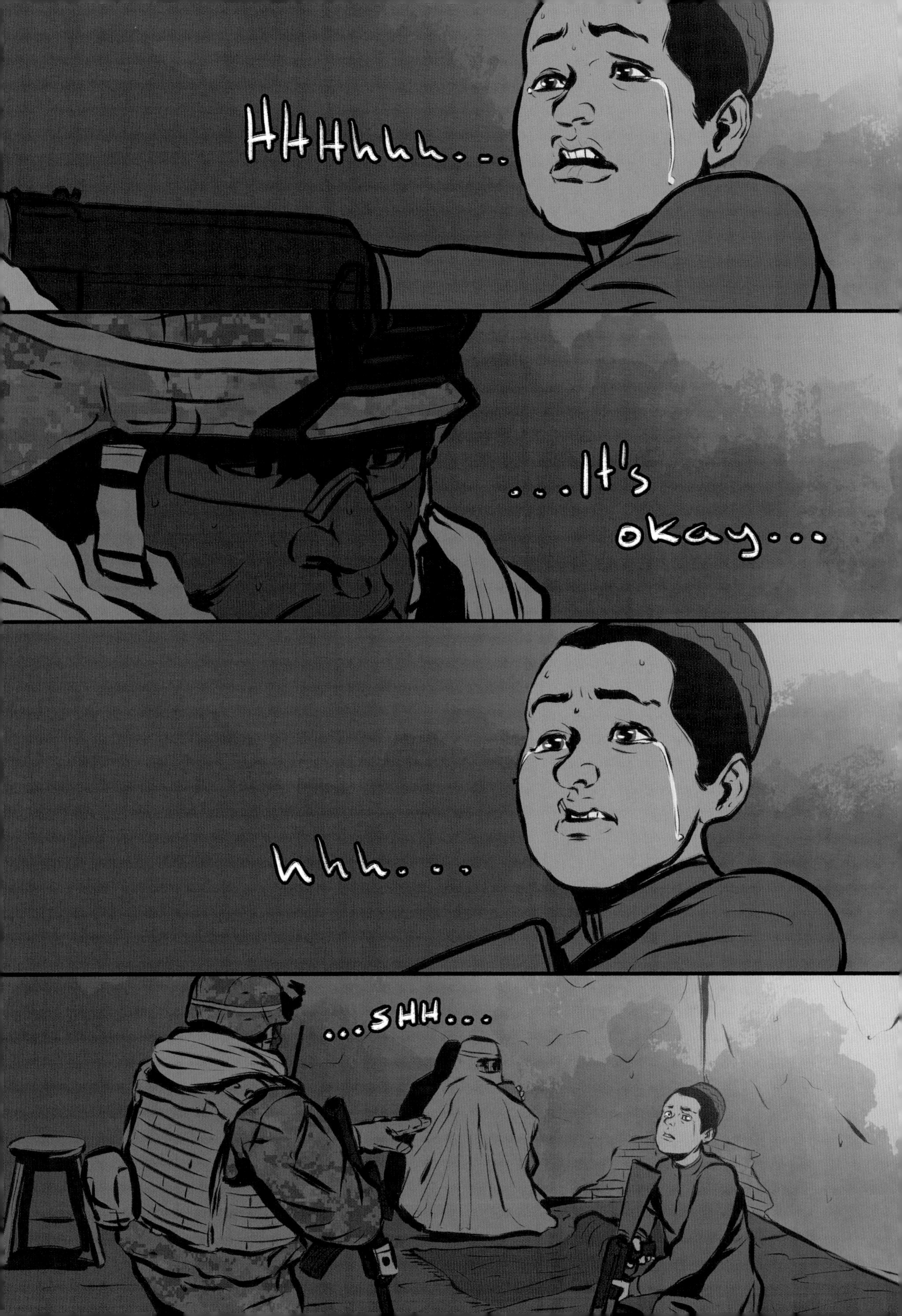
HHHhhh...
...It's okay...
hhh...
...SHH...

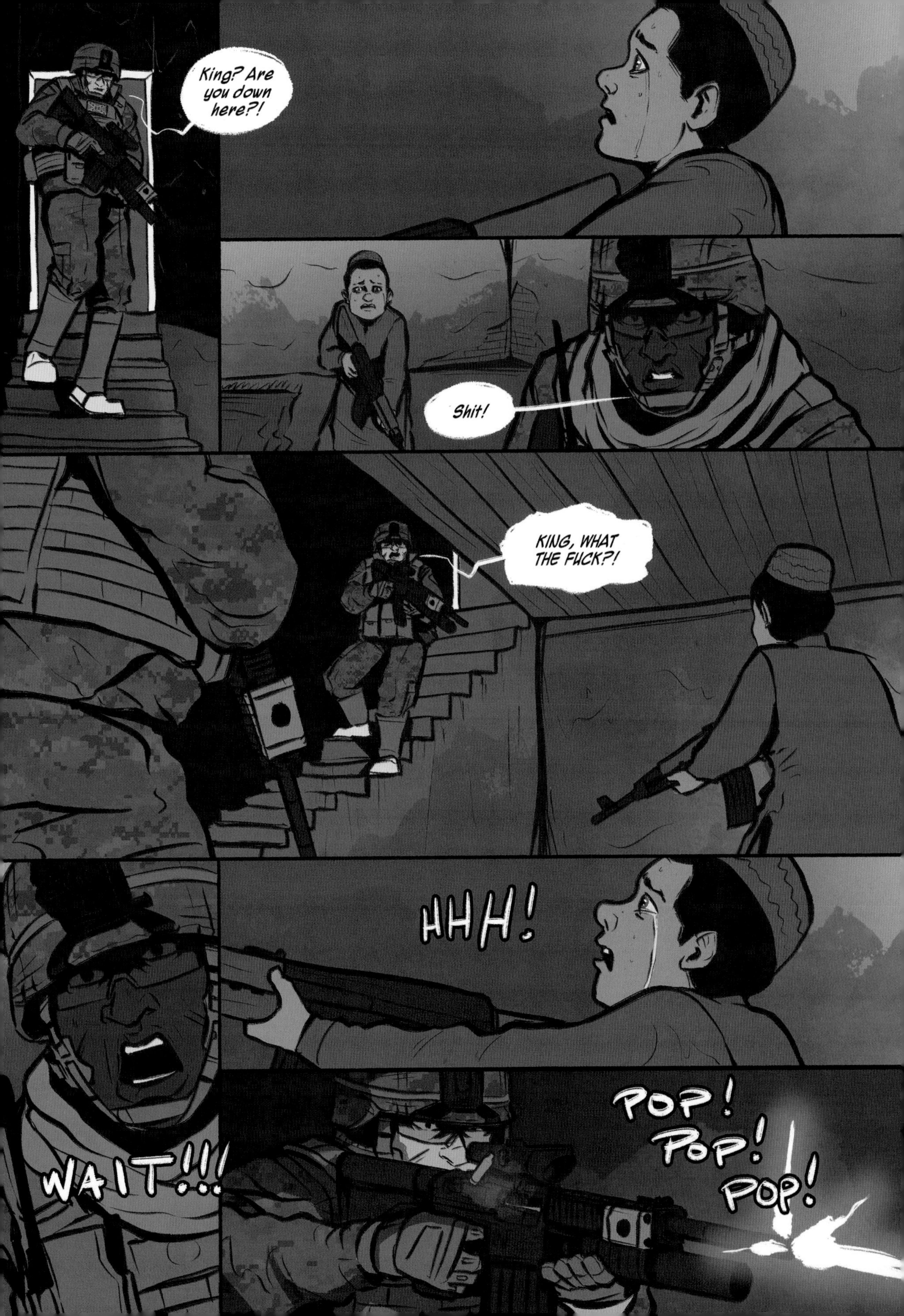
King? Are you down here?!
Shit!
KING, WHAT THE FUCK?!
HHH!
WAIT!!!
POP! POP! POP!

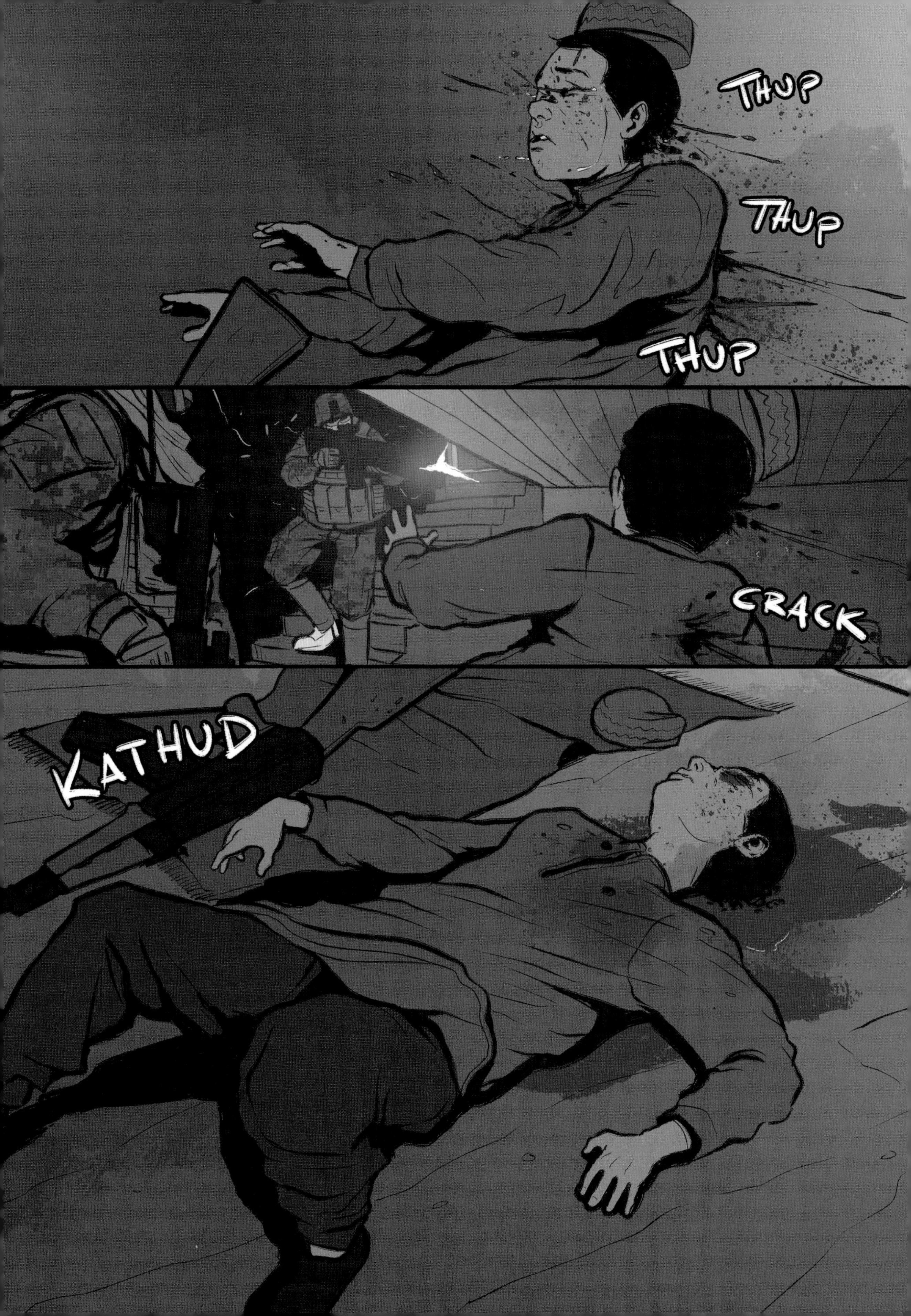
THUP
THUP
THUP
CRACK
KATHUD

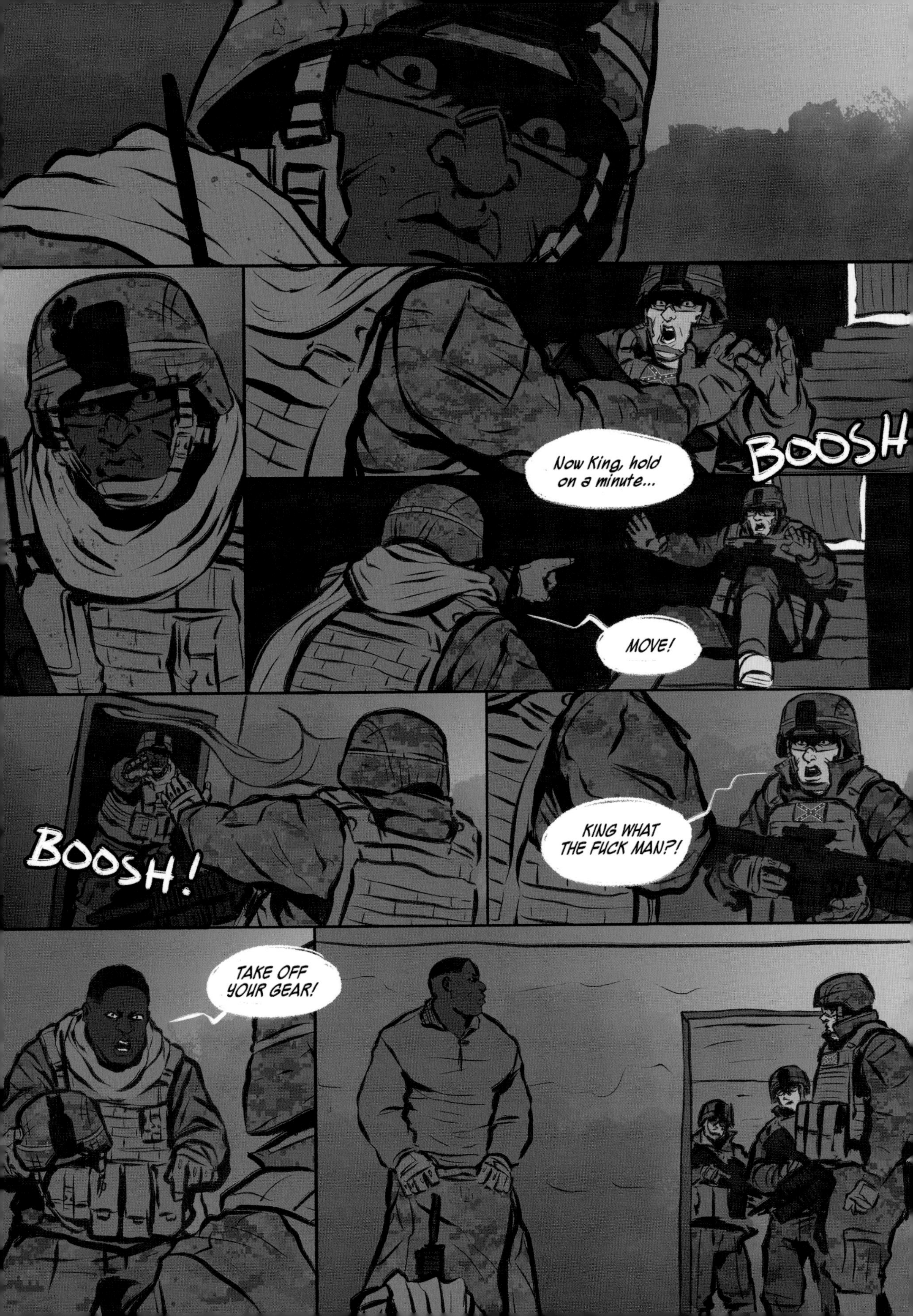
BOOSH
Now King, hold on a minute...
MOVE!
BOOSH!
KING WHAT THE FUCK MAN?!
TAKE OFF YOUR GEAR!

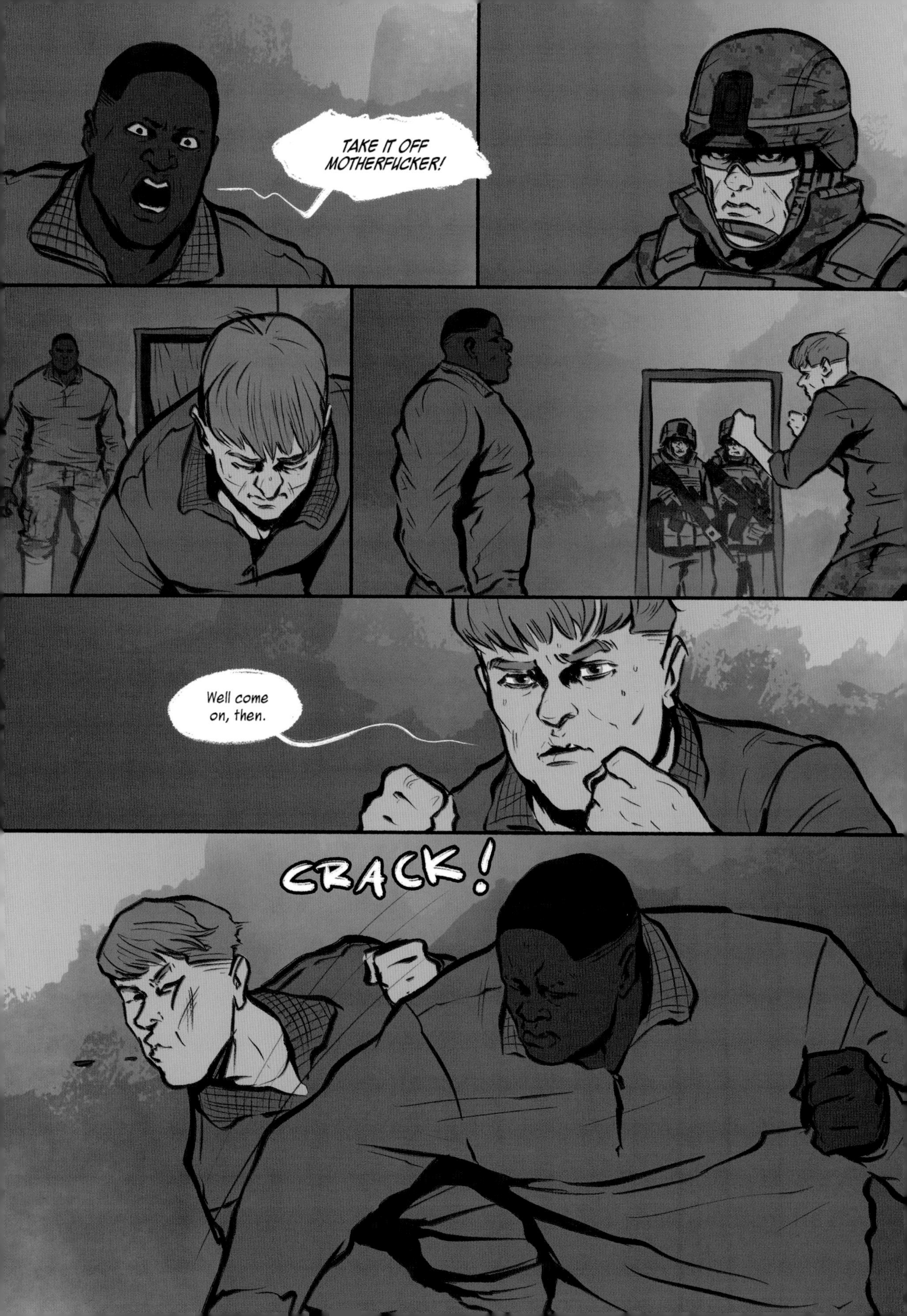
TAKE IT OFF MOTHERFUCKER!
Well come on, then.
CRACK!

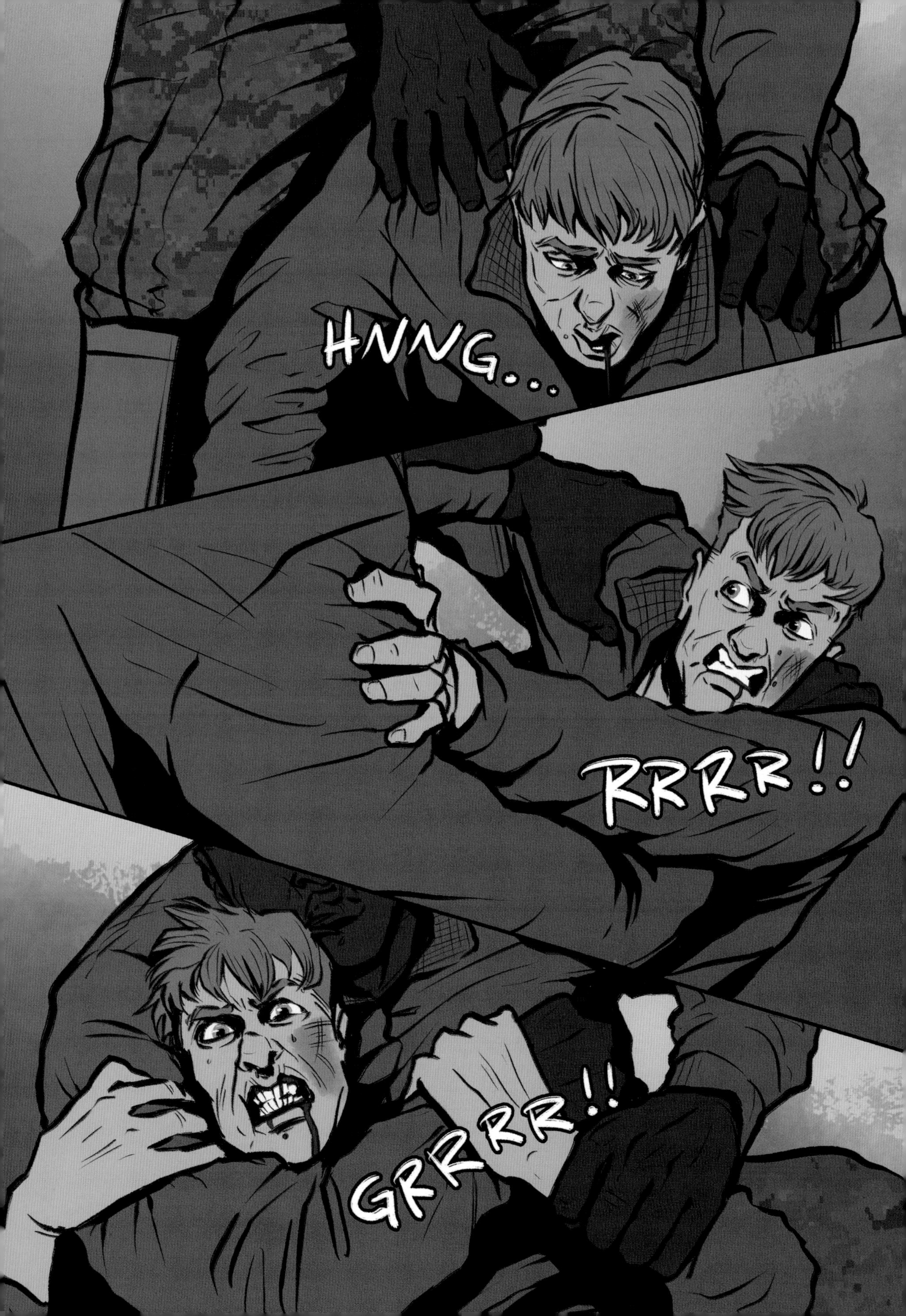
HNNG...
RRRR!!
GRRRR!!

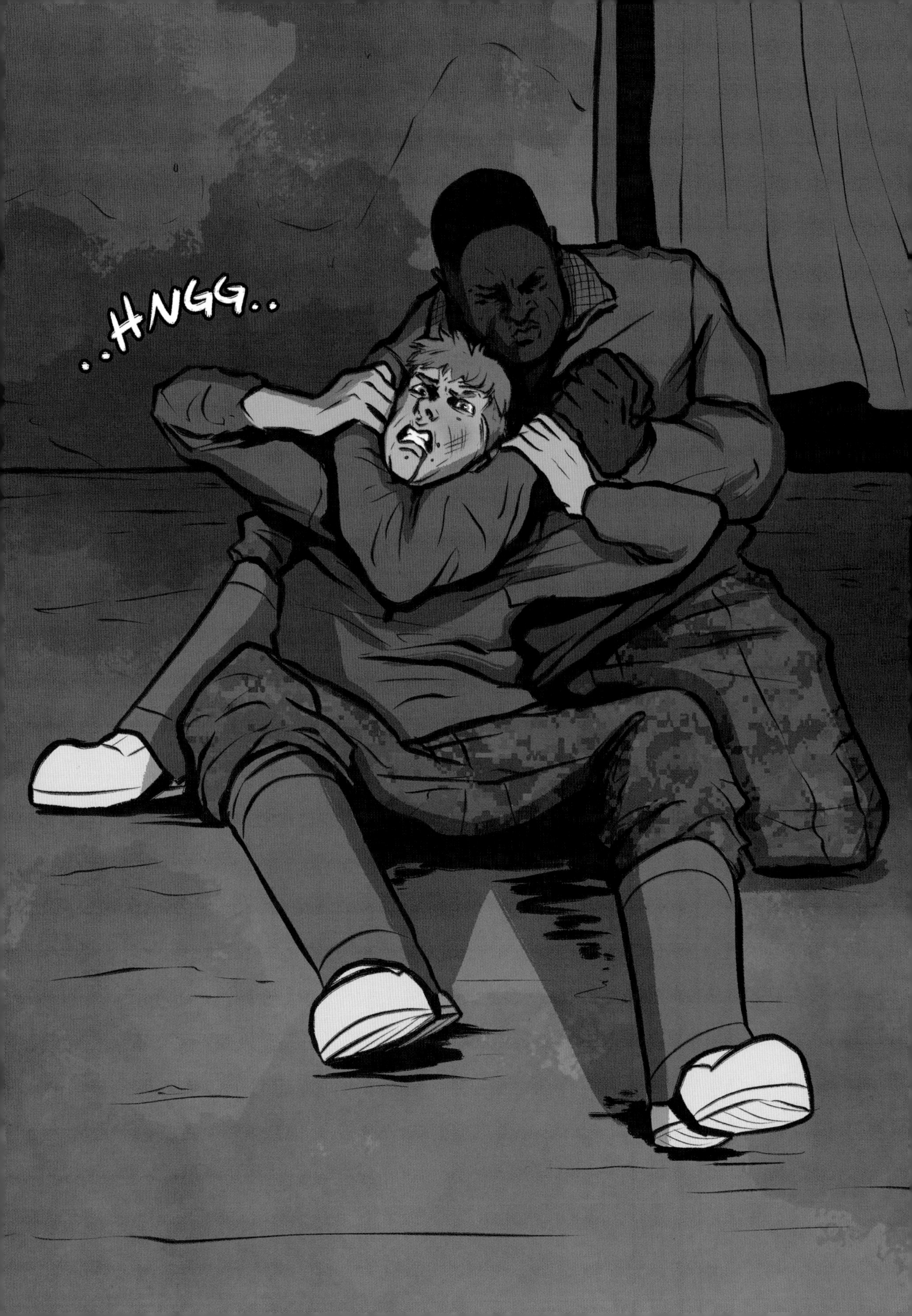
..HNGG..

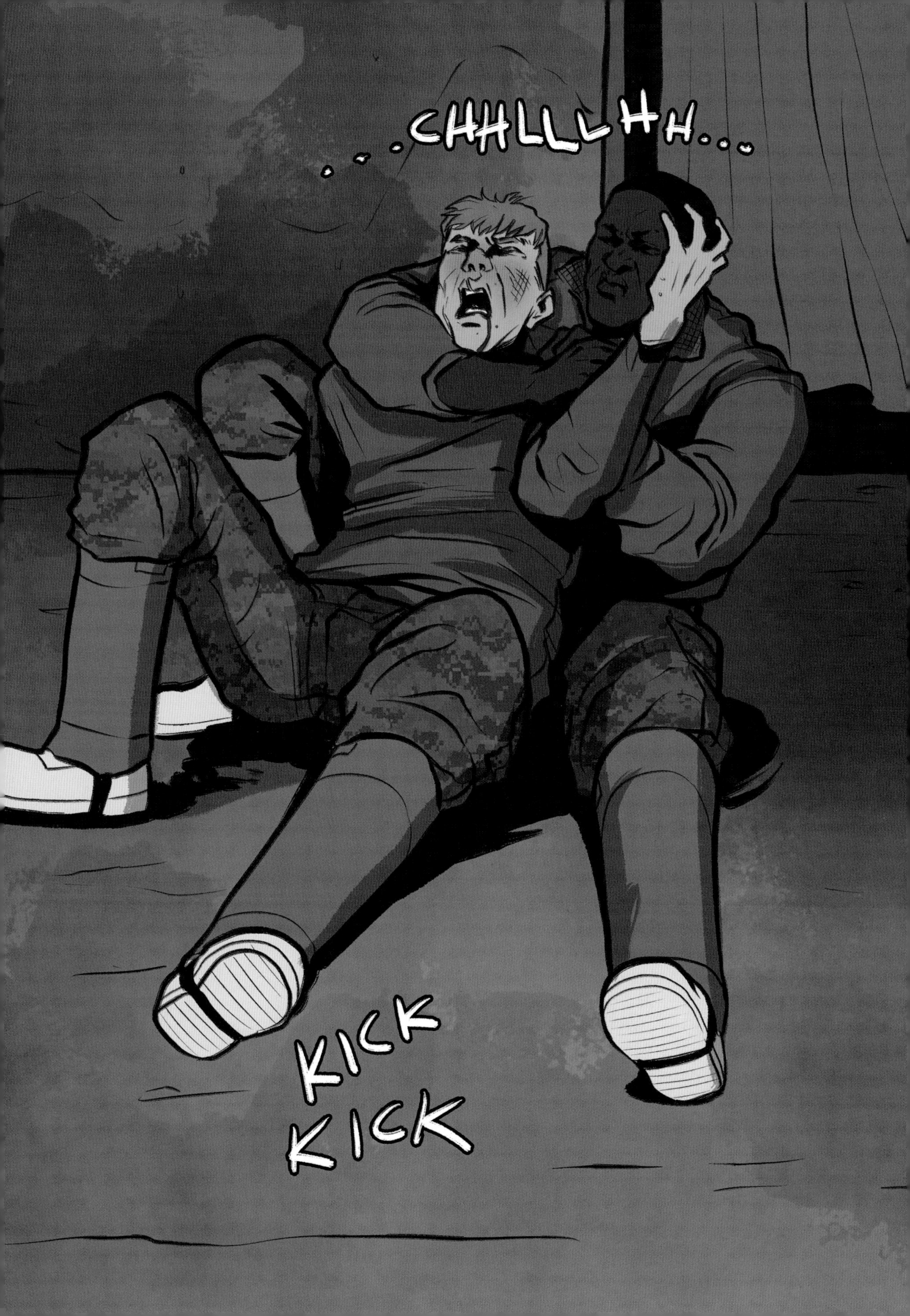

...CHHLLLLHH...
KICK
KICK

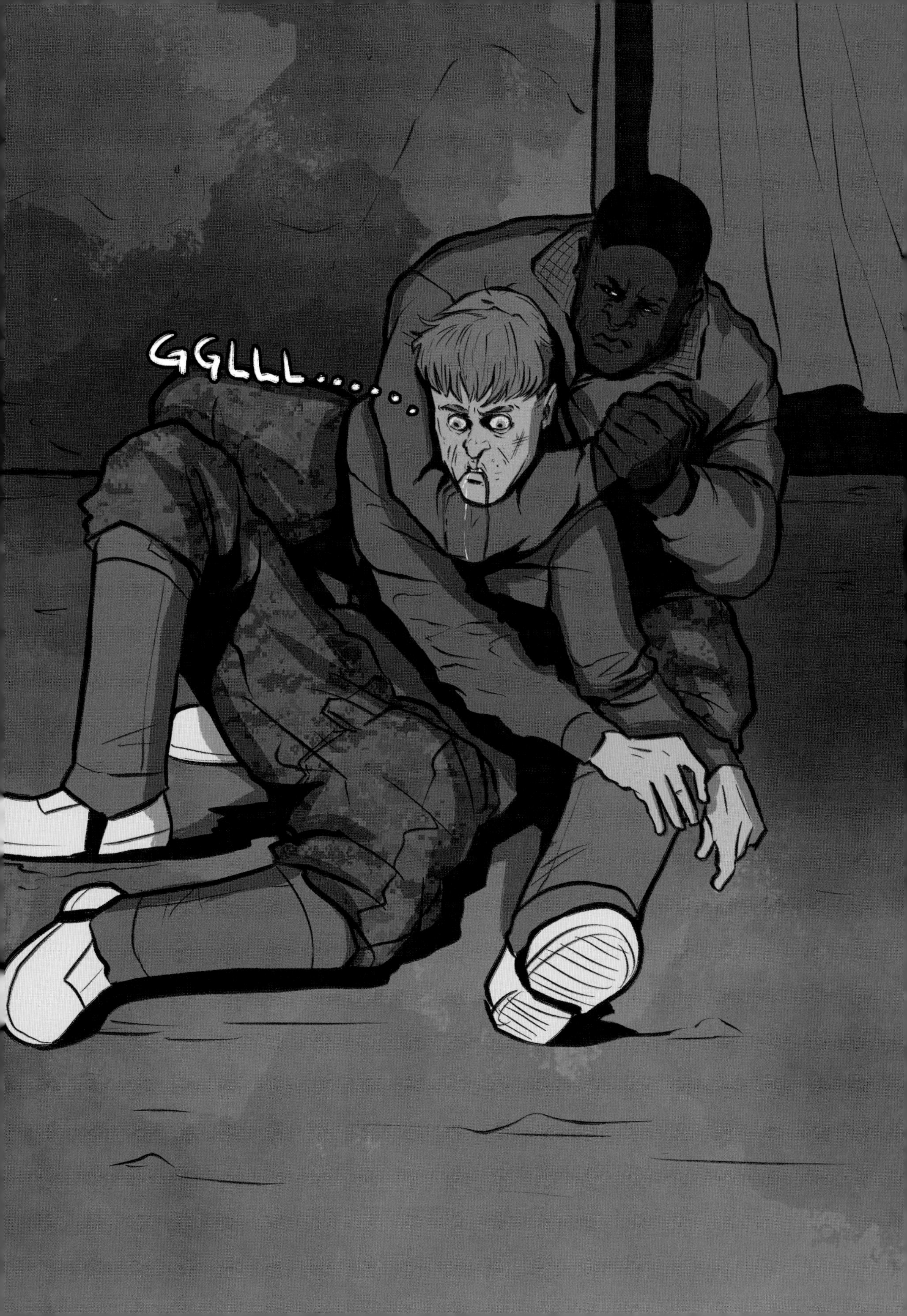
GGLLL.......

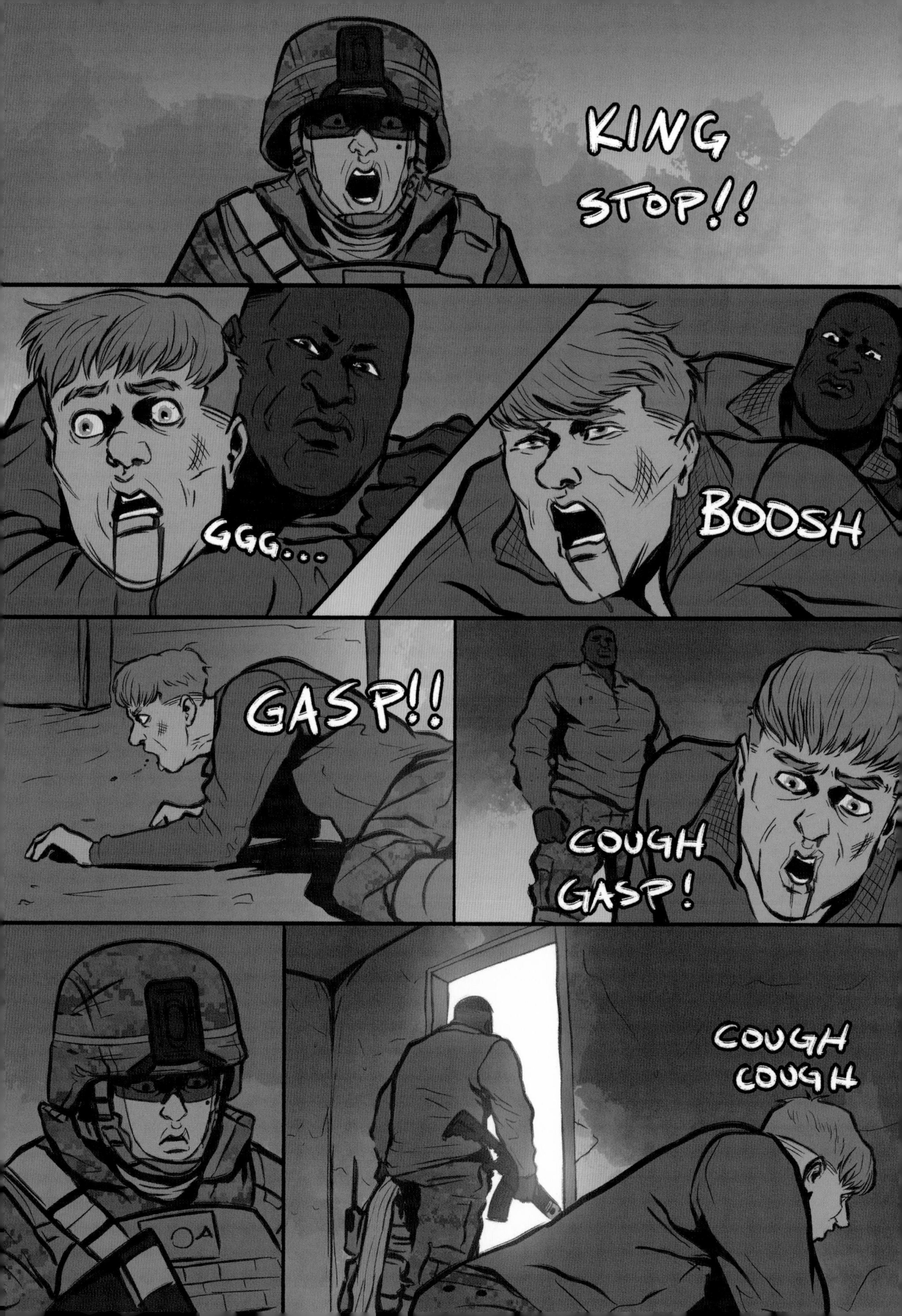
KING
STOP!!
GGG...
BOOSH
GASP!!
COUGH
GASP!
COUGH
COUGH

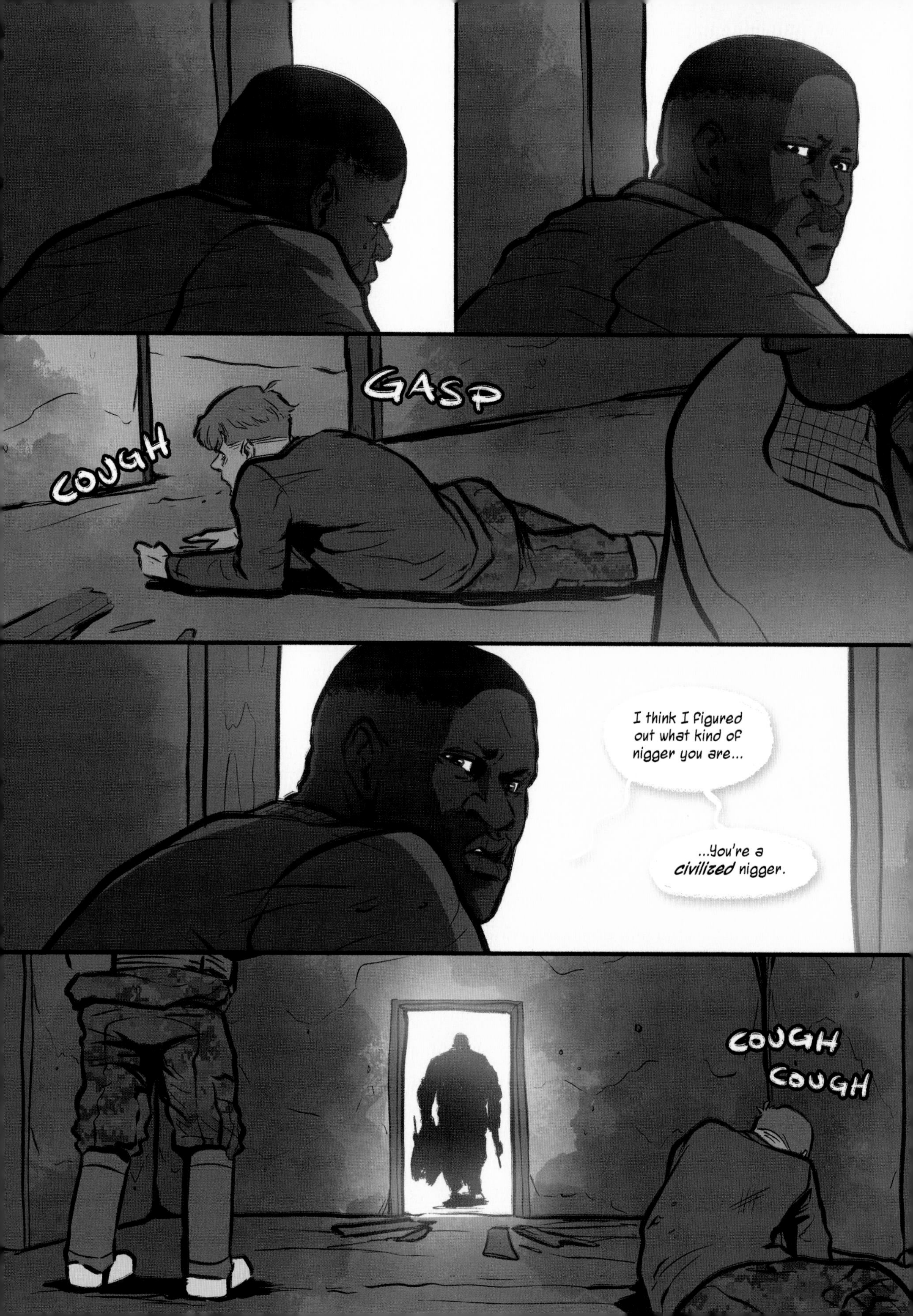
COUGH
GASP
I think I figured out what kind of nigger you are...
...You're a *civilized* nigger.
COUGH
COUGH

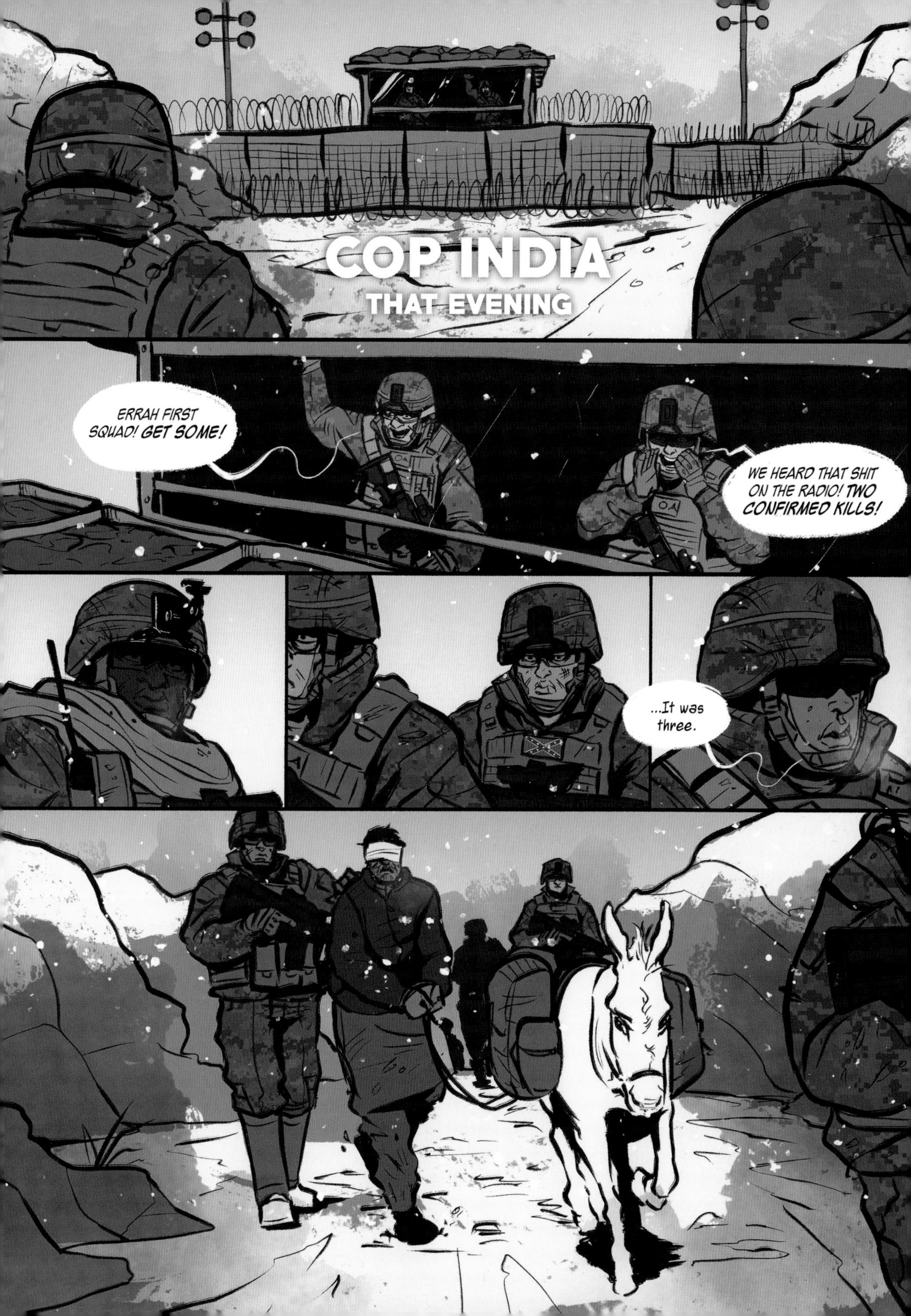
COP INDIA
THAT EVENING
ERRAH FIRST SQUAD! GET SOME!
WE HEARD THAT SHIT ON THE RADIO! TWO CONFIRMED KILLS!
...It was three.

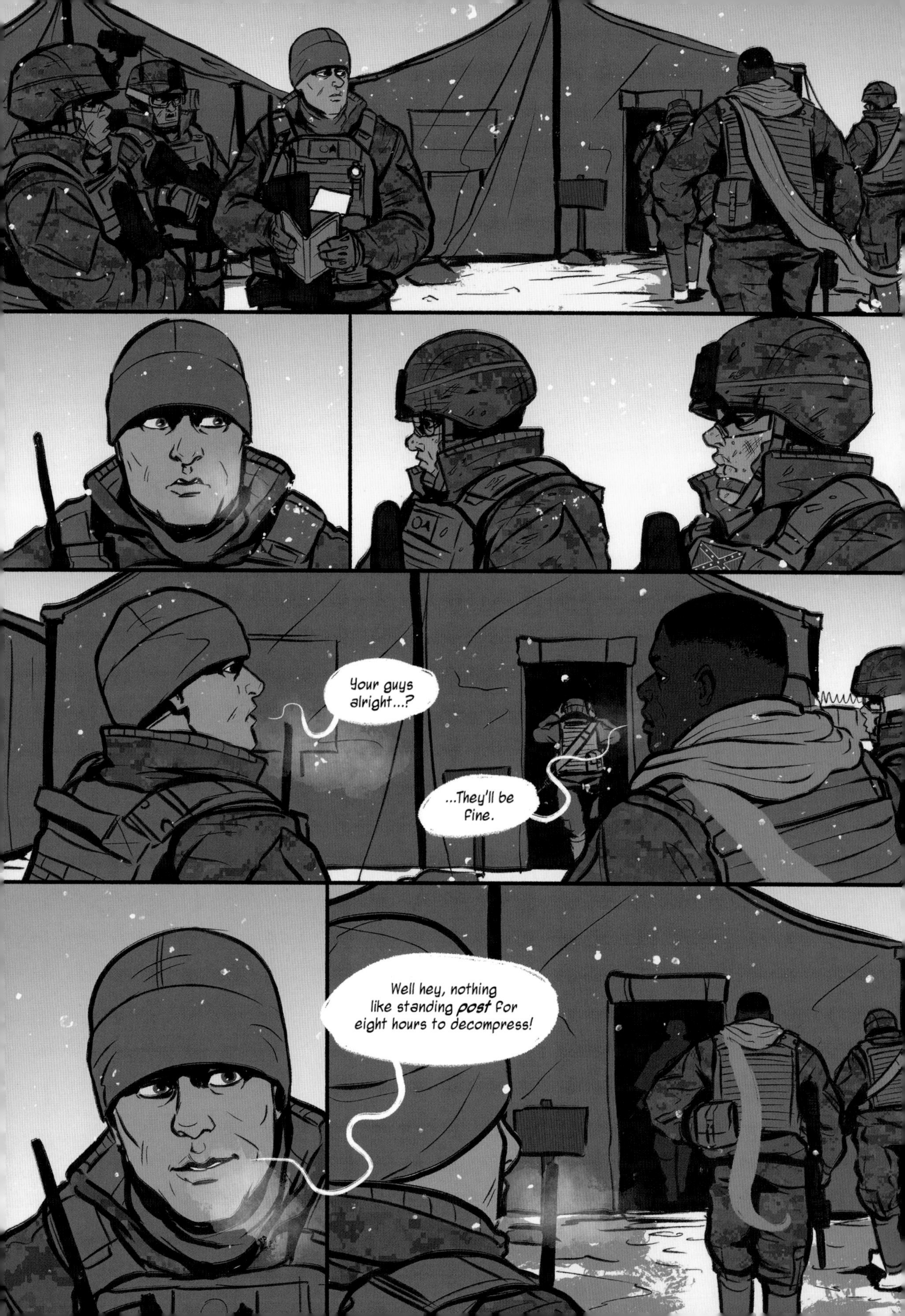

Your guys alright...?
...They'll be fine.
Well hey, nothing like standing *post* for eight hours to decompress!

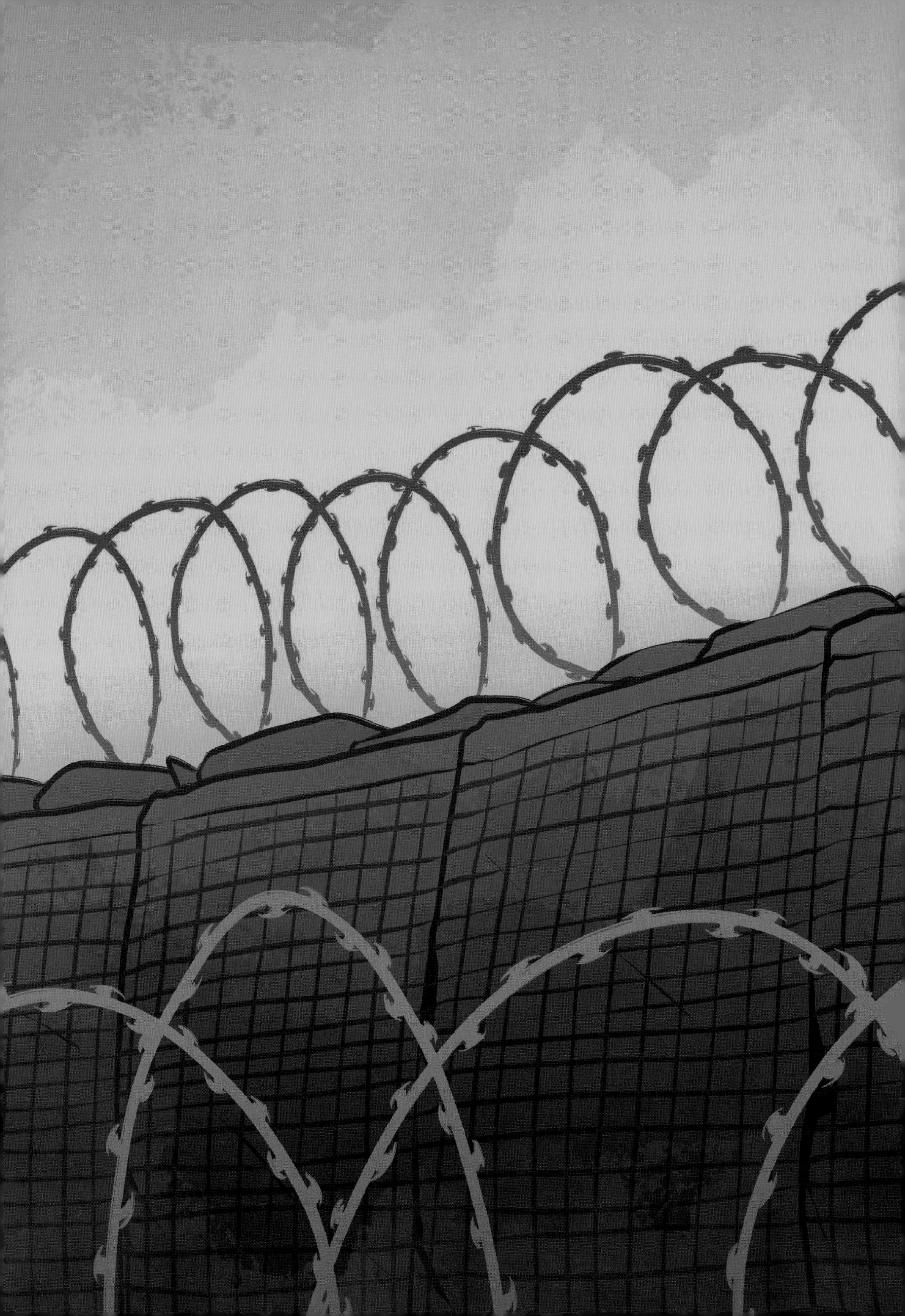

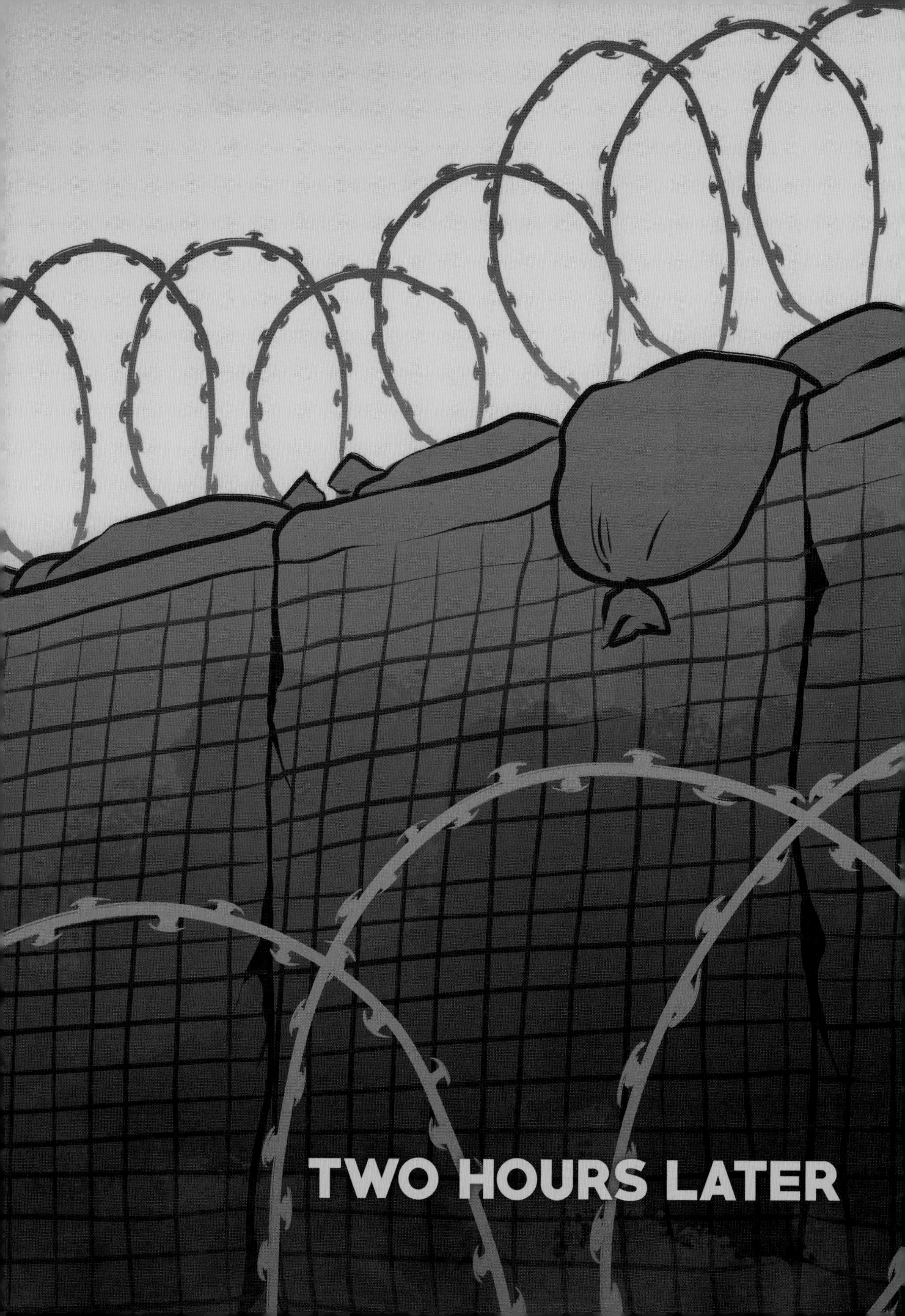
TWO HOURS LATER

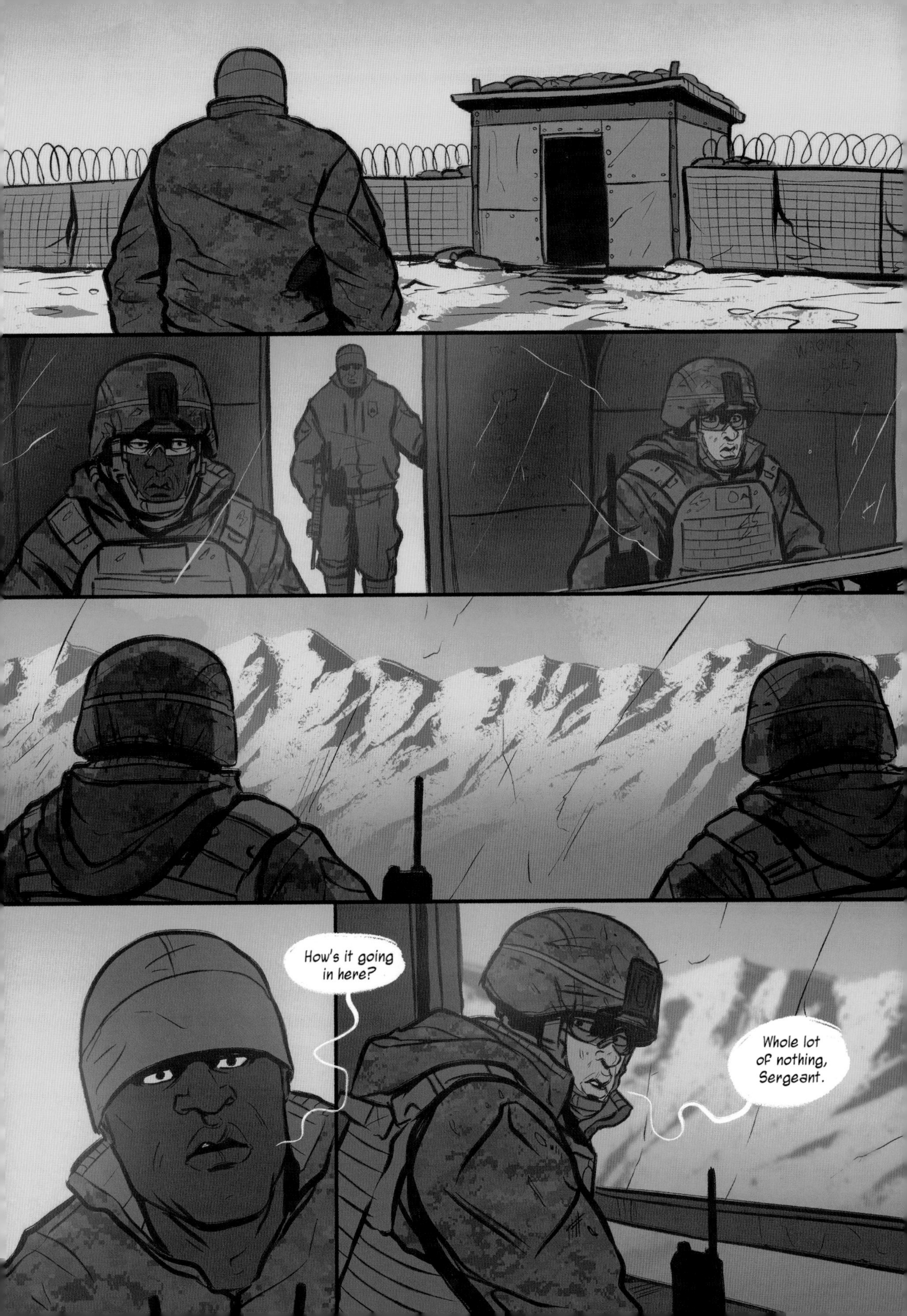
How's it going in here?
Whole lot of nothing, Sergeant.

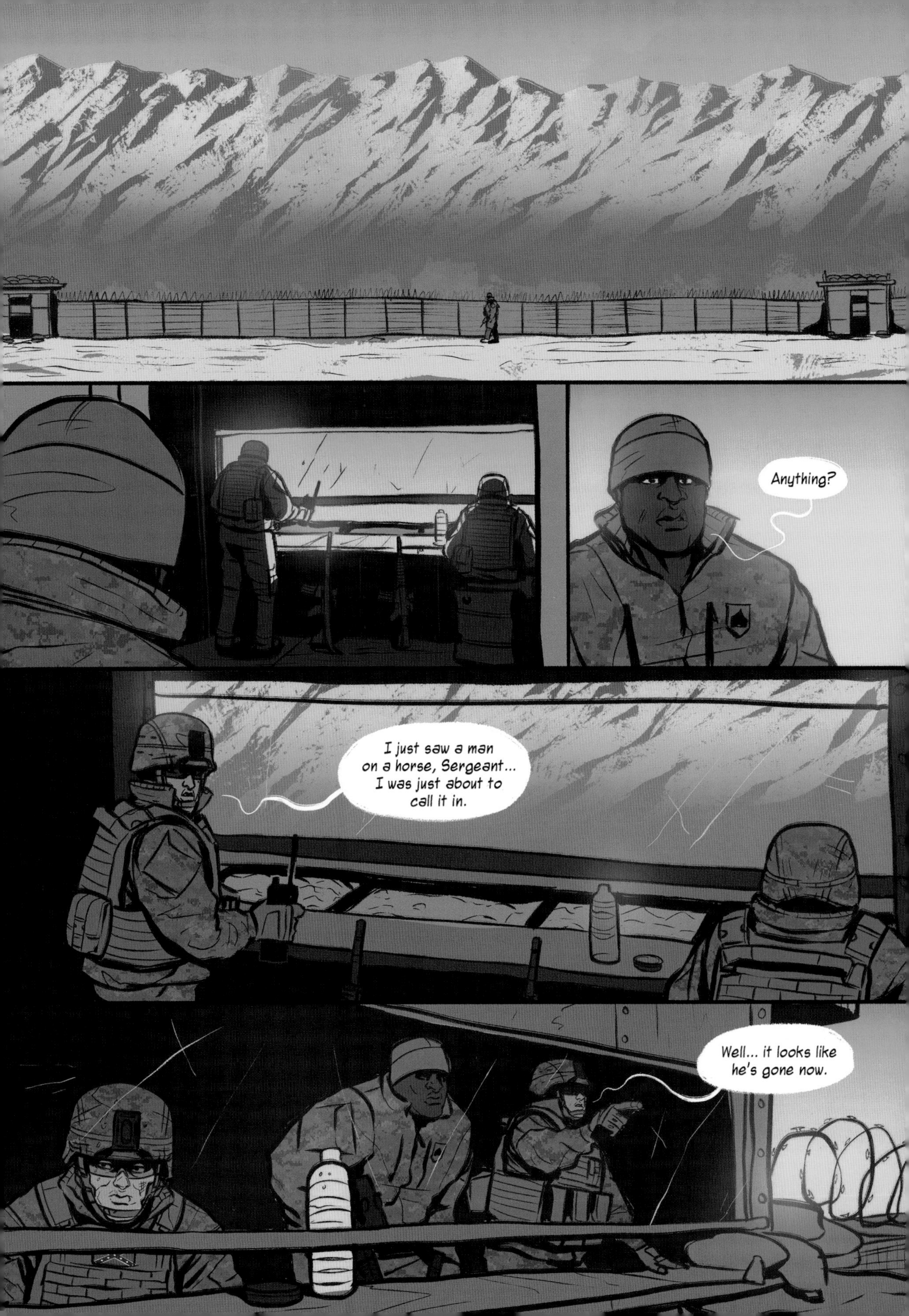
Anything?
I just saw a man on a horse, Sergeant... I was just about to call it in.
Well... it looks like he's gone now.

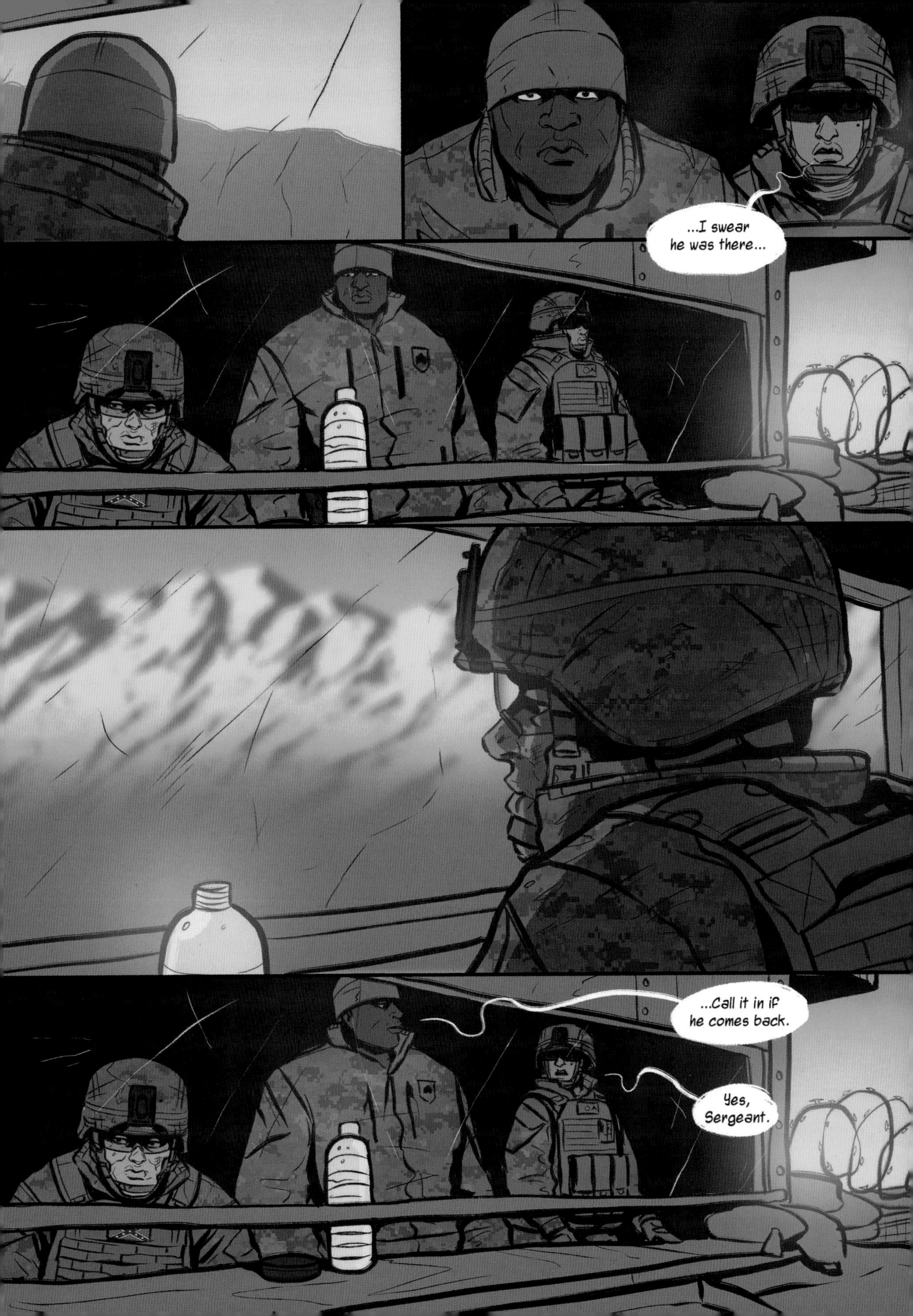
...I swear he was there...
...Call it in if he comes back.
Yes, Sergeant.

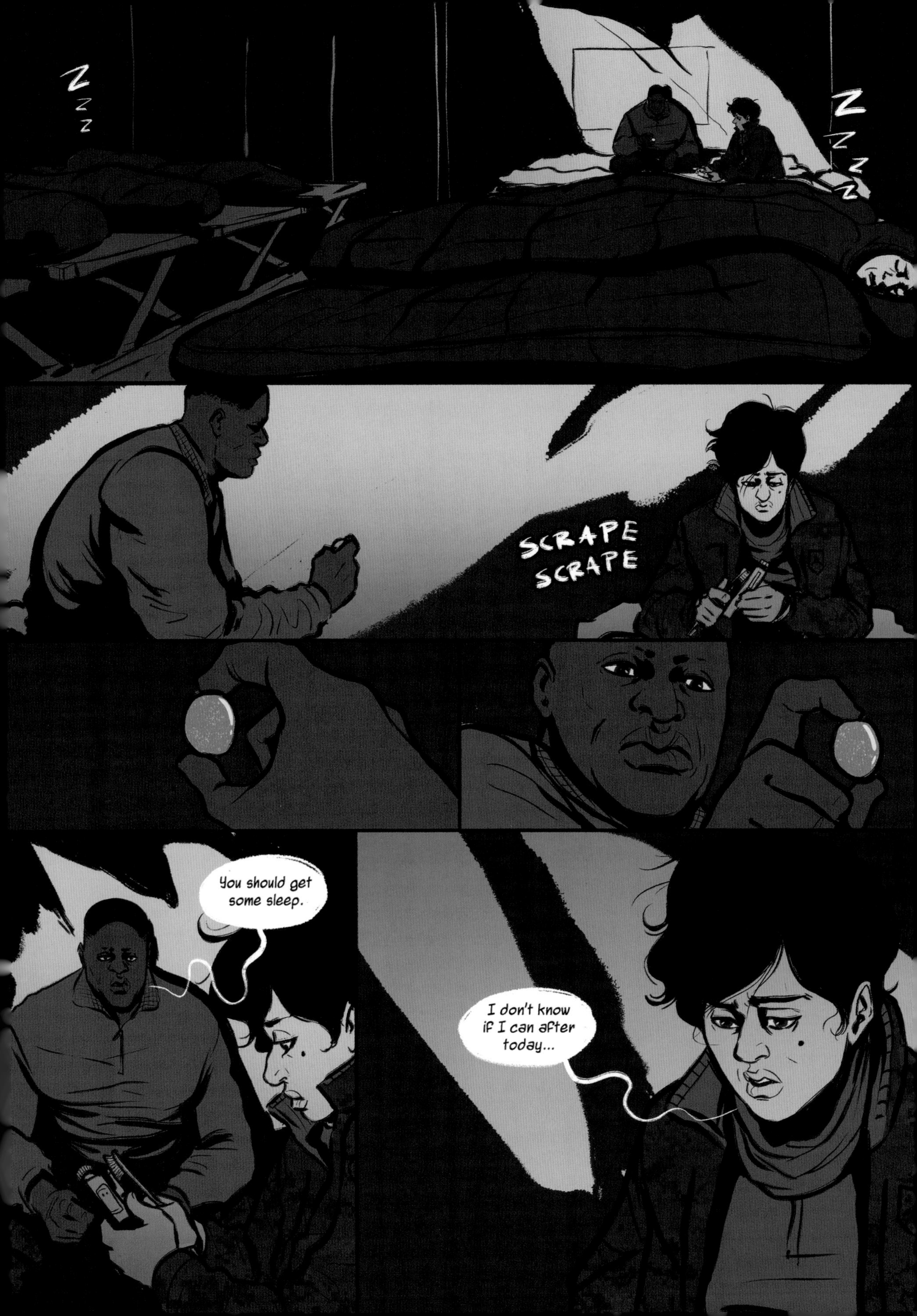
Z Z Z
Z Z Z Z
SCRAPE SCRAPE
You should get some sleep.
I don't know if I can after today...

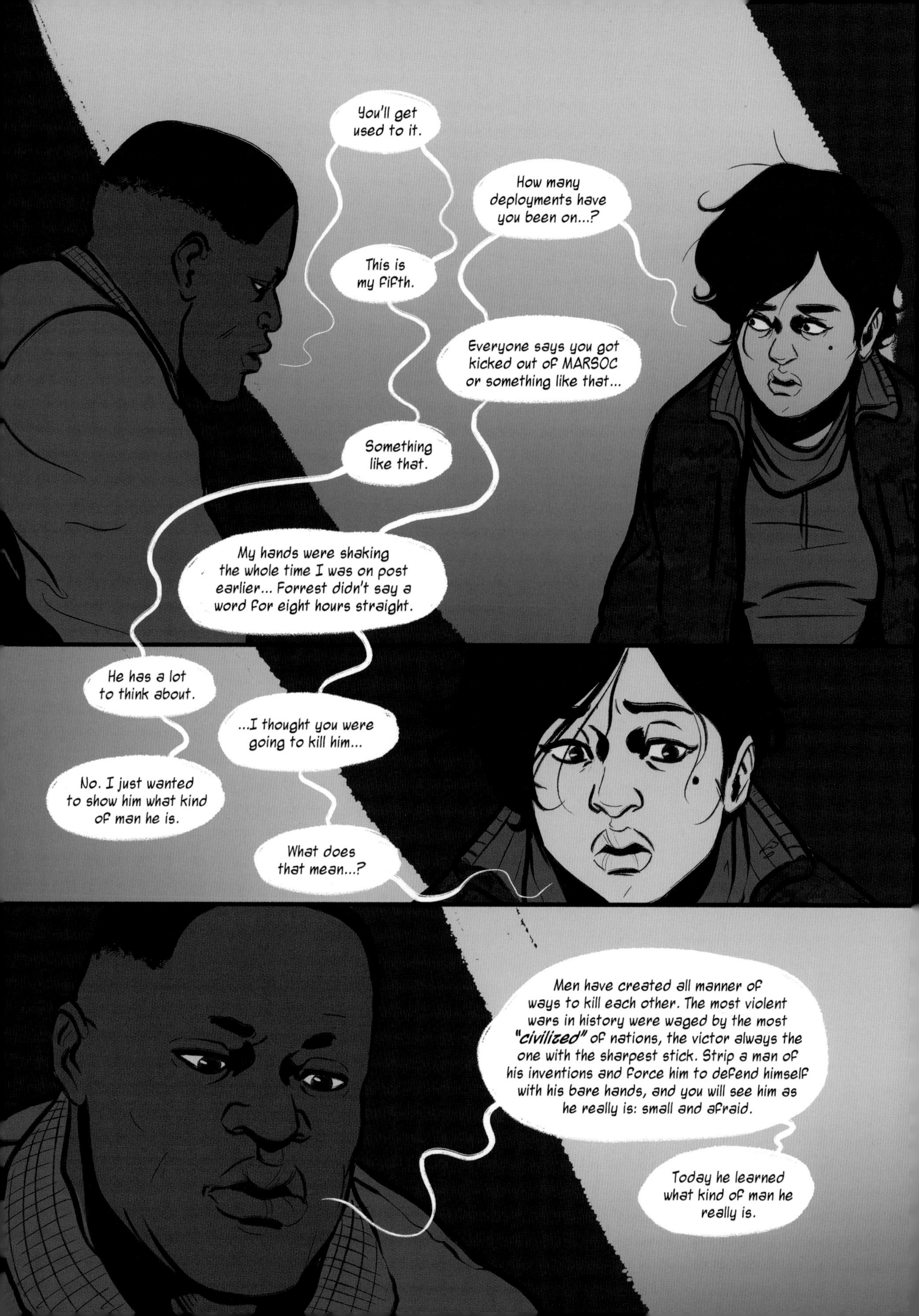
You'll get used to it.
How many deployments have you been on...?
This is my fifth.
Everyone says you got kicked out of MARSOC or something like that...
Something like that.
My hands were shaking the whole time I was on post earlier... Forrest didn't say a word for eight hours straight.
He has a lot to think about.
...I thought you were going to kill him...
No. I just wanted to show him what kind of man he is.
What does that mean...?
Men have created all manner of ways to kill each other. The most violent wars in history were waged by the most "civilized" of nations, the victor always the one with the sharpest stick. Strip a man of his inventions and force him to defend himself with his bare hands, and you will see him as he really is: small and afraid.
Today he learned what kind of man he really is.

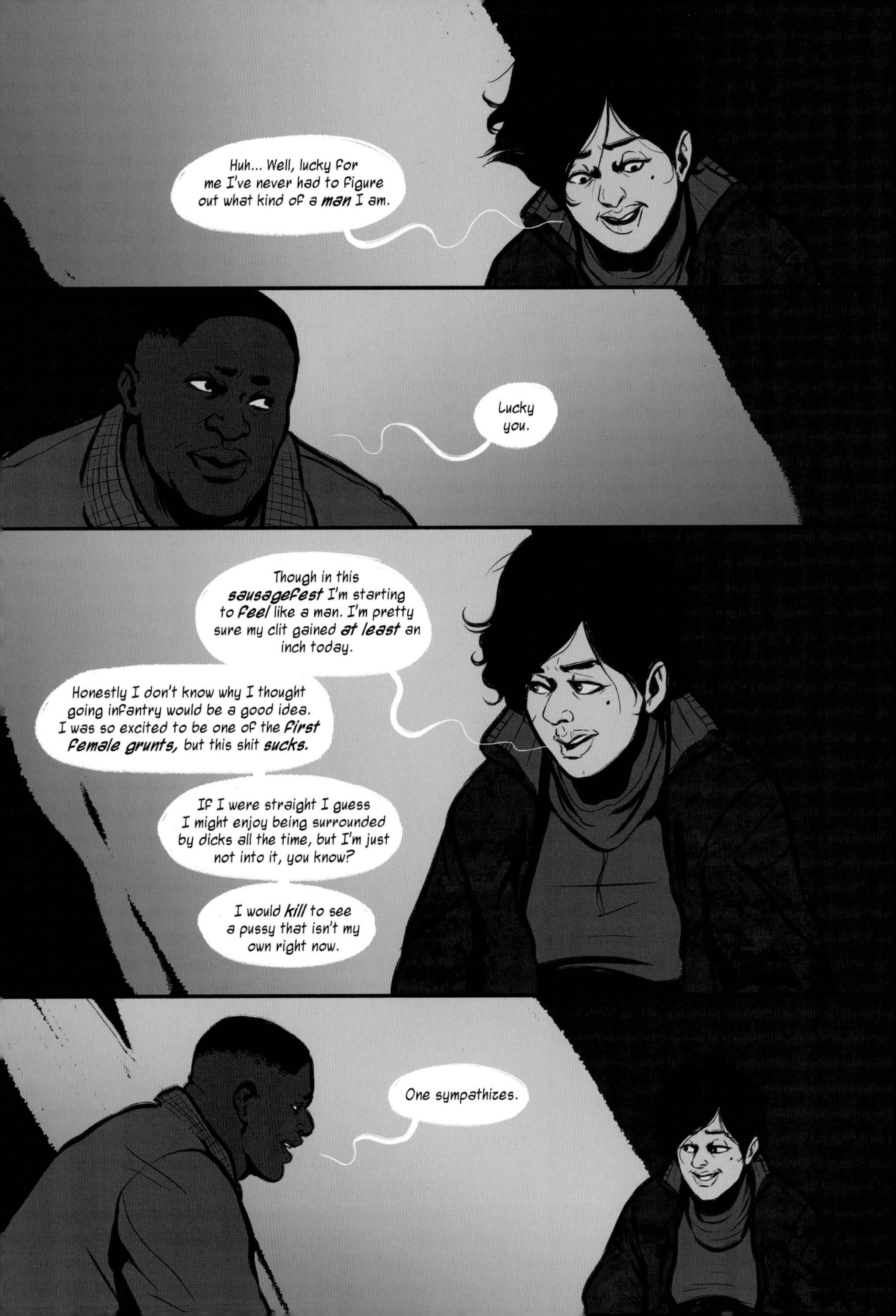
Huh... Well, lucky for me I've never had to figure out what kind of a **man** I am.
Lucky you.
Though in this **sausagefest** I'm starting to **feel** like a man. I'm pretty sure my clit gained **at least** an inch today.
Honestly I don't know why I thought going infantry would be a good idea. I was so excited to be one of the **first female grunts,** but this shit **sucks.**
If I were straight I guess I might enjoy being surrounded by dicks all the time, but I'm just not into it, you know?
I would **kill** to see a pussy that isn't my own right now.
One sympathizes.

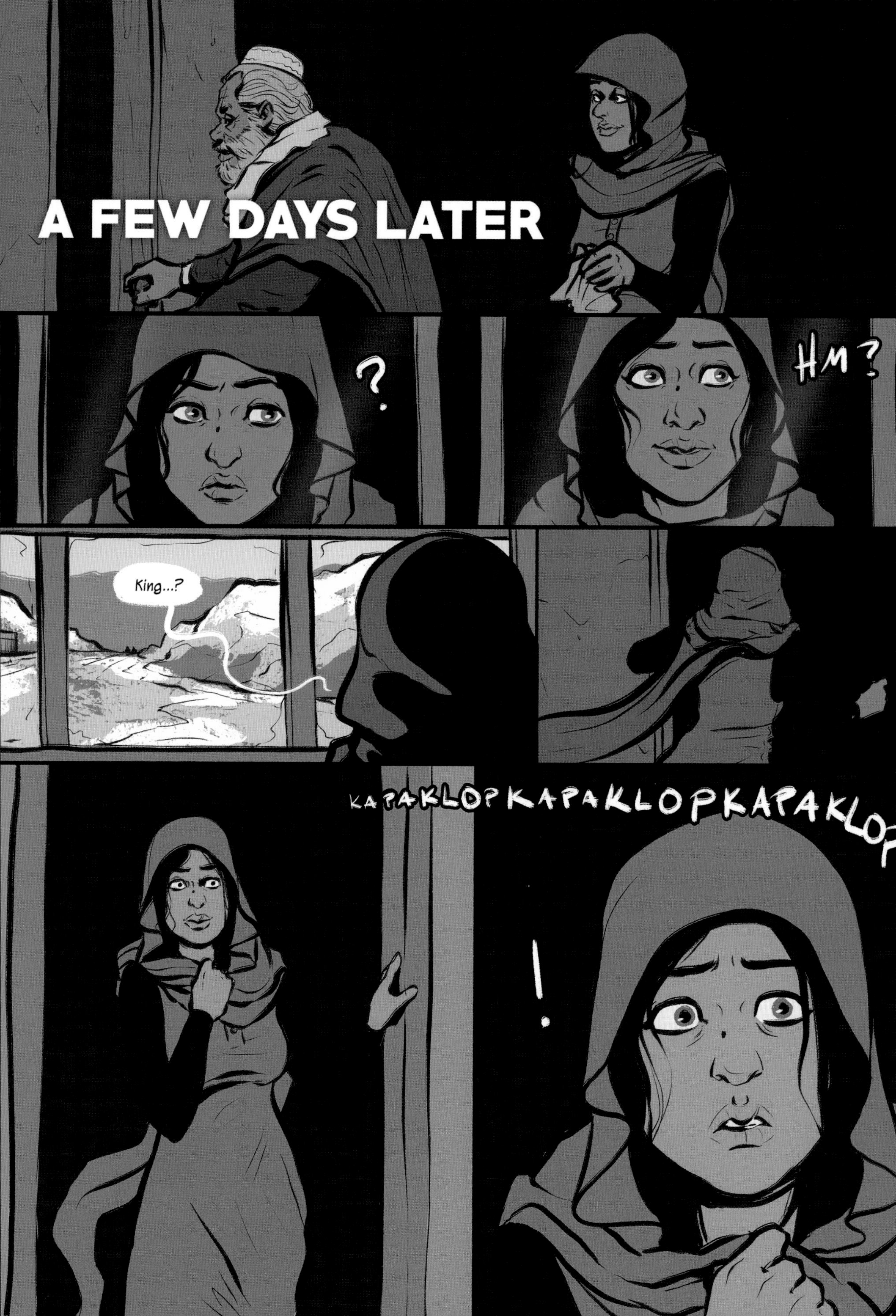
A FEW DAYS LATER
?
HM?
King...?
KAPAKLOPKAPAKLOPKAPAKLOP
!

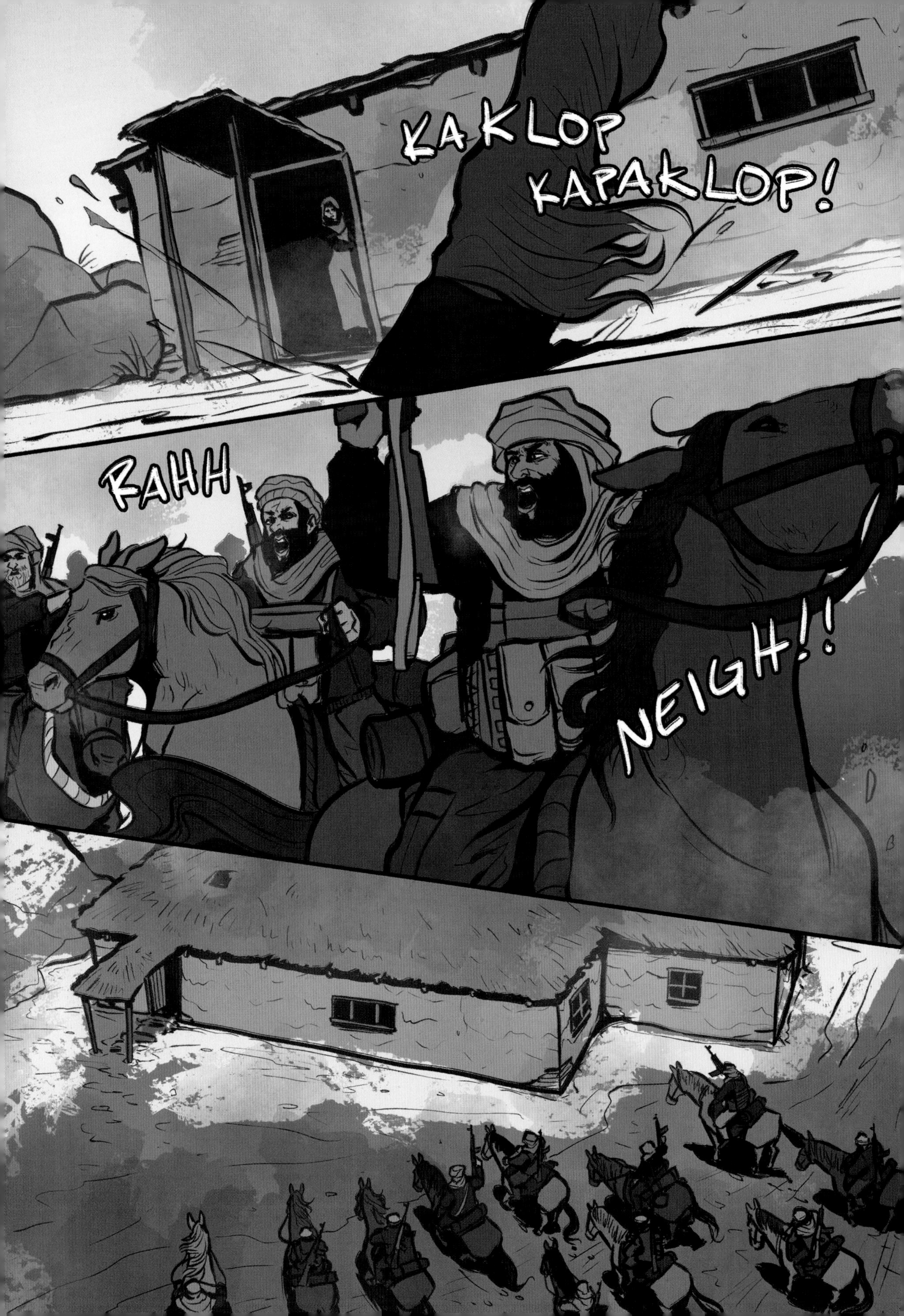
KAKLOP
KAPAKLOP!
RAHH
NEIGH!!

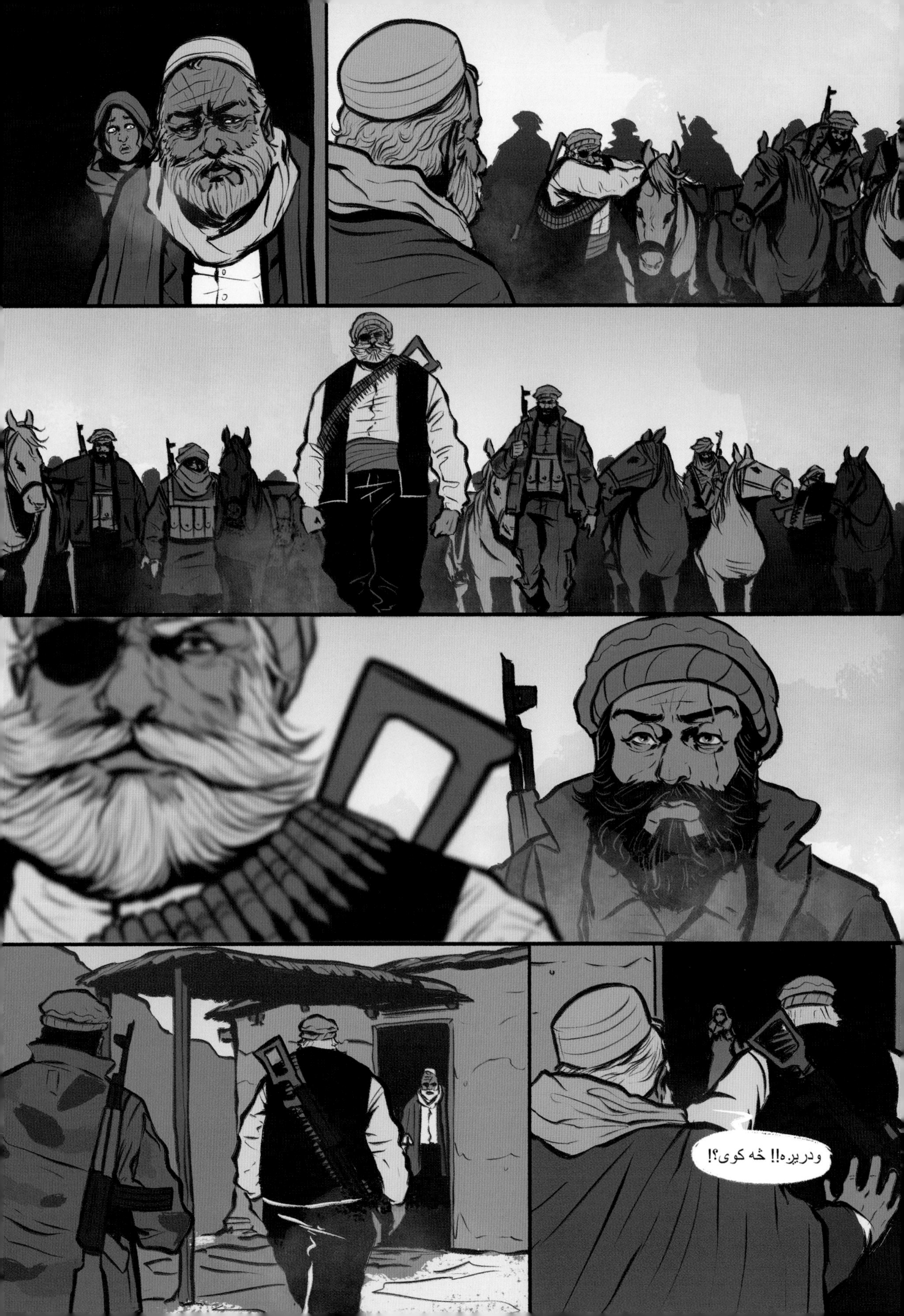
ودریږه!! څه کوی؟!

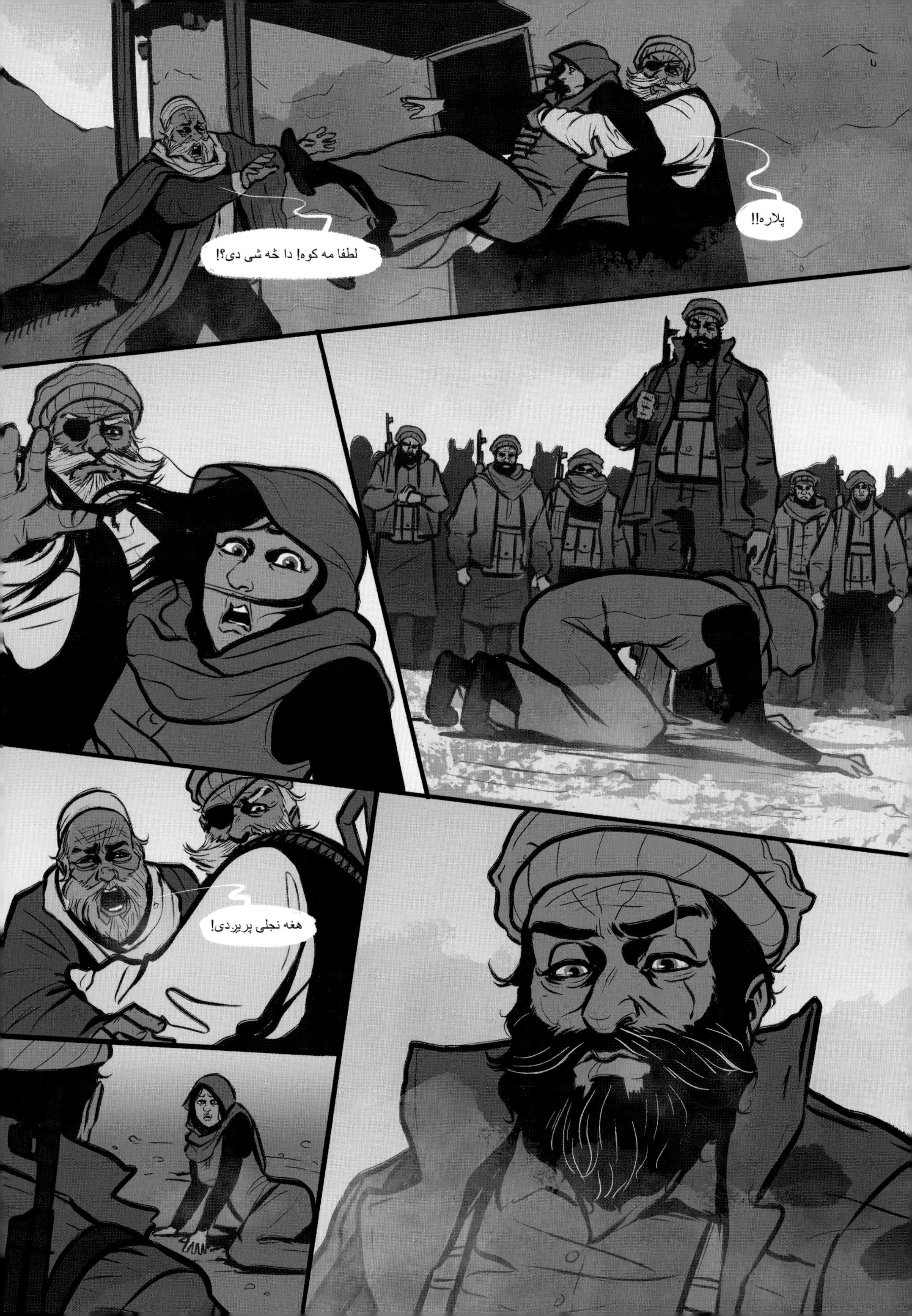
لطفا مه کوه! دا څه شی دی؟!
پلاره!!
هغه نجلی پریږدی!

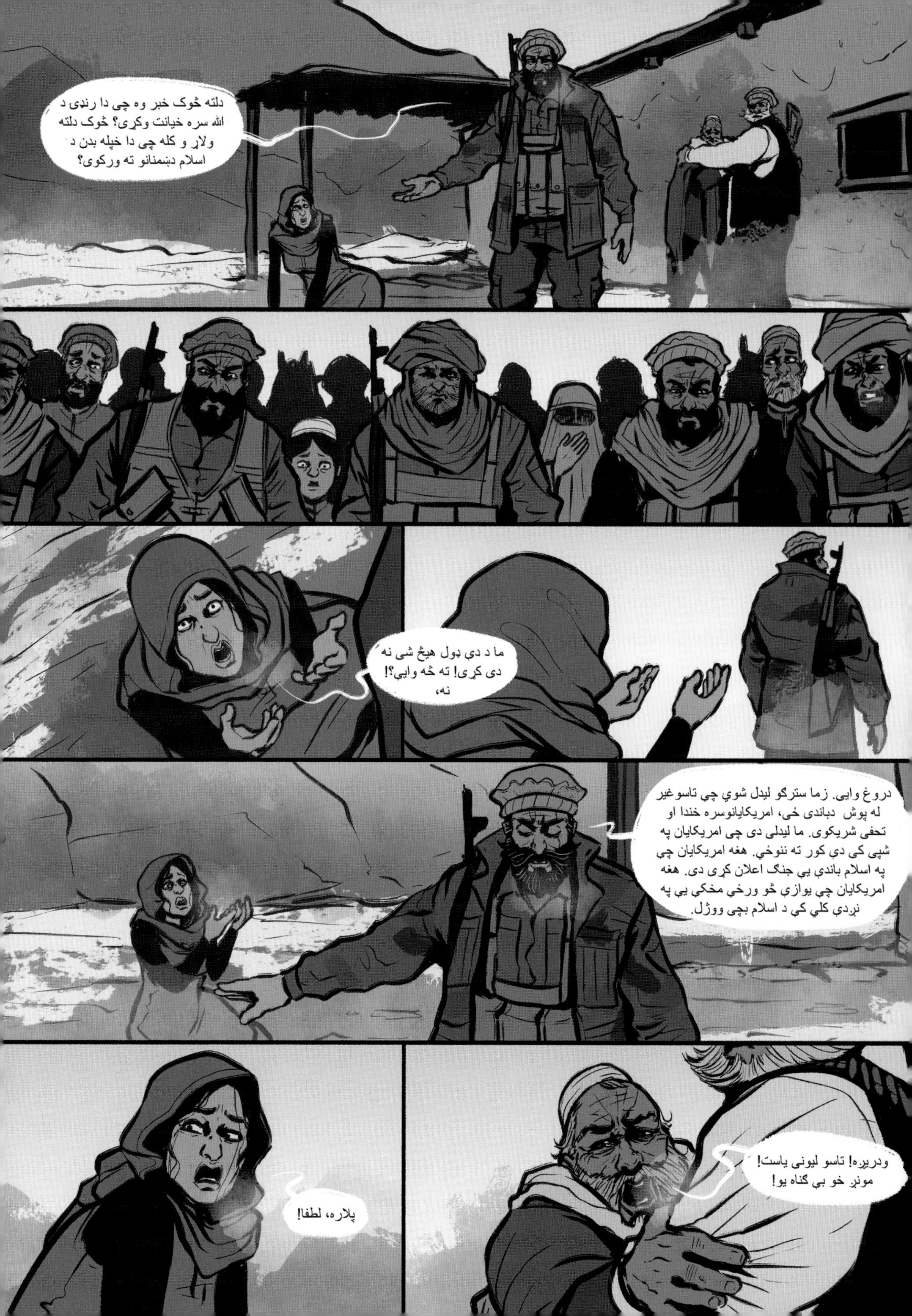
دلته ځوک خبر وه چی دا رندی د الله سره خیانت وکړی؟ ځوک دلته ولاړ و کله چی دا خپله بدن د اسلام دښمنانو ته ورکوی؟
ما د دې ډول هیڅ شی نه دی کړی! ته څه وایې؟! نه،
دروغ وایی. زما سترګو لیدل شوي چي تاسو غیر له پوش دباندی څی، امریکایانوسره خندا او تحفی شریکوی. ما لیدلی دی چی امریکایان په شپی کی دې کور ته ننوځي. هغه امریکایان چي په اسلام باندې یې جنګ اعلان کړی دی. هغه امریکایان چي یوازې څو ورځې مخکې یې په نږدې کلي کې د اسلام بچی ووژل.
پلاره، لطفا!
ودریږه! تاسو لیونی یاست! مونږ خو بې ګناه یو!

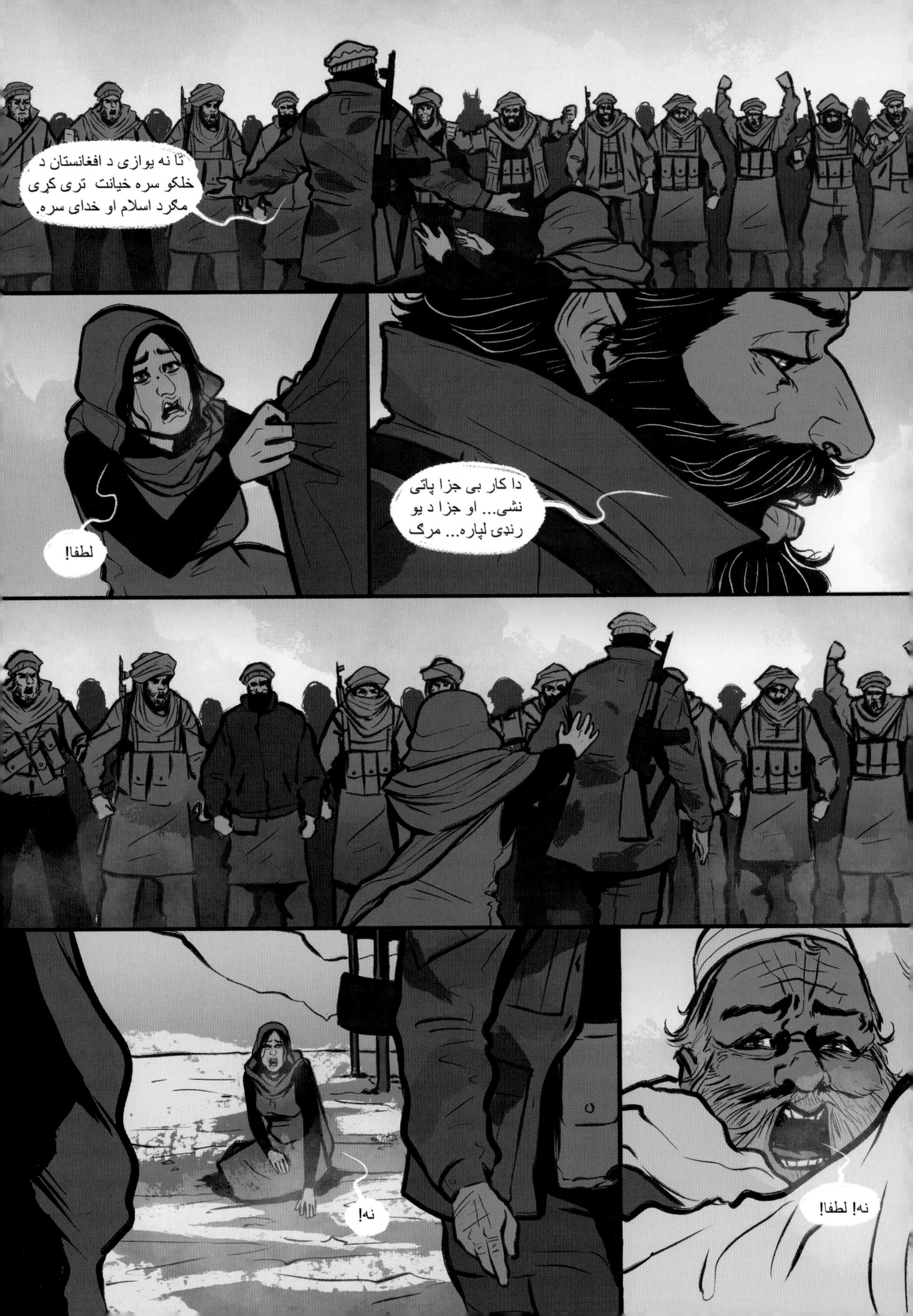
تا نه یوازی د افغانستان د خلکو سره خیانت ترې کړی مګرد اسلام او خدای سره.
لطفا!
دا کار بی جزا پاتی نشی... او جزا د یو رنډی لپاره... مرګ
نه!
نه! لطفا!

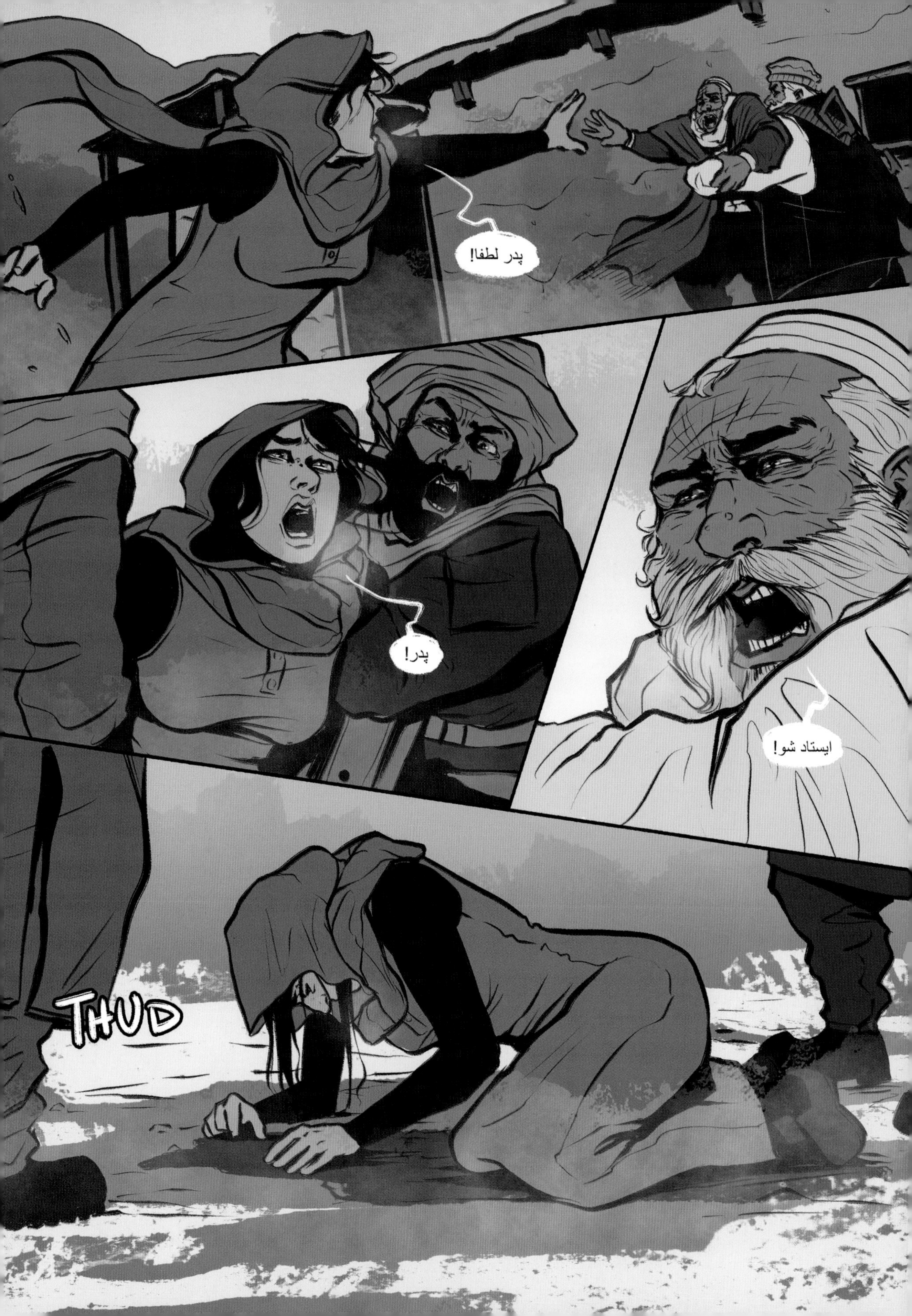
پدر لطفا!
پدر!
ایستاد شو!
THUD

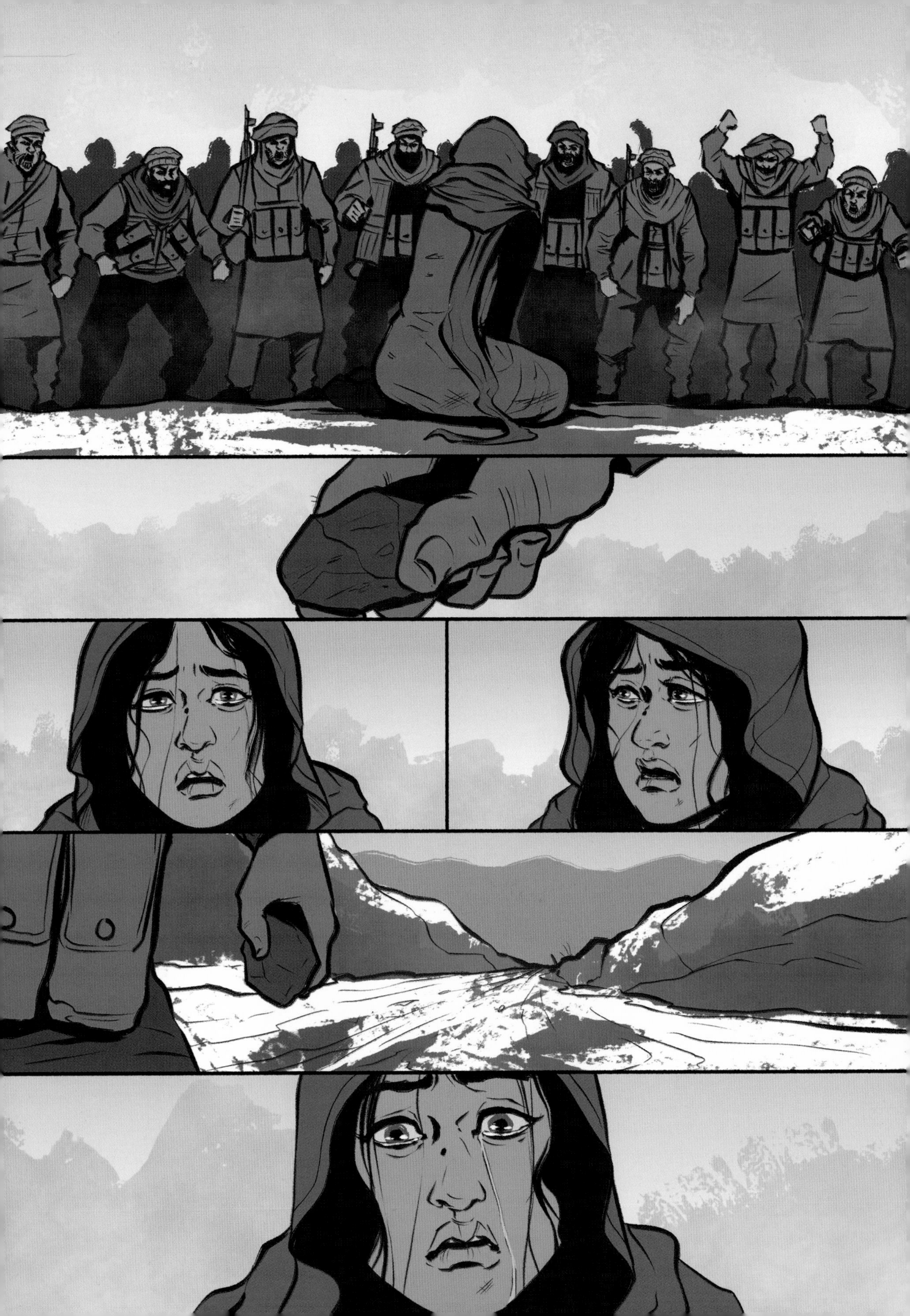

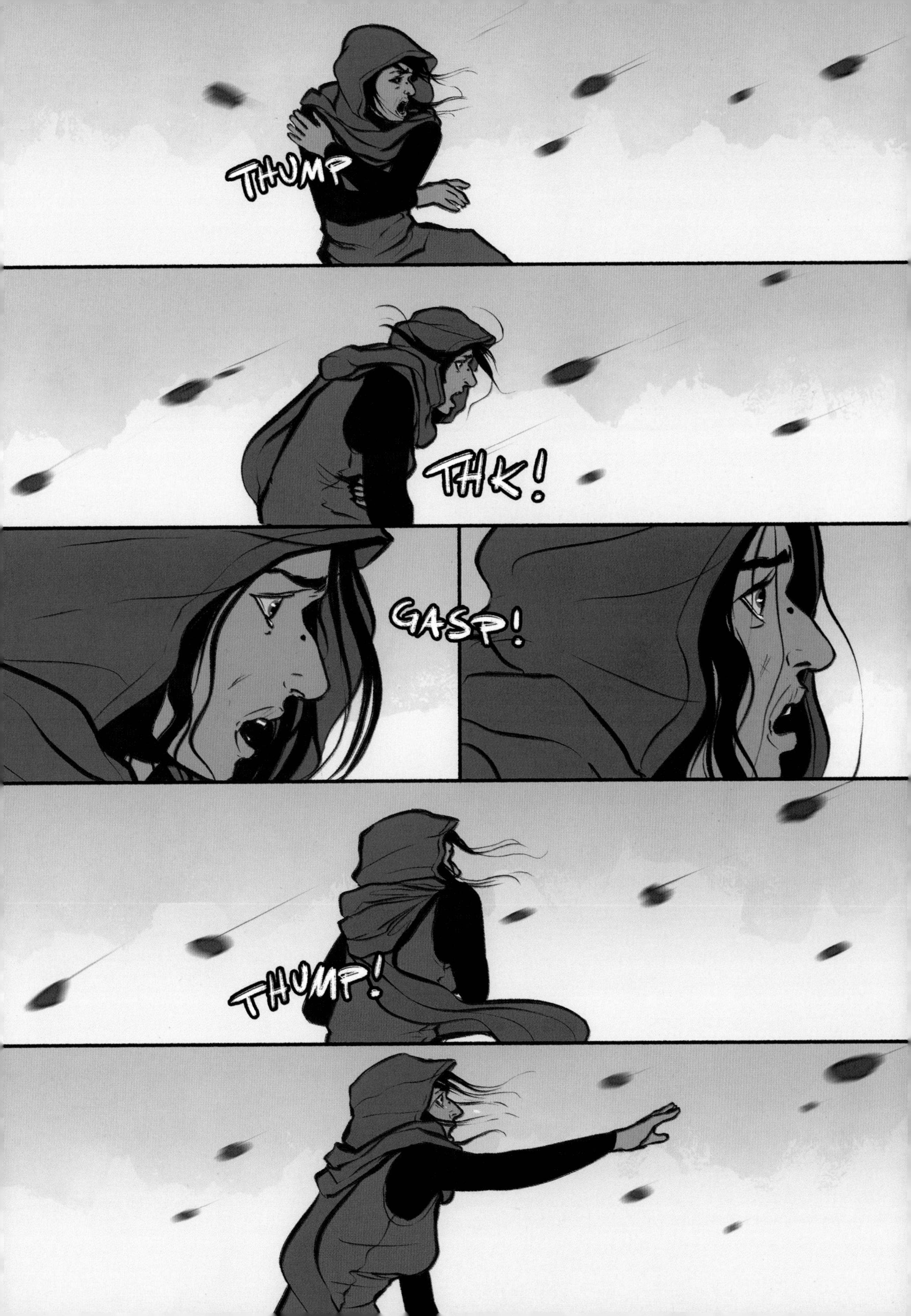
THUMP
THK!
GASP!
THUMP!

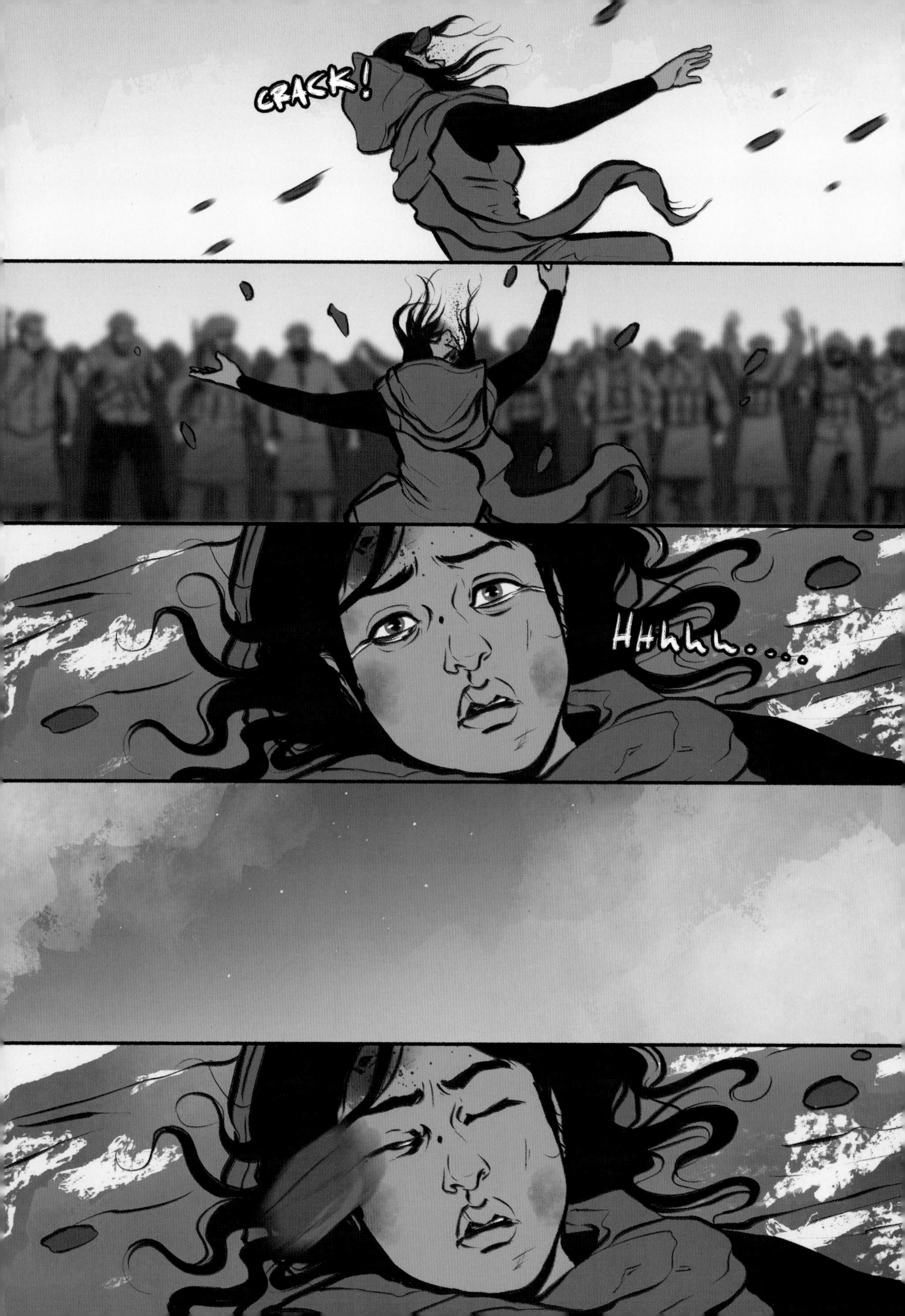
CRACK!
Hhhhh....

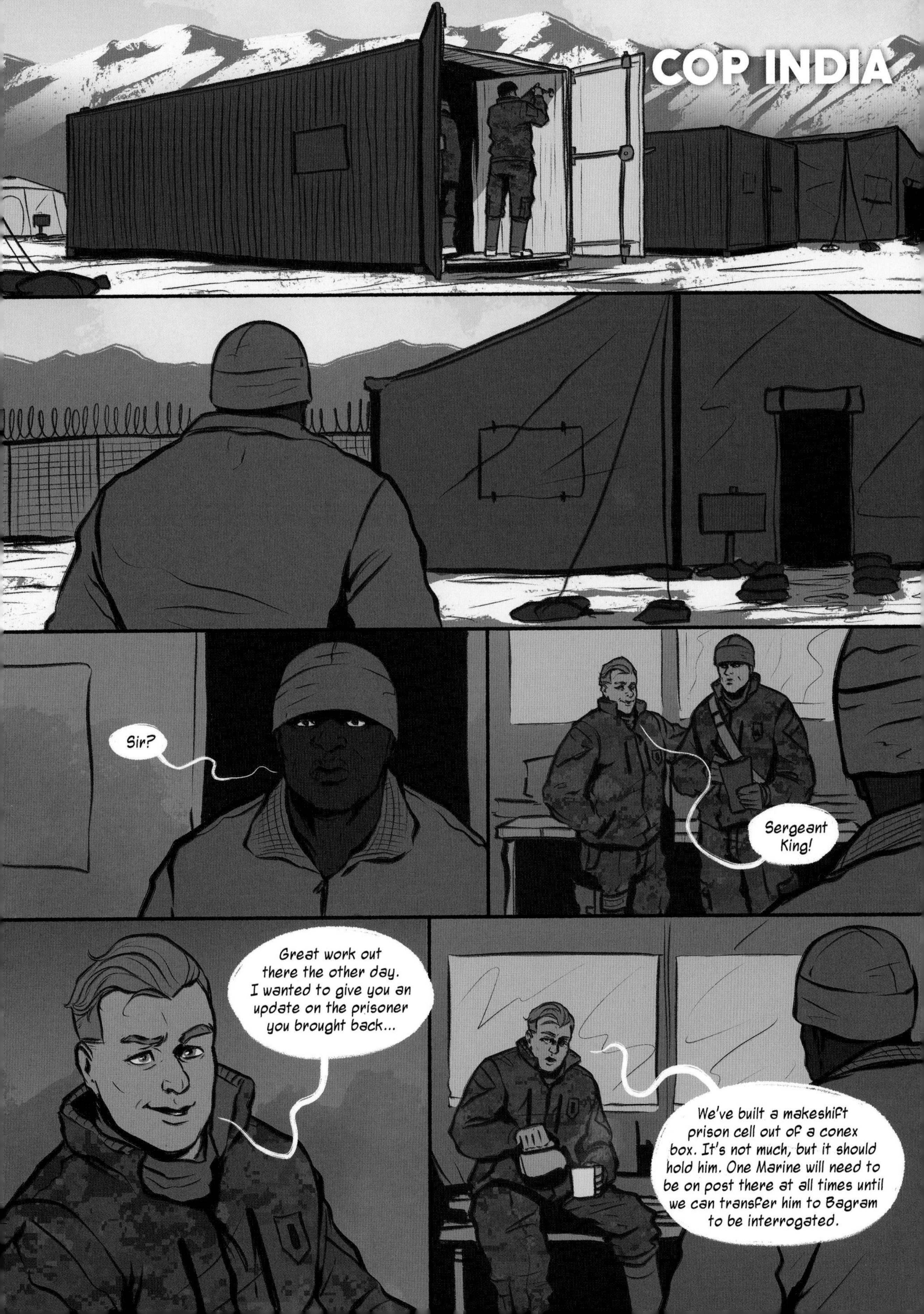
COP INDIA
Sir?
Sergeant King!
Great work out there the other day. I wanted to give you an update on the prisoner you brought back...
We've built a makeshift prison cell out of a conex box. It's not much, but it should hold him. One Marine will need to be on post there at all times until we can transfer him to Bagram to be interrogated.

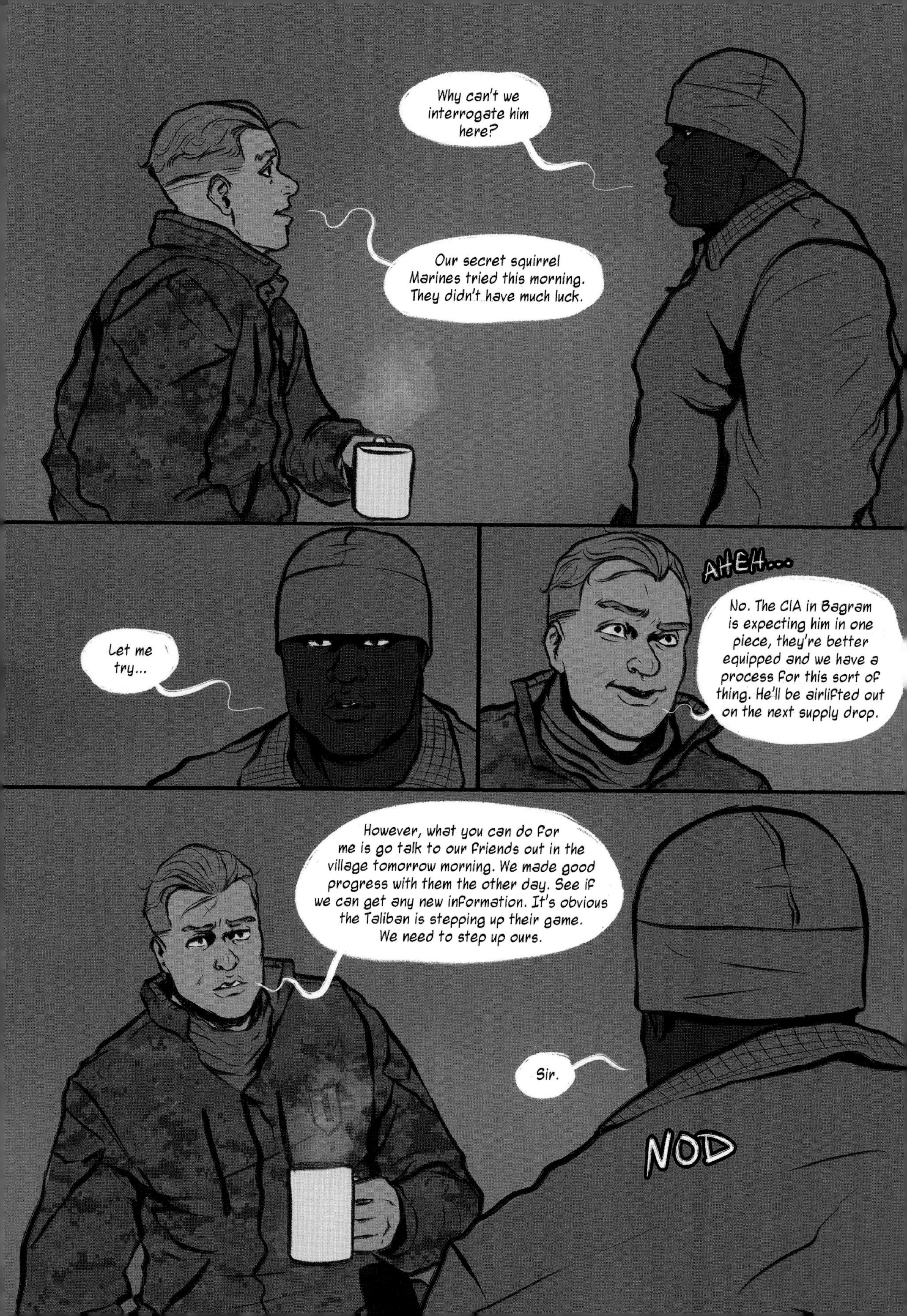
Why can't we interrogate him here?
Our secret squirrel Marines tried this morning. They didn't have much luck.
Let me try...
AHEH...
No. The CIA in Bagram is expecting him in one piece, they're better equipped and we have a process for this sort of thing. He'll be airlifted out on the next supply drop.
However, what you can do for me is go talk to our friends out in the village tomorrow morning. We made good progress with them the other day. See if we can get any new information. It's obvious the Taliban is stepping up their game. We need to step up ours.
Sir.
NOD

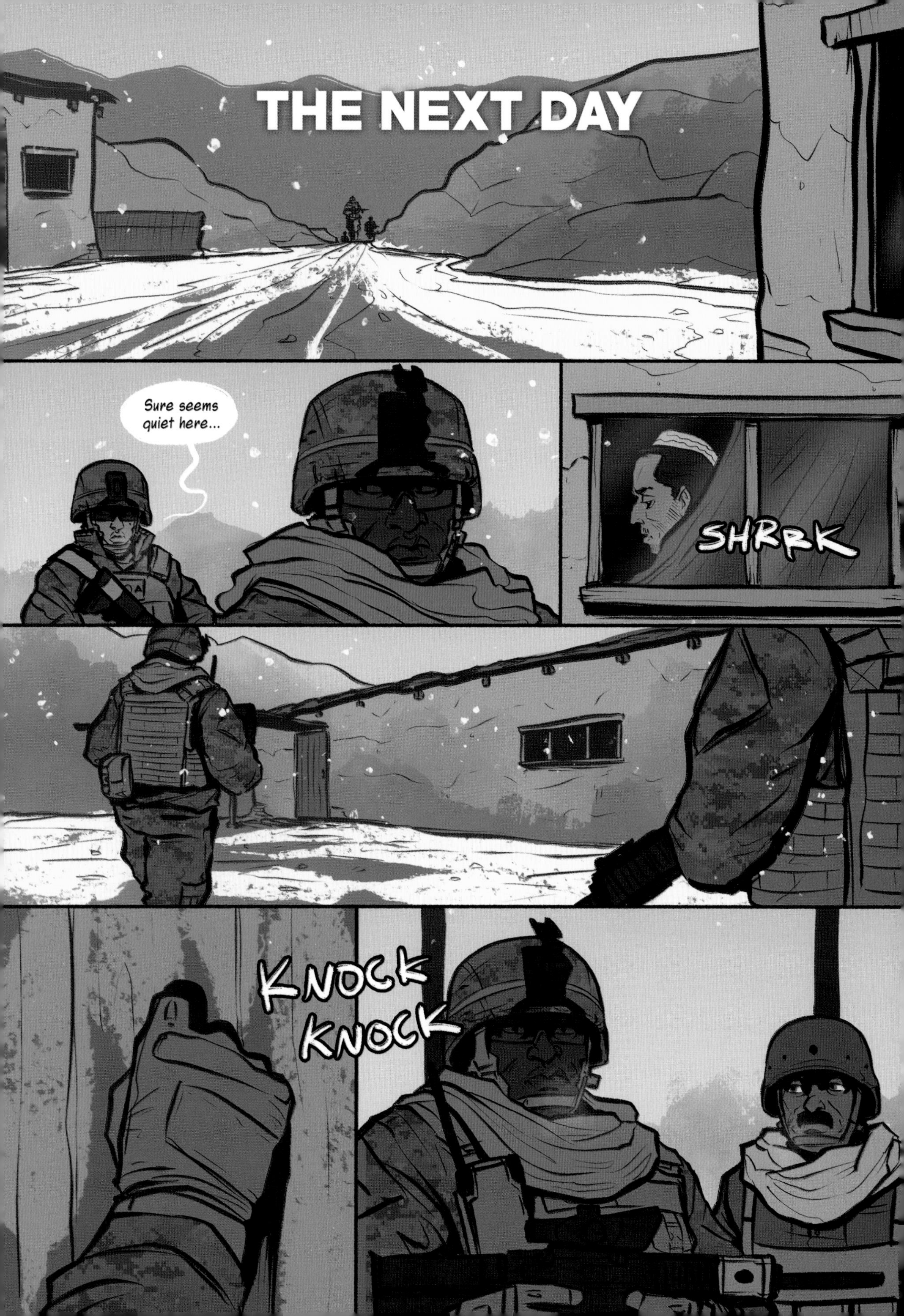
THE NEXT DAY
Sure seems quiet here...
SHRRK
KNOCK KNOCK

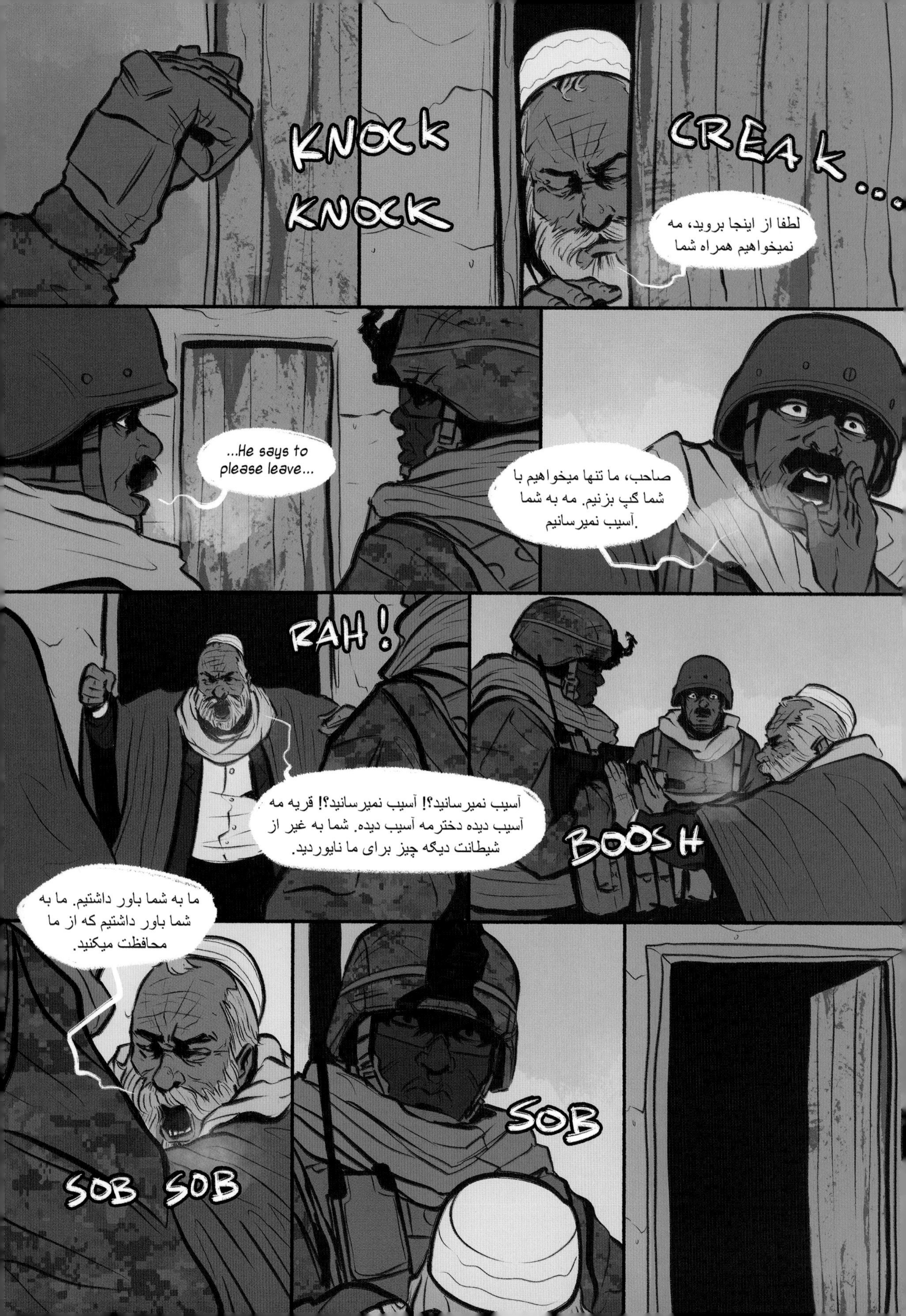
KNOCK KNOCK
CREAK...
لطفا از اینجا بروید، مه نمیخواهیم همراه شما
...He says to please leave...
صاحب، ما تنها میخواهیم با شما گپ بزنیم. مه به شما .آسیب نمیرسانیم
RAH!
آسیب نمیرسانید؟! آسیب نمیرسانید؟! قریه مه آسیب دیده دخترمه آسیب دیده. شما به غیر از شیطانت دیگه چیز برای ما نایوردید.
BOOSH
ما به شما باور داشتیم. ما به شما باور داشتیم که از ما محافظت میکنید.
SOB SOB
SOB

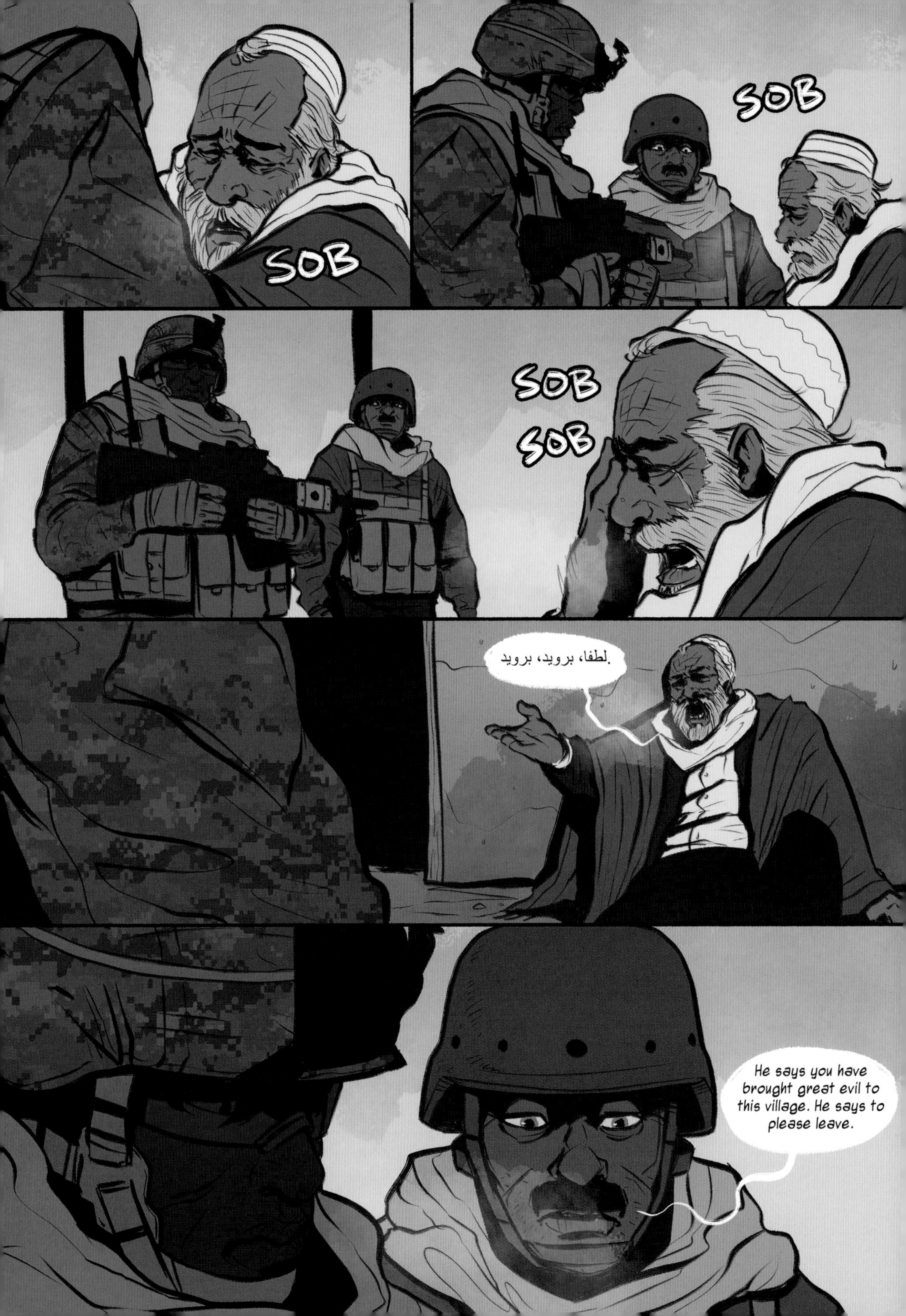
SOB
SOB
SOB
SOB
.لطفا، بروید، بروید
He says you have brought great evil to this village. He says to please leave.

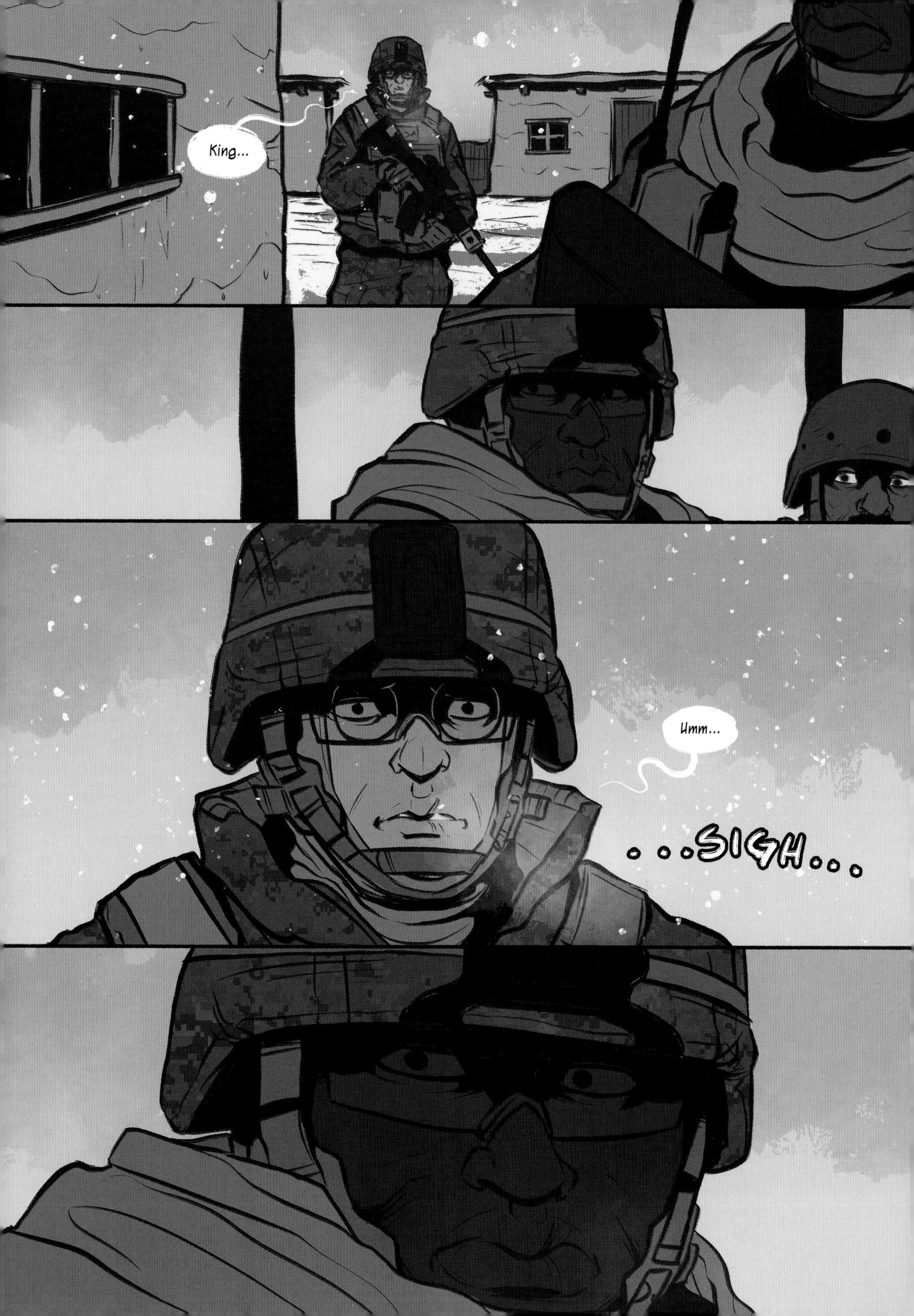
King...
Umm...
...SIGH...

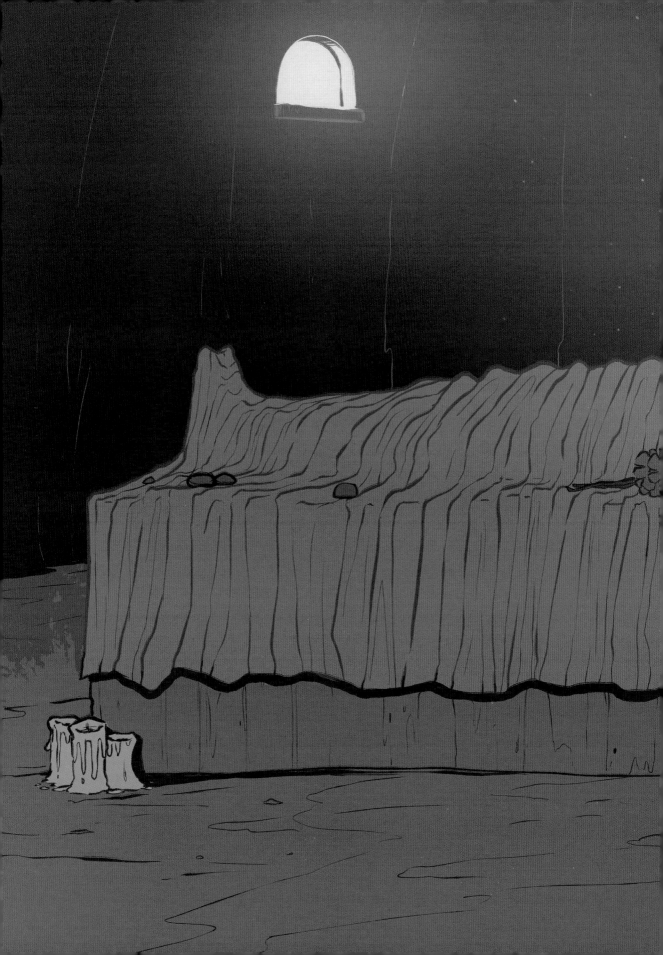

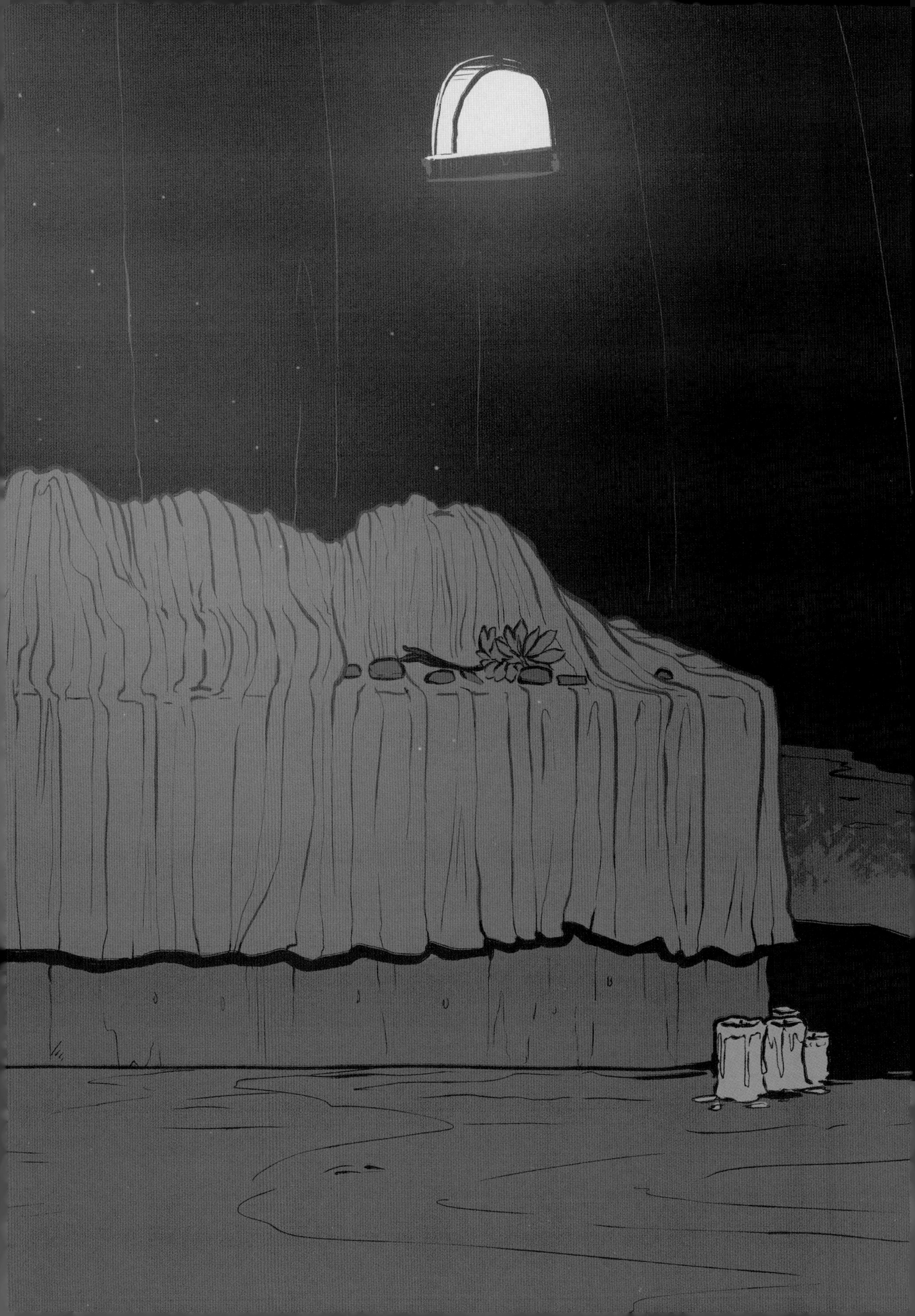

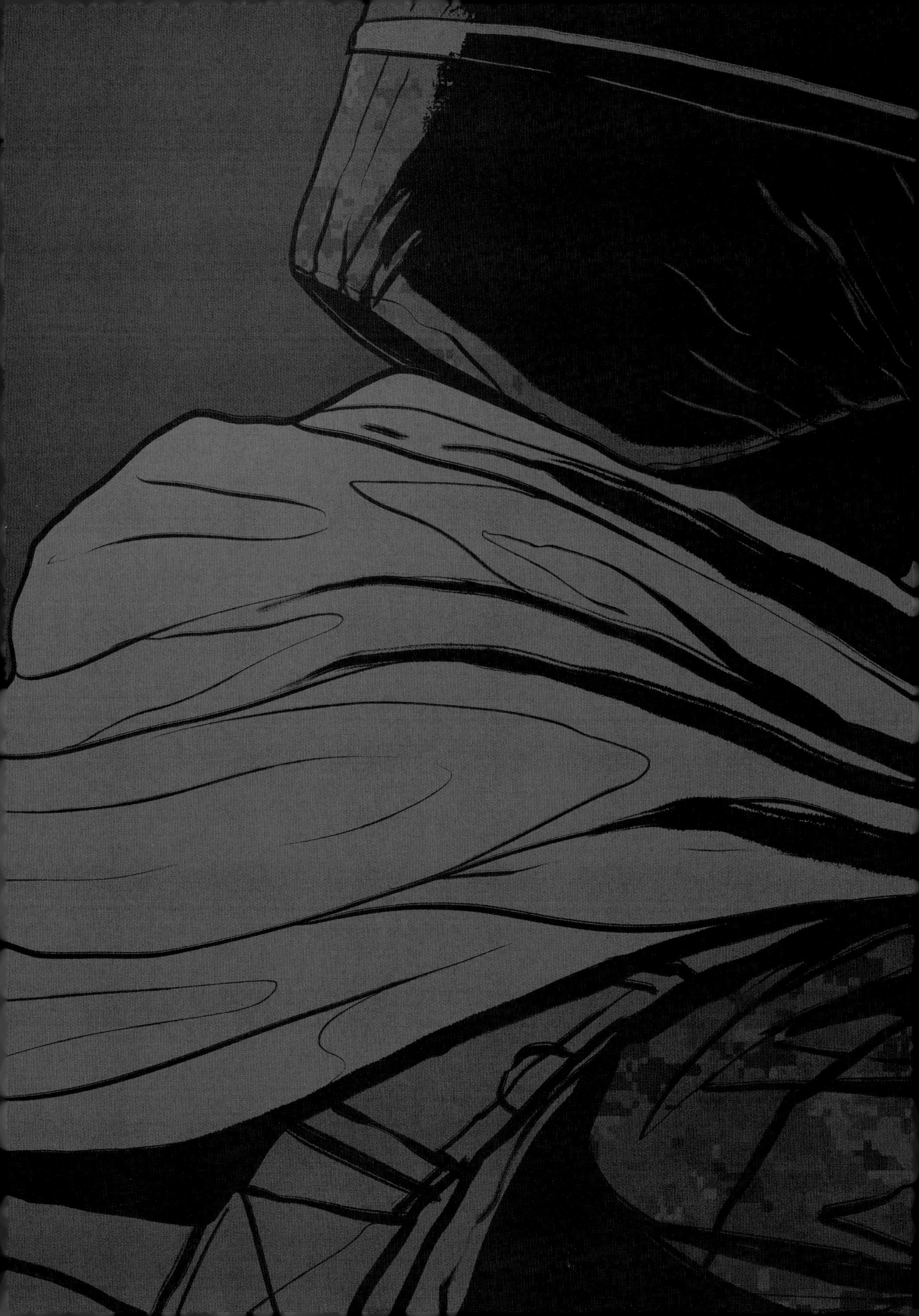

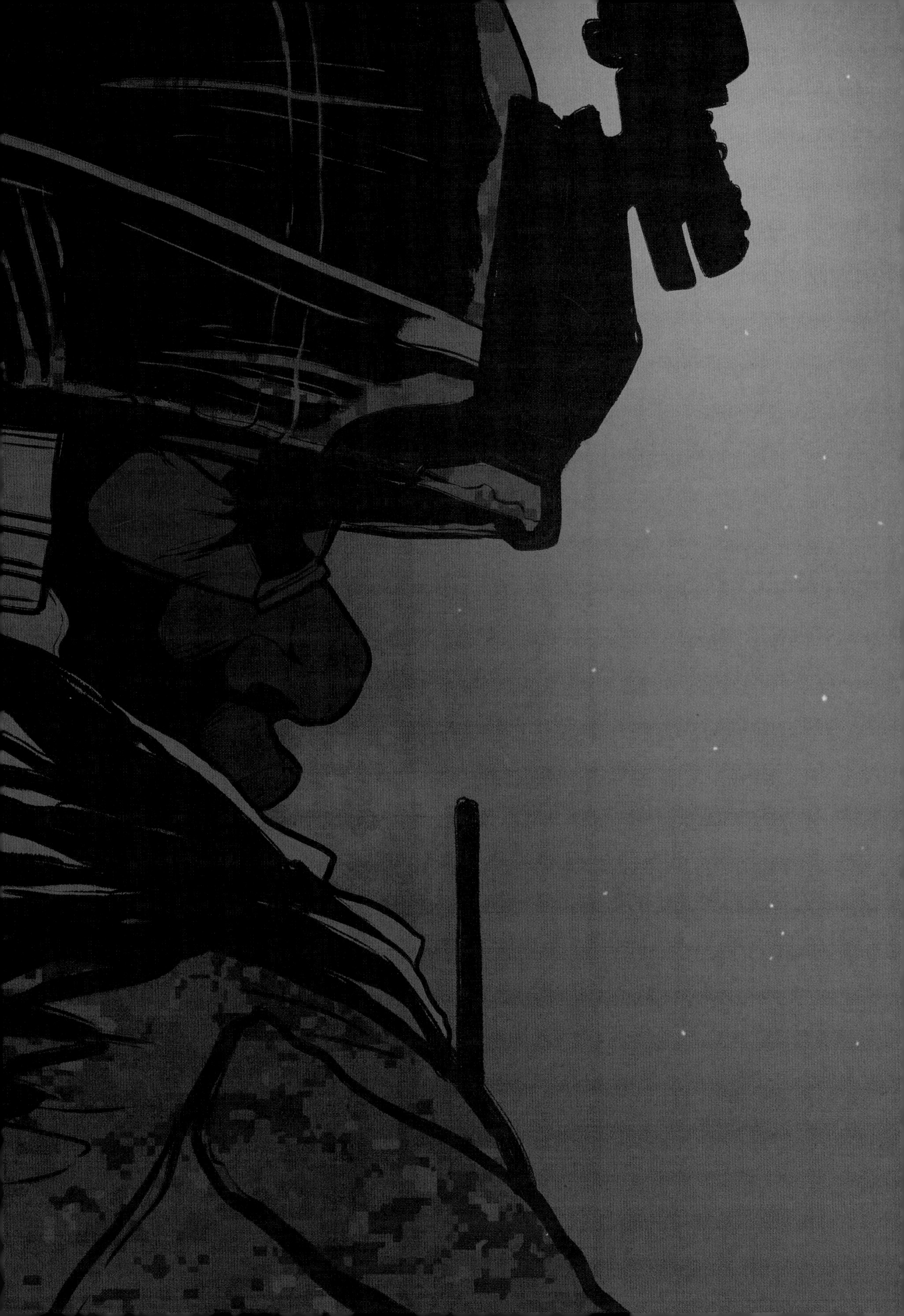

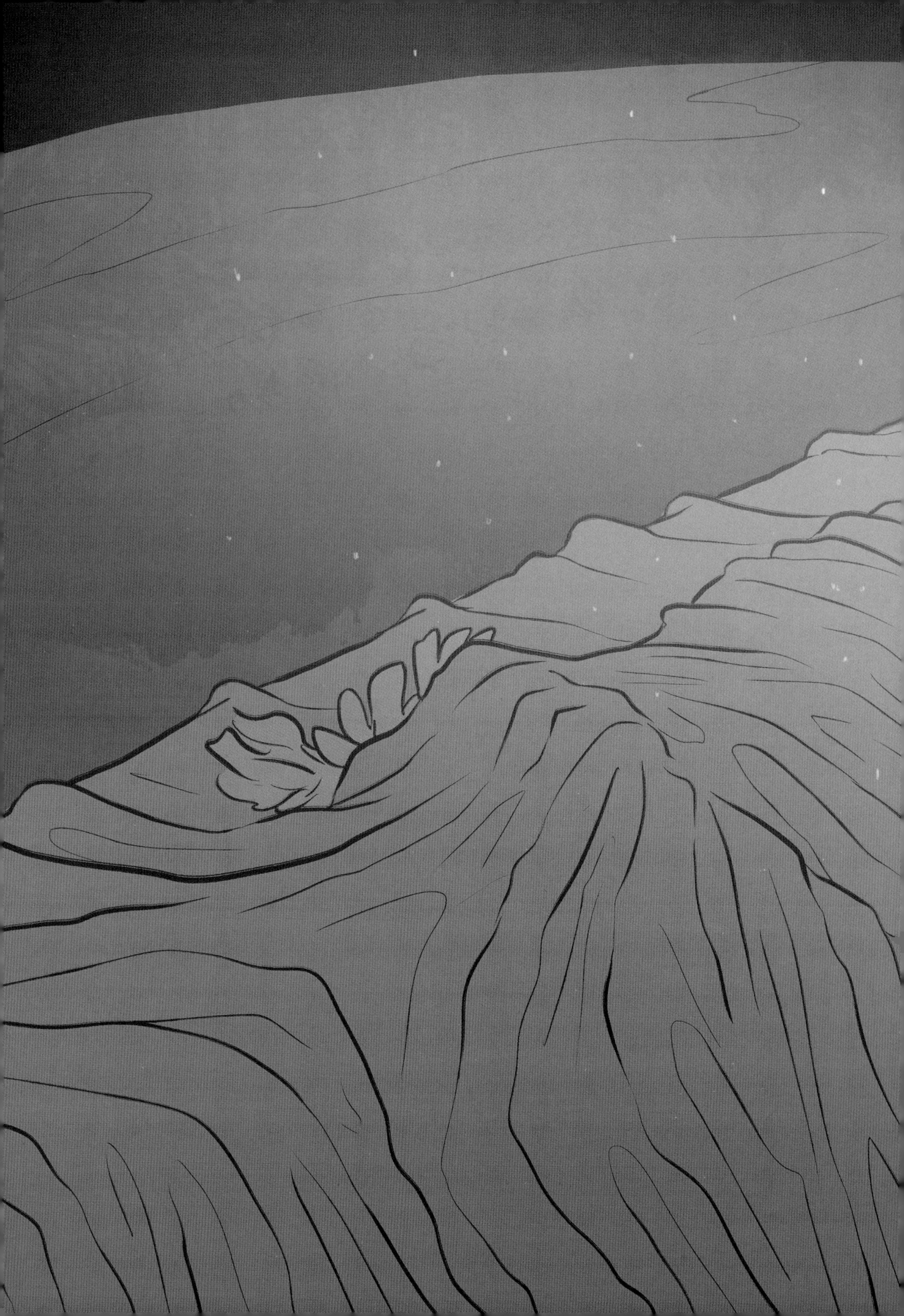

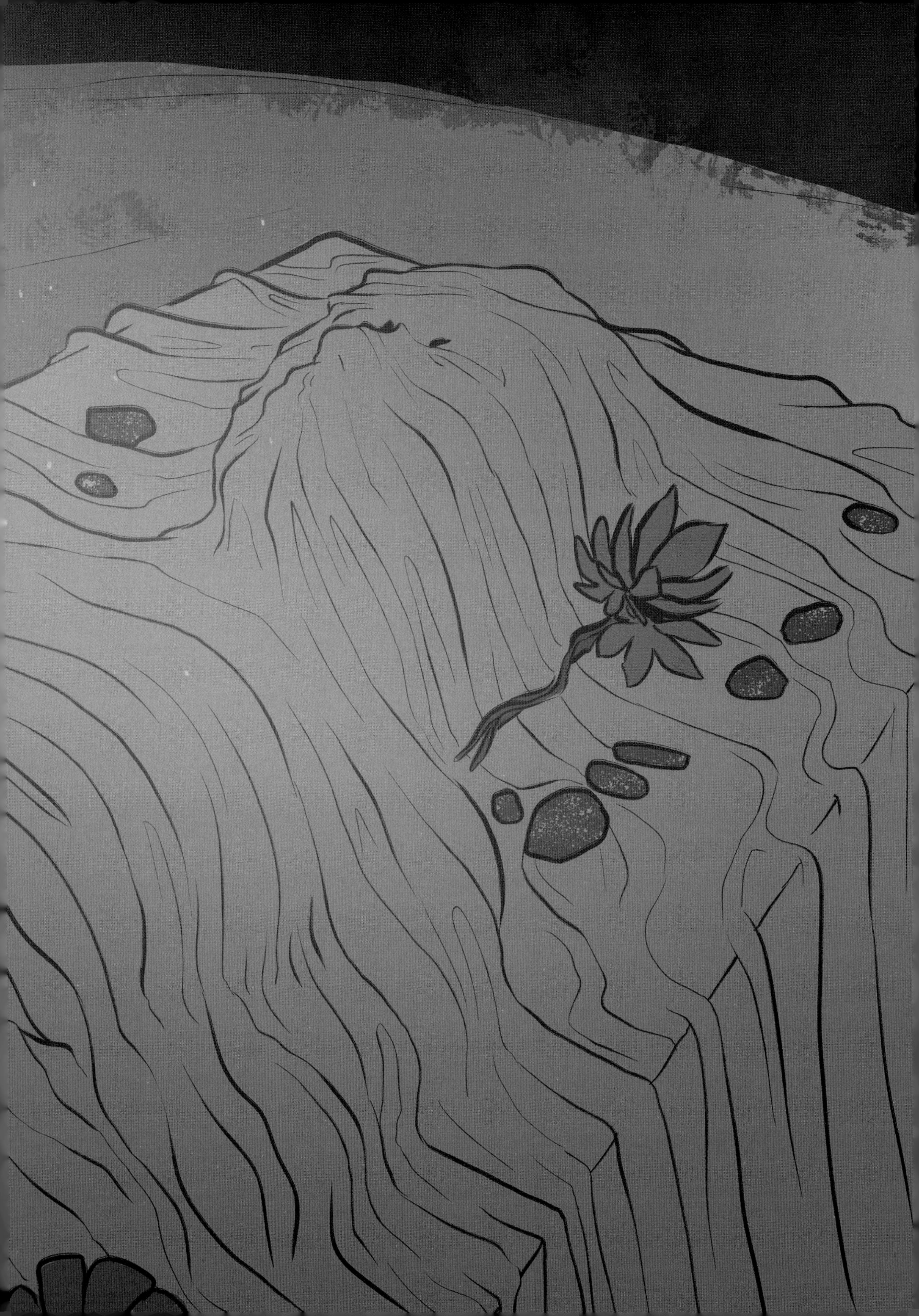

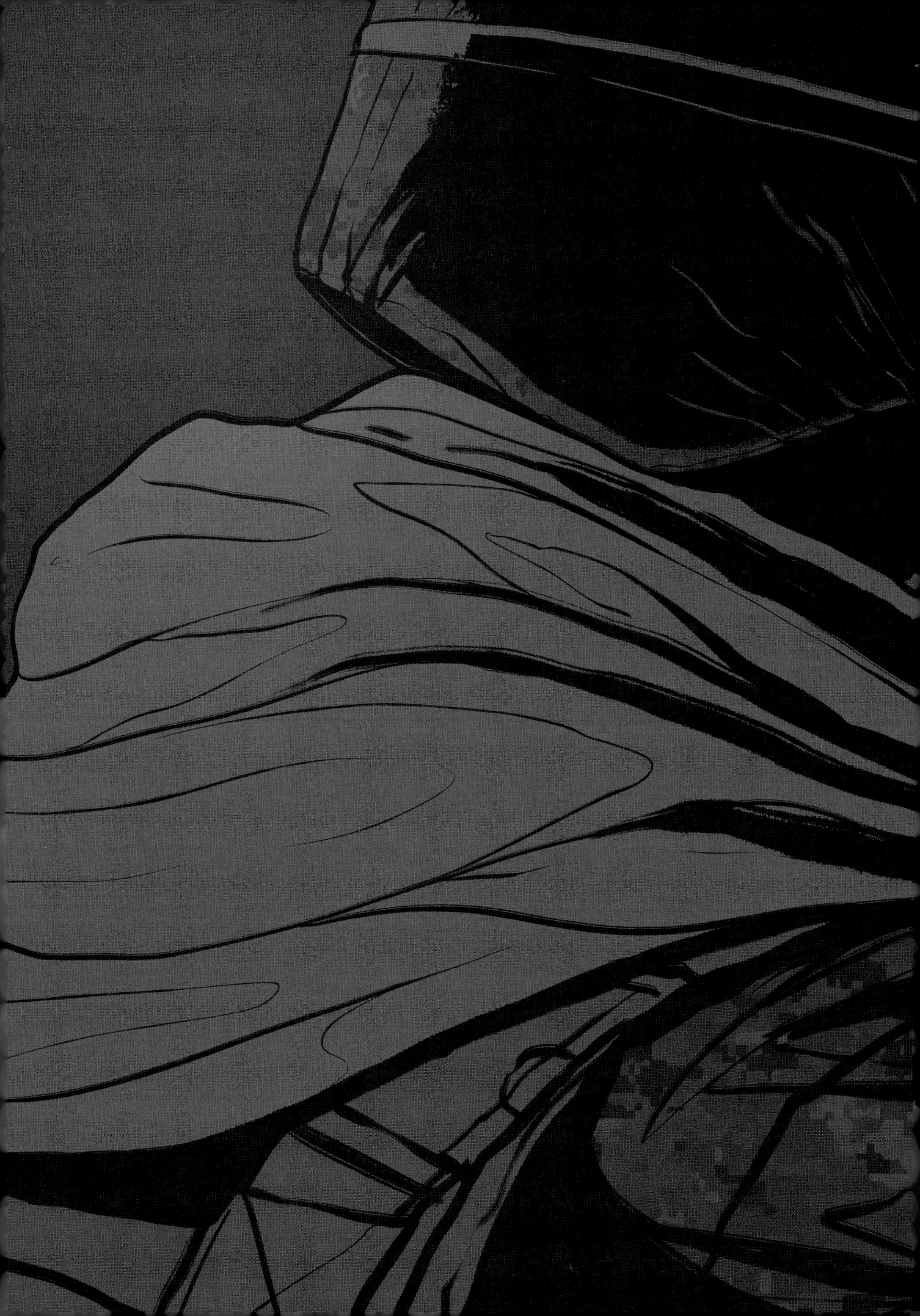

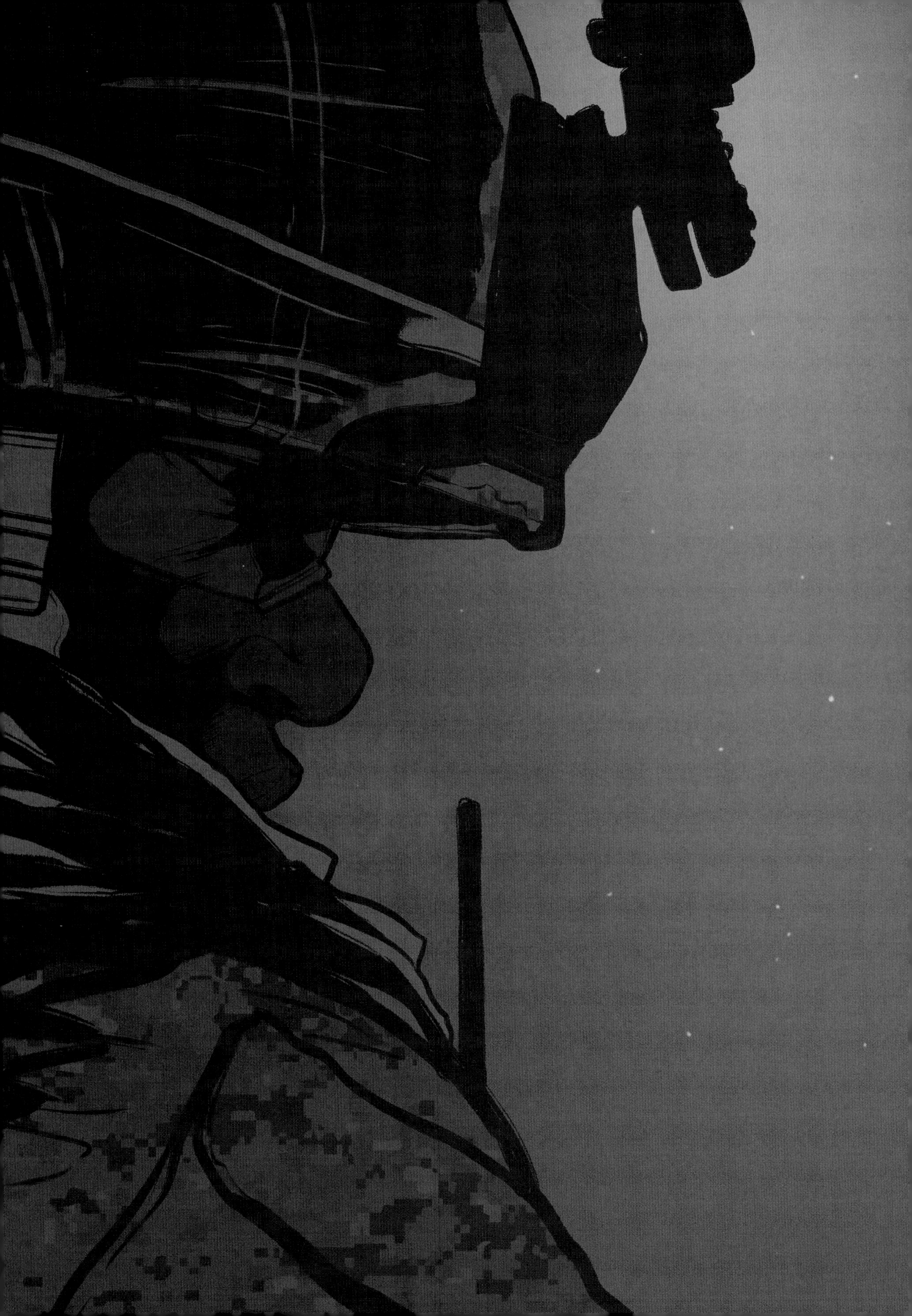

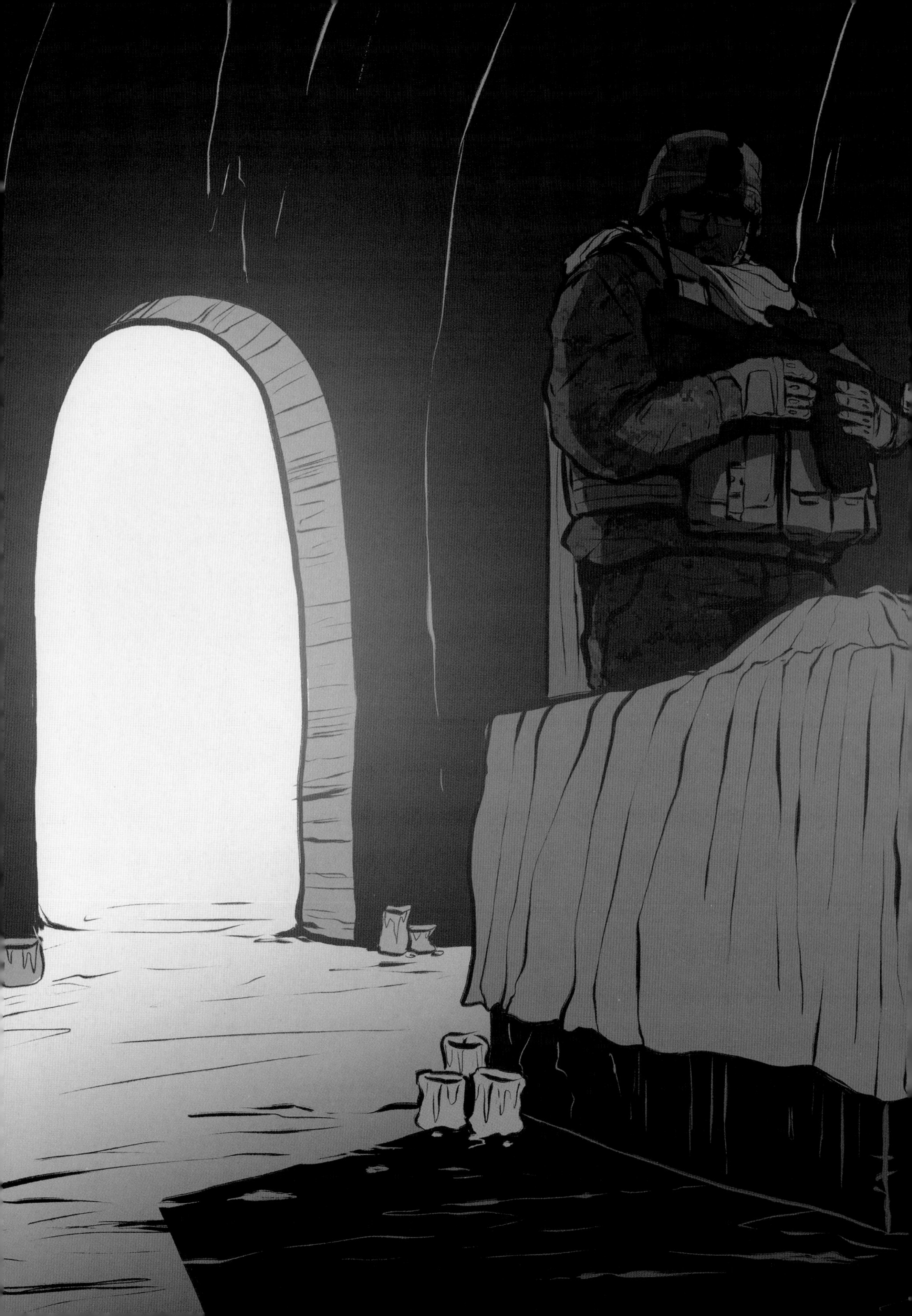

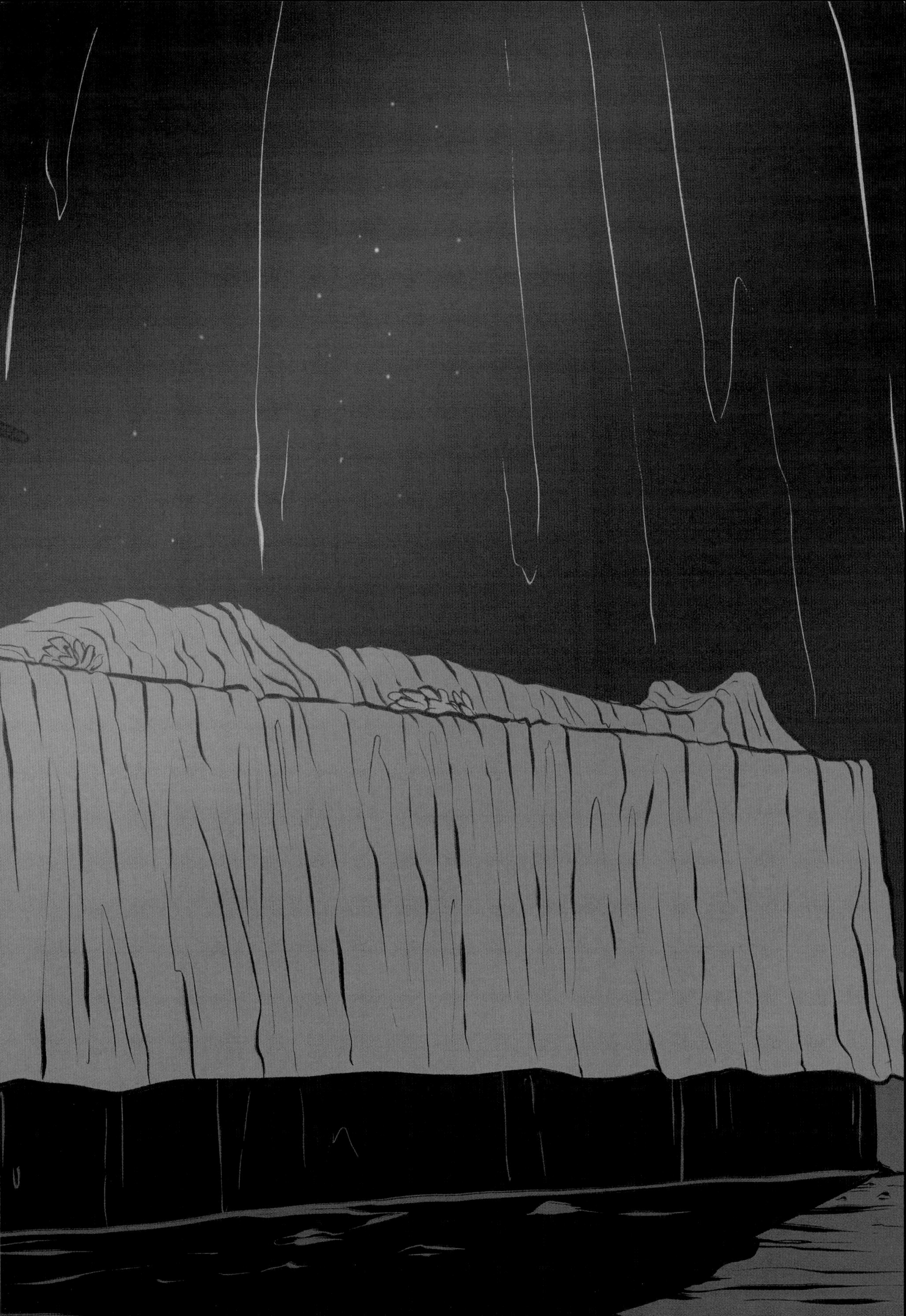

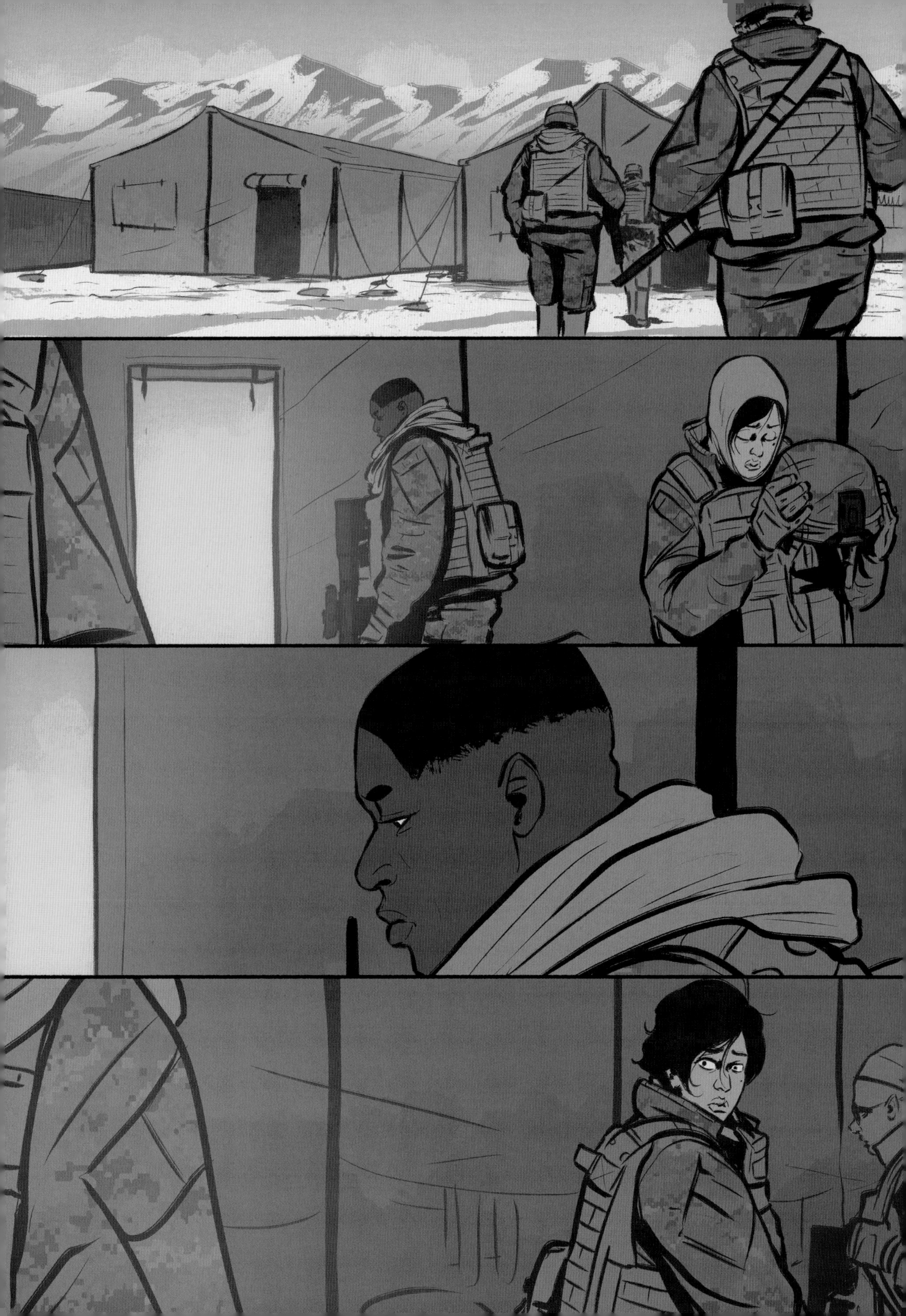

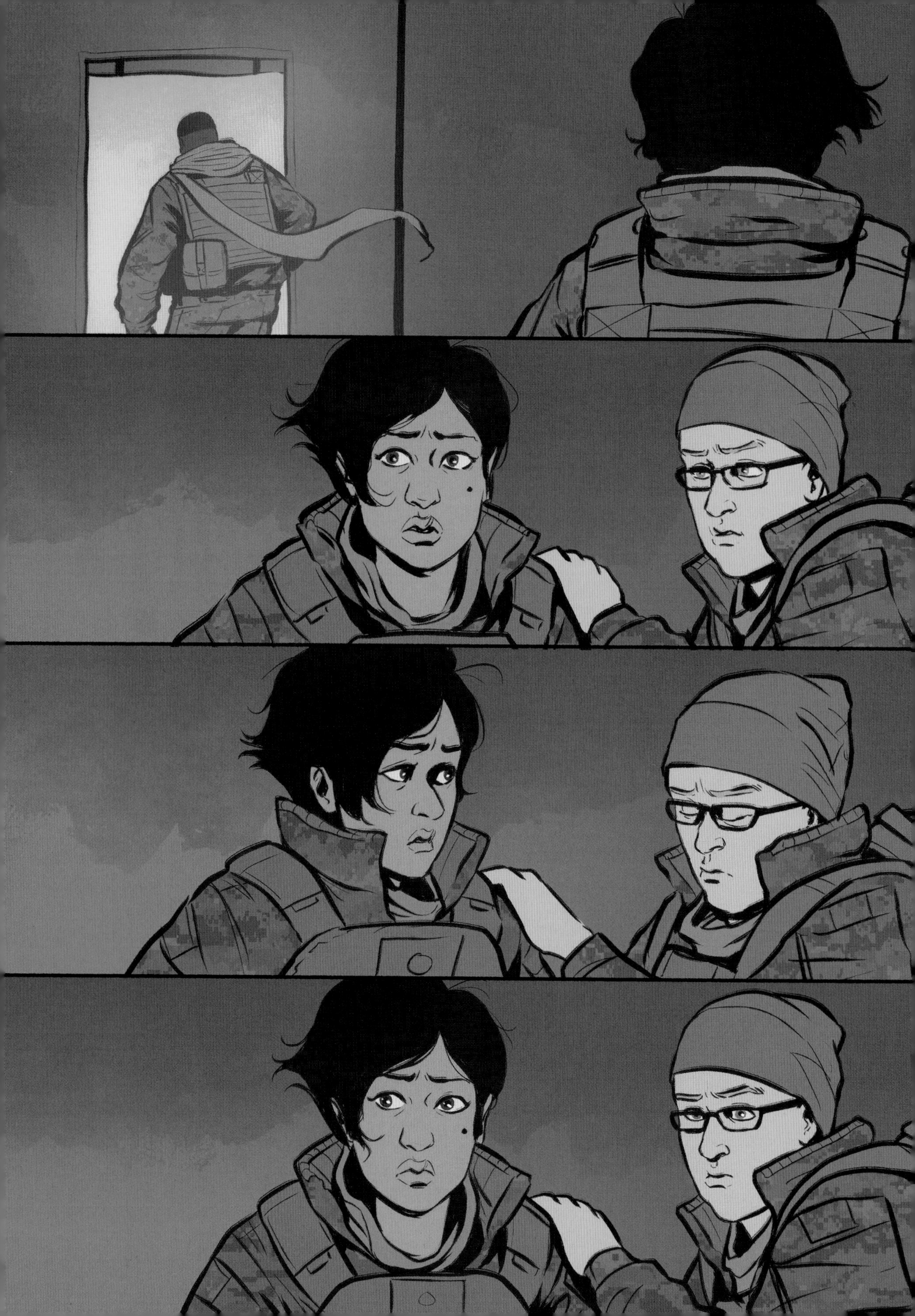

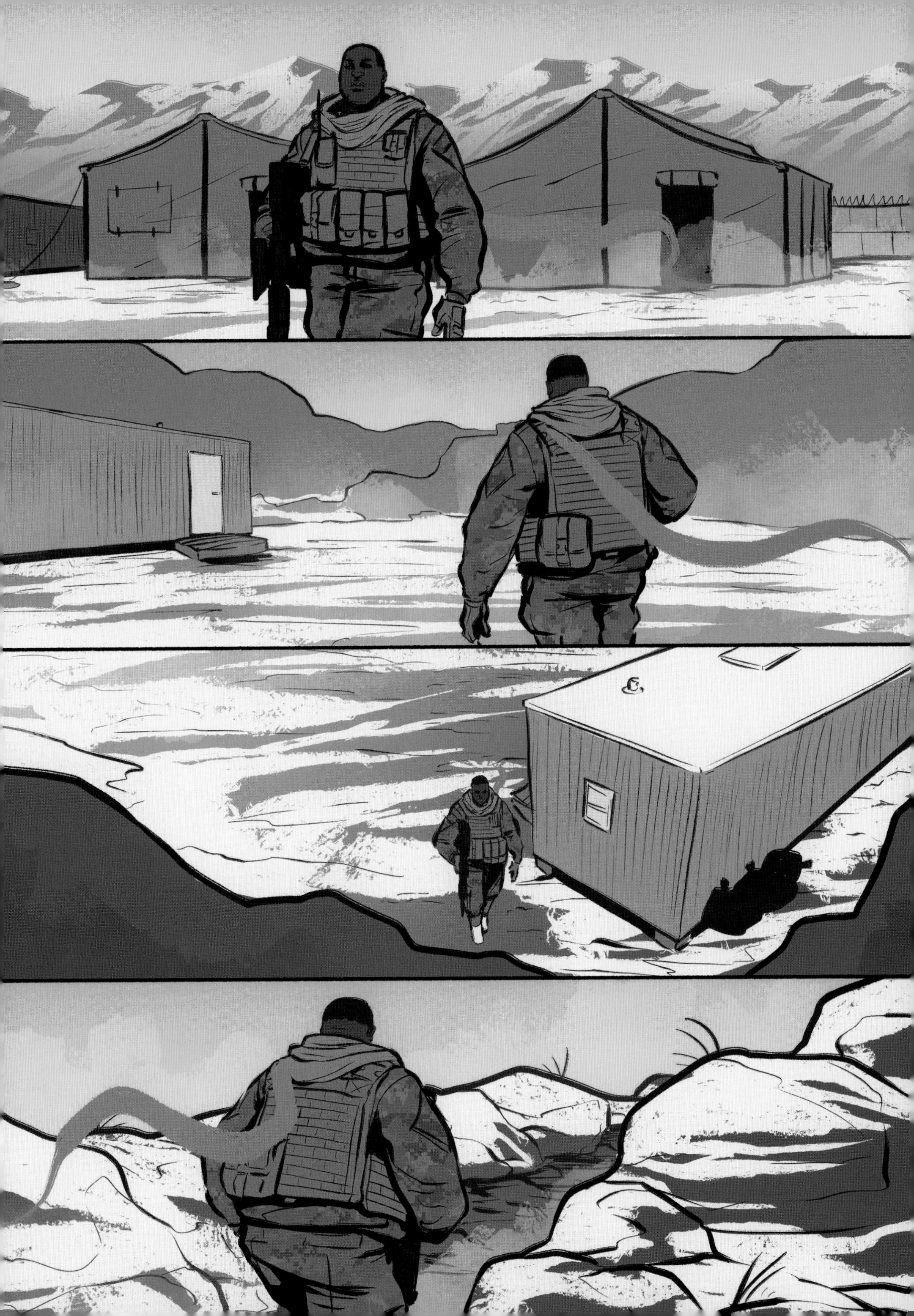

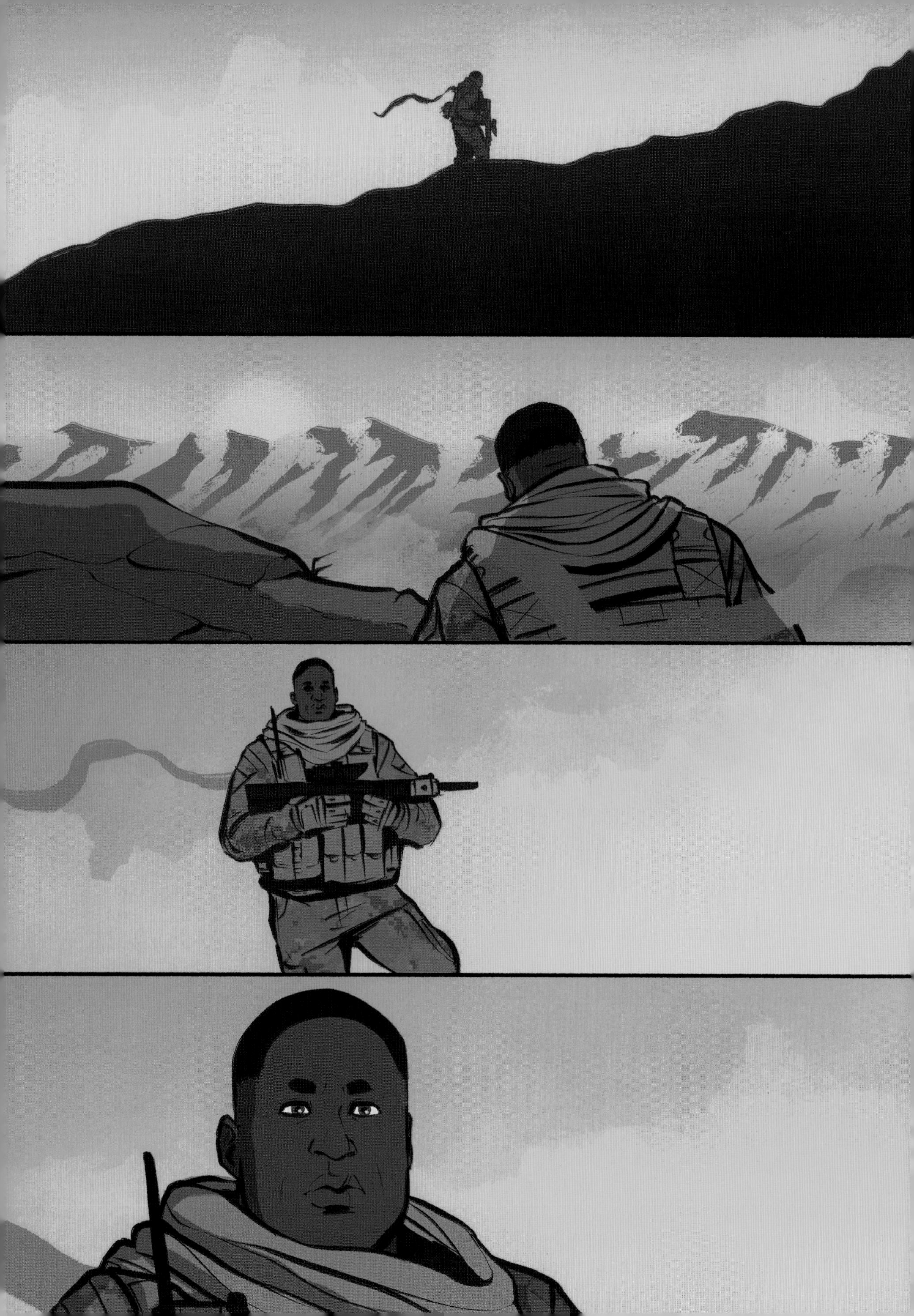

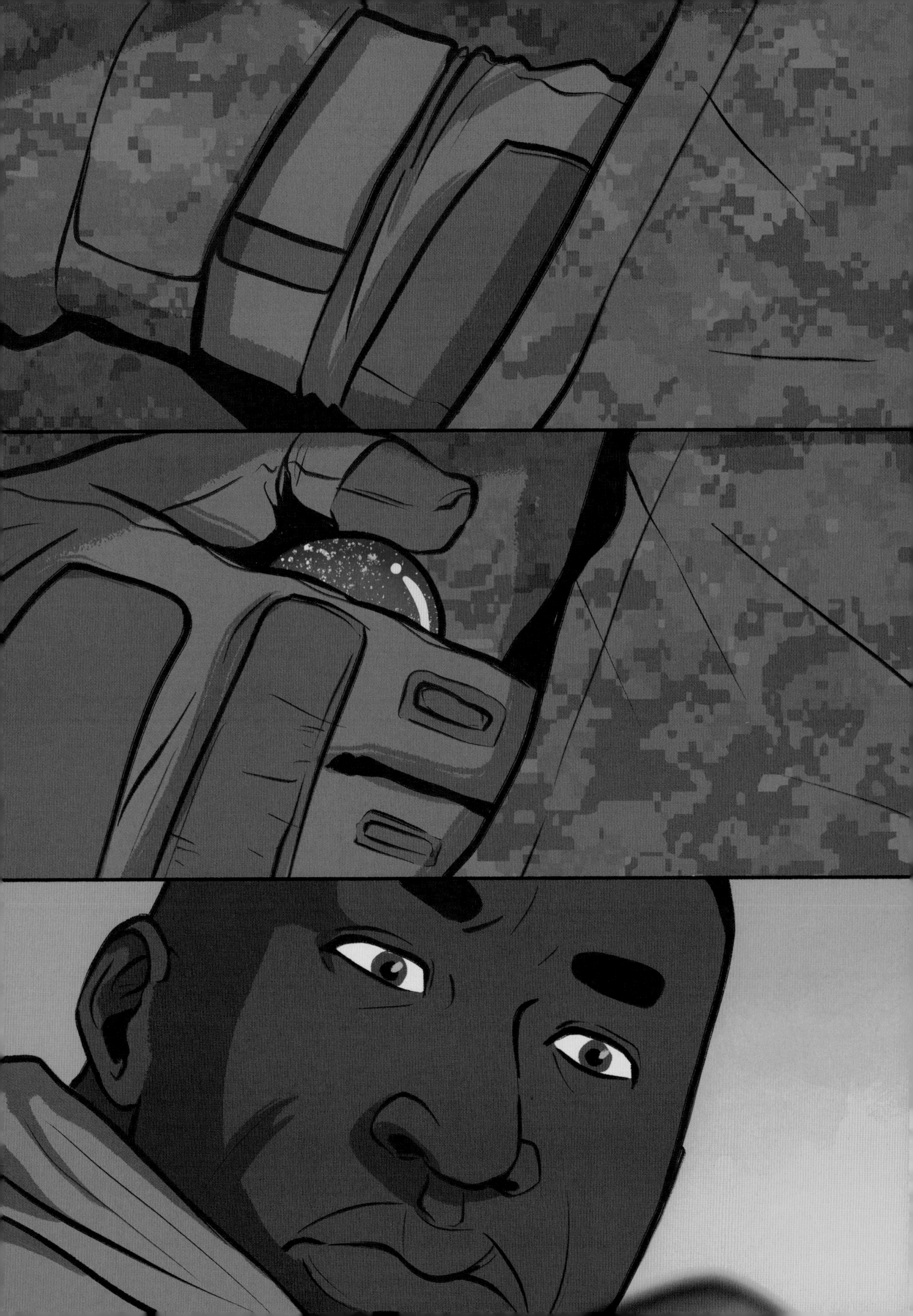

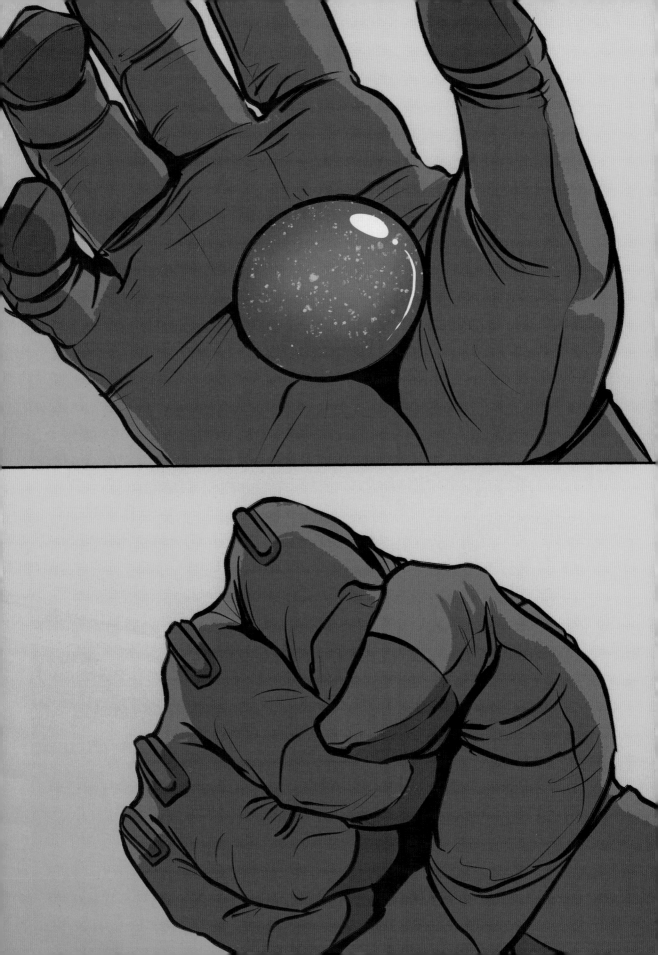

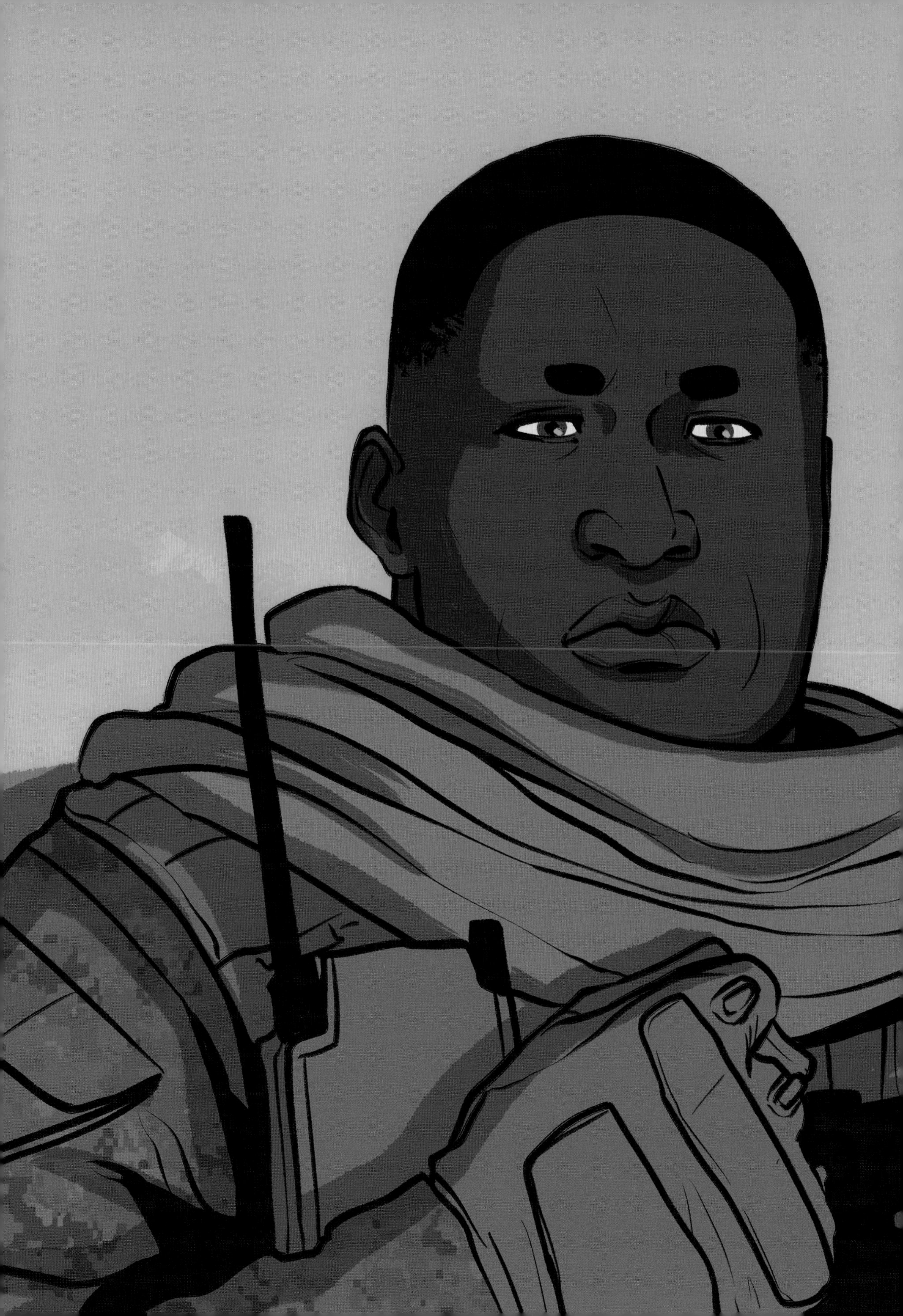

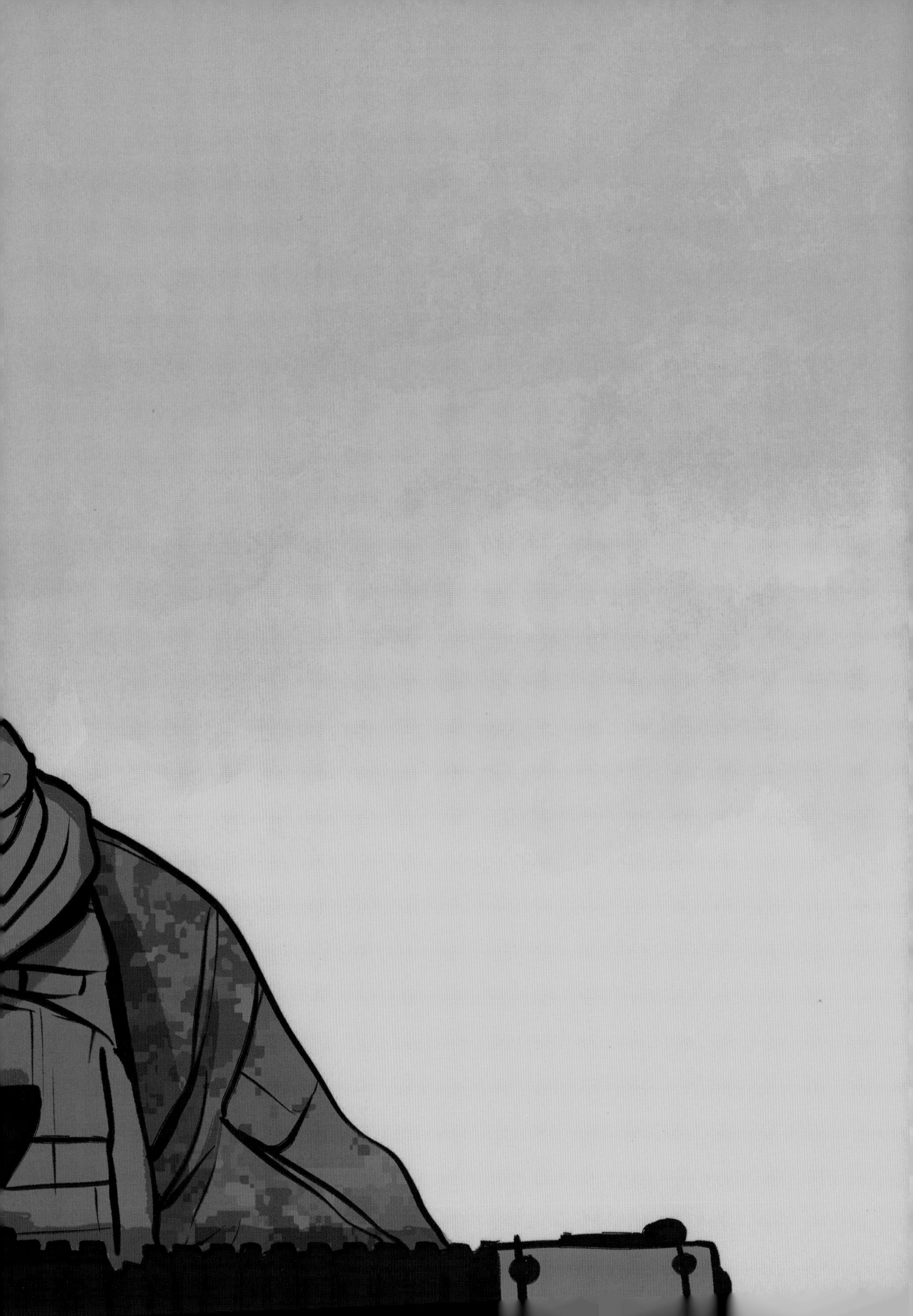

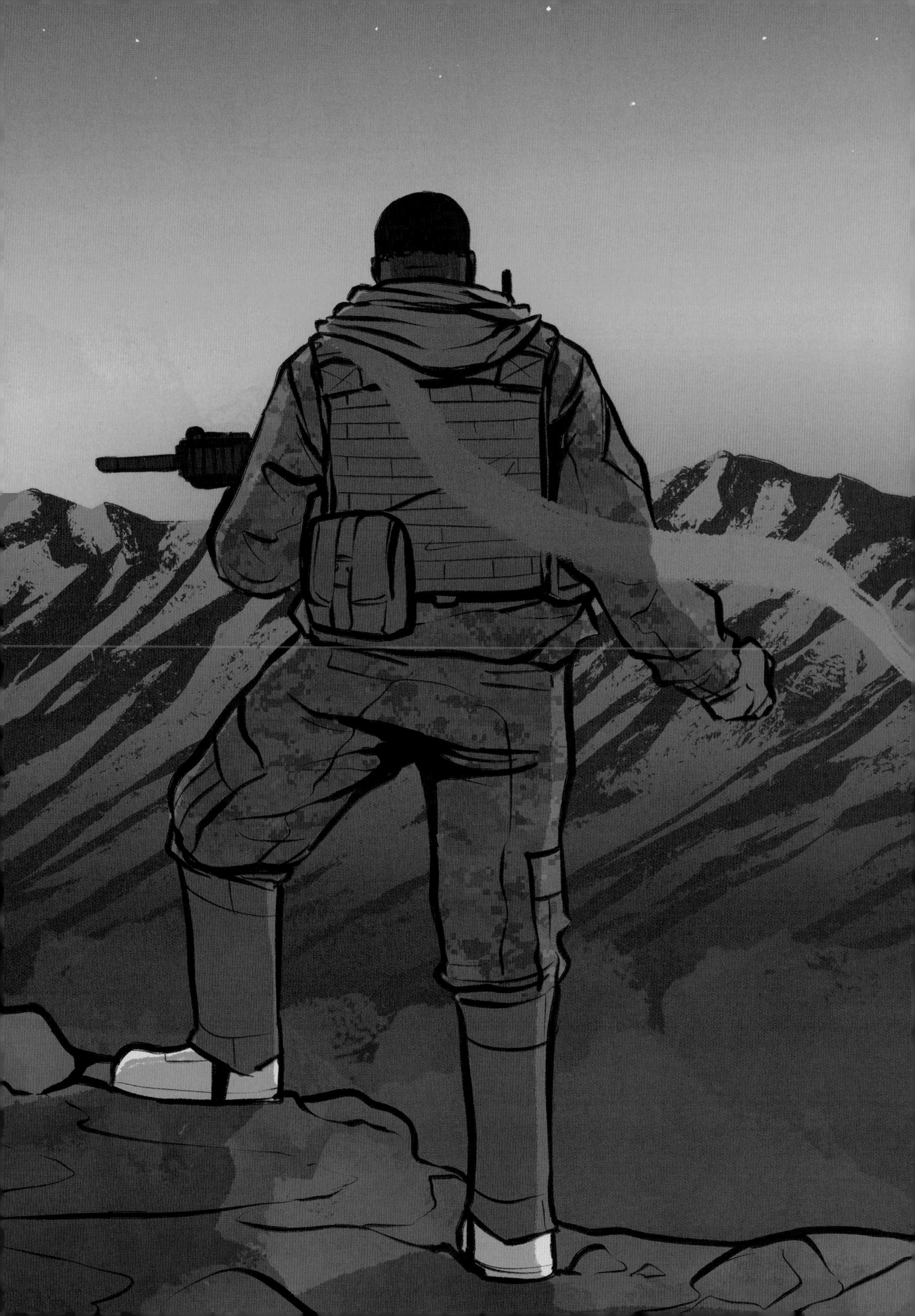

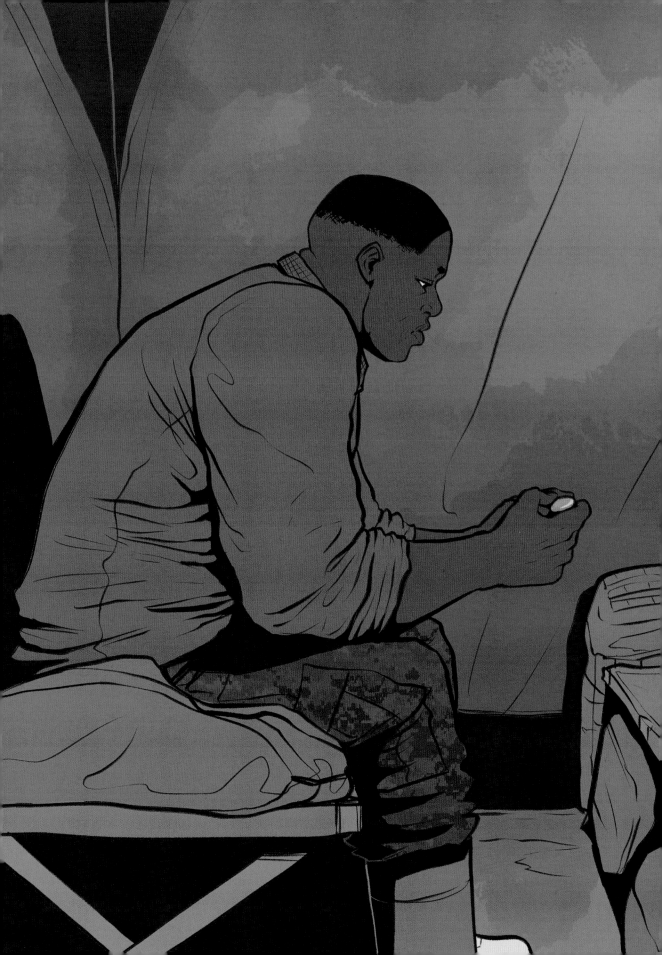

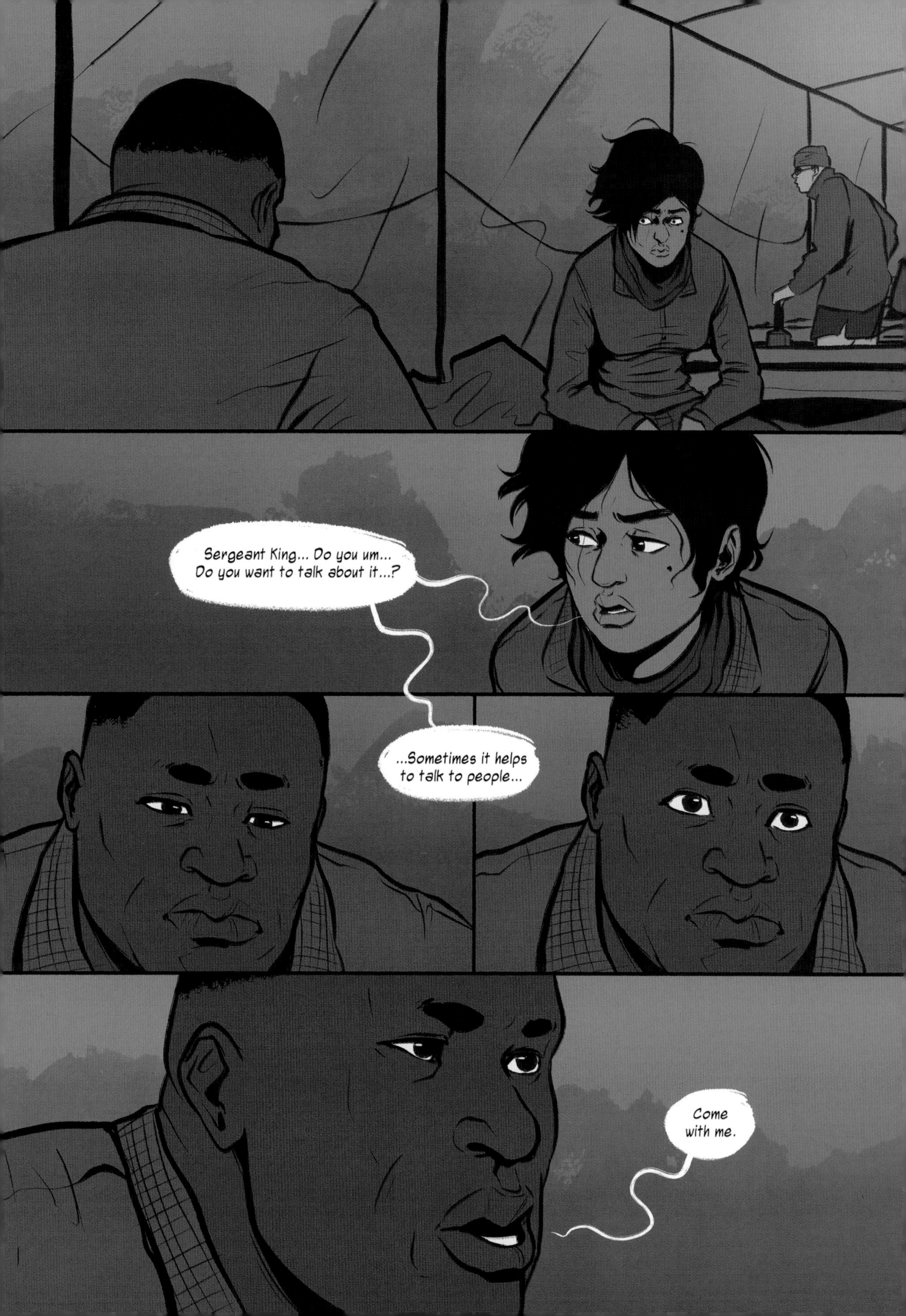
Sergeant King... Do you um... Do you want to talk about it...?
...Sometimes it helps to talk to people...
Come with me.

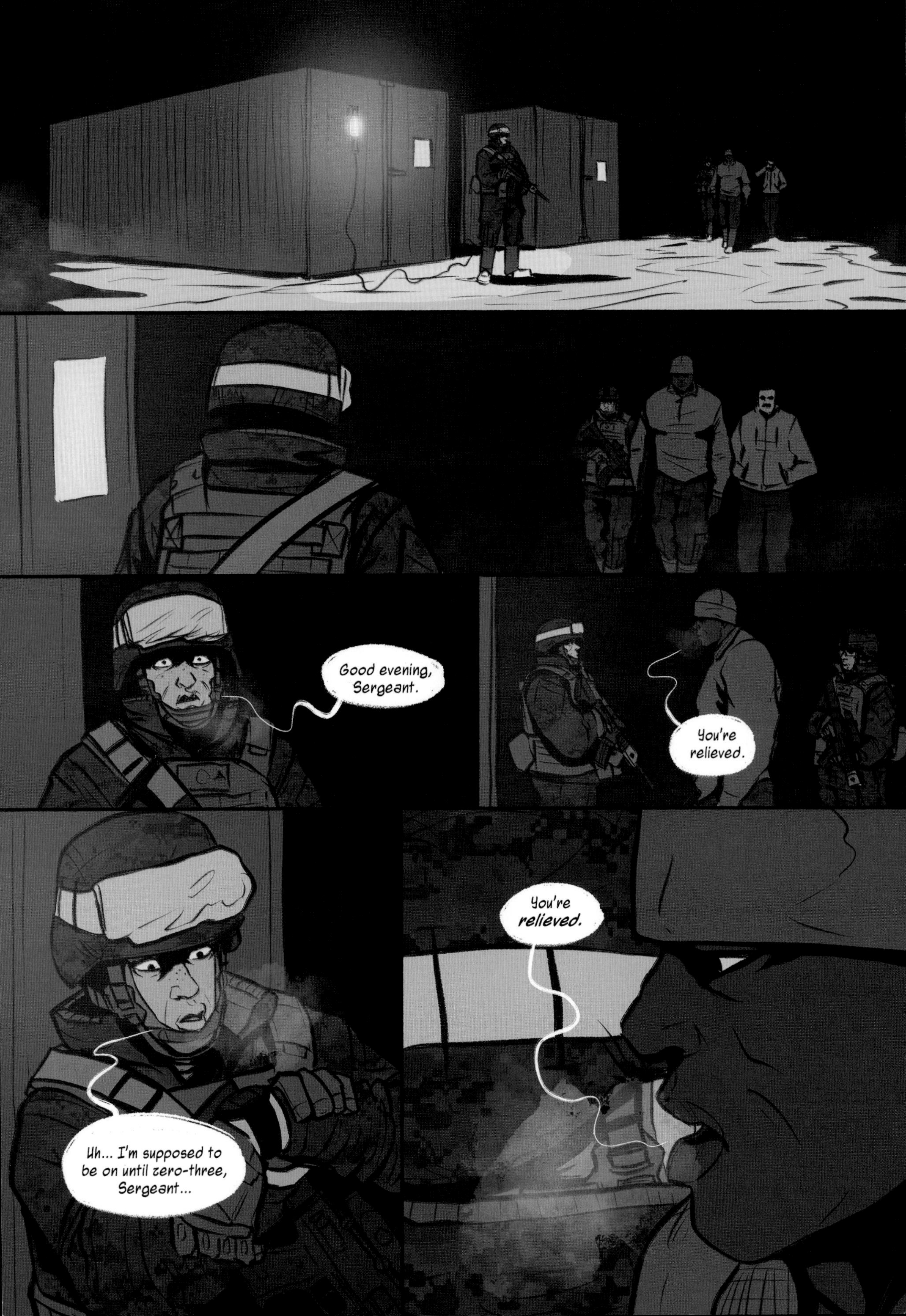
Good evening, Sergeant.
You're relieved.
Uh... I'm supposed to be on until zero-three, Sergeant...
You're *relieved.*

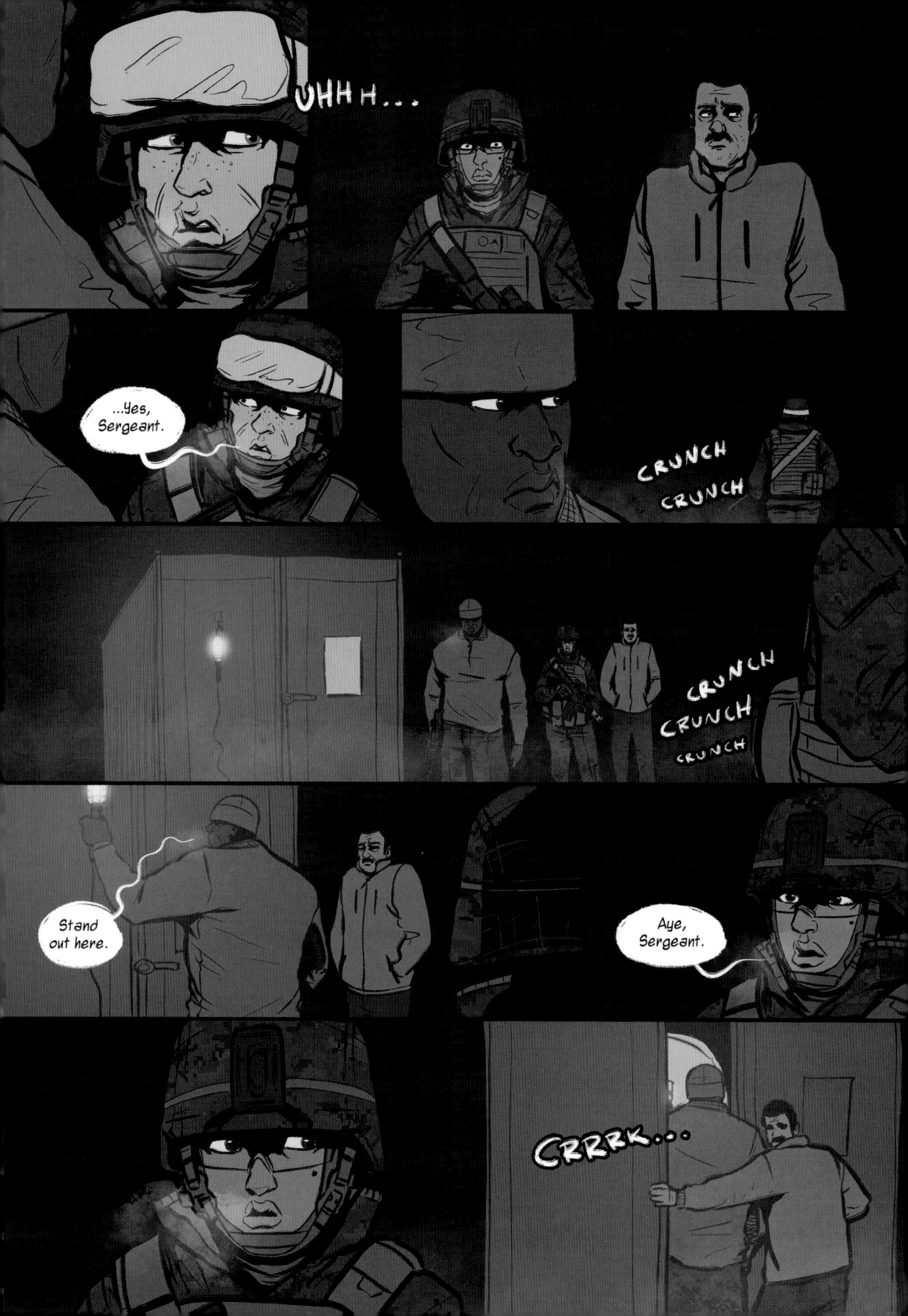
UHHH...
...Yes, Sergeant.
CRUNCH
CRUNCH
CRUNCH
CRUNCH
CRUNCH
Stand out here.
Aye, Sergeant.
CRRRK...

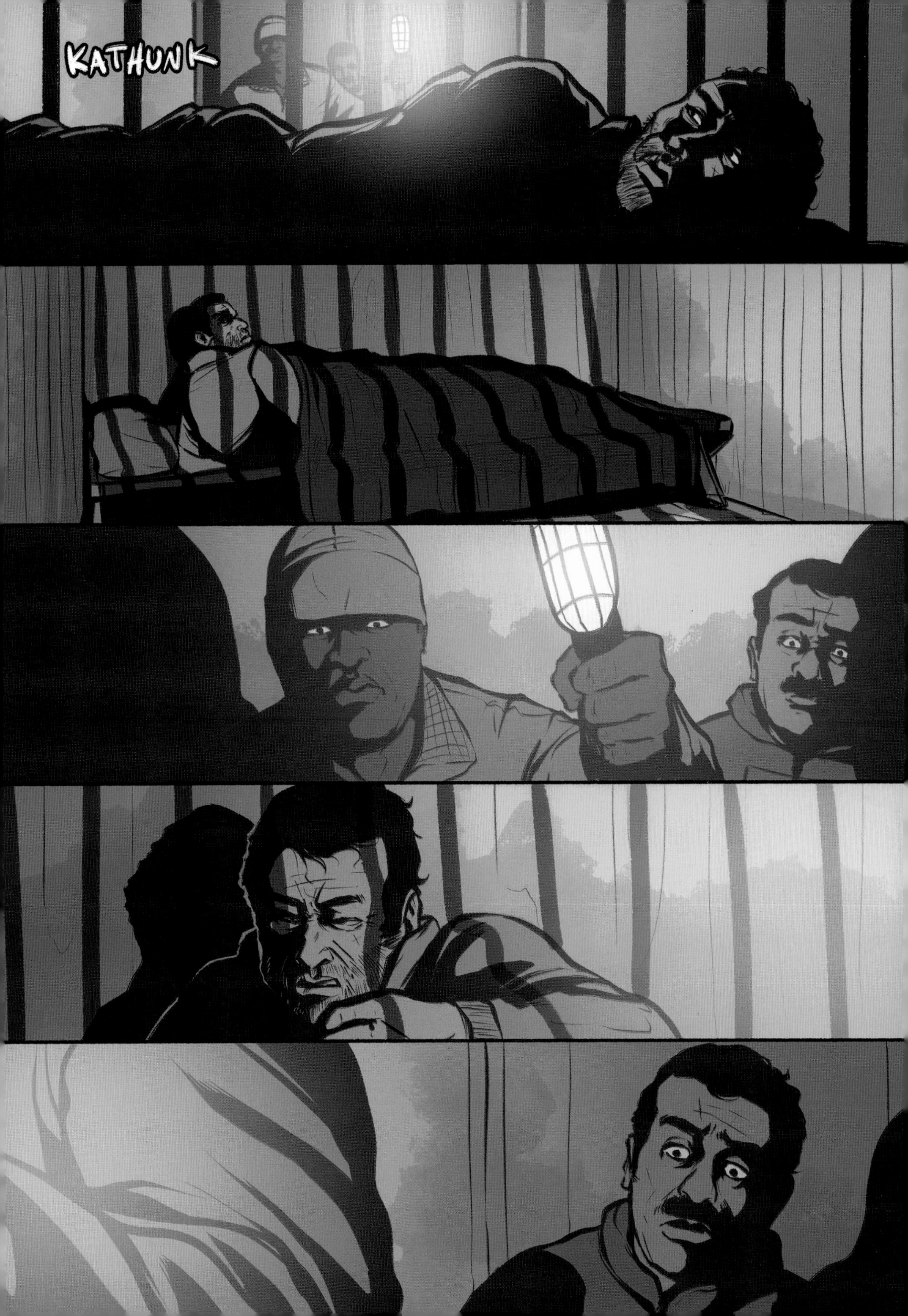
KATHUNK

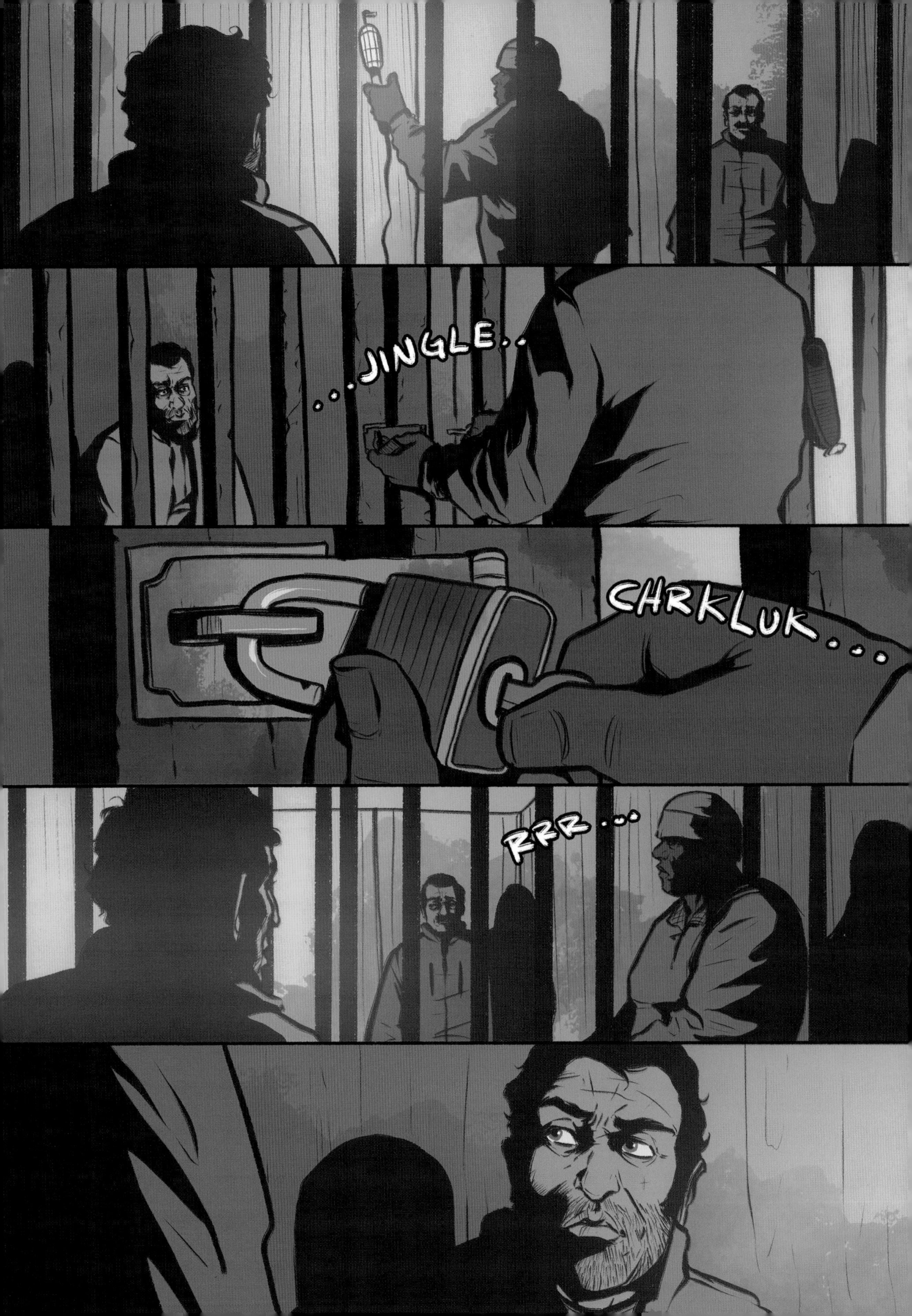
...JINGLE..
CHRKLUK...
RRR...

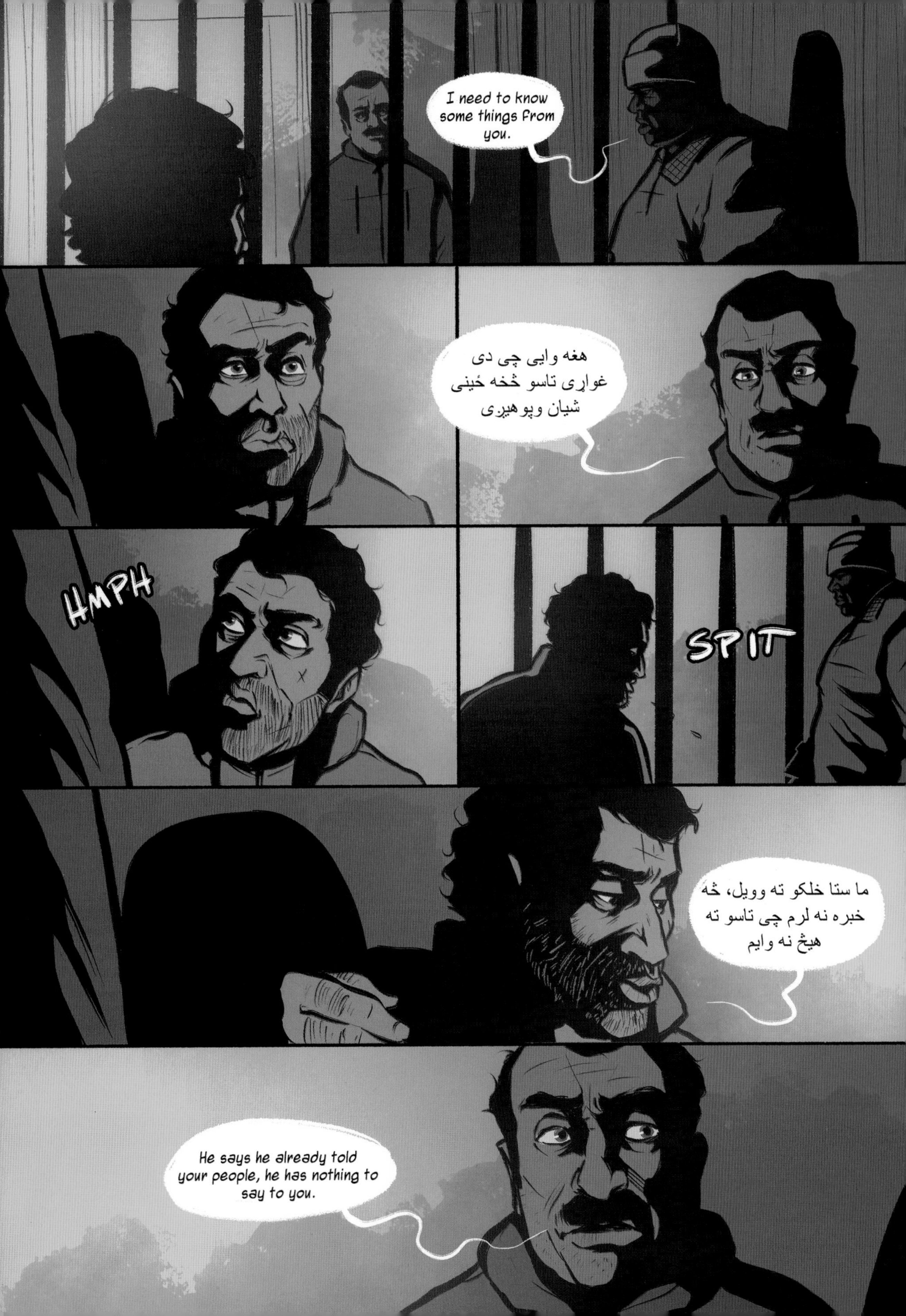
I need to know some things from you.
هغه وایی چی دی غواړی تاسو څخه ځینی شیان وپوهیږی
HMPH
SPIT
ما ستا خلکو ته وویل، څه خبره نه لرم چی تاسو ته هیڅ نه وایم
He says he already told your people, he has nothing to say to you.

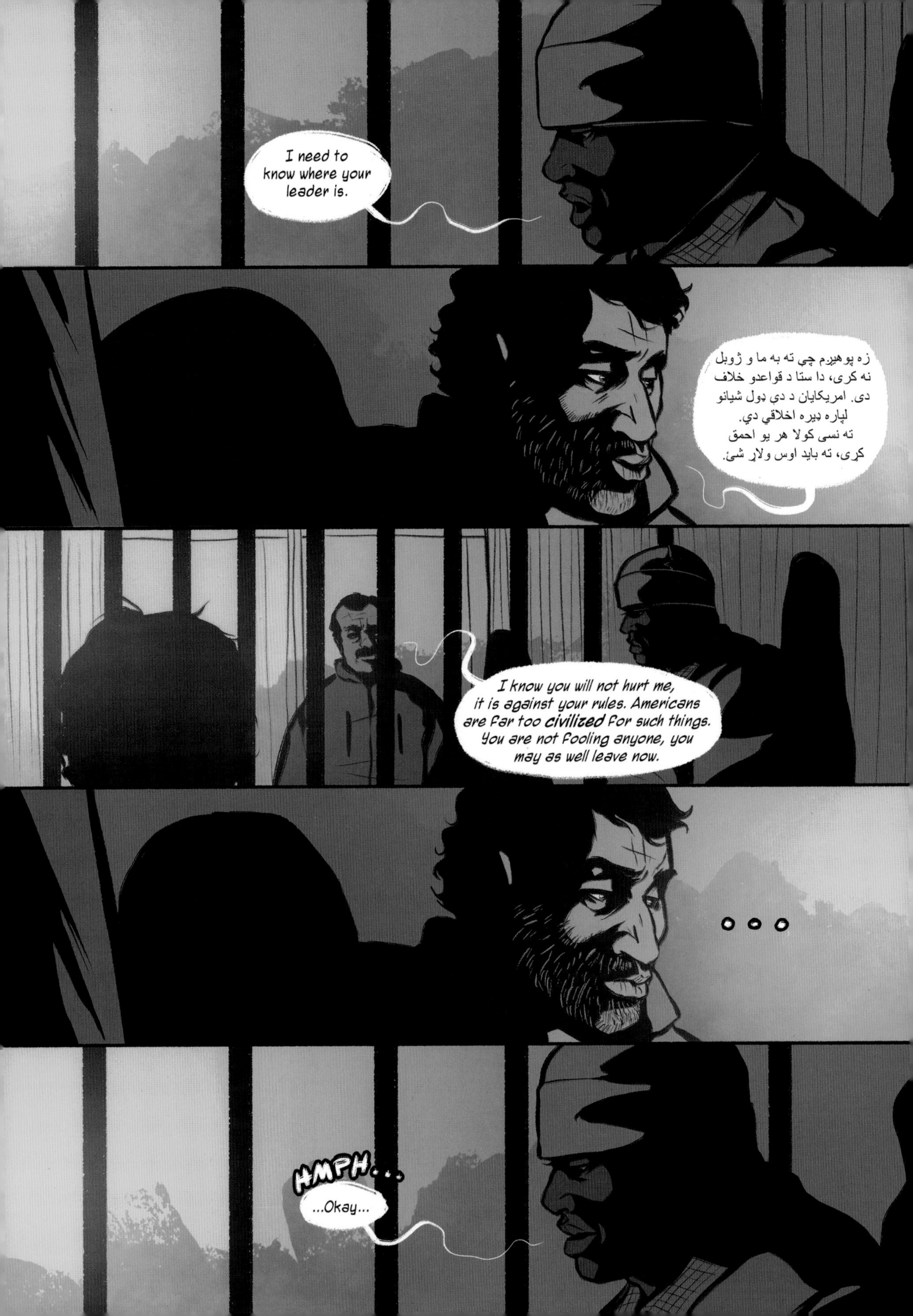
I need to know where your leader is.
زه پوهیږم چې ته به ما و ژوبل نه کړې، دا ستا د قواعدو خلاف دی. امریکایان د دې ډول شیانو لپاره ډېره اخلاقي دي. ته نسی کولا هر یو احمق کړی، ته باید اوس ولاړ شئ.
I know you will not hurt me, it is against your rules. Americans are far too ***civilized*** for such things. You are not fooling anyone, you may as well leave now.
...
HMPH...
...Okay...

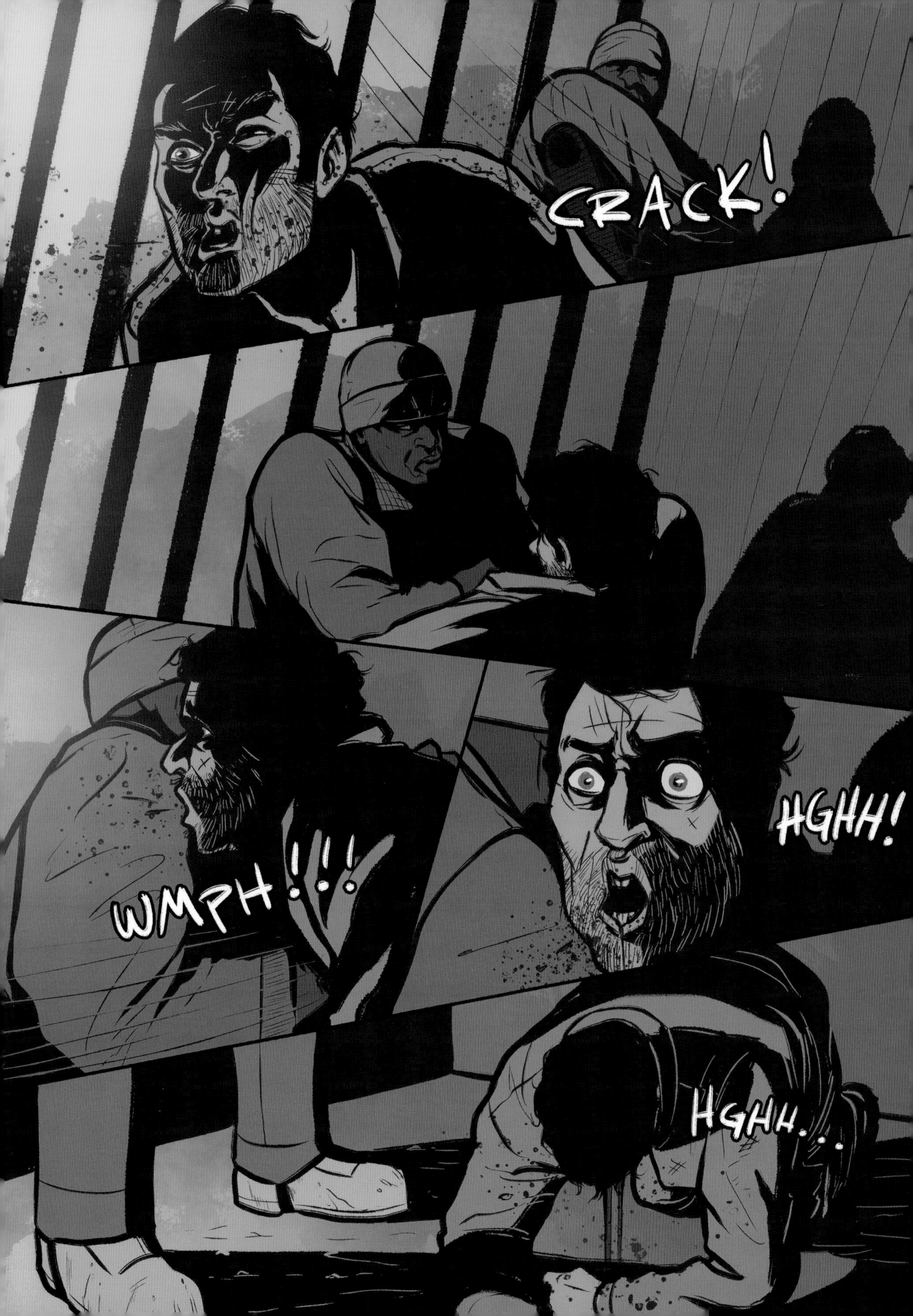
CRACK!
WMPH!!!!
HGHH!
HGHH...

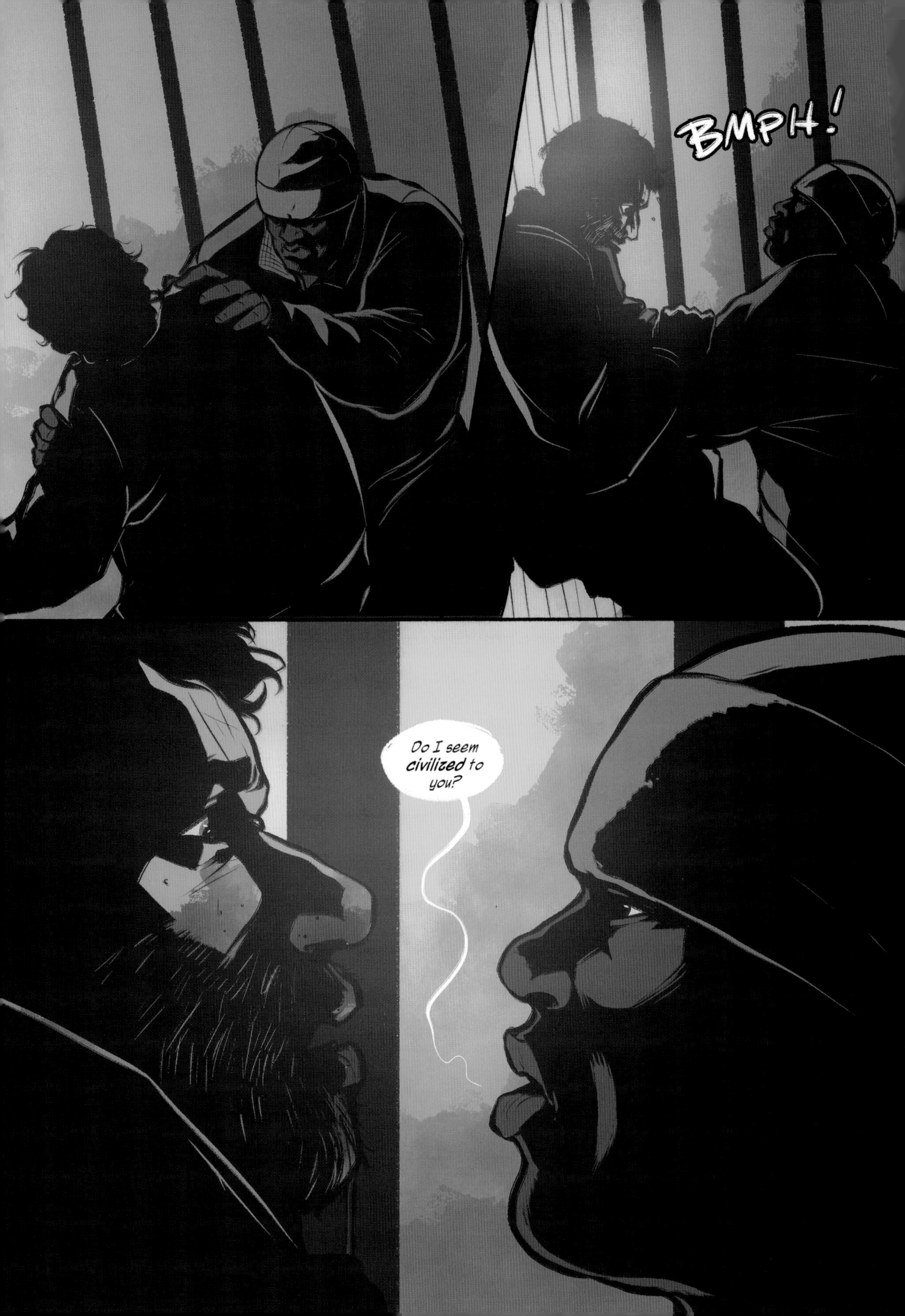
BMPH!
Do I seem civilized to you?

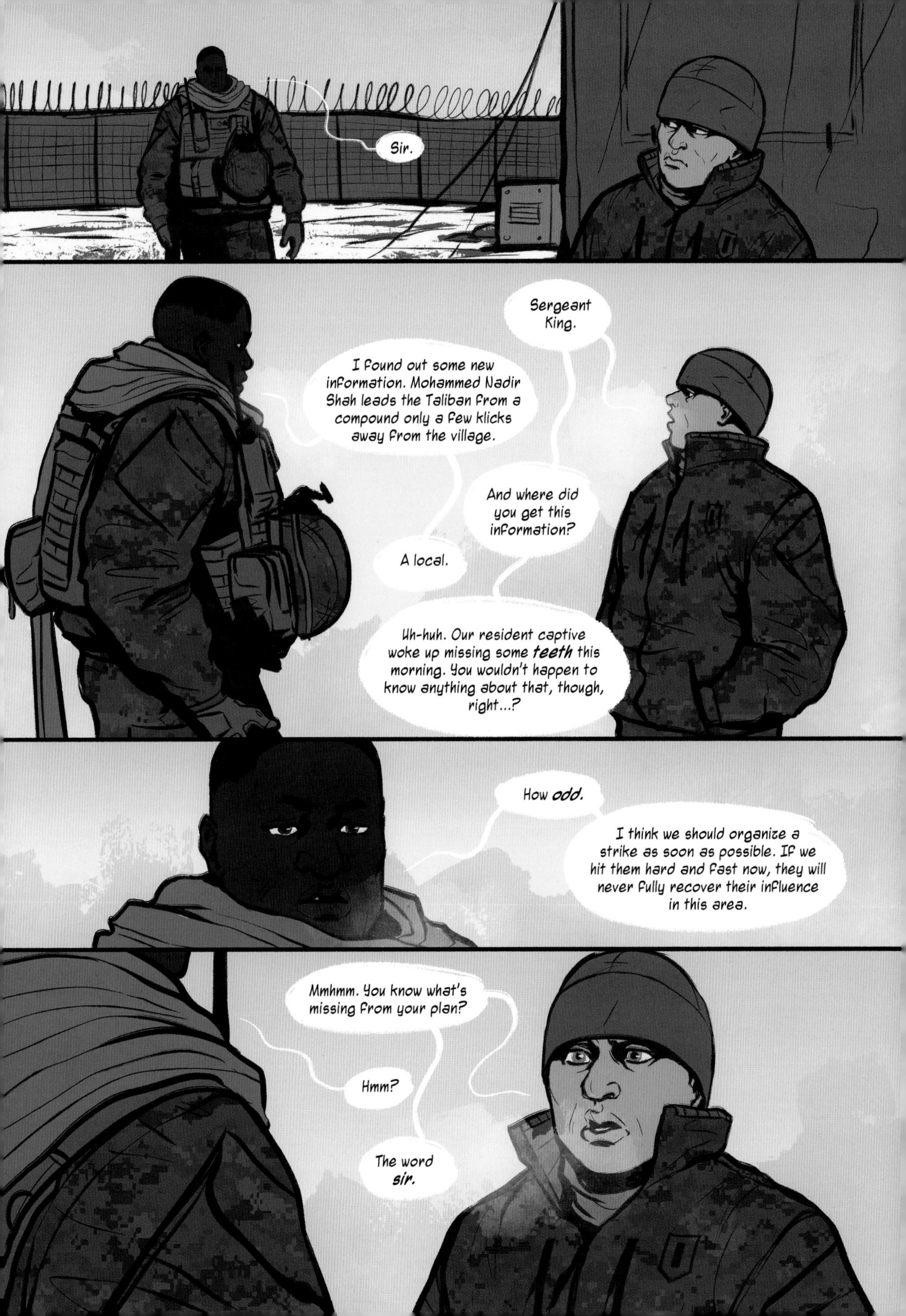
Sir.
Sergeant King.
I found out some new information. Mohammed Nadir Shah leads the Taliban from a compound only a few klicks away from the village.
And where did you get this information?
A local.
Uh-huh. Our resident captive woke up missing some *teeth* this morning. You wouldn't happen to know anything about that, though, right...?
How *odd.*
I think we should organize a strike as soon as possible. If we hit them hard and fast now, they will never fully recover their influence in this area.
Mmhmm. You know what's missing from your plan?
Hmm?
The word *sir.*

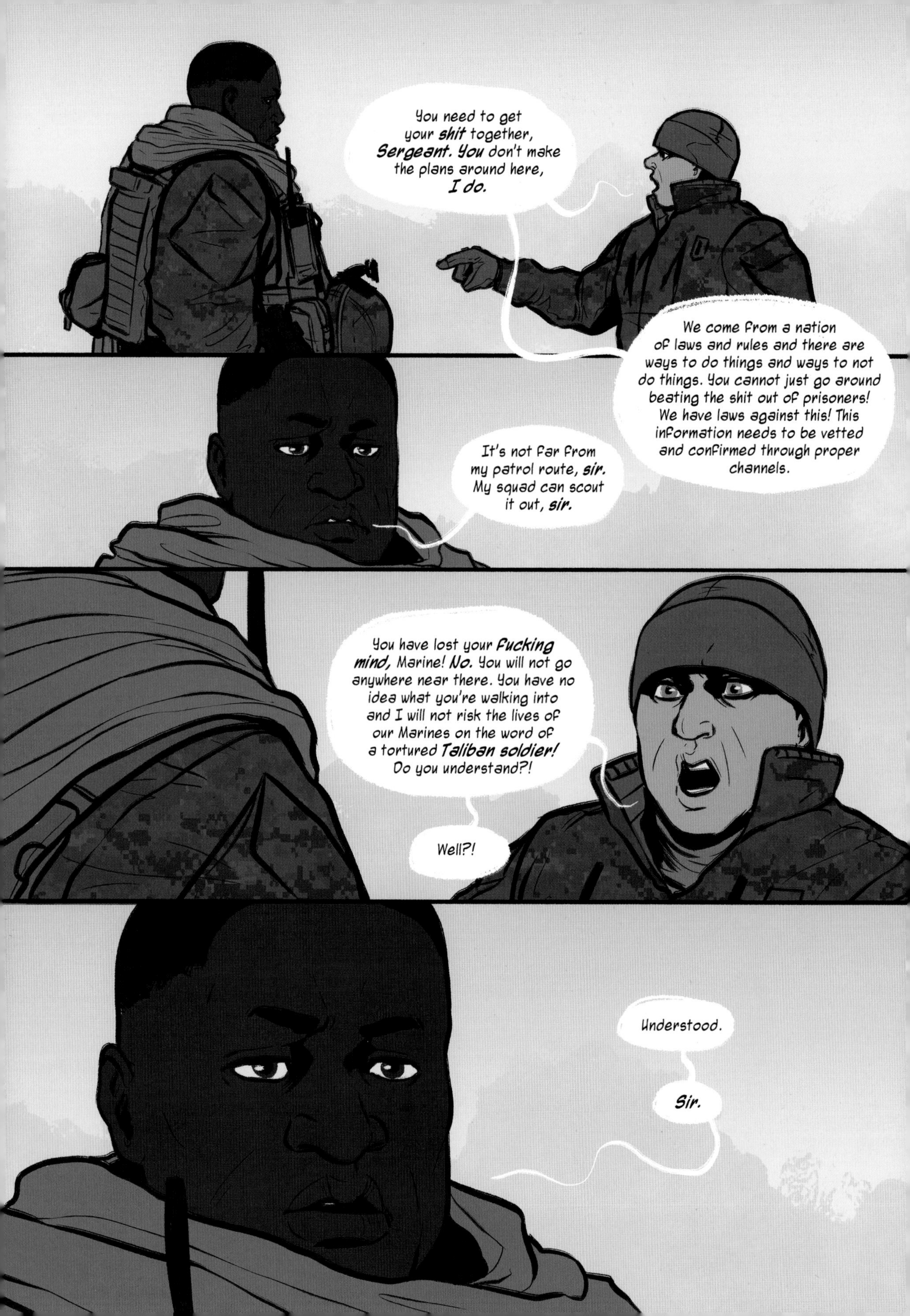
You need to get your ***shit*** together, ***Sergeant. You*** don't make the plans around here, ***I do.***
We come from a nation of laws and rules and there are ways to do things and ways to not do things. You cannot just go around beating the shit out of prisoners! We have laws against this! This information needs to be vetted and confirmed through proper channels.
It's not far from my patrol route, ***sir.*** My squad can scout it out, ***sir.***
You have lost your ***fucking mind,*** Marine! ***No.*** You will not go anywhere near there. You have no idea what you're walking into and I will not risk the lives of our Marines on the word of a tortured ***Taliban soldier!*** Do you understand?!
Well?!
Understood.
Sir.

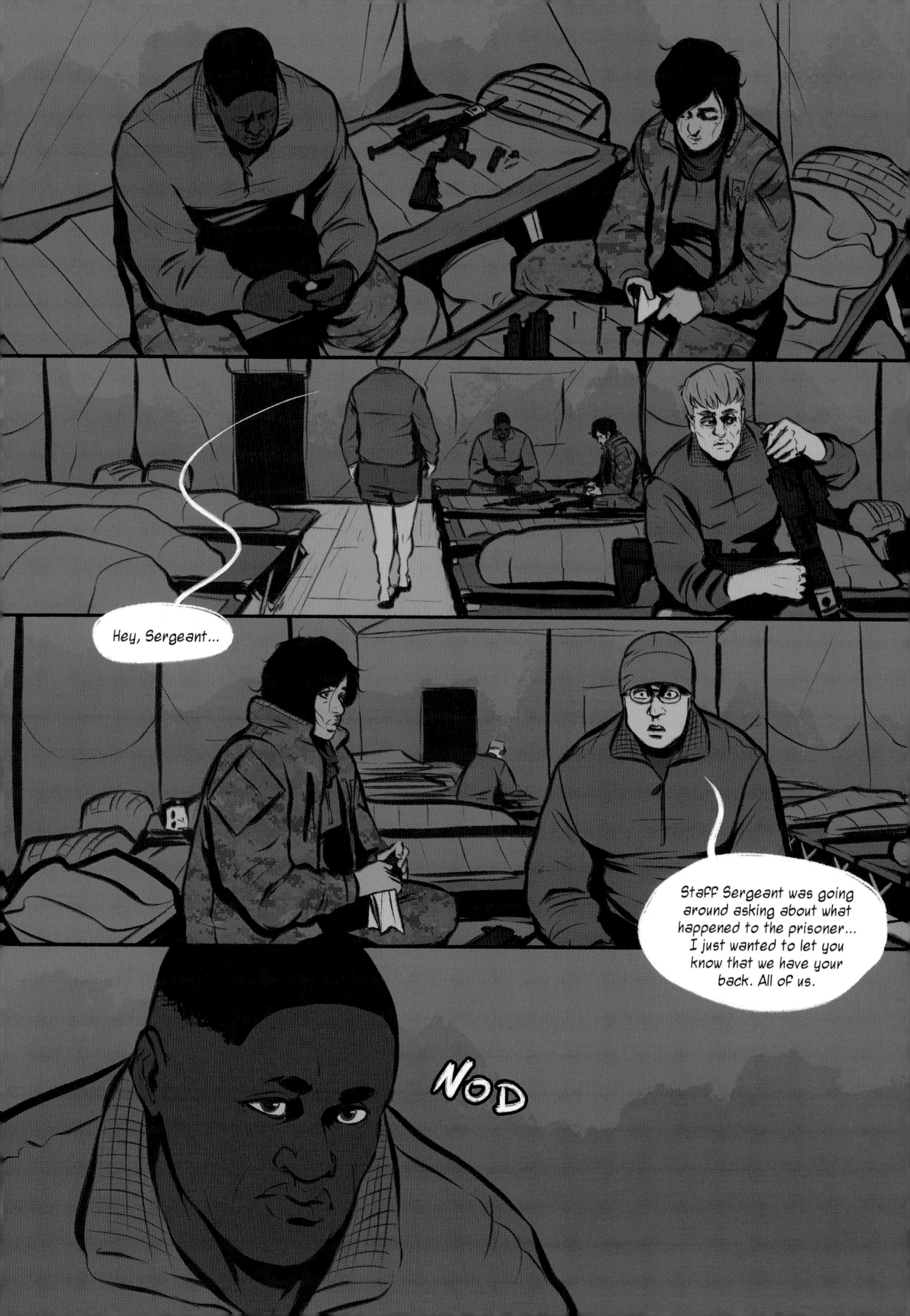
Hey, Sergeant...
Staff Sergeant was going around asking about what happened to the prisoner... I just wanted to let you know that we have your back. All of us.
NOD

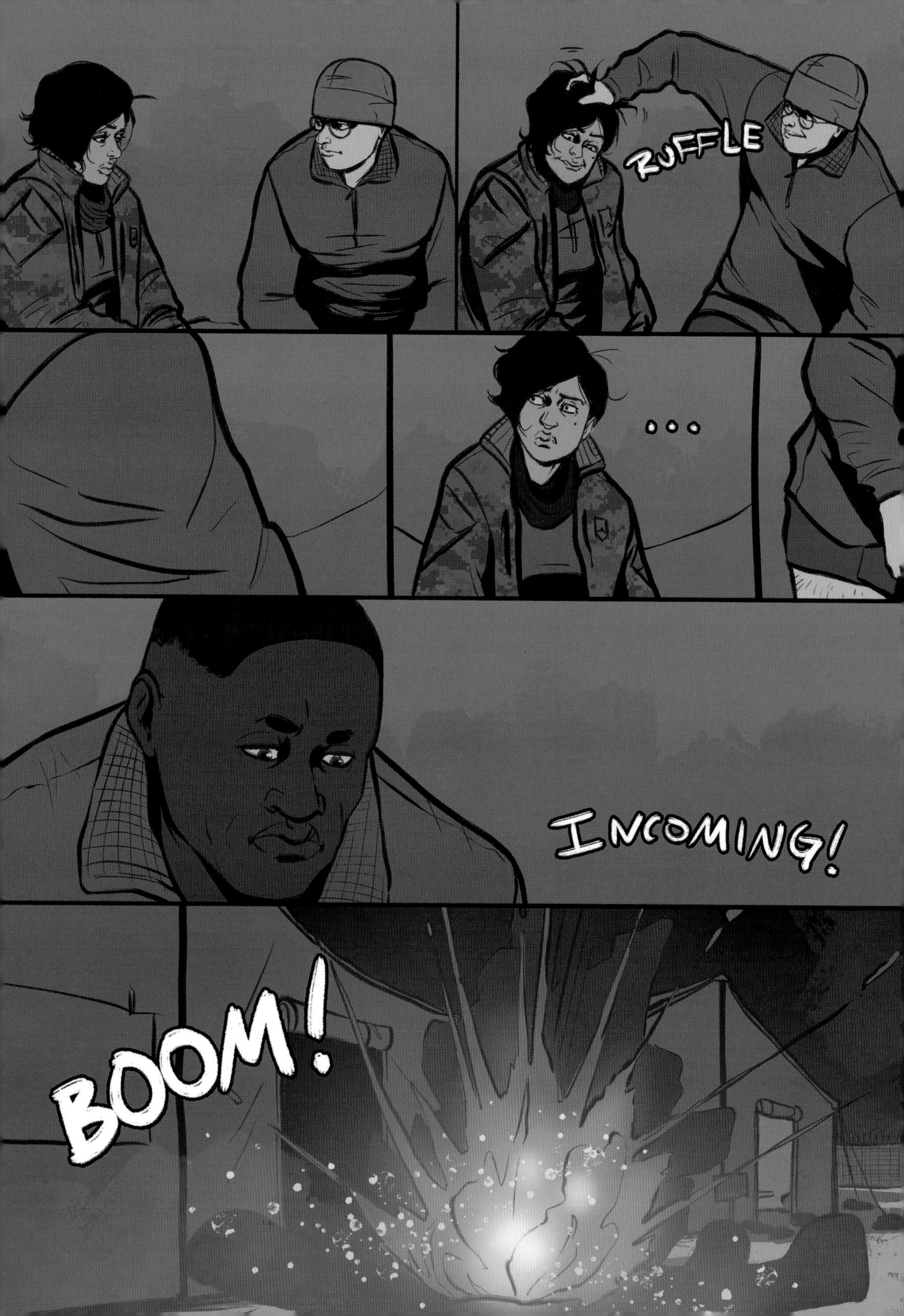
RUFFLE
...
INCOMING!
BOOM!

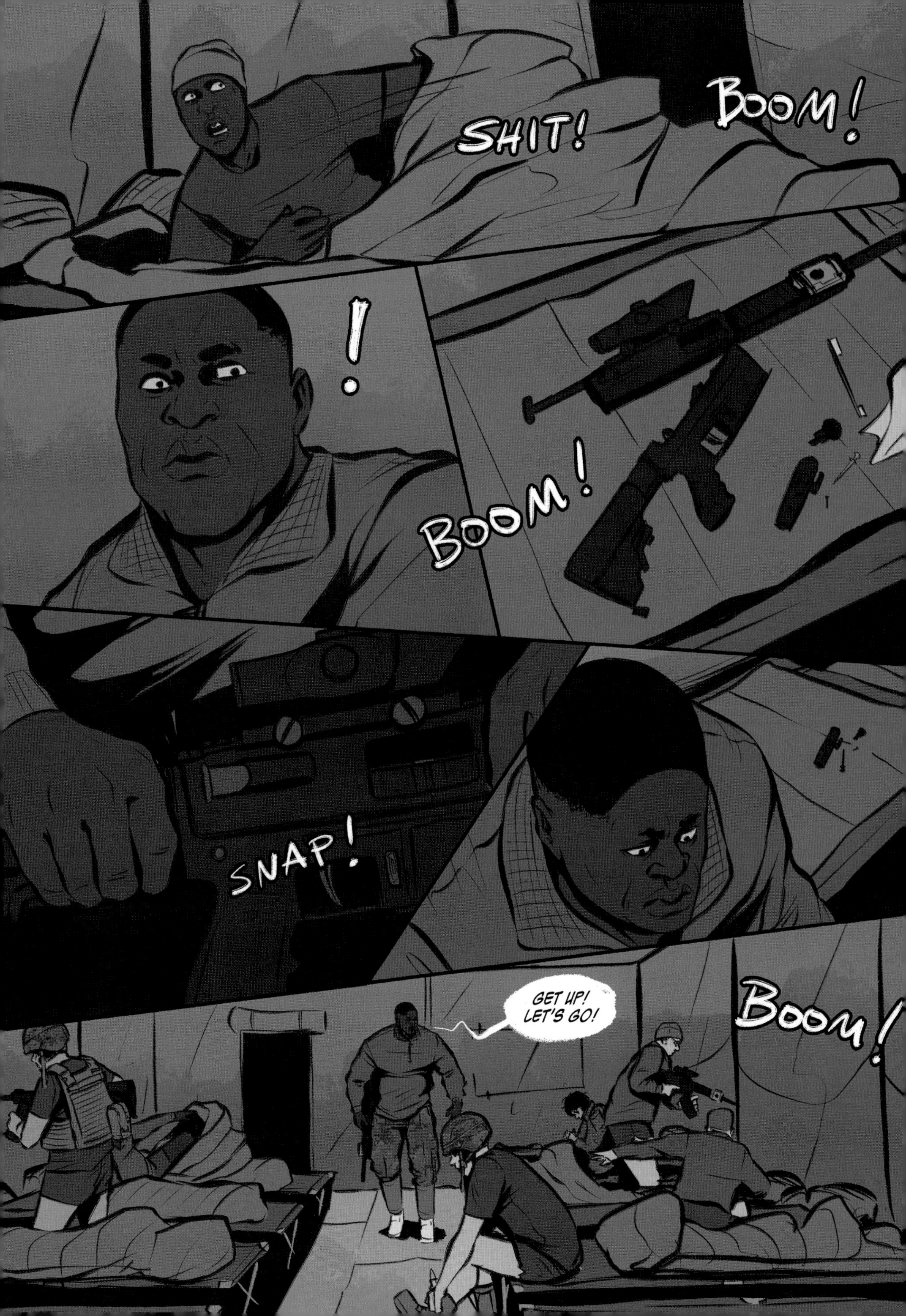
SHIT!
BOOM!
!
BOOM!
SNAP!
GET UP! LET'S GO!
BOOM!

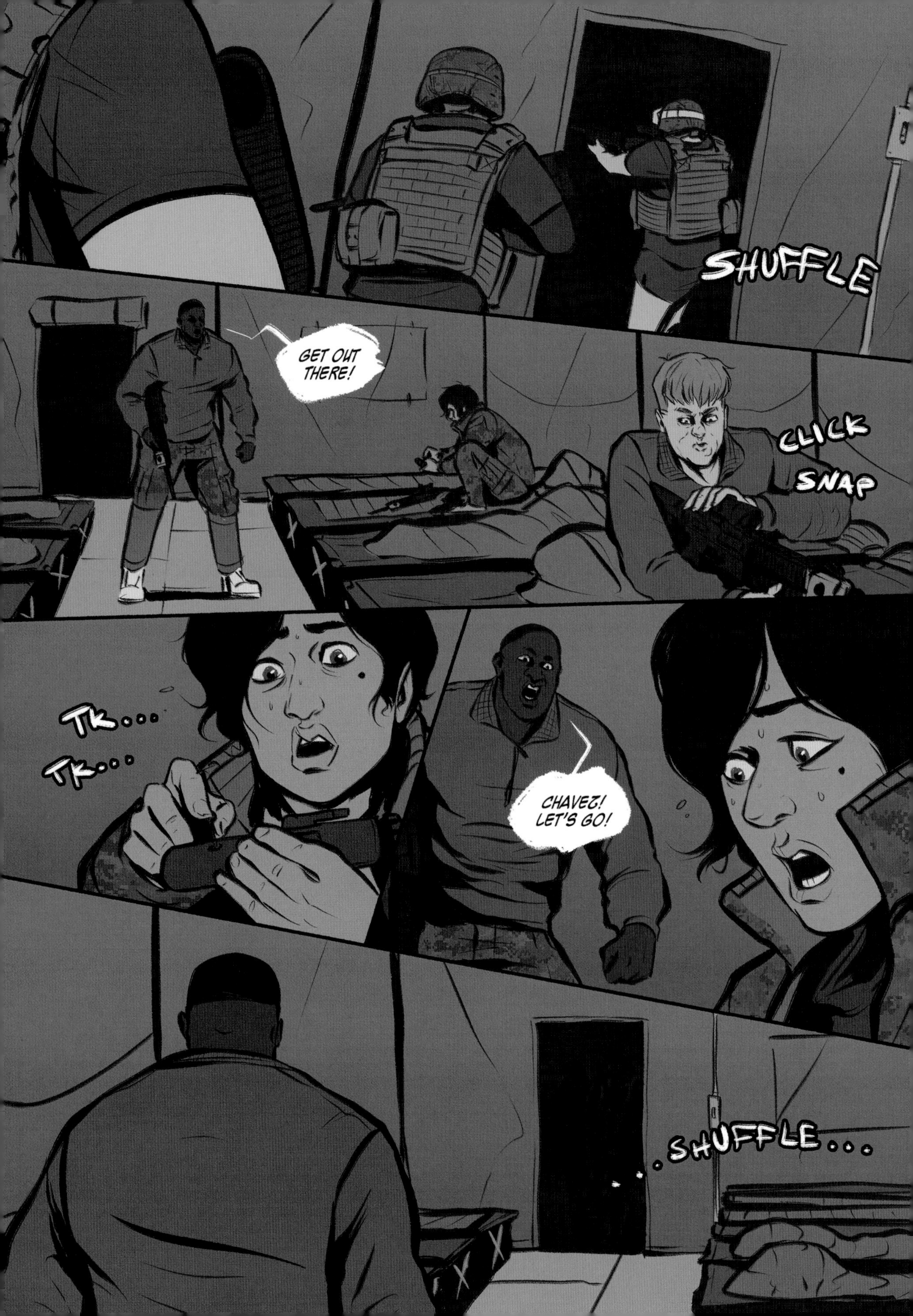
SHUFFLE
GET OUT THERE!
CLICK
SNAP
TK...
TK...
CHAVEZ! LET'S GO!
..SHUFFLE...

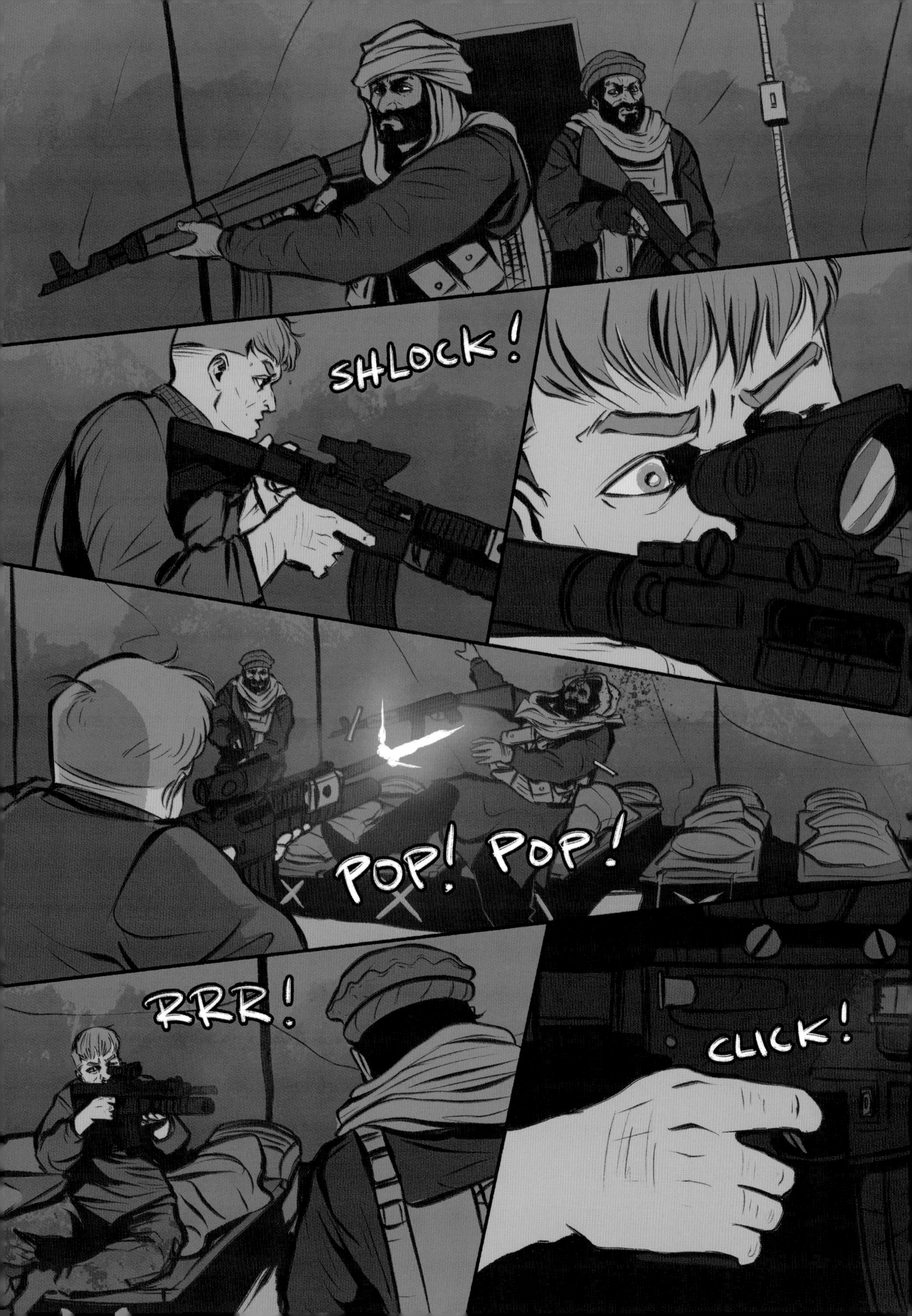
SHLOCK!
POP! POP!
RRR!
CLICK!

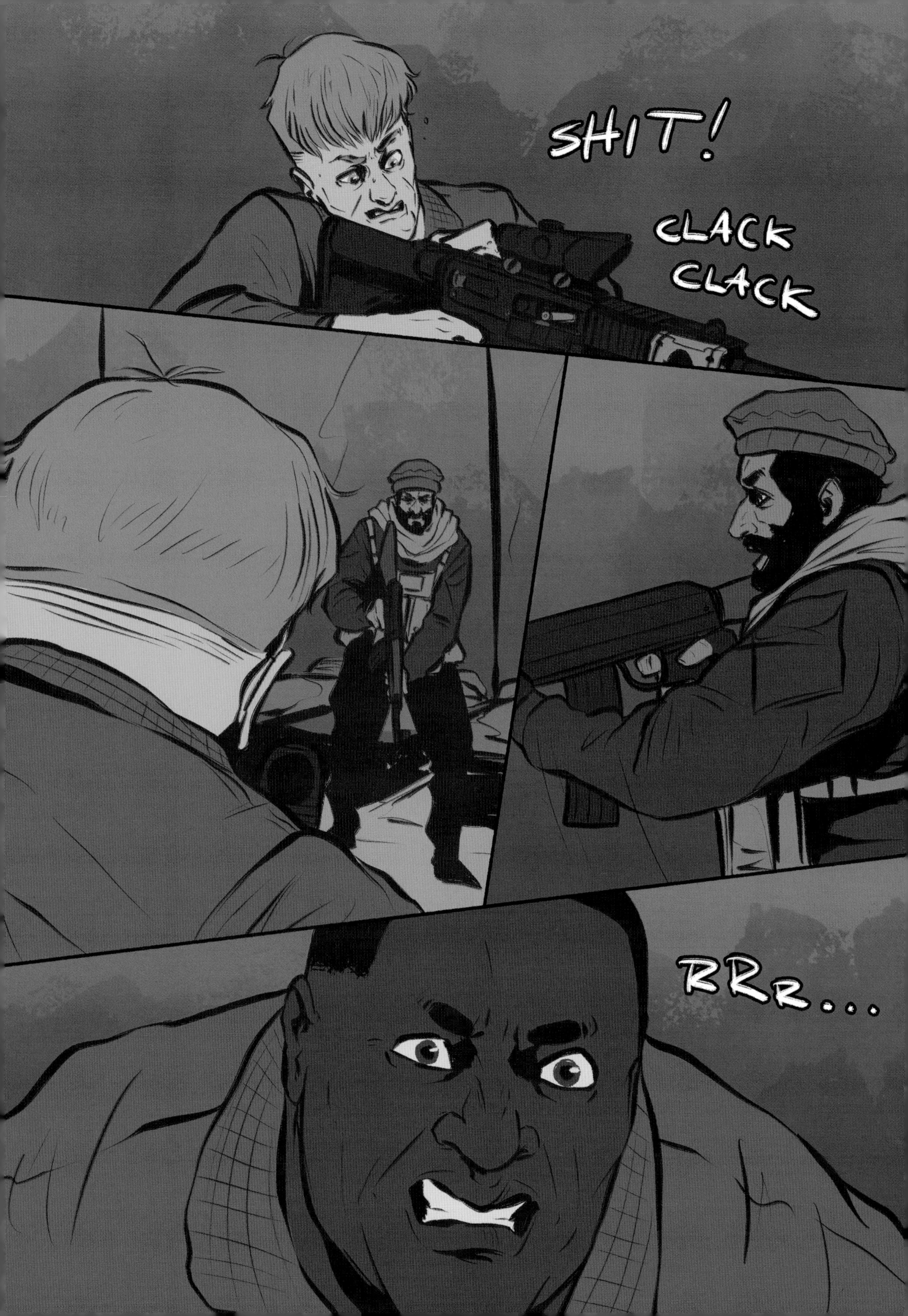
SHIT!
CLACK
CLACK
RRr...

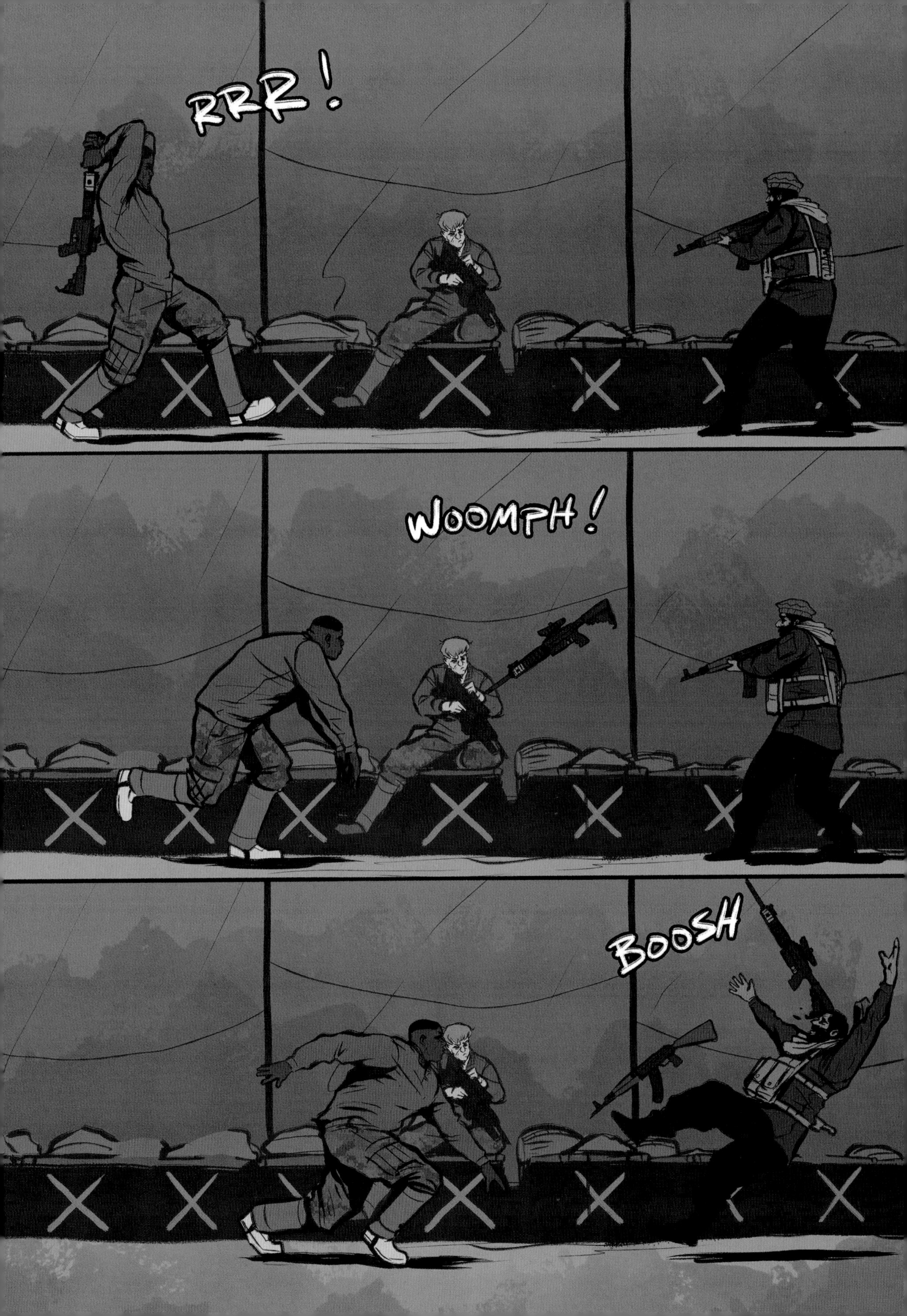
RRR!
WOOMPH!
BOOSH

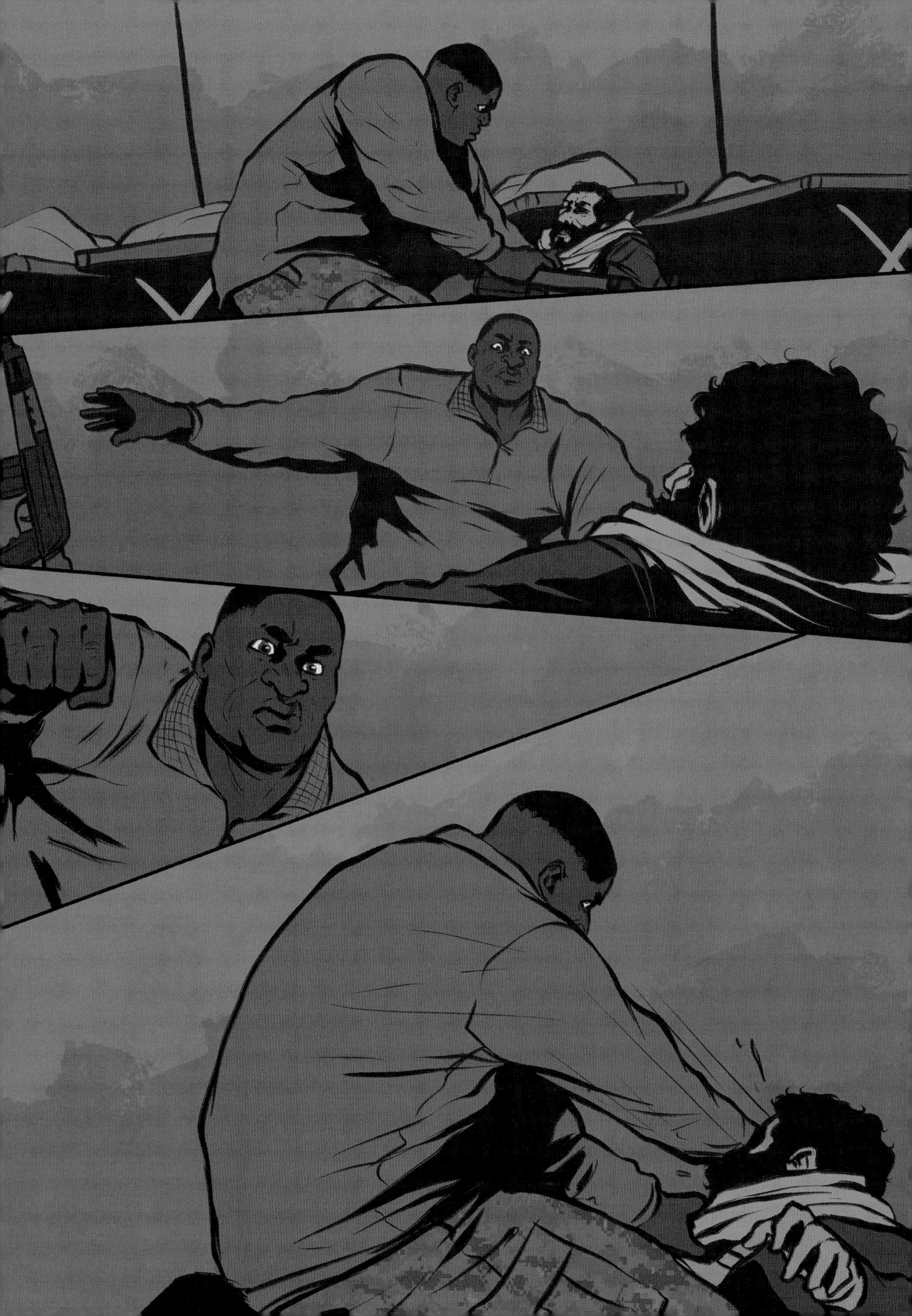

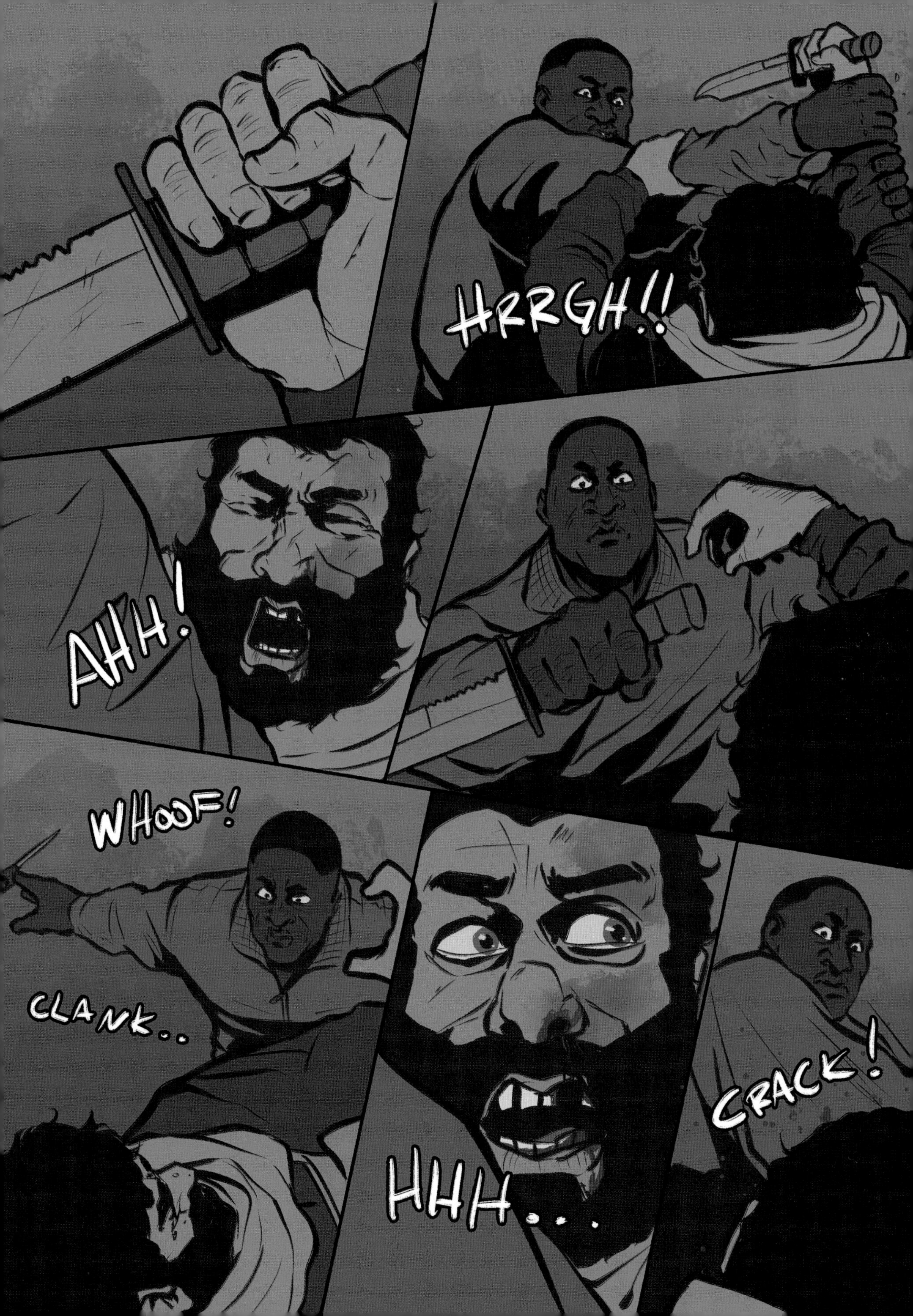
HRRGH!!
AHH!
WHOOF!
CLANK..
HHH...
CRACK!

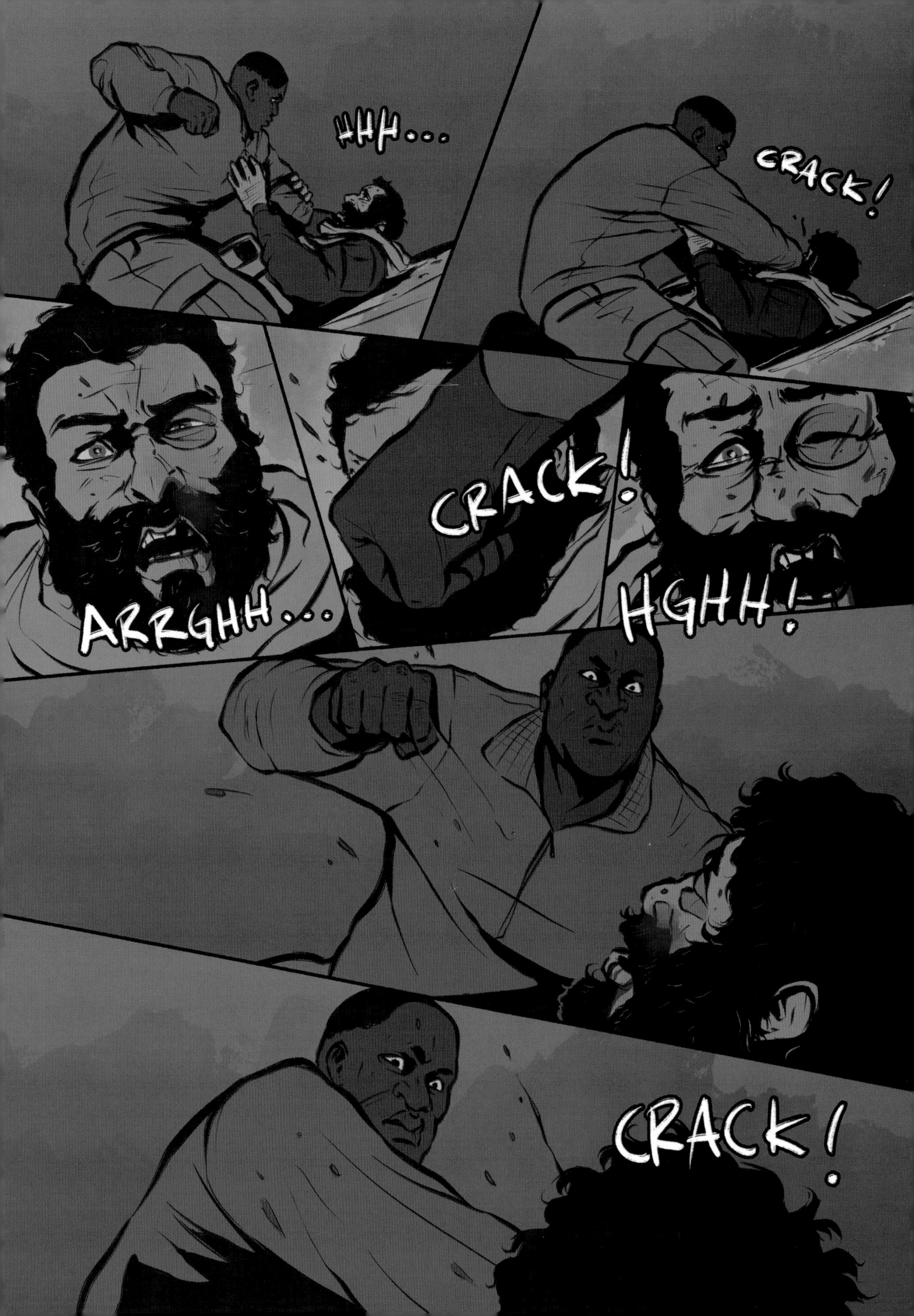
HHH...
CRACK!
ARRGHH...
CRACK!
HGHH!
CRACK!

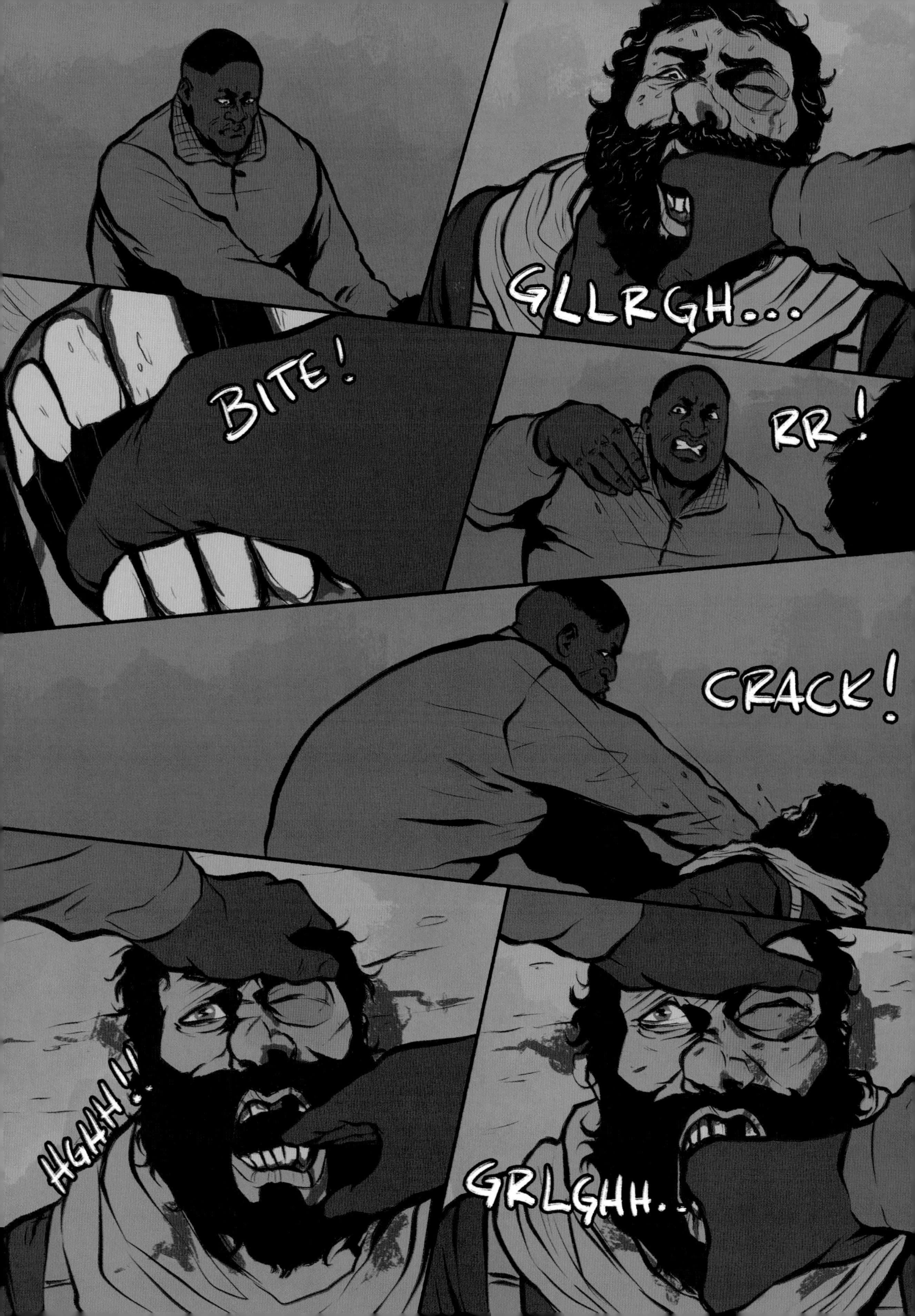
GLLRGH...
BITE!
RR!
CRACK!
HGHH!!
GRLGHH..

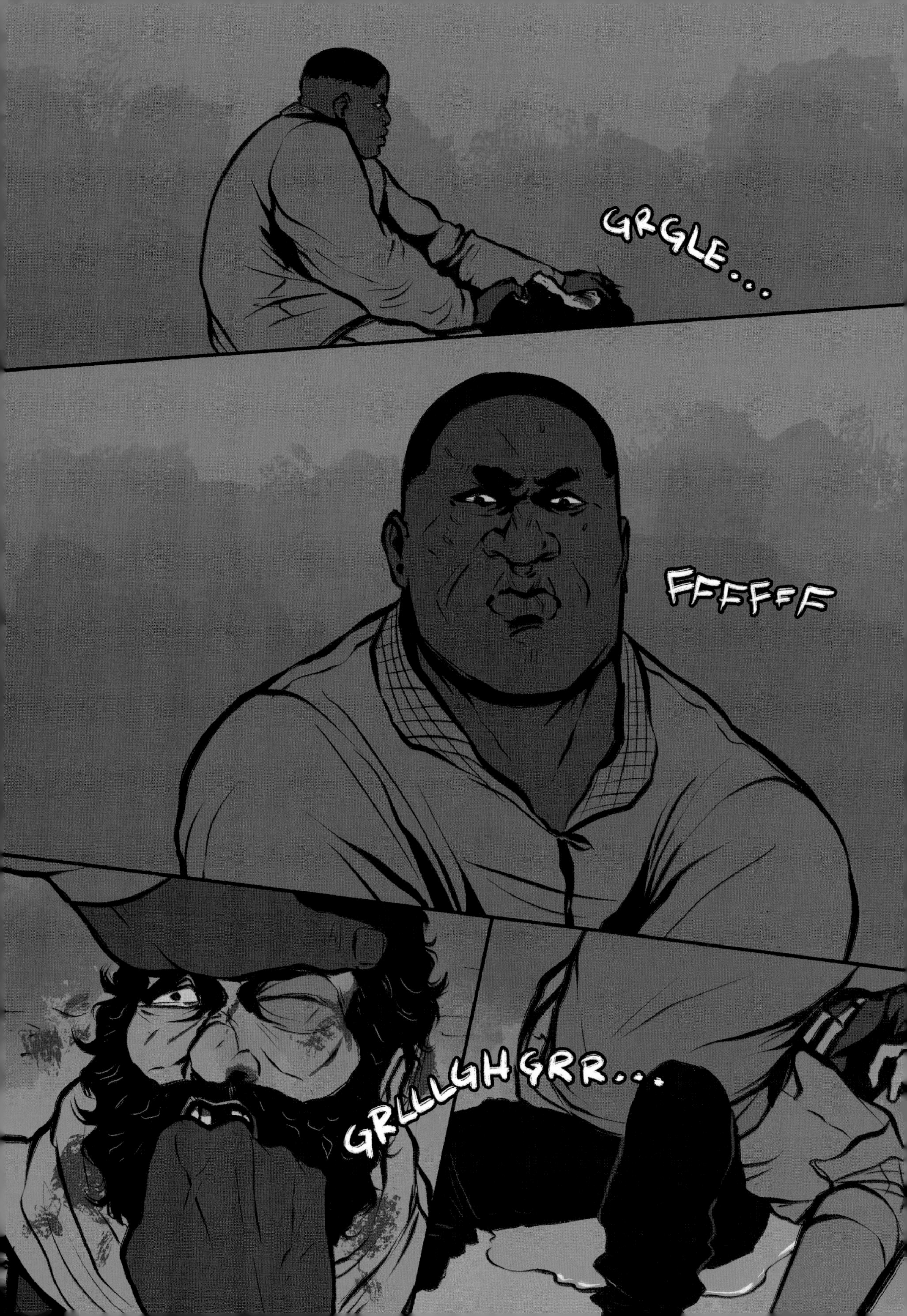
GRGLE...
FFFFFF
GRLLLGHGRR...

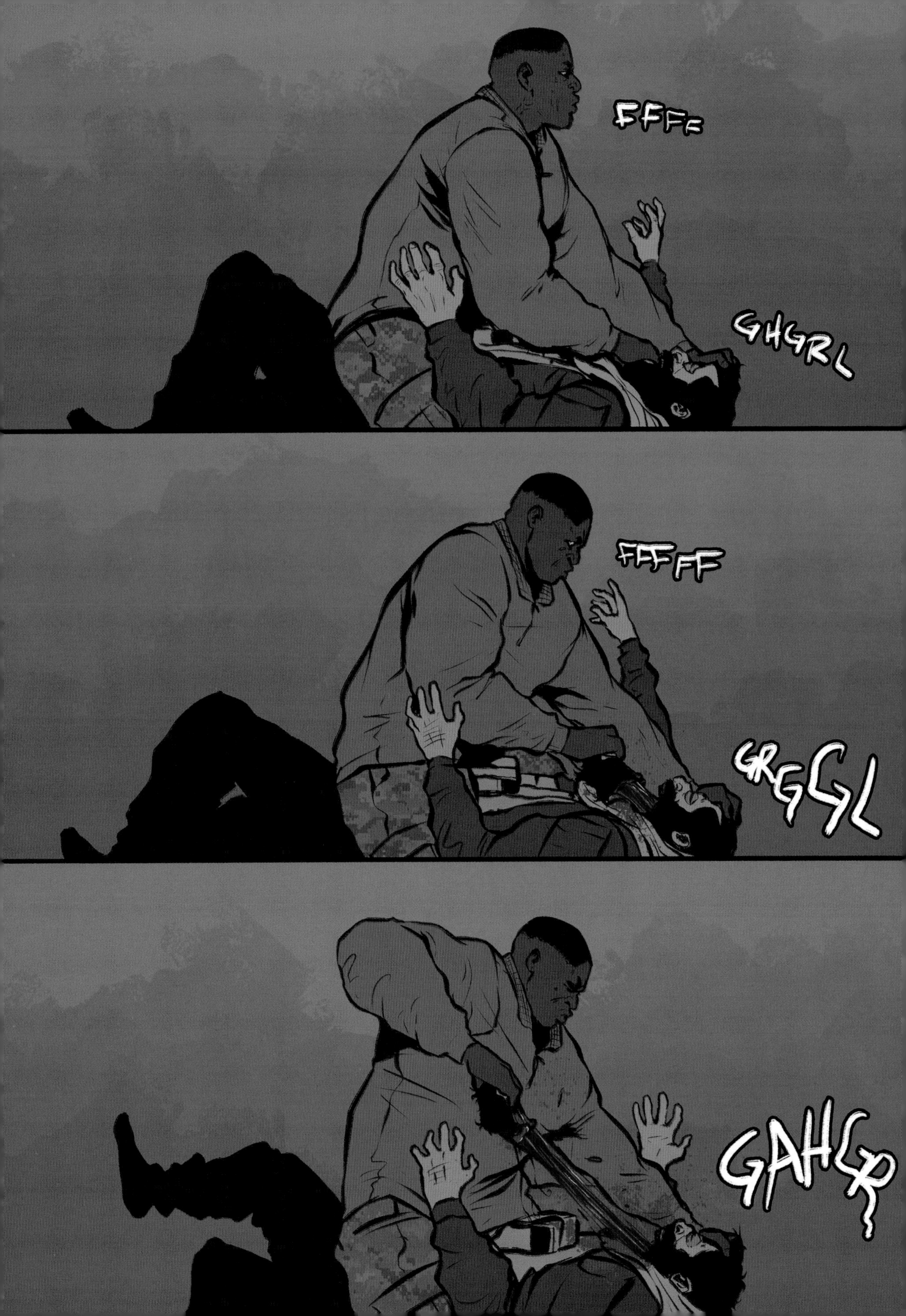
FFFF
GHGRL
FFFFF
GRGGL
GAHGR

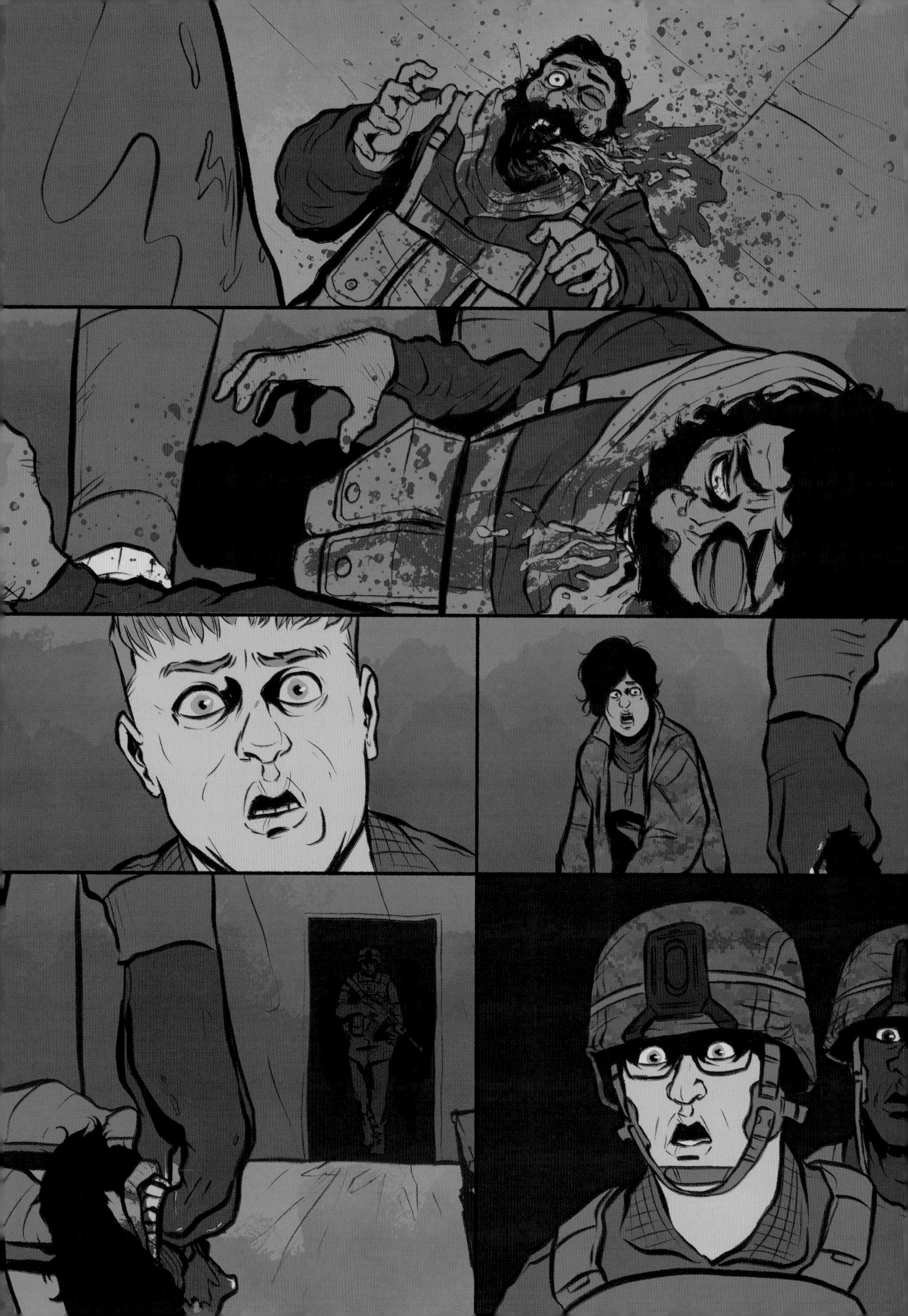

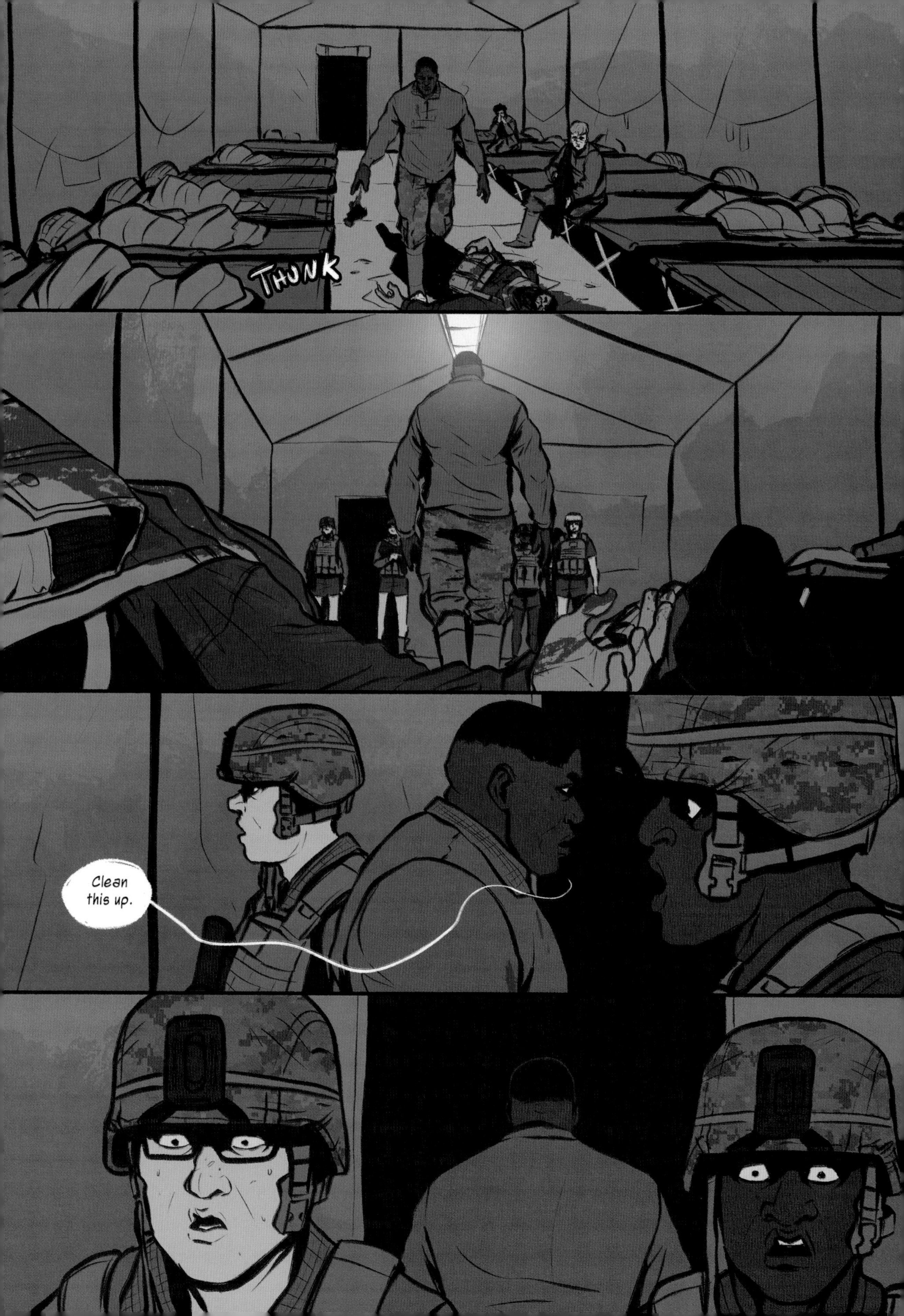
THUNK
Clean this up.

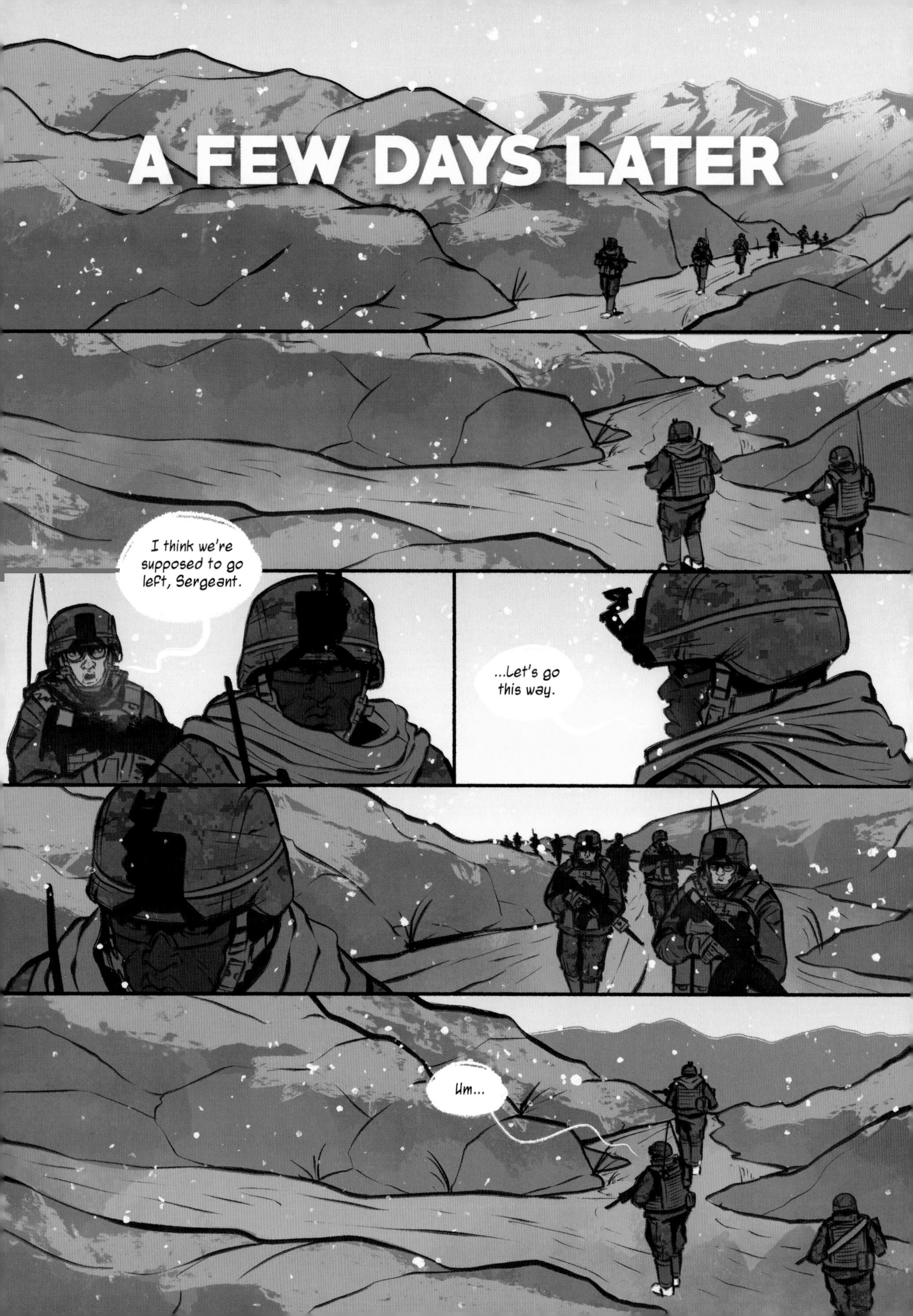
A FEW DAYS LATER
I think we're supposed to go left, Sergeant.
...Let's go this way.
Um...

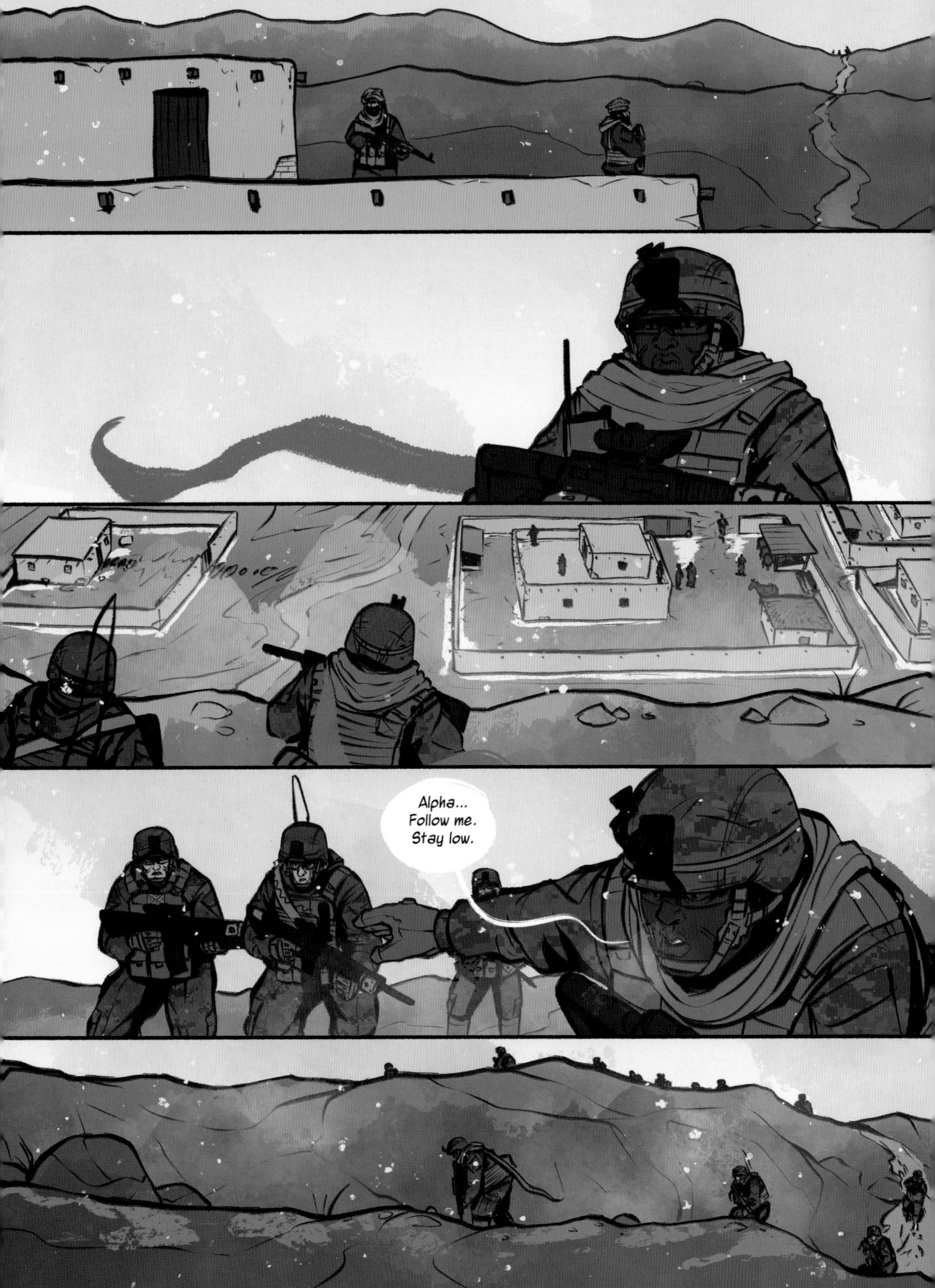
Alpha... Follow me. Stay low.

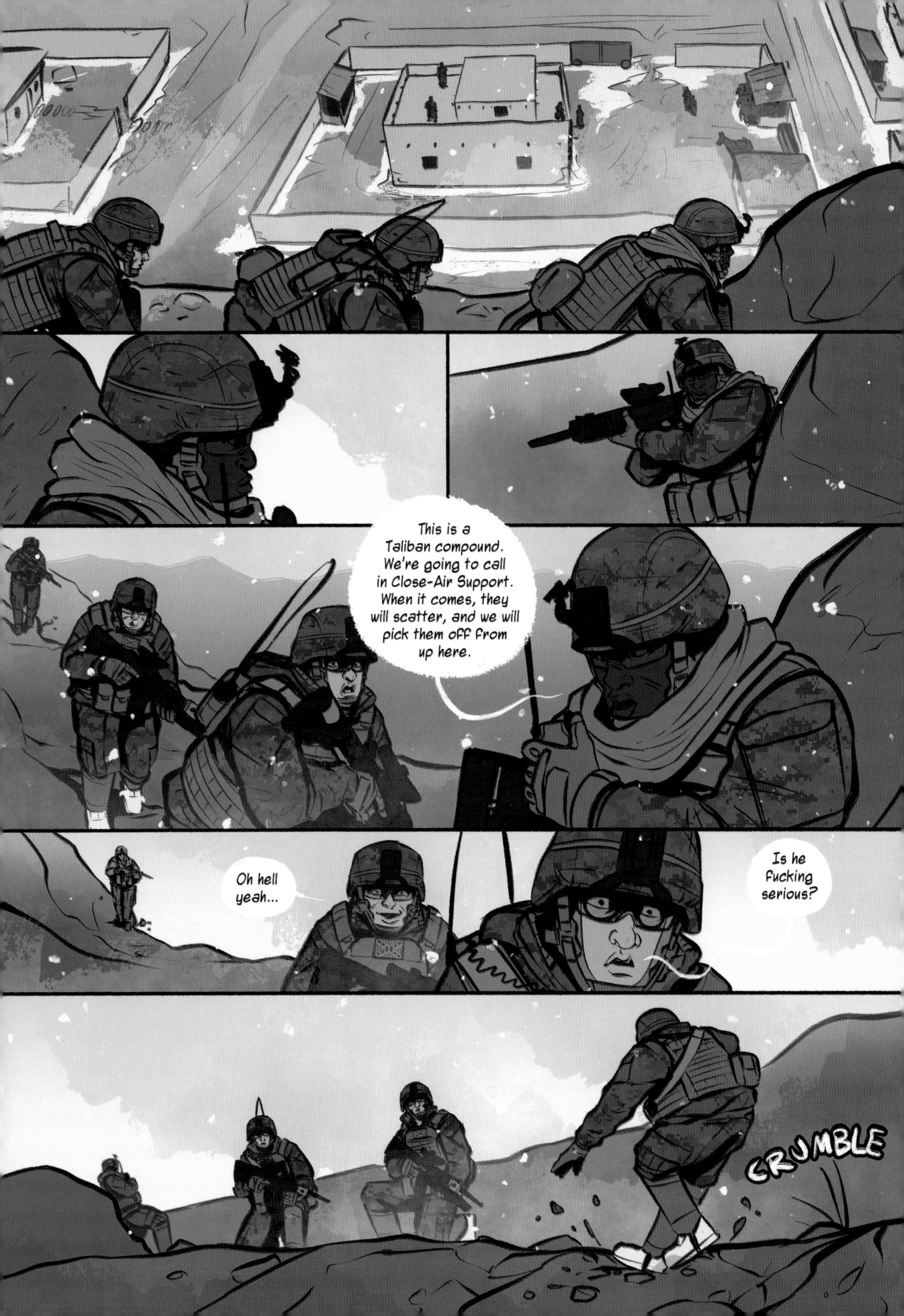

This is a Taliban compound. We're going to call in Close-Air Support. When it comes, they will scatter, and we will pick them off from up here.
Oh hell yeah...
Is he fucking serious?
CRUMBLE

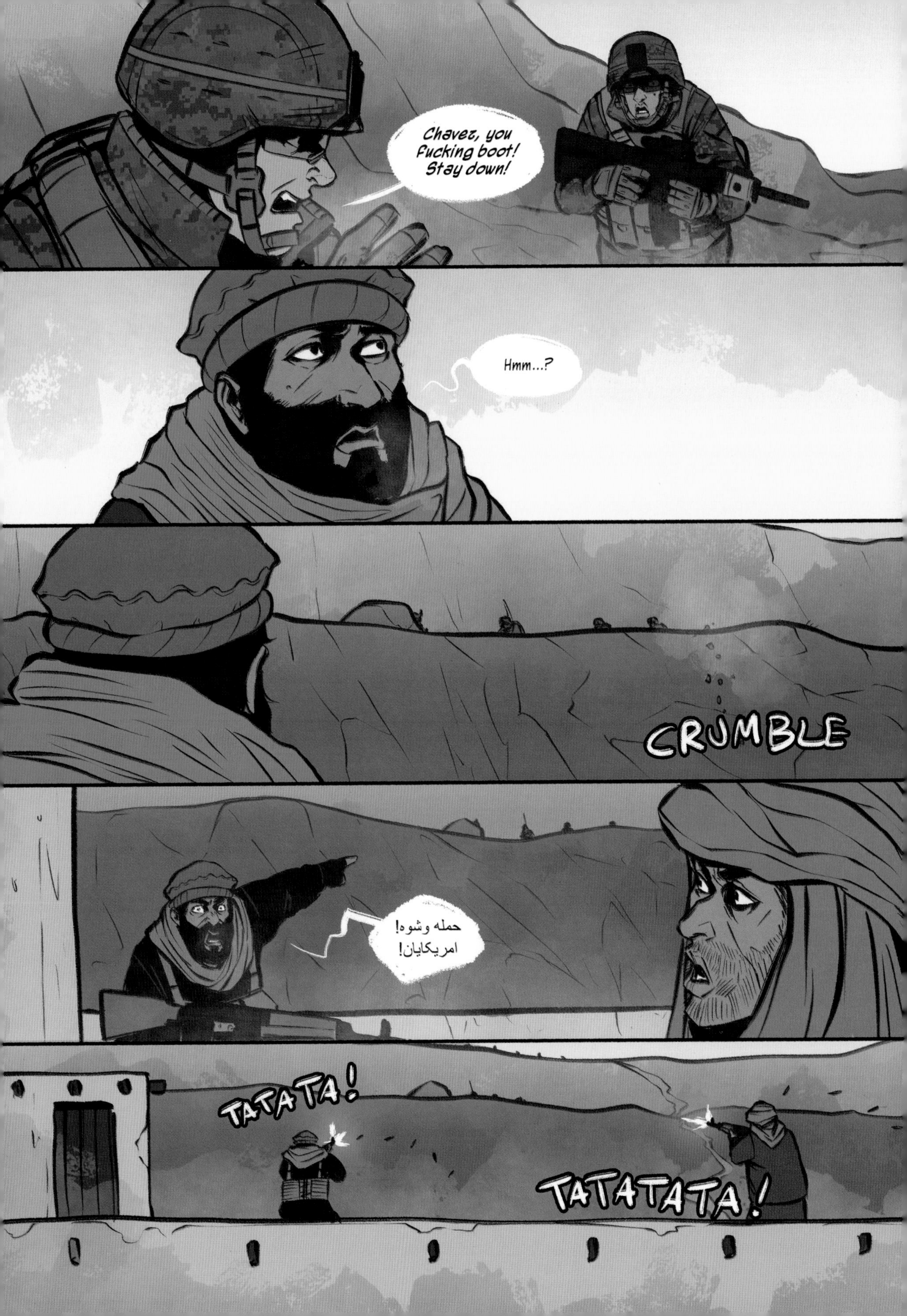

Chavez, you fucking boot! Stay down!
Hmm...?
CRUMBLE
حمله وشوه! امريكايان!
TATATA!
TATATATA!

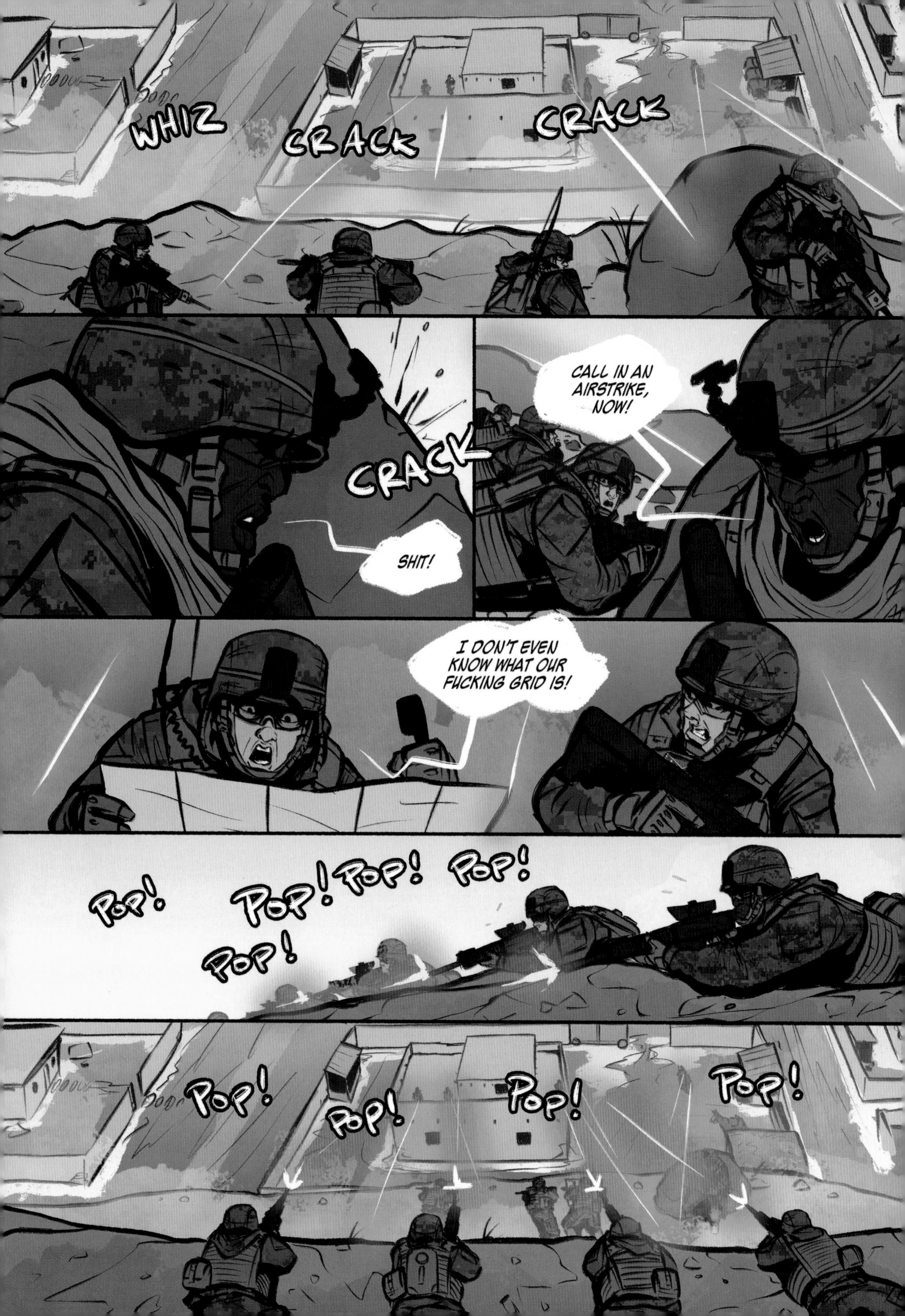
WHIZ
CRACK
CRACK
CRACK
SHIT!
CALL IN AN AIRSTRIKE, NOW!
I DON'T EVEN KNOW WHAT OUR FUCKING GRID IS!
POP! POP! POP! POP!
POP!
POP!
POP!
POP!
POP!

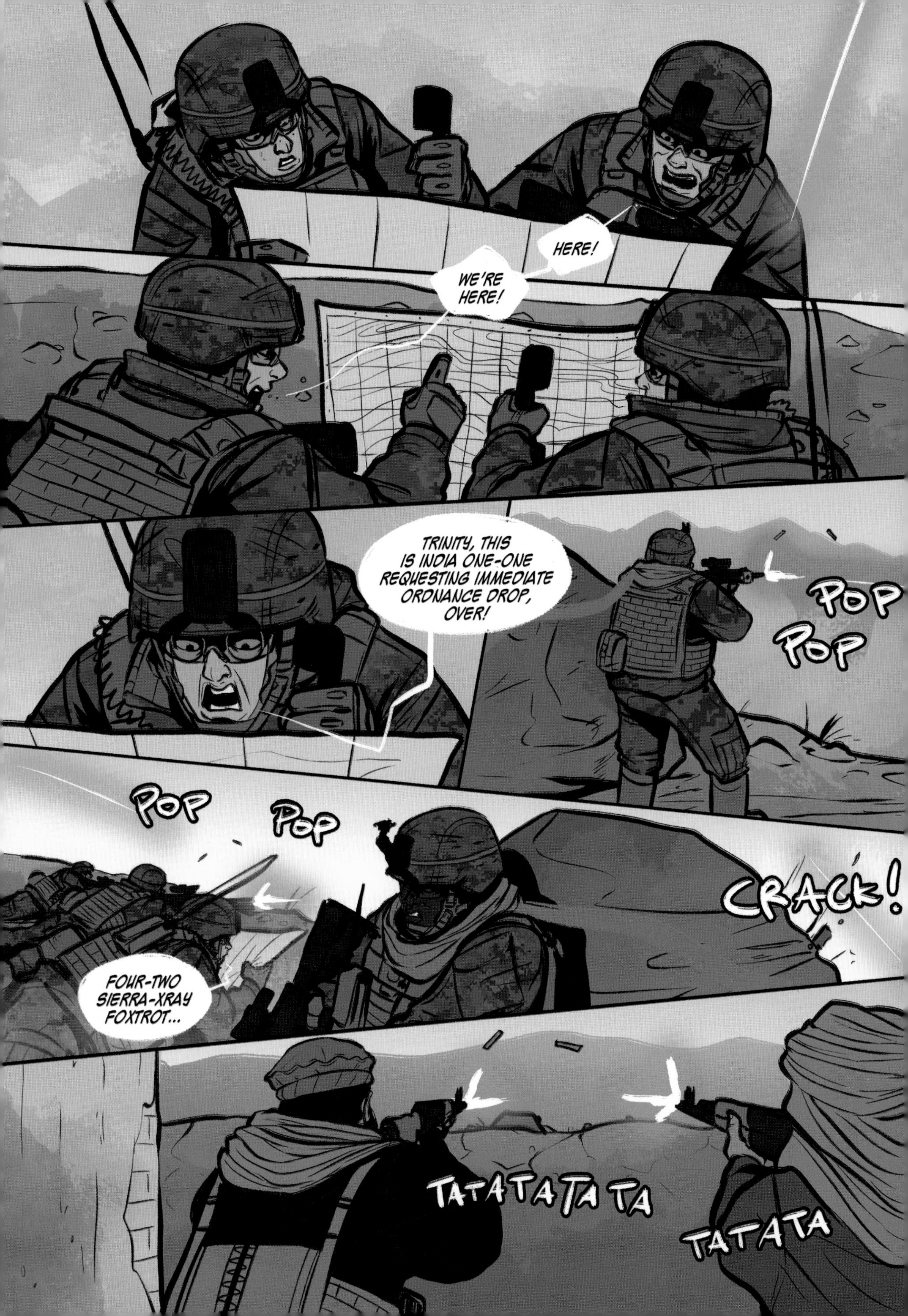
HERE!
WE'RE HERE!
TRINITY, THIS IS INDIA ONE-ONE REQUESTING IMMEDIATE ORDNANCE DROP, OVER!
POP
POP
POP
POP
CRACK!
FOUR-TWO SIERRA-XRAY FOXTROT...
TATATATATA
TATATA

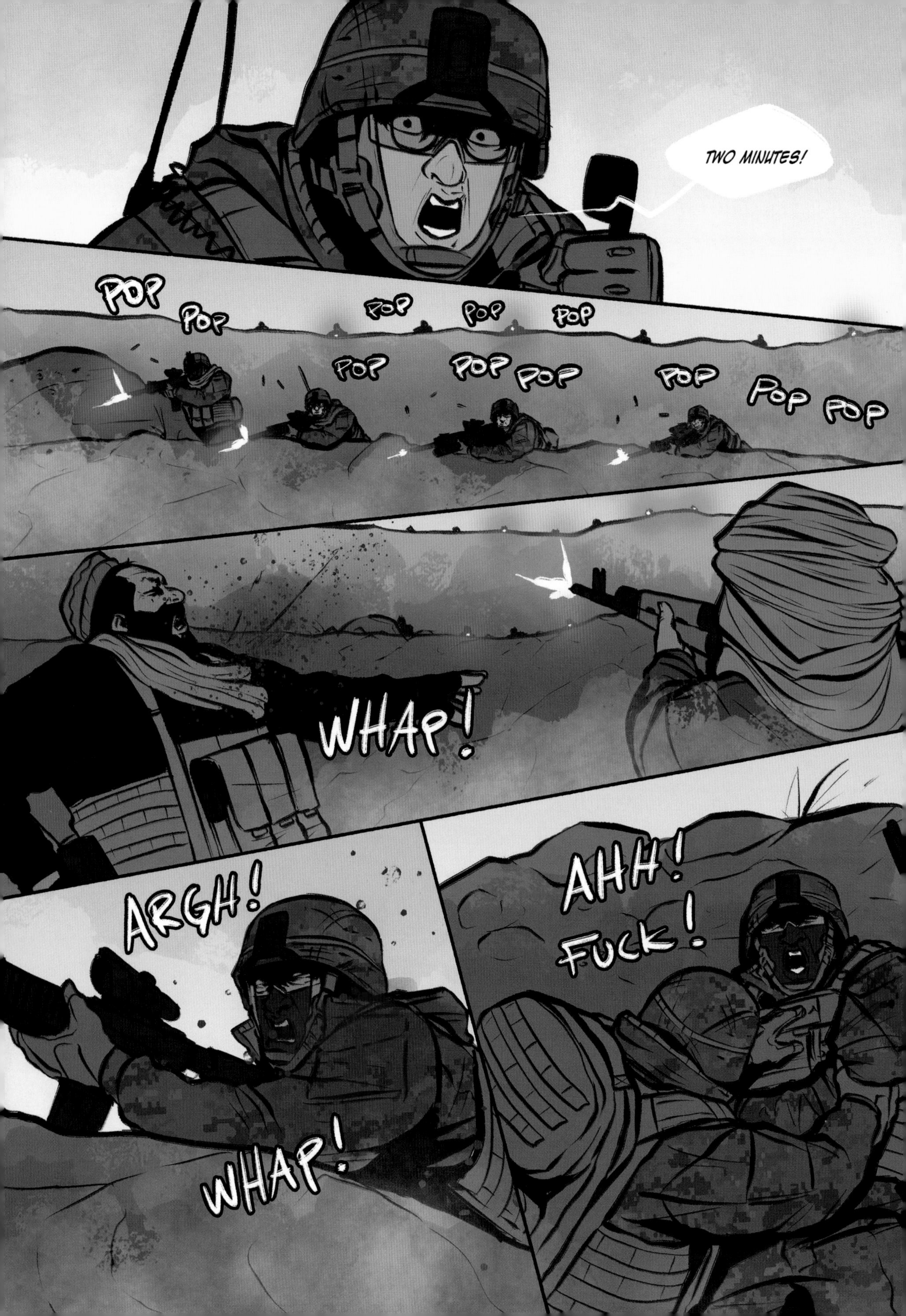
TWO MINUTES!
POP
POP
POP
POP
POP
POP
POP
POP
POP
POP
POP
WHAP!
ARGH!
WHAP!
AHH!
FUCK!

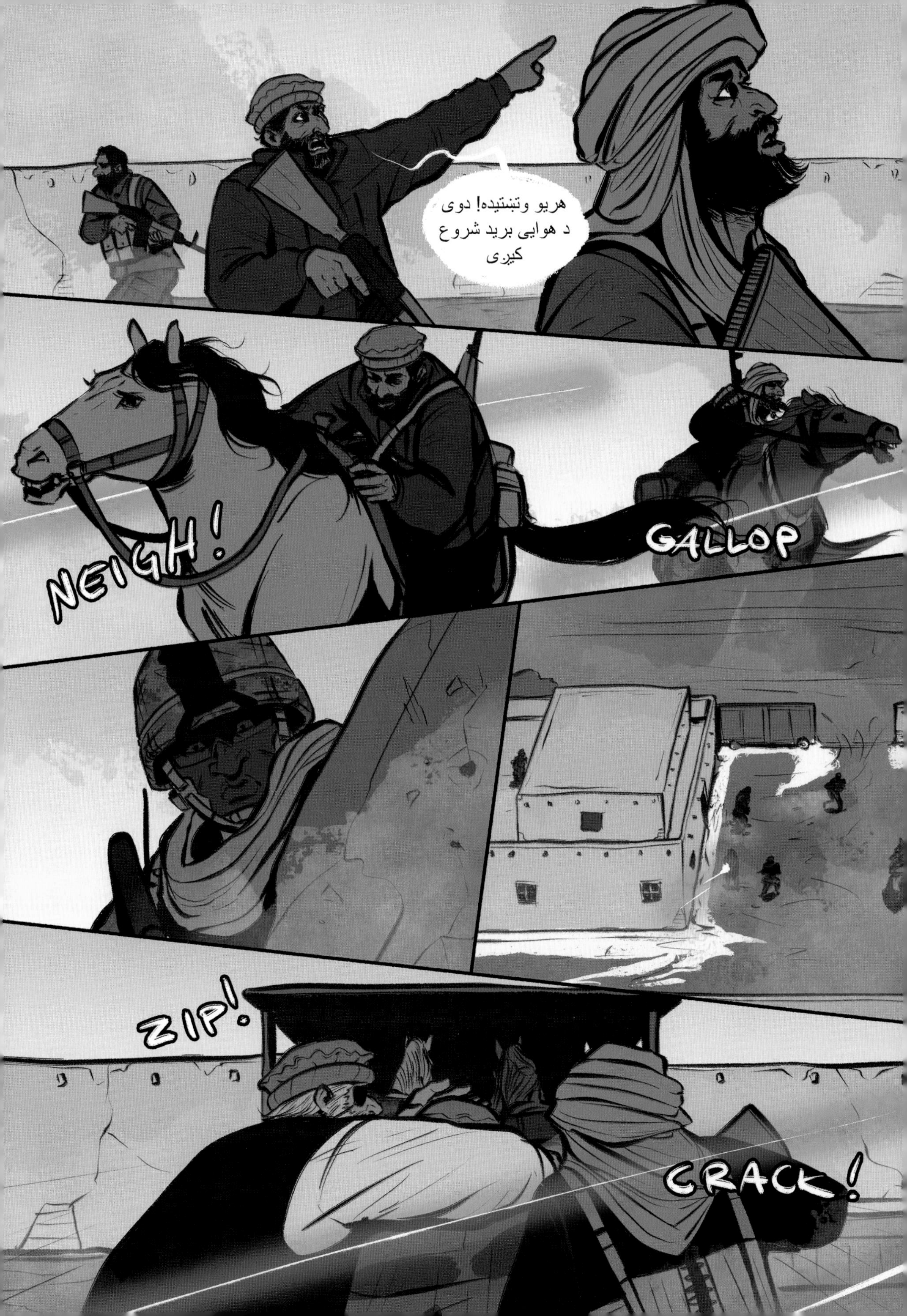
هريو وتښتيده! دوی
د هوايي برید شروع
کیږی
NEIGH!
GALLOP
ZIP!
CRACK!

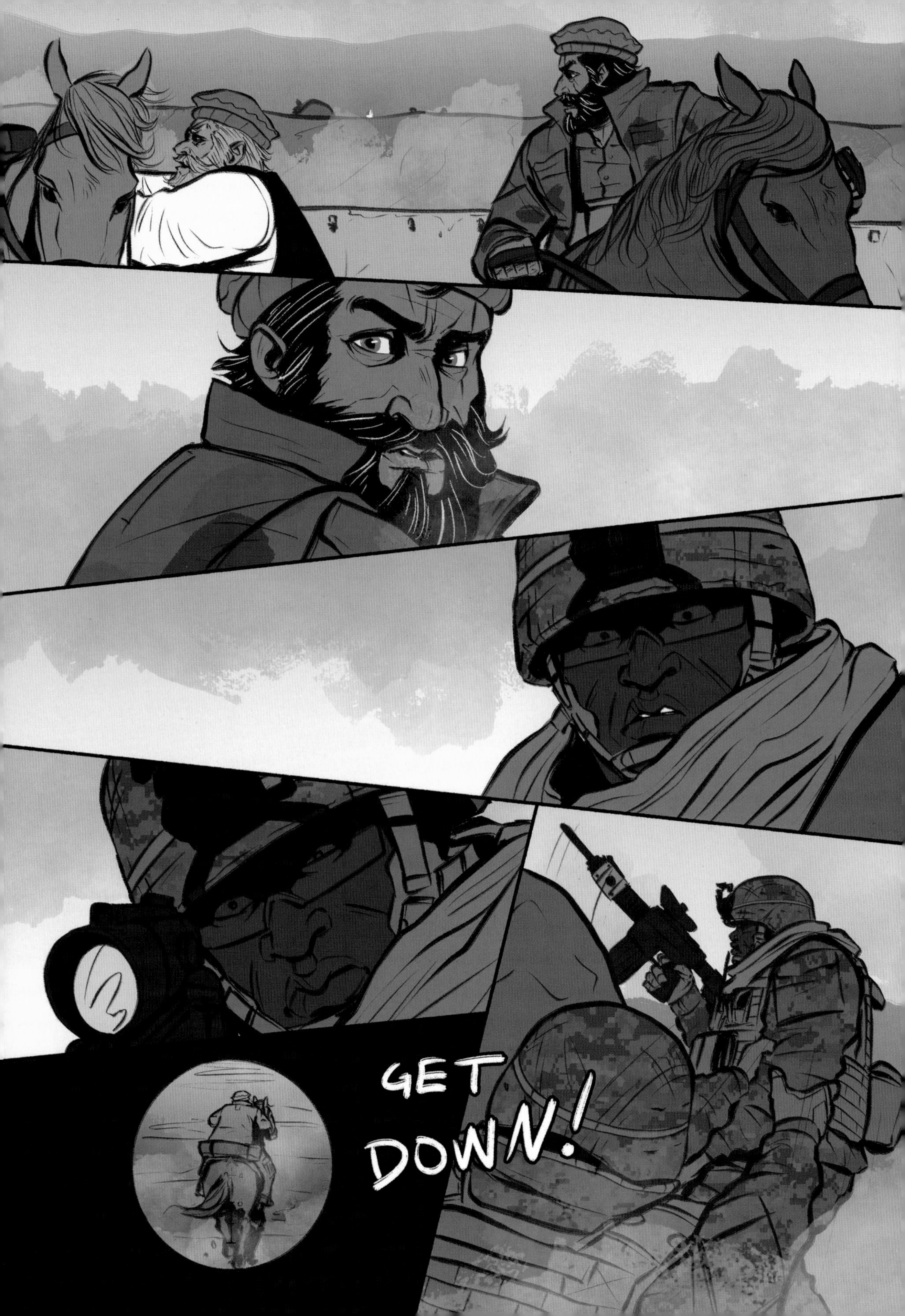
GET DOWN!

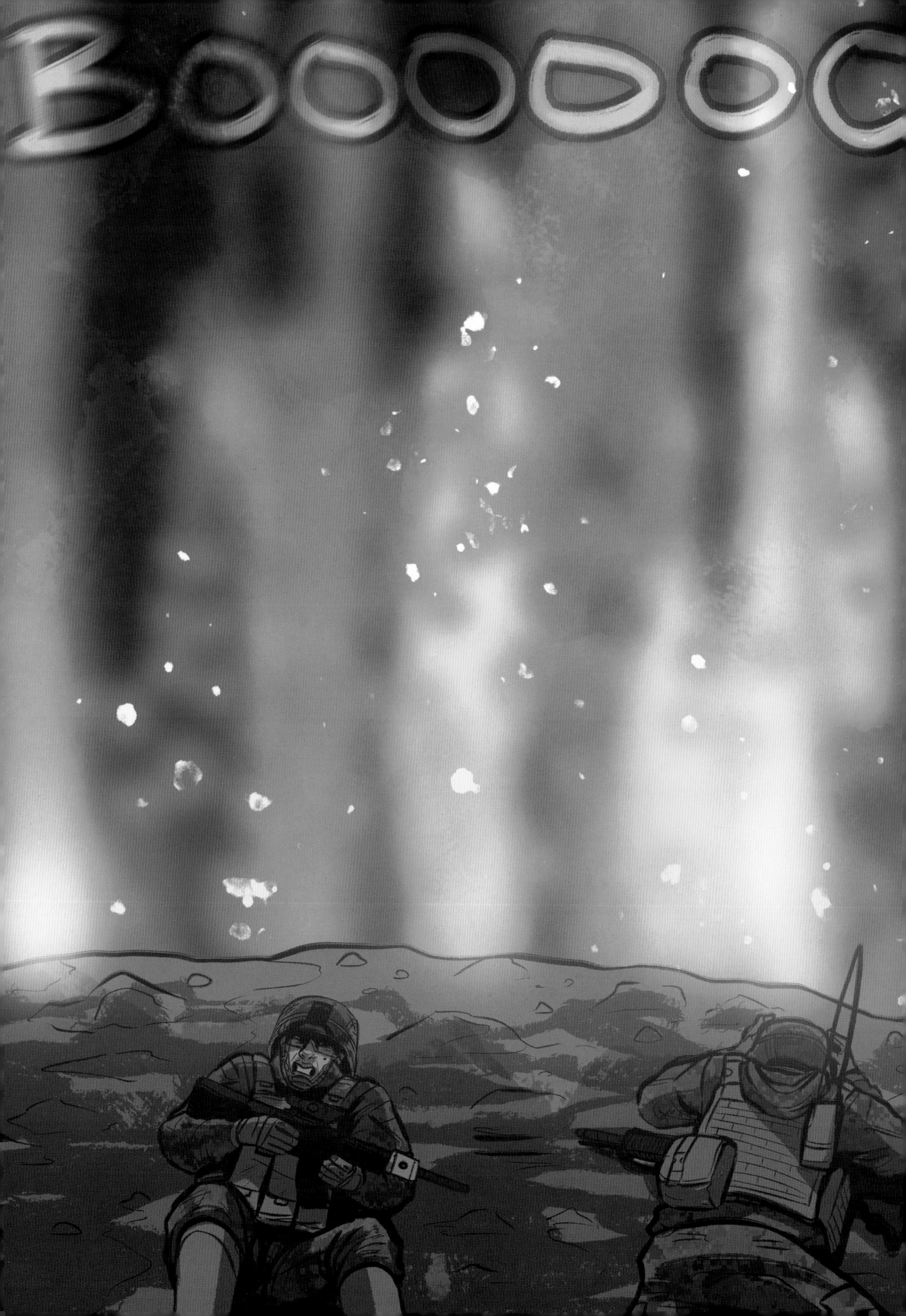
BOOOOOO

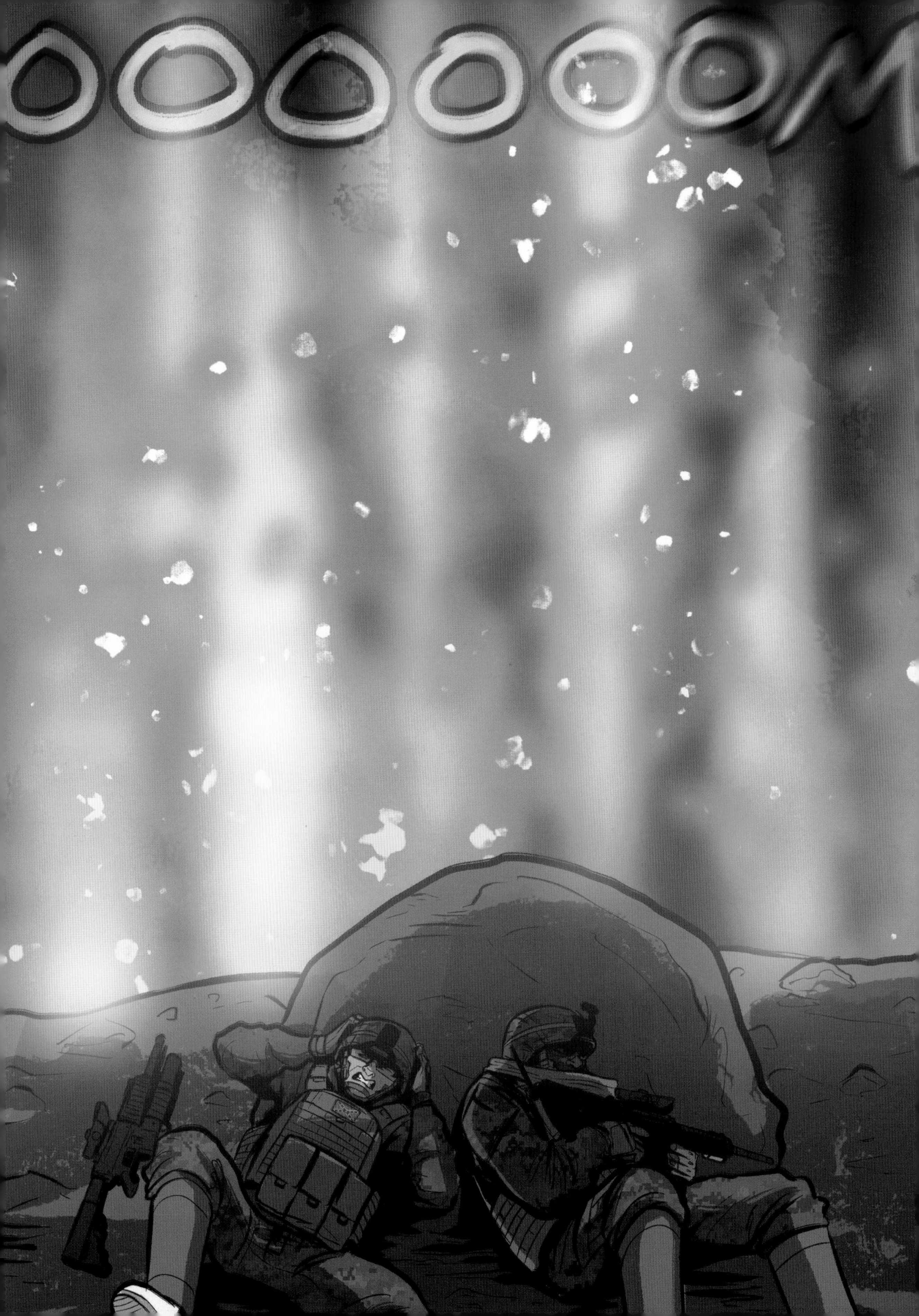
OOOOOOOM

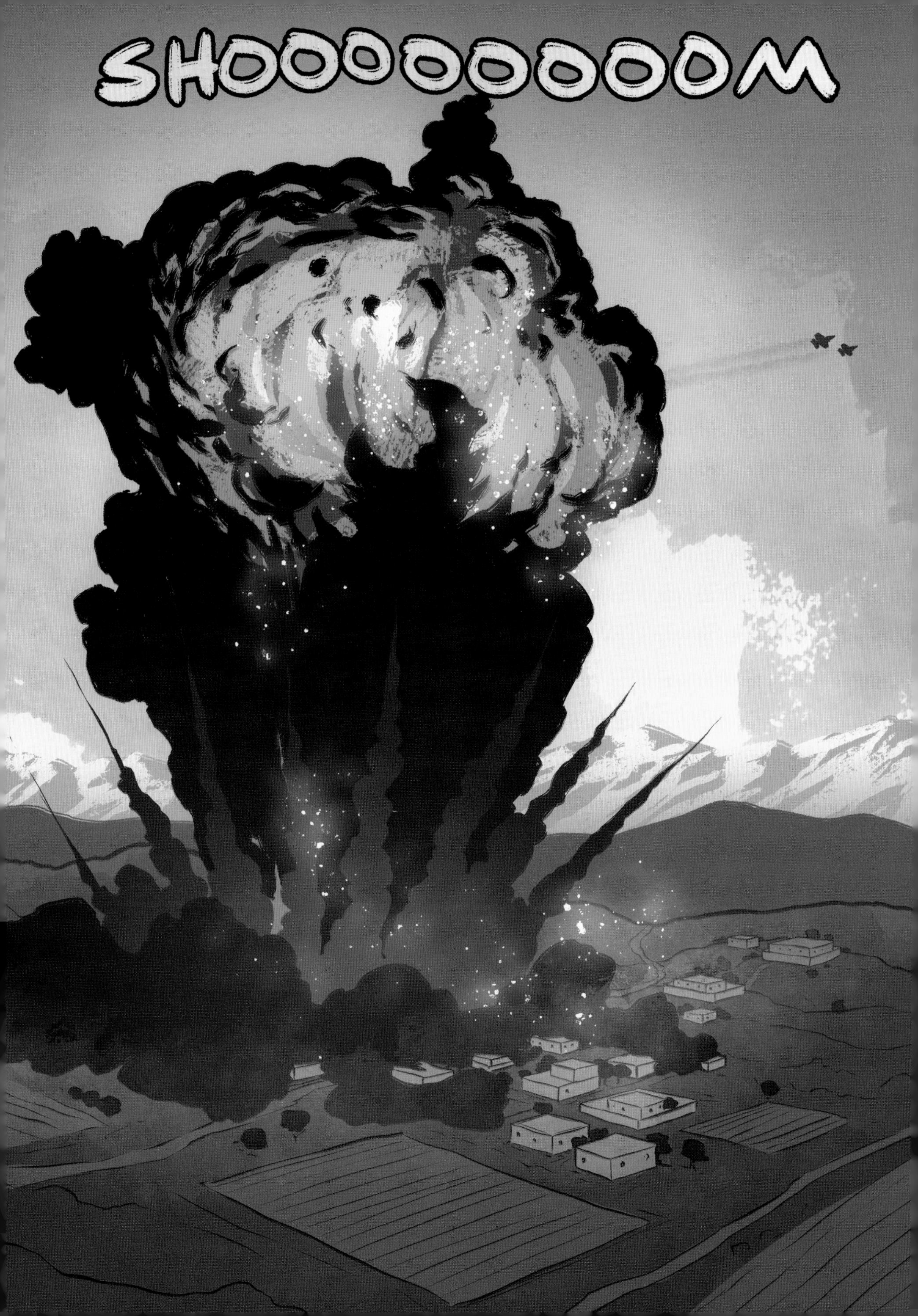
SHOOOOOOOOM

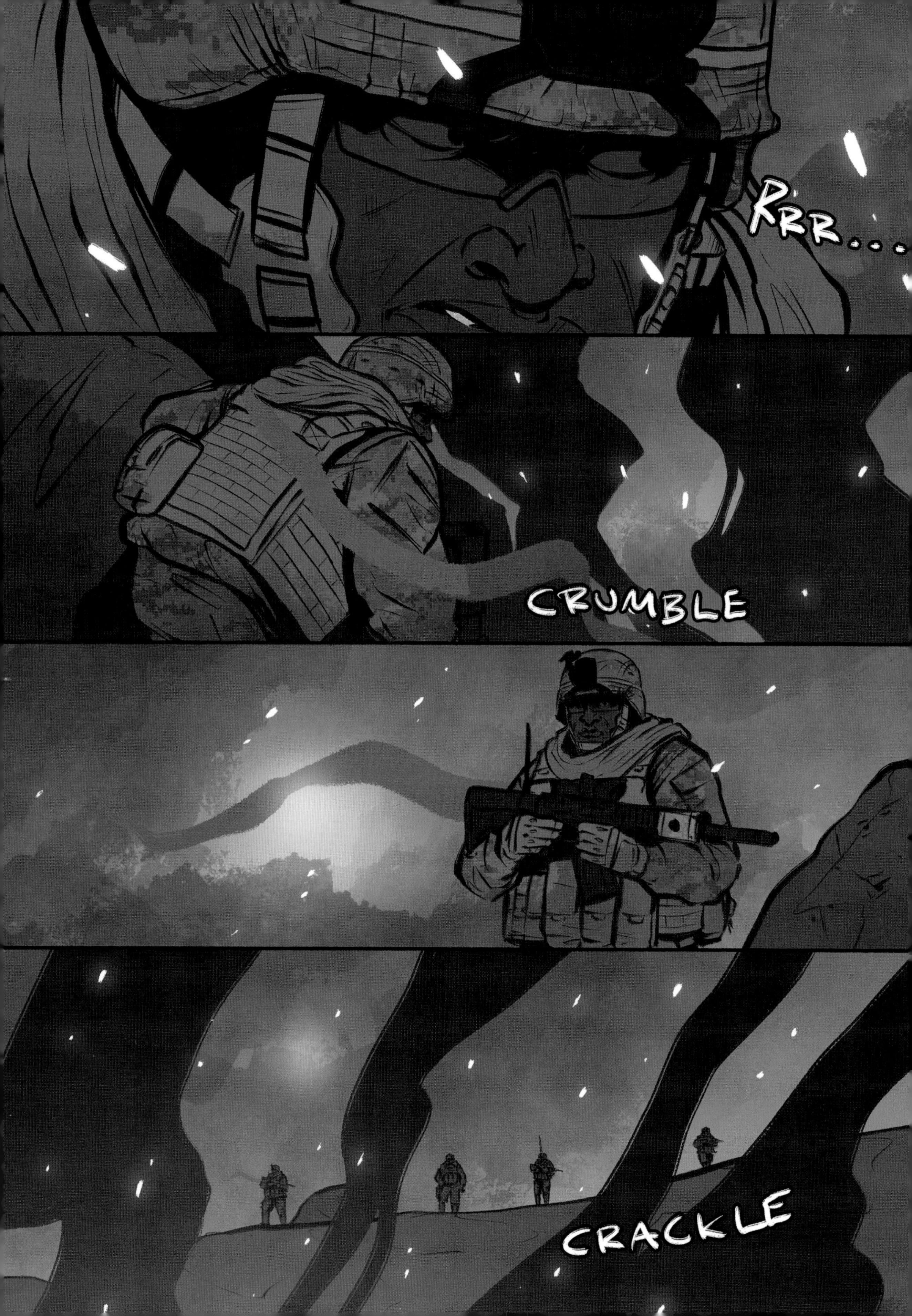
Rrr...
CRUMBLE
CRACKLE

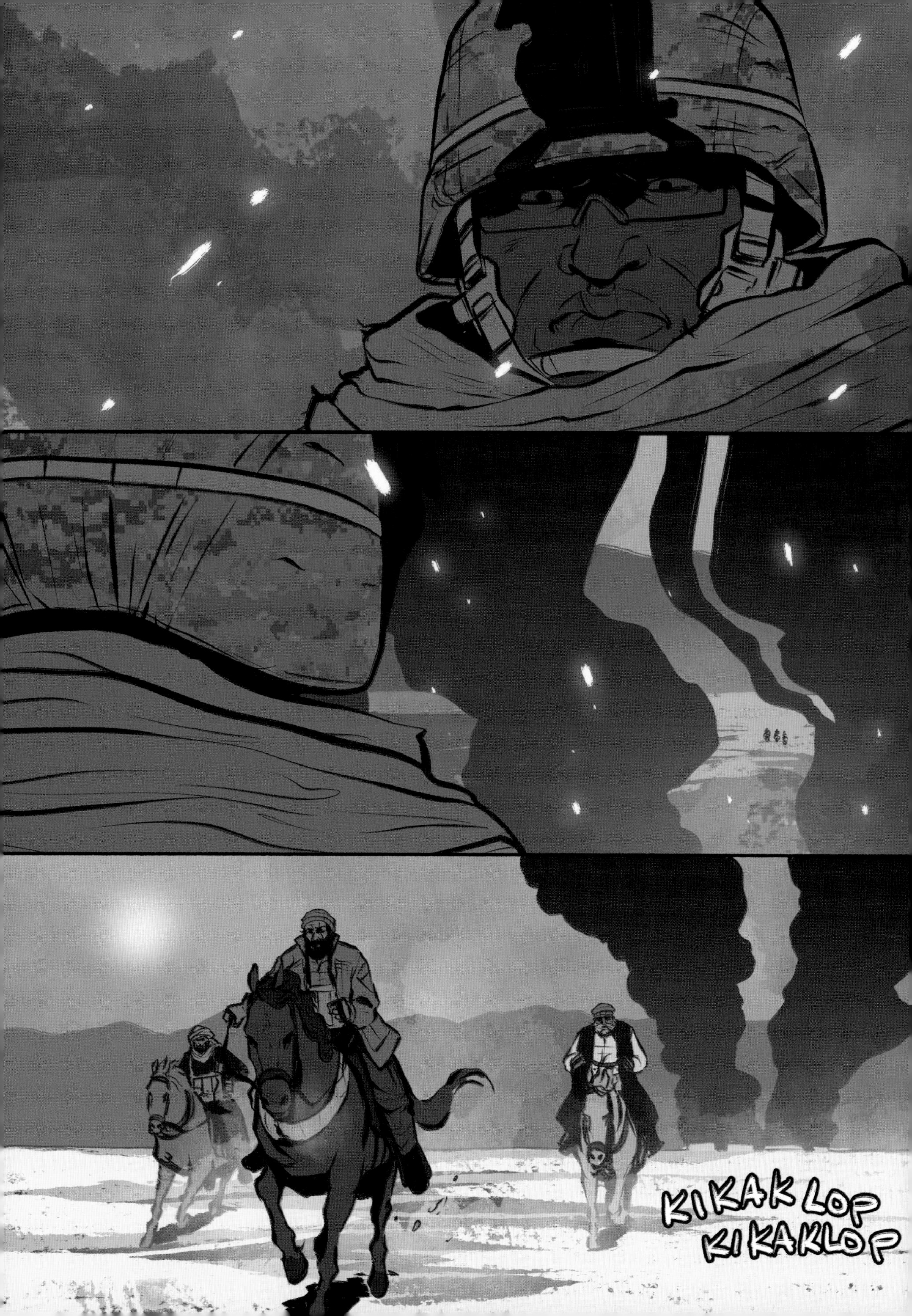
KIKAKLOP
KIKAKLOP

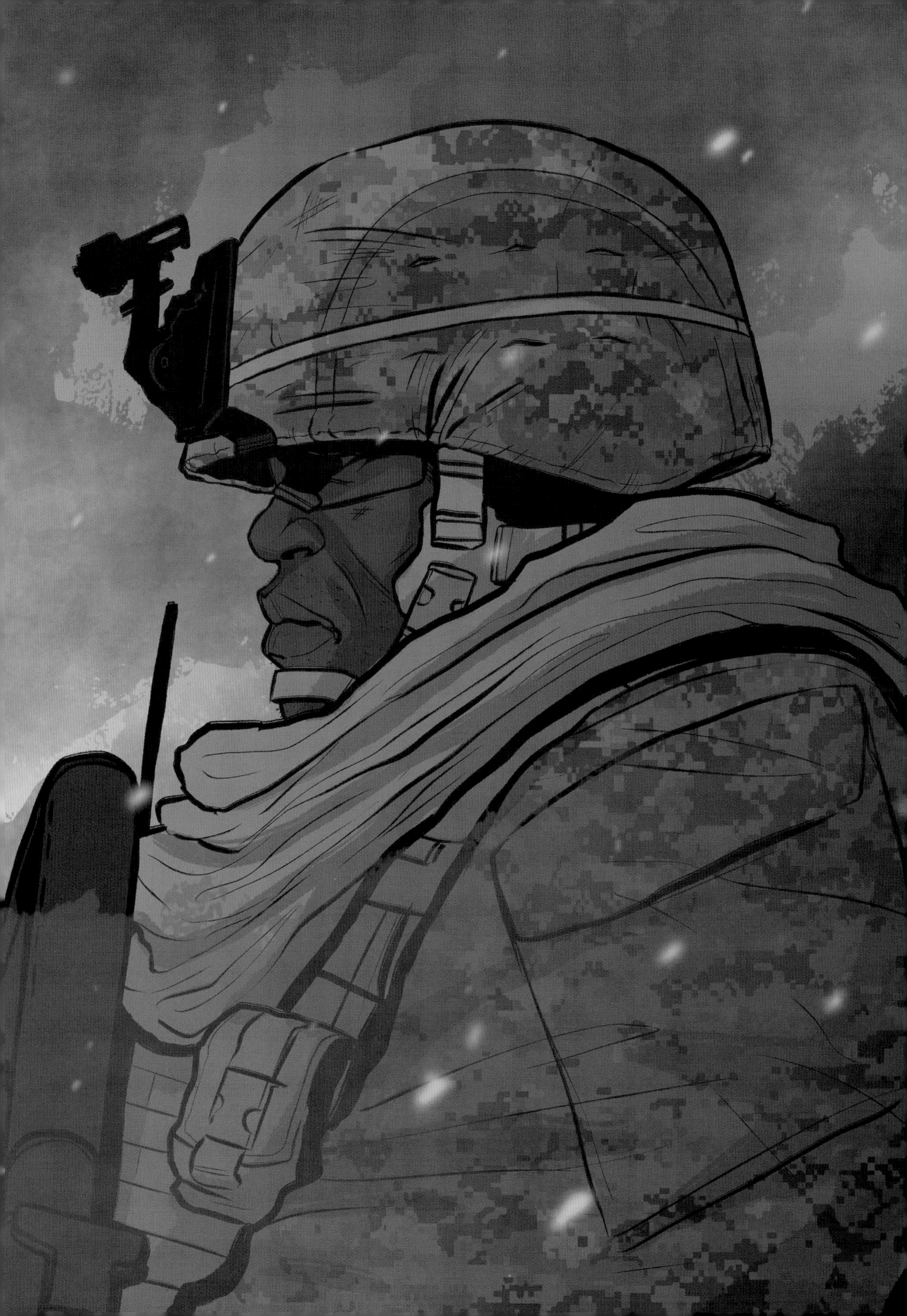

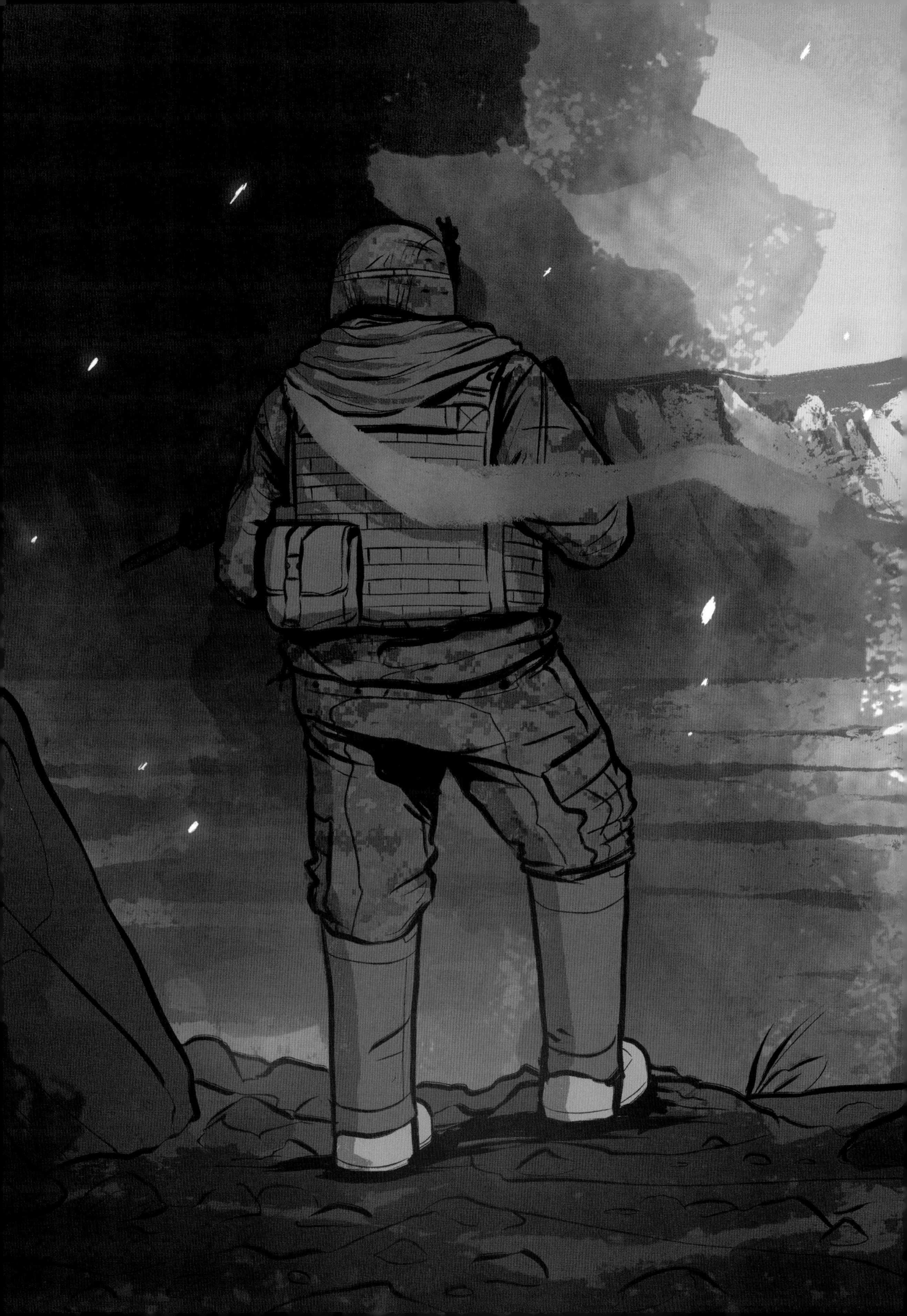

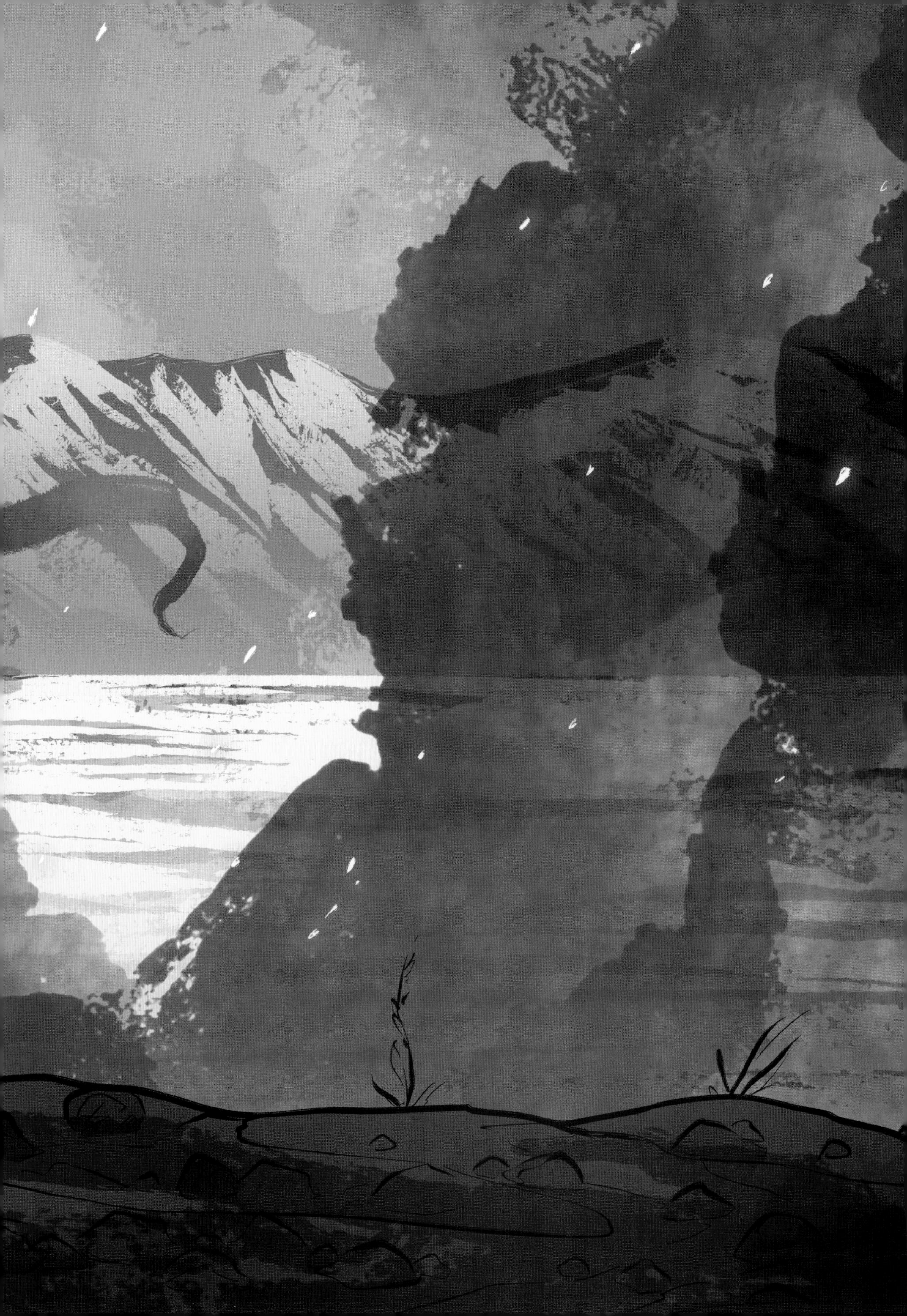

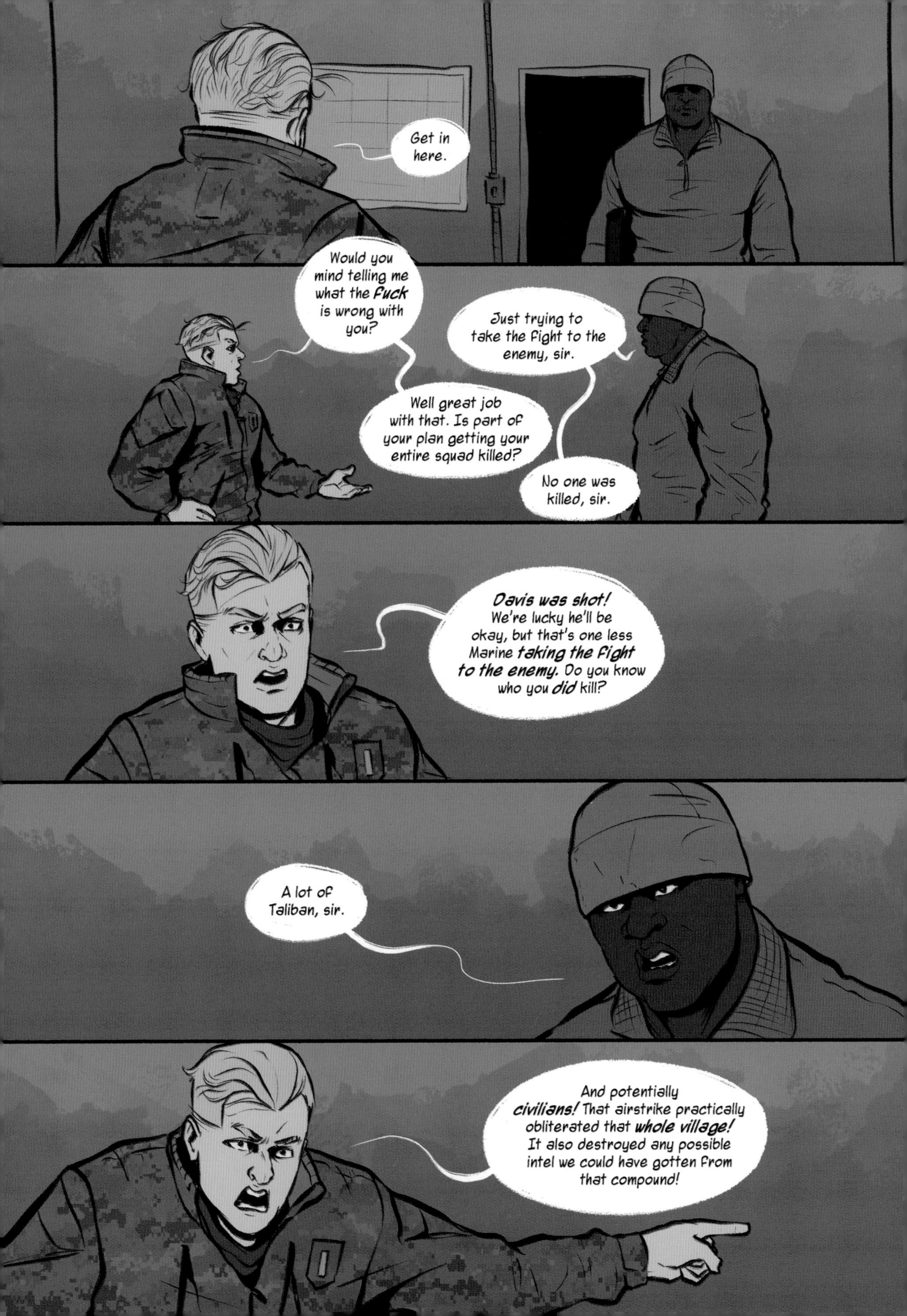
Get in here.
Would you mind telling me what the *fuck* is wrong with you?
Just trying to take the fight to the enemy, sir.
Well great job with that. Is part of your plan getting your entire squad killed?
No one was killed, sir.
Davis was shot! We're lucky he'll be okay, but that's one less Marine *taking the fight to the enemy.* Do you know who you *did* kill?
A lot of Taliban, sir.
And potentially *civilians!* That airstrike practically obliterated that *whole village!* It also destroyed any possible intel we could have gotten from that compound!

I was just doing what we were sent here to do, sir.

Yeah well we have processes and procedures for a reason, King! So Marines and innocent people don't get *fucking killed!*

Innocent people have *already* been killed, sir. We don't have time for processes and procedures.

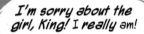

I'm sorry about the girl, King! I *really* am!

...But this can't be about *revenge*, it has to be about the *mission!*

If it is *revenge* or the *mission* that drives me to kill more Taliban, then I don't see what difference it makes to you.

I don't have time for this. I think you and your squad have been through a lot over the last few weeks and you need to take a few days off. Consider your squad grounded until further notice.

You're dismissed.

Sir.

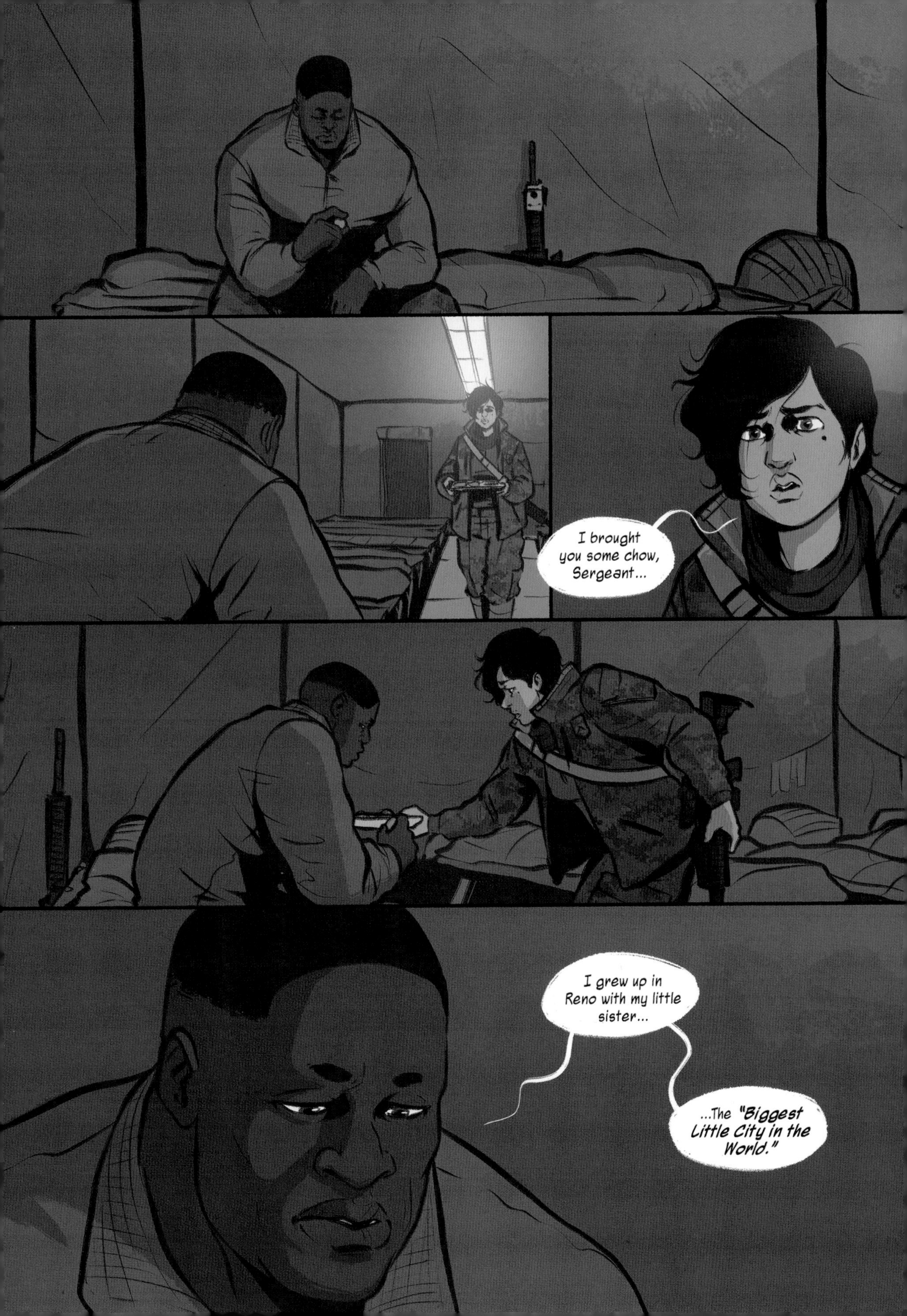
I brought you some chow, Sergeant...
I grew up in Reno with my little sister...
...The "Biggest Little City in the World."

My dad ran off when I was about three. I don't remember him much at all. My mom wasn't much better. I was about ten when she got arrested for meth or turning tricks... or both.
...The state took both me and my sister.
My mom's sister... My aunt... Only other family we had... She lived in Florida. She tried to get custody of us but the state said she wasn't financially stable enough 'cause she was trying to work her way through college.
So we got put in with this foster family in Reno. White couple, big house, the guy worked for the city or something. It seemed too good to be true. Everything was fine for the first few weeks...
...'til he started putting his hands on us. First it was just a slap here, spanking there. Then the belt... then the fist.
He would always find some reason to justify it to himself, and us. He was real particular about cleaning, made us keep the place ***spotless.*** He had this... ***metal urn*** that had his daddy's ashes in it. It was the first thing he checked when he came home, and if it had dust on it or wasn't perfect on the shelf... we'd pay for it.

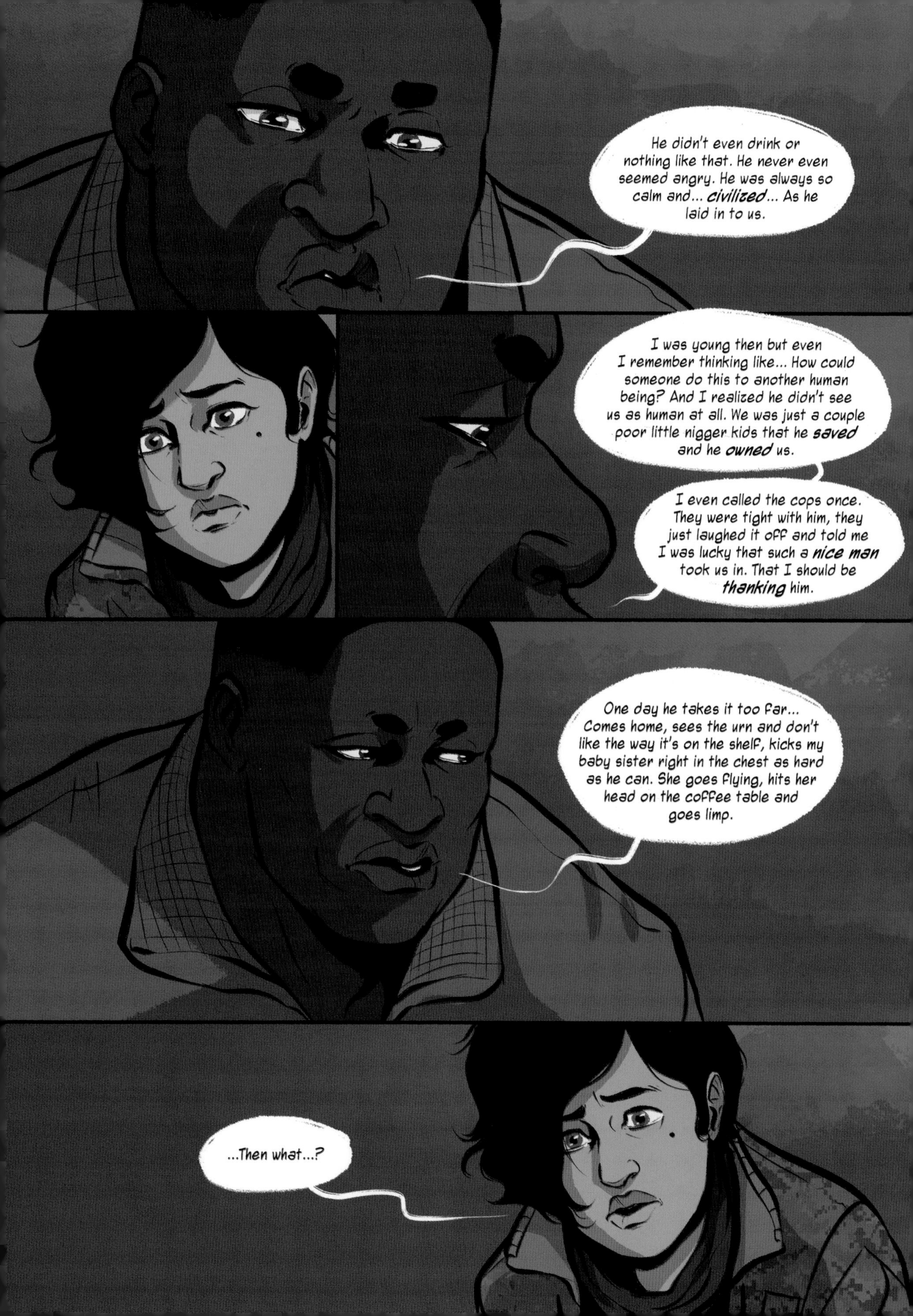
He didn't even drink or nothing like that. He never even seemed angry. He was always so calm and... *civilized*... As he laid in to us.
I was young then but even I remember thinking like... How could someone do this to another human being? And I realized he didn't see us as human at all. We was just a couple poor little nigger kids that he *saved* and he *owned* us.
I even called the cops once. They were tight with him, they just laughed it off and told me I was lucky that such a *nice man* took us in. That I should be *thanking* him.
One day he takes it too far... Comes home, sees the urn and don't like the way it's on the shelf, kicks my baby sister right in the chest as hard as he can. She goes flying, hits her head on the coffee table and goes limp.
...Then what...?

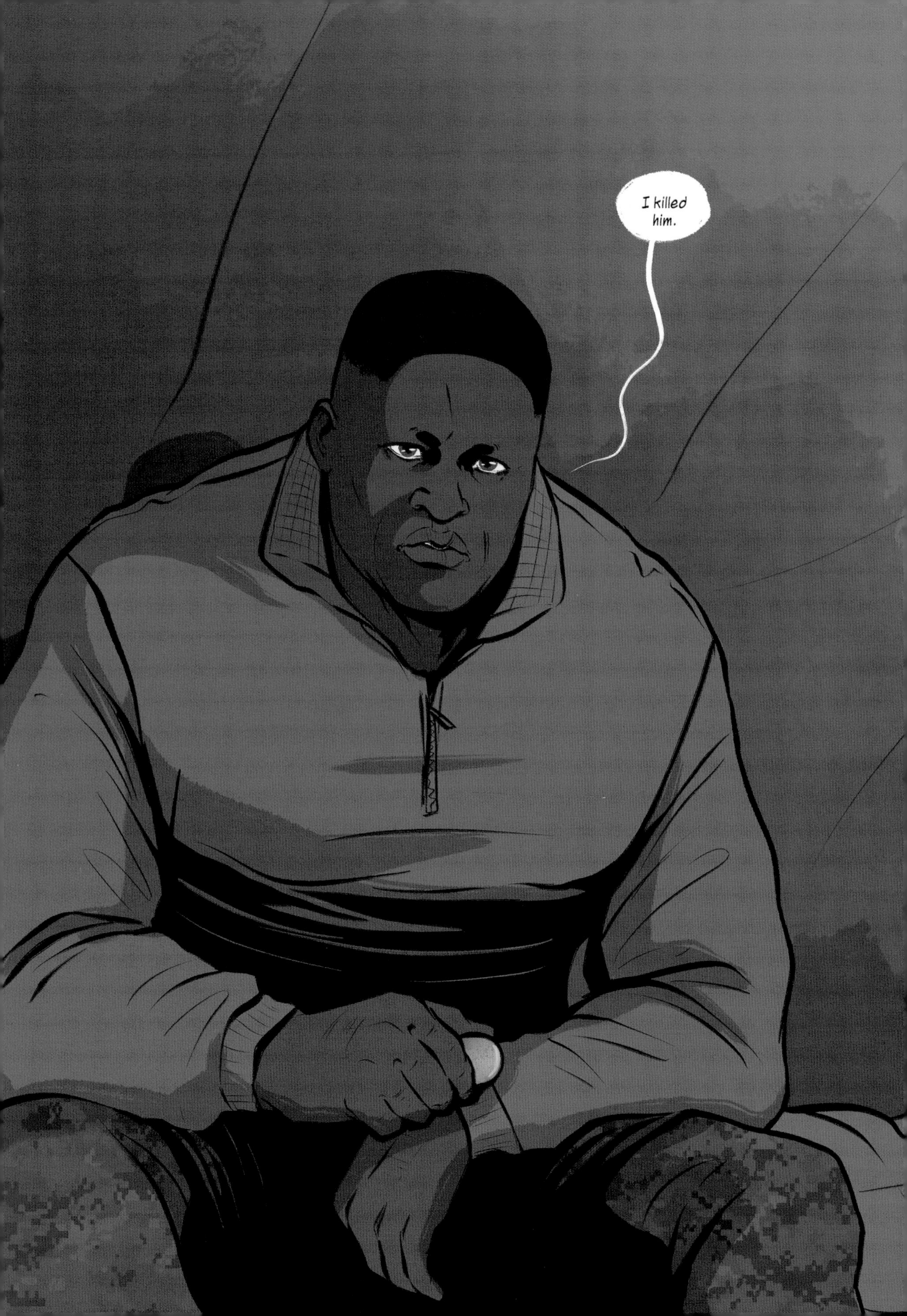
I killed him.

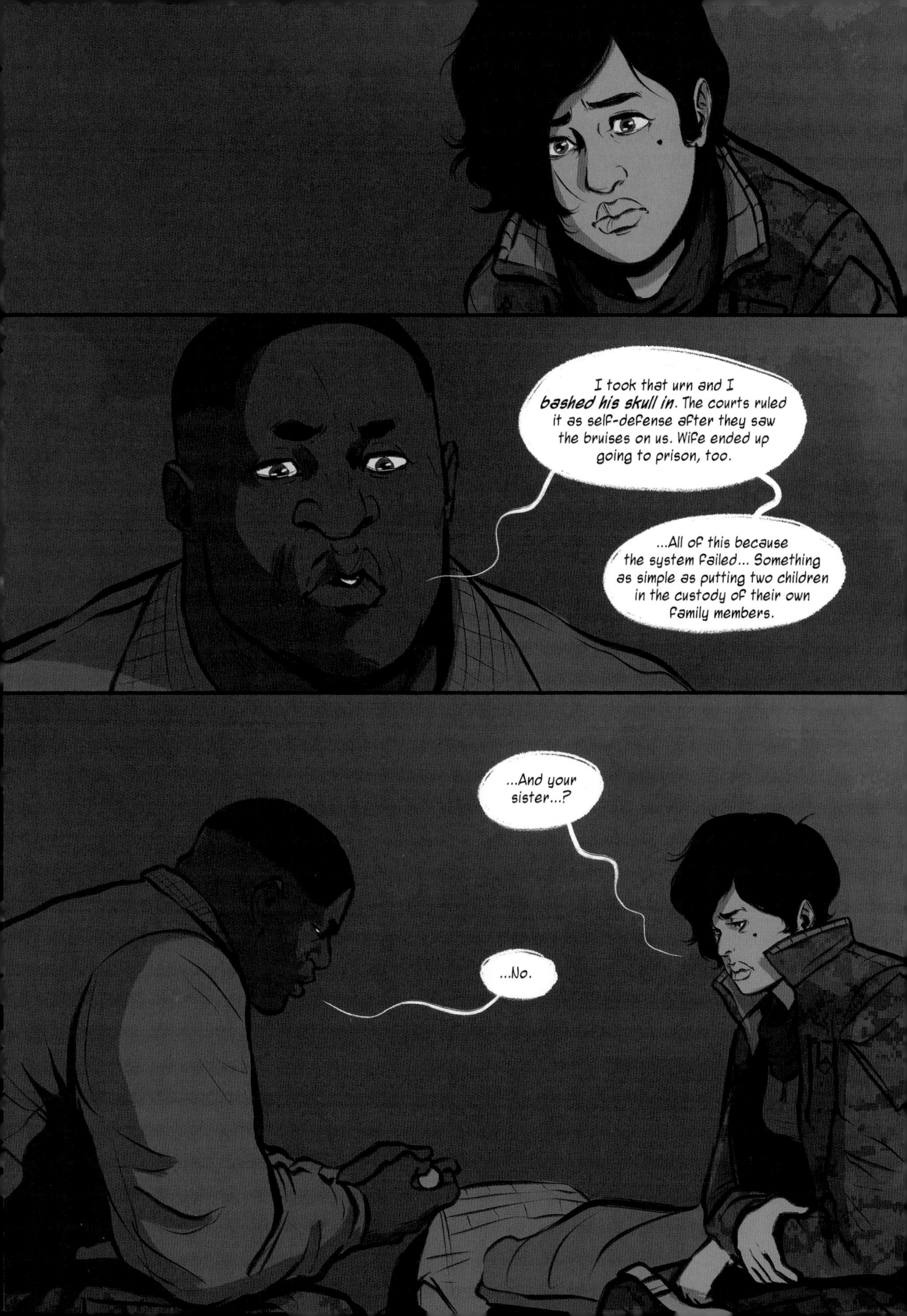
I took that urn and I ***bashed his skull in***. The courts ruled it as self-defense after they saw the bruises on us. Wife ended up going to prison, too.
...All of this because the system failed... Something as simple as putting two children in the custody of their own family members.
...And your sister...?
...No.

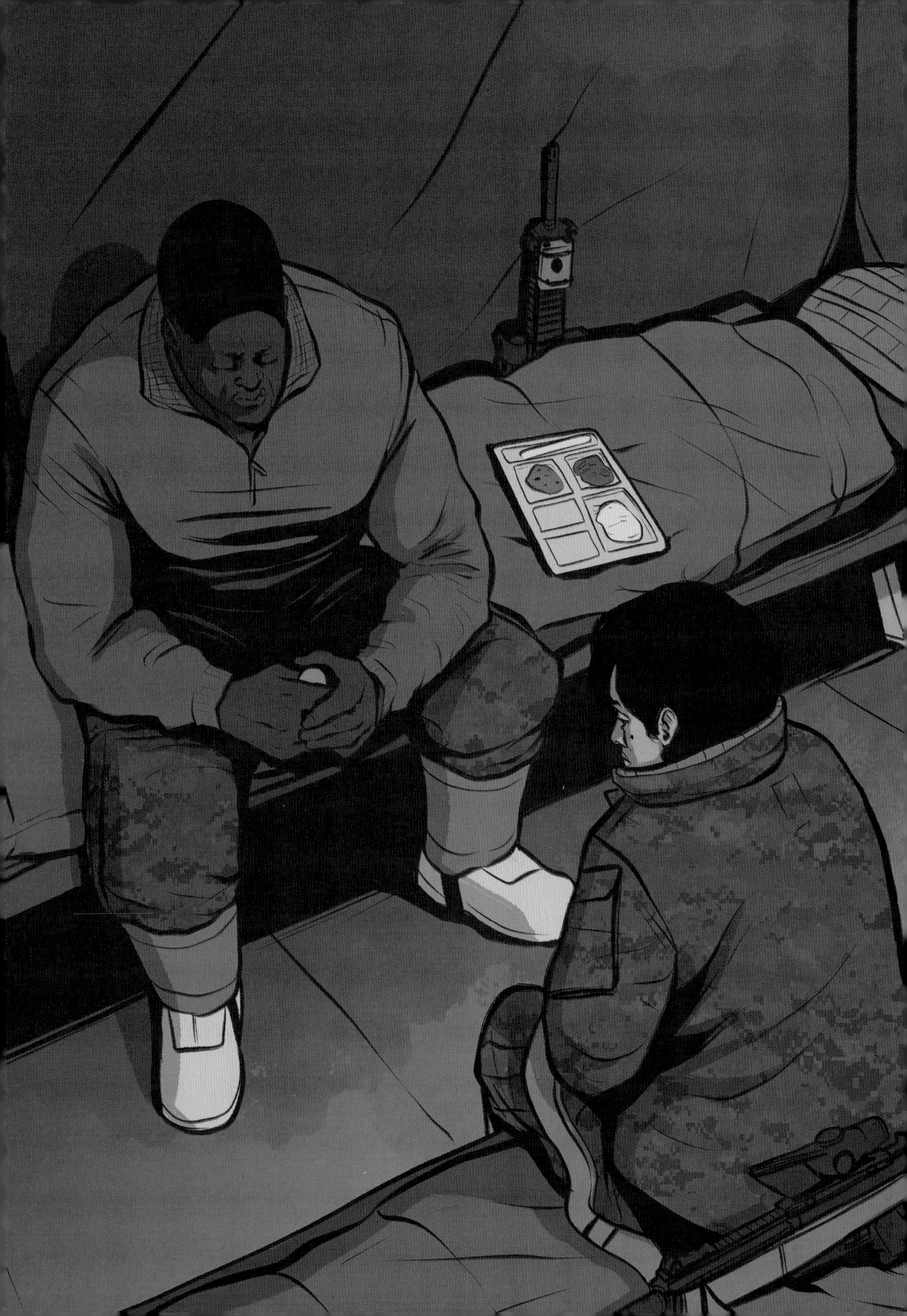

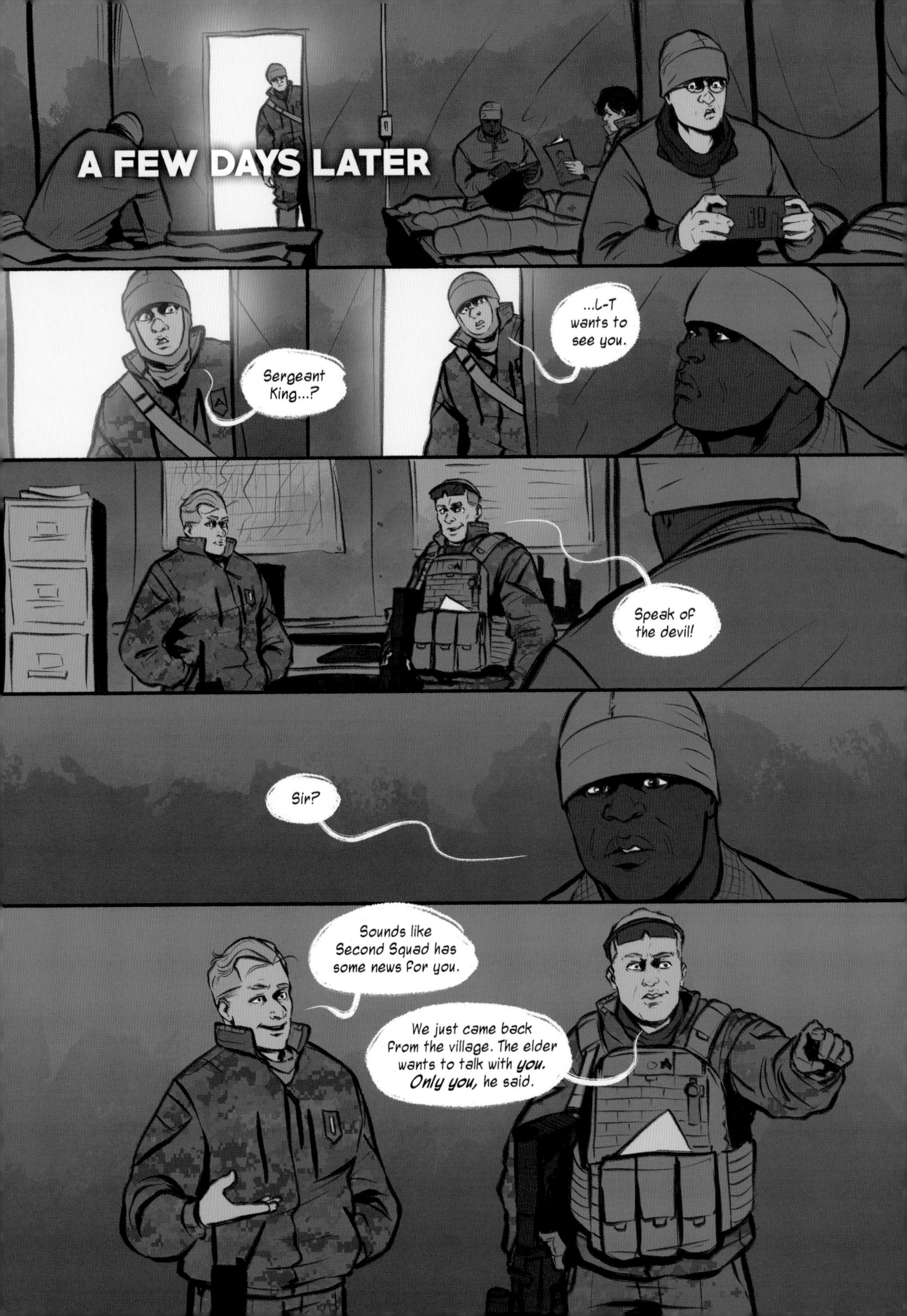
A FEW DAYS LATER
Sergeant King...?
...L-T wants to see you.
Speak of the devil!
Sir?
Sounds like Second Squad has some news for you.
We just came back from the village. The elder wants to talk with *you.* *Only you,* he said.

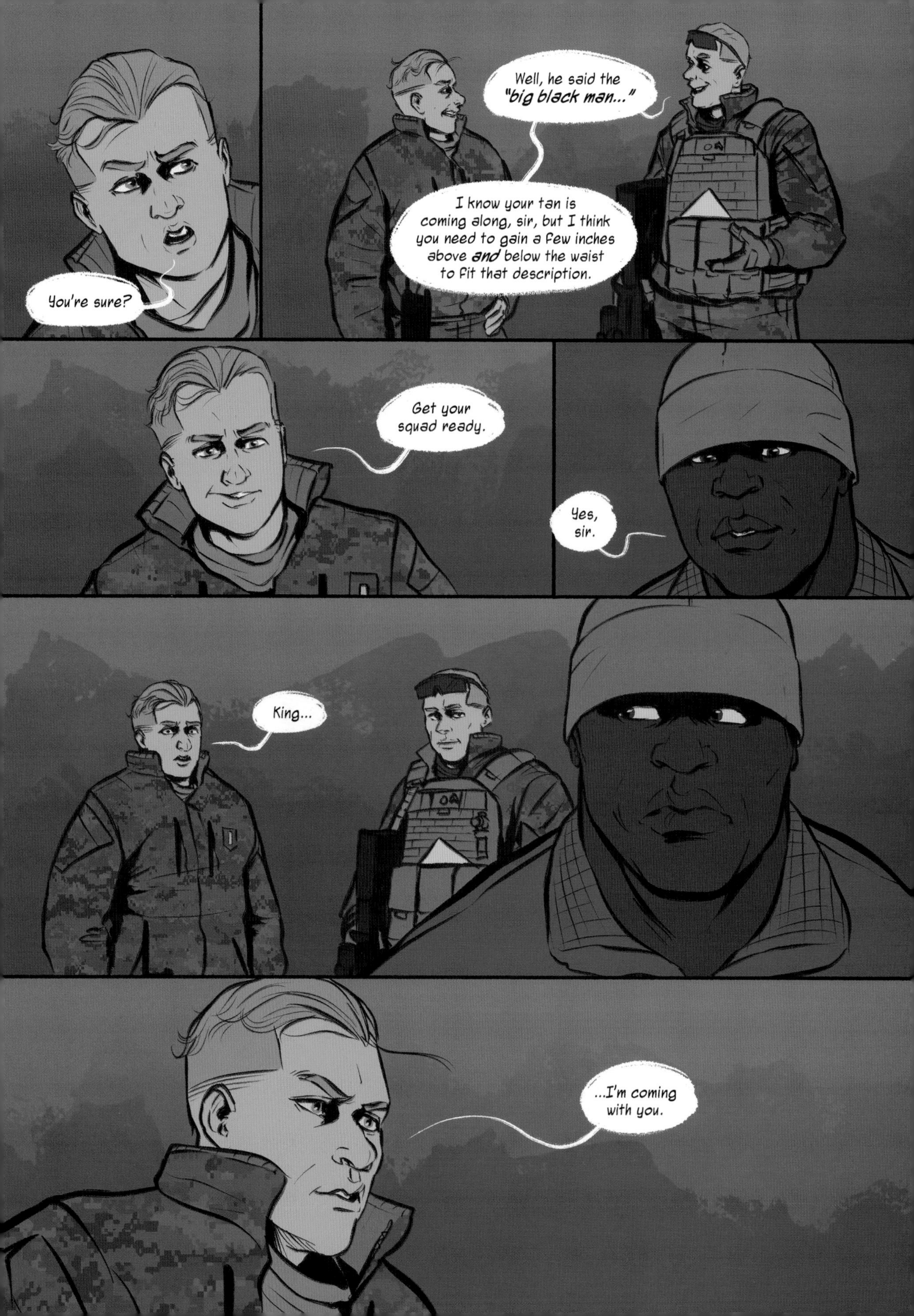
You're sure?
Well, he said the "big black man..."
I know your tan is coming along, sir, but I think you need to gain a few inches above *and* below the waist to fit that description.
Get your squad ready.
Yes, sir.
King...
...I'm coming with you.

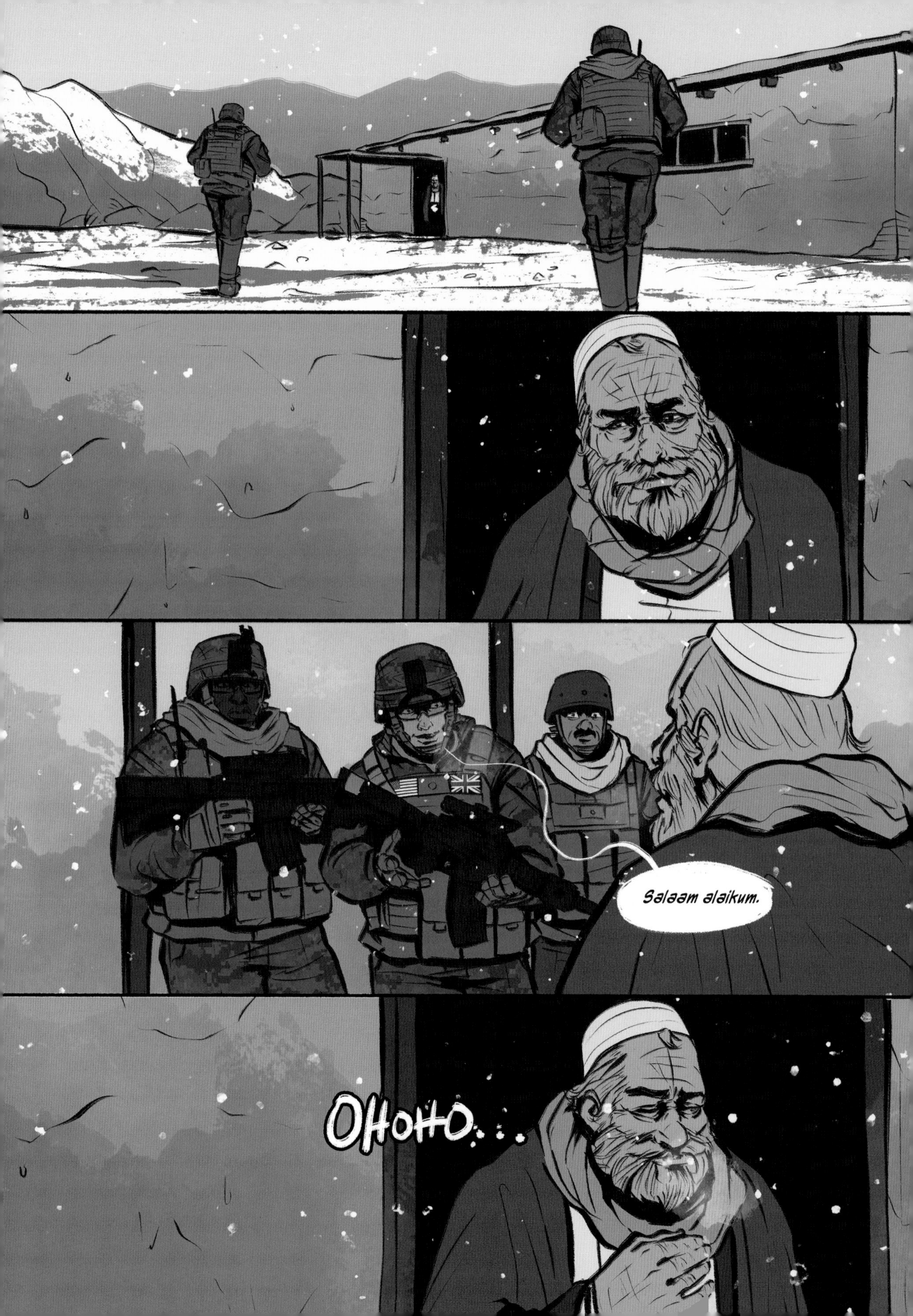
Salaam alaikum.
OHOHO...

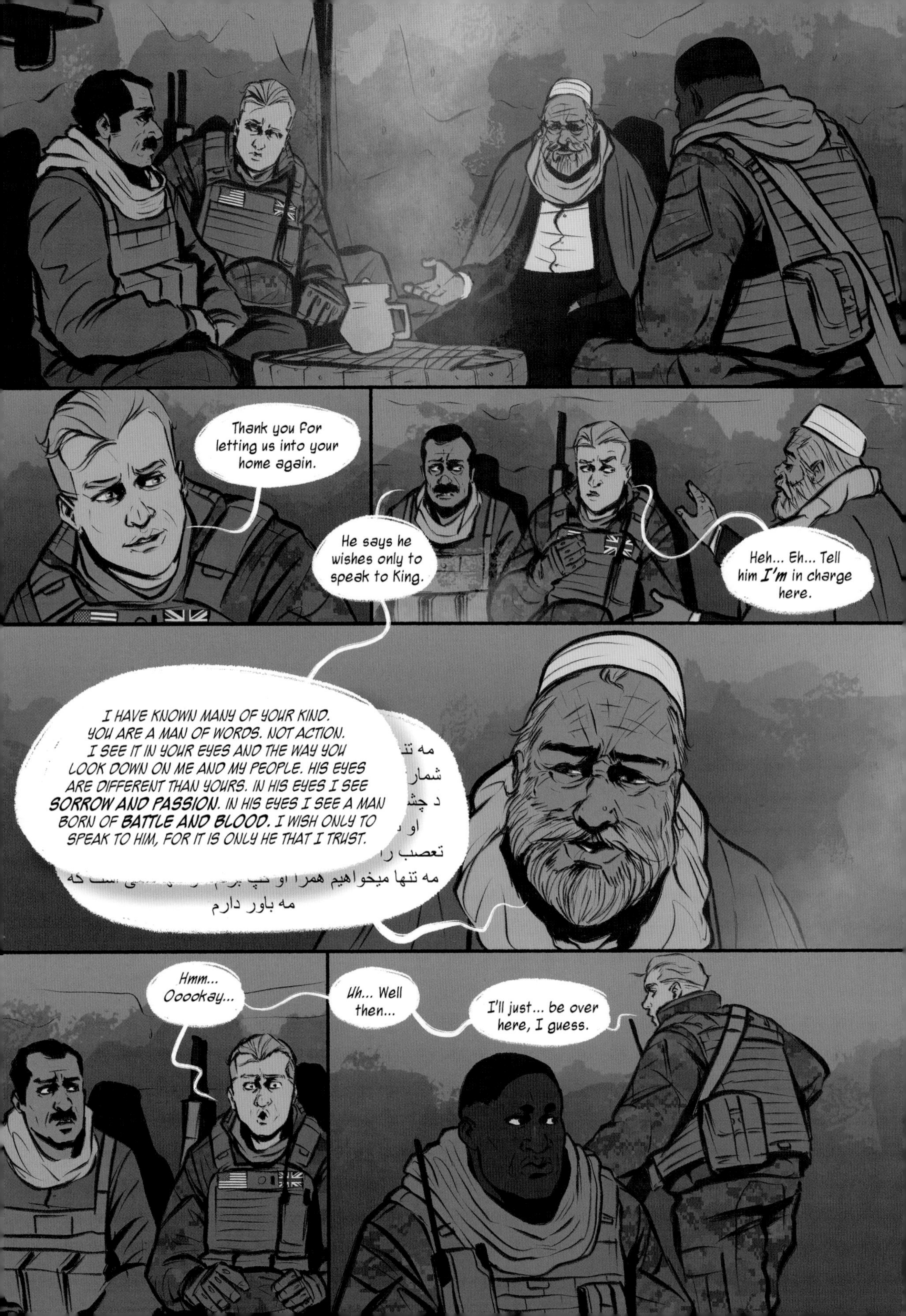
Thank you for letting us into your home again.
He says he wishes only to speak to King.
Heh... Eh... Tell him *I'm* in charge here.
I HAVE KNOWN MANY OF YOUR KIND. YOU ARE A MAN OF WORDS. NOT ACTION. I SEE IT IN YOUR EYES AND THE WAY YOU LOOK DOWN ON ME AND MY PEOPLE. HIS EYES ARE DIFFERENT THAN YOURS. IN HIS EYES I SEE **SORROW AND PASSION**. IN HIS EYES I SEE A MAN BORN OF **BATTLE AND BLOOD.** I WISH ONLY TO SPEAK TO HIM, FOR IT IS ONLY HE THAT I TRUST.
مه باور دارم
Hmm... Ooookay...
Uh... Well then...
I'll just... be over here, I guess.

HUFF

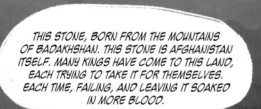

THIS STONE, BORN FROM THE MOUNTAINS OF BADAKHSHAN. THIS STONE IS AFGHANISTAN ITSELF. MANY KINGS HAVE COME TO THIS LAND, EACH TRYING TO TAKE IT FOR THEMSELVES. EACH TIME, FAILING, AND LEAVING IT SOAKED IN MORE BLOOD.

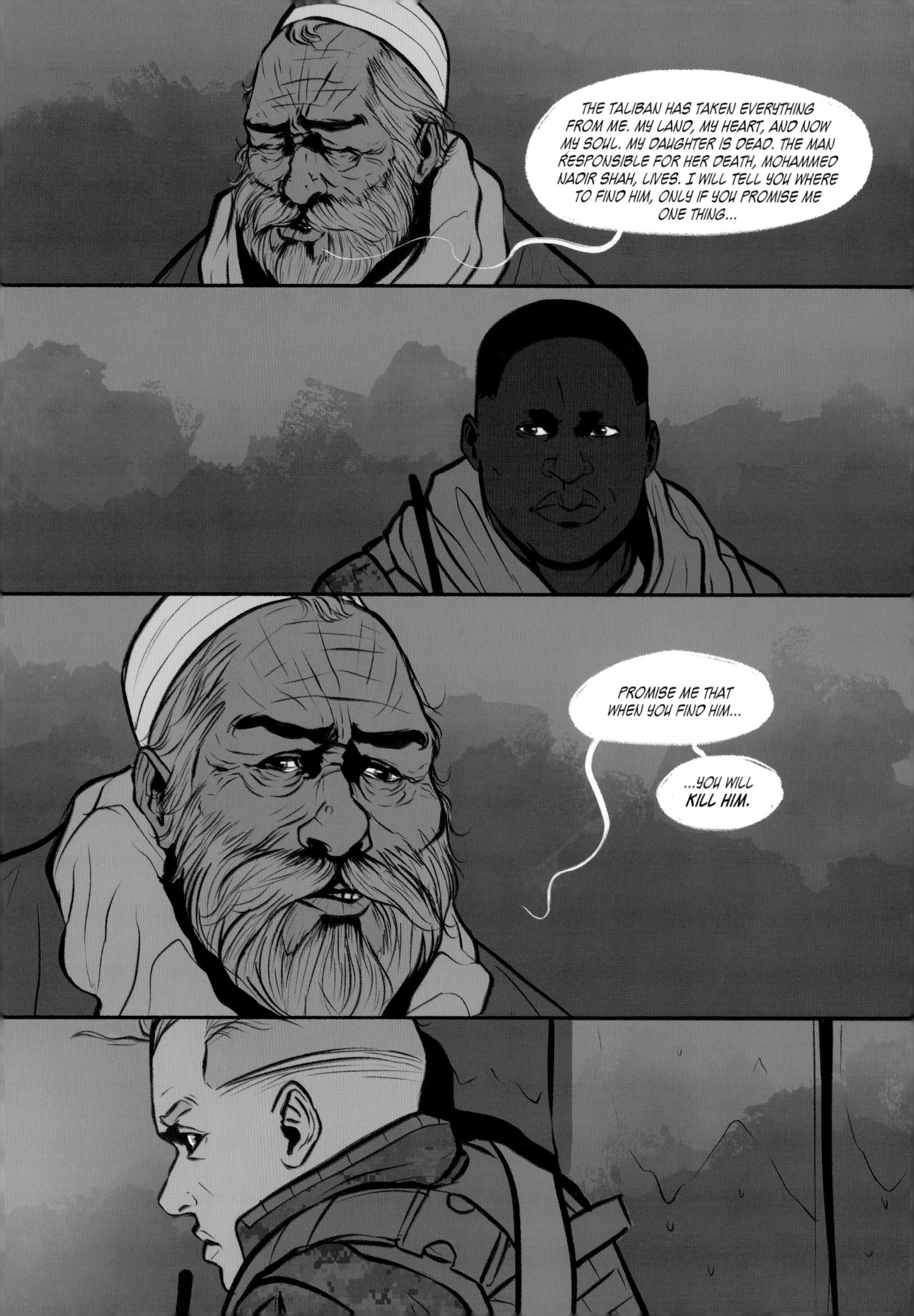
THE TALIBAN HAS TAKEN EVERYTHING FROM ME. MY LAND, MY HEART, AND NOW MY SOUL. MY DAUGHTER IS DEAD. THE MAN RESPONSIBLE FOR HER DEATH, MOHAMMED NADIR SHAH, LIVES. I WILL TELL YOU WHERE TO FIND HIM, ONLY IF YOU PROMISE ME ONE THING...
PROMISE ME THAT WHEN YOU FIND HIM...
...YOU WILL **KILL HIM.**

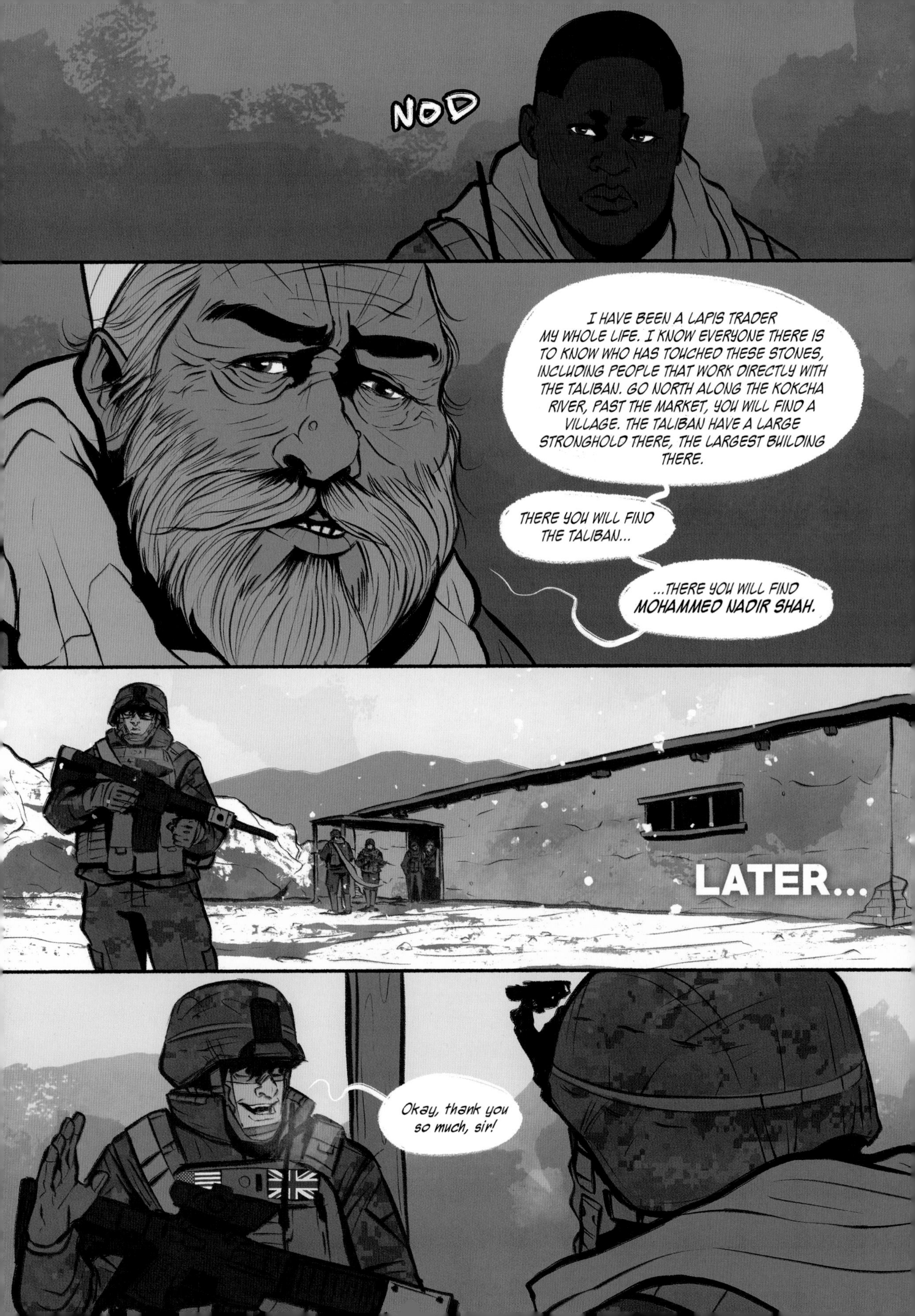
NOD
I HAVE BEEN A LAPIS TRADER MY WHOLE LIFE. I KNOW EVERYONE THERE IS TO KNOW WHO HAS TOUCHED THESE STONES, INCLUDING PEOPLE THAT WORK DIRECTLY WITH THE TALIBAN. GO NORTH ALONG THE KOKCHA RIVER, PAST THE MARKET, YOU WILL FIND A VILLAGE. THE TALIBAN HAVE A LARGE STRONGHOLD THERE, THE LARGEST BUILDING THERE.
THERE YOU WILL FIND THE TALIBAN...
...THERE YOU WILL FIND MOHAMMED NADIR SHAH.
LATER...
Okay, thank you so much, sir!

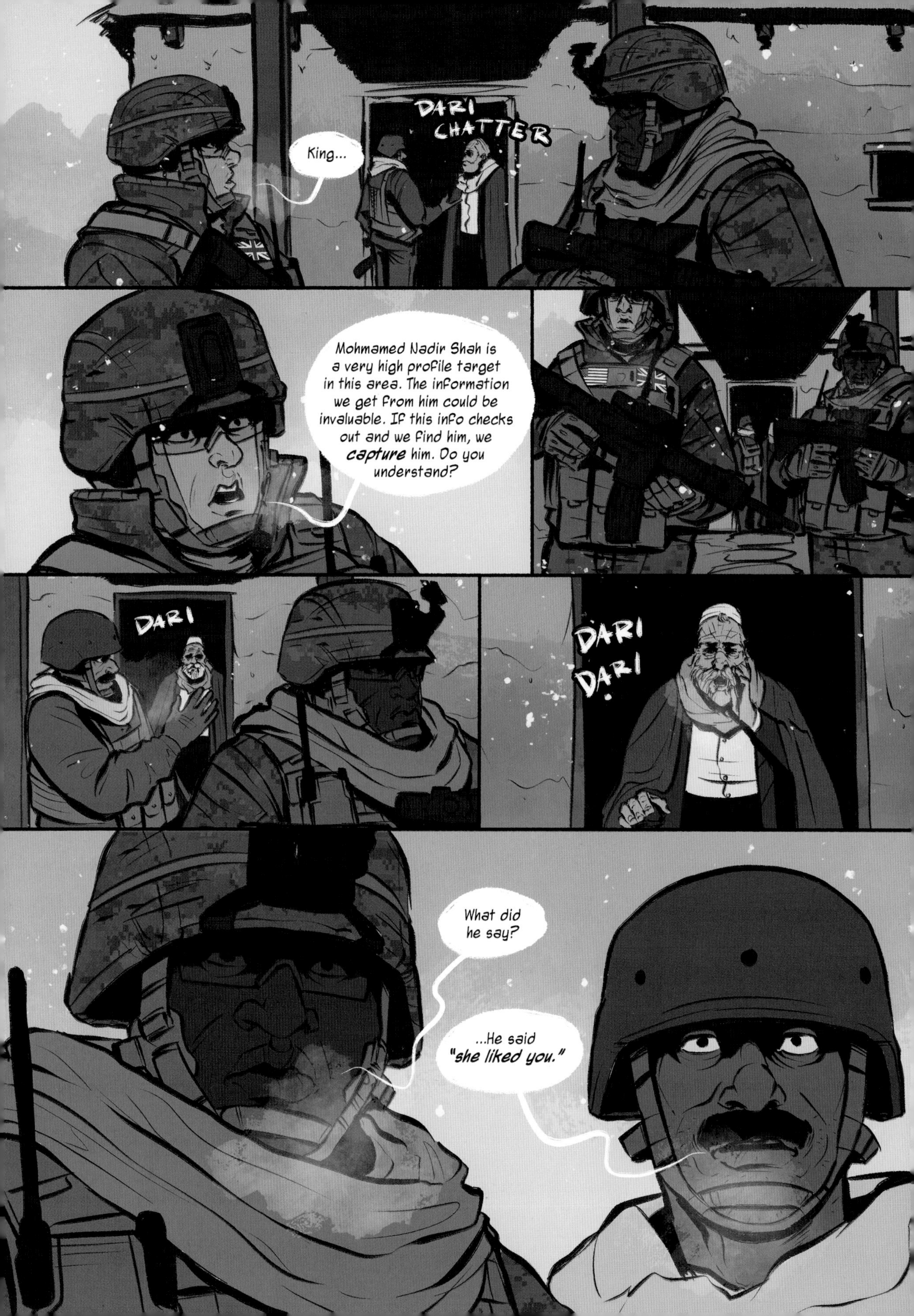
DARI CHATTER
King...
Mohmamed Nadir Shah is a very high profile target in this area. The information we get from him could be invaluable. If this info checks out and we find him, we *capture* him. Do you understand?
DARI
DARI DARI
What did he say?
...He said *"she liked you."*

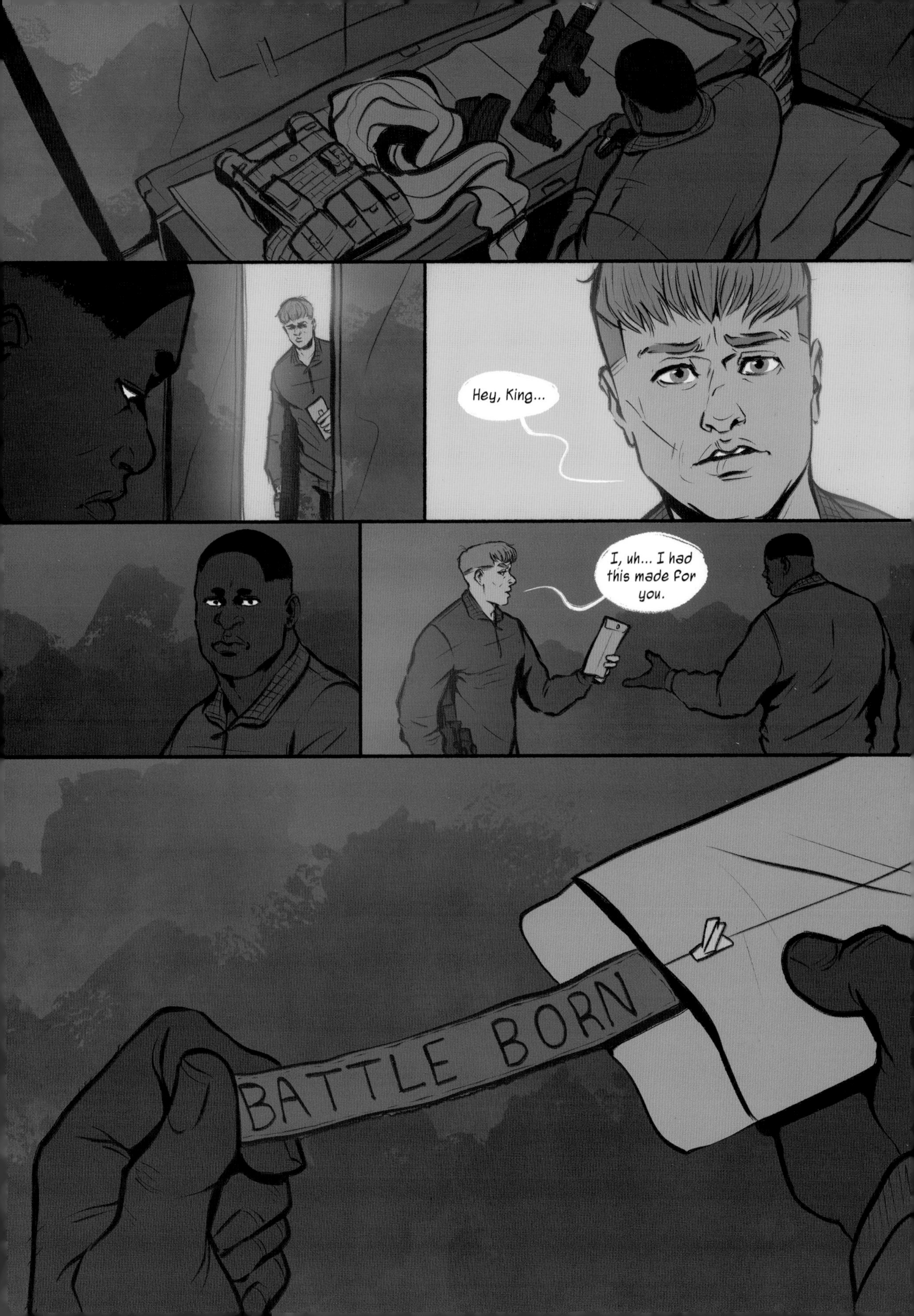
Hey, King...
I, uh... I had this made for you.
BATTLE BORN

I, uh... I just wanted to say sorry for being such an asshole before.
You know why they call Nevada the **Battle Born** state? It gained statehood during the Civil War. It was born in the middle of all of that.
I'm not gonna sit here and suck your dick, but even I know the Civil War was fucked. I know the Confederacy was on the wrong side of history. My family fought and died for it... but I have to respect anyone willing to fight for something. Even if they're wrong.
And I've seen you fight, King. Hell, you **whooped my ass!**
I just wanted you to know that I respect the hell out of that, and um...
Look, I know I'm just a dumb fuckin' redneck, and me and you here, we aint gonna like... **cure racism** or whatever. But also...
HA HA

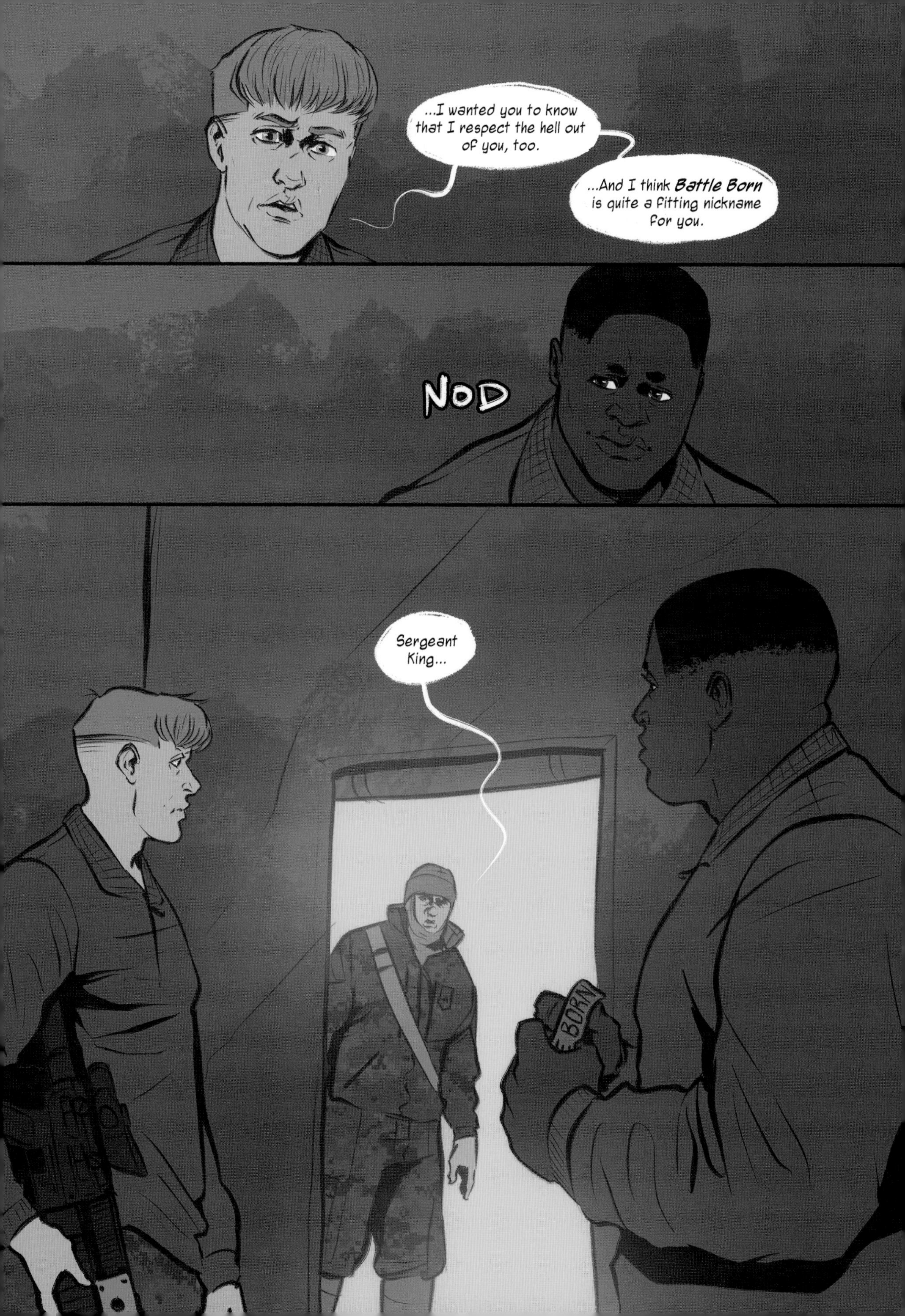
...I wanted you to know that I respect the hell out of you, too.
...And I think *Battle Born* is quite a fitting nickname for you.
NOD
Sergeant King...
BORN

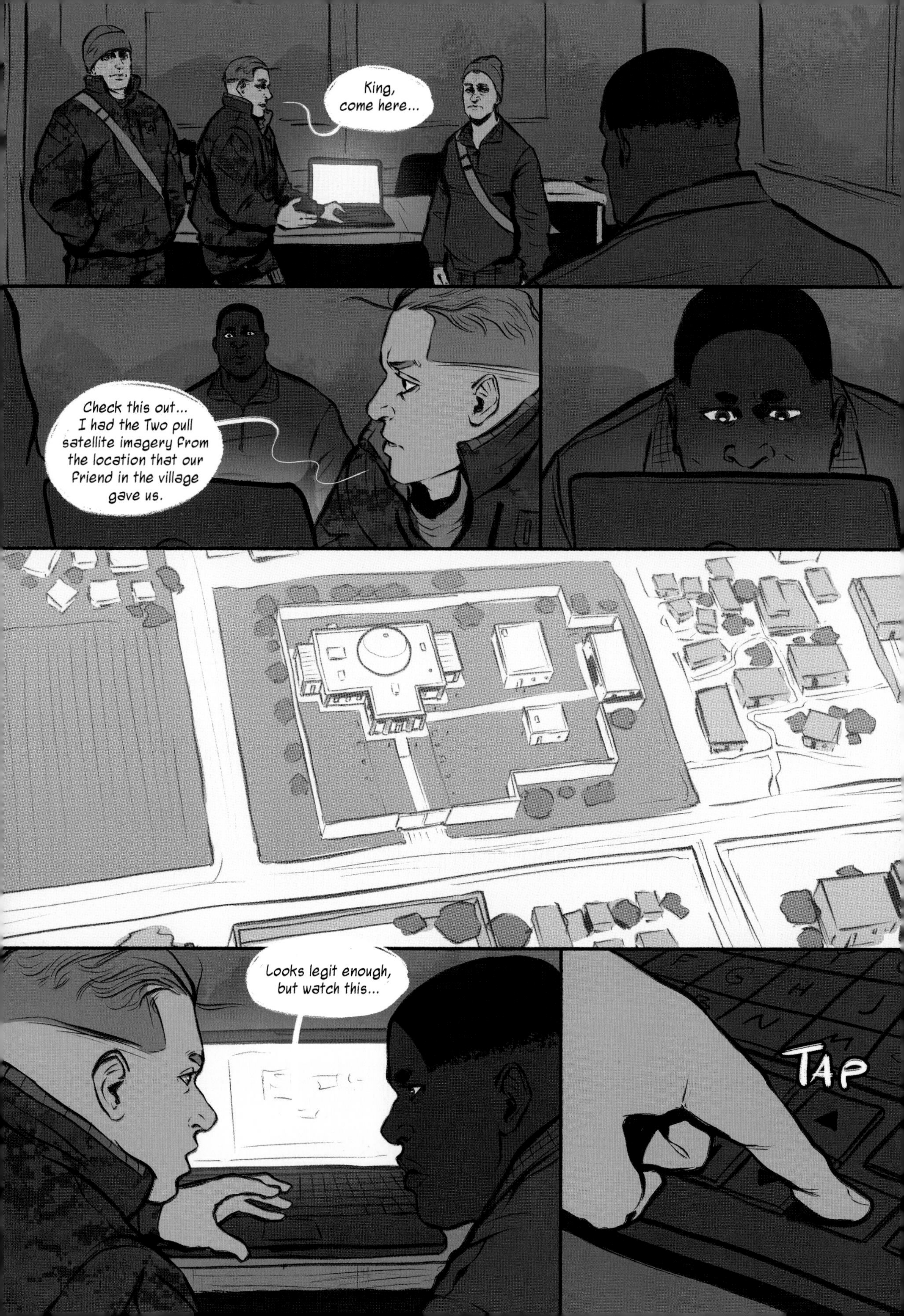
King, come here...
Check this out... I had the Two pull satellite imagery from the location that our friend in the village gave us.
Looks legit enough, but watch this...
TAP

TAP

TAP

We see lots of horses coming in and out of this place, but this footage was taken about an hour after your airstrike blew up the other compound.

Intel says this compound is likely run by another high value target as well. They took in Nadir Shah after his stronghold was destroyed. We've been monitoring it and it looks like he hasn't left yet. If we strike now, we could get two for the price of one, gents.

This place is big, sir. It's gonna take the whole platoon to take it down.

Nothing we can't handle. If we hit 'em hard and fast they won't be able to stop us. If we get 'guns and scout snipers on overwatch, have one squad set outside on security and QRF... One or two squads on the inside could easily take this place. Kill every one of these bearded fucks.

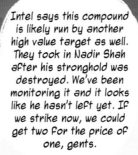

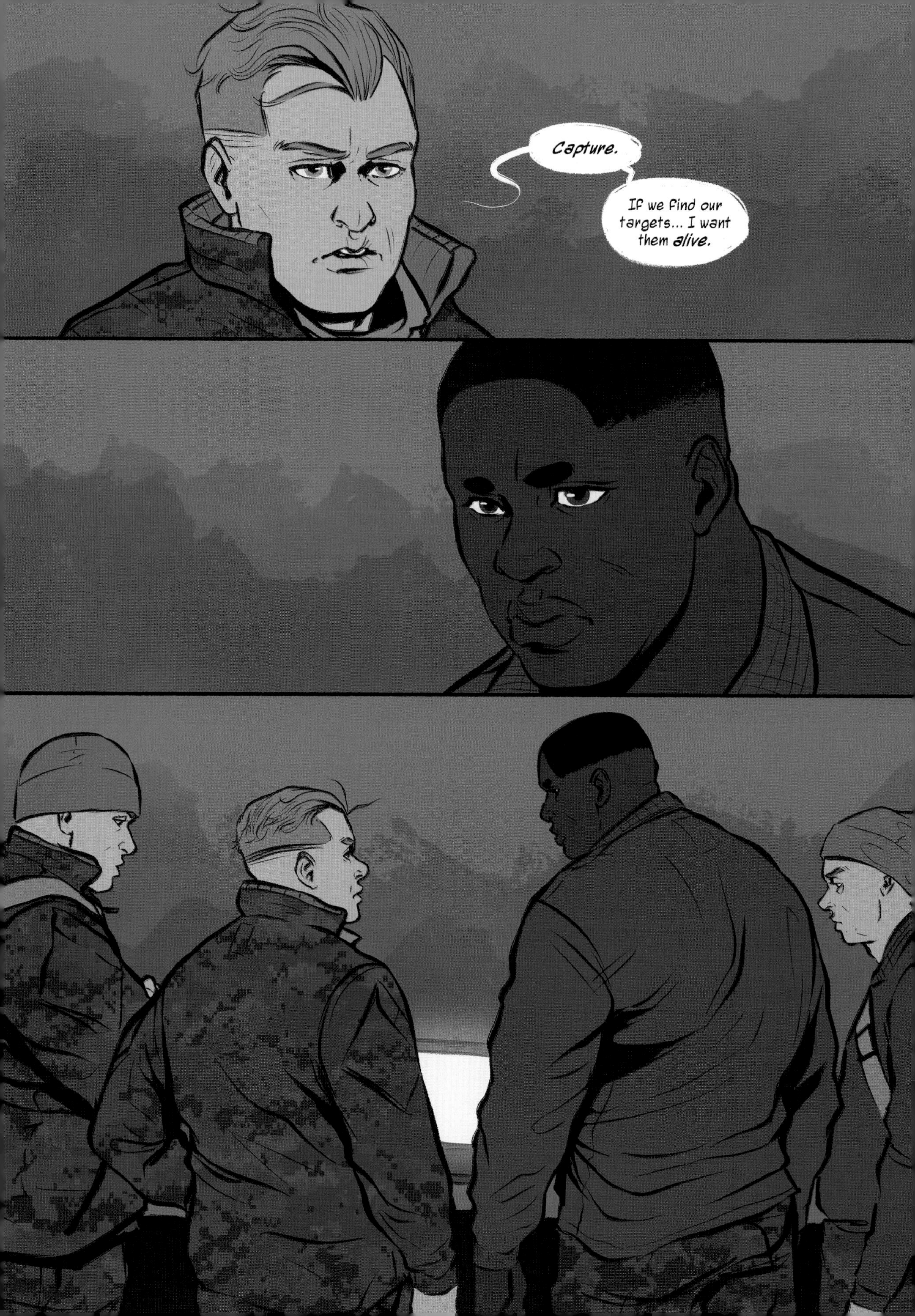
Capture.
If we find our targets... I want them *alive.*

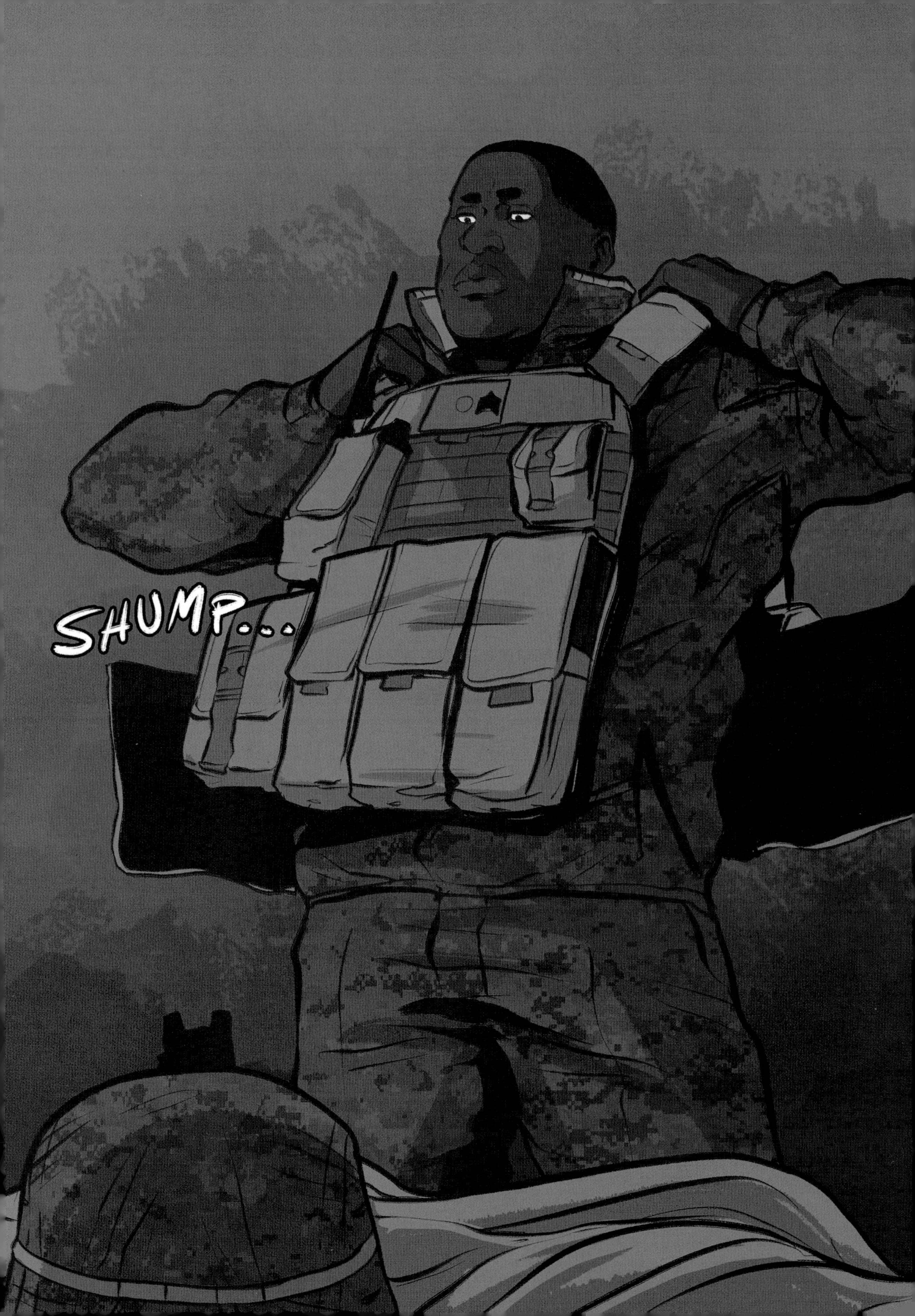
SHUMP...

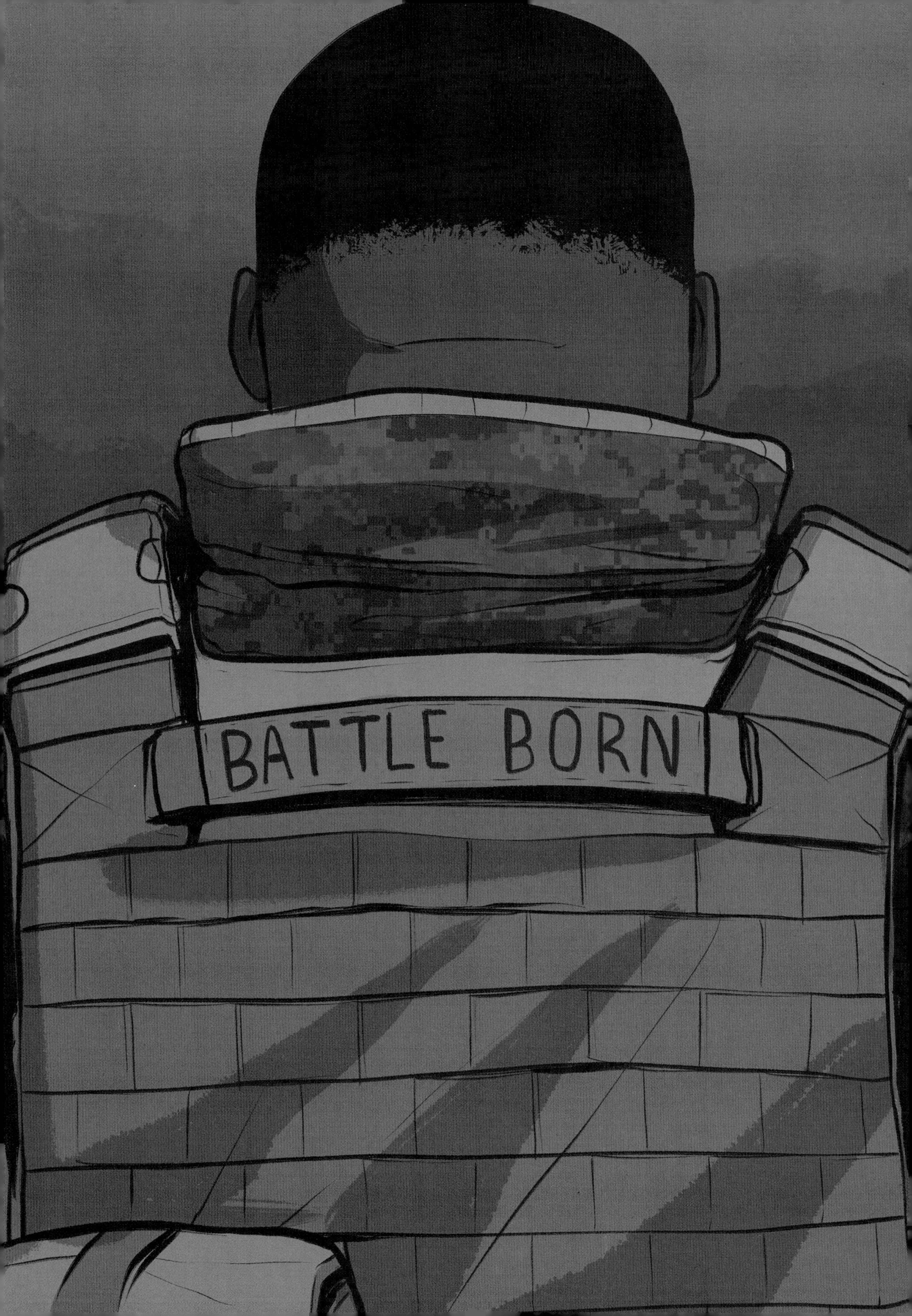
BATTLE BORN

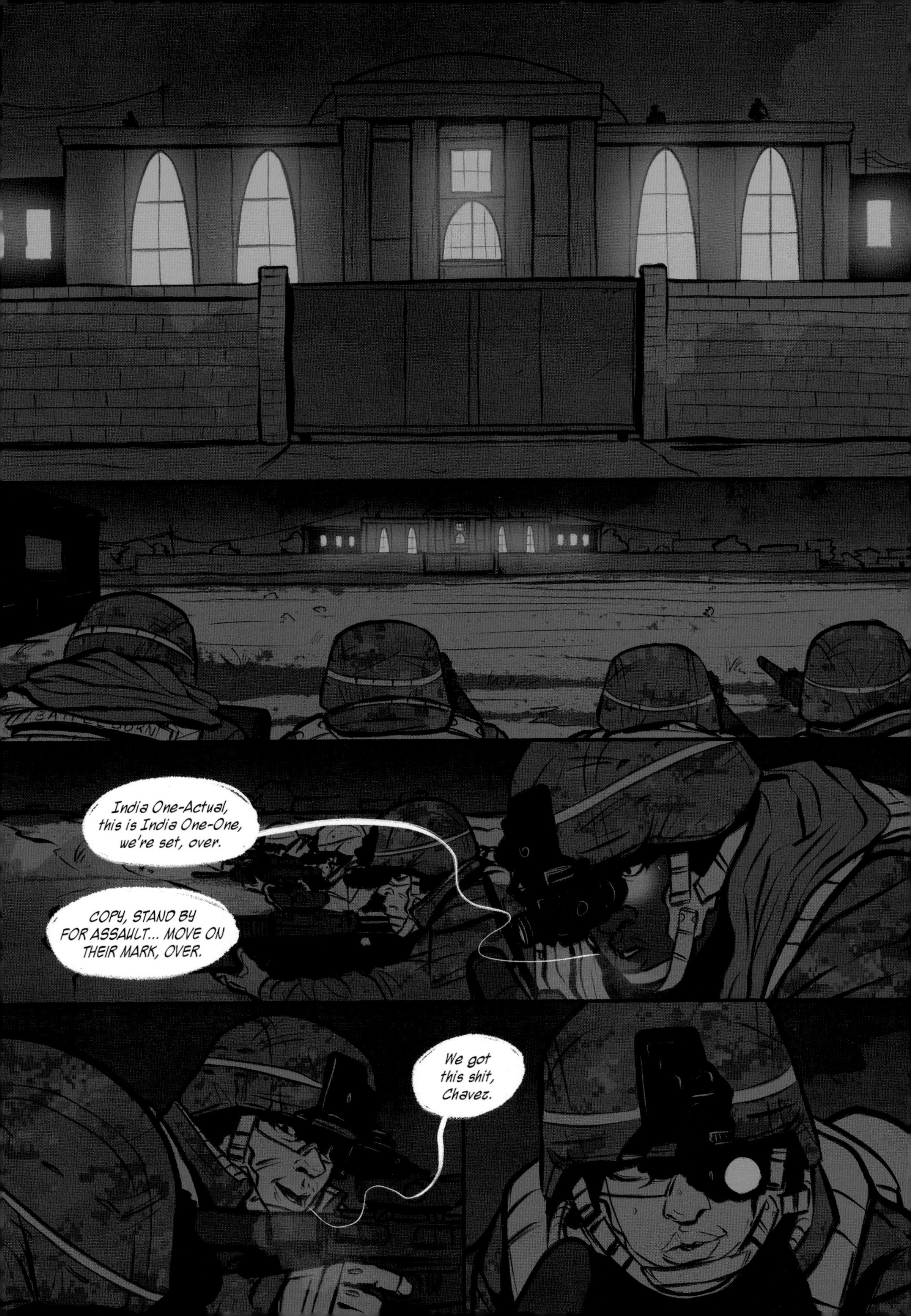
India One-Actual, this is India One-One, we're set, over.
COPY, STAND BY FOR ASSAULT... MOVE ON THEIR MARK, OVER.
We got this shit, Chavez.

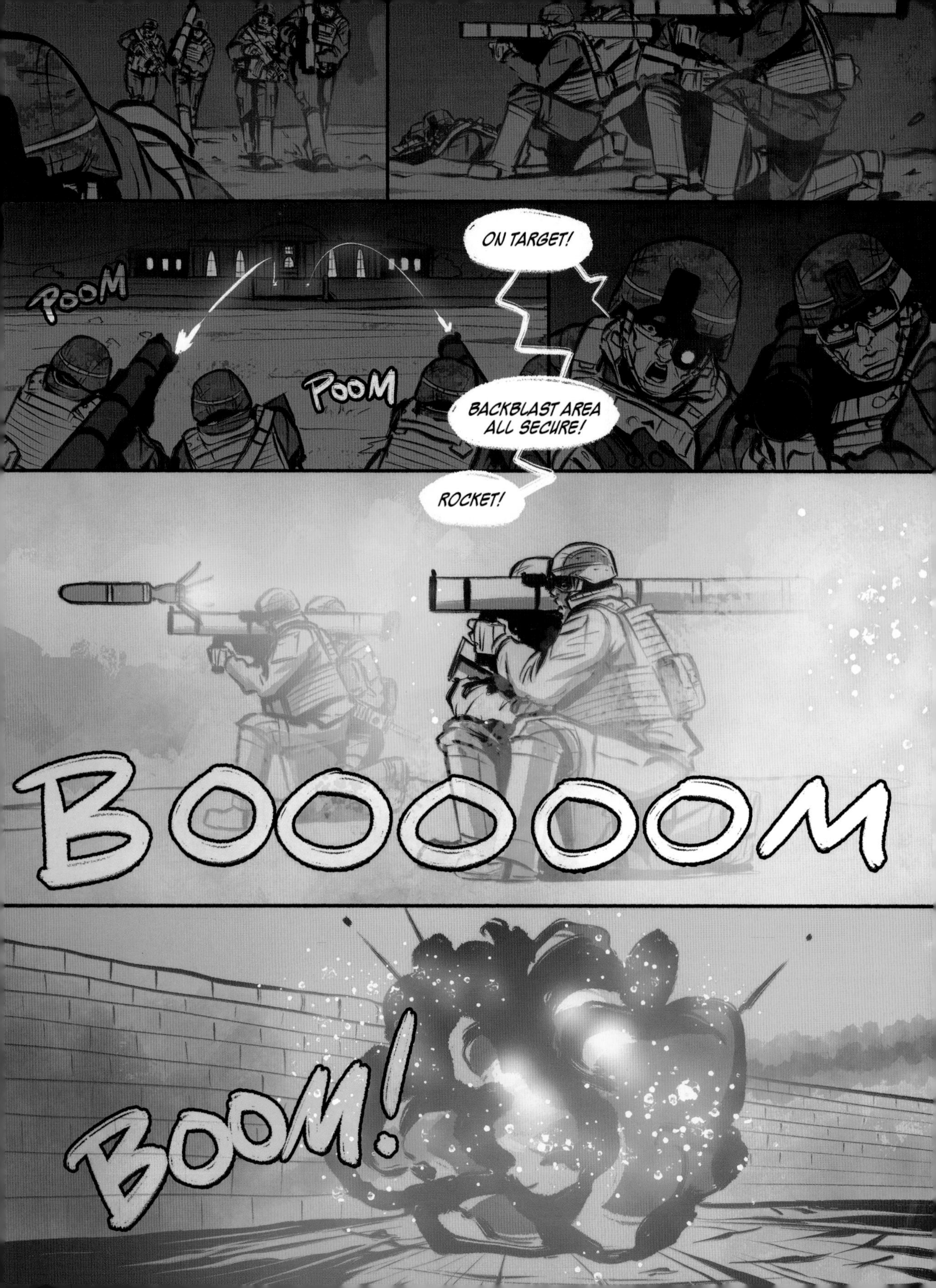
POOM
POOM
ON TARGET!
BACKBLAST AREA ALL SECURE!
ROCKET!
BOOOOOM
BOOM!

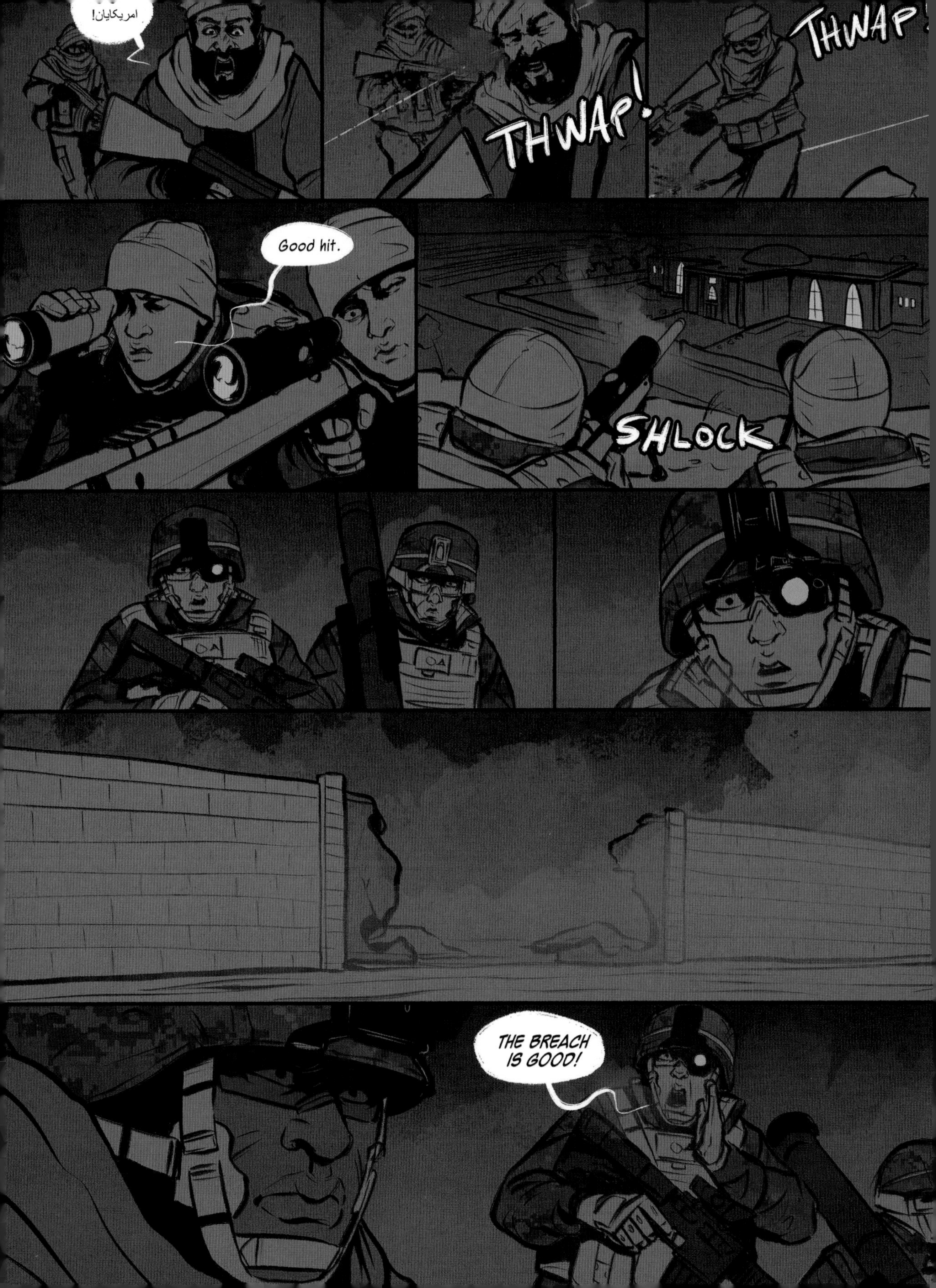
امریکایان!
THWAP!
THWAP!
Good hit.
SHLOCK
THE BREACH IS GOOD!

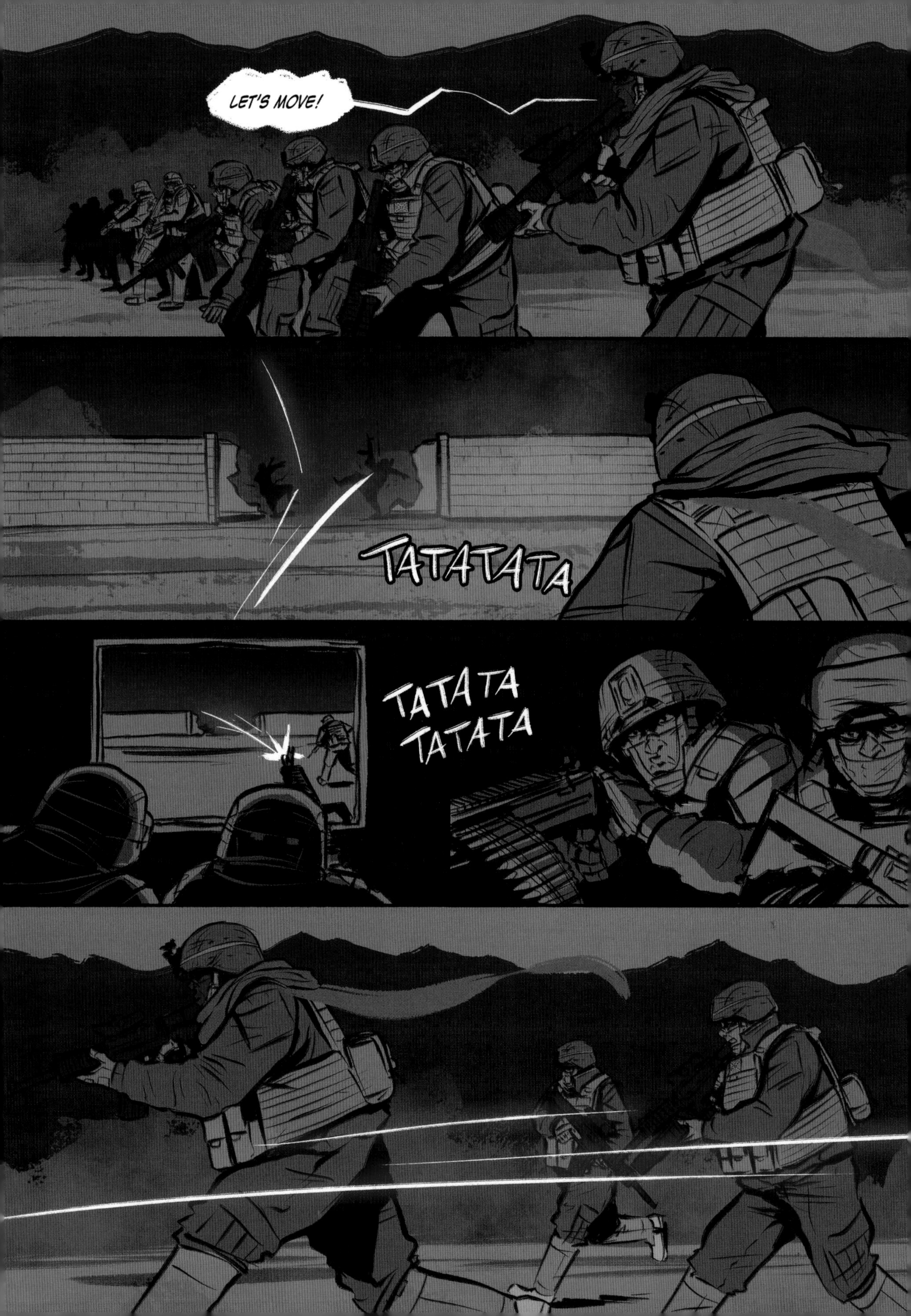
LET'S MOVE!
TATATATA
TATATA
TATATA

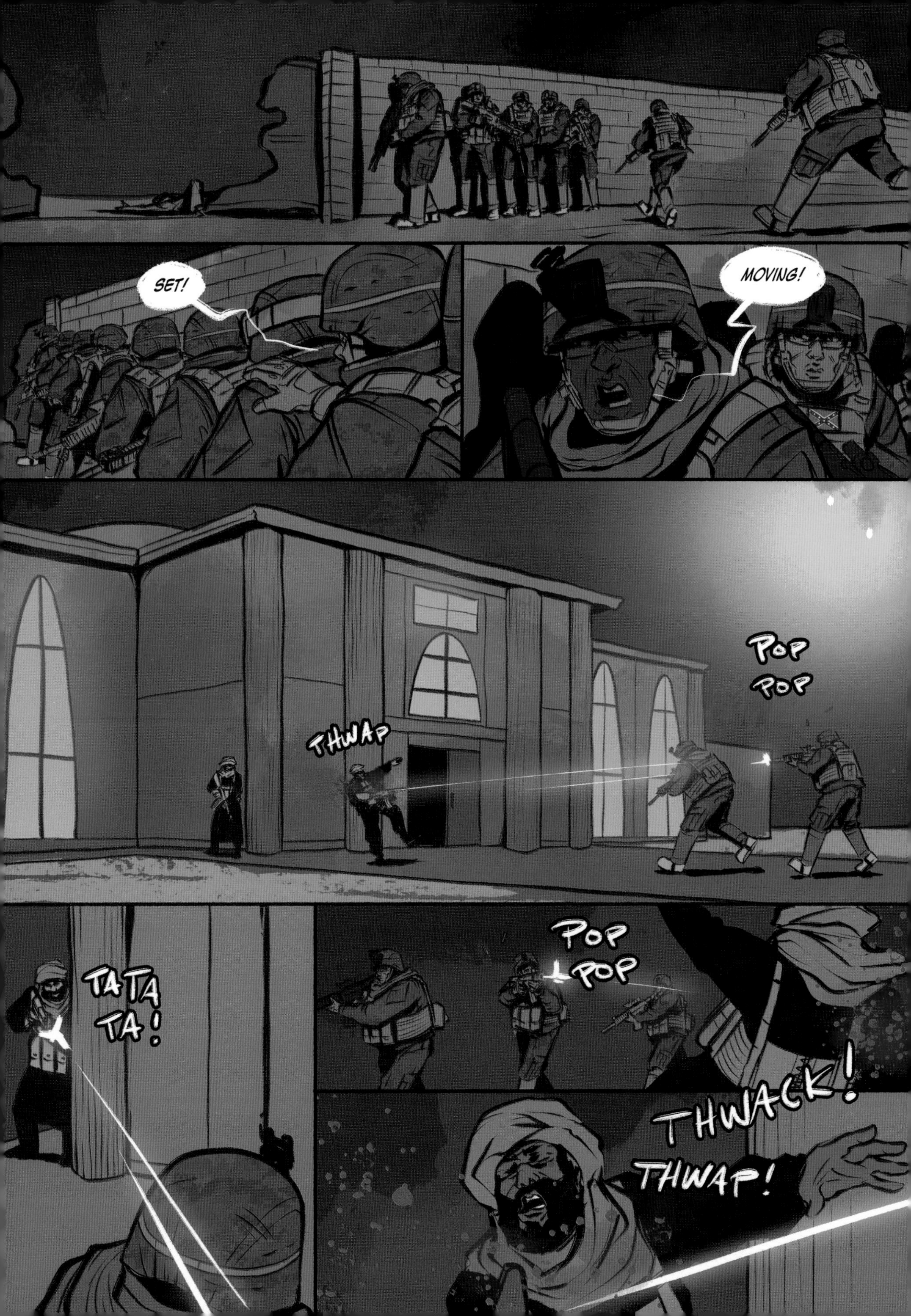
SET!
MOVING!
THWAP
POP
POP
TATA
TA!
POP
POP
THWACK!
THWAP!

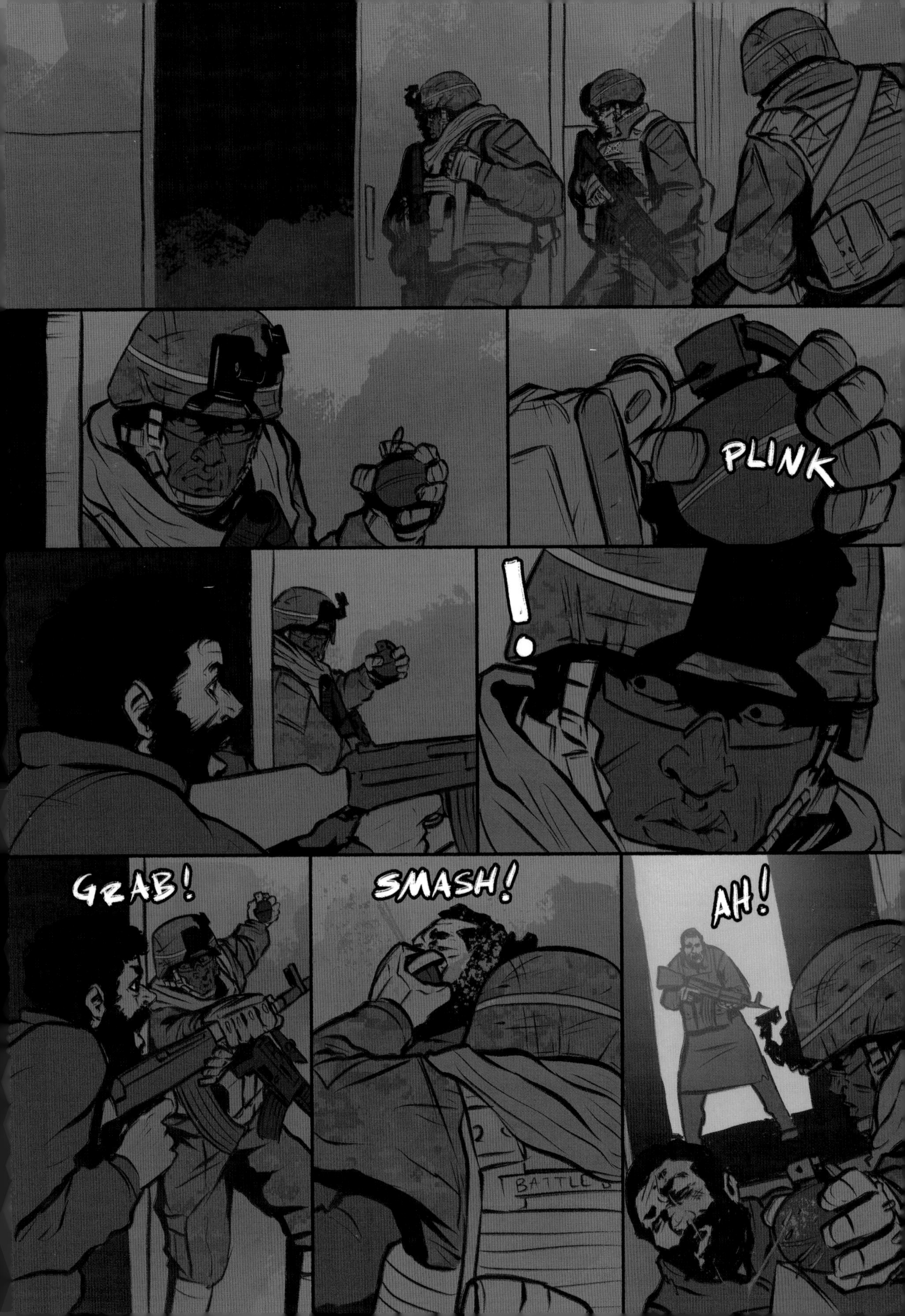
PLINK
!
GRAB!
SMASH!
AH!

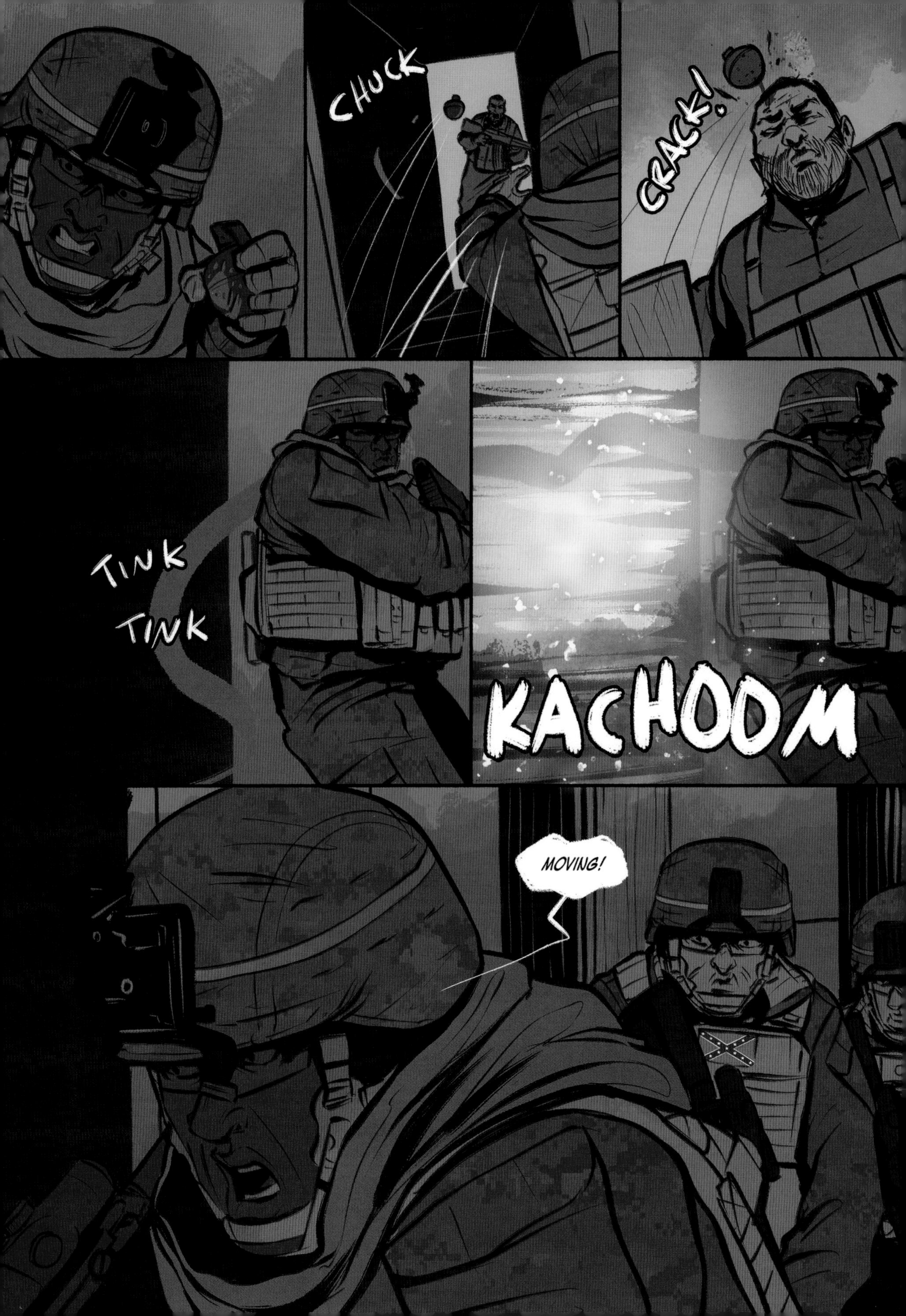
CHUCK
CRACK!
TINK
TINK
KACHOOM
MOVING!

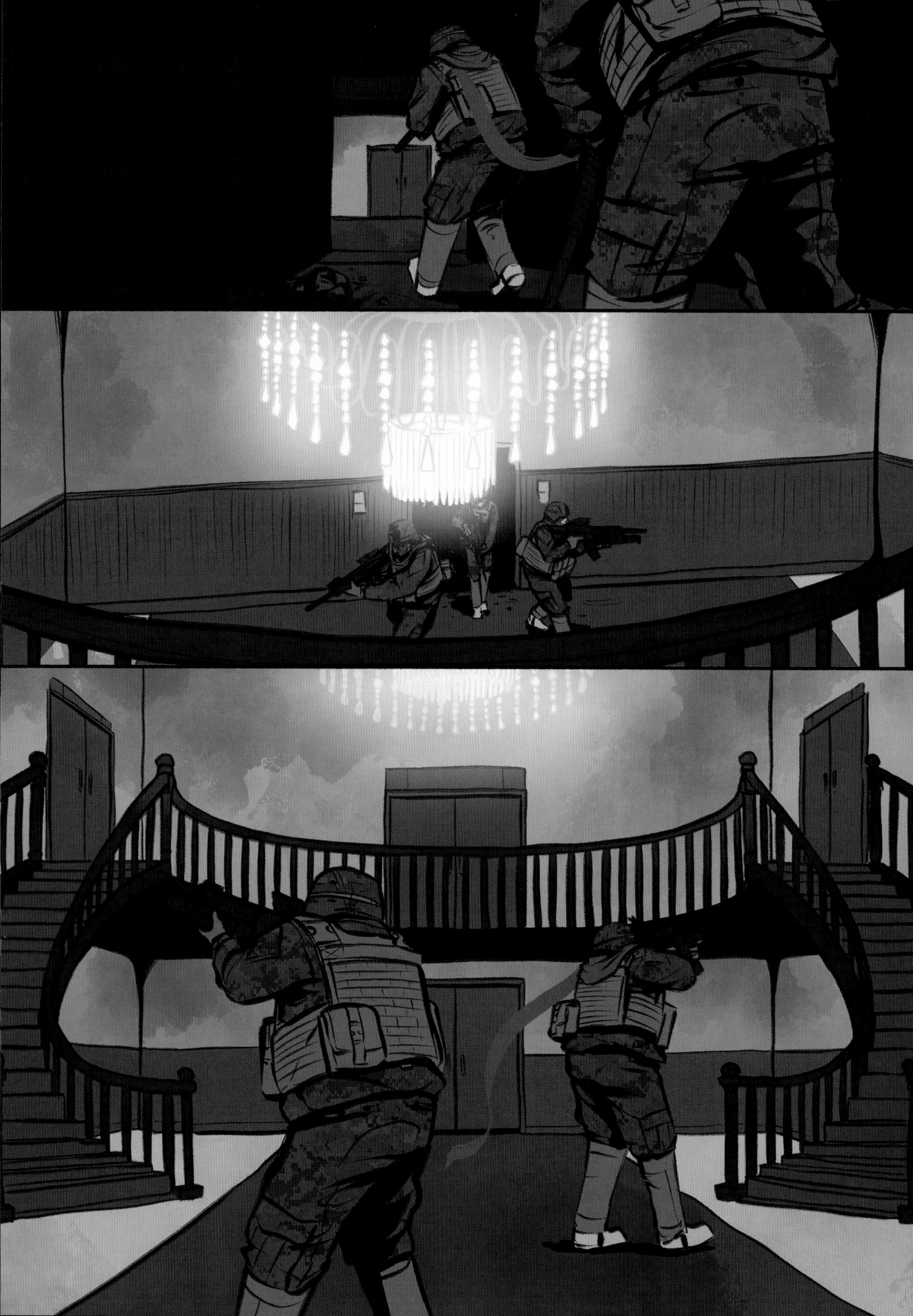

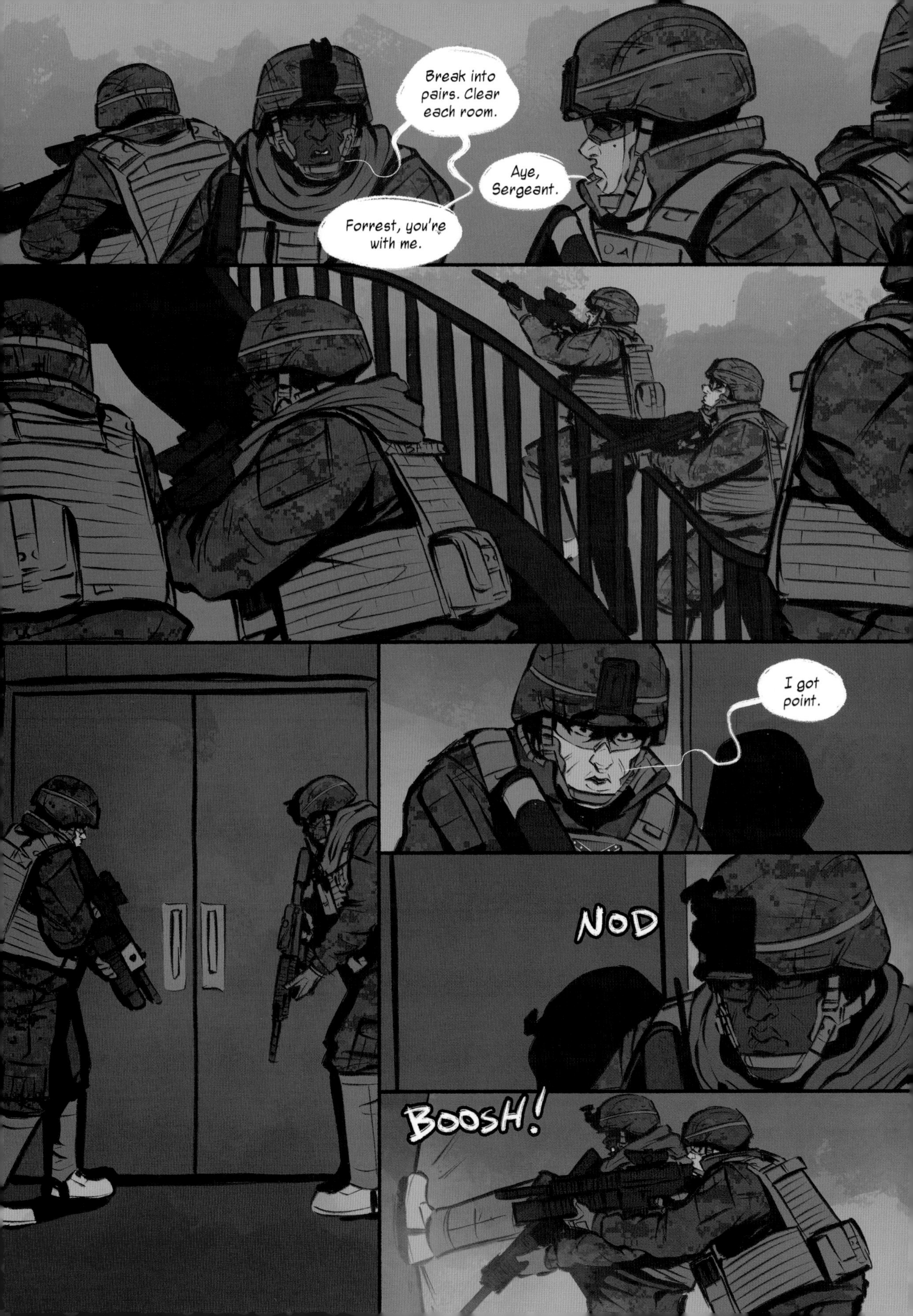
Break into pairs. Clear each room.
Forrest, you're with me.
Aye, Sergeant.
I got point.
NOD
BOOSH!

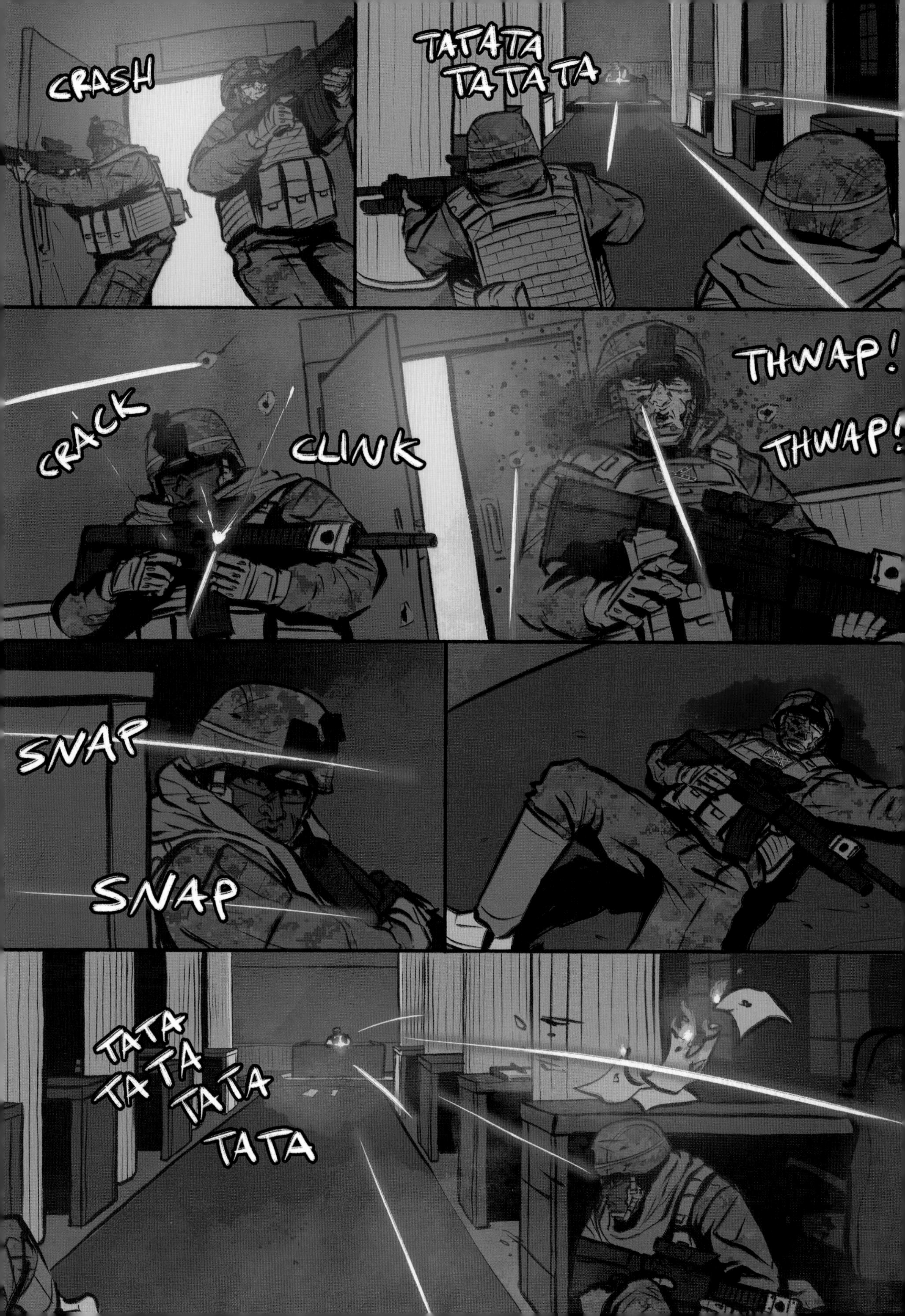
CRASH
TATATA
TATATA
CRACK
CLINK
THWAP!
THWAP!
SNAP
SNAP
TATA
TATA
TATA
TATA

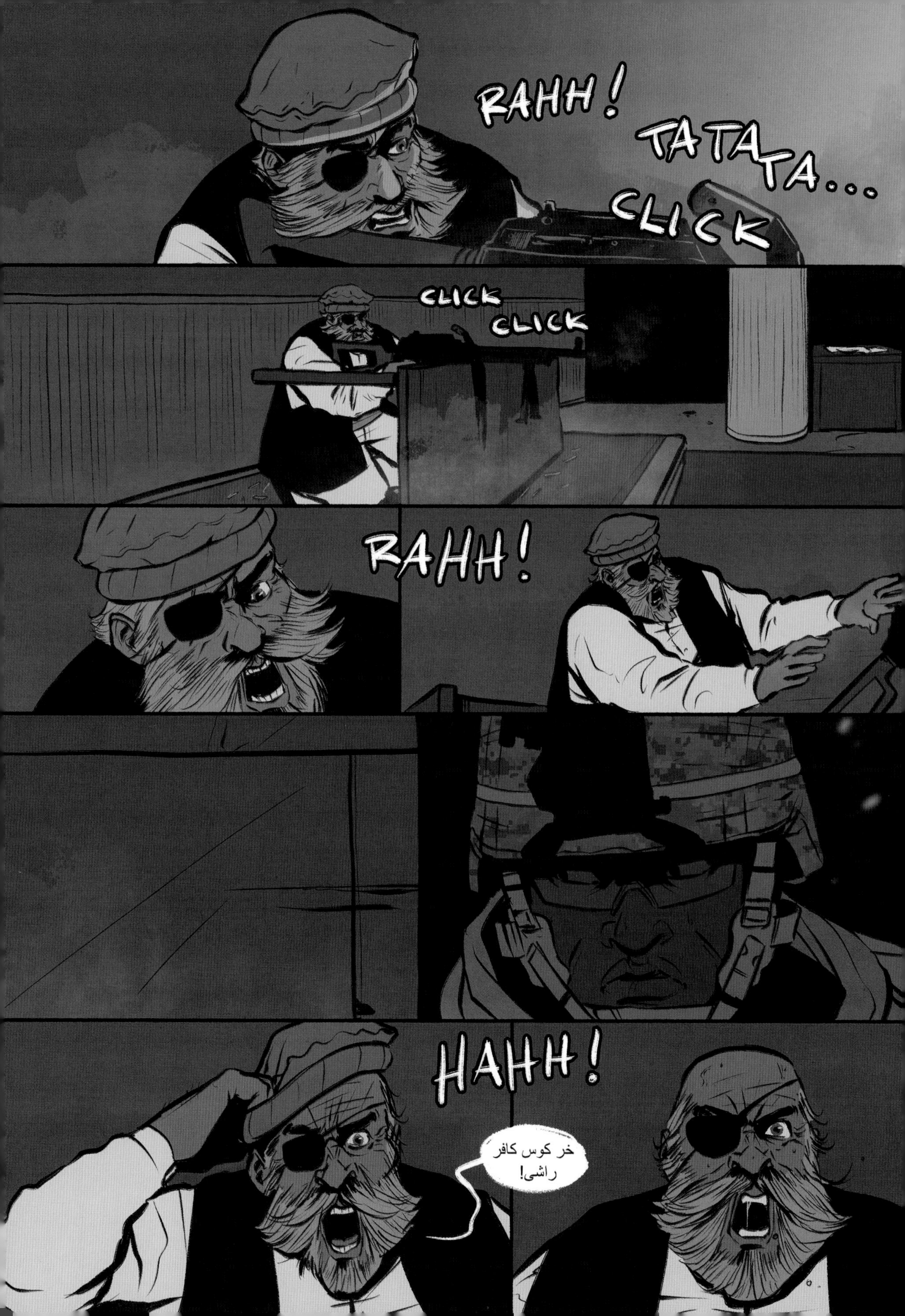
RAHH!
TATATA...
CLICK
CLICK
CLICK
RAHH!
HAHH!
خر کوس کافر
راشی!

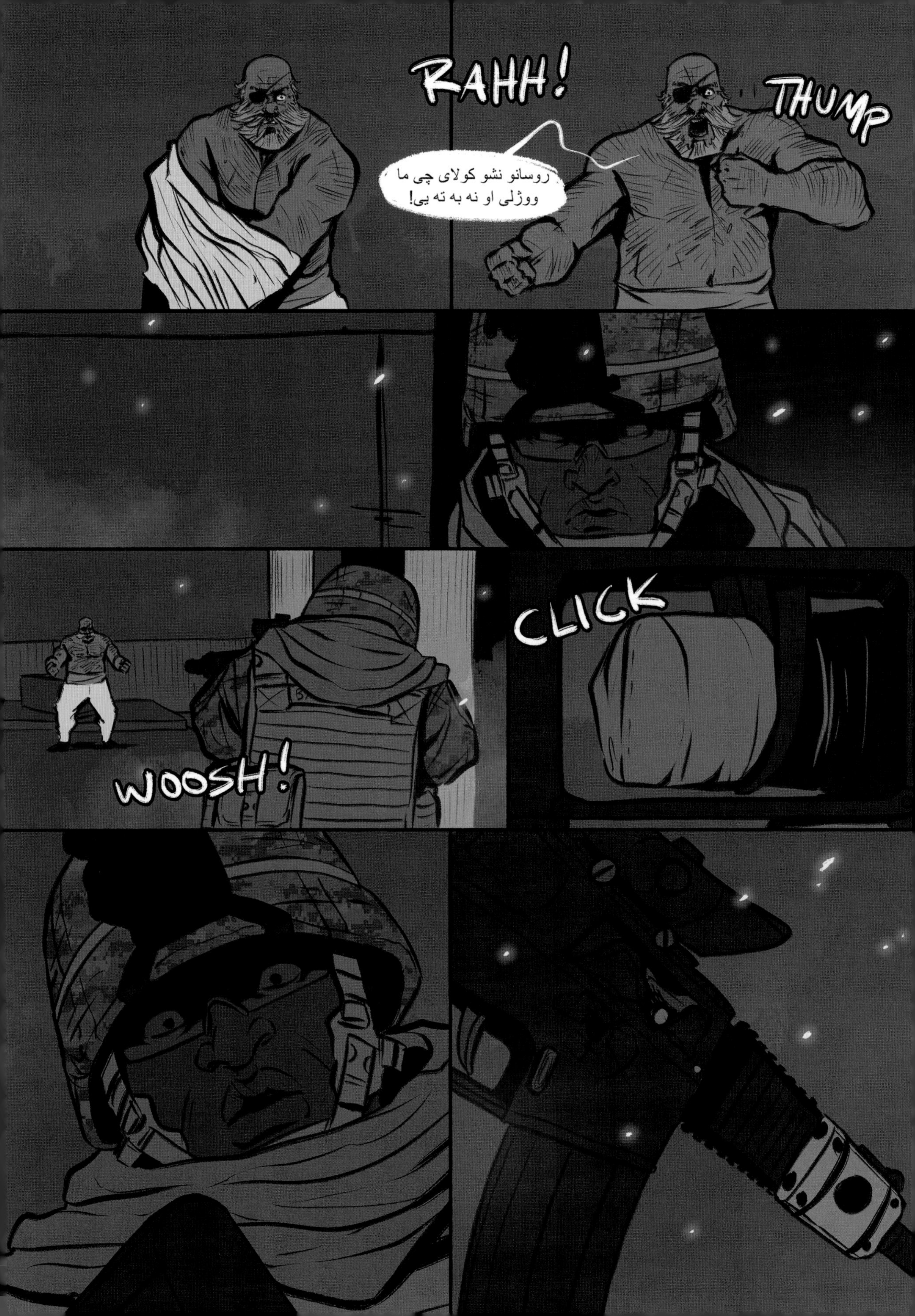
RAHH!
روسانو نشو کولای چی ما ووژلی او نه به ته یی!
THUMP
WOOSH!
CLICK

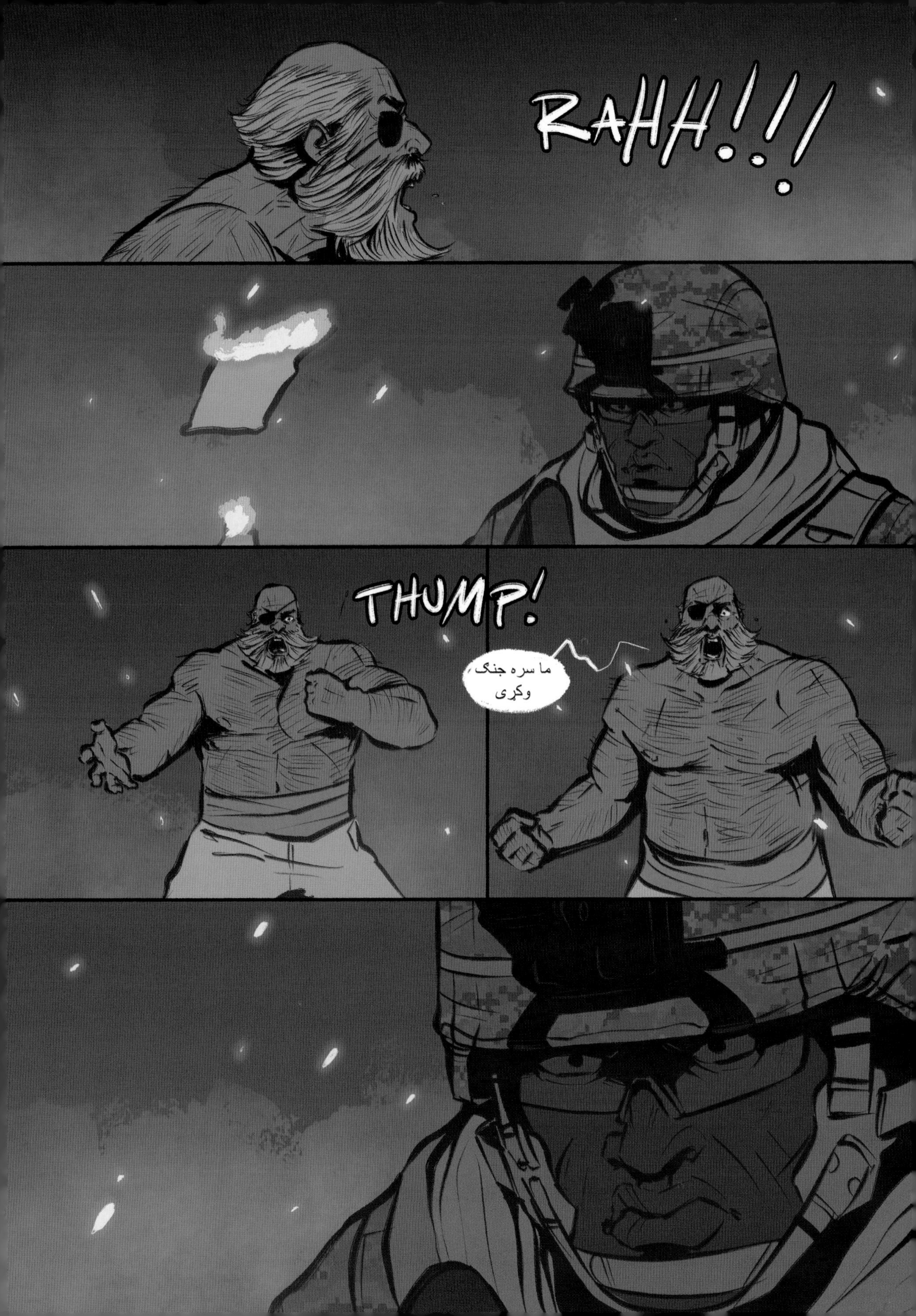
RAHH!!!
THUMP!
ما سره جنګ
وکړی

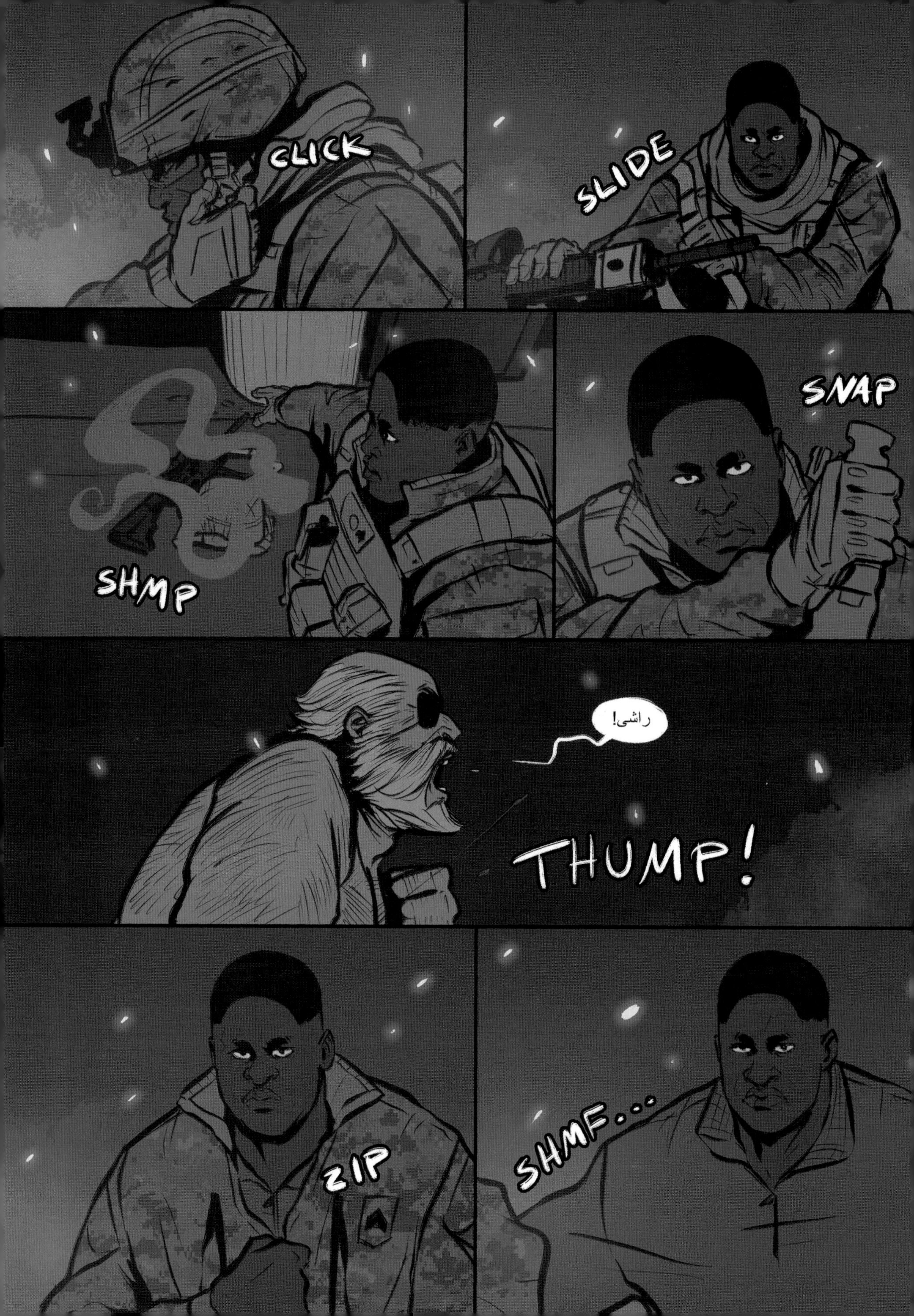
CLICK
SLIDE
SHMP
SNAP
راشی!
THUMP!
ZIP
SHMF...

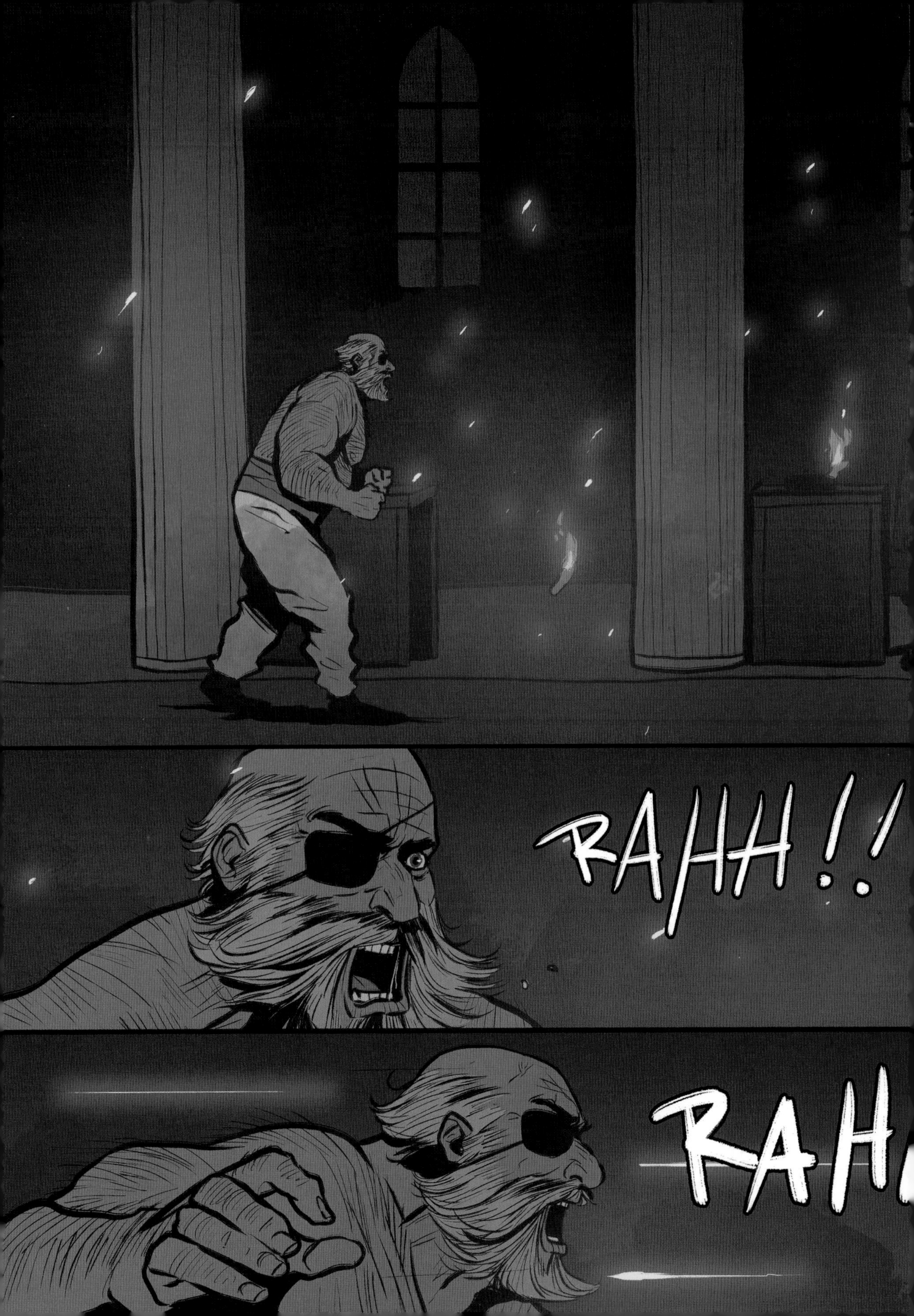
RAHH!!
RAH

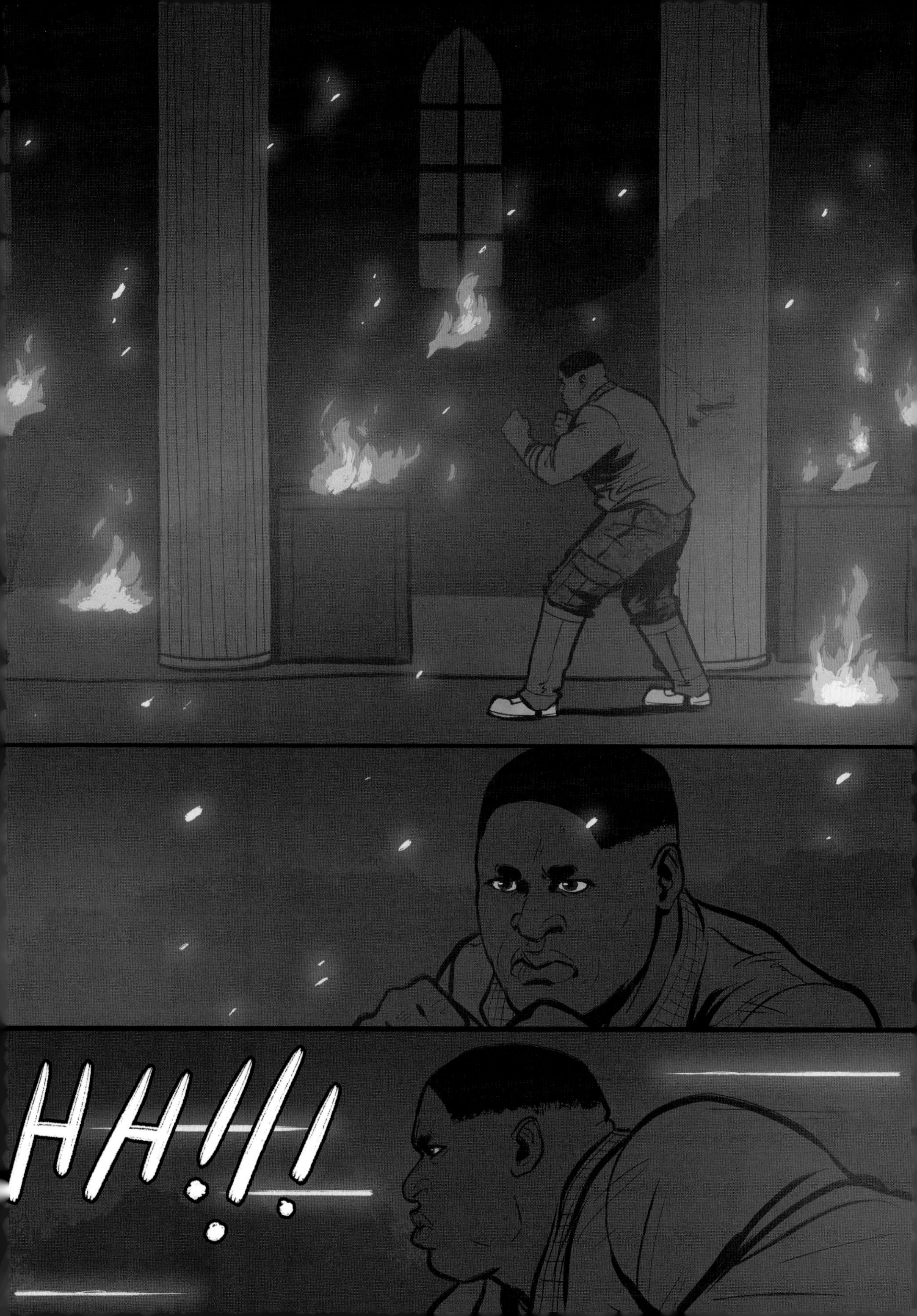
HH!!!

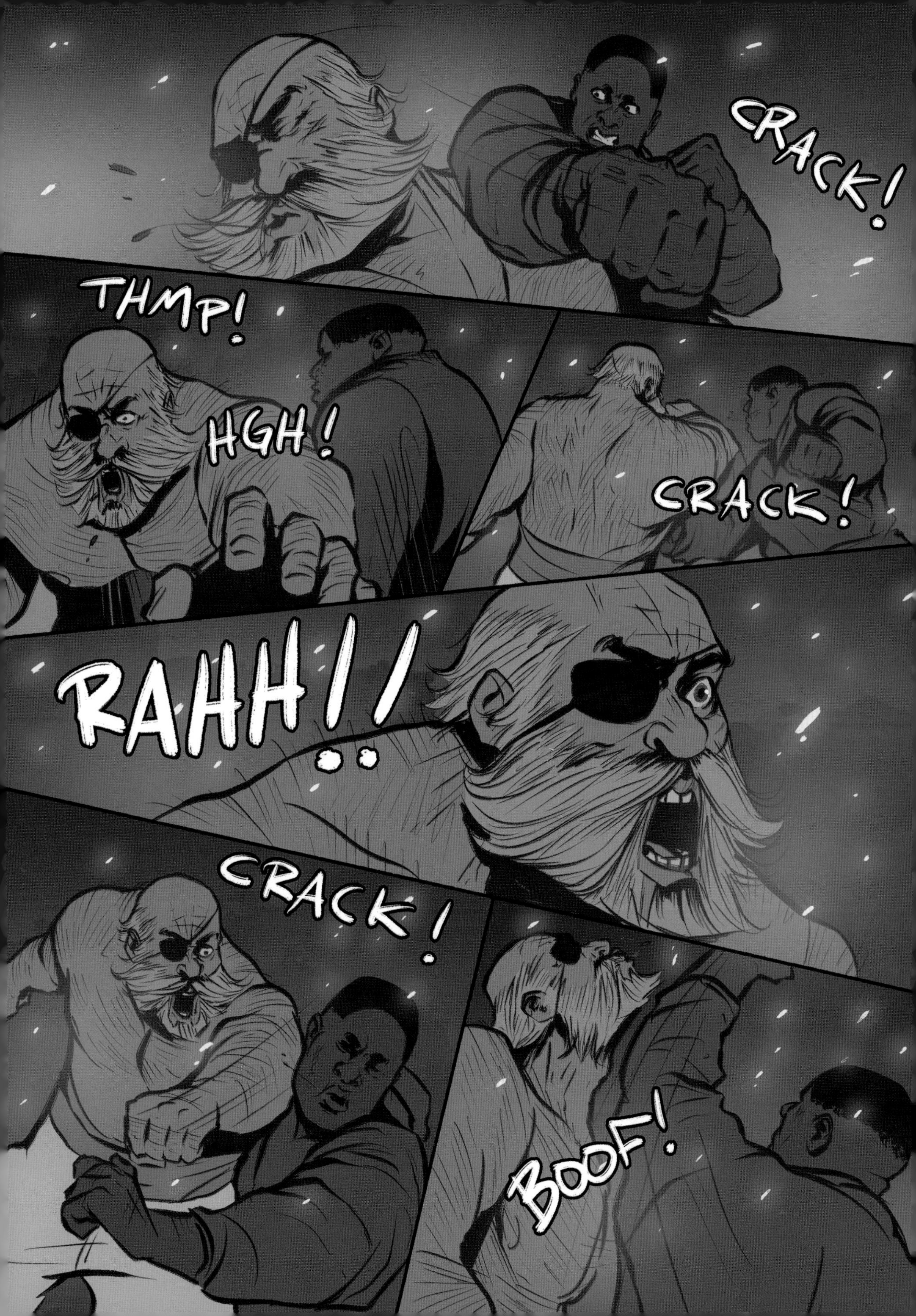
CRACK!
THMP!
HGH!
CRACK!
RAHH!!
CRACK!
BOOF!

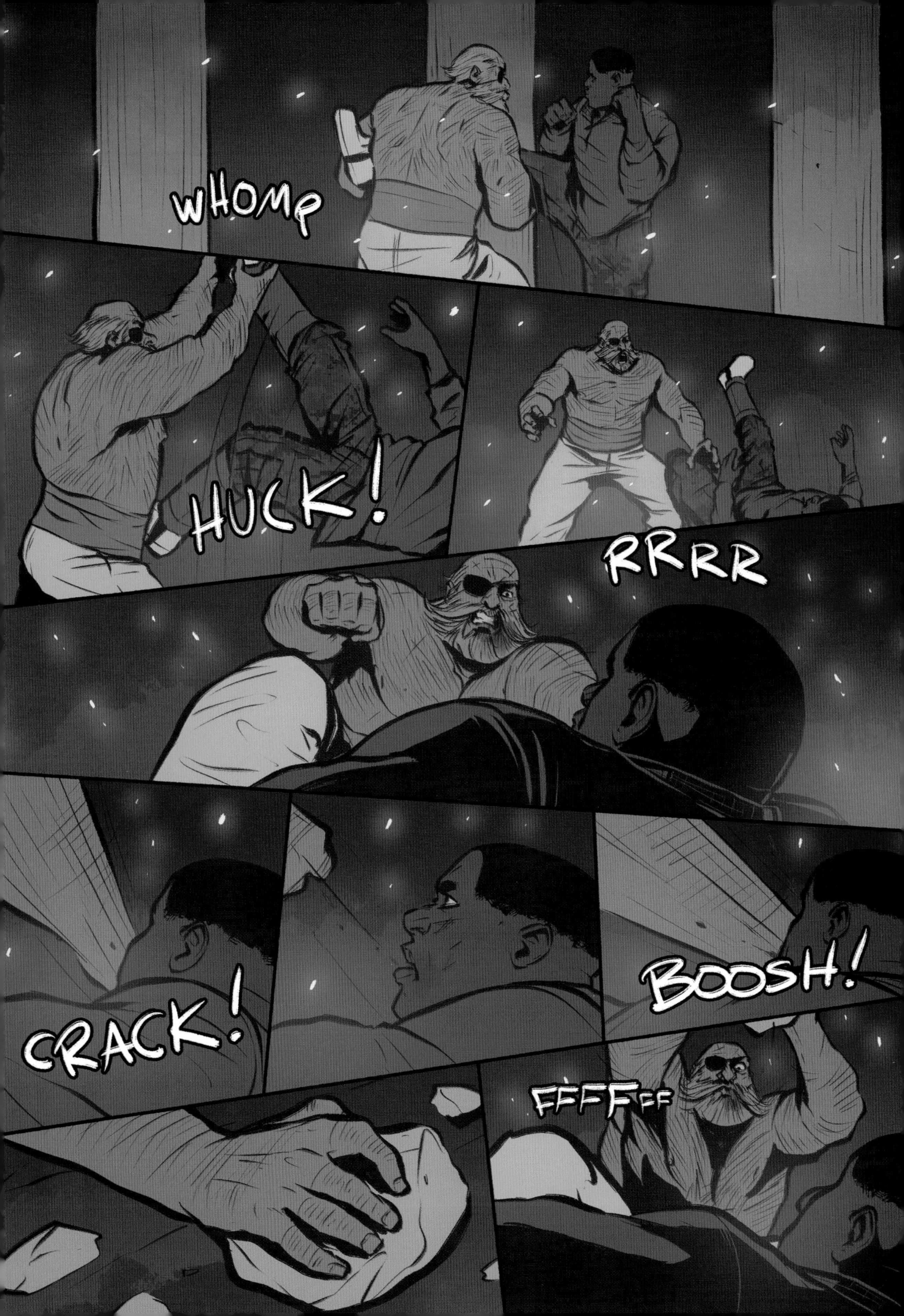
WHOMP
HUCK!
RRRR
CRACK!
BOOSH!
FFFFFF

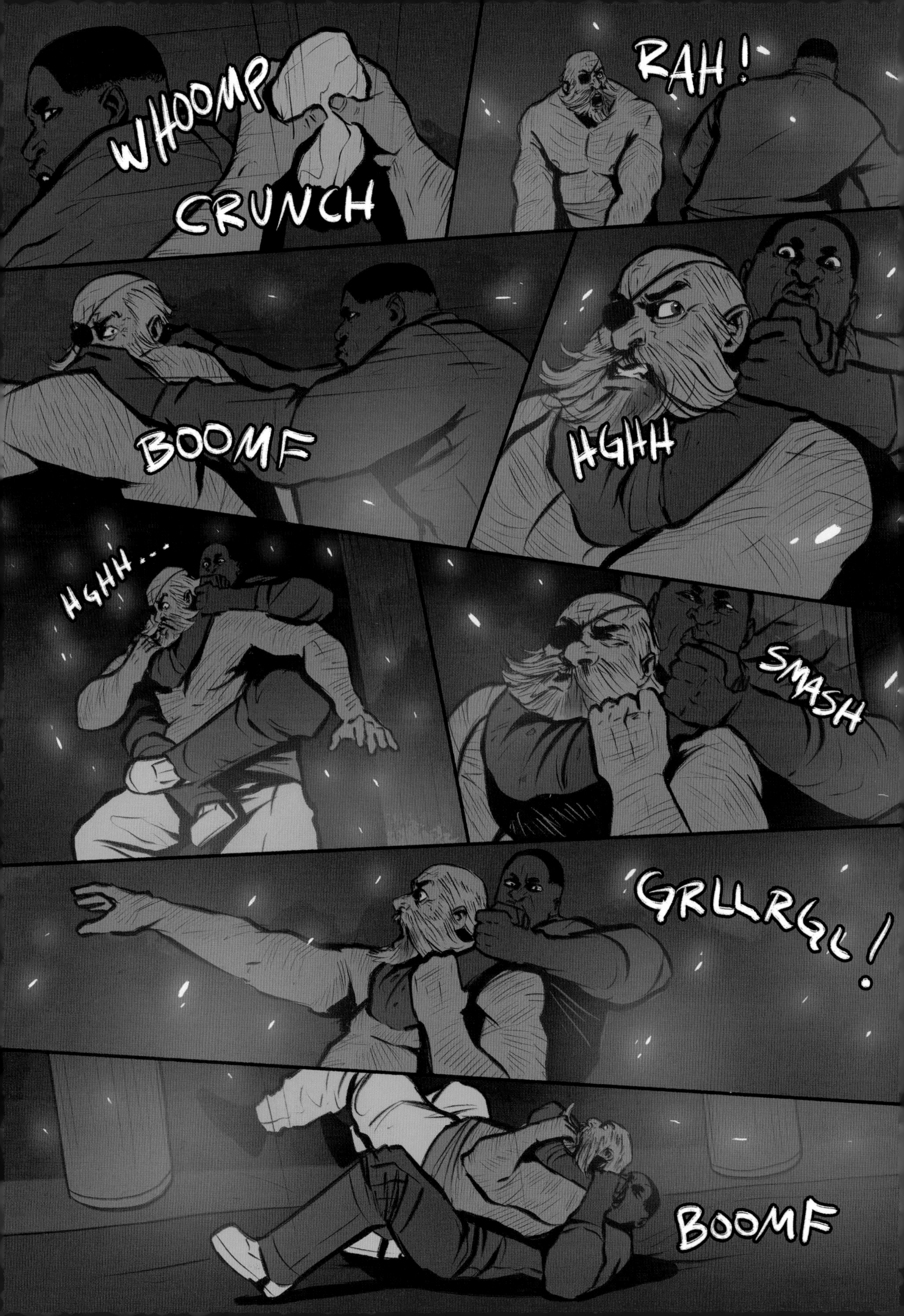
WHOOMP
CRUNCH
RAH!
BOOMF
HGHH
HGHH...
SMASH
GRLLRGL!
BOOMF

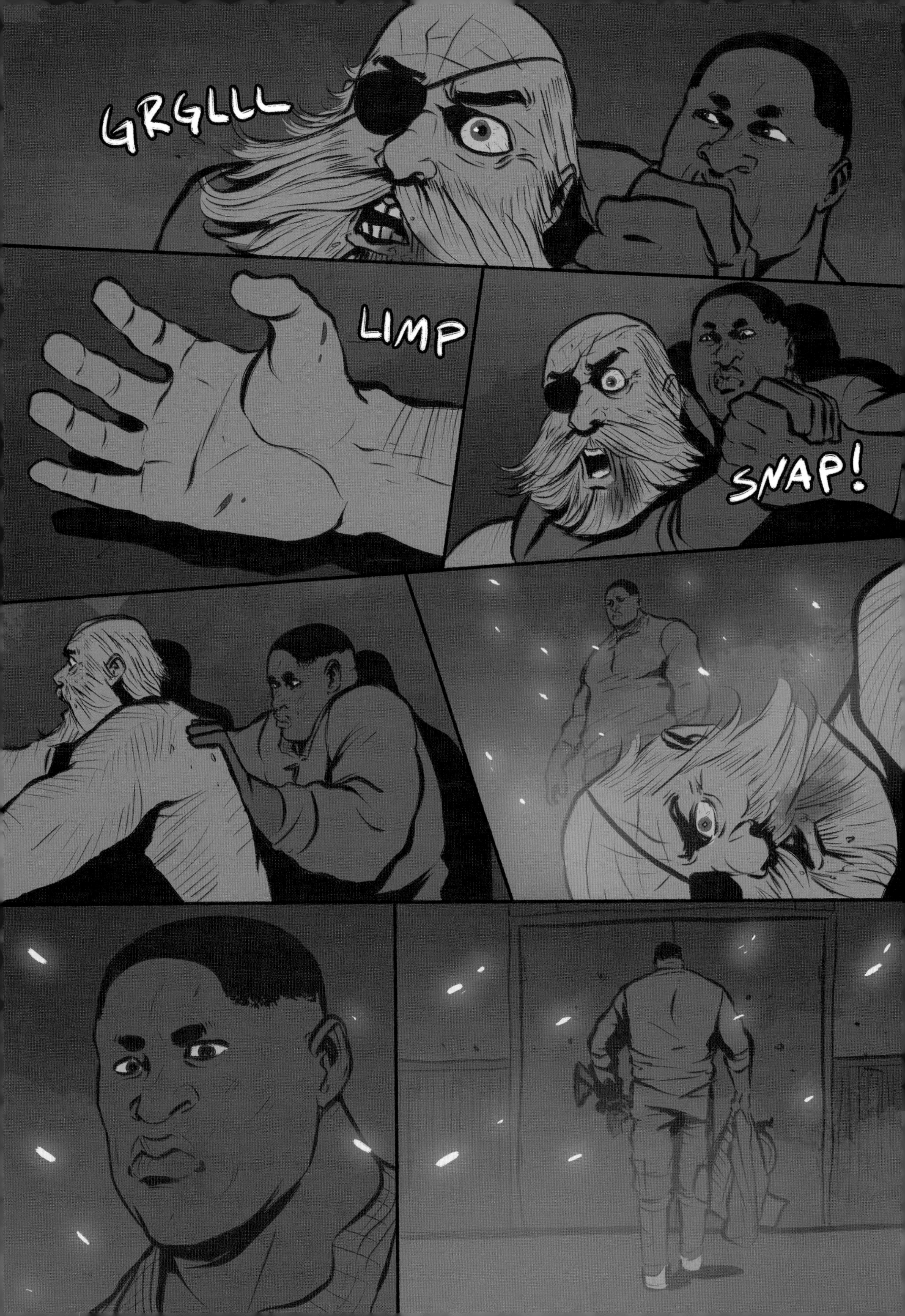
GRGLLL
LIMP
SNAP!

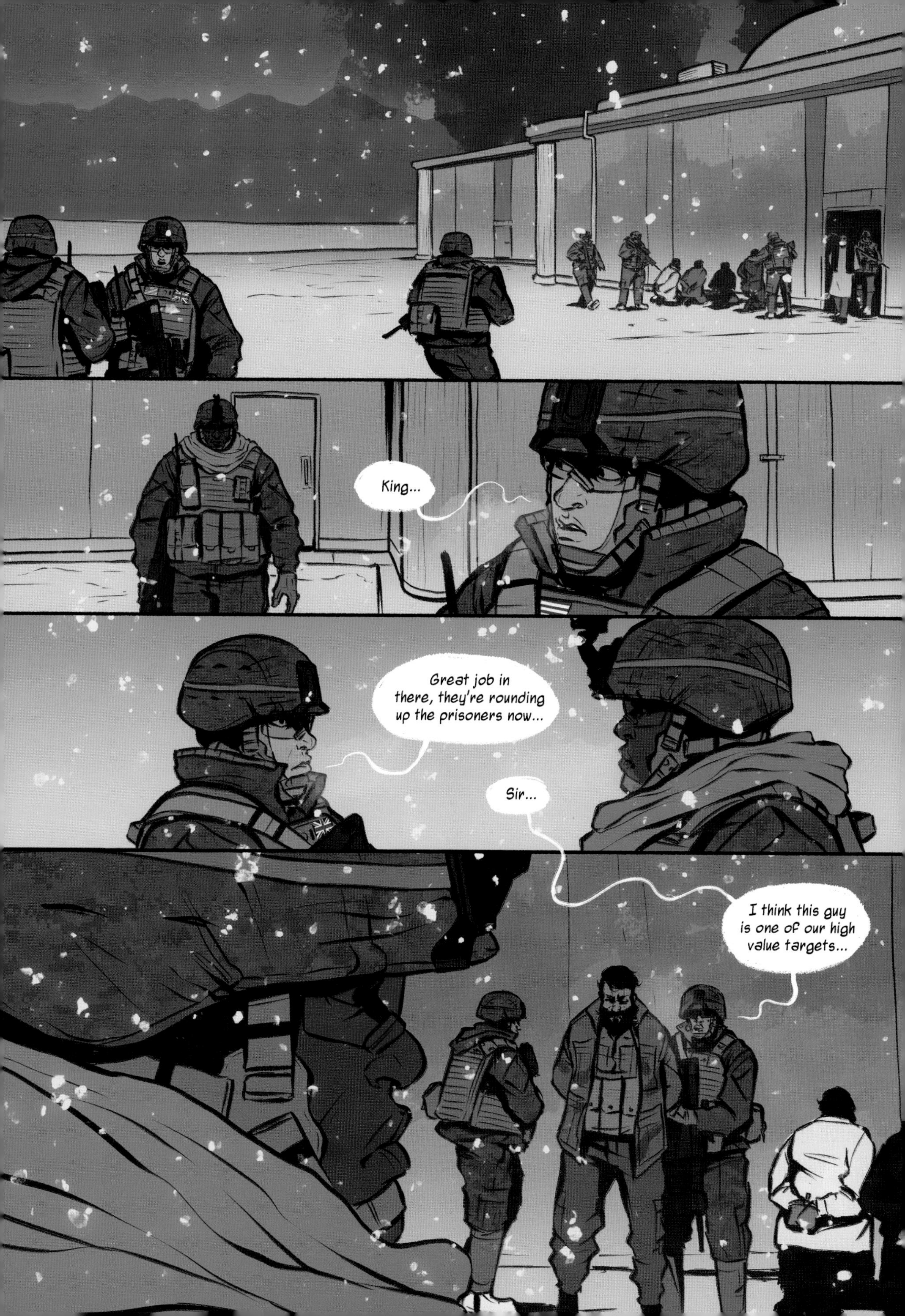
King...
Great job in there, they're rounding up the prisoners now...
Sir...
I think this guy is one of our high value targets...

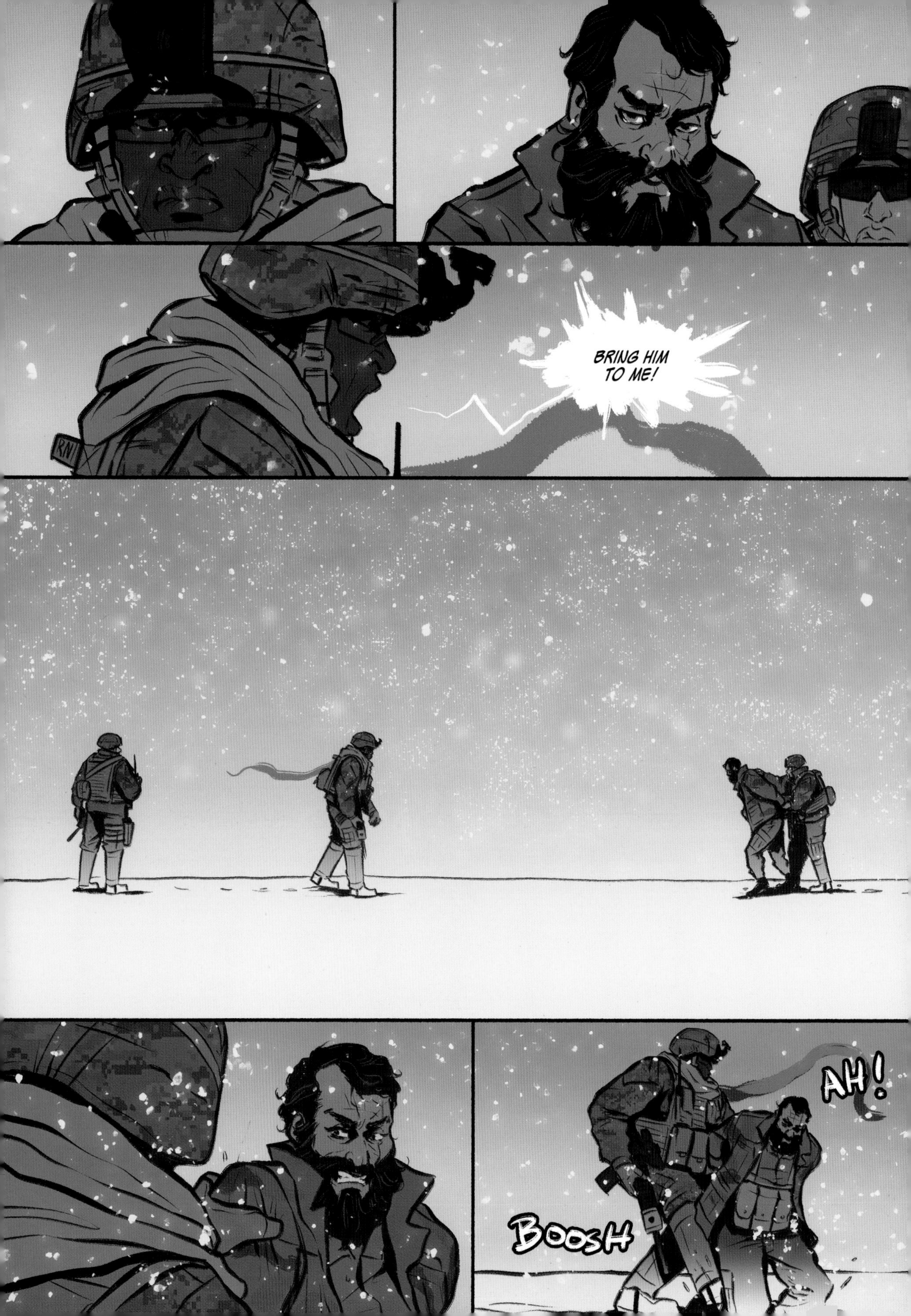
BRING HIM TO ME!
AH!
BOOSH

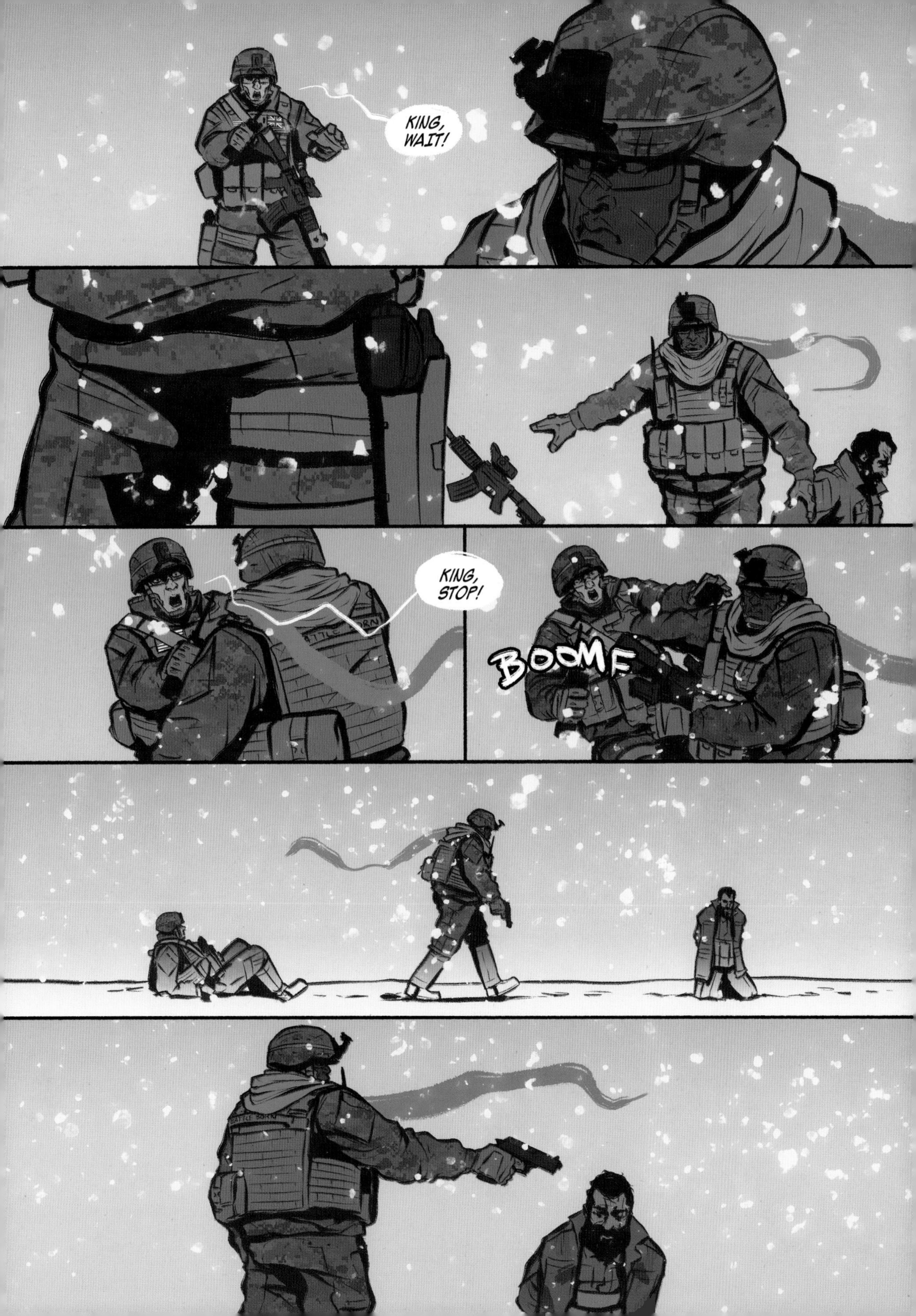
KING, WAIT!
KING, STOP!
BOOMF

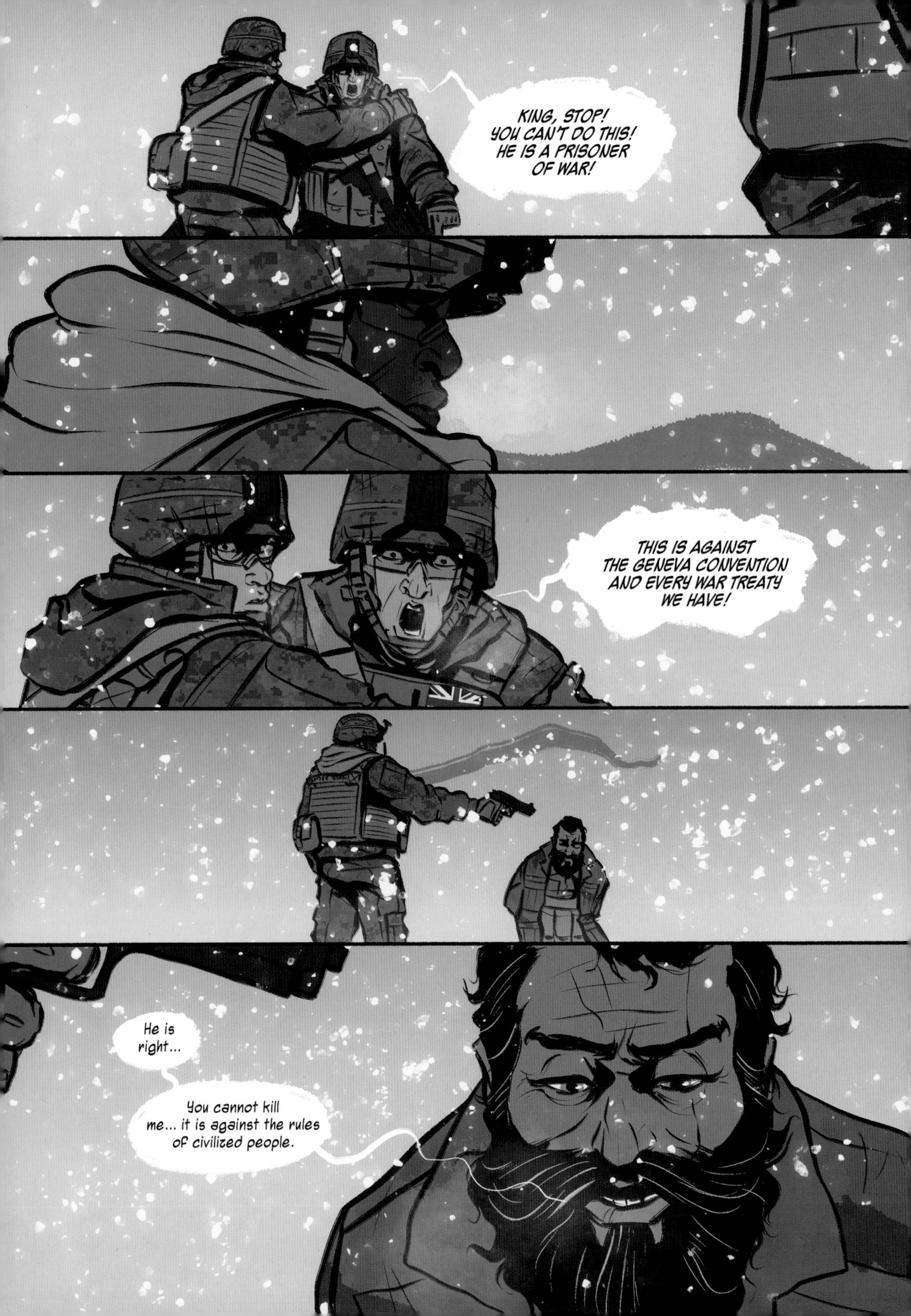
KING, STOP! YOU CAN'T DO THIS! HE IS A PRISONER OF WAR!
THIS IS AGAINST THE GENEVA CONVENTION AND EVERY WAR TREATY WE HAVE!
He is right...
You cannot kill me... it is against the rules of civilized people.

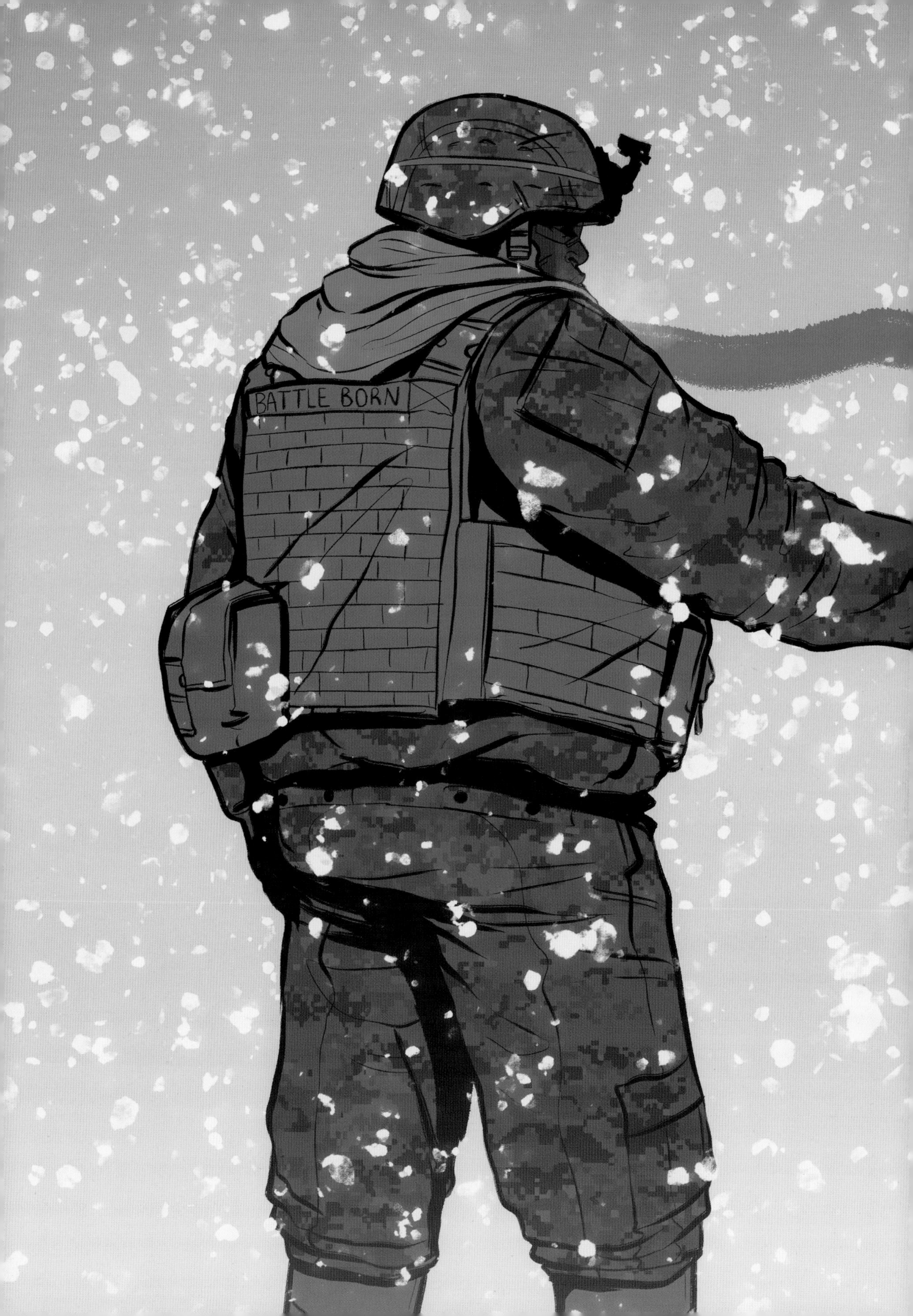
BATTLE BORN

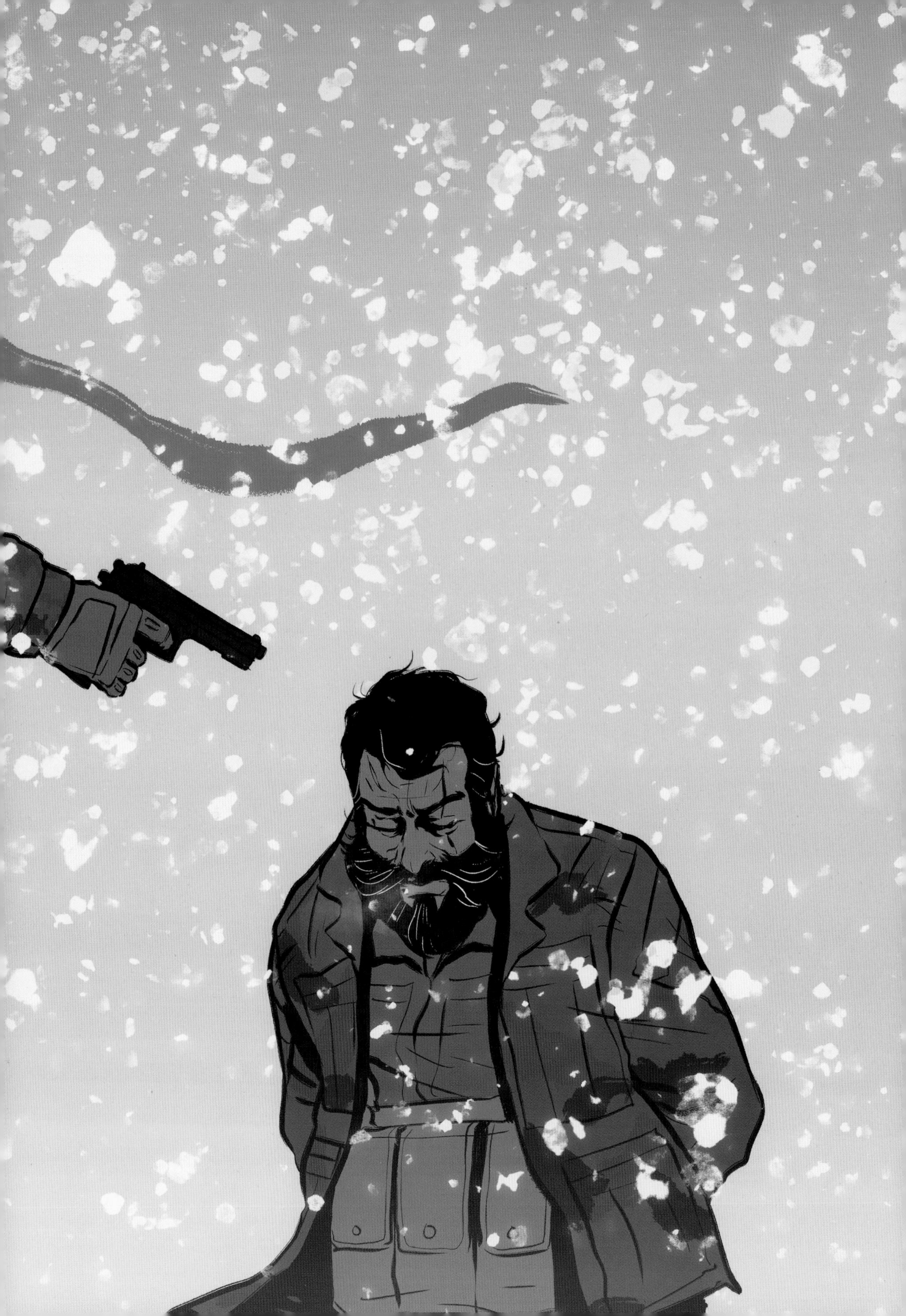

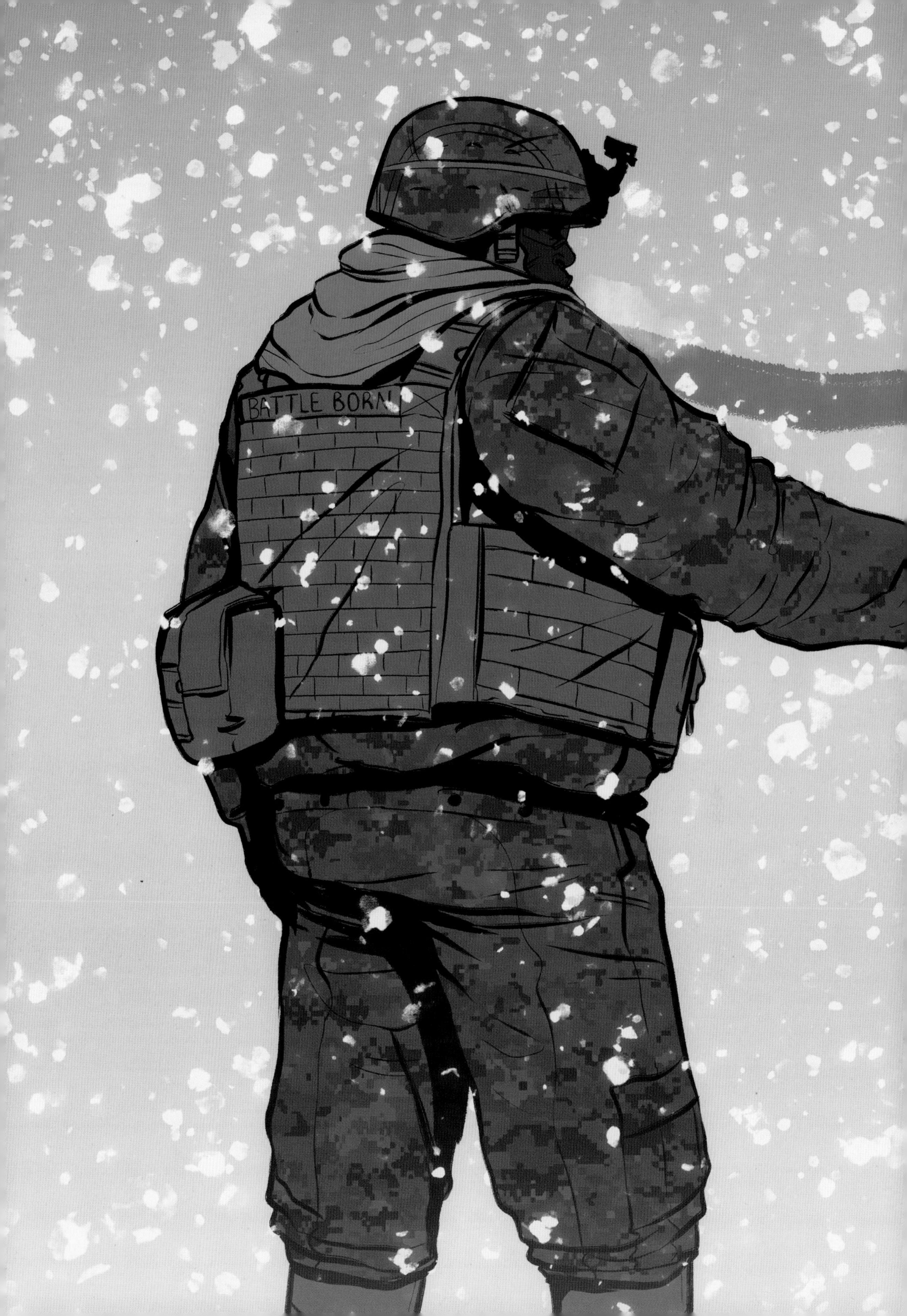
BATTLE BORN

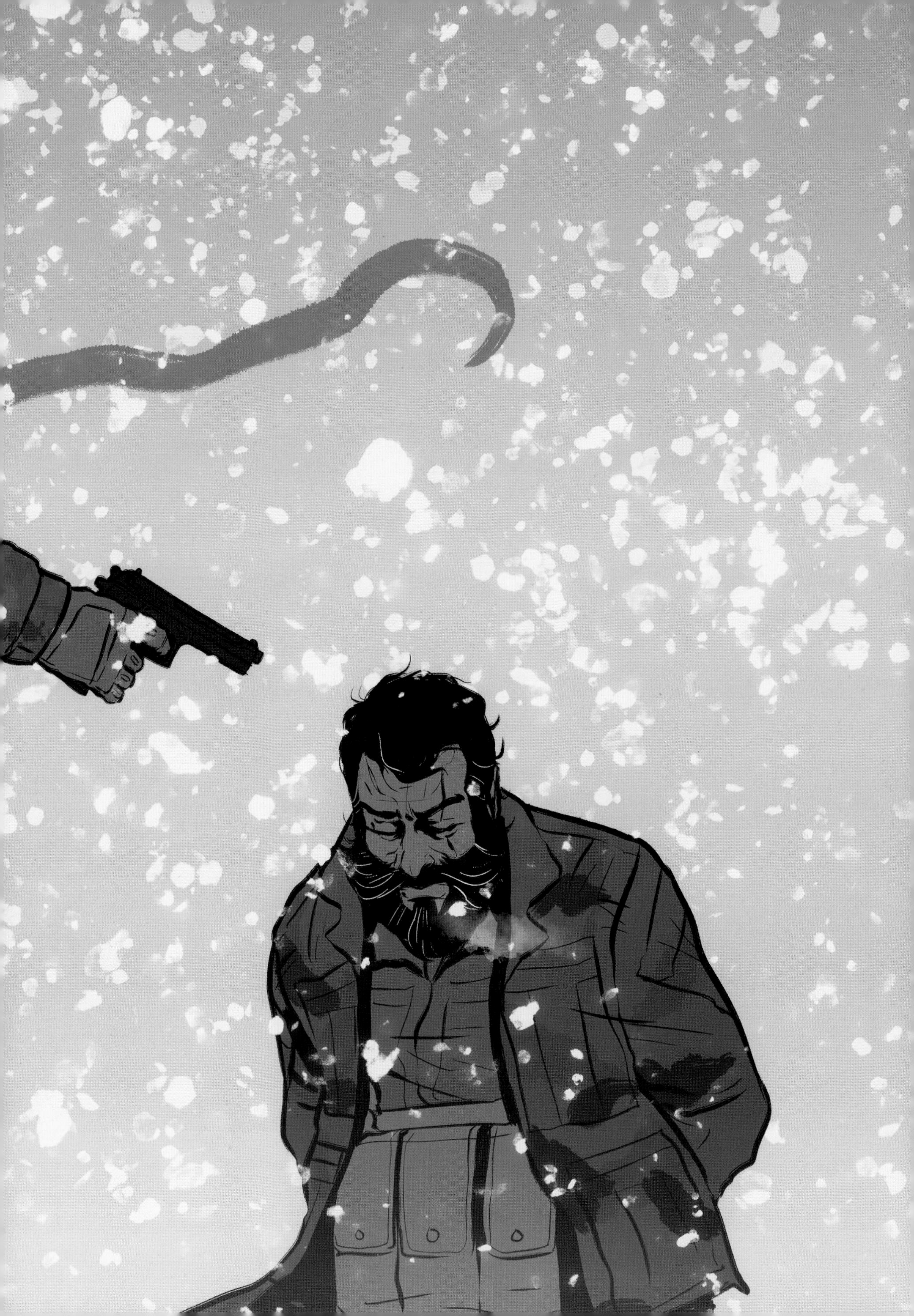

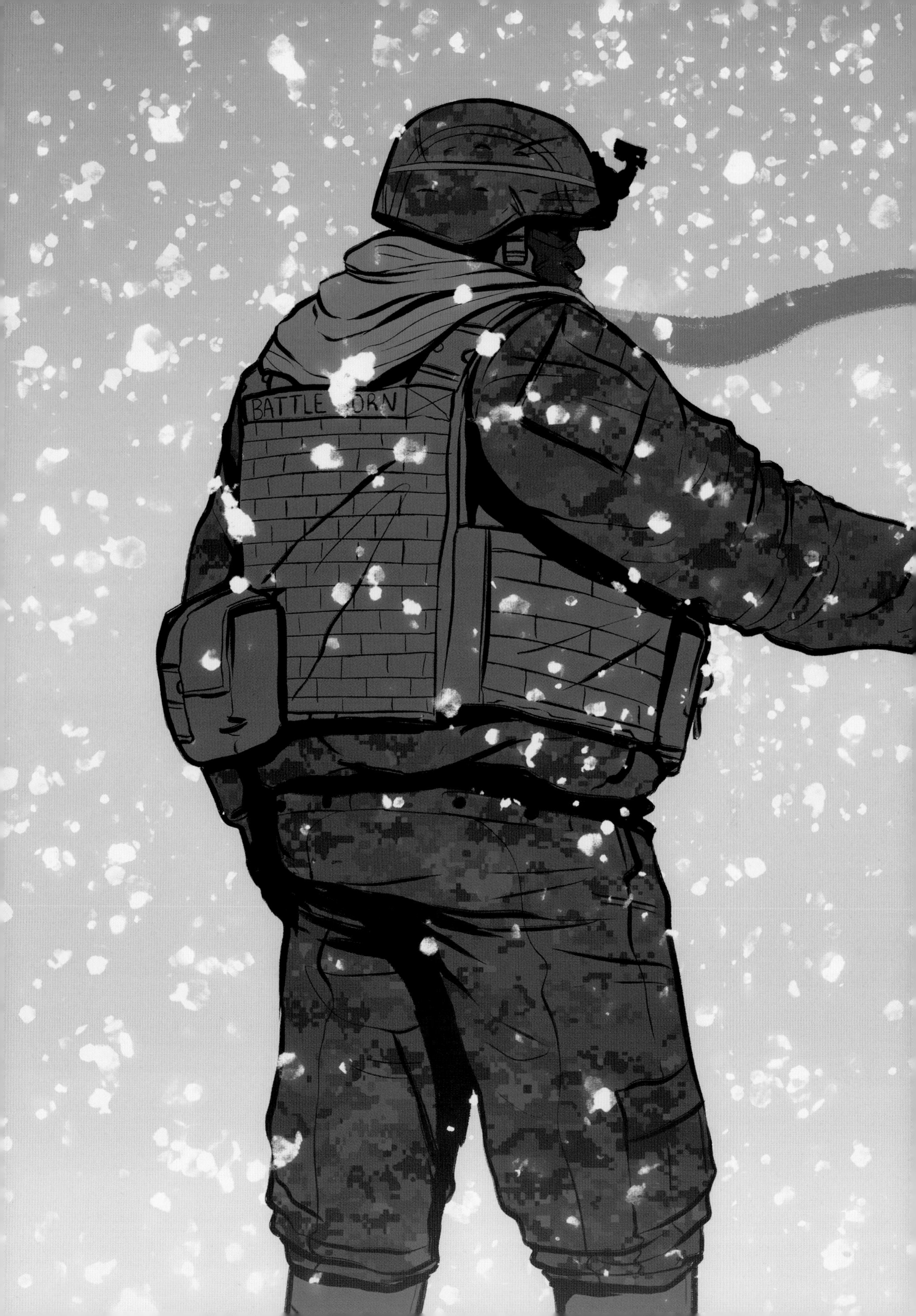
BATTLE

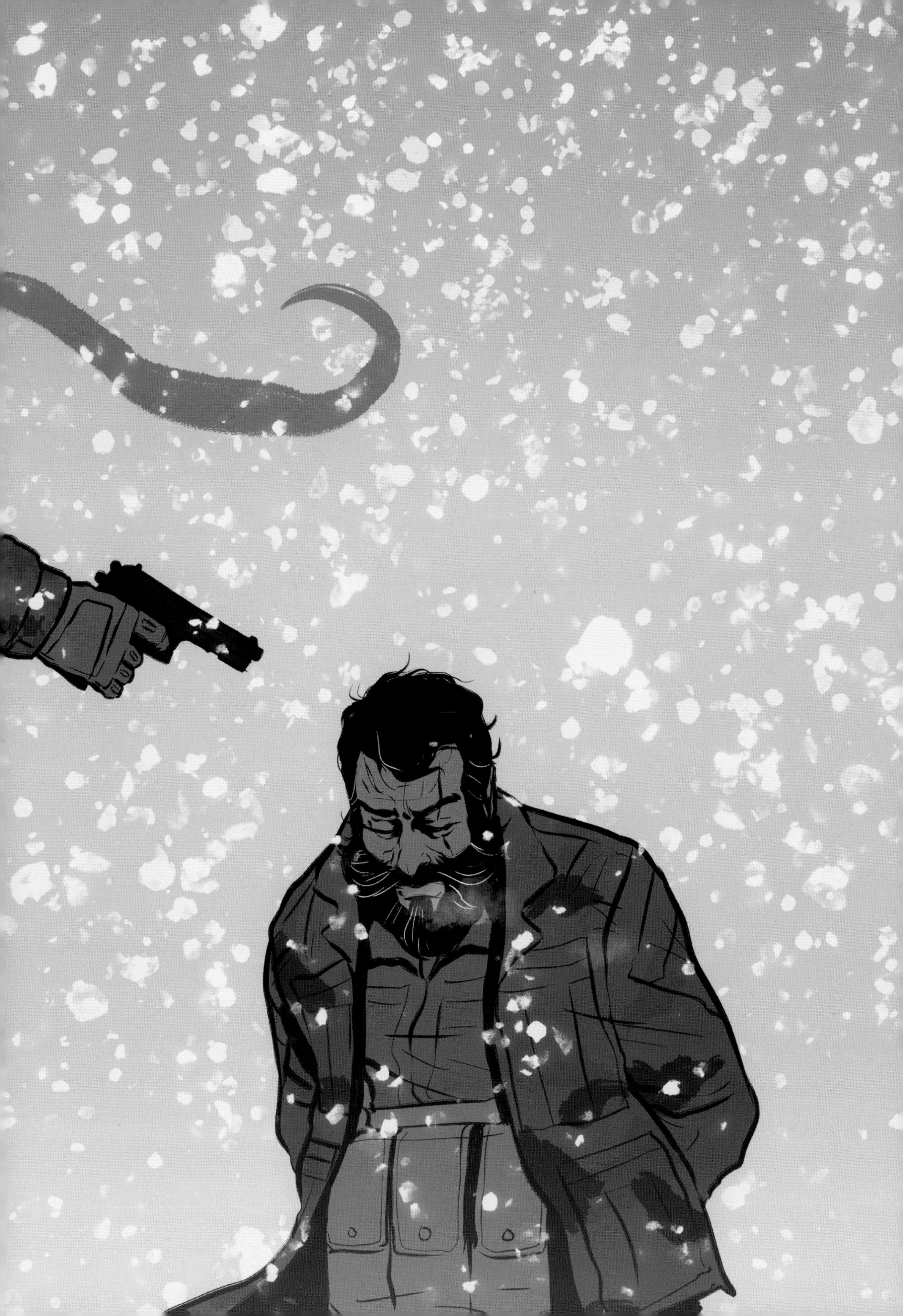

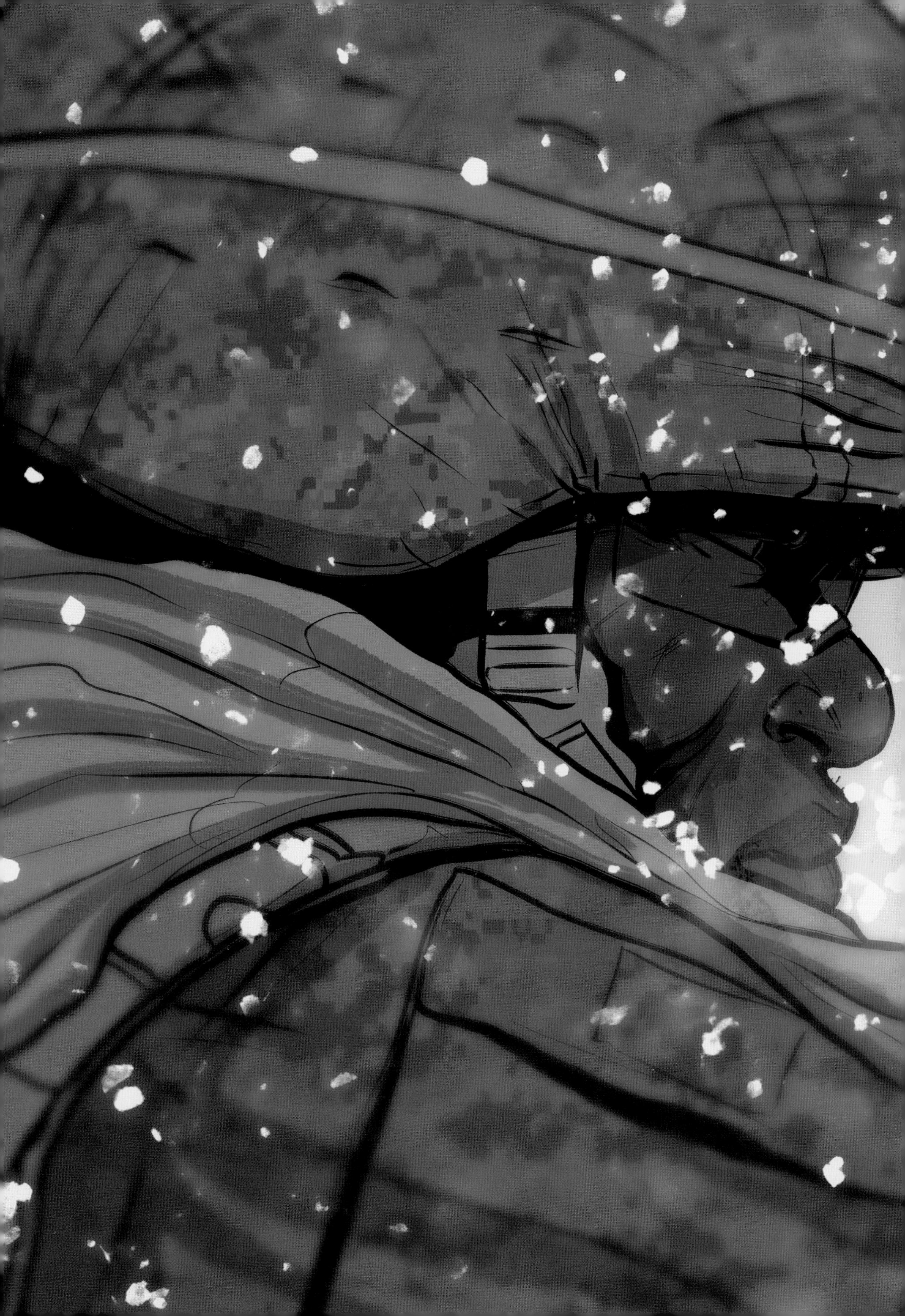

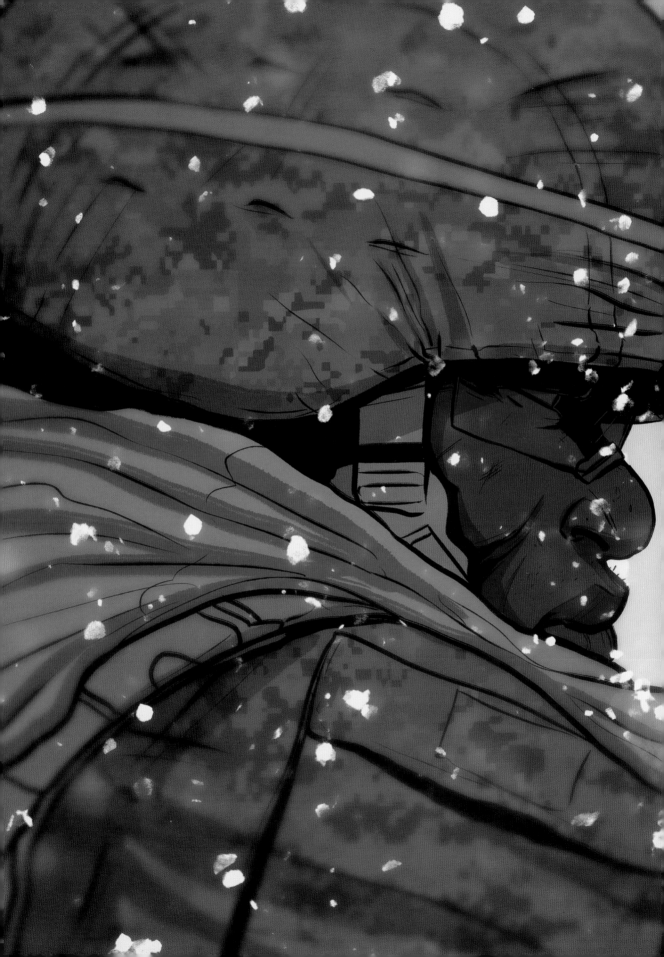

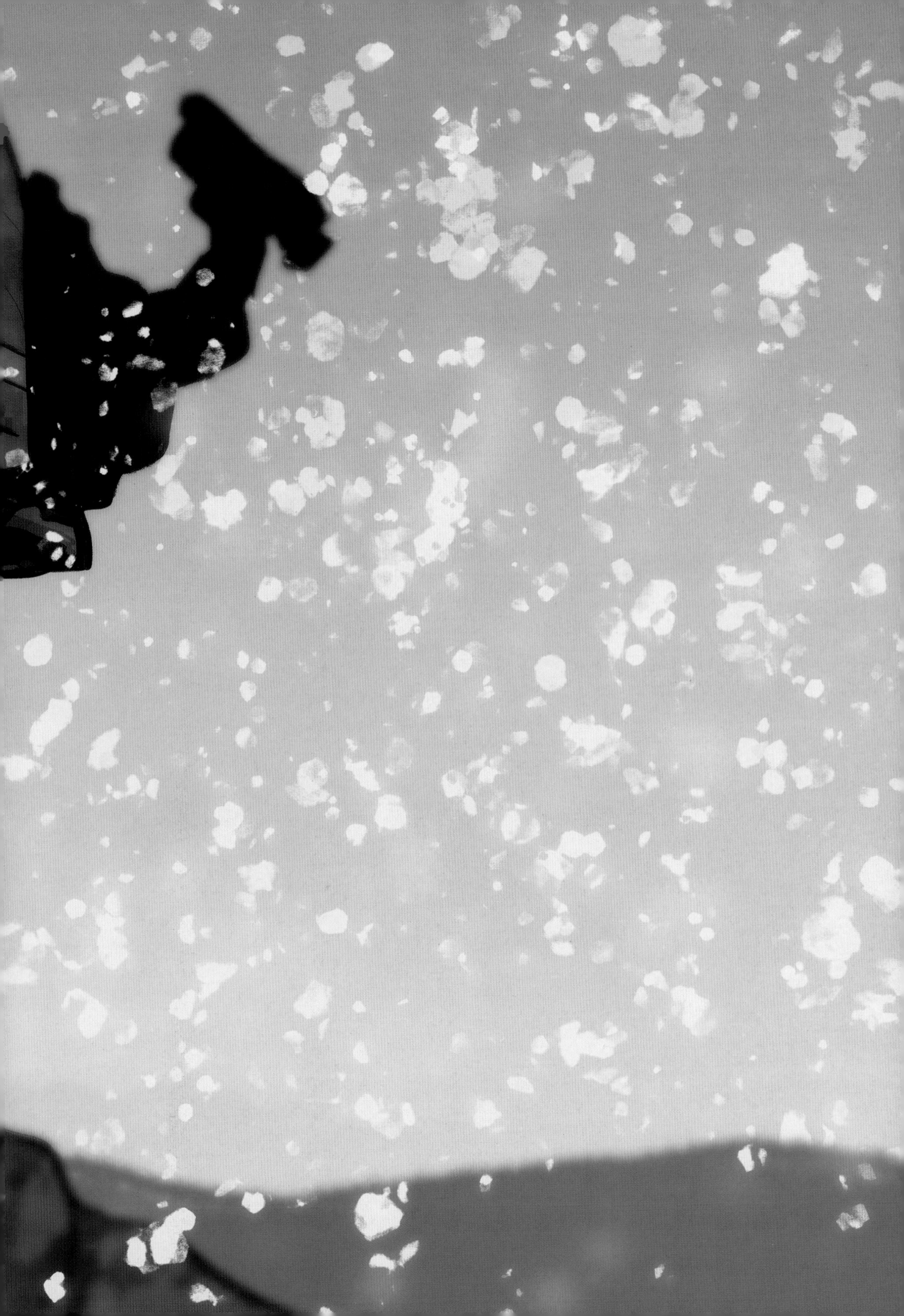

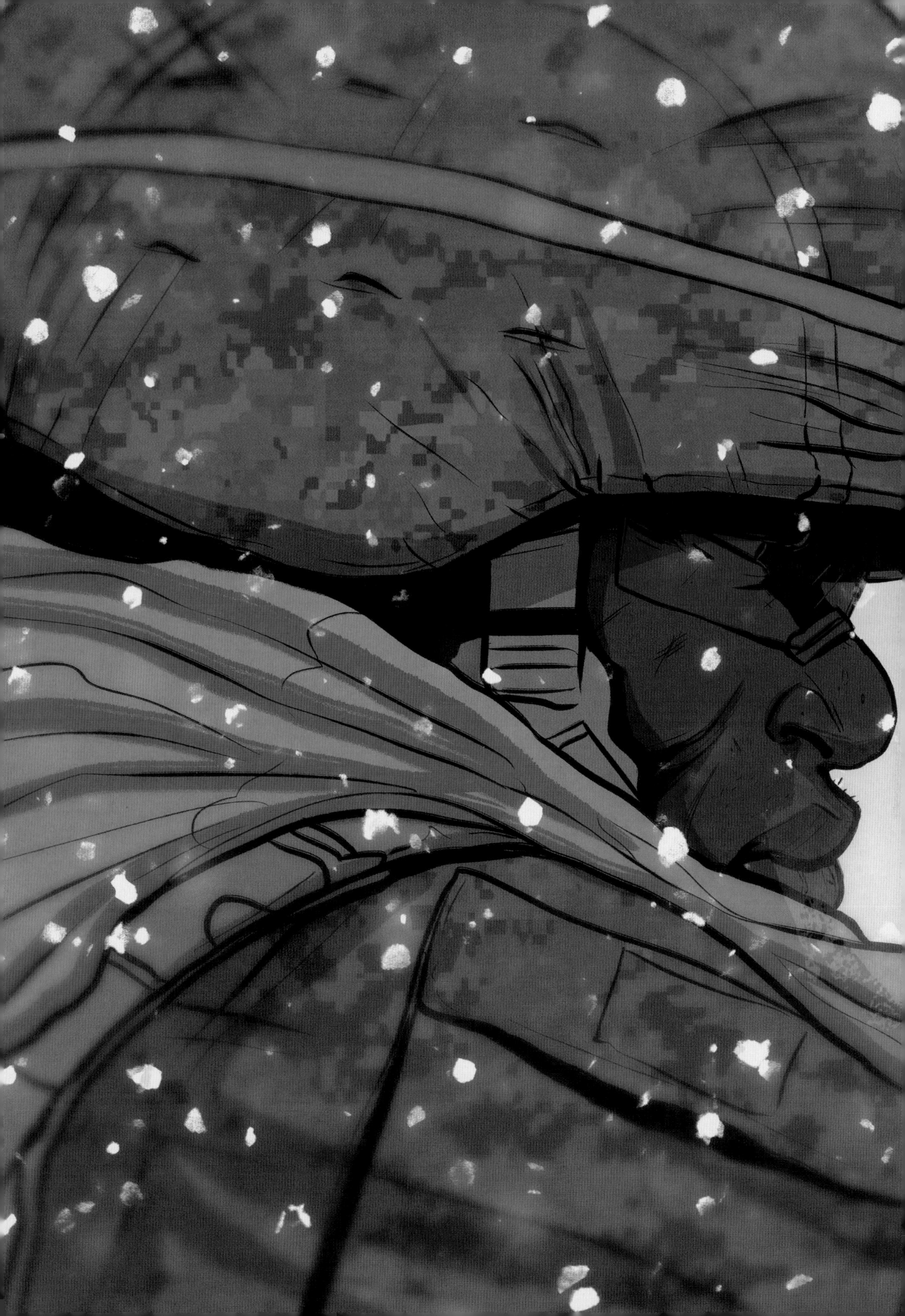

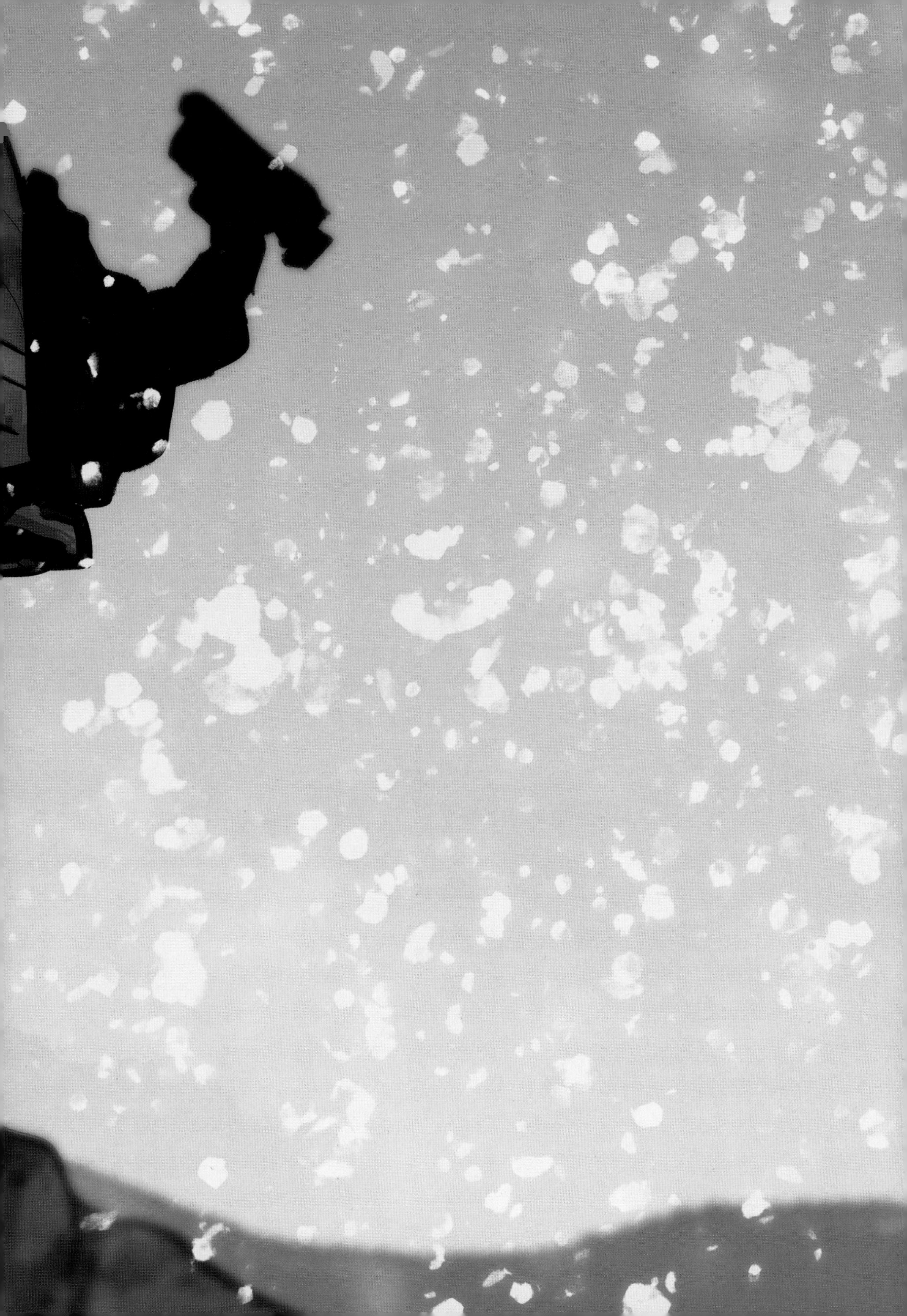

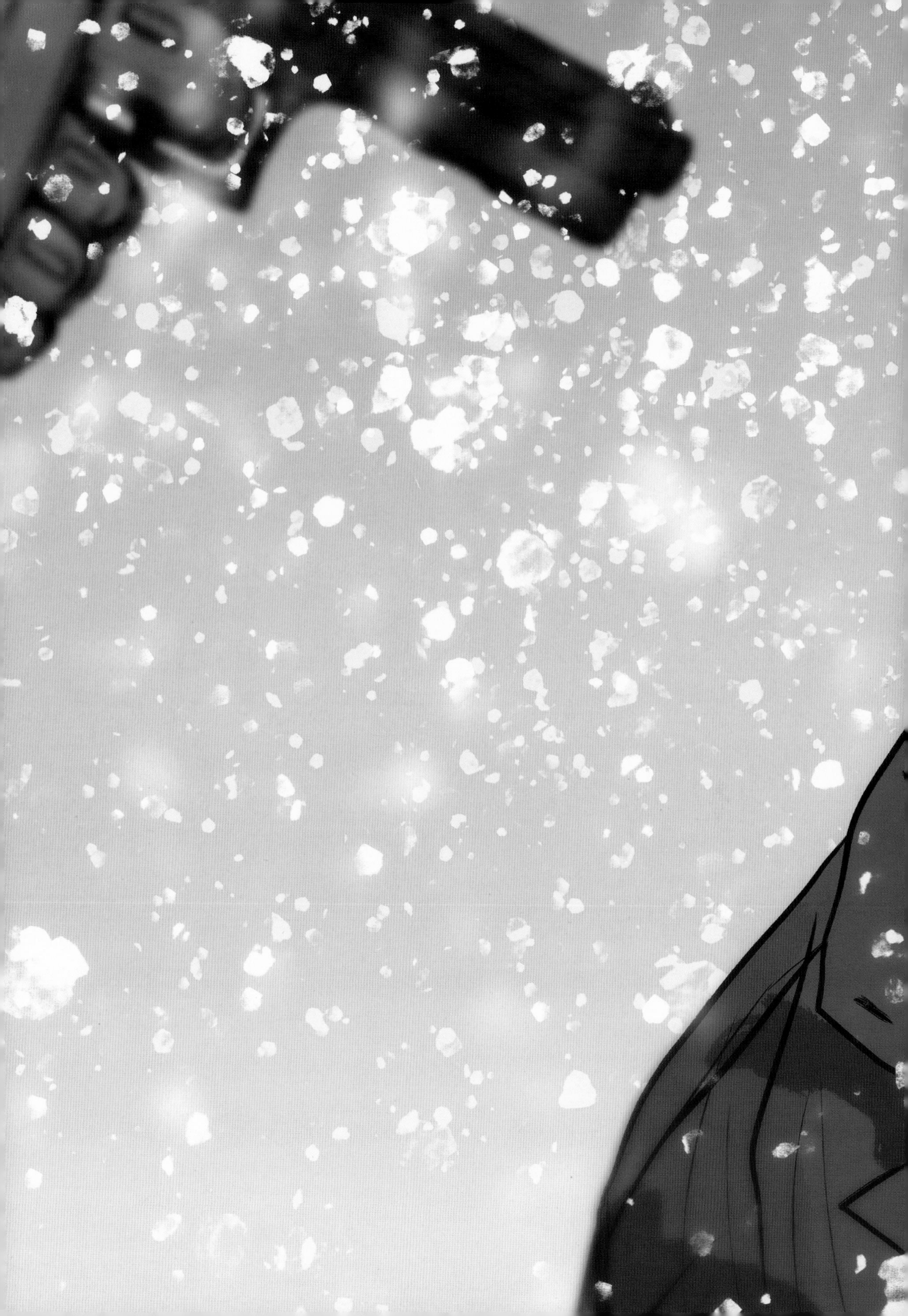

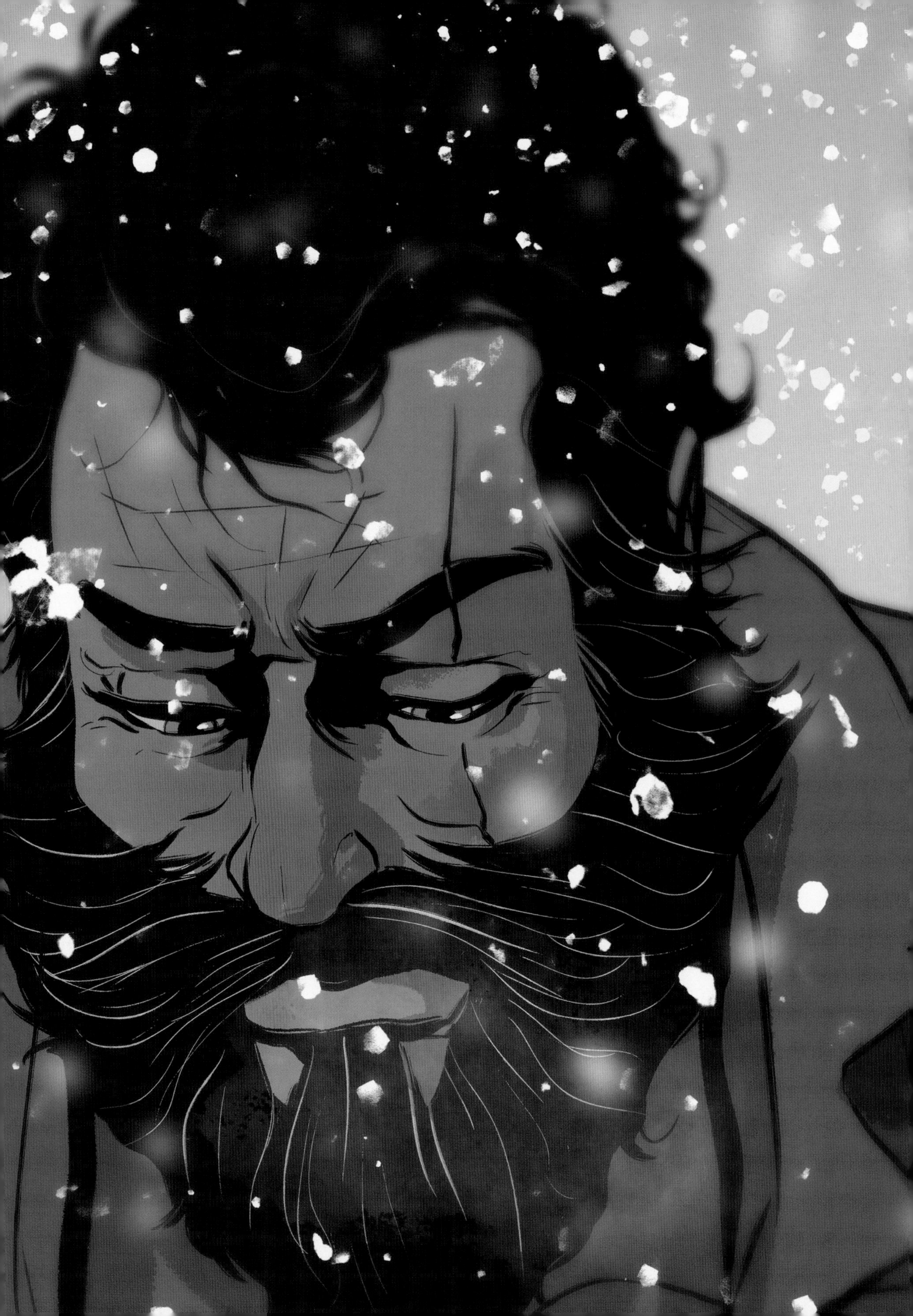

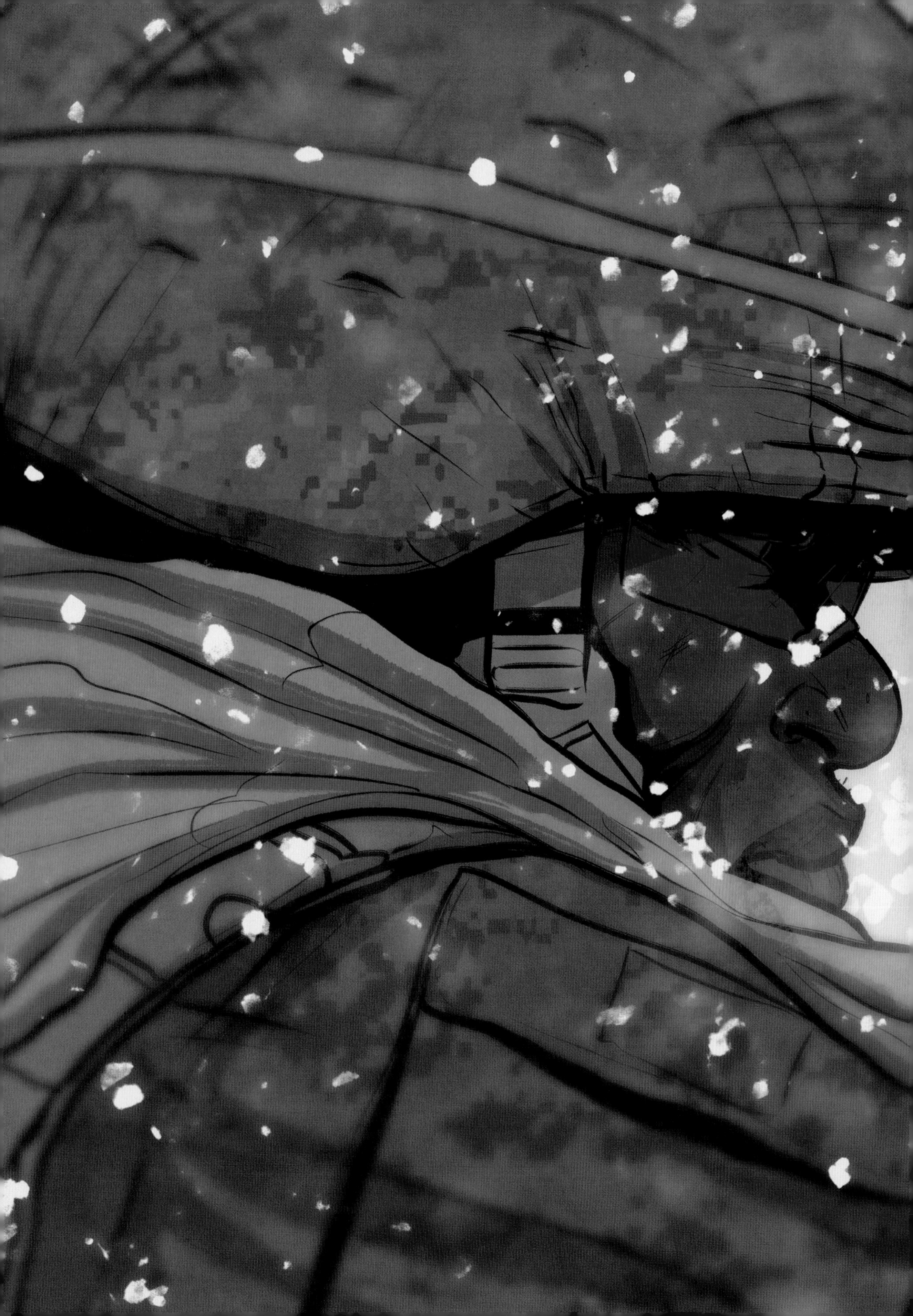

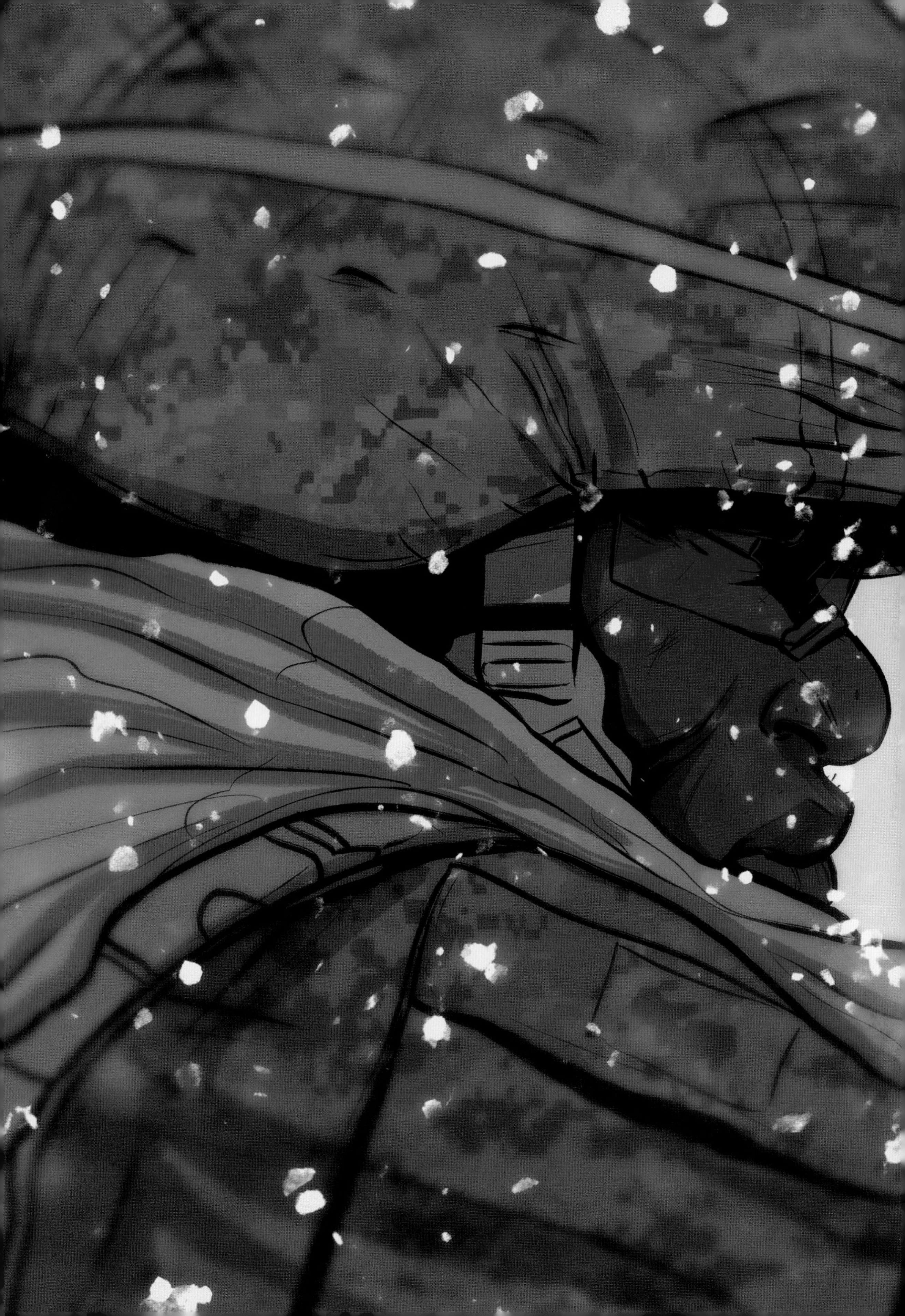

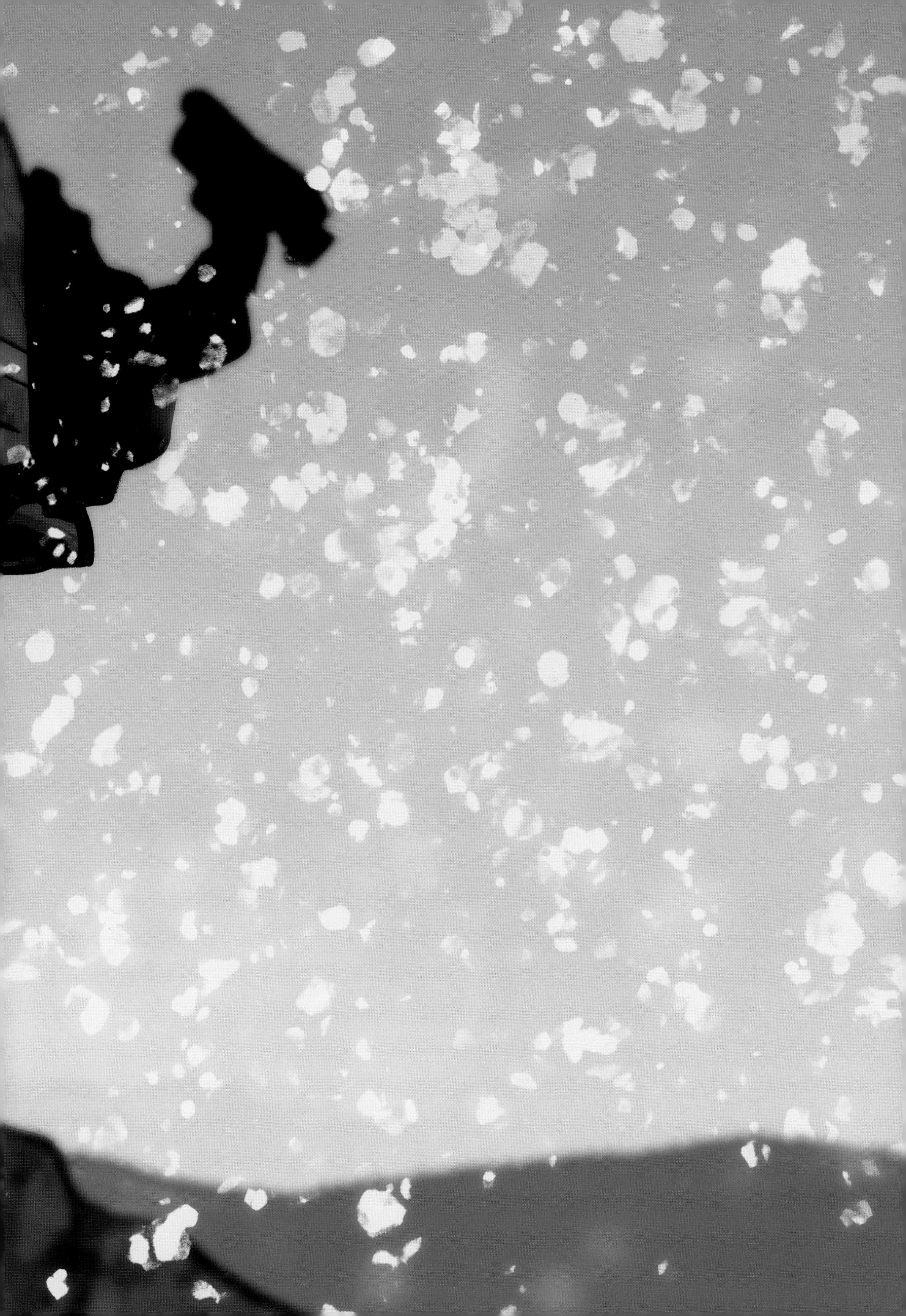

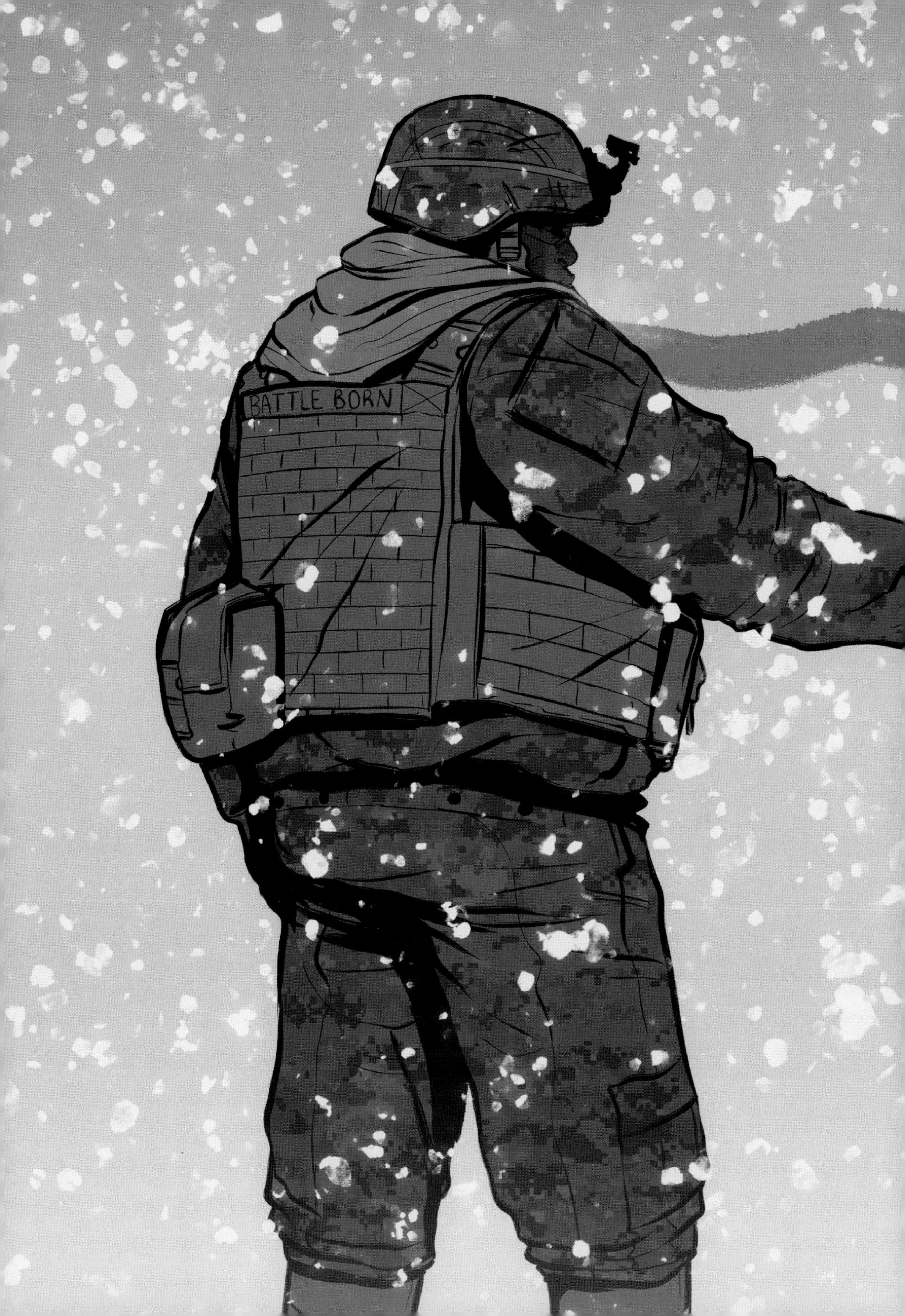
BATTLE BORN

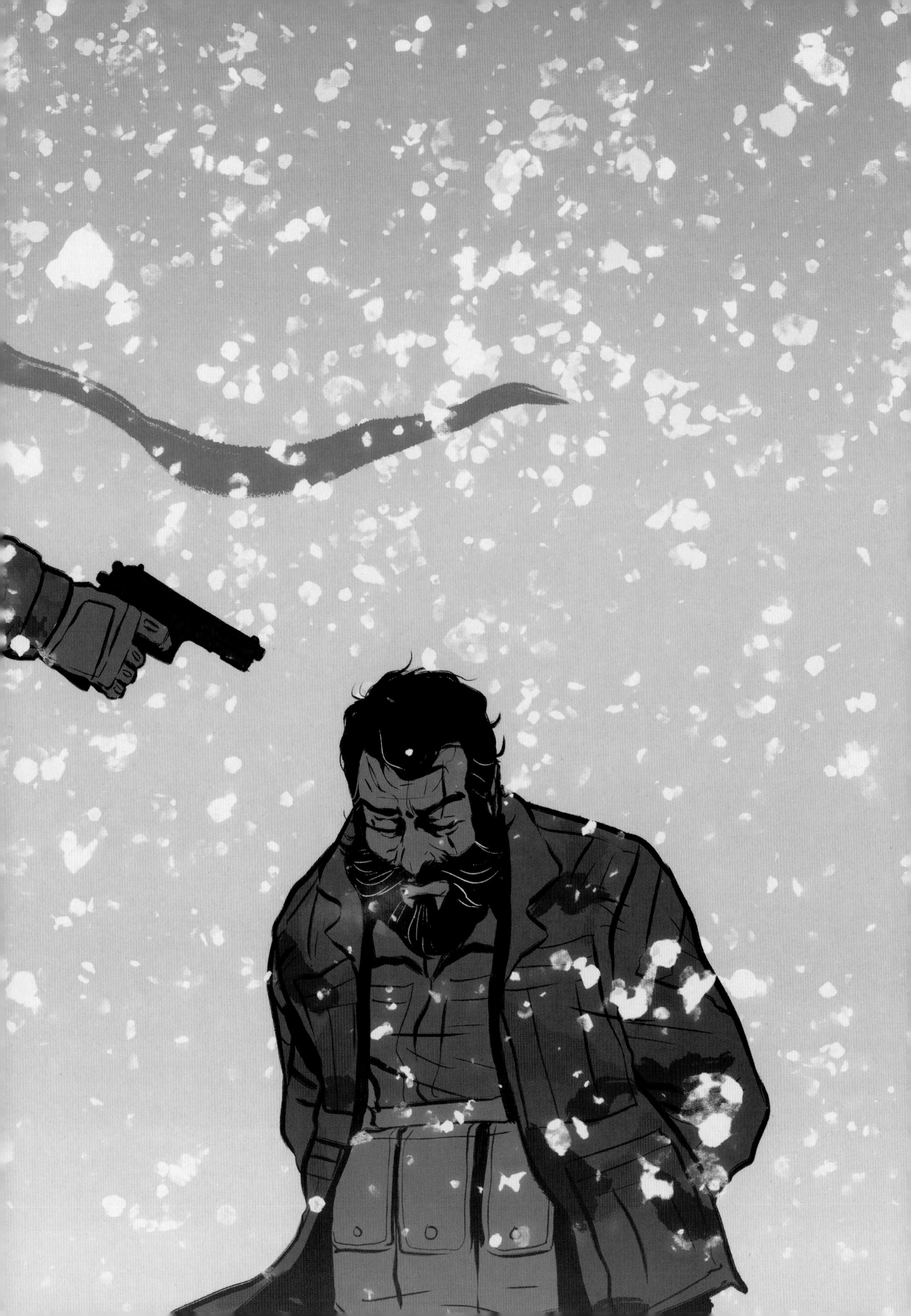

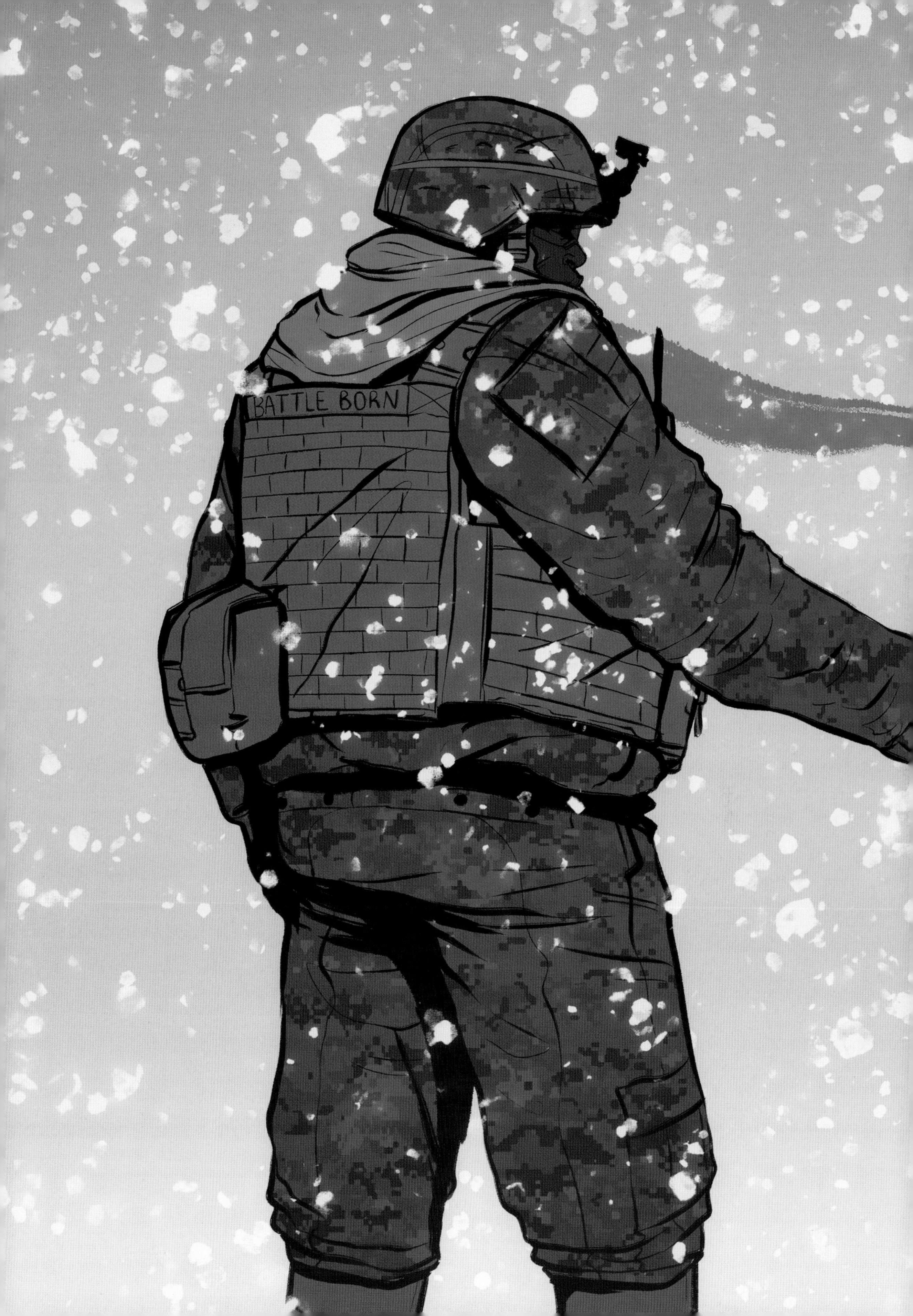
BATTLE BORN

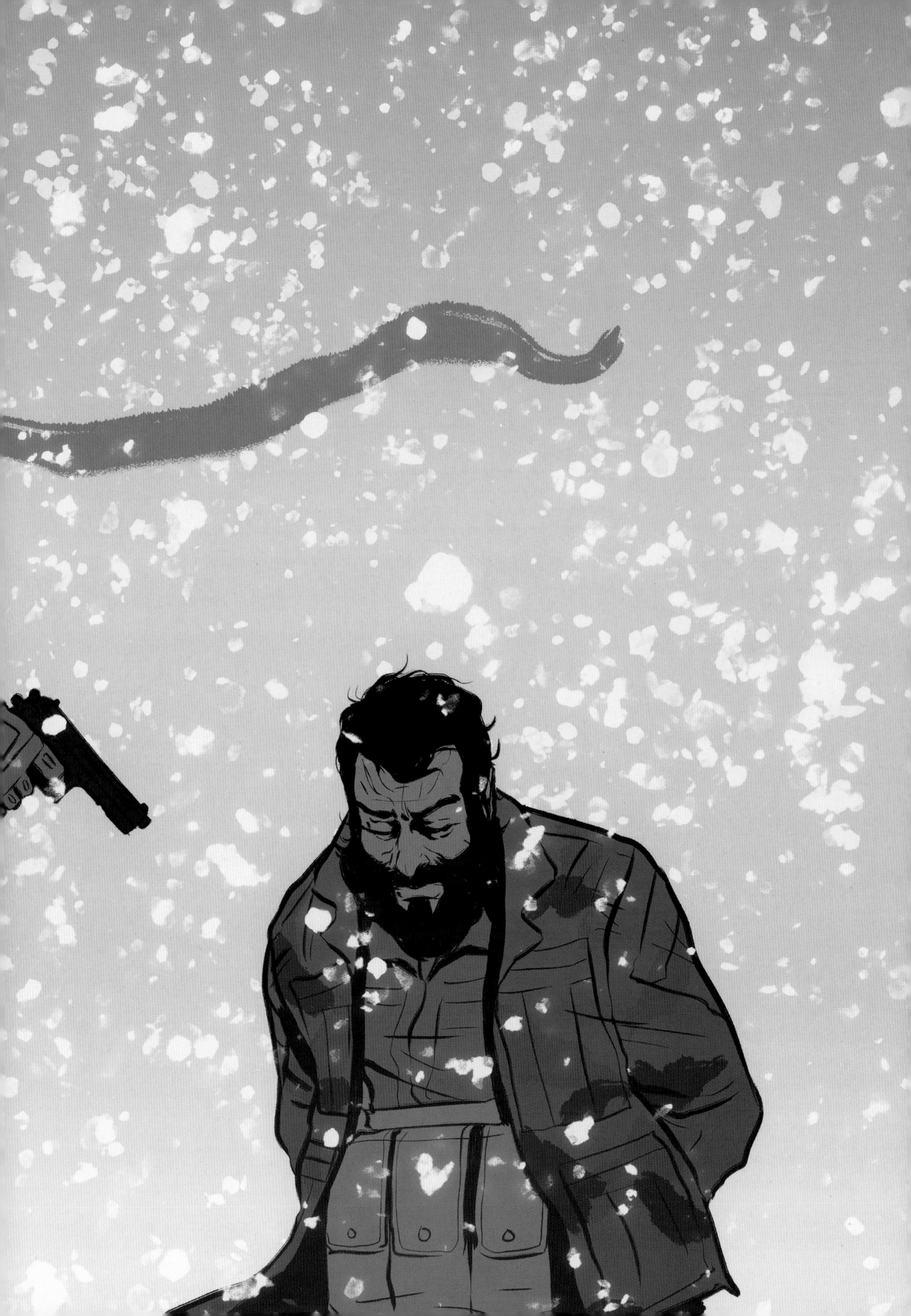

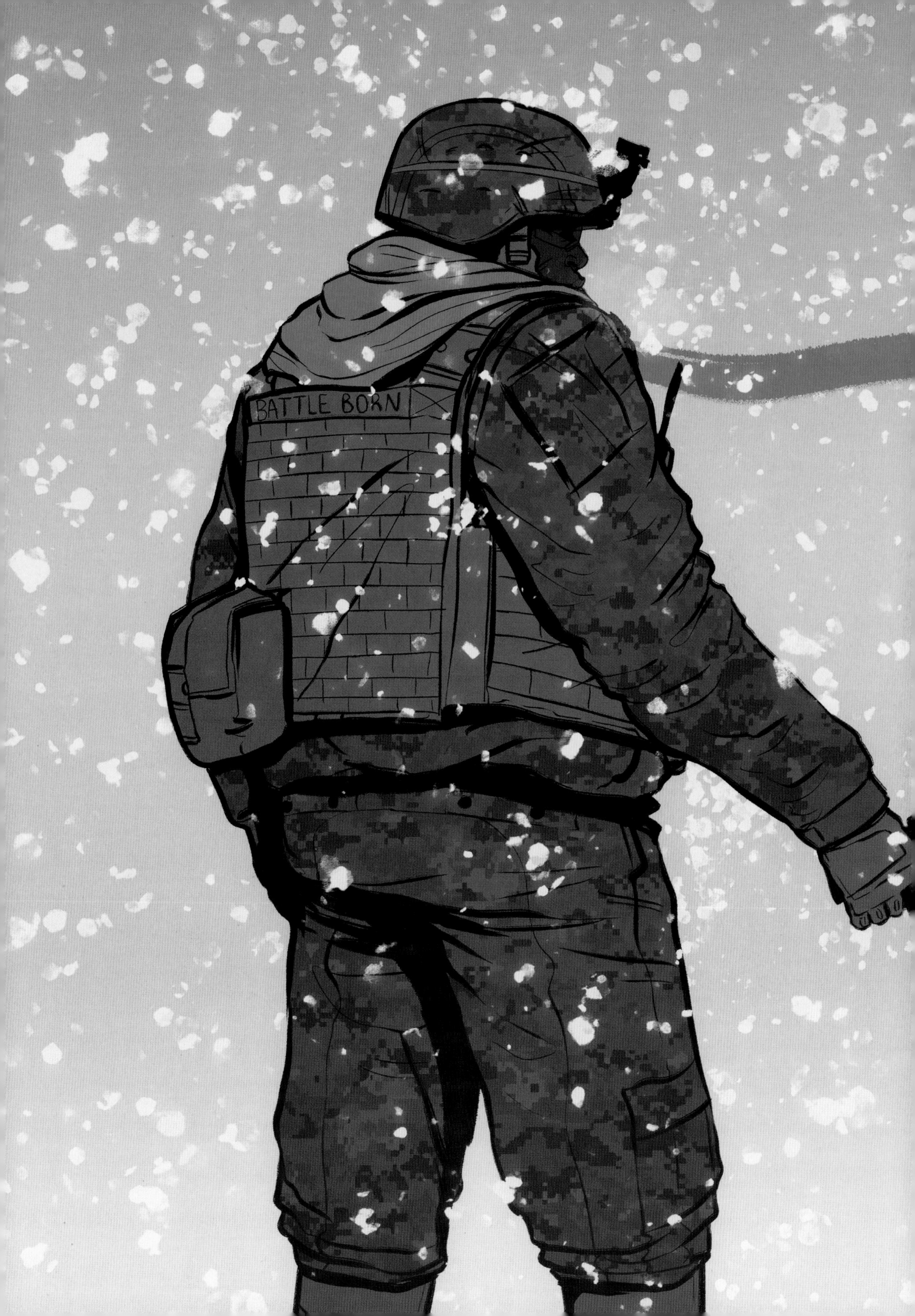
BATTLE BORN

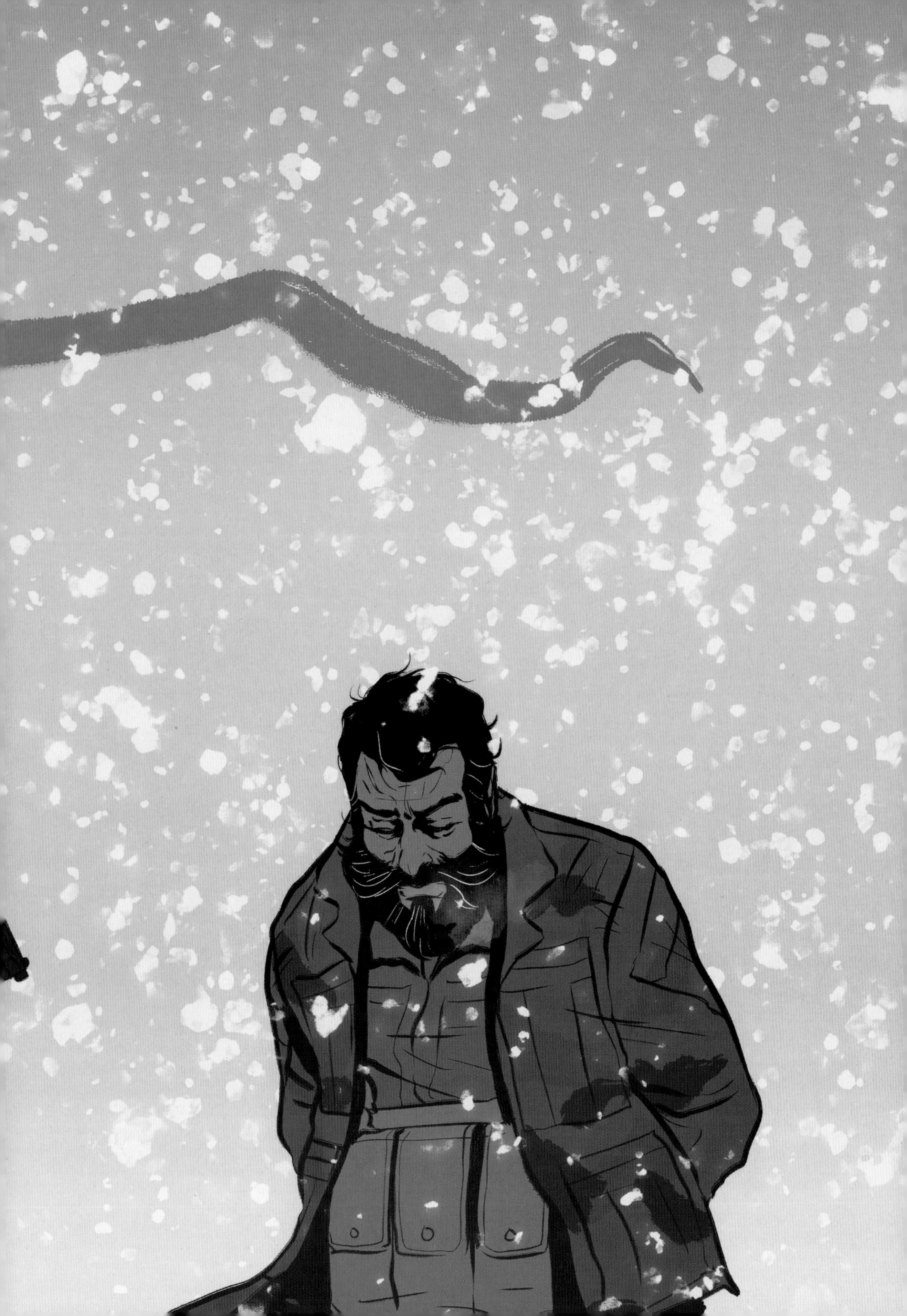

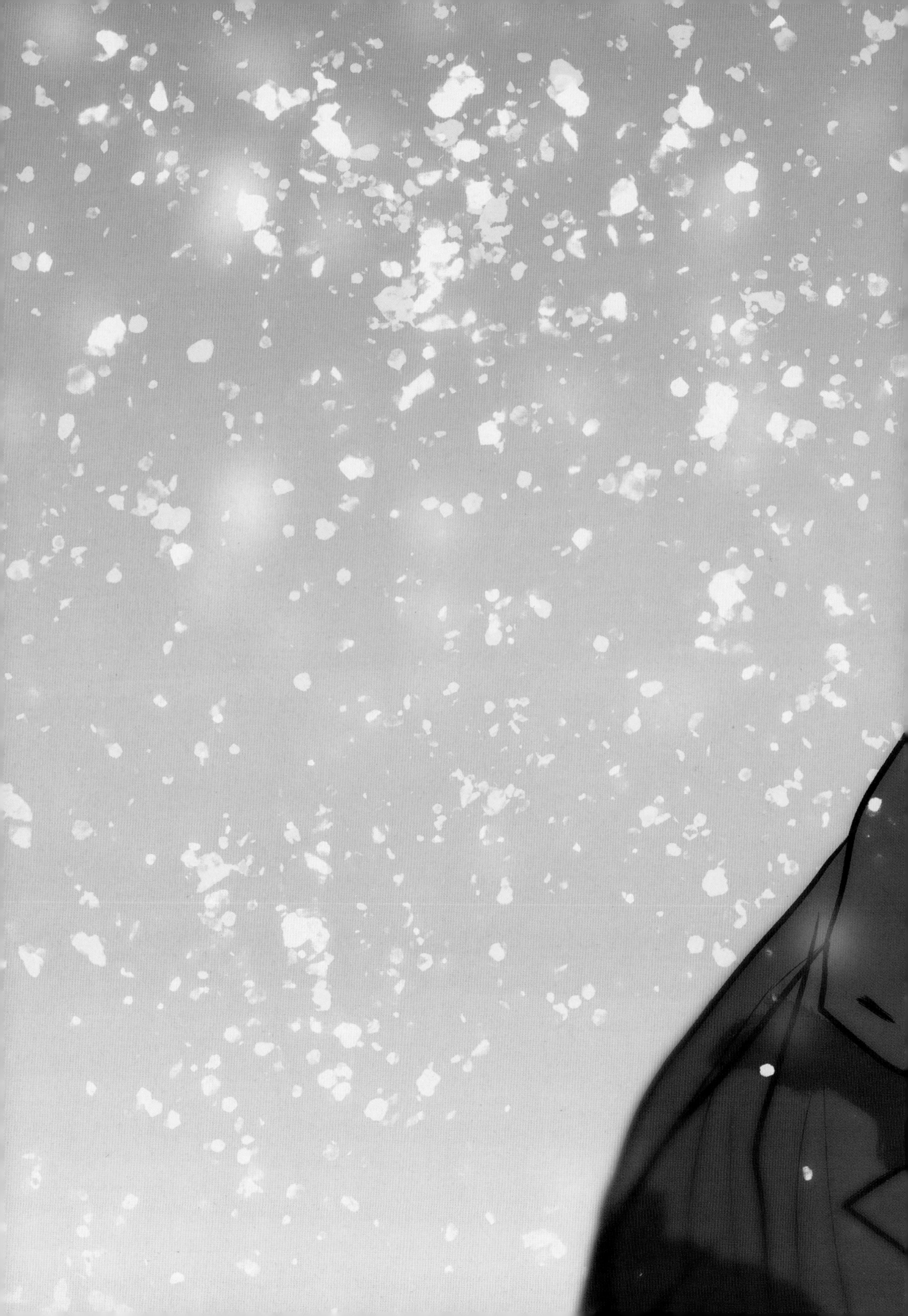

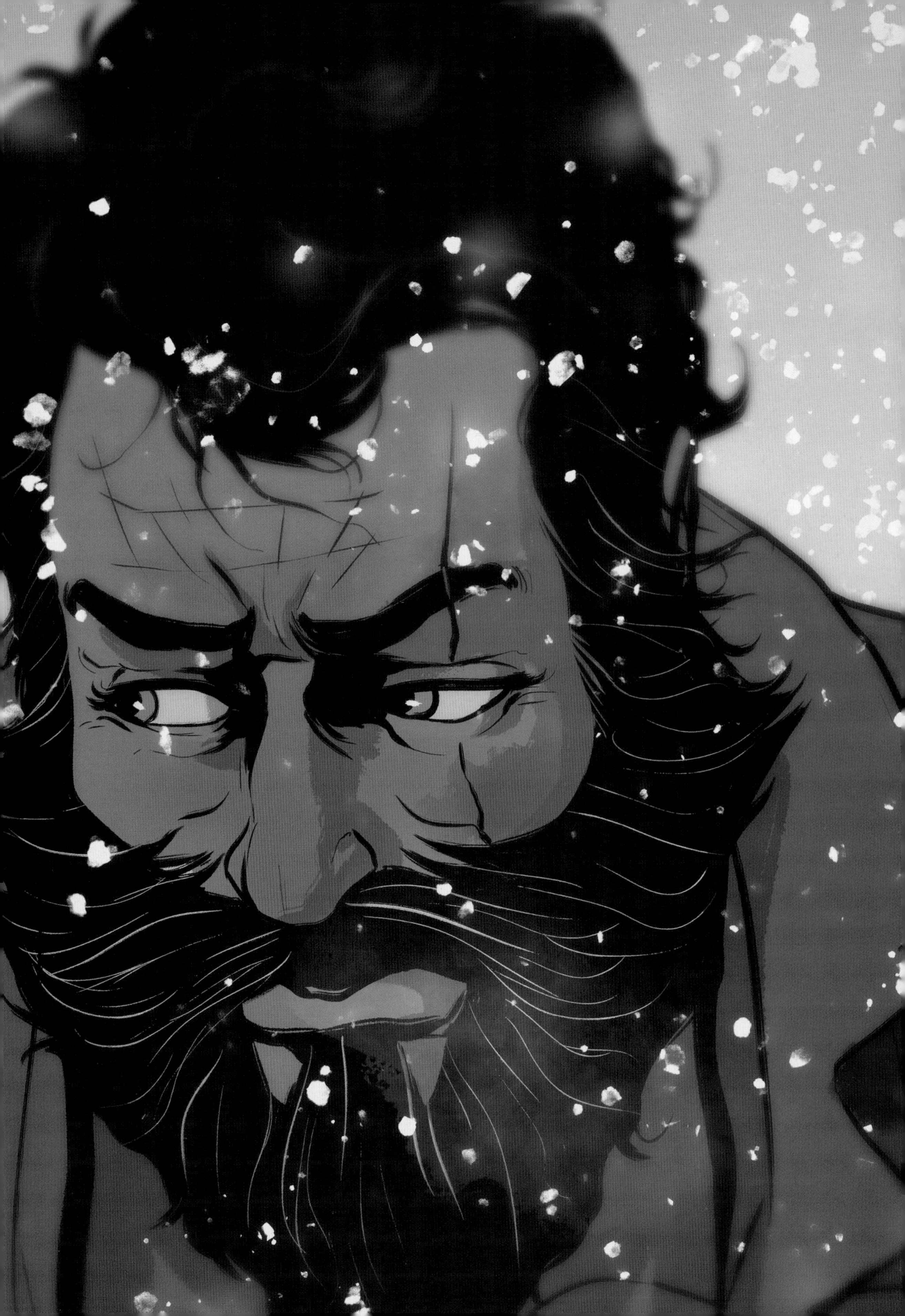

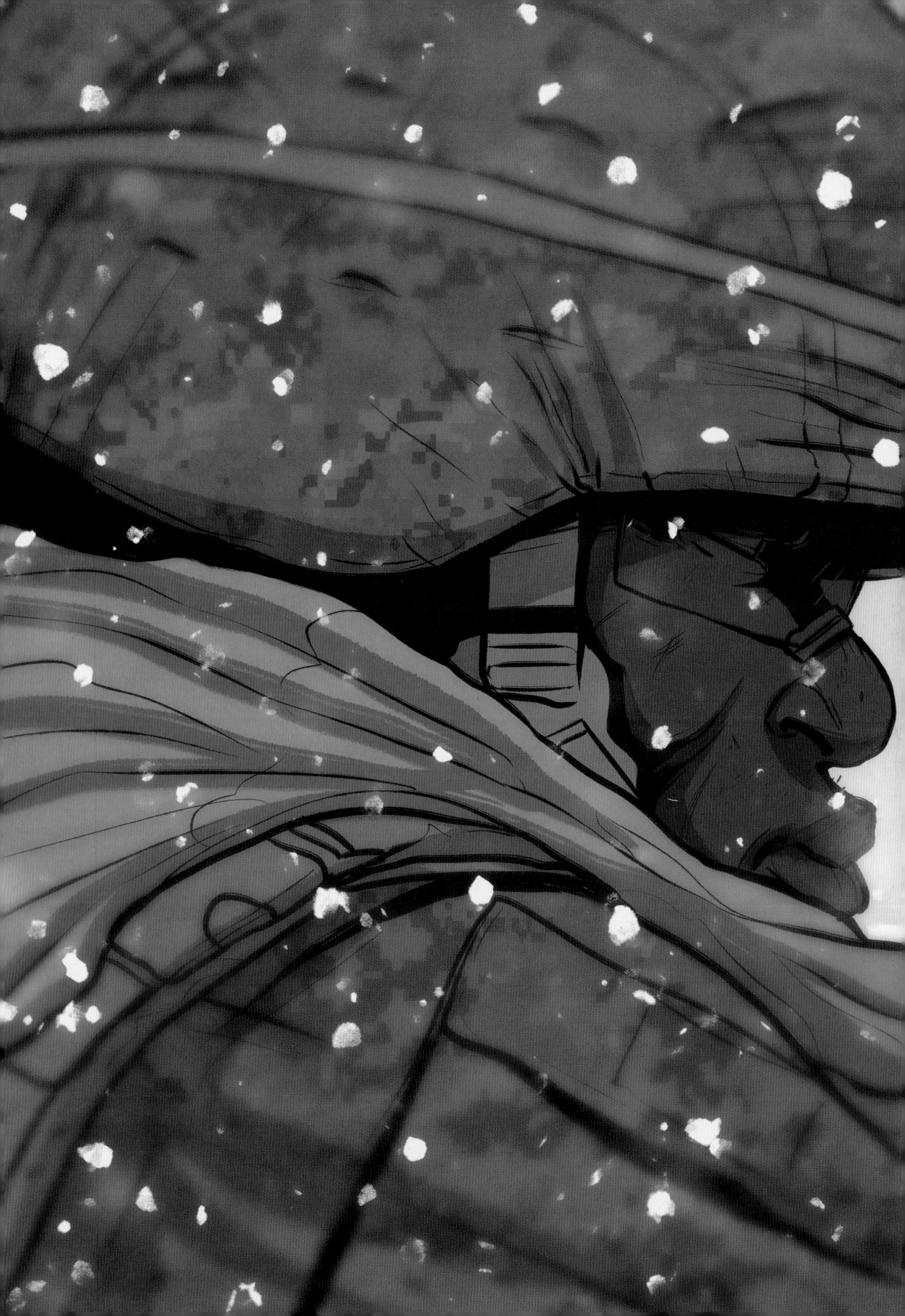

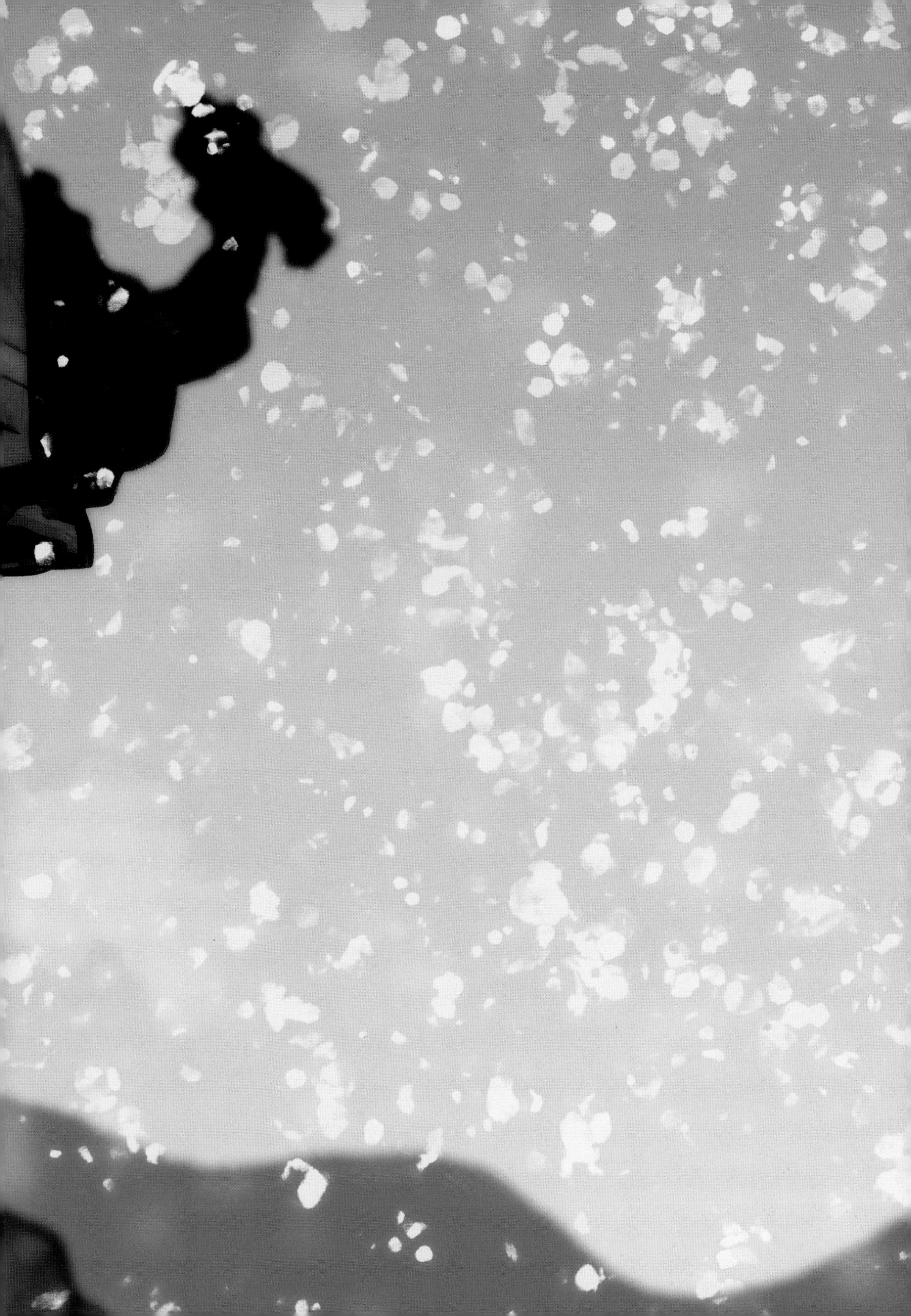

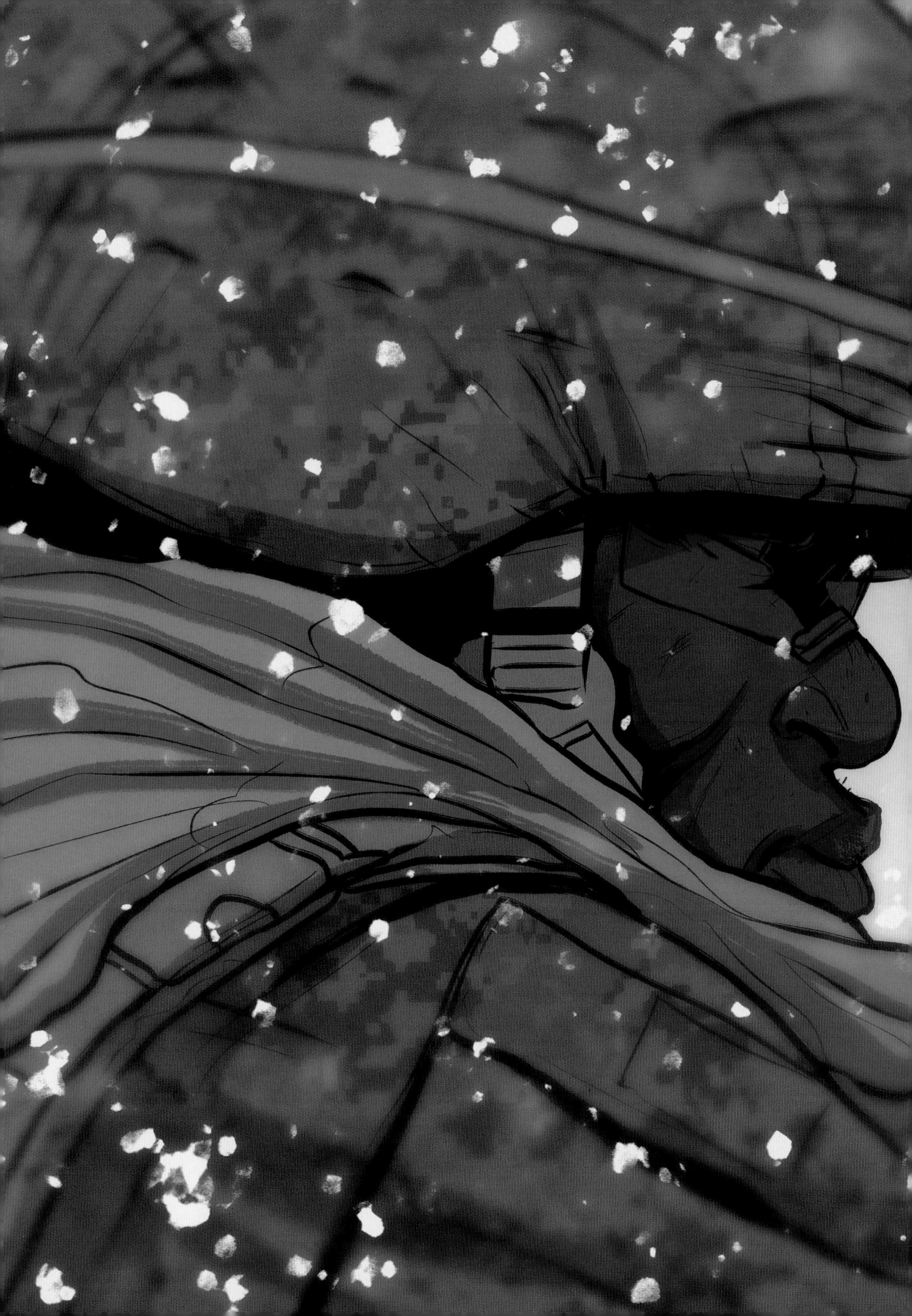

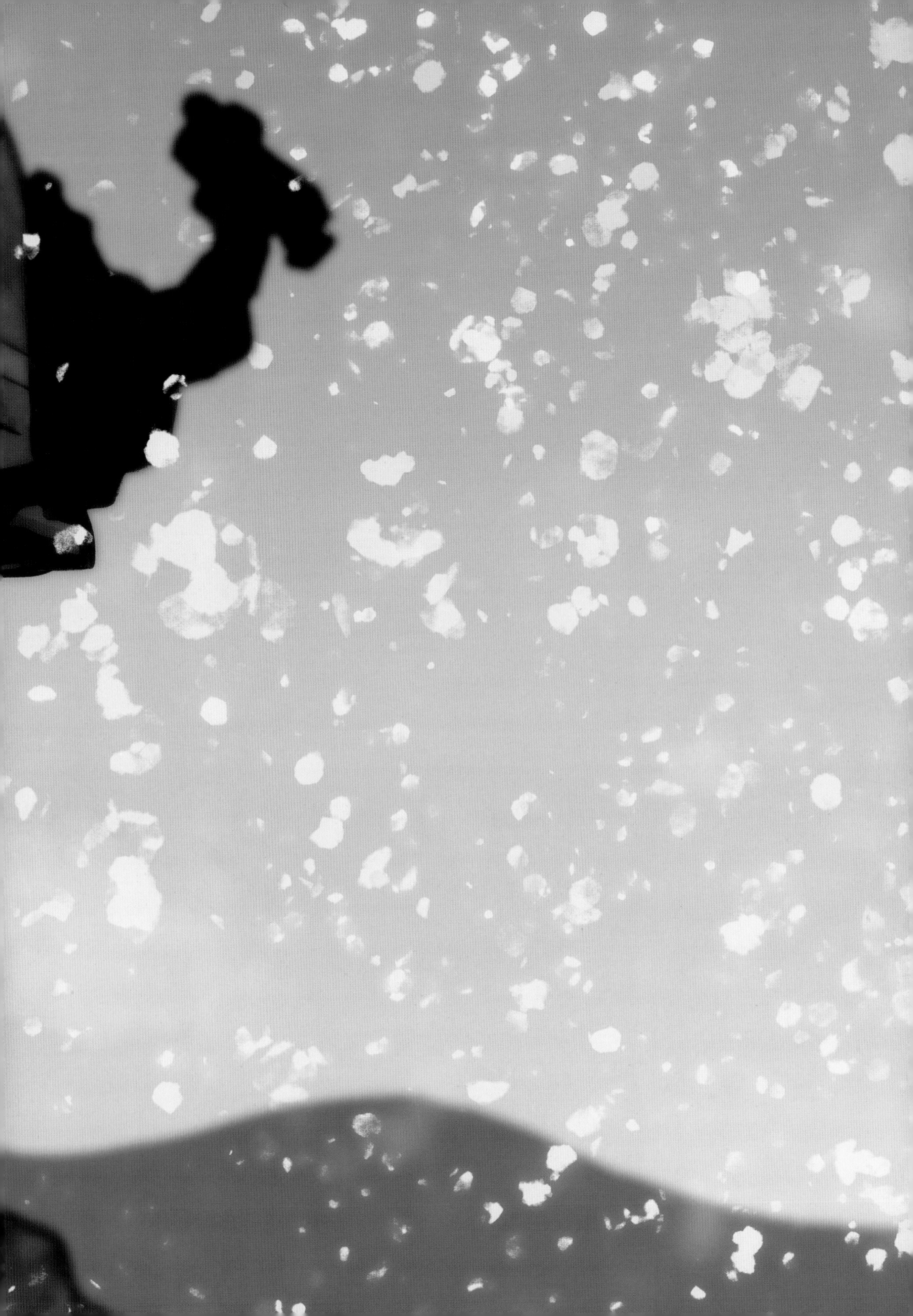

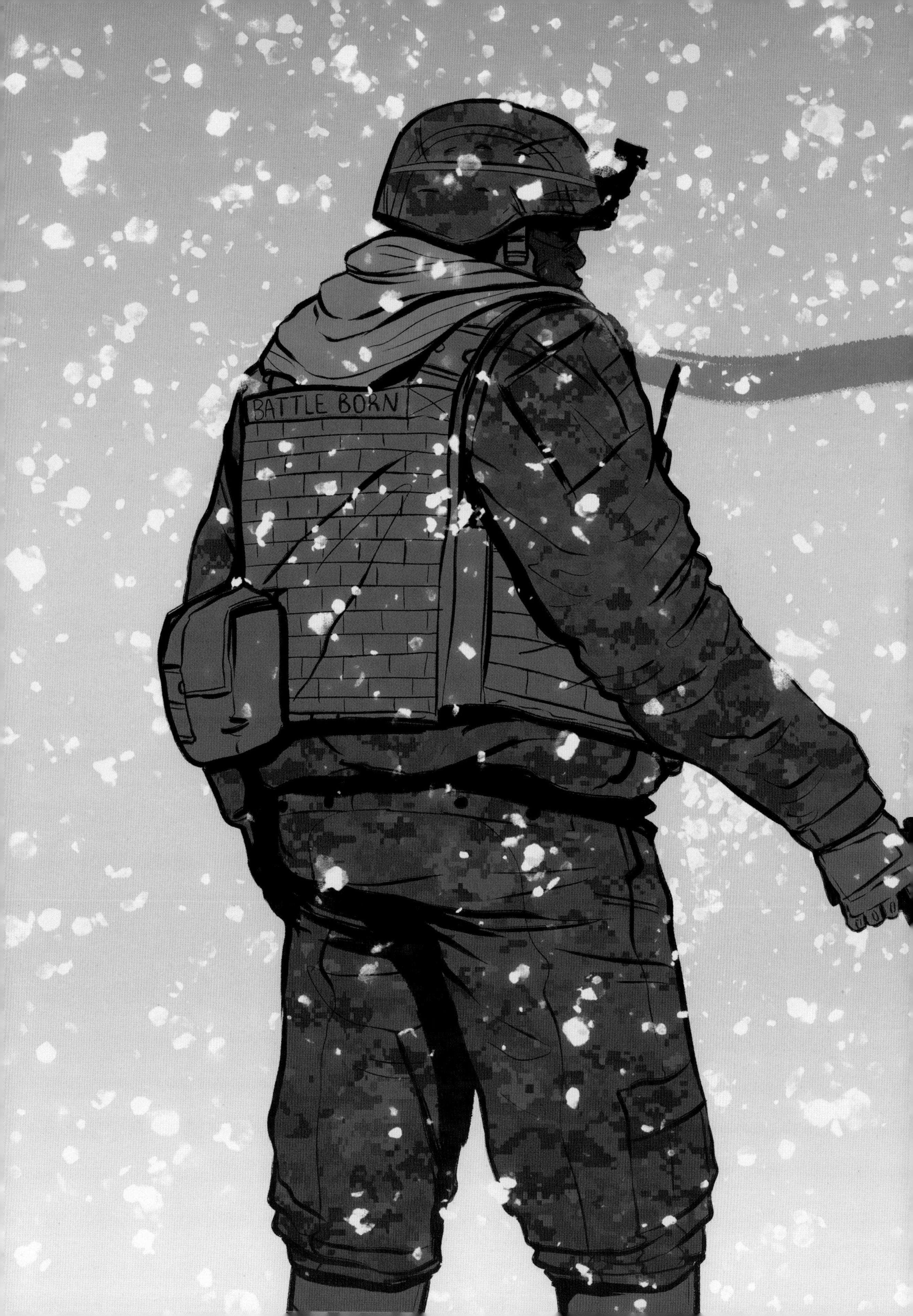
BATTLE BORN

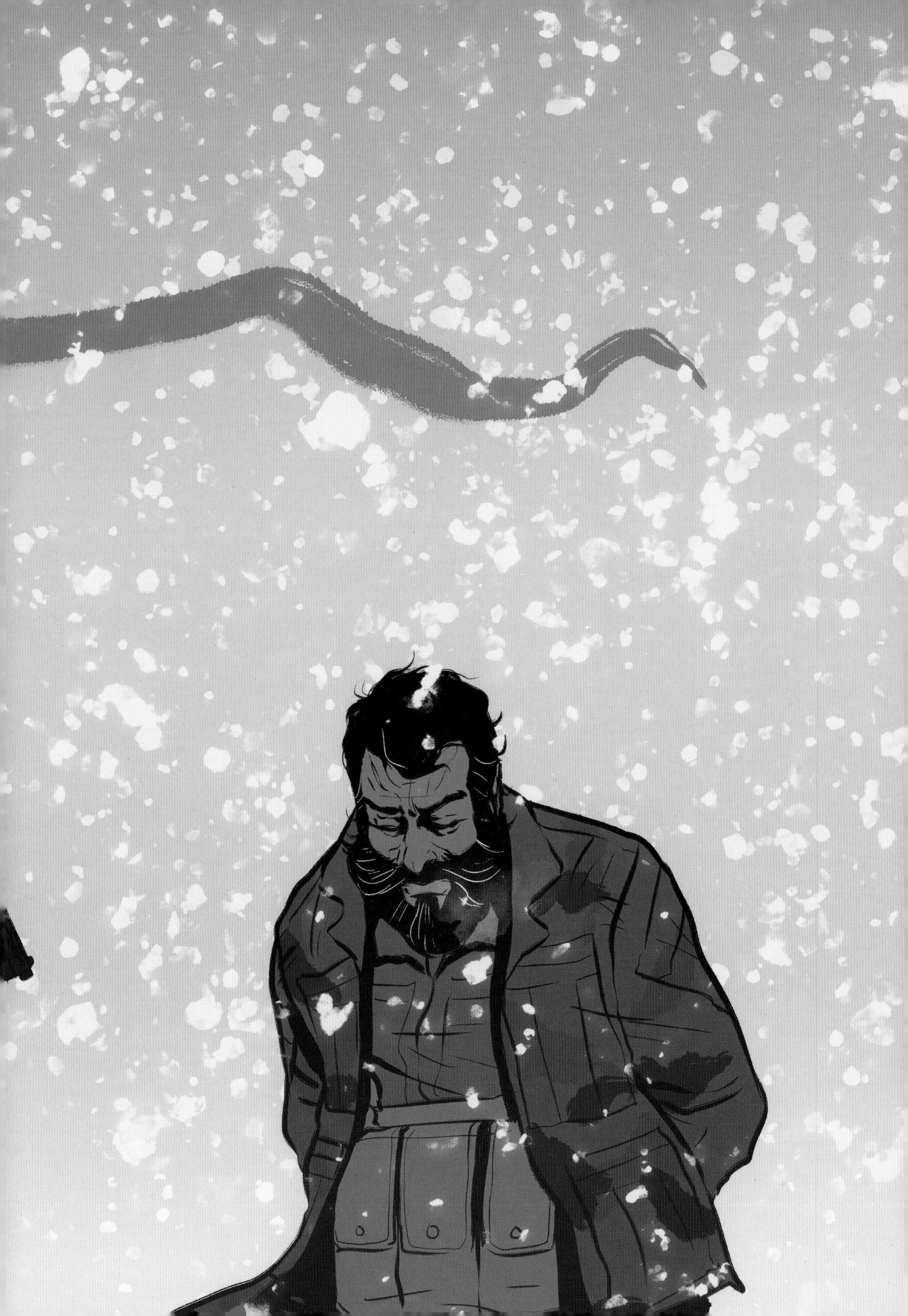

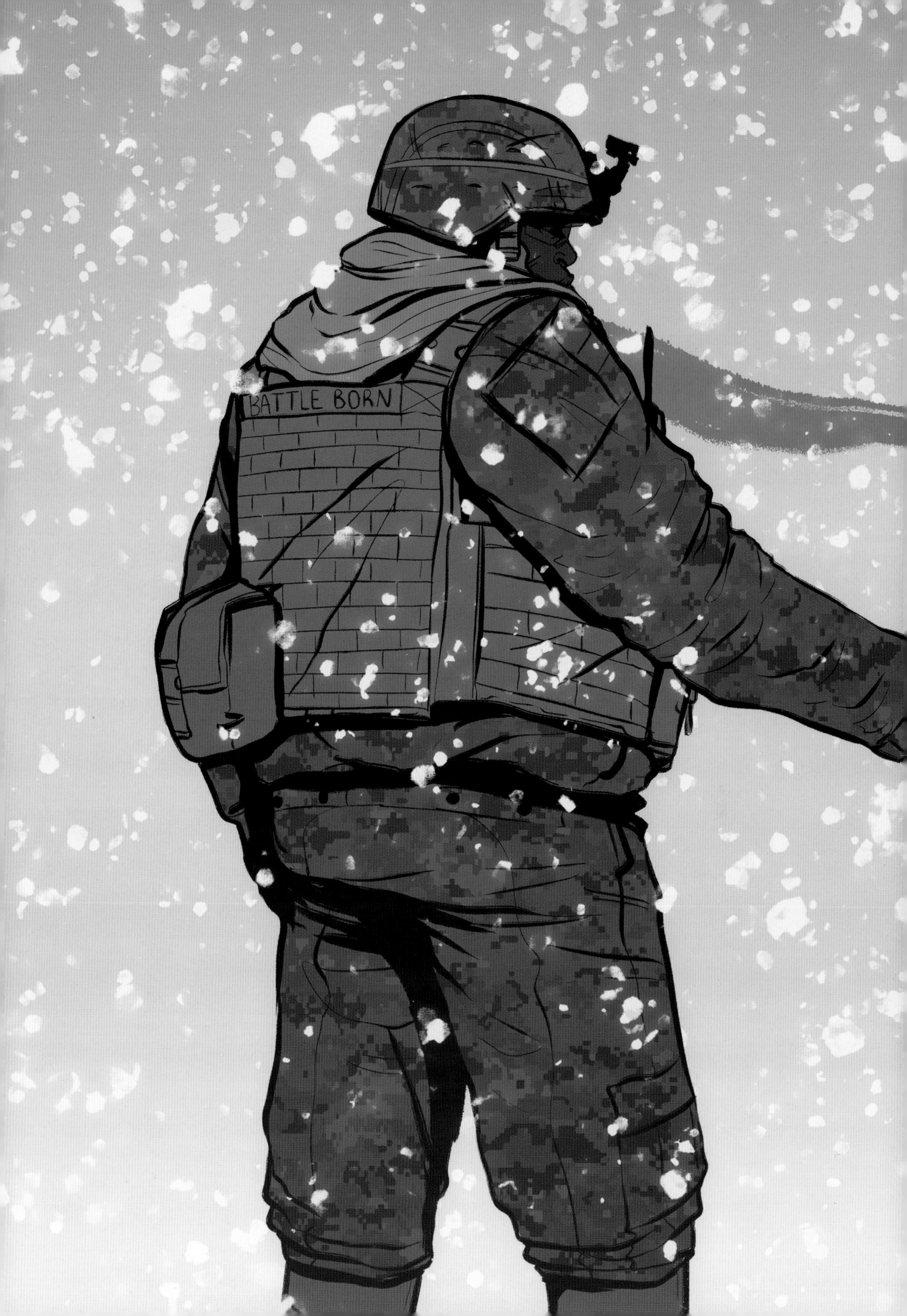
BATTLE BORN

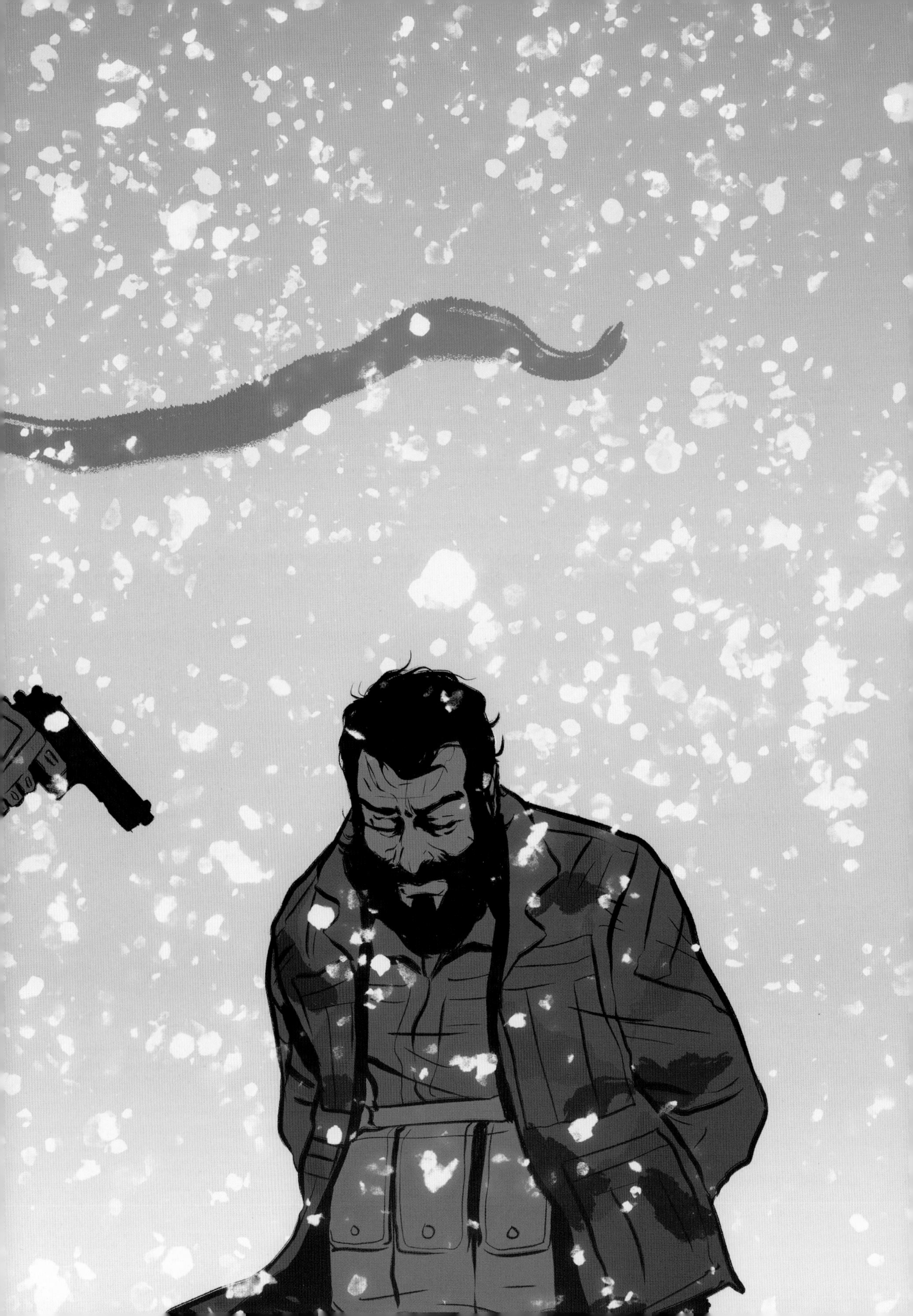

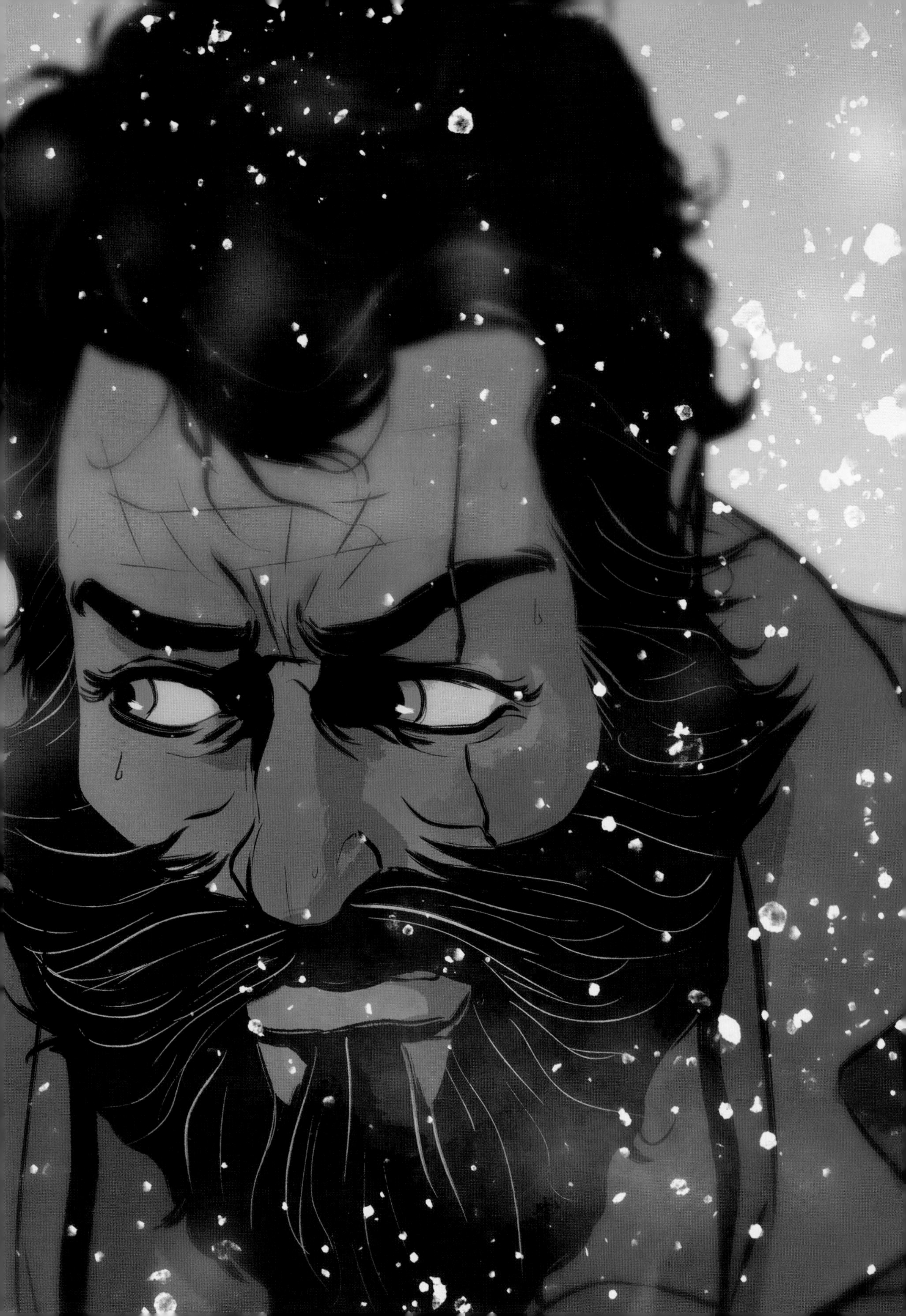

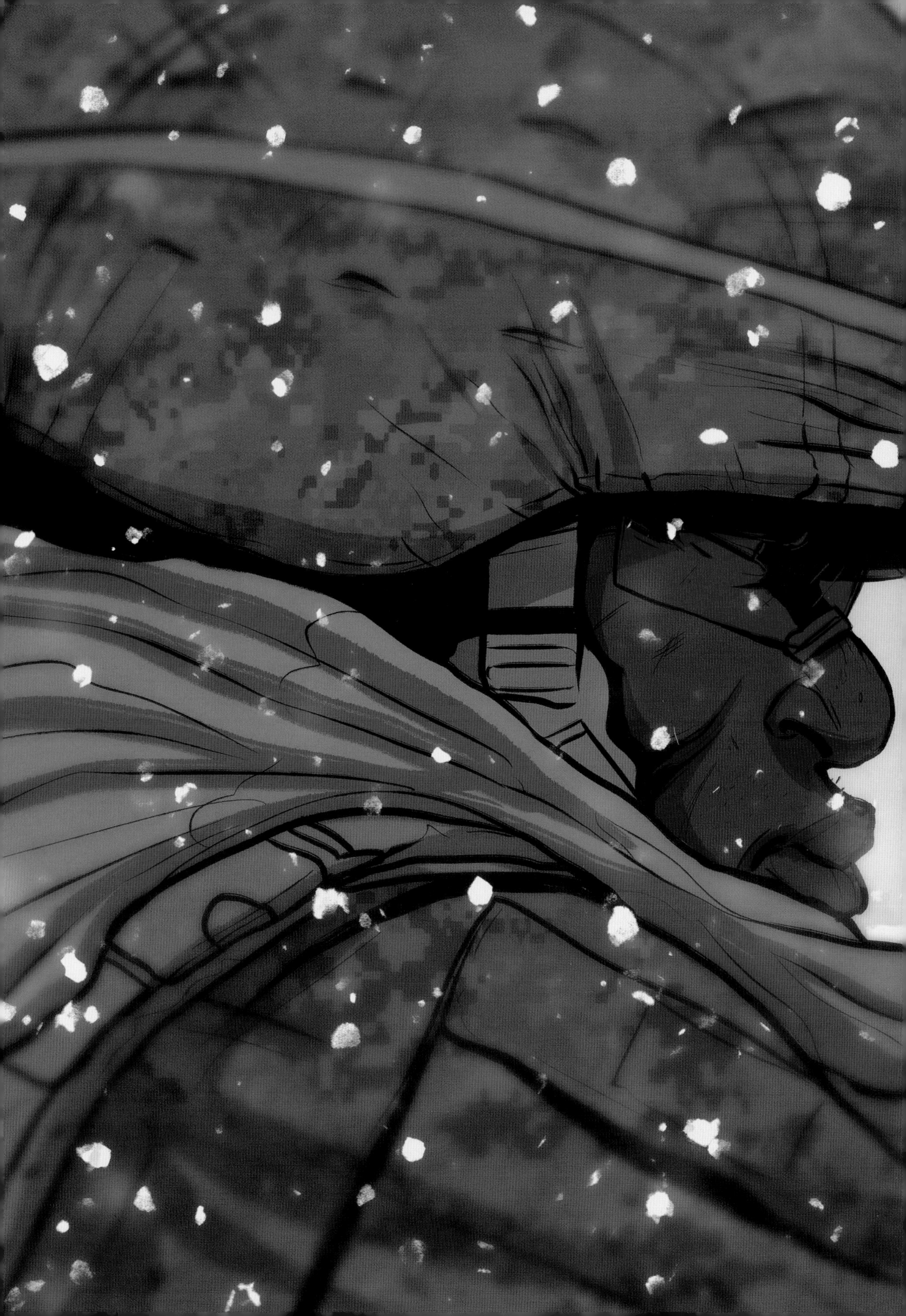

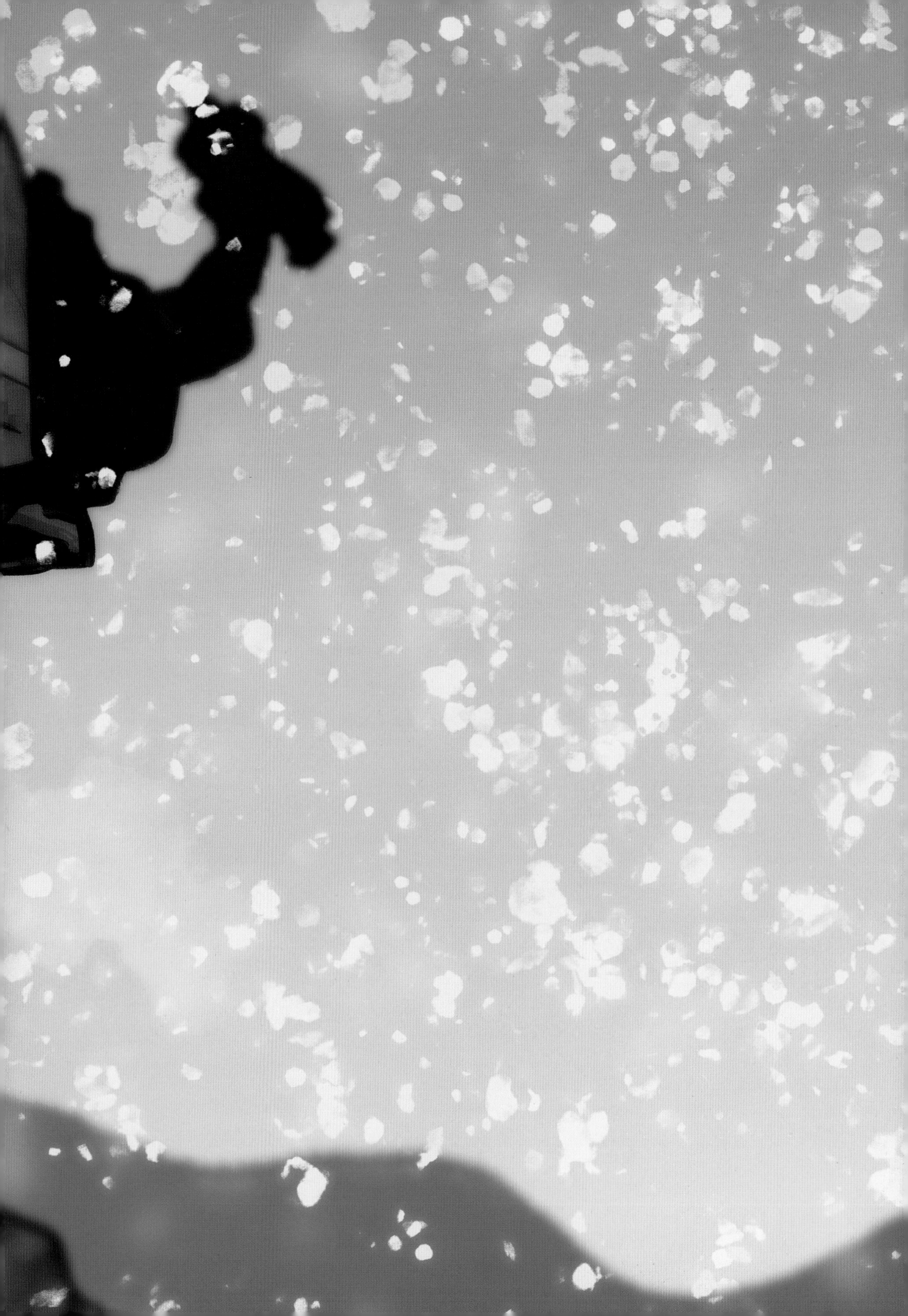

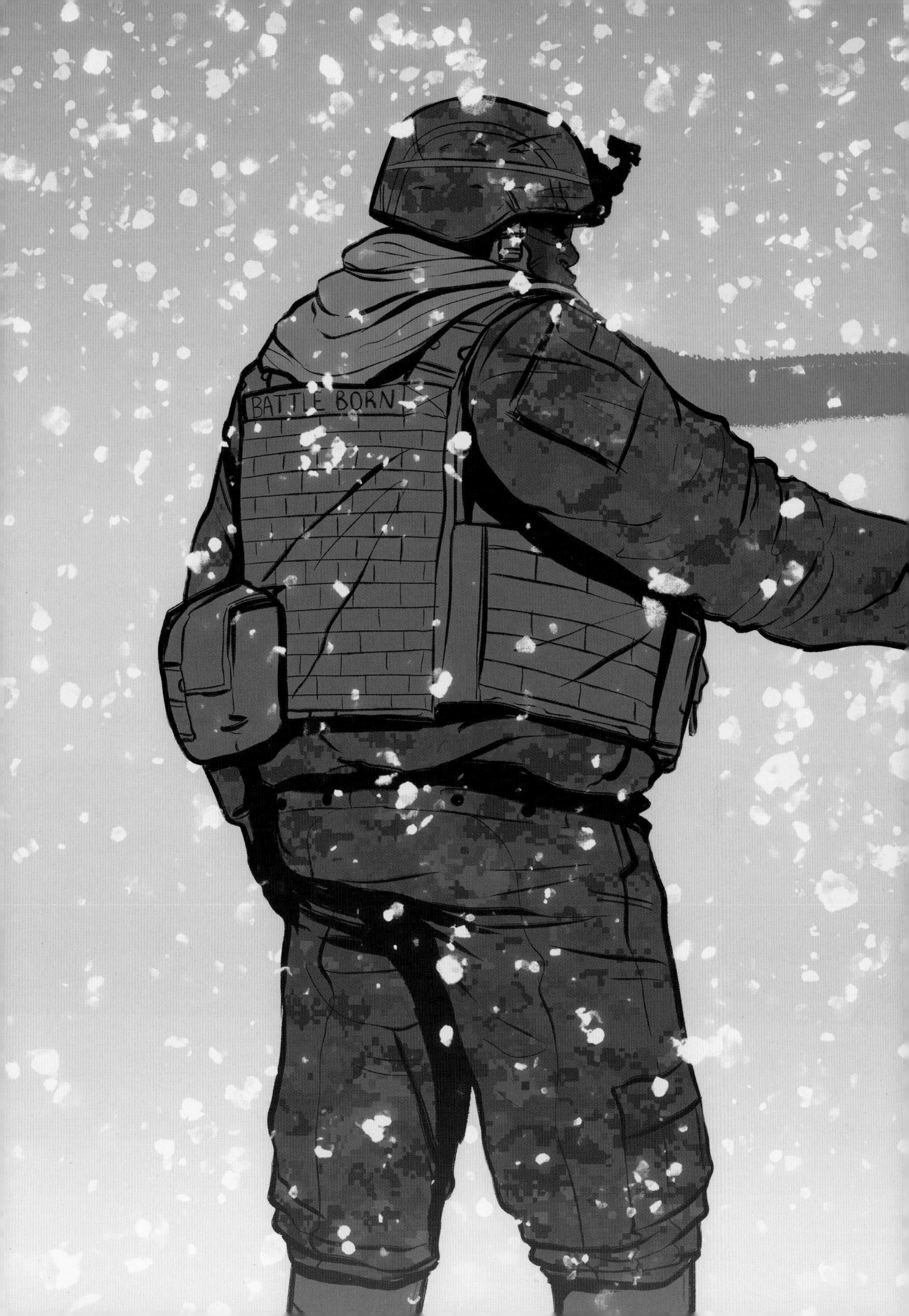
BATTLE BORN

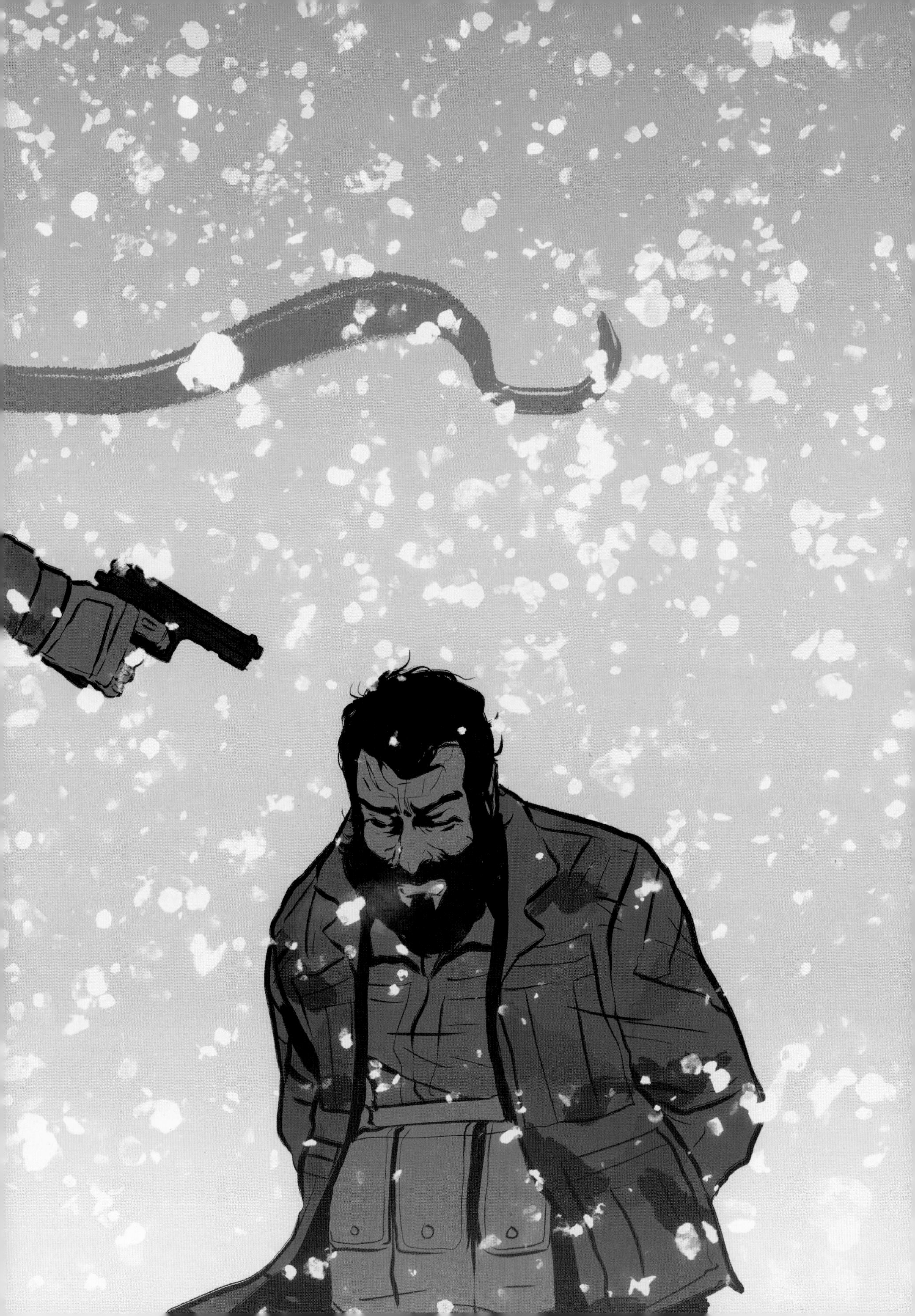

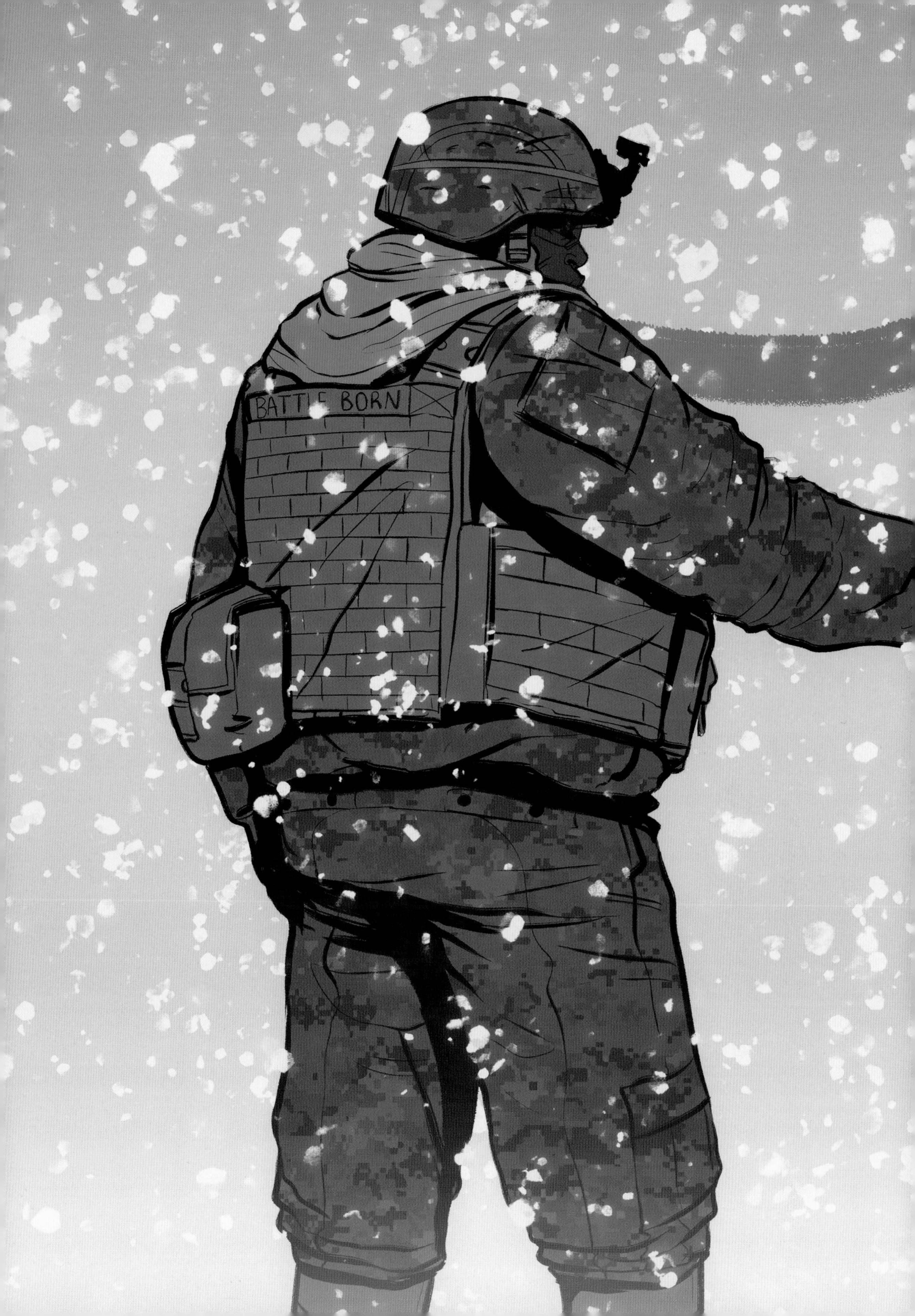
BATTLE BORN

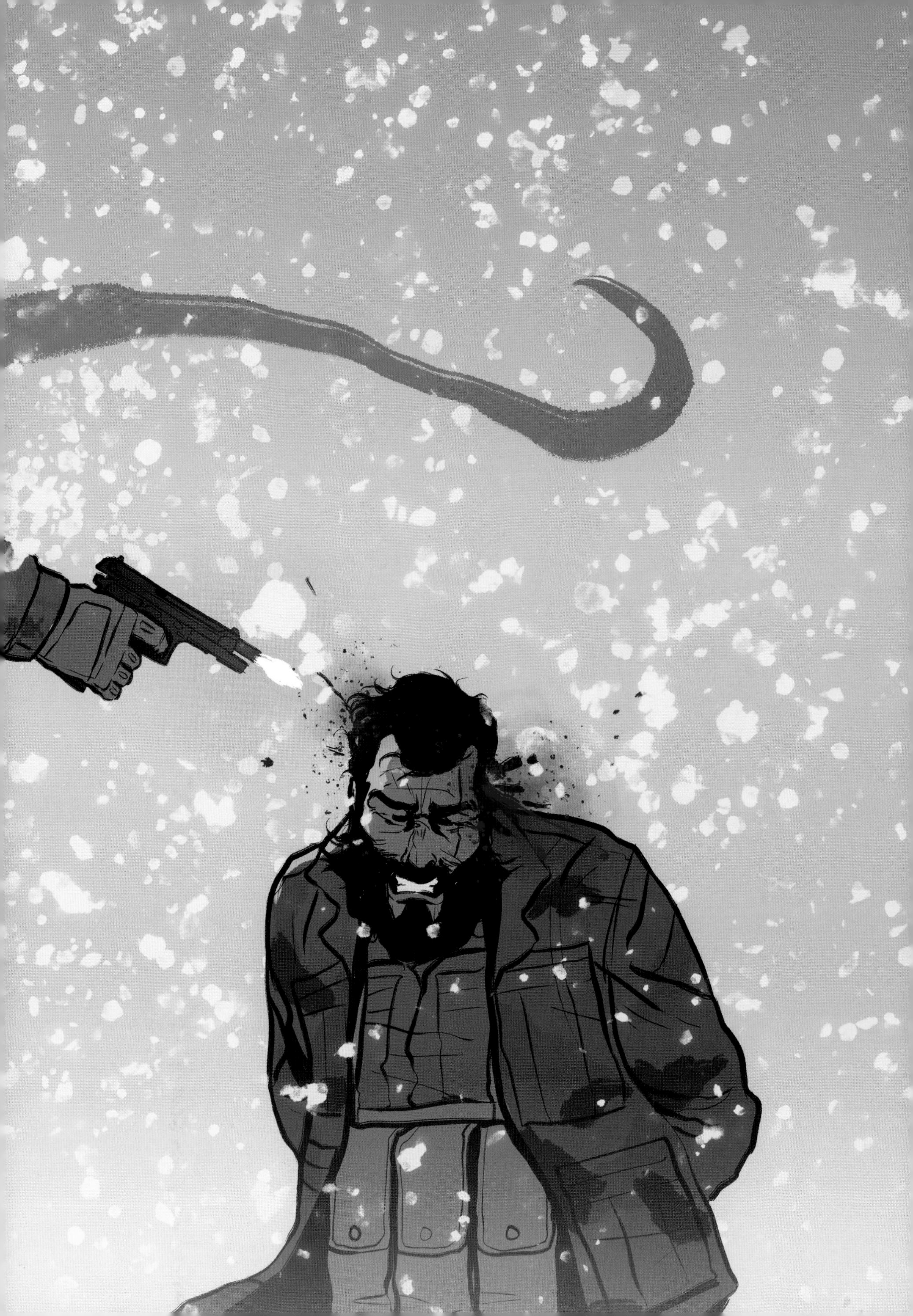

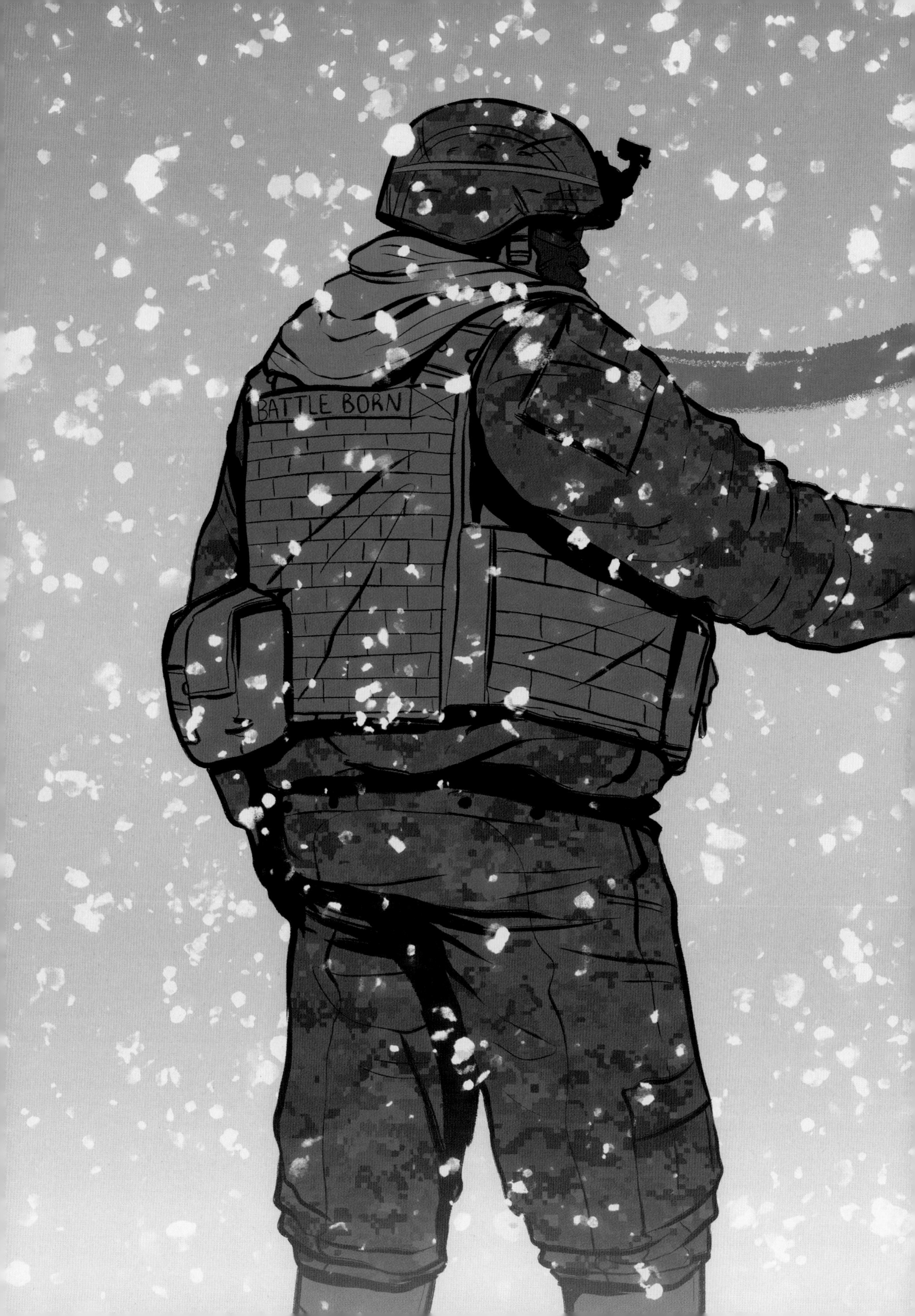
BATTLE BORN

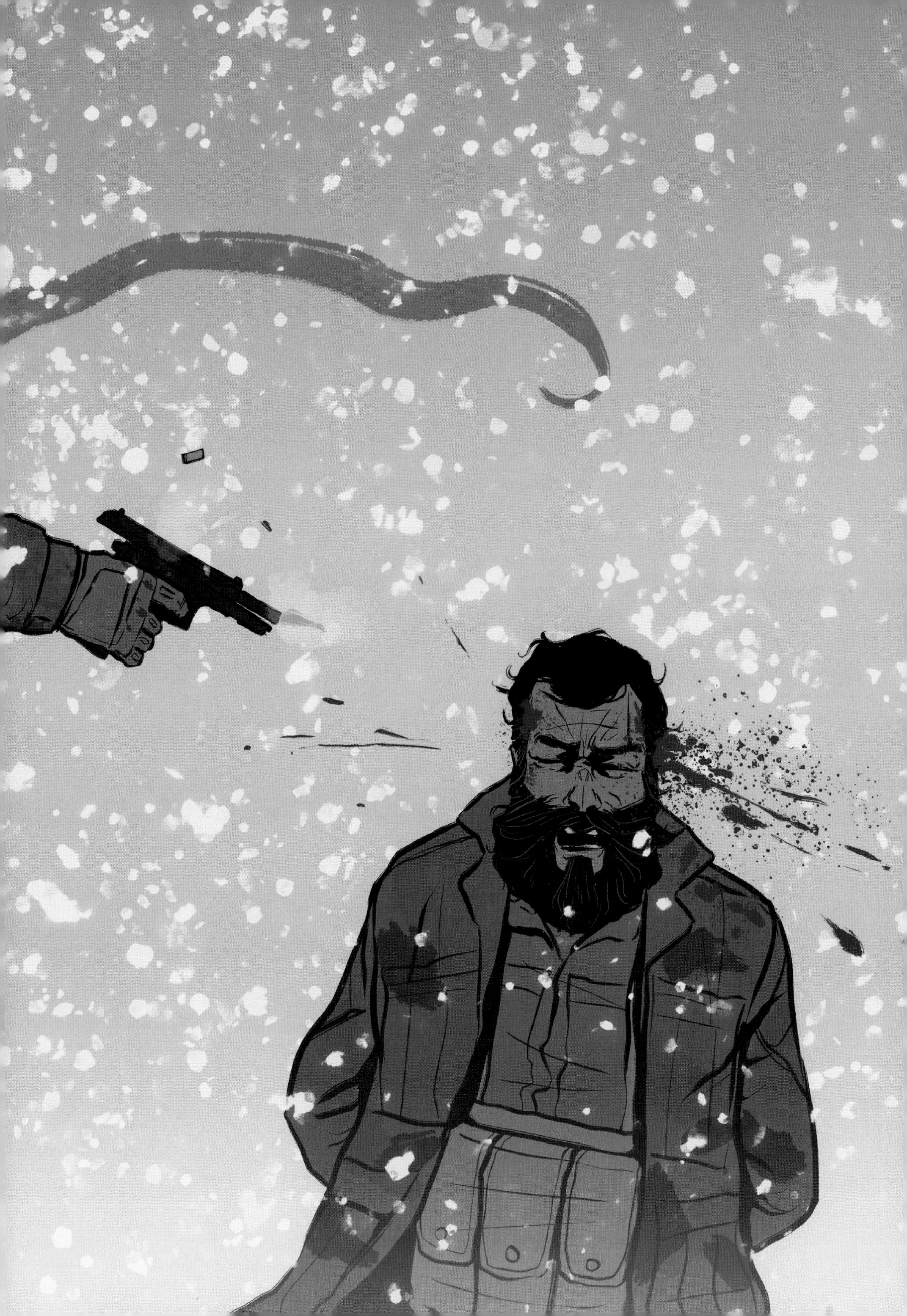

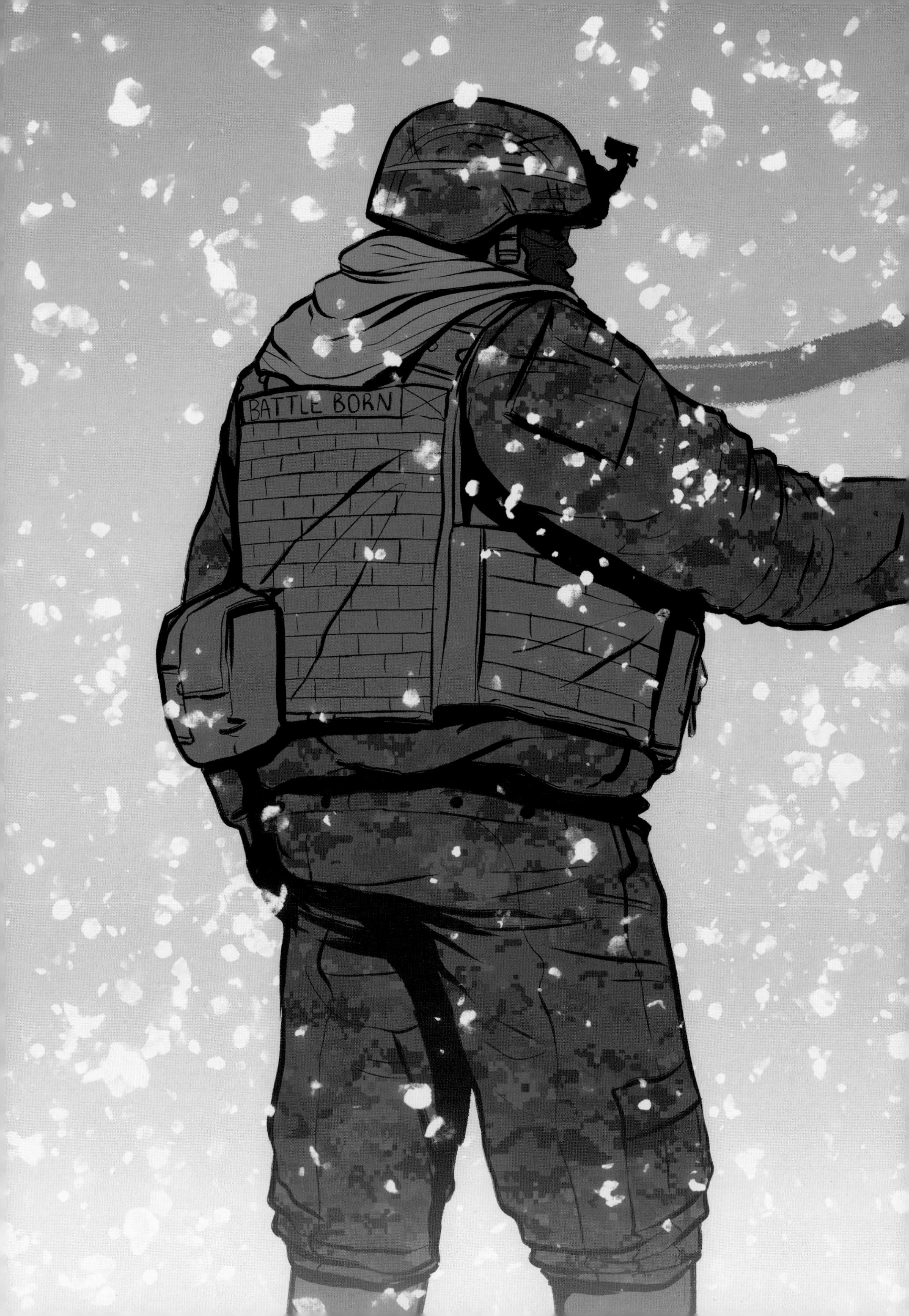
BATTLE BORN

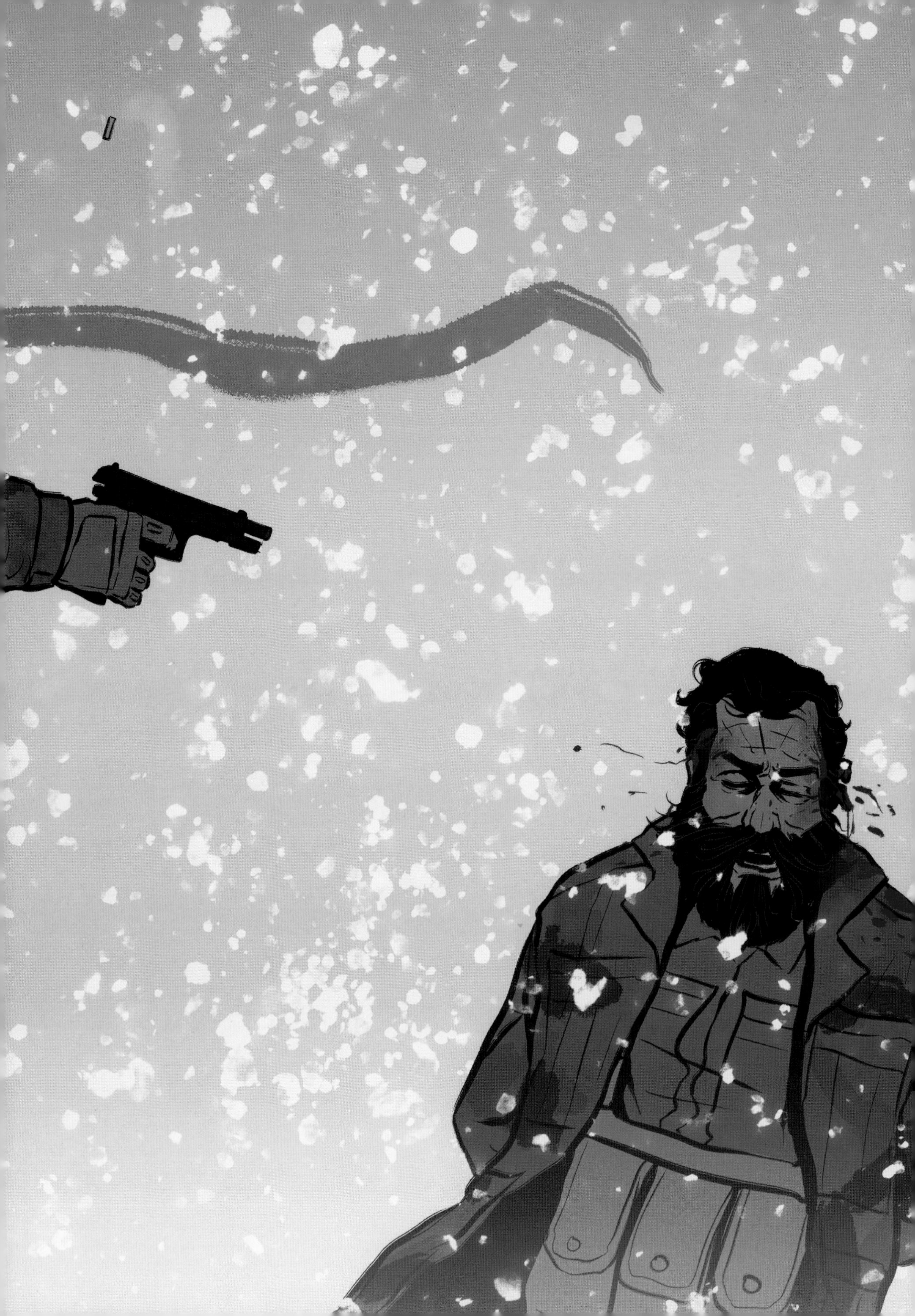

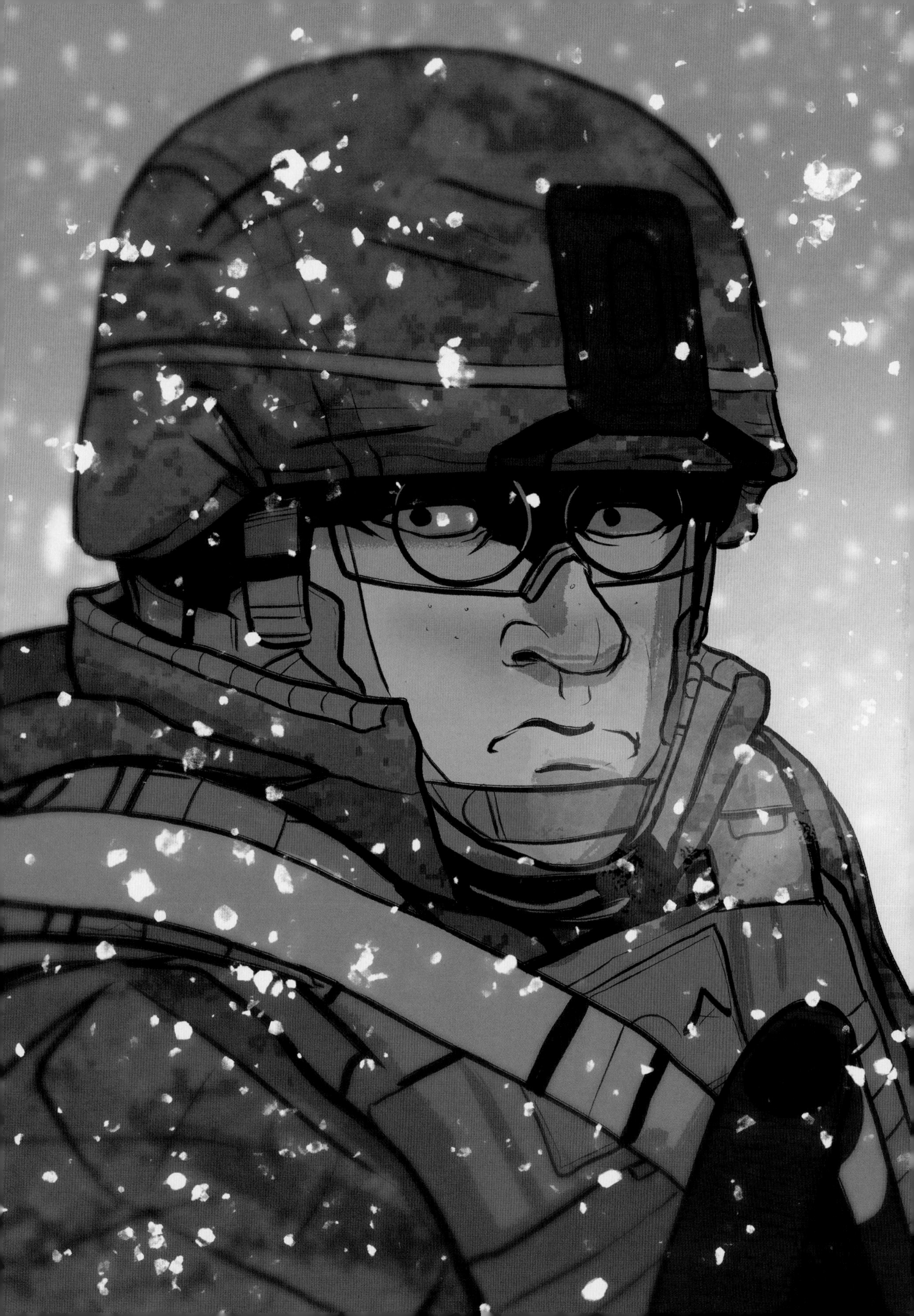

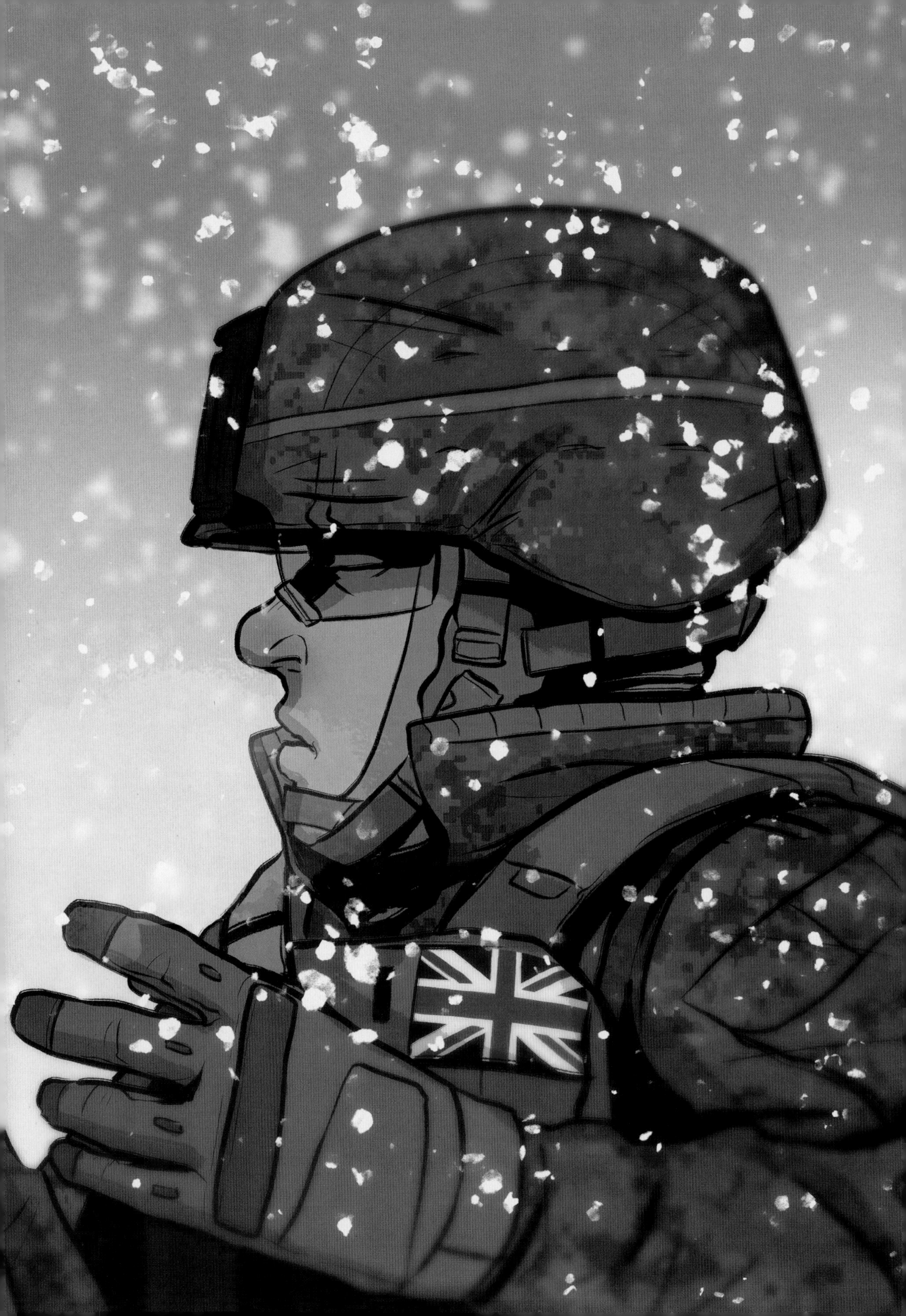

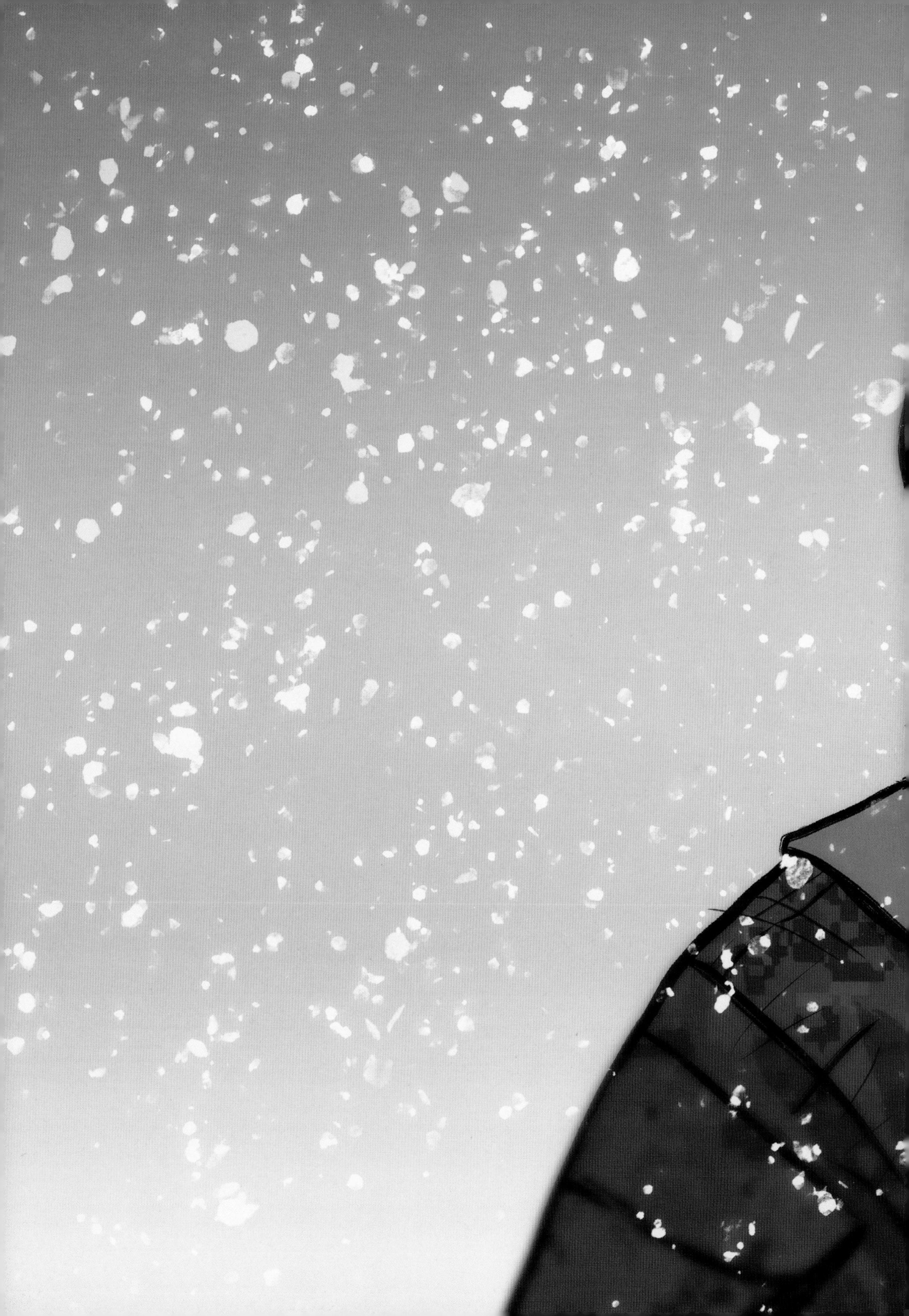

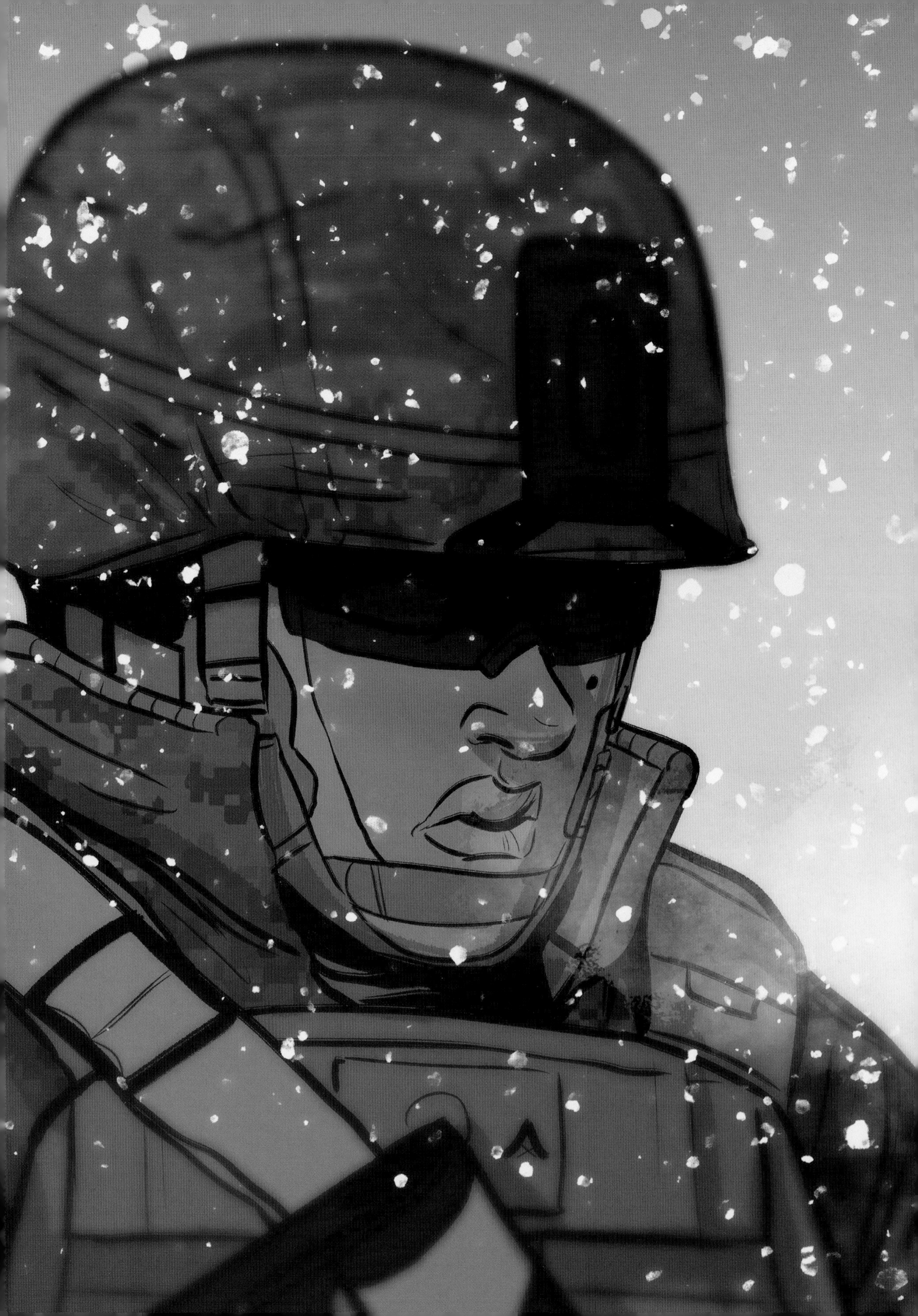

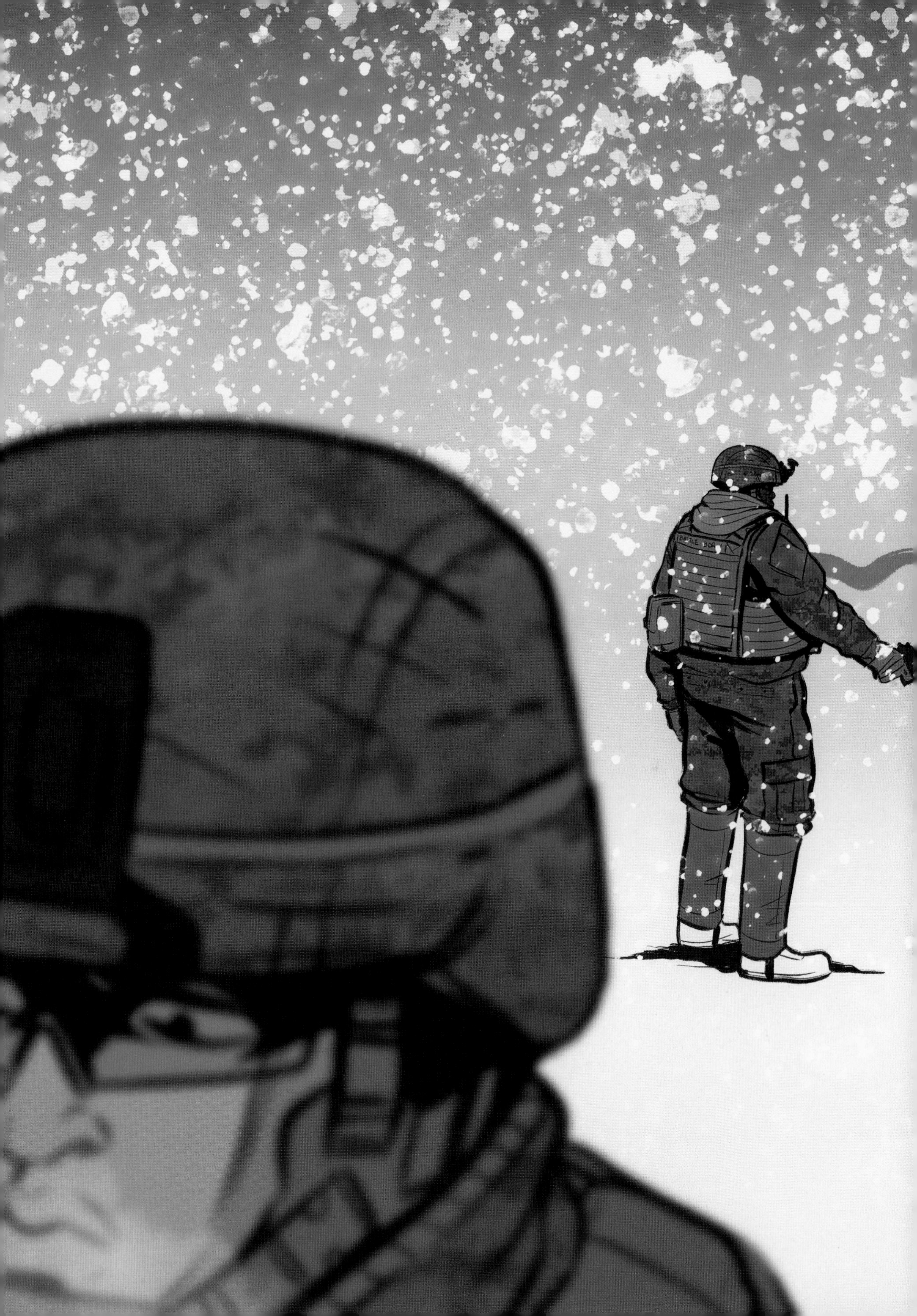

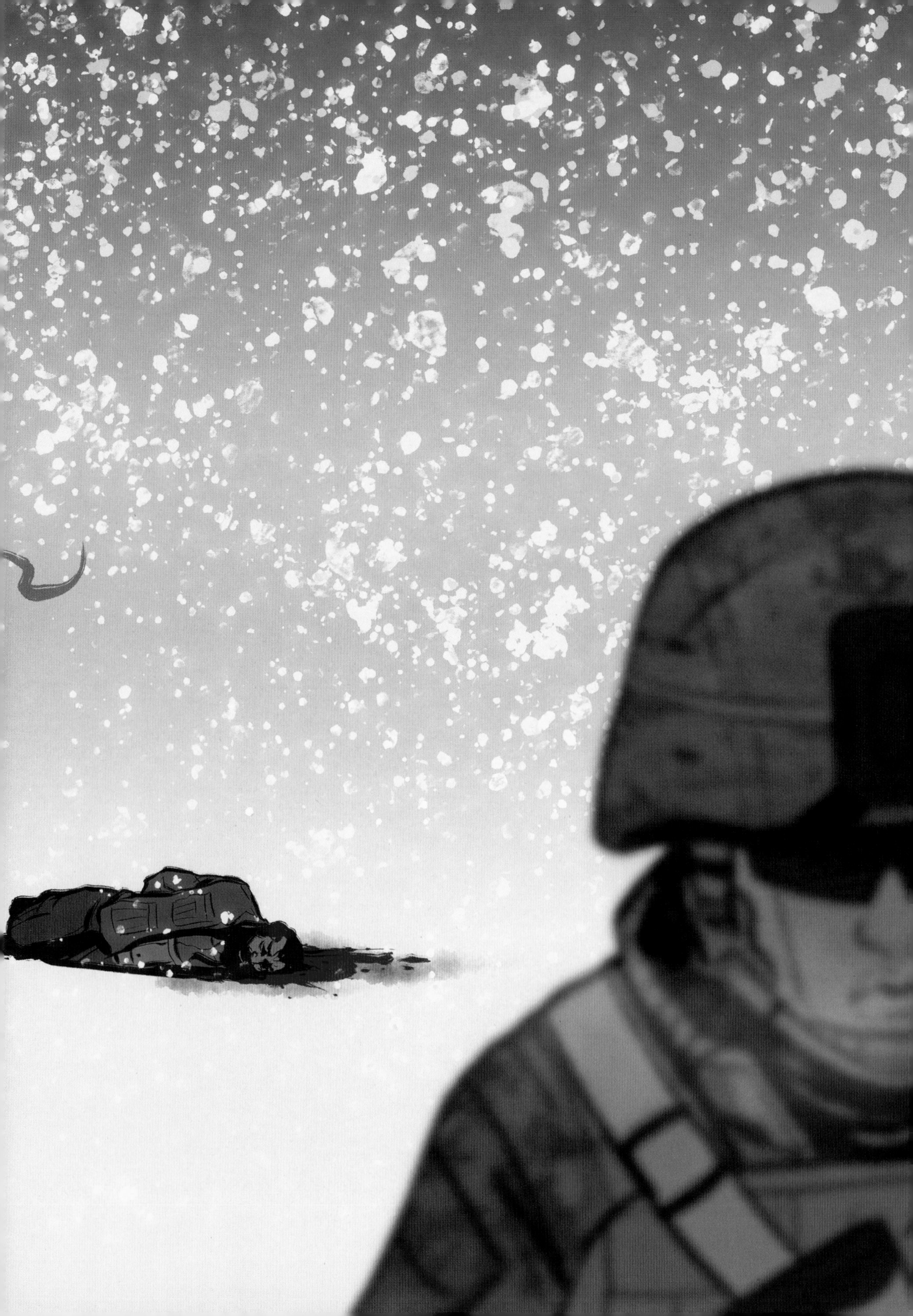

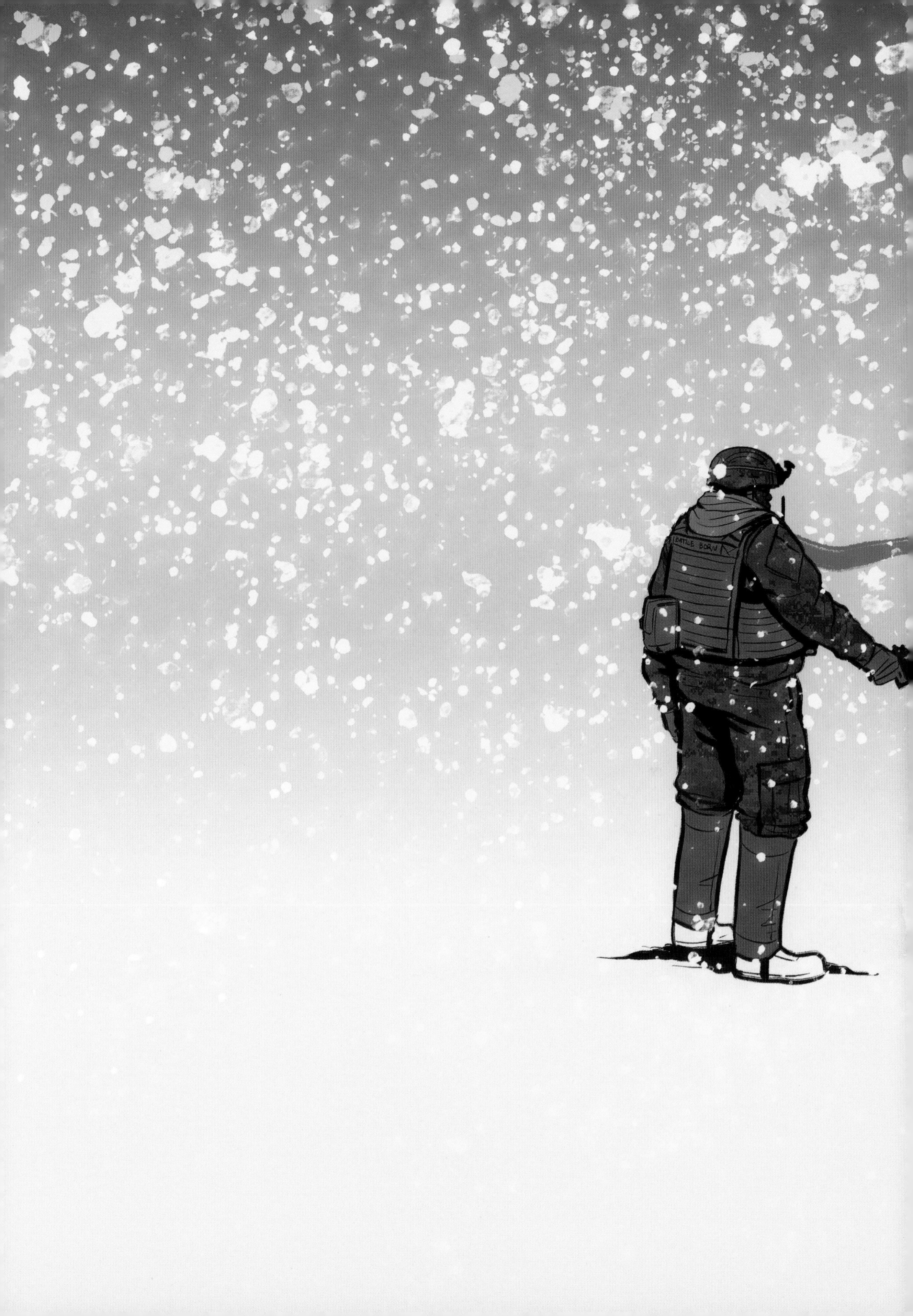
BATTLE BORN

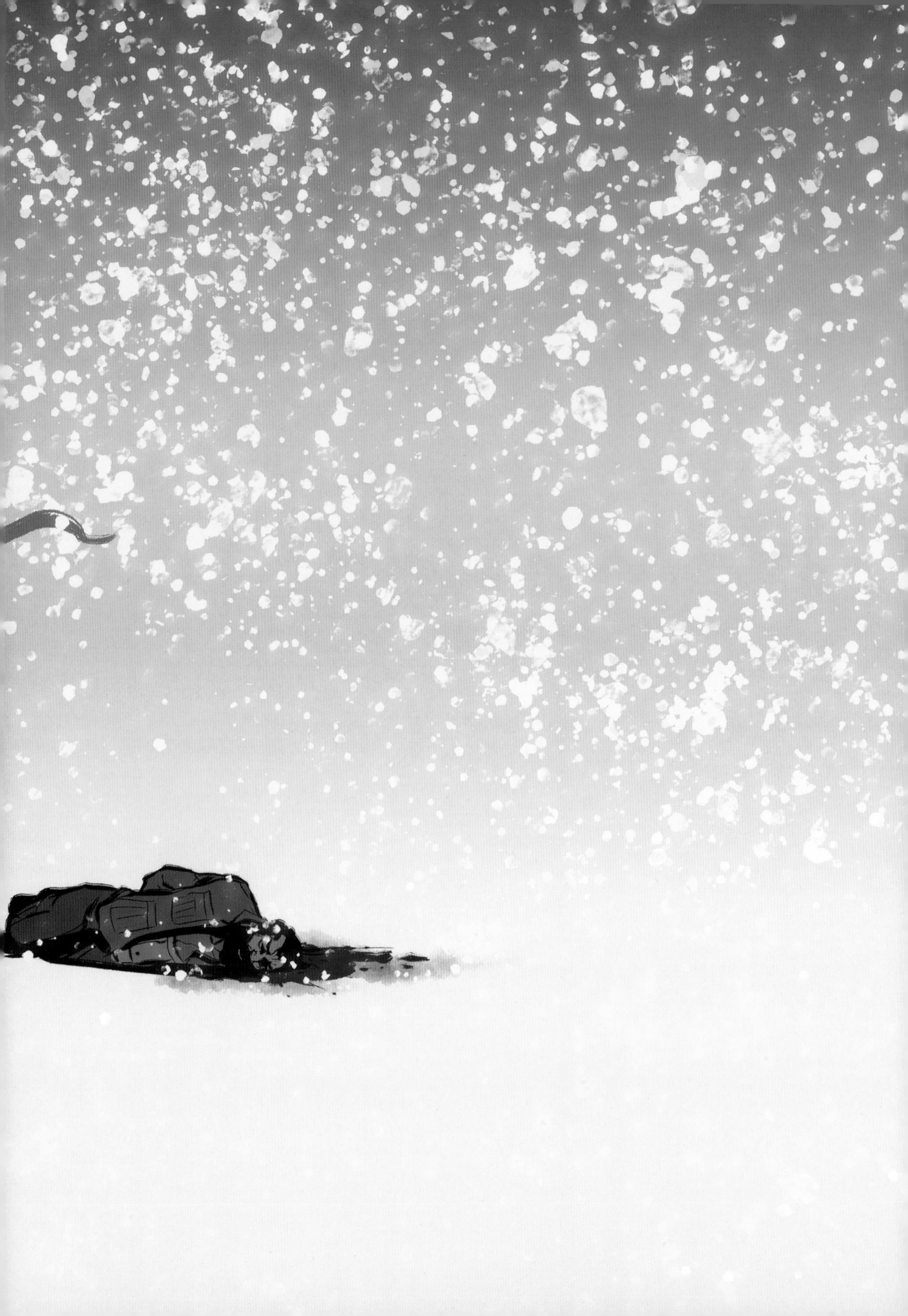

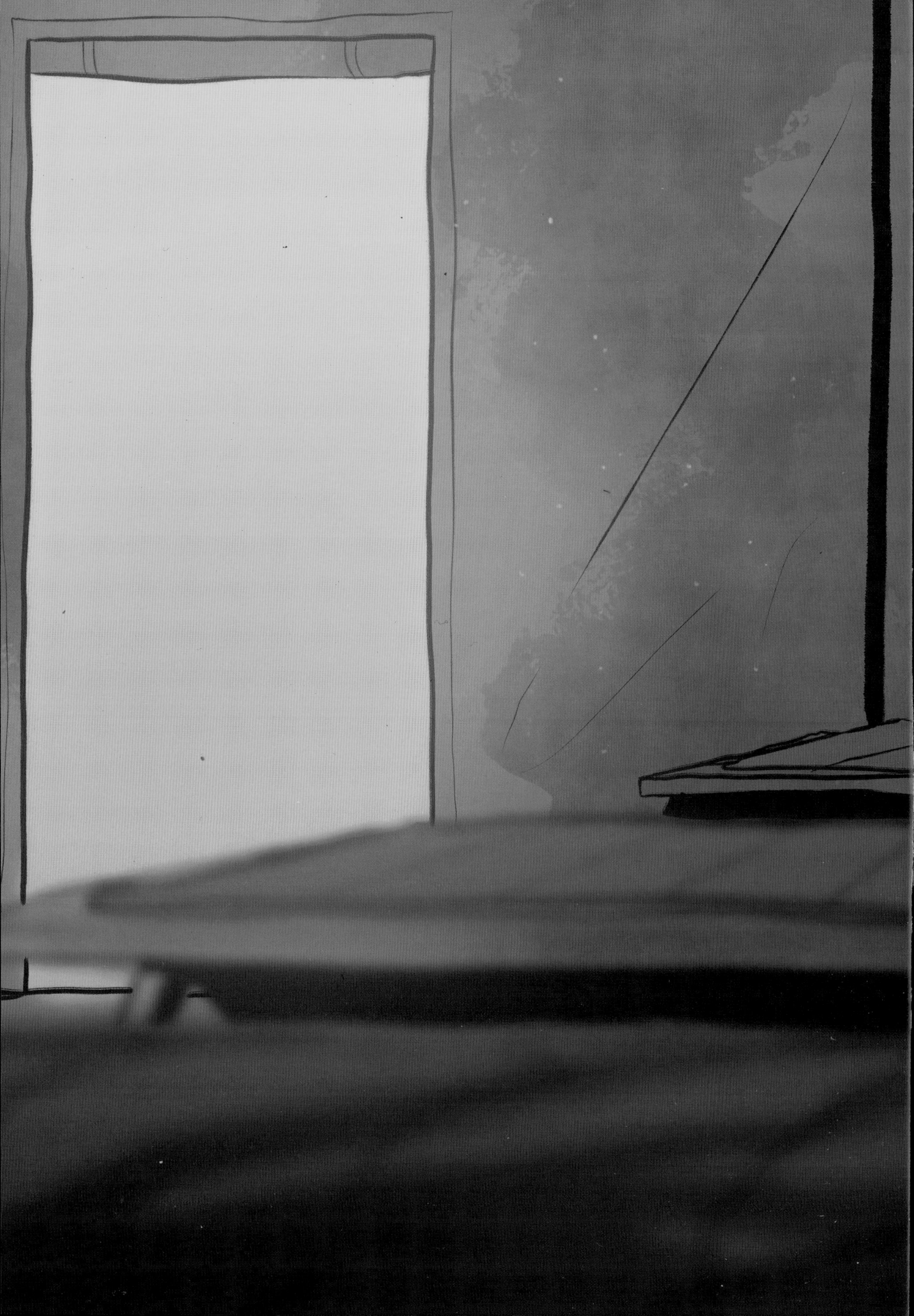

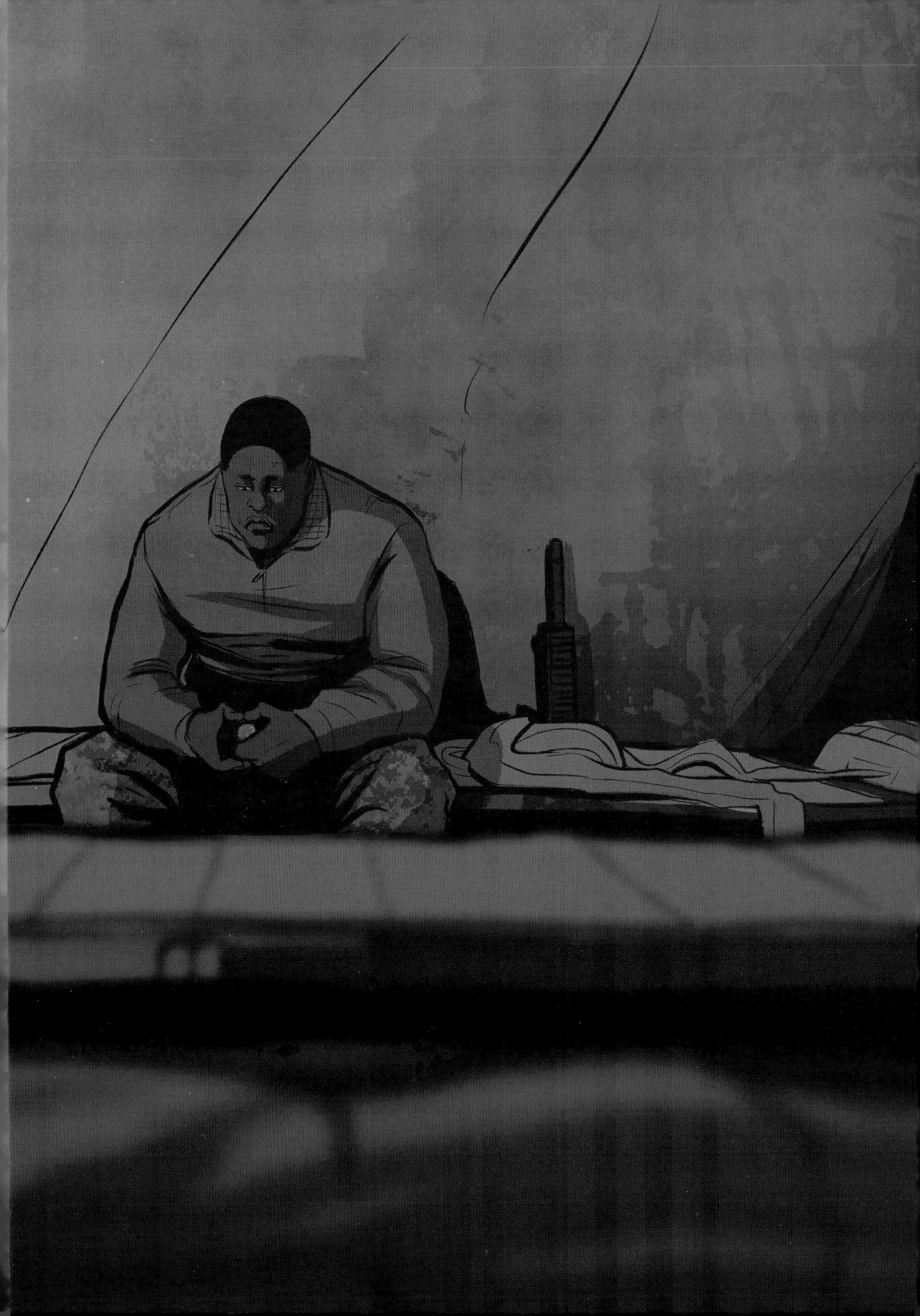

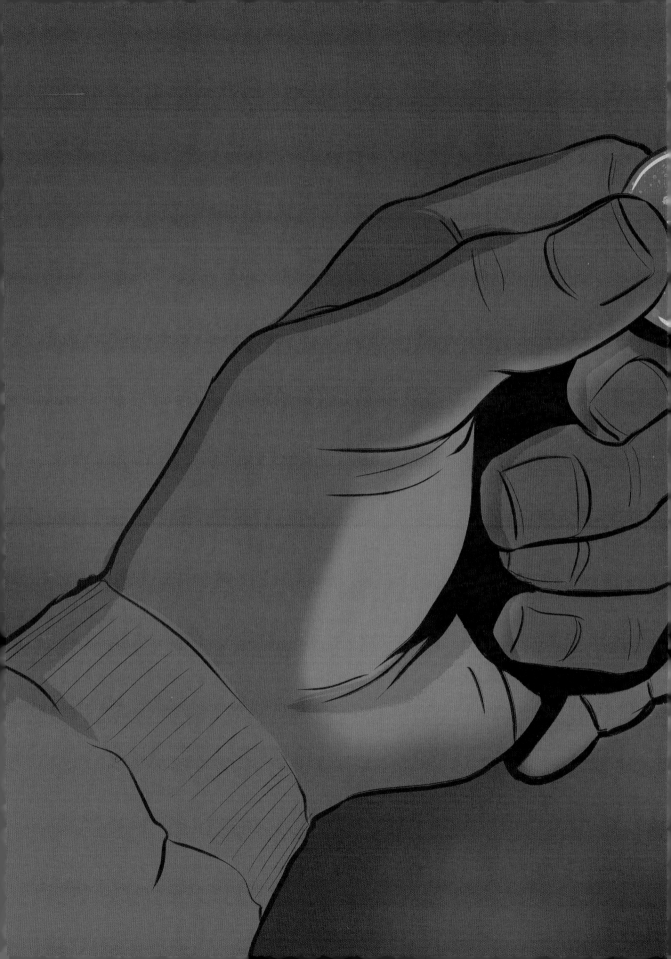

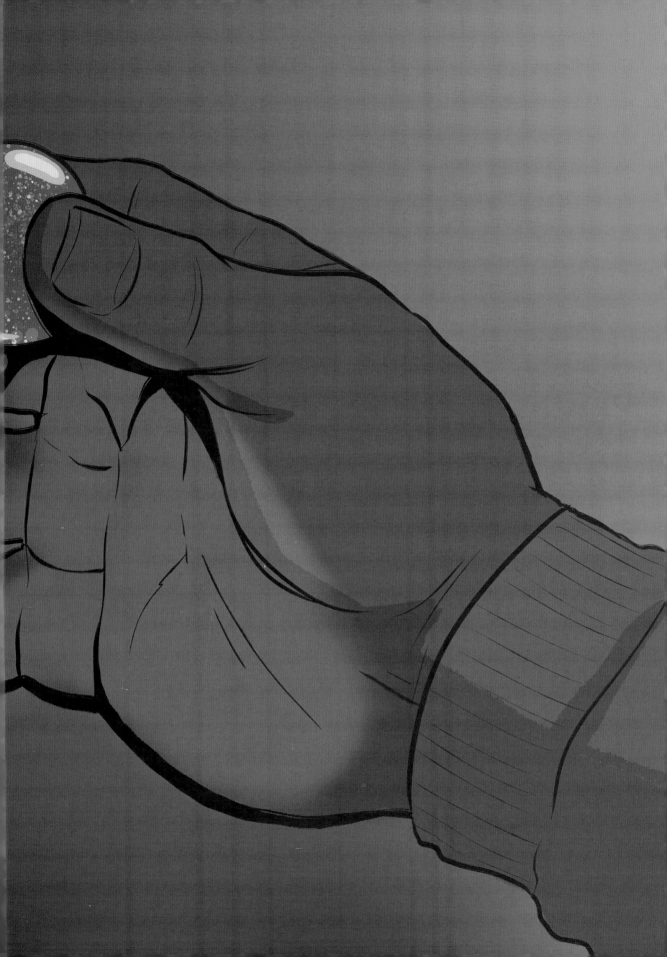

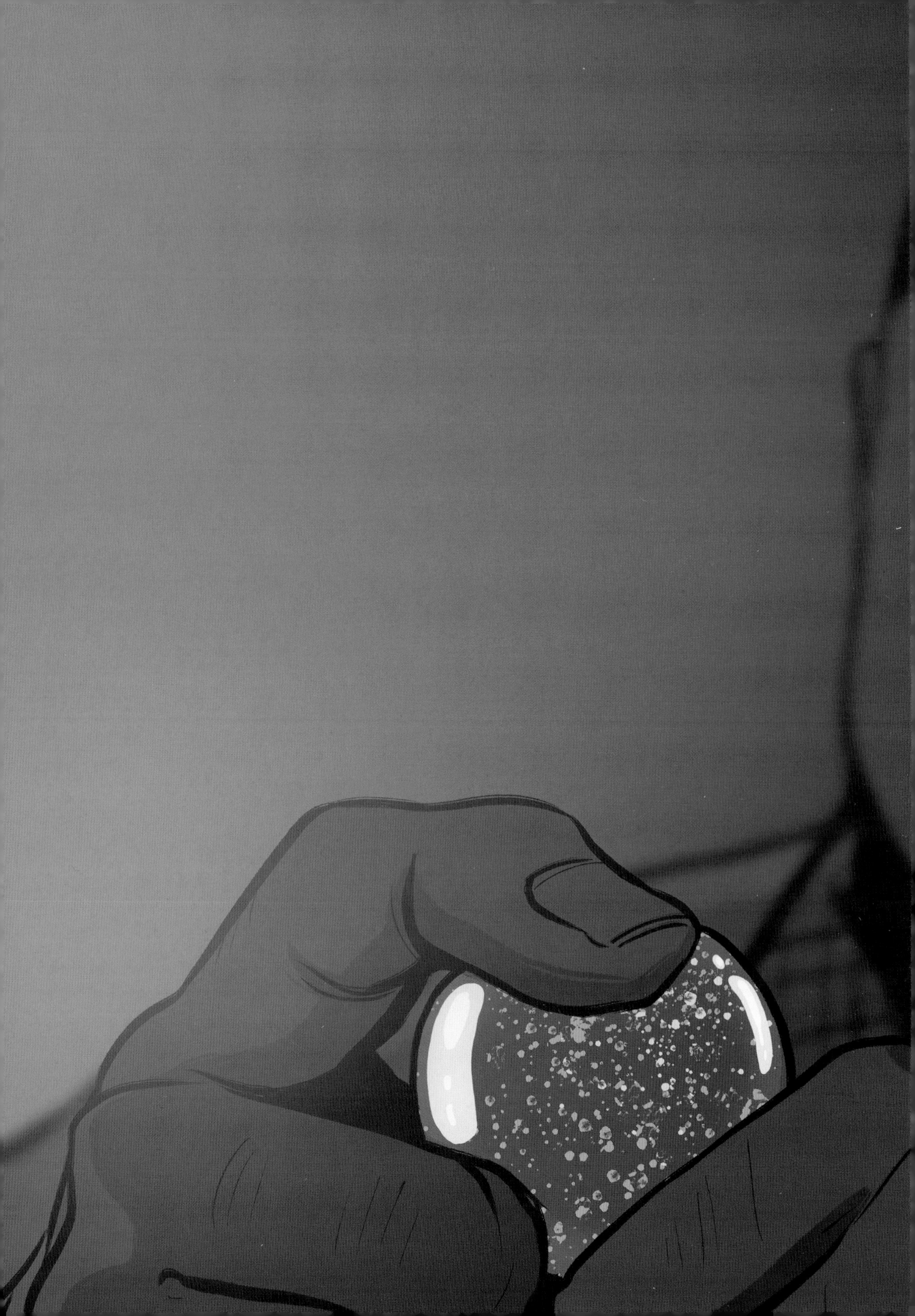

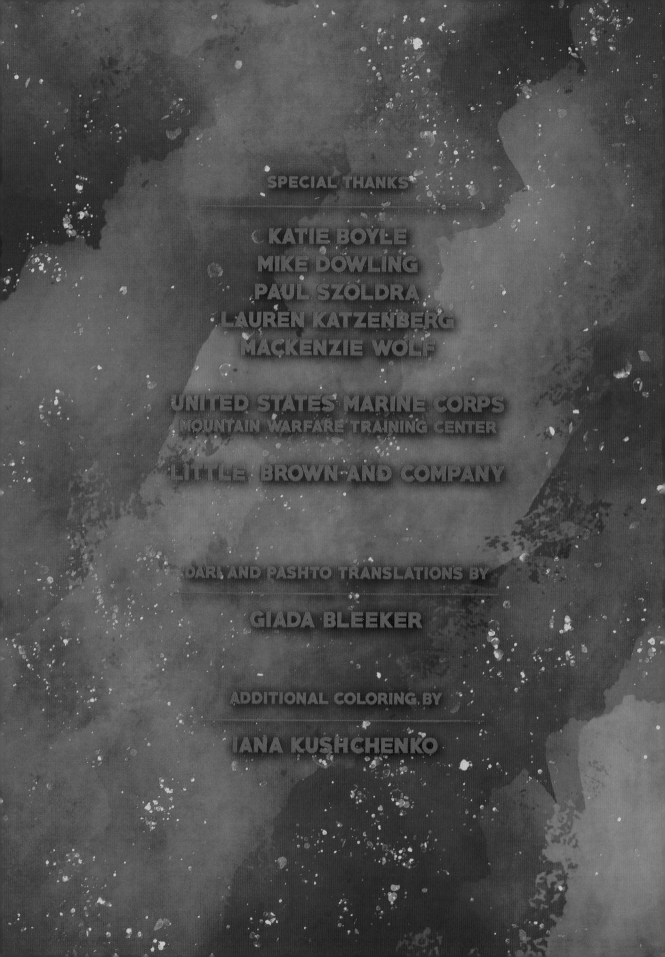

SPECIAL THANKS

KATIE BOYLE
MIKE DOWLING
PAUL SZOLDRA
LAUREN KATZENBERG
MACKENZIE WOLF

UNITED STATES MARINE CORPS
MOUNTAIN WARFARE TRAINING CENTER

LITTLE BROWN AND COMPANY

DARI AND PASHTO TRANSLATIONS BY

GIADA BLEEKER

ADDITIONAL COLORING BY

IANA KUSHCHENKO

BATTLE BORN
LAPIS LAZULI

WRITTEN AND ILLUSTRATED BY

MAXIMILIAN URIARTE

LITTLE, BROWN AND COMPANY
NEW YORK BOSTON LONDON

ALSO BY
MAXIMILIAN URIARTE

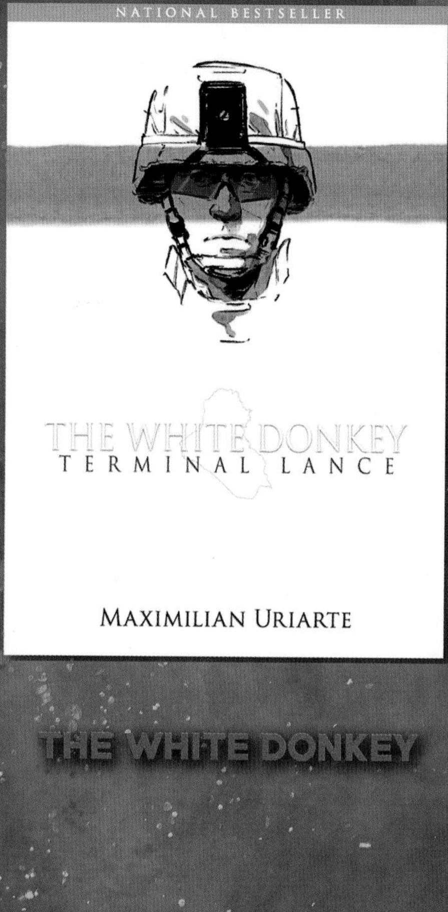
NATIONAL BESTSELLER
THE WHITE DONKEY
TERMINAL LANCE
MAXIMILIAN URIARTE

THE WHITE DONKEY

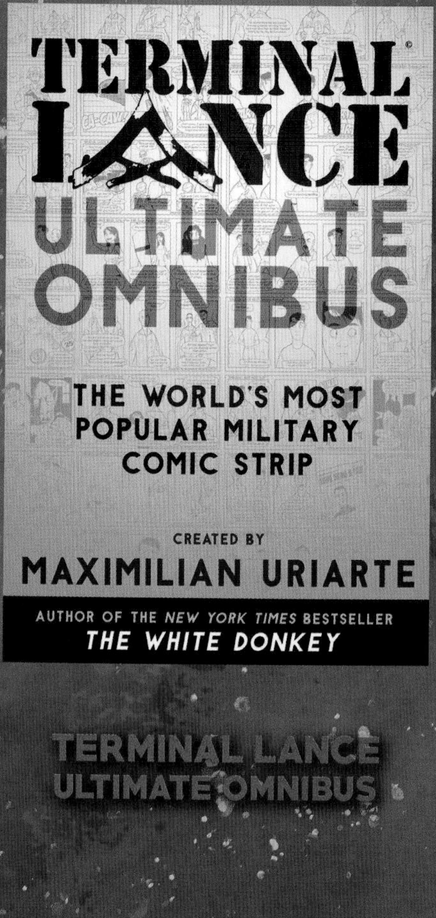
TERMINAL LANCE
ULTIMATE OMNIBUS
THE WORLD'S MOST POPULAR MILITARY COMIC STRIP
CREATED BY
MAXIMILIAN URIARTE
AUTHOR OF THE NEW YORK TIMES BESTSELLER
THE WHITE DONKEY

TERMINAL LANCE
ULTIMATE OMNIBUS

W9-BJZ-316